Cynthia Harrod-Eagles was born and educated in Shepherd's Bush, and had a variety of jobs in the commercial world, starting as a junior cashier at Woolworth's and working her way down to Pensions Officer at the BBC. She won the Young Writers' Award in 1973, and became a full-time writer in 1978. She is the author of over sixty successful novels to date, including twenty-seven volumes of the *Morland Dynasty* series.

Visit the author's website at www.cynthiaharrodeagles.com

Also by Cynthia Harrod-Eagles

The Bill Slider Mysteries

ORCHESTRATED DEATH
DEATH WATCH
NECROCHIP
DEAD END
BLOOD LINES
KILLING TIME
SHALLOW GRAVE
BLOOD SINISTER
GONE TOMORROW
DEAR DEPARTED

The Dynasty Series

THE FOUNDING
THE DARK ROSE
THE PRINCELING
THE OAK APPLE
THE BLACK PEARL
THE LONG SHADOW
THE CHEVALIER
THE MAIDEN
THE FLOOD-TIDE
THE TANGLED THREAD
THE EMPEROR
THE VICTORY
THE REGENCY
THE CAMPAIGNERS
THE RECKONING
THE DEVIL'S HORSE
THE POISON TREE
THE ABYSS
THE HIDDEN SHORE
THE WINTER JOURNEY
THE OUTCAST
THE MIRAGE
THE CAUSE
THE HOMECOMING
THE QUESTION
THE DREAM KINGDOM
THE RESTLESS SEA

CYNTHIA HARROD-EAGLES

The Second Bill Slider Omnibus

Dead End
Blood Lines
Killing Time

TIME WARNER BOOKS

This omnibus edition first published in Great Britain by
Time Warner Books in July 2005

First published separately:
Dead End first published by Little, Brown in 1994

Blood Lines first published by Little, Brown in 1996

Killing Time first published by Little, Brown in 1997

A CIP catalogue record for this book is available from
the British Library.

ISBN 0 7515 3721 7

Typeset in Amasis by Palimpsest Book Production Limited,
Polmont, Stirlingshire

Printed and bound in Great Britain by
Bookmarque Ltd, Croydon, Surrey

Time Warner Books
An imprint of
Time Warner Book Group UK
Brettenham House
Lancaster Place
London WC2E 7EN

www.twbg.co.uk

Contents

Dead End

CHAPTER ONE

The Days of Woes and Rises

When Detective Superintendent 'Mad Ivan' Barrington of Shepherd's Bush nick told you he would make your life a misery unless you accepted a transfer out of his station, you defied him at your peril. As the fount of all paperwork he was in a position to pour out upon you an unending stream of department fertilizer.

Today, for instance, Detective Inspector Bill Slider had been trapped at his desk all morning with a dizzyingly uninteresting report on the connection between stress and absenteeism, which Barrington had given him to précis on a most-urgent basis. As a result, Slider went up so late to lunch that he got the last portion of the 'home-made' lasagne, which had set like crusted rubber in the corner of the oven dish. It was cool, but he dared not ask for it to be heated up again for fear of what it might do to his teeth. Still, the alternative was shepherd's pie, and he'd tried that once.

'Chips with it, love?'

'Yes please.' What other comfort was there in life for a man whose wife and lover had both left him? He sighed, and the canteen helper looked at him tenderly. He had the kind of ruffled, sad-puppy looks that made women want to cosset him.

'I'll give you extra chips, 'cause you had the last bit and it's a bit small.' She shovelled the chips on cosily. 'Gravy, dear?' she asked, already pouring, and then passed his plate over with her thumb planted firmly in the brown bit; but by the time he got to a table the thumbprint had filled in so you could hardly tell. He didn't like gravy on chips – or on lasagne actually – but she had given him extra of that, too, out of compassion. Why did all the wrong people find him irresistible? And he still hadn't finished the report. Mournfully he folded it open beside his plate, speared the driest chip he could see, and continued reading.

Research suggests that disorders with psychosomatic components – headache, indigestion, constipation, diarrhoea, high blood pressure and ulcers – are more frequent among police officers than among citizens generally. What an attractive bunch they sounded, to be sure. He skipped down. *What constitutes stress?* the report asked him in a coy subheading. He was pretty sure it was going to tell him so he didn't answer, and in a minute it did, with an angst league-table two pages long. *Being Taken Hostage by Terrorists* came in at number one, followed by *Confronting a Person with a Gun.* No surprises there. Ah, here was a little light relief, though: *Being Caught Making a Mistake* was apparently more stressful than *Seeing Mutilated Bodies* or *Having to Deal with a Messy Car Accident.* Still, anyone regularly eating in a police canteen got used to dealing with messy accidents.

He pushed the report aside. Was this a fair punishment on a man for refusing to go away and play somewhere else? It wasn't even his fault that he had got so terminally up Barrington's nose. While investigating the chip-shop murder back in May, he had uncovered unsavoury facts about Barrington's former boss who was also, unfortunately for Slider, Barrington's lifelong hero. A man can forgive many things, but not being robbed of his dreams. There was nothing Barrington could do in the disciplinary way, since Slider had only been doing his job, so he had suggested, with all the menace at his command, that Slider should accept a promotion to Chief Inspector and move to Pinner station. Slider had known that he was asking for it when he refused, but that didn't mean he had to like it when he got it.

Of course, the promotion and transfer to Pinner would have meant a pay rise, and money was always an object; but he had never wanted to be a DCI anyway, and he didn't fancy going to an outer station, where life moved at a more leisurely pace. Why, at Pinner they regularly won the Metropolitan Police Beautiful Window-Box competition: they probably had time to read reports like this every day. He liked inner stations like Shepherd's Bush, where you were kept busy. A man needed a stable home-life to be able to cope with the opportunities for introspection left by a slower pace at work, and these days his home-life was about as stable as Michael Jackson's face.

He abandoned the report, sawed a section off the lasagne, and pulled out of his pocket a handbill given to him that morning by his bagman, Detective Sergeant Jim Atherton. It was a flyer for a concert that evening to be given in a local church, St Augustine's, Addison Gardens. A Mahler symphony with a seriously famous conductor, Sir Stefan Radek. Slider was not, like Atherton, a great classical music buff, though he liked some of the famous pieces – Tchaikovsky and Beethoven and *The Planets*, that sort of thing. The only bit of Mahler he'd ever heard he'd thought sounded like an MGM film-track, which was all right in a cinema but not what you'd want to sit through a whole concert of. But the real point here, the reason Atherton had told him about it at all, was that the Royal London Philharmonic – the orchestra which was doing the concert – was the one in which Joanna was a violinist.

Joanna, his lost love. Two and half years ago he had met her while he was on a case, and had – in the police jargon – gone overboard, with a resounding splash. He had been married then for nearly fourteen years and had never even considered being unfaithful before, believing that promises once made should not be broken and wives once chosen should not be forsaken. But he seemed not to be able to help himself, and for two years he had wrestled with guilt and responsibility, desperate to marry Joanna but unable to find a way to tell Irene, his wife, that he wanted to leave her. The worst of all possible worlds for all of them. At last, after a particularly humiliating evening, Joanna had broken it off with him, and had since steadfastly refused to re-attach it.

The really hideous irony was that it was just after Joanna had chucked him that Barrington had suggested, with more than a hint of broken arms about it, that Slider should move to Pinner, which was just down the road from Ruislip and the marital home – 'So nice and handy for you,' Barrington had said menacingly; and Slider for the sake of peace and pension enhancement was on the brink of accepting it as a wise career move, when Irene had announced she was leaving him. He must have had a really horrible conjunction of his ruling planets for these blows all to have fallen together. And it was a sad fact that in his whole life he had only ever been involved with two women, and they had both dropped him in short succession. He'd been left so comprehensively he felt like the slice of cucumber in the garnish on a pub sandwich.

And now Joanna, the lost and longed-for, was playing in a concert just down the road.

'It would be a chance to see her,' Atherton had said beguilingly when he gave Slider the leaflet. 'A chance to talk to her.'

'But she doesn't want to talk to me,' Slider had replied. 'She said so.'

'You don't have to take her word for it. Anyway, Radek conducting Mahler is not to be missed. You know he's the world authority on Mahler?'

'What's he conducting in a church in Shepherd's Bush for, then?' Slider objected.

'I think it's for the restoration fund. He lives just down the road, in Holland Park Avenue. It's a beautiful church,' Atherton added coaxingly.

'Is it?' Slider said unhelpfully.

'And they're rehearsing there this afternoon. Two-thirty to five-thirty.'

Sitting over his cooling lasagne, Slider contemplated the scenario Atherton had been urging on him. The shift ended at four, and unless something came up Slider would be free then. He could stroll down to the church, quite casually, take a look in, wait until they finished rehearsing and then bump into Joanna accidentally on her way out. 'Oh, hello. Fancy a drink? They're just open.' But what if she refused? She had told him she didn't want to see him again, and inviting public humiliation was no way to run a life.

No, he thought, sighing. Better not. He had a lot to do, anyway. There were two more survey reports on his desk for when he'd finished this one, and the car crime statistics to update. He gazed with digestive despair at the lasagne, which had withdrawn reproachfully, like a snubbed woman, under a cloak of hardening gravy. In any case, the jumbo dogknob 'n' beans he had consumed in the canteen for breakfast still lay sad and indigestible in a pool of grease somewhere under his ribs, and he didn't think he ought to add to his problems at this stage. He pushed his chair back and headed for the door, and almost ran into Mackay.

'Oh, there you are, guv.' Mackay's face was alight with pleasure: something wonderful must have happened. 'There's been a shooting in that big church in Addison Gardens, Saint Whatsisname's – one dead. It just came in from the emergency services. Some celeb's got taken out. Right on our ground, too! Luck, eh?'

Slider went cold with fright. 'Anyone else hurt?' he heard himself ask.

'All we've got is that there was a single shot fired, one body, and chummy got away.'

'All right. I'm on my way. Where's Atherton?'

'He's already gone, guv,' Mackay called after his disappearing back.

Atherton was waiting for him out in the yard. Svelte, elegant, creaseless of suit, wearer of silk socks and an aftershave you could only smell when you got close up, outwardly Atherton was nothing like a detective. He and Slider had worked together for a long time now, and Atherton was the nearest thing Slider had to a friend. He was an able man who dissipated his abilities and was far too dedicated to enjoying himself to get on in his career. If he hadn't been so intellectually lazy, he could have been Commissioner by now. If he hadn't been incurably honest, he could have been a top politician.

'We'll go in my car, shall we?' he said. 'It's hell to park up there.'

'Oh, you heard about it, then.'

'I heard.' He gave Slider a quick look and said nothing more until he had edged the car out into the stream of traffic. It wasn't too bad at this time of day – not much of a challenge to a man who loved driving. Not that you could do much real driving in a Ford anyway. He'd really like an Aston Martin, but apart from the price there was the parking problem. In London there was no point in driving anything you would mind getting nicked.

Slider had not spoken, and Atherton glanced sideways at him and had little difficulty in guessing his thoughts. There was not much he didn't know about his guv'nor's home-life, and what he knew he'd never celebrated. That Slider had been married to the wrong woman for sixteen years was bad enough: Irene had no sense of humour and thought that food was something you had to have to stay alive, a combination in Atherton's eyes so unfortunate as to be bizarre. Add to that the fact that the marital home was on an estate in Ruislip, and Atherton had thought things could not get worse for his boss; but getting worse is what things notoriously specialise in. The situation at the moment was, in technical language, a right bugger.

'How are things in the green belt these days?' he asked sympathetically.

Slider didn't look at him. 'It's life, Jim, but not as we know it.'

'It was rotten luck,' Atherton said. 'Ironies of fate, and all that.'

Ironies indeed, Slider thought, running on a now-familiar track. He wouldn't have minded so much if Irene had run off with an Italian waiter or a hunky young milkman, but she had left him for her bridge partner, who was the most boring man who had ever lived. Ernie Newman had the dynamic personality of a man slipping in and out of coma: he had once been a member of Northwood Golf Club but had found the place too swinging for him.

But Irene liked him: he was retired on an enormous company pension and he moved amidst the Volvo set she so admired.

'He's always there. He can spend time with me,' Irene had said; as succinct a commentary on the loneliness of a copper's wife as Slider had ever heard. And when he had protested about Ernie's dullness: 'I've had enough of excitement,' she had said. 'I want a man who thinks *I'm* exciting.' Even in their courting days Slider had never thought Irene exciting. She had always been neat, proper, unimaginative and conventional; but he had to admit that next to Ernie she was Catherine the Great.

She had taken the two children and left Slider in occupation of the house, the ranch-style, modern executive albatross which he had always hated with the pungency of a man who loved architecture forced to live with picture windows and an open-plan staircase. He had only bought it because it was the kind of thing she liked, and she, after all, would have to spend more time in it than him. That was irony for you!

Ernie Newman, a widower, had a five-bedroom detached house in Chalfont, so there was plenty of room for Irene and the children. She had always wanted to live somewhere like

Chalfont. And Ernie was going to pay for Matthew and Kate to go to private school, which was something Irene had long hankered after. Ernie had never had any children of his own – Mavis couldn't, apparently – so he was looking forward to being a father-by-proxy, Irene said. All Slider's masculine instincts had got up on their hind legs at that point, but the concealed knowledge of his own guilt had made it impossible for him to attack. Irene had never found out about Joanna.

And Joanna wouldn't have him back, despite the fact that he was now free. Irony number two. He had more irony than a man with a steel plate in his head. The events of this summer had left him utterly at a loss. What on earth was he supposed to do with the rest of his life? Even work was not enough to fill the void. His sanguine temperament had previously found satisfaction even in the routine plod which made up so much of the job; but burglaries, TDAs, possession and the rest of the malarky had no power now to rouse him from his puzzled misery. He knew as a Christian he ought not to rejoice in murder, but there was nothing like a big case for 'taking you out of yourself', as his mother used to say.

'So how did you know they would be rehearsing this afternoon?' he asked as they rounded the end of Shepherd's Bush Green.

'Joanna told me, of course.'

'Oh.'

Slider resisted the urge to ask where and why Atherton had been talking to Joanna. He had no rights over either of them, and certainly had no right to feel bugged that, having given him the chuck, she continued the friendship with Atherton which only existed because she had been Slider's lover. He turned his mind resolutely away from his own problems.

'I suppose it is Sir Stefan Radek who's been shot? Mackay just said "some big celeb".'

'That's all I heard too. There isn't a soloist, so presumably it's Radek,' Atherton said.

Radek was one of the few serious musicians who had crossed over into general, man-in-the-street fame. He'd even been on tv, Slider remembered. He'd had that series last year, *Classics for Idiots* or whatever it was called, explaining the difference between a concerto and a double-bass with the help of computer graphics and a popular comedian to make it all user-friendly. And now somebody had shot him. That'd teach him to go slumming. All Slider knew about Radek came from a cheery little spoonerism Joanna had told him one night after a concert. 'What's the difference between Radek and Radox? Radox bucks up the feet.' He remembered, too, after another concert when she had been seething about the conductor's iniquities (not Radek, though, someone else), she'd said that if he were found murdered that night there'd be eighty-odd suspects in the orchestra alone. 'Half of us would put our hands up out of sheer gratitude.' She'd been joking, of course; but it made you think. Somebody evidently thought the only good conductor was a dead one, and was prepared to do something about it as well.

St Augustine's was an incongruously big church for the streets it found itself in, hinting at larger, wealthier, or at least more devout congregations in the past. It was nineteenth-century Byzantine, built of soot-smudged pale-red brick with white stone coping, like a dish of slightly burned brawn piped with mashed potato. Inside it was a miniature Westminster Cathedral, cavernous and echoing, with lofty arches lost in shadow, pierced-work lamps, gilded wall and ceiling paintings, windows stained in deep, jewel shades of red and blue and green, and dark-eyed, beardless El Greco saints with narrow hands and melancholy mouths staring from every corner. There were high, wrought-iron gates across the choir, and the orchestra had been set up in the space below them on a low platform. Chairs and music stands and the timps were all that was to be seen. The players themselves had been ushered away somewhere – presumably to whatever place had been set aside for them as dressing-rooms. Slider hoped, anyway, that they had not all disappeared. Like tea, statements were best taken freshly brewed.

He and Atherton walked down the central aisle towards the scene, which was lit by overhead spots so that it stood out from the cave of comparative darkness around, like a gruesome reverse Nativity. The body was sprawled face down on the small podium between the lectern, on which the score lay open, and the long-legged conductor's chair. He had fallen quite neatly without knocking either over, which suggested to Slider that the bullet had not struck him with great force: he had crumpled rather than reeled or been flung off his feet. And in the place of ox and ass there were two people keeping guard over the body: one Slider recognised as the orchestra's fixer, Tony Whittam; the other was a dapper, plumpish, bald man who was kneeling on the floor at the head of the corpse and weeping. Every now and then he wiped the tears from his face unselfconsciously with a large handkerchief held in his left hand; in his right he held the conductor's baton by the point, so that the bulbous end rested on the floor. It looked like the ceremonial reversing of a sword.

As soon as he saw Slider, Tony Whittam stepped towards him with a cry of relief. 'Am I glad to see a friendly face! Are you the official presence?'

'Yes,' said Slider. 'This is on my ground.'

'Well, that's a piece of luck,' Whittam said. His usually genial face was drawn into uncharacteristic lines of shock and anxiety. He was a well-fed, dapper man of fifty-two going on thirty-five, in a light biscuit suit and a tie that would have tried the credibility of a twenty-year old. The orchestra's personnel-manager-cum-agony-aunt was much given to gold jewellery, sported a deeply suspect suntan and an artificially white smile, and altogether had the air of being likely to break out into a flower in the buttonhole at the slightest provocation. He looked like a spiv, but was in fact superb at his job, efficient as a machine and genuinely warm-hearted. Many a time Slider had seen him in the middle of a crowd of musicians, all clutching their diaries, all hoping to get off one date or on another; and he had always managed to spare Slider a glance and a friendly nod while coping patiently with the conflicting demands of, say, Mahler Five and the personal lives of a hundred-odd freelance and therefore temperamental artistes. Perhaps it was unkind mentally to have cast him as an ass.

'Who's this bloke?' Slider asked in an undertone with a gesture of the head towards the ox.

'It's Radek's dresser. He's a bit upset.'

Understatement of the year. 'Dresser?'

'That's what he calls himself. Sort of like his valet, personal servant, whatever. Been with him years. Everyone knows him.' He was, Slider realised, justifying the man's presence.

'Name?'

'Keaton. Arthur Keaton, but everyone calls him Buster.'

'Okay. And where's everybody else?'

'Down in the crypt – that's where the dressing-rooms are, and a sort of band room for coffee and warming-up. I thought it best to keep everyone together until someone came,' he said anxiously. 'Des is with 'em, keeping 'em quiet.' That was Des Riley, orchestral attendant, who set up the platform and loaded and unloaded the instruments – a dark, ripely handsome man dedicated to body-building and fornication. Since orchestral attendants were traditionally known as 'humpers', these would seem to be the two essential qualifications.

'You did just right,' Slider said reassuringly. 'Is everybody all right?'

'Oh yes – I mean they're shocked, as you'd expect, but nobody's hurt.' He nodded significantly, to convey to Slider that by everybody he understood him to mean Joanna.

'Who else was here apart from the musicians?'

'Well, there was Bill Fordham's wife and kid – first horn – they'd come to watch; and Martin Cutts's latest bird, of course; and the verger, he was mucking about back there with some keys,' he gestured with his head towards the back of the church. 'And Georgina, my assistant, but she was through in the vestry making a phone call. They're all down there in the band room. Radek's agent was here earlier, but she'd gone before it happened. And Spaz – he'd already left as well. He's taken the van away – there's nowhere to park it here.' That was Des Riley's assistant, Garry Sparrow, usually known as Gaz the Spaz, a witticism none too subtle for him.

'All right. You've done very well,' Slider said, and crouched to take a look at the body. Radek had been lean and upright, one of those wiry old men who go on for ever and never look much different once they've passed fifty. Slider, musical tyro though he was, recognised him, as he supposed about seventy-five per cent of people would, whether they were music-lovers or not, now that he'd been on the telly. For Radek was not only hugely famous, but physically distinctive. He was very tall, gaunt, and had a great beak of a nose and bushy white eyebrows over heavy-lidded eyes, so that he looked like a half-pissed bird of prey. His shock of over-long white hair was brushed straight back like a lion's mane, but once he got going, it flew about as if it had a life of its own. It was his hallmark; and his photograph – invariably moodily-lit and against a dark background – loured, snarled and brooded famously on a million record-covers, white mane and white hands spiked against the blackness, the archetypal image of the super-maestro.

Today he was dressed in civvies of course – fawn slacks, with a black roll-neck sweater tucked into them, leather moccasins and, my God, pale yellow socks.

'He doesn't look as impressive as he does in white tie and tails,' Slider murmured to Atherton.

'Nobody looks their best dead,' Atherton reminded him.

There was no doubt he was dead, at any rate, Slider thought. Radek's face was pale grey, with a touch of blue about nose and lips, and the skin looked unpleasantly moist, like sweating cheese. His eyes were open and fixed, staring as no eyes ever stared in life, and his lips were drawn back from old-man's long yellow teeth as though he were baring them in defiance. There was a bitter smell of sweat about him, a whiff of after-shave, and underneath that a faint, unclean smell, which Slider associated with mortality. Radek was lying more or less in the recovery position, one leg slightly drawn up, and both his hands were clenched – the right lying beside his head, the other, caught under him, seemingly locked onto the cloth of his roll-neck.

The entry wound was in the right lower side at the back, just above the belt of his slacks; quite a neat hole, surrounded by a blood stain. Slider examined the podium and slipped his fingers in underneath the body, but there was no blood and seemingly no hole on the other side.

'No exit wound,' he said.

'Still inside?' Atherton said.

'Presumably. He must have been hit at extreme range.'

'Or else it was deflected.'

Slider grunted agreement, and stood up, turning to Whittam. 'All right – you saw what happened?'

'Well, yes,' Whittam said unwillingly, as though it might incriminate him. 'I was standing at the side, over there, making sure everyone was in place, just waiting for Radek to start. Once they were off, I was going to join Georgina in the vestry. I'd got a lot to do, and it was a late kick-off already.'

'Why was that?' Atherton put in. 'I'd heard Radek was a stickler for punctuality.'

'He is. Woe betide the musician who's late. He won't step on the platform if anyone's missing.'

'But he's not punctual himself?' Slider asked.

'Oh he is usually. But he was in a rotten mood today. He'd had me up and down to the dressing-room half a dozen times, complaining about everything, and Des couldn't get away. He treats him like a personal servant, you know, despite—' He gestured with his head towards Keaton, who was still kneeling beside his dead master like Greyfriar's Bobby. 'Then when he finally deigned to come upstairs he stood over there by the vestry telling me the arrangements he wanted for tonight, as if we hadn't gone over them ten times already. Bloody temperamental celebrities! I tell you, dear old Norman Del Mar was never like that.'

'All right. Go on,' Slider urged. He wanted to get the general picture before the rest of the team arrived and the scene fragmented.

'Well, he got up on the podium and lifted his stick, and everyone got ready, and he just sort of stood there a minute – working himself up to start, I suppose. And then there was this bang – like a big heavy door slamming. It made my heart sink: I thought it was the verger frigging around up the back, and there's nothing a conductor hates more than someone making a noise at a moment like that. Breaks his artistic concentration, you see. I expected him to turn round and bawl me out for it, but he just crumpled up and fell. And then Martin Cutts's bird screamed, and old Buster came running past me shrieking like a hen, and it was only then I sort of put two and two together and realised he'd been shot. I ran over, but it was obvious he was dead.'

'Did you see who did it?'

'No, that was the trouble, you see – everyone was looking at Radek. By the time I even thought to look round the bloke had gone, whoever he was, and it was the same for all of us. But the verger was up the back, as I said. I think he may have seen him.'

'Doctor's just arriving, guv,' Atherton murmured, looking over his shoulder towards the door. 'And it looks like the photographer behind him.'

Slider glanced back. 'All right,' he said. 'We've got about a hundred people downstairs to interview. We're going to need the cavalry. Call home and get everyone here who can read and write.'

'And McLaren as well, sir?'

'Get on with it. And when you've done that, see if Niobe here's fit to speak yet.' He turned to Whittam. 'Can you take him somewhere and find him a cup of tea or something? The doctor will want to get to the body.'

Whittam jumped eagerly at the chance to be useful. 'Yes, of course. I'll take him in the vestry. It's nice and quiet there.'

'How do I get downstairs?' Slider asked.

'Over there, that door,' he pointed to the opposite side from the vestry. 'You can't go wrong, it doesn't go anywhere else.'

The door led onto a dank corridor which ran the length of the church. It was lined with an assortment of stacking chairs, elderly cupboards, and cardboard boxes full of mildewed bunting, torn crêpe paper decorations, remnants of junior nativity play costumes, and other bits of typical church-hall junk. Looking right, he saw at the far end a door onto the street, and beside it another door leading back into the body of the church; turning his head to the left he saw stone steps leading down, and a whiff of cigarette smoke and a murmur of voices told him he was facing the right way. At the bottom was another corridor, and immediately to his left the doorway into a large room furnished with sundry chairs, trestle tables, mirrors, and a ballet barre across one end which was largely obscured by coats. A tea urn and trays of cups and saucers filled one table, and the orchestra was hanging around, making itself as comfortable as it could in the manner of people accustomed to being kept hanging around in various dismal locations all round the world. They were chatting, dozing, smoking, reading and, in the furthest corner where the trombone section lurked, playing cards on somebody's upturned instrument case. Joanna called it the airport terminal syndrome, with the emphasis on the terminal.

Joanna was sitting on the massive old-fashioned radiator right next to the door, her legs dangling, her hands knotted loosely between her knees, her head resting against the wall, her eyes closed. She seemed very pale, and the lines around her eyes and mouth looked more pronounced than he remembered. He wondered how close she had been to the podium, how shocked she had been. He was so glad to see her it took him a moment or two to find his voice.

'You shouldn't sit on radiators,' he said quietly. 'You'll get chilblains.'

Her eyes flew open. She stared at him almost blankly, and then, to his relief, there was a softening of her expression which, whatever it betokened, was on the side of pleasure rather than dismay.

'Well,' she said, 'if it isn't the mild-mannered Bill Slider.'

CHAPTER TWO

The Dog it was That Died

'You're looking rather pale,' Slider said.

'I've just seen someone killed,' she said. 'You think with television news reports – Bosnia, Northern Ireland and everything – that you've seen it all. But it's different in real life. One moment there's a real human being standing there, just a couple of feet away from you, and the next—' She shook her head. 'How do you ever get used to it?'

'We don't,' he answered, divining that she meant the question personally. 'If we stopped minding, we'd stop being effective. The flippant remarks are meant to fool us, you know, not you.'

'Poor Bill,' she said.

He wished he could take that as encouragement; but he had work to do. 'How close were you to the podium?'

'I was sitting at number four. Close enough, thank you.'

'You've been promoted,' he discovered with delight. The front four in the first violin section were permanent positions, while the rest of the section moved up and down on a rota system so as to share the work evenly. 'What does that make you?'

'Deputy principal,' she said shortly.

'That's wonderful. Why didn't you—?' But of course he knew why she hadn't told him. He altered course hastily. 'Well, I'm just thankful you weren't hurt. There was only one shot, is that right?'

She raised an enquiring eyebrow. 'Am I being a witness now?'

'You are a witness, like it or not. But you can be especially helpful to us – to me – because you know what we need. You know—'

'My methods, Watson,' she finished for him. 'All right, what do you want to know?'

'Start with your version of the incident.'

'Well, Radek came out from the vestry—'

'I thought he had a dressing-room down here?'

'He did, but there's another set of stairs down from the vestry. The conductor, and soloists if any, go up and down that way to avoid having to rub shoulders with the great unwashed, namely us. I've done concerts here before, you see. I know all about it.'

He smiled because she had anticipated his question. 'You see?' he said elliptically.

'I've already accepted the premise,' she said, giving him a firm look. 'You're not bright enough to put a scam by me.'

'Thanks. I understand Radek was late starting.'

'A bit.'

'Was that unusual?'

She shrugged. 'He's usually punctual, but they're a law to themselves, you know, conductors. It's our job to wait for them, not vice versa. It was only five minutes anyway. It was two thirty-five by my watch when he stepped onto the platform.'

'Did he seem as usual when he came on?'

She made an equivocal face. 'I didn't notice anything specific, but I wasn't particularly looking. He was always an ugly, bad-tempered old bastard, not the sort you gaze at rapturously. He seemed to be in a bad mood, but that was nothing unusual.'

'All right, go on.'

'Well, he crossed the platform, got up on the podium, opened the score, picked up his stick—' He could see her watching it replay in her mind.

'From where?'

'He'd put it down on the lectern while he opened the score. Oh, and he took out his handkerchief and wiped the sweat off his face. He always sweated a lot. It could be pretty nasty sitting up front. He'd flick his head to get his hair out of his eyes, and drops of sweat would fly.'

'Yuck.'

'Exactly. Anyway, he wiped his face, put his hanky away, picked up his stick and said, "Mahler".'

'Telling you which piece you were going to rehearse?'

'Of course. So he waited for everyone to find their place and get their instruments up. And then—' She hesitated.

'Go on. However it seemed to you.'

'Well, he stopped with his stick up, just staring at nothing, frowning. He might have been communing with his muse, I suppose, assuming the nasty old thing had one, but it didn't quite look like that. He looked more as if he'd remembered something bad, like he'd left the gas on or he ought to have paid his VAT yesterday or something. He put his hand up and pulled his roll-neck – like this – as if he was loosening it, like a nervous gesture.' She looked at Slider. 'I don't want to make too much of it, because it all happened so quickly, but it was something I noticed.'

'You think he was expecting something to happen?'

'God, I don't know. He looked as though he had something on his mind, that's all I can say.'

'All right. Go on.'

'Well, then everything seemed to happen at once. There was a terrific bang. I think someone out in the church shouted "No!" and someone else screamed. Radek dropped his stick and crumpled up, fell forward. It all happened in an instant. He was on the floor while the echoes were still bumping about in the roof.'

'Did you know it was a gunshot?'

'Oh yes. I don't know why, because I've never heard a gun fired in real life, but I knew it was a gun. Of course I looked that way, and I saw a man in a light brown coat and a hat with a big brim up at the back by the main door. It was too far away for me to see any detail, but he was just standing there, staring. Then he turned and ran for it. There's a small door within the large one, and he went out through that and was gone. It was all over in a second.'

'Did you see what he did with the gun?'

She frowned. 'I didn't see the gun. I think – I'm not sure – he had his hand in his pocket.'

'Did you recognise him?'

She shook her head. 'Too far away, and too dark. We were under the lights, you see. And he had a hat on.'

'So you don't even really know that it was a man?'

She thought about that. 'I assumed it was. I suppose it might have been a woman, but if it was, it was a woman hoping to pass for a man. It wasn't a female shape.'

'Okay, what happened next?'

'Old Buster came rushing over from the vestry side, screaming, almost before Radek hit the floor. Tony Whittam was behind him, and they crouched over the body, and I think Tony said "He's dead", or something like that. Des Riley came halfway, and then went back into the vestry, presumably to call the emergency services.'

'How did everyone else react?'

'Everyone was very quiet, apart from Martin Cutts's bird, who was sobbing as if it had happened to her. It's funny, in films everyone rushes about shrieking and fighting to get out, but here nobody moved or made a sound. I suppose we were all too shocked. Then Bill Fordham jumped up and went running out to his wife and kid to make sure they were all right.' She made a wry face. 'Of course Brian Tusser – the first trombone – asked in a loud voice if it meant the concert would be cancelled, and would we still get paid, but he's just a despicable scrote. I mean, I suppose we all thought it, but he had to go and actually say it aloud.'

'I suppose that means no-one in the orchestra would have reason to kill Radek? He was a benefactor to you, really.'

'I wouldn't go that far,' she said hastily.

'Wasn't he generally liked?'

'Not by musicians. He was rude, unpleasant, arrogant, conceited, and had delusions of godhead. If he'd been a good conductor we could have forgiven him, but as it was—'

'Not a good conductor? But he was famous!'

'Not synonymous terms, I'm afraid. The critics loved him, but what do they know? On the box he was erratic and his technique was non-existent, but he'd got too famous for any of us to criticise. We had to carry him and cover up for his cock-ups; and then if we managed in spite of him to give a good performance, he got all the praise *and* got paid about a hundred times what any of us got for the same concert. So what was to like?'

'Was he really that bad?'

'Are you kidding me! You've heard me complain about conductors before.'

'Yes, but everyone complains about bosses. It's a way of getting through life. Was Radek really worse than anyone else?'

'Well, just to give you an example, we rehearsed the Mahler yesterday at Morley College, and he brought the entire second fiddle section in in the wrong place *twice*. Then he was so rude to the principal second – you know, Sue Caversham? – that he reduced her to tears, and that's not easy to do, because Sue's a tough cookie – you have to be, to be a woman and get to the front desk. And then the bastard threatened that if it went wrong again today she'd lose her job. I mean, what was she supposed to do? If she hadn't followed him in, if she'd hung back and come in at the right place, he'd have bawled her out just the same.'

'Can he do that? Get one of you sacked?'

She made a face. 'Not officially. We're all self-employed, as you know. Officially we are the orchestra and the orchestra is a self-governing body, so it's *us* who hire *him*. But in reality a man as powerful as him can do what he likes, and the management won't cross him for fear of losing his favour.'

'But if he's so terrible, why do you have him at all?'

'He's got recording contracts,' she said simply. 'It's work, you see, what we exist for. The contracts go where he goes, and if he doesn't like us, he'll take them to another orchestra. So we have to kiss his boots. *Had* to, I should say,' she remembered. 'All contracts are now cancelled, by order of the Great Agent in the Sky.'

Slider was silent a moment, absorbing all this. 'So there may have been people with reason to want to kill him?'

'Almost everyone he's ever met, I should say. Old Buster must have been the only creature on the planet that loved him.'

'Well, thank you. You've been most helpful,' he said, but it came out sounding coolly official, and it broke the mood between them. He looked at her, felt awkward, and saw her feeling awkward back.

'That's all right. Just doing my duty as a citizen,' she said flippantly.

He plunged, suicidally. 'Oh Jo, can't we—?'

'Now don't start that again, please. You know my feelings. Can't we leave it at that?'

'No, we can't,' he said, a little angrily, and she looked surprised. 'It's crazy to ruin both our lives like this, when—'

'My life isn't ruined, thank you very much,' she interrupted stiffly.

'Well mine is!'

'That's not my fault.'

'I never said it was. Did I ever blame anyone but me? I do understand your position, but—'

'No, I don't think you do,' she said with feeling. 'You think I'm cutting off my nose to spite my face—'

'I *don't*!'

'—but you altered the basis of our whole relationship. Look at it from my point of view: for two years you keep me dangling in limbo, and then when you find yourself all alone with no-one to come home to at the end of the day, you can't get to me quick enough.' She looked away unhappily. 'Maybe you just want a housekeeper, and any woman would do. Someone to wash your socks.'

'I don't want you for that. How can you think it?'

'Well of course *you* don't think you do,' she said, quite kindly. 'But I don't know that our being together would make us happy. And I'm not sure I want to take a chance on which of us is right.'

She said 'I'm not sure' rather than 'I don't want to', he noticed. It was little enough to pin his hopes on, but it was all he had; and besides, with a serious case to run, now was the time for consolidation rather than trail-blazing.

'All right,' he said meekly, 'but you will help me with this case, won't you? You know how helpful you can be to me, someone who knows the music scene, and knows my world; one foot in each camp so to speak—'

'If you want a native interpreter, Jim Atherton knows the music scene,' she said shortly.

'But I don't fancy him.'

It was probably a stupid time to risk a joke. Cancel probably: she was looking at him with narrow suspicion.

'I told you, you can't put a scam past me. I'm a witness, and I'll do my duty as a citizen, but that's all. This isn't a foot in the door, Bill. It's over between you and me.'

'Between you and me, maybe, but not between me and you,' he said painfully.

'I'm sorry,' she said, and she looked as if she meant just that.

'For it to work, I would have to have come first with you, and I didn't. You can't change that.'

The troops had arrived and were disposed about the band-room taking statements, which would later all have to be read and evaluated. Talk about making work for yourself, Atherton thought, coming back up to the vestry; but at least most of them would be short. 'I didn't see anything, can I go now?' The police doctor who had come to pronounce Radek's life extinct also pronounced Keaton unfit for further questioning, gave him a tranquilliser, and recommended he be sent home. Atherton could see for himself that the old boy was past anything at the moment: he sat pale and trembling like a vanilla blancmange, and any time he tried to speak it spilled over into helpless tears again.

'We'll get you a taxi to take you home,' Atherton said. 'Is there someone we can contact for you, who can come and be with you?'

That brought more tears. Keaton, it seemed, had lived alone with Radek, doing everything for him, and going home to the empty house was going to be painful.

'Is there somewhere else you'd prefer to go?'

But no, when he managed to get the words out, Keaton made it plain he wanted to go home. 'I just want to be alone. You're very kind, but I need to be alone.'

Atherton let it go, and Whittam went to look for a taxi. 'We'll have to come and see you, and ask you some questions,' Atherton said. Keaton raised sodden eyes. 'You must be the person who knew Sir Stefan best. You can help us understand the situation.'

'Very well,' Keaton said wearily.

'Can you tell us who his next of kin is?'

'His daughter,' Keaton said. 'Fay Coleraine. She's his only relative. Do you want her telephone number?'

Atherton took it down. 'We'll break the news to her,' he said. 'I'm sure you won't feel like doing it.'

'Thank you,' Keaton whispered. 'You're very kind.'

'I must just ask you now, before you go – did you see the man who did it?'

'I – I caught a glimpse. I was more – more concerned – with Sir Stefan.'

'I understand. But did you recognise the man?' A shake of the head. 'Have you ever seen him before?'

'No. I told you, I only caught a glimpse of him.'

'Do you know of anyone who might have wanted to harm Sir Stefan? Had he any enemies?'

Another shake of the head. 'No. How could he have? He was a wonderful man. A great artist. The nation loved him.'

The nation was not in the frame, Atherton thought; but there was evidently no point in pursuing it now. Whittam came back in. 'We've got a cab at the door. Do you want me to come with you, Buster?'

Keaton shook his head numbly. Whittam glanced at Atherton, who shrugged minutely. It was only five minutes away, and the man had said he wanted to be alone. One had to assume that adults could decide such things for themselves.

'I'll see you into the cab, anyway,' Whittam said kindly, and put his hand under Keaton's elbow to help him to his feet. The old boy did look very doddery, but that might have been the trank taking effect.

'We'll call on you tomorrow morning, Mr Keaton, if that's all right,' Atherton said. 'Just to ask you a few questions.'

Keaton turned and fixed Atherton with a red and angry eye. 'Find him,' he said in an unexpectedly strong voice. 'Find the man who did this terrible thing.'

'We will,' Atherton said, and Keaton gave him a nod and shuffled away on Whittam's motherly arm.

Atherton went downstairs to Radek's dressing-room. Some effort had been made here to soften the ecclesiastical grimness of the basement: the bare brick walls had been painted with cream gloss, and there was crimson carpet on the floor, whose sumptuousness was only marred by the number of component pieces it was in. It must have been an extremely narrow left-over – presumably a spare bit from an aisle somewhere. There was a table against one wall, with an upright chair before it and a large mirror on the wall over it, with a strip light above. A four-hook coat rail was fixed to the wall in the corner behind the door, and a dark overcoat was hanging on it – presumably Radek's. Against the wall opposite the mirror was an ancient armchair, and a smaller table on which stood a water carafe and a tumbler. Both were empty and dry, presumably put there in readiness for the evening. On the other side of the table was a minimalist two-seater sofa, upholstered in a rather loud purple and orange velours which went with the crimson carpet like sardines and blancmange. Its apparent lack of conviction as a sofa suggested it might turn into an equally unsatisfactory bed, as though performing two functions badly were the same as performing one well. On the sofa was a large, double-depth briefcase, open, and a narrow black fibreglass briefcase, closed.

A second door opposite the first led to a small, damp-smelling bathroom which contained an open-fronted shower cubicle with a fixed head and no curtain (fat lot of use, Atherton commented inwardly), a lavatory pedestal, a hand-basin fixed to the wall with a mirror above it, a thin roller-towel hanging on wooden rollers to the side of it, and a metal waste-paper basket on the floor. Still, he thought, it was luxury compared with what the orchestra had, which was two identical rooms between eighty of them, and an extra unisex loo in the passage with a wet floor and a cistern which took eighteen minutes to refill after flushing.

The light was on in Radek's bathroom; the soap and towel had been used, and in the bin there were several used tissues, a crumpled paper bag from Boots containing the outer cardboard container from a new tube of Germoloids, a smeary wad of cotton-wool, and a used baby bud. Atherton turned hastily away and went back into the dressing-room. He examined the overcoat first: navy cashmere and wool, silk lining, Austin Reed label inside. Smart but not ostentatious. In the pockets were a plastic comb, not very clean, a pair of washleather gloves, old and worn comfortable, a South Bank car park ticket dated a week ago, a handkerchief, unused, and three anonymous boiled sweets in plain wrappers, the sort that hang about in cute wicker baskets round the tills of certain restaurants.

He abandoned the coat and went to look at the two cases. The small one contained two conductor's batons in a contoured velvet interior designed to hold three. Atherton lifted out one side of the contouring, and underneath found a snapshot of a young woman on a beach holding up a very fat baby to the camera. It was obviously an old photograph: judging by the unconvincing colours and the white border round the picture he'd place it in the early seventies. There was also, curiously, a paper drinks coaster bearing in curly script the name *The*

Ootsy-Tootsy Club (shouldn't that be Hotsy-Totsy? he frowned) and underneath in small letters *Ningpo Street, Kowloon.* He turned it over. On the back in melting Biro was written *Beda* and *3–671111*, presumably a telephone number. He slipped it gently into his pocket.

The briefcase contained three scores, a notebook with a lot of musical scribble – notes in both senses on interpretations – and that day's *Grauniad*; an engagements diary pretty well filled in for the year; some correspondence from the agent concerning today's concert; a quantity of laudatory cuttings (did he read them before going on, to stiffen his resolve?); a clean pair of socks; a battered metal glasses case containing a pair of spectacles with gold frames; a sponge bag containing toothbrush, toothpaste, nail brush, face-cloth, dental floss and baby buds; a packet of laxative chewing-gum, opened, one stick missing; a packet of twelve Phensic, opened, two missing; a packet of twenty-four Actal, opened, six missing; and a bottle of milk of magnesia, in its box, but half empty and very crusty about the neck, as though it were regularly swigged from rather than poured into a spoon.

'A regular little pharmacopoeia,' Atherton said aloud.

'That's one word for him,' said Des, appearing at the open door at that moment. 'Des for Desirable' he sometimes introduced himself, and he wasn't quite joking; and somehow – irritatingly – his conviction that women couldn't resist him tended to be borne out by women themselves. He was tall and well-built, with glossy, insistent black eyes, and if he wasn't handsome he at least had thick dark hair and all his own teeth, which gleamed between full lips and in contrast with his year-round, gypsy-swarthy tan. He was wearing today an almost transparent cheesecloth shirt, artfully tight across his pectorals and open far enough down to reveal a glimpse of black shiny hair with a cute little solid gold ingot on a chain nestling amongst it. His trousers were also tight enough to have made further contraception unnecessary, outlining his fierce gluteal muscles behind and leaving everything to be desired at the front.

Atherton knew him by reputation from Joanna and one or two other musicians, and had met him a few times when hanging around waiting for Joanna, with or without Slider.

He was friendly enough, so secure in his own irresistibility that he didn't regard other men as rivals but as also-rans.

'Hullo,' Atherton said. 'Did you want me?'

'Come for the old bugger's goods and chattels,' Des said, gesturing towards the briefcases. 'Old Buster's howling for 'em.'

'I thought he'd gone.'

'Got as far as the cab and realised he'd left 'em behind. Didn't want anyone pawing through the Holy Grail, so Tony asked me to come and get 'em.'

'I'll have to make a note of the contents first,' Atherton said. 'It looks as though he was a bit of a hypochondriac,' he added, glancing at the pills he still held in his hands. Des after all was the person in the orchestra who probably had most to do with Radek.

'Tell me about it! The ailments were as unattractive as the man: constipation, piles, bad breath!'

'By his works shall ye know him,' Atherton suggested.

'Yeah,' Des said with enthusiasm. 'That's what made him late this afternoon, you know – one of the things.'

'What, bad breath?'

Des grinned. 'He was stuck on the loo, moaning. I came in looking for him just as he was coming out with his tube of Germoloids in his hand. Old Buster was furious. He's a real vicar's daughter, Buster – doesn't like the mention of anything rude like toilets or botties, especially in connection with His Majesty. Screamed at me like a parrot when I came in – "Can't you knock?" As if I didn't know enough about his precious lord and master! I felt like telling him a few truths!'

'What sort of truths?'

Des looked sly. 'Well, it's me he comes to for his little comforts when we're on tour – Buster wouldn't approve. I always have to have a couple of cans of lager waiting for him when he comes off – and the odd spot of something stronger.'

'Like what, for instance?' Atherton asked.

The dark eyelashes fluttered down delicately. 'Well, I can't tell you, can I, you being a copper? But let's say it's white and you can smoke it, but it ain't Rothmans.'

'That's all right,' Atherton said. 'That's nothing to do with me. What else did you get for him?'

'He asked me to get him girls sometimes. Or boys, depending

where we were. I didn't much care for that,' he added, giving Atherton a full stare, 'but my job wouldn't last long if I crossed the maestros, so I just shut my mouth and do my best. Of course, he tipped me well, but money doesn't make up for being used as a pimp, does it?'

Atherton agreed sincerely, while mentally recalibrating the words. He was pretty sure that Des would do anything in the world for a sufficient wad of wonga, and never turn a hair. 'So he was bisexual, was he?'

Des shrugged. 'Not really. More like indiscriminate. He was married once, you know,' he added, 'but his wife died. There was a bit of a scandal about that at the time, I don't know if you remember, because she committed suicide. Don't blame her, though. Imagine waking up married to him.'

'You didn't like him, then?'

'He was a disgusting old man. I didn't like having to hang around him saying yes sir, no sir. Treated people like dirt. He was vindictive too. There's quite a few people in the business he's ruined. He's even tried to get rid of Spaz, the poor little bleeder, but I struck at that,' he finished proudly. 'Told him Spaz was my assistant and nobody but me was going to sack him. He took it from me, because he knew I meant what I said. And he knew I knew too much about him. But I've kept Spaz out of his face ever since.'

'What did Spaz do to annoy him?' Atherton asked.

'Old Radek wanted to have a little feel of the family jewels one time, and Spaz refused him,' Des said. 'Mind you, I told Spaz it was his own fault for going in there on his own. He should have come to me. I'd told him that more than once. Let me deal with the temperamental ones, I said. I suppose he got ambitious.' He suddenly remembered his errand. 'Gawd, what am I doing standing here chatting? Buster'll be foaming at the mouth. Here, give us the bags, will you.'

'I've nearly finished,' Atherton said, writing unhurriedly. 'Go on talking. I'm sure there's lots you can tell me about the late lamented. Like who wanted to kill him, for instance.'

'Can't help you there,' Des said cheerily, 'though if I meet the bastard that did it I'll buy him a pint. Anyway, you know where to find me.'

'If you think of anything, anything at all—'

'Yeah. I'll call you,' Des said. 'I've watched the cops shows on the telly. It's always the most obvious suspect that done it, but that puts me at the head of the queue, and it wasn't me.'

Atherton stared reflectively into the space left by the humper's departure. 'The world's a stage, the light is in one's eyes,' he mused, 'the auditorium is extremely dark. The more dishonest get the larger rise; the more offensive make the greater mark. Right on, Hilaire old son. Dog bites man, no story; but it seems some or other man has bitten back.' He sighed. 'I only fear we may be going to be spoilt for choice.'

CHAPTER THREE

Do Not Go, Gentle, into that Good Knight

'How did you get on with the verger?' Slider asked, placating the inner man with a cheese salad roll. Because of the call-out he'd missed lunch entirely, one of the few things to be grateful for that day.

Atherton had a smoked salmon sandwich, but that was Atherton all over. 'He's not going to be much use on the description front. He didn't really get much of a look at the bloke, what with the dim lighting, the hat and the haste.'

'Sounds like the title of a detective novel. Are we going to get a videofit out of it?'

''Fraid not. All he can tell us is that the bloke was wearing a camel-coloured duffel coat and a brown trilby-type hat with a wide brim. He was young, say between eighteen and twenty-eight, white, and slightly built.'

'Terrific.'

'Narrows the field to, say, about thirteen million people.' Atherton stretched out his legs and crossed his ankles, reaching behind him to the window-sill where he'd put his cup. 'But the duffel coat may help. Who wears a duffel coat nowadays?'

'Bird watchers?'

'Sartorial ignoramuses. Talking of which—' He broke off as the door opened and McLaren put his head around it.

'There was a phone message for you earlier, guv.' He looked at the remains of Slider's cheese roll as automatically as a construction worker looks at a passing woman's chest. 'A Mrs Hislop-Ivory, and would you phone her back.'

'I don't know any Hislop-Ivory. What was it about?'

'She didn't say.'

'Did she leave a number?'

'Er, no.'

'Are you sure of the name?'

'I wrote it down,' he said, as though that helped.

'Oh well, I suppose she'll ring again if it's important.' Hislop-Ivory sounded like fund-raising, or a complaint about neighbours' parking. 'Is Mr Barrington in?'

'Just came in, guv,' McLaren said, glad to be helpful.

'I thought I smelled the brimstone,' Atherton murmured. When McLaren had gone, he said, 'Anyway, to resume, the verger didn't see the bloke come in. He may even have been there for some time, hovering around in the back – though I doubt it. If you were going to shoot someone, you wouldn't hang around beforehand waiting to be recognised, would you?'

'Not unless you were trying to screw up your courage,' Slider suggested. 'When did the verger first see the villain?'

'He was up in the gallery checking on the seating for the concert when he suddenly remembered the door onto the street from that passage that runs down the side of the church.'

'Yes, I know it.'

'Well, he couldn't remember if he'd locked the door, and he didn't want people to be able to wander in off the street and down to the dressing-rooms without being seen. So he came down from the gallery, crossed the church – the stairway to the gallery is on the opposite side from the passage—'

'And was the villain there, then?'

'He didn't see him. So probably no. He went through into the passage, checked the street door – which was locked, by the way – and then came back out into the body of the church. That's when he first saw chummy, standing in the centre aisle, level with the last row of chairs.'

'Doing what?'

'Just standing there with his hands in his pockets, looking at the orchestra. Verger goes past him, heading back towards the gallery to finish the job he was doing; so his back's to chummy now. He's just reached the door when he hears the gunshot. Verger looks round at chummy, sees him with the gun in his hand, just standing there staring, presumably at Radek. Frozen – as is the verger – with fright. Then chummy turns and legs it, stuffing the gun into his pocket as he goes, and out through the street door. Verger hesitates, wondering if he should give chase—'

'I should bloody well think not,' Slider said. 'Chasing armed killers can seriously damage your health.'

'Civilians don't always think as clearly as us,' said Atherton. 'Anyway, he decided his duty was to the living and ran the other way.'

'So the likelihood is that the killer came in during the moments when the verger was checking the passage door. Straight in and out job.' He frowned in thought.

'So what now?' Atherton said after a moment.

'As I see it,' Slider said, 'Radek was a famous man, and shootings are rare. Possibilities are that the killer was (a) a random homicidal maniac who wandered in off the street, (b) a non-random homicidal maniac like the one who killed John Lennon, (c) someone who knew Radek and had a beef against him, and (d) someone doing it on someone else's behalf. Now given that (a) and (b) are the least likely, thank God, in this country, (c) is still the most likely, by several streets.'

'But there's still a chance it could be (d).'

'A chance. But what sort of hired killer does the job in broad daylight in front of a hundred witnesses? And shooting from that distance? Hand-guns are notoriously inaccurate. From that distance he could just as easily have missed as hit the target.'

'Yes, but (d) doesn't have to be a hired killer in the professional sense. It could be someone acting on somebody's behalf without their knowledge – taking revenge for them or something.'

'Yes, it's possible. My bet is that it will turn out to be a domestic, though.'

'I'd still like to compile a list of all the people who had a grudge against him.'

'From what we've heard, it'll be a long list.' He screwed up the bag his roll had come in and potted it into the bin. 'Let's see how Anderson has got on with the computer. Then I shall have to go and see Mr Barrington.'

As he entered the Hall of the Demon King, Slider thought Barrington was looking strained and unwell. He was walking up and down the room in his usual menacing way, but there was something jerky and irritable about the movement; and when he turned and placed his hands on the desk to lean on them and glare, Slider saw that his cuticles were ragged, as though he'd been biting them. He wondered privately if Mad Ivan were cracking up at last. All that suppressed anger must eventually rot your brain.

It was Slider who had asked to see Barrington, but Barrington got in first. 'You do realise, I hope, that this station, like every other, has to run on a budget?'

'Yes, sir.'

'And that misappropriation of publicly owned resources is theft, plain and simple. You understand that?'

'Sir,' said Slider neutrally. Wisps of steam were beginning to emerge from Barrington's ears. Slider tucked his head down in anticipation of the explosion.

Barrington straightened up to his full impressive height. 'I walked into the CID room yesterday afternoon and found one of your firm – Mackay – making a private telephone call to his wife. He finished it fairly rapidly when he saw me, of course, but after he put the receiver down I waited in vain for him to offer to pay for the call. I'm still waiting. I suppose it's too much to hope that he's made the offer to you?'

Slider was put off his stroke. 'The men sometimes have to phone home to say they're going to be late, sir—'

'It's still a private call, made on the office phone.'

'I'm sure they don't abuse the privilege—'

'Privilege! Is that what you call it?' Barrington paced, and Slider watched. This had the flavour of psychosis about it, all right, full and fruity. 'I call it dishonesty. Theft is theft, and there's no difference in kind between stealing the price of a phone call and stealing from the petty cash. It's only a matter of degree.'

'It has been the custom, sir—' Slider began hopelessly, but Barrington whipped round and glared at him.

'The custom to condone theft? I think not. It has been slackness. Indiscipline. Carelessness. Officers of the law, whatever their rank, must be scrupulous in their behaviour, at all times, and at all levels. From now on, there will be *no* private telephone calls made on office telephones.'

'Sir.'

'If they want to call their wives or girlfriends or mothers or bookmakers, they can go downstairs and use the payphone. That's what it's there for. Do you understand?'

'Sir,' Slider said again. It was all very depressing. The man had clearly lost touch with reality. Once Slider told the troops, they'd dial till they puked out of sheer defiance, and he'd have to avoid catching them at it.

'This applies to all ranks,' Barrington snapped, perhaps detecting some slight lack of enthusiasm in Slider's mien.

'I understand, sir,' said Slider. 'May I talk to you about something else now? I did want to report on the Radek murder case.'

Barrington looked blank for a moment, like a man who's been smacked on the side of the head unexpectedly by a golf-ball. Then he sat down abruptly at his desk. 'I was wondering when you'd get round to that,' he said sharply. 'Well, carry on.'

Sighing inwardly, Slider carried on.

'Forensic aren't going to be able to help us on this one,' he concluded. 'There's nothing at the scene to identify the killer amongst all the hundreds of footprints and fingerprints. We've interviewed everyone who was present, but all the accounts are pretty much the same and no-one has much to contribute. Only the verger was close enough even to get a glimpse of the face under the hat, and he didn't see enough to know the man again. But we'll assemble what description we can, and we've started the door-to-door. I think this is a case where posters may help, too – someone must have seen him in the street either before or afterwards. We could be ready to go on the television for this evening's news, the local for preference, if you think it's worth it with what little we've got.'

He paused enquiringly, but Barrington only stared at him briefly as though he hadn't been listening, and then said, 'Go on.'

Slider continued. 'In case it was a random killing we've run a computer check, but nothing's come up. Description and MO don't tally with anyone on the streets at the moment – though that doesn't rule out someone with no record, of course.'

Barrington grunted.

'The post is scheduled for tomorrow afternoon. We had a bit of trouble, Freddie Cameron being away on holiday, what with the general shortage of forensic pathologists. But at least it ought to be quite straightforward – there's no mystery about the cause of death, after all. Anyway, there's a man at Thomas's, name of James: he's young but he's got some gunshot wound experience—'

'James? Yes. I know him.' Slider made a politely enquiring noise. 'I met him once or twice when I was up in Nottingham.' The Nottingham forensic lab dealt with all the specialist firearms enquiries outside the Met area. 'He's a good man. I didn't know he was at Thomas's now.'

Slider nodded and continued. 'Regarding the gun, sir, I've got two teams combing the area at the moment – front gardens, basements, rubbish bins and so on – but in view of the fact that chummy put the piece in his pocket, I'm not hopeful. In my experience either they throw it away immediately in a panic, or they hang on to it and dump it or stash it when they get home. And we don't know where home may be, of course. But my gut feeling is that this murder will probably turn out to be a domestic, and it's just a matter of finding out who wanted him dead. I think once we talk to the family we'll latch onto something fairly quickly.'

Barrington stopped at that, and turned to look at Slider thoughtfully, pulling out his lower lip with his finger and thumb in the unattractive way of someone who doesn't realise he's doing it.

'You see this as an old-fashioned police job, do you?' he asked suddenly.

Slider was puzzled. 'Sir?'

'This case. Means, motive and opportunity. Dedicated plodding. Is that how you see it?'

Slider hadn't a clue what he was talking about, and he didn't like it. This was so unlike Barrington-talk he had an obscure sense of trouble approaching.

'I wouldn't say that exactly, sir,' he said cautiously. 'All I mean is that I don't think it was a random killing. It might be as simple as money. From what I understand of the music world, conductors earn a lot of money. Radek must have been a very wealthy man.'

'I've had a call, you see, from Bob Moston at 6 AMIP,' Barrington said.

'I see,' said Slider non-committally. The Area Major Incident Pool handled the particularly complex or high-profile cases. It remained to be seen whether this would prove to be either, but a glory-hungry AMIP boss or a responsibility-shy local boss might insist on passing the case upwards.

'Radek was rather a media honey last year,' Barrington went on, 'though he's not particularly in the news at the moment.' He will be after today, Slider thought. 'But you just never know with the press. There's a romantic side to it – the single shot fired in a dark church – which might catch their imagination. On the other hand—'

He let it hang. On the other hand, Slider filled in for himself, it might be cast into the shade by a newly discovered Soap Star's Secret Love-Nest Shock, or MP In Baby Alligator Abuse Scandal.

'Is Mr Moston anxious to take the case, sir?' Slider asked.

Barrington looked surprised. 'Oh. No. On the contrary. Two of his SIOs are *hors de combat* at the moment.' French yet, thought Slider. 'And the other three are already involved in more than one case each. He's asking whether we're likely to be sending this case up to him, because he'd probably have to tackle it himself if we did. So I want your assessment. Can you handle it here?'

If you leave me alone, I can. Slider, the brave captain, tilted his clean-cut English chin at the stern and critical general. 'I think so, sir. At the moment there's no media pressure, and we've no reason yet to think it's going to be a sticker. I've got a good team, and Atherton's pretty *au fait* with the music scene.' You're not the only one who knows French, chum.

'You – er – have a contact in the orchestra concerned, I believe?' Barrington said with unexpected delicacy. 'Is that likely to cause a problem?'

How the hell did he know that? 'Quite the contrary, sir.' He couldn't really risk *au contraire*, not so soon. 'It should be a useful source of information. Though I must point out that there's no indication the orchestra was anything but an accidental witness.'

'Very well. We'll keep the case, then. And we'll keep off the television for the time being. I think the likelihood of gain is outweighed by the disadvantage of the publicity.' Barrington got up and began pacing again. 'And I'll handle the press on this one. I want you to have a free hand.'

Free to win fame or to fuck up. 'Thank you, sir,' Slider said.

Barrington paced, and Slider began to feel restless. He had better things to do than to wait on Mad Ivan's thought processes.

'Will that be all, sir?' he prompted, Jeeves-like.

Barrington turned and stared thoughtfully at him. 'Yes. Carry on. But don't forget what I said. Discipline, and attention to detail. You can't run a successful campaign without them.'

'Yes, sir,' Slider said dutifully, and removed himself. Definitely cracking up, he thought. And who was likely to get the rubble coming down on his head?

Radek's house, now the house of sorrow, was one of those large, handsome, four-storeyed, nineteenth-century town-houses, white stone rendering over yellow London brick, porch with white pillars, steps up over a semi-basement. It was one of a terrace set back a little from Holland Park Avenue, with a private access road divided from the common pavement by iron railings, a shrubbery and a row of ancient plane trees seventy feet high. They soared with magnificent disproportion over the little cars and the little people down in the street, like members of an alien culture so advanced it did not even need to acknowledge the host infestation.

Inside the house was gracious and beautiful in a way that you simply had to be born to money to achieve. Slider appreciated, but knew he could never have emulated it, even if he won the pools. It was as many light years away from the Sunday supplement, Marilyn Cripps good-taste of Irene's wistful dreams as *that* was from the Ruislip Moderne she was fleeing so hard, poor thing. And oddly enough, Buster Keaton fitted into it, and looked not nearly so odd amidst the quiet elegance as he had in the ordinary world. He was short, stout and shiningly bald, but his features held the remnants of what must once have been a remarkable beauty, and he moved among the glowing treasures with the ease of custom.

'Yes, it is a lovely house,' Keaton said, leading Slider into the first-floor drawing-room. 'I have been very happy here. I count myself fortunate to have been able to share all this, as well as the life of a great genius.' In himself he was immaculate, clean enough to have eaten off, and even indoors and at a time like this was dressed in grey flannels with a knife-edge crease, pale blue shirt, striped tie and navy blazer.

'Was Sir Stefan a genius?' Slider asked. Keaton looked at him sharply, and he smiled disarmingly. 'I'm afraid I don't know much about music.'

Keaton examined him for bona fides, and his hackles slowly lowered. 'Yes. Yes, he was a genius. It's a word that's over-used and often misapplied, but in his case it was justified. He was a man of rare and extraordinary talent. Of course like most geniuses he was misunderstood by lesser people.'

'In what way?'

'Oh, they sometimes thought him rude and intolerant. I've heard the things people say – musicians – but they didn't understand. He lived to serve Music: he didn't have the time or energy to worry about their petty feelings.' He settled himself on the end of a chaise-longue, sitting very upright, his back unsupported, and waved Slider to a chair. 'Of course his dedication took its toll of him. Not that he counted the cost: he never spared himself. But it was killing him.'

'Killing him?'

Keaton's large pale eyes seemed to widen further. 'His heart,' he said. 'He was not a well man. I've been trying for eighteen months to persuade him to do less, to go into semi-retirement, but he couldn't live without his work. "If I go tomorrow," he'd say to me, "I want to go with my stick in my hand."' Slider began to detect a very faint residual Yorkshire accent in the otherwise cultured tones. It seemed to grow with the increasing cosiness of the prose-style. 'I warned him. I said, "You're not as young as you used to be. Take it easy," I said. "Does it matter if you do one concert a week instead of two or three?" Well, he did slow down a bit, but not as much as I wanted him to. And now—' the eyes shone with tears, 'and now he's gone, even if it was the way he wanted.' He had to pause a moment to regain control. 'He could have gone at any time, I knew that,' he went on, shaking his head slowly. 'I shouldn't be surprised.'

Slider was sitting forward, hands clasped between his knees, staring at the carpet while he listened. Now he looked up. 'But it wasn't his heart that killed him, Mr Keaton.'

For a moment Keaton looked quite blank, as though he'd been spoken to in a foreign language. Then he drew out a handkerchief and slowly and carefully wiped his eyes. 'No,' he said. 'I was forgetting. You must forgive me. This has been such a dreadful shock for me, I hardly know what I'm thinking.'

'You'd been with Sir Stefan a long time,' said Slider, to get him going again.

'More than forty years,' he answered with a touch of mournful pride. 'It was June 1953 when my wife and I joined him. Of course he wasn't *Sir* Stefan in those days, but he was already world-famous. We came as a couple. My wife was cook-housekeeper and I was chauffeur-handyman.'

'Your wife?'

A gleam of something appeared in the depths of Keaton's eyes at the interjection – perhaps annoyance or even amusement that Slider had obviously been writing him down as a lifelong bachelor.

'My wife Doreen died in 1960.' He spread his hands in a little deprecatory gesture. 'I was not always as you see me now. In my youth I was thought quite handsome. Let me show you.'

He got up and went across the room to a bureau, opened a drawer, and took out a large photograph album. As he walked back, he turned the pages over and then turned it round and presented it to Slider open, holding it for him rather than entrusting it to his grasp. Alone on the page was an eleven-by-eight black-and-white print of a smiling young woman in the rolled-over hairstyle and high-shouldered print dress of the forties. Her arm was linked through that of a young man in a double-breasted suit, his thin light hair Brylcreemed down and his pale eyes almost disappearing by some trick of the light. They were standing on grass and amid shrubs, and in the background was part of a building, the sort of vast Victorian pile which usually turned out to be either a private school or a lunatic asylum – not, Slider thought, that there was always much difference. Yes, he had been good-looking. A little on the short side, perhaps, but women didn't usually mind that too much.

'What's this place?' he asked.

'Fitzpayne School,' Keaton replied. 'Not my *alma mater*, I hasten to add. I taught there after the war.'

'Classics?' Slider suggested, following the Latin clue.

Again that faint gleam. 'Biology. Botany was my subject, but I taught zoology as well. I shouldn't have liked to be known as The Bot Master.'

Slider smiled dutifully at what was obviously a well-rehearsed joke. He could just see Keaton telling it daringly over the sherry at parents' evenings, to indulgent and faintly shocked laughter.

'What did you do during the war?'

'I was at university. Cambridge. I did research there for the Ministry of Food as part of my degree – how to make two ears of wheat grow where one grew before, that sort of thing.'

It was said defensively, as though he had been accused of dodging the call-up. Slider decided to ease one sting with another. 'You're obviously an educated man. What made you give up teaching to become a chauffeur? Didn't you find it rather a come-down to go into service?'

Keaton looked away for a moment, and Slider thought he might have gone too far; but after a moment he said, without apparent offence, 'I didn't enjoy teaching. I didn't really like children, you see, especially little boys – their minds are so undisciplined. And then I decided I wanted to write. I suppose most of us feel we have a book in us somewhere, don't we?' Slider assented dishonestly. He had never had the least urge to write – real life, at least in his case, being a lot stranger than fiction.

'But of course I needed some kind of employment to keep me until I made my fortune,' Keaton went on with a little self-deprecatory smile, 'and when I saw the advertisement for a couple for Sir Stefan's house, it seemed like the answer to a prayer. Accommodation was such a problem after the war, you see, with so much of the housing stock destroyed by the Blitz and no money left in the kitty to replace it. Doreen and I looked at some rooms, but the ones we could have afforded would have given me acute spiritual pain to live in.'

Slider nodded sympathetically. 'And the advertisement related to this house, did it?'

'Yes. The Radeks had just moved in here. His wife, Lady Susan, inherited it from her father.' He smiled faintly. 'When I took the job on, I looked on it as a part-time job. I thought I'd have plenty of time to myself to write. But it was impossible to live under the same roof as Sir Stefan and stay aloof, especially after his wife died. Little by little I was drawn in, and eventually – when Doreen died as well – he became my whole life.' His eyes were distant again, and shining. 'Serving him so that he could serve Music. It was a great cause. I have been part of something noble and valuable. My life has not been wasted.'

The old-fashioned ideal of service, Slider thought, half amused, half admiring. Nowadays no-one would publicly espouse it for fear of being thought a prat, though it was still what drew most of the recruits into the police service. But the fashion was to claim to be cynical and self-serving. It was quite refreshing talking to old Buster, he thought.

'Tell me about Sir Stefan,' he asked now. 'He wasn't English, was he?'

Keaton gave Slider a sharp look. 'He was a British citizen, and proud of it,' he said almost crossly. 'He was knighted for his services to music, and they don't give knighthoods to foreigners, you know.'

'I'm sorry, I didn't mean to suggest – but his name doesn't sound English. I thought I read somewhere that he was of Czech origin.'

'Polish,' Keaton corrected shortly. 'But he took nationality in 1950. He came to England with his mother after the fall of Poland, when his father was killed. Stefan joined the infantry in 1940 and fought right through the war. He finished as a major and won the MC. He had a very good war.' Keaton was obviously immensely proud of Radek's record. Slider had the feeling he'd get shown the medals if he wasn't careful. 'He didn't have to fight, you know. They wouldn't have called him up. And he risked more than most people to do it, because he was already a brilliant musician. Imagine if he'd been blinded, or deafened, or lost a hand? For him, it was a great personal sacrifice to put his career to one side for five years.'

'And why did he?'

'Duty,' said Keaton simply. 'He felt that music couldn't exist in the same world with the Nazis. To give himself to music would be pointless if they were not destroyed.'

A truly noble, selfless man, Slider thought. Can this be the same Radek I've been hearing about, or is it just a case of power corrupting absolutely?

'Did he have any family? His wife is dead, I think you said?'

'Lady Susan died in 1959. It was tragic – they were devoted, you know. He never married again. There was just one child, Fenella – but she's always called Fay. She was born in 1950.

She married Alec Coleraine, the solicitor, and they've just the one son, Marcus.'

'How did Sir Stefan get on with them? Were they close?'

Keaton pursed his lips. 'Stefan adored Fay, but she was always a headstrong girl, and they often quarrelled. He didn't want her to marry Alec Coleraine – didn't think he was good enough for her – which he wasn't in my opinion. But she waited until she was twenty-one and then told her father he couldn't stop her any more. Well, Stefan put a brave face on it, and they were always very loving when they met without Alec, but if Alec was around there was friction.' He paused as though hearing himself, and added, 'It was nothing serious, though, just family bickerings.'

'It happens in the best of families,' Slider said reassuringly.

Keaton went on confidentially. 'Stefan didn't like the way they were bringing up Marcus. Between them they spoiled him, gave him everything he wanted, and when Sir Stefan tried to instil a bit of discipline in the boy, they'd take his side. So of course, he always knew he could appeal to his mother and father against his grandfather, and there's nothing spoils a child quicker. Sir Stefan did his best; he wanted Marcus to come and stay with us much more often, but Alec wouldn't let him. I'm afraid,' he added, as though forced to reveal a deeply unpalatable truth, 'that Alec Coleraine doesn't regard music as a proper thing to spend one's life on. Marcus could have been a talented soloist, but his father thought it was prissy to play the violin. He wanted him to go into a profession and make lots of money – as if that was the test of manhood, how many zeros you have in your bank balance. Well, he's only got himself to blame if the boy's turning out wild.' He sighed. 'But it all added to the strain on Stefan. It all helped wear him out.'

'Has there been any specific cause of quarrel between them recently?' Slider asked.

Keaton opened his eyes wide. 'Good lord no! This is just ordinary family tensions I'm talking about. I hope you aren't suggesting that Alec Coleraine would ever dream of—?' The tears came again quite suddenly. 'Oh dear, I'm sorry. Just for a minute I'd forgotten. I just can't believe he's – the thought of *anyone* doing such a thing is so very—'

He disappeared into his handkerchief.

'This is all so distressing for you,' Slider said kindly after a moment. 'Can I make you a cup of tea or something? If you just tell me where the kitchen is—?'

'Oh, no, no thank you,' Keaton said through the muffling folds. In a moment he re-emerged, blew his nose and straightened his shoulders and his tie, with his generation's desire always to keep up appearance. 'No, I'll do it. I should have offered you something, I'm sorry. Will you have some tea now? Or would you like something stronger?'

Slider thought it would give the old man time and privacy to compose himself, so he said, 'Thank you, tea would be very nice. Are you sure I can't make it for you?'

'No, no, that would never do. Besides, I know where everything is. I shan't be long.'

He went out, and Slider stood up and walked across to look out of the window. Here at the back of the house was a handsome, high-walled garden with several magnificent trees, and a stretch of lawn which curved back and forth round borders and archipelagos of herbaceous plants and shrubs. From ground level, he thought, it would present an artfully simple appearance of intriguing vistas and inviting walks. He could see that the planting had been done to present blocks of sympathetic colour in the way that was fashionable nowadays: no cottage-garden riot of oranges, purples and yellows, no eye-bashing cheerfulness of vermilion muddled up with magenta. Just below him, for instance, was a long bed planted with nothing but blue flowers set amongst silvery foliage: at the back tall spires of delphinium, rocket and Mexican lupins were having their second flowering; in front of them pale flax, deep-blue cornflowers and feathery love-in-a-mist; and to the front of the bed the lower-growing blue salvia, cherry pie, cranesbill, and an edging of clumps of campanula. It was exquisite and restful, the outdoor equivalent of the cool, elegant drawing-room he was standing in.

That was the kind of gardening that he'd always wanted the time and space to do, and never had. It was the frustrated architect in him, he supposed. When he was younger, when he'd had time to spare, he'd enjoyed going to visit great houses and walking round their gardens, gathering ideas. It had bored the children rigid, though Irene had liked looking round the houses, as long as they were fully furnished and no older than eighteenth century. But she had no interest in gardening – or anything to do with the outdoors, really. She, having been born there, saw no romance in the countryside: she regarded it with suspicion and dislike as a source of mud, creepy-crawlies and rude animals. To her the modern world was the apogee of civilisation, for there was no need for a person ever to step out of doors (except from building to car and car to building again) or to encounter the inconveniently dirty habits of old mother Gaia. A centrally-heated, double-glazed conservatory was as near to God in a garden as she wanted to get.

Well, he thought, now she'd gone and the garden was his to do again. Perhaps a resuscitation of his interest in gardening would help to fill all the lonely hours ahead of him. It looked as though it would have to do it for Buster, who seemed to have nothing else.

A sound made Slider turn. He saw Keaton coming in with a large tray, and hastened over in case he needed a table cleared. But Keaton anticipated the move and said, 'I can manage quite well, thank you. I'm used to this.'

He had tidied away the evidence of his tears, but he looked frightfully old and worn – pale in cheek and blue-shadowed around the eyes. I wouldn't be surprised, Slider thought, if the old boy didn't last much longer. It was often the way when people lived closely together for a long time, that one could not outlive the other.

'I'm sorry to have to put you through this,' Slider said. 'Just a few more questions, and then I'll leave you in peace.'

'You must do your job,' Keaton said, sorting out the tray. 'We all have to do our duty. How do you like your tea?'

When they were both settled with their cups, Slider said, 'I'd like you to tell me, if you would, about Sir Stefan's friends. Who was there who was close to him?'

Keaton shook his head almost reprovingly. 'You've got the wrong idea. I told you he was dedicated to his work; it took up all his time and his spiritual energy. There was nothing left over for anything else. Friends, socialising and such, would have been a useless drain on him. He didn't have time to go to *parties*, you know.' He spoke the word witheringly. 'It was all he could do to keep up with his daughter and her family.'

'But he couldn't spend every moment of every day working?'

'Indeed he could,' Keaton said. 'You have no idea the amount of preparation that has to go into giving a concert. Studying the music, reading, learning the score, communing with his spirit, preparing himself to give *of* himself so that the great work of a man long dead might come to life again. Even the time he was forced to spend giving interviews, having his photograph taken, making speeches, attending banquets – all that sort of thing – he deeply begrudged.' He looked at Slider sternly. 'It's not just a matter of standing up and wiggling a stick, you know. That's the trouble with the world today – everything is slipshod, everything is geared to what will just do. It's not "how good can I make it", it's "how little can I get away with" – even amongst professional musicians. There's no dedication to excellence any more.'

He was getting annoyed. Slider hastened to placate him. 'I know he must have been a dedicated man. But surely he must sometimes have had to relax and – recharge the batteries, so to speak.'

Keaton shrugged. 'To stay quietly here at home was enough. A simple meal, civilised conversation, a walk in the garden – they were his pleasures. He didn't hanker after the noise and racket of the modern world.'

Slider swallowed that with his tea. 'The garden is magnificent,' he said.

'Sir Stefan loved it. It was my pleasure to create a beautiful place for him to rest in.'

'Are you the gardener? I'm impressed.'

Keaton gave a modest smile. 'Gardening has always been my great love, and my relaxation. Sir Stefan generously gave me a free hand.'

'He couldn't have regretted it. It's beautiful,' Slider said, and Keaton warmed in the obvious sincerity.

'I have help,' he confessed. 'A man comes in to mow the lawn and do the heavy work. But what you see is my creation. I still plant and prune and propagate. And I do a little research work now and then, just to keep my mind active. Stefan built me a large greenhouse and shed down at the bottom. I'm trying to develop a new iris.' His mouth trembled. 'If it was accepted, I was going to name it after him. Oh dear!'

'I'm astonished you've had time to keep the garden looking so lovely, as well as looking after Sir Stefan.'

'Oh, I didn't go everywhere with him. To concerts, yes, but

not always to rehearsals and recording sessions. So I have a little time for my other tasks. I do the cooking; you know, when we're at home, take care of his clothes, keep his personal correspondence – not that there's much of that. It's enough to keep me busy.' He had slipped back into the present tense. Adjustment was not going to come easily to him, Slider thought with compassion.

'Did you always go with him on tour?'

'Always. He couldn't have done without me for more than a few hours. And it was doubly important that someone who understood his delicate state of health was on hand.'

On the spur of the moment Slider decided to slip one in. 'What is the Ootsy Tootsy Club?' he asked casually.

Keaton's eyes snapped to attention. 'I don't know what you mean.'

'It's in Hong Kong. You went to Hong Kong recently, didn't you?'

'Last October. A triumphant tour – but exhausting. The heat and humidity never suited him.'

'And the Ootsy Tootsy Club?'

'I don't know any such club,' Keaton said coldly. 'Why should you think I do? It sounds ridiculous. What has it to do with anything?'

Slider said soothingly, 'It's impossible in these cases to tell what might be helpful. We often have to ask what seem like pointless questions.'

'Have to? Why do you have to?' Keaton said irritably.

'We have to find out who killed him. You want us to catch the man who did it, don't you?'

'Will it bring Stefan back to life?' Keaton said petulantly. 'Then no, I don't care about it. Leave him to his conscience and to God.'

'I'm afraid we're not allowed to do that,' Slider said gently. He stood up. 'I won't trouble you any more now, Mr Keaton, but I may have to come back another time. I hope you won't mind.'

Keaton shrugged. 'I shall be here. There's nowhere else to go now, anyway.'

On the way to the door Slider said, 'Oh, by the way, I imagine that Sir Stefan must have been a very wealthy man?'

'Yes,' said Keaton without emphasis. 'His agent dealt with

the financial side of things. I suggest you talk to her about it.'

'Thank you, I will. But I wondered if you knew how his property was left. Had he made a Will?'

'Oh yes, some time ago. There was nothing complicated about it. This house and most of the contents come to me. Everything else goes to his daughter.'

'Bah, humbug!' Atherton said, perching himself precariously on the edge of his overflowing desk.

'Thank you, Ebenezer. Would you care to be more specific?'

'Radek, a selfless, dedicated genius? Bah, humbug!'

'Oh, that. You members of the younger generation are distressingly cynical. I've often thought it.'

'Anyone'd be cynical after what I've been hearing about Radek from various members of the orchestra. Whose version is right, I wonder, the dresser's or the musicians'?'

Slider shrugged. 'As in all things, the truth probably lies somewhere between the two.'

'Perhaps, but what about Radek's naughty habits? Do you think Keaton didn't know about them, or didn't want to know? Or was Des Riley making it all up?'

'He saw red when I mentioned the club in Hong Kong,' Slider said. 'I think he didn't want to know, because it interfered with his vision of holiness.'

'You didn't think it was all a bit too good to be true, Buster's hero-worship?' Atherton suggested.

'Oh no. I think he's genuine. But it's possible he needed to believe Radek was a saint, to make himself feel more important. Otherwise he was just a glorified domestic servant. I mean, dedicating your life to someone is a bit pointless if that person isn't something out of the ordinary.'

'I dunno,' Atherton said, 'women do it all the time. And look how I've dedicated myself to you.'

'Yes, but then I am out of the ordinary.'

'True, oh King. So, how do you fancy the son-in-law for villain?'

'He's a solicitor,' Slider mentioned.

'Case proved, then,' Atherton said simply.

'Seriously!'

'Seriously, the daughter does stand to inherit a fairish fortune

– though owing to that wicked Married Woman's Property Act, it remains hers to dispose of.'

'The good old money motive,' said Slider. 'I always feel more comfortable when we get down to the *cui bono*. But the daughter's got the same motive as her husband, and a less legal mind.'

'Maybe it was the daughter then. Under a hat a slightly built young man could be a woman, and a gunning down in public does smack rather of female hysteria.'

'I don't know how you've lived to your ripe age, saying non-pc things like that. I wonder how much of a motive the money was, though,' Slider mused. 'We must find out what he was worth and exactly how he left it.'

'It makes you glad you've got nothing to leave,' Atherton said.

'I suppose so.' He looked at his watch. 'Just time for a quick bite before the post mortem.'

'Crown and Sceptre? It's on the way, more or less.'

'Okay. I don't know though,' Slider added, humpty-dumpty-like, as they started down the stairs, 'it would be nice to know you could go on being useful after you were dead.'

'We all do that.'

'We do?' Slider asked incautiously.

'Organic fertilizer. Nothing is wasted,' Atherton smirked. 'And think of all those maggots. Fishermen would pay good money for 'em.'

'Police humour is so childish,' Slider sighed reprovingly.

'At least it's *gentle* humour,' Atherton said, and it took Slider a moment or two to catch up with that one.

CHAPTER FOUR

The Late Ex Man

It was strange going to a post mortem and not seeing Freddie Cameron. He and Slider had known each other for years, and had worked together on many a case. In the natural course of things, since there were less than seven hundred murders a year altogether, there were few forensic pathologists with homicide experience, and since everyone wanted an expert, the same ones tended to be called in every time. It was bad luck, really, Freddie being away just at this moment. Forensic pathologists shouldn't have holidays. Slider hoped this new man knew his onions.

Things were already under way when Slider and Atherton arrived: the photographer had finished, the body had been undressed, and Mackay, as exhibits officer, was bagging the clothes. The body was now lying face-down on the slab, and the new man, James, was hovering over it. He was in his thirties, tall and powerful, with a rather pale and slightly alien face whose strangeness Slider eventually tracked down to the large pale-green eyes, which were slightly too shallow and too far apart to look as if he had originated on this planet. His brown hair was very long and straight, and he wore it in a pony-tail down his back tied with a leather thong. He also wore earrings, tiny gold star-shaped studs, and had a faint Birmingham accent, which may or may not have accounted for the other strangenesses. He was as different in looks from Freddie Cameron as could be, right down to the denims he wore under his lab coat and rubber apron; but true to his species, he was sucking a peppermint when Slider and Atherton walked in. All corpses smell: it's only a matter of how much.

'Hullo,' he said cheerfully. 'Are you the Investigating Officer? I don't think we've met before.'

Slider introduced himself and Atherton. 'Freddie usually does my posts.'

'Oh, the ineffable Freddie! Great bloke. Where is he, then?'

'On holiday. Antigua, I think.'

'Blimey, he must be doing all right. A long weekend in Selly Oak is all I can run to.'

Slider smiled. 'This could be a turning point in your career, carving a big celeb.'

'Yeah, I do nice work. I'll give him a pretty scar.' He turned briskly to his assistant. 'Okay, let's have him over.'

With the trained strength of hill rescuers, they flipped the body over onto its back, and suddenly the likeness of Sir Stefan Radek was before Slider's eyes, the familiarity of the hawk-nosed face, but an unfamiliar colour, and unmistakably dead. Only the white hair, flying and silky, looked alive – as indeed, in a way it still was. The flesh looked not like flesh, but like some extremely realistic plastic; the old-man's body, blue-white and hairless, shamefully naked, exposed in this final humiliation, was not him, exactly, but like him, as, say, a Spitting Image puppet is meant to be. Gaunt, grotesque, veined of arm and yellow of foot, it waited for the knife and the ritual disembowelment.

James surveyed it thoughtfully. 'Funny, I saw him conduct only last year, in Birmingham. Took my mum and dad. He looked like a sort of god up there, waving his arms about.'

'Sic transit,' said Atherton.

'And then some,' James returned reverently. 'And talking of transit, come and have a look at this. I've read about 'em, but I hadn't actually seen one before. Look, it's your exit wound. See that?'

While not necessarily wanting to have it personalised, Slider had a particular interest in the exit wound. 'I didn't think there was one.' He bent closer. There seemed to be a scratch-like abrasion, v-shaped in form, in the flesh padding the waist on the right side. 'Is that it? It's just a couple of scratches.'

'Ah,' said James, as though it were a personal triumph, 'but look at this.' He took up a probe and, inserting it into the apex, gently retracted a triangular flap of skin. 'There's your exit wound, see? As I said, I've read about this in the manual, but this is the first time I've actually handled one. It happens when the bullet's lost so much velocity, it only just has the force to sort of plop out through the skin; and the skin, being naturally elastic, springs back together and hides the hole. It must have been fired at extreme range.'

'I think it was,' Slider said. 'It must have been about sixty feet. So what happened to the bullet? We thought it was still inside.'

'It was in his underpants. We found it when we stripped him. Here,' and he reached over to the side table and picked up a plastic bag, in which the nasty little object reposed. 'You'll want to send that off to ballistics. Chris Priest's your man. Tell him Laddo sends his best. We've often worked on the same shooting. We were both at Nottingham in our palmy days.'

'Laddo?' Slider queried out of a fog of thought.

James made a face. 'My mother had me christened Ladislaw. What would you have done? A cruel thing to do to a helpless little babe in arms, I always thought. And talking of arms, did you notice the left hand? Nice little example of cadaveric spasm.'

'Oh yes, he was clutching the neck of his sweater, wasn't he?' Slider remembered.

'Yeah. It was the real thing all right. Had quite a job to disentangle him.'

'Isn't cadaveric spasm a sign of great emotion or fear at the time of death?' Atherton asked.

'Or violent activity,' James answered. 'You often find it in drownings for instance, where the victim's struggling to survive – bits of weed clutched in the fingers and so on. Or in assaults, of course – scraps of torn clothing. Nothing to help you here, though, I'm afraid. No nice shred of shirt with a handy name-tag sewn in to guide you to the villain.'

'I'm never that lucky,' Slider said.

'Well, let's get started. I'll have the exit wound out first,' James said, cutting himself a neat square. 'I'm making a collection of entry and exit wounds – got nearly fifty now. It won't tell us a lot we don't know already in this case, of course, but if you can tell me exactly how far away the killer was standing, and how high off the ground the victim was, I can give you an estimate of his height.'

'Thank you,' Slider said. 'Every little helps.'

The pathologist worked in silence for a while. With a few long, powerful strokes of the scalpel he opened up the corpse as easily as Slider opened his morning mail, and examined the evidence of the bullet's path. 'Well now,' he said at last, 'you see why God gave us all love-handles. This little sucker passed through the meat of the waist without touching any vital organs. Mind you, at the speed it was travelling, if it had hit any obstruction it probably would have stopped right there, but as it was, it just slipped out the other side. Hardly did any damage at all. If he'd been a young man, he'd be sitting up in his hospital bed by now yelling for Lucozade.'

'So what killed him?' Atherton asked. 'Shock?'

'One way or another, yes, I expect so. We'll see.'

'I understand he had a heart condition,' Slider said.

'That'd help, of course,' James said. 'Though he looks a fit old boy. Not bad musculature for his age. It must be a healthy way of life, waving your arms around in public.'

'It is,' Atherton said. 'Look at Monteux: at the age of ninety-two his contract with the LSO expired, and he wouldn't accept a renewal for anything less than fifteen years. Conductors are famous for living to ripe old ages.'

'If they don't get gunned down,' said Laddo, with a grin. 'I should look for a hostile critic if I were you.' He cut out the heart, took it to the sink and sliced into it, washing out the chambers and examining them. 'Well, it all looks normal to me. No sign of any heart disease.'

'Are you sure?' Slider said. 'I was definitely told he had a weak heart.'

'Quite sure. Some normal wear and deterioration, due to age, but otherwise it looks in very good shape, considering.'

'So what killed him?'

'Tell you in a minute, when I've finished. Let's get the old loaf out, shall we?'

The removal of the brain was the part Atherton liked least, and he always kept a trivial question or remark ready so that he could turn away and engage the nearest person in conversation to drown the buzzing of the bone saw. Slider, though, watched impassively. Once the first cuts had been made the corpse lost all resemblance to a human being in his eyes; but then he'd been brought up on a farm.

Some time later James straightened up, flexed his fingers

in a satisfied way, and said, 'That's it then. Syncope, caused by shock.'

'QED,' said Atherton.

'Come again?'

'Queer'e died, isn't it?'

James's face cleared. 'Oh, there's nothing mysterious about it, especially given his age. He was – what – seventy-something?'

'Seventy-two,' Slider said.

'Well, there you are, then. At his age shock is not to be sniffed at. The physical insult together with the psychological trauma of being shot were quite enough to cause the old CNS to shut down, and Bob's your uncle. It's still down to the gunshot, even if the bullet didn't hit anything vital.'

'It's still murder then,' Atherton said. 'That's a relief. I didn't want to be wasting my talents on a mere assault.'

On the way out Slider paused by Mackay. 'Anything in his pockets?'

'A handkerchief, a pencil stub and some loose change.' He displayed the plastic bags. 'Nothing interesting, guv.'

'I thought at least he'd have the decency to be harbouring a signed blackmail demand,' Atherton complained as they stepped out into the blessed fresh traffic fumes, 'or a cassette recording of a death threat. Oh well.'

'Life is never easy.'

'You speak as one who knows. Will you drive or shall I?'

'Such exquisite grammar,' Slider marvelled. 'You drive, dear. I want to think.'

'Okay. Where to?'

'Home, James. Back to the factory.'

'So Radek didn't have a heart problem,' Atherton said a moment later as they took their place in the Fulham Palace Road traffic queue. 'I wonder if Keaton made it up, or if he really believed it.'

'I think he really believed it. My bet would be that Radek told him he had a weak heart in order to keep Keaton in line. Might even have pulled the old sudden spasm stunt in the middle of an argument he was afraid he was losing. Ill health can be a wonderful weapon, and heart's the best of all. From what I've heard of him so far, it's the kind of manipulative thing Radek would pull.'

* * *

McLaren called out to Slider indistinctly as they passed the door of the CID room – indistinctly because he had his face in a chicken salad bap about the size of a baby's head. It looked like one of those circus acts where a man attempts to put his head in a lion's mouth. Slider's sympathies had always been with the lion in such cases.

'Oh, guv, that woman phoned again,' he managed to say.

'What, Mrs Hislop-Ivory? Did you take her number this time?'

He looked blank. 'She said you knew it.'

Slider snarled silently. 'If I knew it, would I have asked you for it? Did she say what she wanted this time?'

'Only would you phone her back. She sounded quite shirty about it,' he added helpfully.

'If she rings again, find out what she wants, and *get the number*. Do you want me to write you instructions?'

'No, guv,' McLaren said, spraying mayonnaise-soaked shreds of lettuce over his desk. 'I'll get it next time.'

'And don't you know Mr Barrington doesn't like anyone eating in the office?' he said.

'He's gone out,' McLaren said simply.

Slider felt it was time to be stern. 'That's no excuse.'

'Sorry, guv, but it was getting so late and there's so much to do, I thought I'd better not stop. Only I've followed up that telephone number in Hong Kong—' He paused seductively.

'Where's Mr Barrington gone?' Slider asked, unseduced.

'Press conference,' said McLaren. 'This phone number—'

'Yes?'

'Turns out to be the central tourist information office. And Beda was a girl who used to work there, only she's moved on now. Confidentially, the office manager hinted she'd been on the game in her spare time – amateur, like – and that's what she left to do, full time. More money in it.'

'I suppose someone at the club tipped Radek off about her,' Atherton said.

'So why did he keep the number afterwards?' Slider wondered. 'Was she so important to him?'

'Probably accidental,' Atherton suggested. 'Des Riley said he was in the habit of sticking bits of paper in the back of his baton case for safe-keeping and having a periodic clear-out, so probably that one just slipped the net.'

'Anyway, guv, this bird at the tourist office knew about the club all right. A bit sniffy about it, she was – not the sort of place they recommend, she said. But it confirms what Riley said about Radek's habits. D'you want it followed up any further?'

'What else have you got on hand?' Slider asked.

'All the possible sightings of chummy. We've got the first lot of phone-ins sorted, and the most promising have got him proceeding up Addison Gardens and left into Richmond Way. So he could have been heading for the station.'

'He could.'

'He still had his hat on, and he was looking upset, according to one eye-witness,' McLaren added with satisfaction. 'So if he did go down the tube, someone'll be bound to've clocked him.'

'All right, stick with that,' said Slider. He turned to Mackay, 'Anything on the gun search?'

'Nothing, guv. He must have kept it in his pocket. When'll we get the ballistics report?'

'Tomorrow, with any luck. But it's not going to help us much until we've got a suspect. Keep plugging on.' He turned to Atherton. 'I think you'd better go and talk to Radek's agent. You speak the lingo. It's me for the daughter, I think. What do we know about her?'

'Born 1950, went to Benenden School, very posh; has her own interior design business called Fenella, office in Hampstead, charges telephone numbers to tell the rich and shameless what colour to paint their dadoes. Married to a solicitor, Alec Coleraine of Coleraine and Antrobus, but uses her maiden name in business. And as you probably wouldn't know, not being a *Hello!* man, she features quite a bit in the society columns. Knows everyone; does over the houses of the glitterati and gets invited to their parties as a consequence. Very smart, and I gather reading between the lines as hard as nails in the business way.'

'Oh good,' said Slider wearily. 'She sounds just my type.'

At first Atherton took Kate Apwey, of Parker, Pool and Law, to be what he called a Victoria, meaning a good-looking, desperately smart, well-spoken but slightly daffy girl of the sort often found in publicity offices, who succeed without any particular abilities largely by getting on well with people and knowing how to behave at promotional parties. She was certainly easy on the eye, well groomed, and talked in the obligatory rapid, lightly slurred, upper-class falsetto, full of ums and sorts-ofs and other aids to well-bred inarticulacy. Atherton, who loved language, wanted to strangle her within ten seconds of meeting her, and wondered what she was doing working in an agency at all, unless it be a branch of Jackson-Stops; but ramming his fists into his pockets and sticking it out, he discovered that there was more to her than met the eye, and supposed belatedly that there would have to be if she had been Radek's agent for the last five years.

'He's a tremendous loss to us,' she said brightly. 'We've had him on our books for nearly eleven years now, ever since he sort of quarrelled with Holton and Watson, and he's been um, very, very lucrative indeed. We handle everything for him – concerts, recordings, personal appearances, everything really. His work-load is phenomenal. But I could book him ten times over for every date. Everyone wants him. He's very big box-office.'

'So tell me, why was he doing a concert at St Augustine's Church? That's a bit down-market for him, isn't it? Surely they couldn't have been paying him his usual fee?'

'No, he wasn't getting a fee at all – though I'm not supposed to tell anyone that. He didn't want anyone to know. He said if anyone found out he'd be swamped with begging letters.'

'He didn't like doing charity work, then?'

'Not at all. He hated it. He said no-one helped him when he had nothing, he had to look after himself, so everyone else could do the same.'

'So why was he doing this concert, then?'

'It was for his daughter,' she said. The notion seemed to puzzle her. 'She asked him to do it for the restoration fund, and he agreed. He said it was a once-only thing. It surprised me quite a bit, because it wasn't really his style, if you know what I mean; but I suppose he wanted to please her. He did care about her, I suppose.'

'That can't be bad, can it? Did you like him?'

She hesitated over the answer to that. 'Oh, well – he earns us so much money he's entitled to be sort of particular. He makes his own conditions, sort of thing.'

'Which are?'

She hesitated again. 'He wanted me to um handle him personally. To be available all the time, you know? No substitutes allowed and no excuses.' She reflected glumly for a moment. 'It made it difficult for me to have any private life of my own. I mean, men friends are not sort of understanding when you're called out at short notice at night to hold someone's hand for them.'

'But it was worth it to you?'

'It was my job,' she said snippily.

'And you were glad to serve the cause of music?' Atherton suggested smoothly. 'To be handmaid to the great genius of the podium was enough reward for giving up your private life?'

She looked at him askance, and rather pink. 'Um, not really.'

'You did it for the money, then?'

Now she blushed. 'Look, it's my job, all right? He wanted me, and if I'd refused he'd have got me sacked, and I'd never have got another job as good as this one. And it wasn't going to be for ever anyway.'

'He wanted you, did he?' Atherton said with bland interest. 'I'm sorry, I didn't realise when you said he wanted you to handle him personally that you meant it literally. Lots of evening work, was it? Organ recitals, that sort of thing?' He thought she would get angry, but though her colour remained high, she looked at him steadily.

'What business is it of yours?' she asked.

He reassessed her rapidly. 'I apologise. But I have to know exactly how the land lay. And it's better if I hear all about you *from* you, isn't it? That way you can be sure I hear the truth.' She stared at him, her brain evidently working behind her impassive eyes. 'Did he ask you to sleep with him?'

'Yes,' she said after a pause.

'And did you?'

A longer pause. 'Yes,' she said at last. It was difficult to tell what she felt about that.

'For the money? Or to keep your job?'

She seemed to make up her mind about something. 'Look, whatever he was in ordinary life, he was a great conductor, a world-class celebrity, and there's something about a man like that. At the end of a concert, especially on a tour, when he's just come down off the platform and the audience is going mad out there, there's a sort of atmosphere. I mean there's a sort of, like, electricity about him.'

'He was on a high, and the excitement transmitted itself to you. So when he asked you back to his hotel room you felt honoured to be asked.'

She looked at him doubtfully. 'Sort of. How do you know?'

'I love music. I go to concerts,' he said. 'I can understand that you might go willingly, at least the first time. Where was that, by the way?'

'Frankfurt.'

'And you went to bed with him.'

There was a long silence. He thought she might not answer, but suddenly it burst out. 'It was horrible! He was so old, and he smelled, and the things he wanted me to do—! It was like you said at first, I was sort of excited, he was a celebrity. But it wore off, and then there I was in this hotel room with this horrible old man.' She put her hands to her face, pulling the skin of her cheeks back with her knuckles. 'Afterwards,' she went on, 'he gave me a lot of money, and said how good I was, and he'd tell my boss I was terrific at my job. Well, I wanted to get on. And anyway, I knew – I mean, it was obvious what he meant. He said he'd say I was so good he wanted me to look after him all the time—'

'You thought he was hinting that if you refused him next time he'd tell them you were no good and get rid of you.'

'It was no hint. He'd have done it all right,' she said almost indignantly.

'So you went on sleeping with him to order, to keep your job.'

'It wasn't often,' she said in self-justification; and then, the horror returning to her eyes: 'It was just – having it hanging over me. Not knowing when. But I was saving the money. And when I had enough—' She stopped abruptly.

He waited to see if she'd go on, and when she didn't, he said, 'You said it wasn't going to be for ever. What did you mean by that?'

She flicked an alarmed glance at him, and then looked away. 'Nothing really. Well, I mean, he was an old man, wasn't he? He couldn't live for ever.'

'You were hoping he'd die?'

'No, not hoping. But sooner or later he'd have to, wouldn't he? Or retire.'

'You have a boyfriend?' She nodded, either doubtfully or reluctantly. 'Did he know about your relations with Radek?'

'I never actually told him about – he knew I had to be with him at concerts and things – but he sort of guessed, or assumed. So I didn't deny it. I mean, I wouldn't have lied to him.'

'He didn't like it?'

'No, of course not.'

'You had rows about it?'

'Sometimes. Steve loses his temper, but it doesn't mean anything. I mean, he's soon over it.'

'Did he know Radek gave you money?'

'We were saving up for a house,' she said with wonderful inconsequence.

'You and Steve were going to get married?'

'Eventually. But I wanted to carry on working. I told Steve that. He understood that. My career is important to me.'

'But you couldn't go on sleeping with Radek once you were married, could you? And if you refused him, you'd lose your job.' She didn't answer, looking away from him, biting her lips. 'But of a dilemma for you,' he said warmly.

'He was a hateful old man,' she said suddenly, fiercely. 'He knew how I felt, but he liked tormenting people. I'm glad he's dead. Whoever killed him did a public service.'

Back in his car, Atherton consulted a copy of the orchestra's schedule which Tony Whittam had given him and reckoned there was just time to catch one of the orchestra members before she left for an evening session at Abbey Road. He drove to Joanna's flat in Turnham Green, and found her in, but not alone.

'I'm giving Sue a lift to the studio. You know Sue Caversham, don't you?'

'We have met,' Atherton said, accepting the offered hand of the principal second violin. She was a nice-looking, strongly built woman in her forties with very shiny brown hair and a wide mouth and an air of being secretly amused by everything, which some might have found daunting, but which Atherton found inviting.

'Briefly,' she said. 'It wasn't you who took my statement, more's the pity.'

'We've just finished a late lunch,' Joanna said, 'but I can get you some cheese and biscuits if you're hungry. Policemen are always hungry,' she added to Sue. 'It's all that brain activity.'

'No thanks,' Atherton said, and then, 'What sort of cheese?'

'Dolcelatte.'

'And Carr's water biscuits? Yes please, then.'

'Not another foodie!' Sue laughed as Joanna departed to get the cheese. 'I'm always so impressed with Jo, all the cooking she does. We just had the most marvellous pasta, and the sauce wasn't even ready-made. Me, I have difficulty opening a tin.'

'Don't you *like* food?' Atherton boggled in horror.

'Love it, but when I get home from work, if it doesn't get on the plate of its own accord, it's too much effort. I get a piece of bread out of the fridge, or if I'm in unexpectedly good shape I pour out a bowl of cereal.'

'Is playing the violin really so exhausting?' Atherton asked disapprovingly.

'No, I'm just bone lazy,' Sue said comfortably. 'Also it depends what you're playing and who for. Some conductors make life harder than others.'

'Like the late unlamented?' Atherton asked. 'Can a conductor make that much difference?'

'He can if he's a nasty, self-obsessed, vindictive old sod, and I use the word advisedly, like Radek,' Sue said. Joanna, returning, looked amused.

Atherton caught her eye and said, '*De mortuis*?'

'*Non est disputandum*,' she finished for him. 'Here we are. Cheese, biscuits, and I've even found you a glass of wine. Left over from last night, so it's not too old.'

'Ah, Château Hot Tin Roof,' Atherton said, holding it up to the light. 'Were you going to use it for cooking?'

'Snob,' said Joanna. 'You don't have to drink it.'

'I'm sure it's delightful,' he said hastily. 'Reverting to the subject, are all conductors hated?'

'Oh no,' Sue said quickly. 'Barbirolli, for instance, was a lovely old geezer. He used to share his sandwiches on the coach. And Pritchard *never* forgot to thank you, or to stand you up if you'd had something tricky to do.'

'But then there are those like Lupton – when he gets lost he just bottles out and stops conducting. Gets you into a mess and expects you to get him out of it,' Joanna offered. 'And Farnese, who's so convinced he's a genius he takes the parts home and *rewrites* them. I mean, actually changes notes, never mind annotations.'

Sue put in, 'You know the old saying, don't you: what's the difference between a bull and an orchestra?'

'Tell me.'

'A bull has the horns at the front and the arse at the back.'

Atherton snorted crumbs. 'You're my sort of woman. Tell me, didn't you have a blow-up recently with the arse in question?'

'Yes, and very nasty it was.' She made a face. 'Six point six on the Sphincter scale. I thought I'd had it, actually. Our management is as wet as a fortnight in Cardiff, they never stick up for us – as poor old Bob Preston found out.'

'Who's he?'

Sue and Joanna exchanged glances, and Joanna shrugged and took up the story. 'He's – or he was – our co-principal trumpet. We did a *Messiah* with Radek a couple of months ago, and Bob always does the solo in "The Trumpet Shall Sound" because the principal, Les, doesn't like playing D trumpet parts. Everyone who conducts us knows that, and Bob's very good – *Messiah*'s his specialty. But that wouldn't do for bloody old Radek. He said he wasn't having any mere *co*-principal doing a solo under his magnificent direction.'

'The fact was that he wanted to promote one of his little protégés,' Sue put in. 'He's always got some wunderkind he's discovered tucked up his sleeve, and when they get famous, he's there hovering in the background taking half the glory. Anyway, there was this boy-wonder trumpeter, Lev Polowski—'

'Polish, or Russian of Polish extraction, so he felt entitled,' Joanna explained.

'So he said Bob was off the case. There was a big row, and Bob stood up to Radek, the twonk.'

'Brave but foolish,' Atherton commented.

'The upshot was that Radek said he wouldn't have Bob in the orchestra any more,' Sue finished. 'He told the management if they didn't chuck Bob he'd take his contracts elsewhere, so poor old Bob got the big E.'

'Do you think Radek would have carried out his threat?' Atherton asked.

Joanna looked at him. 'Nice point. I think he just might have – he was megalomaniac enough. And besides, he'd never want for work. He could command any fees he liked, and any orchestra in the world would fight to have him. So the management had no leverage. Couldn't take the chance.'

'What's happened to Bob now?' Atherton asked.

Sue shrugged. 'He's freelancing when he can get work, but it's hard for trumpeters. You don't need many of them per orchestra, and there's hardly any solo work. I've seen him once or twice. He's very depressed.'

'So he has a real grudge against Radek?' Atherton said.

The two women gave the impression of suddenly sitting bolt upright. 'Oh hang on,' Sue protested, 'you can't think Bob would murder the old bastard because of that?'

'I'm not thinking it, I'm canvassing possibilities,' Atherton said blandly.

'It's not a possibility. If I'd thought you'd suspect him, I'd never have told you about it,' Sue said angrily.

Joanna was watching her with faint amusement, having gone down this path herself long before. 'I should have known these questions weren't all random,' she said. 'It doesn't matter, Sue. They'd find out anyway. Better he hears it from someone who can give them a balanced picture.'

'All the same—'

'And if Bob had murdered Radek, you wouldn't want him to get away with it, would you?'

'Yes, but Bob—'

'I know. The idea's ludicrous. He wouldn't hurt a fly.'

'You might as well suspect me,' Sue said, looking defiantly at Atherton. 'After all, I had a row with Radek just the day before he was killed.'

'I have taken that into account,' Atherton said smoothly. Sue went scarlet, and Joanna stepped in.

'What he means is he doesn't think that would be enough motive for you to actually want to kill Radek,' she said firmly. 'Isn't that right, Jim?'

'Oh, I think I can eliminate you,' Atherton said generously. 'After all, you wouldn't have had time to hire the killer.'

Sue stared for a moment, and then burst into laughter.

'You rotten sod. I'm keeping score now. You'll pay for that.'

'I do hope so,' Atherton said warmly. 'You must let me cook for you some time. Joanna will tell you I'm a noted cook.'

'That sounds good to me,' Sue said. 'What about tonight, after the session?'

'Brilliant idea! If I can get off early enough, I could do you a *boeuf en croûte*. It's what I call casing the joint.'

'Oh God!' Sue groaned in protest. 'What am I getting myself into?'

Joanna looked from her face to his and back, and suddenly felt rather left out of things.

CHAPTER FIVE

How Green was my Volvo

Slider finally ran Radek's daughter to earth in Hampstead, in a house she was redecorating. Her little van, painted ecology green with a nice curly Fenella in crimson lettering edged with black on the side, was parked on the paved hardstanding (what had once been the front garden) behind a Volvo estate and a dark blue Jaguar XJ which made Slider whimper. He'd always wanted one. He parked his own shabby Vauxhall across the front, blocking them all in, since there wasn't anywhere else to put it: the streets here were only about one car wide. The tall, narrow, eighteenth-century house would have made him whimper too, if it had been anywhere else, but Hampstead was one of those places, like Greenwich Village, you either adored or didn't.

The door was opened to him by a maid, and that was something you couldn't often say nowadays. She was foreign, of course – something east of Clacton, he surmised – and, smiling as if she hadn't understood a word he said, she invited him to wait in the hall with a gesture as graceful as part of a temple dance, and disappeared upstairs. The house was very quiet: all he could hear was the measured sound of a long-case clock ticking somewhere out of sight, and once a creak of a floorboard from upstairs. It gave him the feeling that he had sometimes had as a child, when he had been ill in bed on a schoolday: that everyone in the whole world had gone away somewhere, to another planet, perhaps, leaving him absolutely alone.

To distract himself he examined the letters on the hall table and discovered that the house belonged to a Famous Writer (of the Booker as opposed to the Airport type), so famous even he had heard of her. A quick poke about in the mental files suggested that she was married to an almost equally famous Historian who was now Arts Editor of one of the serious newspapers. That accounted for the money, at least. What they could want with redecorating he couldn't imagine – everything looked immaculate – unless it was somehow deductible.

At last the maid came downstairs again, and with another uncomprehending smile and lovely gesture said, 'Please,' and led him upstairs. She showed him into a beautiful double drawing-room, where Mrs Coleraine and the Famous Writer were standing at the window examining fabric samples. The writer was tall and rangey with big teeth and big hair and a large, jolly voice which left her eyes untouched by humour or humanity. Slider had been abused, insulted and even spat at by many a potential interviewee, but it was a long time since he had been made to feel that he ought to have gone round by the tradesman's entrance.

'Ah yes, Inspector,' she said witheringly, like a heart surgeon looking down at the nit nurse, 'come in. You want to see Mrs Coleraine, I understand. I can't imagine why you couldn't have waited until this evening when she's at home, but I dare say you have your reasons. Something tremendously urgent, I suppose?'

Slider declined to be drawn, and merely gave her a humble smile. She turned to her companion.

'Fay, my dear, I suppose I had better leave you to it, but I shall only be upstairs in my bedroom.' In case I attack her, Slider thought. 'I am beginning to incline towards the green. The raw silk is so lovely I can't resist it. Can we think along those lines? What I'm looking for is a sort of *underwater* feeling. We can talk about textures later.' When this horrid little man has gone, said her glance, and she bestowed a gigantic smile on Mrs Coleraine, large enough to last her till she came back, and went out of the room.

Fay Coleraine turned to Slider. She was a tall woman, but being much more lightly made than the Famous Writer had appeared small in her company. She had a sweet, worn face in which he could find no likeness to Radek except for the height of the cheekbones and the heaviness of the eyelids; on her they looked beautiful rather than menacing. Her hair was strawberry blonde, short and set in the sweeping waves that women of a certain age always seem to adopt, revealing her ear-lobes in which small pearls were set. She was wearing black slacks and a black silk blouse, with a black and white scarf in the neckline which was twisted in and under a string of very good pearls. Slider couldn't tell if it were a uniform for her work, a concession to mourning, or merely a random choice of clothes, but she looked smart, attractive and expensive.

'I'm sorry to interrupt you at your work,' he said, and she smiled a kind smile that made him want to take her out to tea and tell her not to worry about anything.

'Don't mind Maggie. She doesn't mean to trample. Was it something urgent?'

'Not urgent, in that sense, but trails do get cold, and the sooner we ask our questions the better. I did call your house, but they told me you were working today.'

She almost shrugged. 'I thought it better to keep busy. There didn't seem any reason to stay at home; and Maggie's hard to pin down.'

'I won't keep you long,' Slider said, and she gestured towards a brocaded chaise longue.

'Oh, don't worry, take whatever time you need. Shall we sit down? Though I'm not sure what help I can be. I simply can't imagine who would do such a dreadful thing. I've racked my brains, but I can't think of anyone who hated my father that badly. You're sure it wasn't just one of those random things, like the Hungerford massacre?'

'We don't think so. It doesn't look like it. The symptoms are wrong.'

She sighed. 'Well, you must know, of course.'

'I'm very sorry. It must have been a terrible shock for you.'

She sat forward a little, folding her hands together and trapping them between her knees in a rather girlish gesture. 'It was, of course, but I must be absolutely frank with you and say that I didn't like my father very much. I don't think anyone did, except Buster. But then I don't think my father wanted to be liked. Worshipped was good enough for him.'

'Your mother must have liked him,' he suggested.

'Oh, I don't think so. Swept off her feet by him, more like.' She looked at him from under her eyelids. 'He wasn't a nice man, you know. He was mean and spiteful. He liked tormenting people and playing them off against each other. He used to do it with Mummy and me, and with Mummy and Dodo—'

'Dodo?'

'That was Mrs Keaton – Doreen Keaton. I called her Dodo. She was our cook-housekeeper when I was little.'

'You were – what – three years old when the Keatons came to work for your parents?'

She nodded. 'We'd just moved into the Holland Park house. It's the first home I remember – we were in a flat before, in Kensington. My grandfather died and left everything to Mummy, including the house. She was the only child, and my grandparents were only-children too, so I was very short of relatives. And then Mummy died when I was only nine.'

'That's very sad. I'm so sorry.'

She looked at him as if to see whether he really was, and then nodded, accepting his interest. 'I loved her so much, and that's when I really started to hate my father. Because he drove her to it, you know.'

'No, I don't know. What did she die of?'

'It was an overdose of sleeping pills. Well, of course, she wouldn't have had any sleeping pills if my father hadn't been such a beast to her. They brought it in as an accident at the inquest, but I believe – I still believe – it was suicide. And Dodo did as well.'

'Did she say so to you?'

'Not in so many words, but she told me that it wasn't an accident. And on her deathbed she said to me that "things were not as they seemed". Those were her words.'

'Did she look after you when your mother died?'

'Yes, she was very good to me. I don't know how I would have coped if she hadn't been there. But she died less than a year after Mummy. It wasn't really surprising, she was such a pale, wispy sort of creature, always full of aches and pains – though she never complained. She just soldiered on, cooking and cleaning and looking after me. Do you know, I have no memory of her laughing? Smiling, yes, but not laughing. Isn't that sad?'

'What did she die of?'

'Gastroenteritis. It just got worse and worse over a couple of days, and then they took her into hospital, but it was too late.

Nowadays I suppose they would have been able to save her. It amazes me to think how far medical science has advanced in just thirty years.'

'You must have missed her very much. Who looked after you then?'

'Oh, well, after that my father wanted to get rid of me, of course – I would have got in the way of his career – so he sent me off to boarding school. Do you really want to hear all this? It hasn't anything to do with this awful business,' she said abruptly.

'If you don't mind,' he said. 'It helps if I have the whole picture. Sometimes something can have a completely different meaning if you can put it in context.'

'Well, if you're sure. Where was I?'

'You went to boarding school. Who looked after you in the holidays – or did you spend them at school too?'

'Oh no, I came home in the holidays. Buster looked after me. He didn't trot round after my father quite as much in those days.'

'Did you like him?'

'Buster? Oh yes, he was all right. He was very kind to me, really. I always remember he used to make me Shrewsbury biscuits, because I'd once said I liked them. I'd got them mixed up with Garibaldis, and every school hols he'd have a batch of them ready for me when I got home, so I had to eat them, even though I didn't like them much, rather than hurt his feelings.'

She smiled, and Slider smiled back. 'Your father didn't marry again?'

'No. To tell you the truth, I don't think he'd have married the first time if Mummy hadn't had money. He didn't really want any competition, you know.'

'With whom?'

'With anyone. If he was married people would always say, "Oh, and how is your wife?" Divided attention, you see.'

'Yes, I see.'

'He had Buster to take care of him, and Buster was better than a wife. He didn't have to remember Buster's birthday or buy him flowers.'

'He does seem very devoted.'

'Oh, he is. Poor old thing. He'll be so lost without Daddy.' It was the first time, Slider noticed, that she had said 'Daddy' instead of 'my father'. 'He's like a faithful old dog. A bit creepy almost, I sometimes used to think, the way he dedicated himself to him. But now they've grown old together they're a bit more on equal terms. They fight like cat and dog, you know. It's quite funny sometimes, as long as you're out of range. They sling plates at each other like a married couple.'

Slider inched in a delicate question. 'The relationship between them – was it ever – was Buster more than—?'

She cut him off, looking genuinely shocked, and even a little annoyed. 'Good God no! Oh, I know nowadays it's the first thing anyone thinks, and it does make me cross. There was nothing like that between them. My father may have been a swine, but he was perfectly normal.'

'I was really asking more from Buster's side.'

'He was married too, you seem to forget. Of course he was normal.'

'It doesn't always follow.'

She looked at him, and then sniffed. 'I suppose not. But I assure you Buster wasn't – isn't – like that. He thinks my father's a genius, that's all.'

'And was he?'

She noticed the change of tense. 'I keep forgetting. He was always such a larger-than-life figure, it's hard to remember he's gone. Well, I don't know – a genius? Yes, I suppose he was. If I hadn't been his daughter I probably would have worshipped him too. I do love music, you know. But by the time I was old enough to leave home, I'd had enough of the world of music, if you follow.' Slider nodded. 'That's why I married Alec.' She smiled. 'Alec's a musical ignoramus. He wouldn't know Schubert from Schoenberg. It was so refreshing! And it drove my father mad, of course. He absolutely forbade me to marry, so I waited until I was twenty-one and then thumbed my nose at him. He never really forgave me.'

He couldn't tell how she felt about that. He asked, 'What were relations like between you and your father? Recently, I mean.'

'He didn't really care about me, not as a person. But I was *his* child, you know, so he wanted me to do well so that he could bathe in reflected glory. He was very into all that. Buster said a clever thing once – that my father never discarded, he only added to his hand. If he'd ever talent-spotted anyone or helped them in their career, they were his for life, and he expected them to go on being grateful and referring to his influence in all future interviews. He didn't much care for my business – he thought it was frivolous – but when I did well at it and made lots of money and became famous in my own small way, he liked to claim the credit.'

'How did he do that?'

'He brought me up to have good taste, of course, and taught me to stand on my own two feet and be tough, which made me a good businesswoman. And his fame rubbed off on me, so that people used me because they wanted to say their house was done over by Sir Stefan Radek's daughter.' She smiled tautly. 'All nonsense, of course, but I stopped arguing with him. If it made him happy.'

'Did you see much of him?'

'No, not really. I suppose it averaged out at about once a month. Family occasions, and the odd invitation if he felt we would do him credit. I didn't pop in. For one thing he was hardly ever at home – although he had slowed down a bit in the last year or two. Buster's influence, I think. And for another, we always ended up quarrelling, and it wore me out.'

'What did you quarrel about?'

She hesitated just perceptibly. 'Alec, usually. He thought he wasn't good enough for me. He always wanted me to admit I'd made a mistake and that he'd been right, that I should have listened to Daddy's advice, that sort of thing. I know I oughtn't to have risen to it, but my father had ways of getting to you. He had a vicious tongue.'

'How did your husband get on with him?'

'He didn't mind him so much. Well, he hadn't had to put up with him all his life, had he? He didn't like my father criticising the way we brought Marcus up – that's our son – but he was better at holding his tongue than I was.'

'You have only the one child?'

'Yes. We'd have liked more, but—' She shrugged. 'We're very short of family altogether. It's like a chronic condition. Alec always wanted a large family, but all he has is me and Marcus, and a godson he's rather fond of. I suppose that's why he's tended to spoil Marcus. He gives in to him much too easily. He's so soft with him he would never even let me punish him, and of course a child soon learns he can play one parent off against the other.' She stopped, and stared thoughtfully at the carpet, pursuing a private thought.

After a moment Slider said, 'When was the last time you saw your father? Can you remember?'

'Oh yes. It was three weeks ago, on my birthday. We went there for dinner. I did speak to him on the phone last week about the concert – it's a pet cause of mine, the St Augustine's Restoration Fund. I was rather surprised he agreed to do it. To be frank, I think Buster persuaded him in the hope that it would bring us closer together. He always cherished the hope that we'd be reconciled into one big happy family.'

'But it was kind of your father to do it. It shows he cared for you.'

'Does it? I expect he just wanted people to think what a wonderful person he was, to do it for charity.'

Slider felt a first twinge of indignation on Radek's behalf, that his gesture was being so undervalued. But perhaps it was a case of too little, too late. After all, he didn't know how Radek had treated his daughter all his life. 'And your husband?' he asked. 'When was the last time he saw your father?'

'It would be the same time, of course. Alec didn't go visiting without me. What a funny question.'

'Oh, I thought they might meet in town or something. Your husband's office is in town, isn't it?'

'Yes, in Bedford Street, just off the Strand. But Alec and my father weren't friendly like that. I've told you, Alec doesn't like music. They had nothing to say to each other.'

'I understand,' Slider said. 'Now, you've said you have no idea of anyone who might want to kill your father?'

'None at all. The idea's ludicrous. Oh, lots of people disliked him, but it takes more than that, doesn't it?'

'Yes, usually,' Slider said. 'Did he have any interests or activities outside of music?'

'Never, to my knowledge. Music was his whole life. It left no time for anything else.'

'Did he have any close friends that you knew of?'

'He didn't have any friends of any sort.'

'What about the people he'd helped? You said he liked them to keep up with him.'

'Yes, but that wasn't friendship. He liked them to keep telling everyone he had been a forming influence on them. Sometimes he got invited to their special concerts, or to the parties afterwards, and sometimes he went. Sometimes he invited them in the same way, if they were hot enough property. But he didn't entertain at home, and I've never known him go to a private dinner or party. He always said he hadn't time to waste on purely social events.'

The Famous Writer appeared in the door. 'I say, I wonder could you move your car?' she said to Slider, in the sort of way she might have asked him to take his boots off the sofa. 'It's rather blocking us all in.'

'Yes, of course,' Slider said meekly, standing up. Mrs Coleraine stood too, and gave the writer a slightly puzzled look, by which Slider understood that the interruption was contrived, his welcome having been deemed to have been outstayed. 'I've more or less finished now, anyway.'

'I'm afraid it hasn't got you anywhere,' Mrs Coleraine said contritely. 'I wish I could help you more, but I really can't.'

'That's all right,' Slider said. 'It all helps to build up the picture. And if anything should occur to you, please give me a ring. The smallest thing may be of help, so don't think you'll be wasting our time.'

'I'm sure she wouldn't think that,' the writer said, baring her teeth. 'Would you, Fay darling?'

Fay darling seemed to think that was on the verge of being rude, and she put out her hand to Slider and said, 'If you need to speak to me again, I'll be glad to give you all the time you want.'

Slider took the hand. It was warm and dry and firm. 'Thank you,' he said. He really didn't think he could suspect her. She had hated her father, blamed him for her mother's death, resented his criticism of her husband, but Slider just couldn't imagine her shooting him in that silly, half-arsed way. On the other hand, in a silly, half-arsed way was the only way she would be likely to be able to do it, given she was an honourable citizen and Radek was her father. And she had stood to gain a vast amount of money by his death. Well, she'd have got it anyway, eventually, so there was no need to hurry him along. Unless he'd threatened to change his Will. Or unless she had some absolutely urgent need that couldn't wait. Hadn't old Buster said the son was a bit of a wild thing? Maybe he'd got himself into some trouble that needed a large sum of money to sort out. He must find out. And, sadly, find out where she'd been on Wednesday. But he'd be glad to discover she had a watertight alibi.

The maid was waiting outside the drawing-room door to show him out, proving it had not been a random interruption. He followed her downstairs and she opened the door for him and held it, making a graceful gesture with the other, an exquisite temple-maiden's version of the good old A & C.

'Lovely technique,' he said, bowing to her as he passed.

She smiled a smile of complete incomprehension. 'Please,' she said.

Slider pulled up on the hardstanding outside his house and let himself in, shoving the front door against an interesting-looking heap. It turned out, however, to consist of two local freebie newspapers, an envelope for postal film-developing, a coupon for a free half-bottle of wine with any two adult meals ordered at the Ruislip Harvester ('for a limited period only, not to be used in conjunction with any other promotional offer' – did that mean that after the limited period it could be used in conjunction with another promotional offer? You simply couldn't trust people's punctuation these days) and the spectacular offer of a free watch and inclusion in the *Reader's Digest* prize draw. Open now! You may already have won £100,000! You never know your luck! I bloody do, Slider thought, gathering the ex-rainforest together and heading for the kitchen. As they say in the Job, I'm so unlucky I could fall in a barrel of tits and come out sucking my thumb.

The house smelled strange, a marginally sub-pleasant odour which he could not pin down, somewhere between margarine and Shake'n'Vac, with a hint of cold plimsolls thrown in. There was a chill echo about it, too: it was strange to come home and find the television not on – as if, like a fifth member of the family, it had left him too. The house was still fully furnished – Irene had taken nothing except her and the children's personal belongings, and the new wicker conservatory furniture she loved so much – but that only made it worse. Chairs and carpets without personal clutter gave it the feeling of an institution; a sort of kindly brutality designed to wipe out your inconvenient personality traits. Strange how the word 'home' could have two such opposite connotations.

He had only come to change his clothes and have an urgent reunion with his deodorant stick. He dumped the papers on the kitchen table and debated making a quick cup of tea, but the inhospitality of the kitchen daunted him. The dishcloth draped over the tap had dried into a hoop, and the last footmark he had made on the lino-tiled floor (Monday, putting the dustbin out – it hadn't rained since) reproached him mutely where it had dried. Sherlock of the Homes could have deduced a thing or two about him from that: this man is five-foot-eight, weighs ten stone, wears rubber soles, and his wife is away.

It had never really been *his* home, he reflected; but, oddly, was much less so now that Irene and the children were gone. He hadn't spent much time here in the weeks since it happened. He stayed long at work, ate out, and once or twice had managed to sleep out, too. He hated waking up in the morning to find himself curled up on 'his' side of the otherwise empty bed. It made him feel like a prat, but even when he deliberately started off in the middle he migrated in his sleep out of obedience to habit.

O'Flaherty, uniformed sergeant at Shepherd's Bush and one of Slider's oldest friends, knew his circumstances and had several times invited Slider back to supper. His wife was a noted cook of the steak-and-kidney pie, Irish stew and jammy pud school; aided by the Guinness intake, it accounted for O'Flaherty's shape and his nickname of Flatulent Fergus. But they both made Slider welcome, and after one particularly indulgent evening, Fergus had pressed him to stay the night.

'I don't like to think of you sittin' around like an undescended testicle in that empty house o' yours. We got loads a room, now the kids are gone. You can have Brendan's room – less clutter than in the girls'.' And when Slider had argued politely, 'Ah sure God, would you sit down and have another drink? It won't take Margery a minute to put some sheets on.'

So Slider had stayed the night in a sagging single bed, which had a hollow in the middle you could have parked a Mini in (the effect of years of having been used as a trampoline, as the father in him rather than the detective recognised) in a tiny room with Superman wallpaper and Muppet bedlinen. It was a night of crowded dreams peopled with caped crusaders and woolly monsters, amongst whom he searched in vain for someone without ever knowing who it was. He woke late and unrefreshed, and had felt both ashamed and comforted when he found that Margery had washed and ironed his shirt for him while he slept. She refused to be thanked, as if it were the most natural thing in the world for her to do. The kindness of strangers got him where he was most vulnerable. He felt like Blanche.

Drifting back from the memories to the present, Slider suddenly wanted to be out of here. The place was like a corpse waiting for the post mortem to begin. He went upstairs, had a quick shower, and changed his work suit for cords and a sweater, and then went into the familiar annoying routine of trying to find a pair of socks that matched and didn't have holes in them. What did they make socks out of nowadays, anyway? In a fit of fury he pulled the drawer out and up-ended it on the bed. As he rummaged he heard Joanna in his memory saying, 'You only want a housekeeper. Someone to wash your socks.' She was right in a way, but it was not really the sock-washing, it was more a case of needing something solid somewhere in a life that was otherwise fraught with peril and uncertainty. When the house was sold he would really have to accept that his marriage was over, and that there was nowhere he belonged and no-one who wanted him. It was not a prospect he relished.

There were enough coppers who lived bachelor lives, and got by very well in their own individual ways. Atherton for one. He lived in the part of Kilburn so extensively done up it dared to call itself West Hampstead, in a Victorian terraced cottage which he shared with a former tomcat called Oedipus. Atherton was an archetypal bachelor, Slider thought: being otherwise alone in the world, he dedicated his leisure and disposable income to putting his body into nice things and nice things into his body. Bathing, dressing, eating, drinking and mating – not necessarily in that order of preference – were his pleasures, and he took them very seriously. Slider remembered that Joanna had once said Atherton was in danger of becoming a caricature of himself. Precise, almost dilettantish in his enjoyments, he had already probably gone past the point where he was likely to be able to make the transition from bachelorhood into marriage, even if he wanted to. That he wanted to was moot: his reputation was envied amongst the younger coppers. Awap – Anything With A Pulse – they called him behind his back.

It was a pity, given Atherton's freedom from domestic cares, that he wasn't a career man, Slider thought, rolling over-ventilated socks together and throwing them back in the drawer, whence they would return to haunt him one day. Dickson had once told Atherton that as a policeman he suffered from the disadvantage of too much education – an insult rated very differently by insulter and insultee. Too much of a smartarse, was the general opinion. But Slider believed it was more a spiritual malaise that held Atherton back: an inability to take things seriously, which itself was a function of the chronic outsiderism they all suffered from. Grown like callus to protect the tender places of the soul, it performed a useful function in keeping them sane while dealing with the world's worst madness; but excessive growth could deform. There were lame coppers in plenty; Slider was sometimes afraid his friend was becoming one of them.

Or, to put it another way, if all coppers were odd, those who lived alone were easily the oddest. And he, Slider, was going to join them. He saw himself in years to come living in a small place of his own (it would have to be small, after Irene had had her share of the dead albatross) with his own few, well-liked things around him. Pottering about in his off-duty hours. Cooking for himself. Gardening maybe. Taking up his architectural drawing again, perhaps. Growing more idiosyncratically himself year by year, as people do who have no-one to rub the nobbly bits smooth against. He could see himself ten years on, greyer and more leathery, spreading a little in shapeless sweaters and half-moon glasses, full of annoying little habits of speech and gesture. But probably in the end not discontented – not absolutely.

That was the worst part. He didn't want it that way. He had not been built with that in mind. He abandoned the sock quest, feeling useless and helpless, mourning the awful waste of the situation. How had it come to this? All those years of dull faithfulness, for Irene's sake, for the children's sake, and now they'd all fled like wet nestlings under Ernie's protective wing. It was as though the gods were playing some elaborate practical joke on him. His life was falling apart. He wandered out into the passage and looked down at the stairs – narrow, low-ceilinged, joining the top to the bottom of a house built out of margarine boxes and spit. Everything had been designed in a spirit of meanness, with no consideration but to push back a little further the limits of human tolerance. He had only bought it for Irene's sake, and now she was gone, and he was left with the house. Ha ha, good one, Life.

He walked two steps and pushed open the door of Matthew's room. The furniture was all there, but the room was stripped of his personality, except for the paler patches on the walls where he had taken down his posters of state-of-the-art jet fighters. He must have done it in some haste, because on one wall there was a drawing-pin left in, holding a small triangle of dark shiny paper. Absently, Slider removed it and sat down on the bed with it in his hand.

He had no-one to blame but himself, he thought – as though that made anything better. He had married Irene, knowing what she was like. He had remained a policeman, knowing what it did to home lives. He had followed his career while his children grew distant from him and his wife grew first bored and then resentful. And if she had run off with another man, well, hadn't he been unfaithful to her first, even if she didn't know about it? And hadn't he neglected her until – what an indictment! – even Ernie Newman looked attractive? What kind of a rôle model would Ernie provide for his teenage son, he wondered? Better than his own father, probably: Ernie would always be there, boring, pedantic, costive, but indisputably *there*, and Matthew would forget the Dad who had taught him to bowl overarm and take a fish off a hook without damaging it. And Kate—

He had forgotten he was holding the drawing-pin, and fiddling with it, he accidentally drove it into his thumb. He looked down in surprise and hurt. The dark triangle of paper came from Matthew's absolutely favourite poster, the moodily lit, seriously brill picture of a Stealth jet: he'd be really upset that he'd torn it getting it off the wall.

Suddenly, and with shocking vividness, Slider remembered a moment from his own childhood. It was not long after his grandmother, Dad's mother, had died. He was standing in the kitchen of their dank little cottage: winter and summer it always smelled of water, standing or running, mossy or soapy. In the dresser drawer he'd found the picture Gran had given him at Christmas, printed on card in soft, Walt Disney colours: Jesus the Good Shepherd, in a blue robe, with a crook, surrounded by sheep, children, and a brown-and-white collie. He'd loved it when she gave it to him, had thought it lost, and found it again: a moment of joy. But then he remembered she was dead, and suddenly the picture seemed unimportant, stupid, hatefully trivial. In a violent gesture, instantly regretted, he had torn it in two and flung it on the floor. Then Dad came in. He didn't immediately say anything, just picked up the two pieces and held them against each other, looking at them in a silence that made Slider suddenly terrified that he might be going to cry. But Dads never cry. At last he said, 'Never mind, son. We can put it together again with sticky-tape. It won't show from the front.' And suddenly the boy Slider had found himself weeping, his face pressed to Dad's rough, hairy, horse-smelling jacket, his arms round Dad's stringy waist; weeping as though he'd never stop, because then he knew for the first time, really knew, that nothing could make life the way it had been again.

It had been the beginning of the loneliness of growing up. In every life there comes a moment when the individual realises for the first time how separate and untouchable they are, alone in sin and alone in sadness; after that a wholeness is gone, and pleasures, though they may be many, can never be taken for granted. In his mind's eye he could see Matthew taking down his posters, and, in spite of all his care, tearing the corner off his favourite one. Sitting alone on his son's bed, Slider felt his loss as though it were his own. He would have cried, except that Dads don't.

CHAPTER SIX

Turner Blind Eye

It's a human habit which persists in the face of any amount of disappointed experience to imagine, on first hearing a person's name, what they are going to look like. Slider saw Alec Colcraine as a tall, lean, thick-blond-haired sort of name; distinguishedly handsome, perhaps going just a little romantically grey at the temples – silver threads among the gold, tra-la. One thing he wasn't expecting, and it turned out to be the one thing you simply couldn't help noticing on meeting him, was that Alec Coleraine was short. Slider was not a tall man, but as Coleraine advanced hospitably across the carpet of his office to greet him, Slider overtopped him by a good two inches.

'Inspector Slider? How do you do?'

'I'm grateful to you for seeing me at short notice,' Slider said, shaking hands. The hand was small, too: he was built in proportion. 'I hope I haven't kept you here inconveniently.'

'No, no, I had plenty to do. I don't usually leave the office until sixish, anyway. Besides, my convenience is hardly important in a matter as grave as this, is it?'

'I wish everyone I had to speak to thought like that,' Slider said with a smile. While all this making nice was going on, he was studying the face. Coleraine was one of those men who by dint of a small-featured, boyish face and a good head of hair (brown, with a coppery glint) managed to look a good ten years younger than they really were. It was when you came to the eyes that you found the age, but as long as they were crinkled up in a pleasant smile, it was easy to miss it. But on further examination there was something about these eyes that Slider associated with disability or long childhood illness. It was hard to pin it down – it was something to do with the skin around them, a faintly freckled pallor, the unexpected deepness of the fine lines – but he would not have been surprised to learn that Coleraine had suffered from polio or had had a bad accident which had resulted in years of plaster casts and traction. There was nothing visibly wrong with him, however. He was good-looking, with regular, Grecian features, powerful about the chest and shoulders, and he moved and spoke with the sparky briskness that often lumbered short men with the Napoleon-syndrome label.

As they went through their preliminary chatting, Slider could see that he had considerable charm, and could understand why Fay Coleraine had wanted him. Probably a great many women would want him, he thought – that combination of boyishness and power could be intoxicating. But as Coleraine talked, Slider detected a harshness about the shapes the mouth and eyes made; charm and dynamism overlaid a brittleness, as if he had spent his life defending a vulnerable place by keeping it hidden. There was an edge to the voice, too, which Slider found almost unpleasant. But he knew Coleraine didn't like music: perhaps it was simply that he was tone deaf.

Eventually they got on to the subject of Radek. 'What did you think of your father-in-law?' Slider asked. He was seated in an antiqued leather chair, buttoned to within an inch of its life, on one side of the vast reproduction Georgian desk. Coleraine, on the other side, sat well back in an executive swivel that pivoted through so many planes it could have done service as a flight simulator. Slider had accepted the offer of whisky, and was nursing a dangerously large measure of Glenmorangie in a vast cut-glass tumbler so heavy it was going to take both hands to get it up to his mouth. Everything in the office seemed to have been chosen to declare that if money was no object, good taste certainly wasn't either.

'I don't really care for that kind of music,' Coleraine answered, 'so I don't know whether he was a genius or only fabulously successful. He was certainly the latter. But the *cognoscenti* seem to think he was one of the world's all-time greats, too, so who am I to argue?'

'I meant, what did you think of him as a person,' Slider said patiently, aware that Coleraine knew perfectly well what he had meant. Was this just another game of bait-the-policeman – a favoured pastime amongst some members of the middle classes, who cherished the Father-Christmas belief that all coppers were thick – or was he putting off an evil moment?

'Oh, I see.' Coleraine seemed to consider for a moment. 'Well, he wasn't an easy person to like,' he said at last. 'Not that he cared whether he was or not. He liked to play power games with people, as long as the odds were stacked for him to win – and let's face it, when a man is as rich and important as Stefan, they usually are.' He had put rich first, Slider noted. Was that accidental or a significant psychological marker – what they called in more technical police language, a bit of a dead give-away? Coleraine went on, 'It was sad, really: being who he was, he could have done so much good; but he was arrogant and selfish and mean. It seemed such a waste.'

'I suppose he was a very wealthy man?'

'Oh, I didn't mean "mean" in that sense,' Coleraine said hastily – too hastily to avoid the clumsiness of the sentence. 'Fay and I have plenty of our own. We both have successful businesses which we built up entirely ourselves, without any help from Stefan.'

'You think he ought to have helped you?'

Coleraine looked confused, as Slider meant him to be, by the near-sequitur, and hesitated over the possible paths out of the apparent misunderstanding. 'Look, I wasn't interested in my father-in-law's money. I want you to realise that. I've done all right for myself,' he said, with a vague wave of the glass at his surroundings. 'It was the way he treated Fay that I didn't like,' he went on with an air of being absolutely fair. 'I mean, when we were first married. That's all in the past now, of course.'

'How did he treat your wife?'

Coleraine frowned at the question. 'I don't want you thinking this is some festering sore. It's ancient history now. And in fact, I got on pretty well with the old boy at the end. He wasn't half so bad if you stood up to him and let him know you didn't give a damn what he thought of you.'

'You were on friendly terms with him, then?'

'Yes, he wasn't such an ogre really.'

'You visited him quite a lot, I suppose?'

'No, not a great deal. Just now and then. From time to time,' he said with diminishing eagerness. 'He wasn't the sort of man you'd drop in on out of pleasure.' Slider was interested that Coleraine seemed to think it mattered what he thought of his relationship with Radek. He was trying to create an impression, or perhaps trying not to create another impression. Now why was that?

'So what did you drop in on him out of?' he asked.

'Oh, for God's sake,' Coleraine said impatiently, lifting one hand towards his brow in an uncompleted gesture. 'I wasn't in the habit of dropping in on him. All I'm trying to say is that I got on all right with the old boy, but we weren't great chums, all right?'

Slider smiled enigmatically. 'How did he treat your wife when you were first married?' he reverted. Coleraine didn't answer for a moment, looking annoyed, or perhaps rattled, and Slider went on, 'I understand he didn't approve of the marriage? Or didn't approve of you?'

'Who told you that? Oh, never mind. The fact is Stefan wouldn't have approved of Fay marrying anyone. He wanted to keep her to himself.'

'But he'd sent her away to school, hadn't he, to be rid of her?'

'He could hardly keep her at home once his wife died,' Coleraine objected. 'With no-one to look after her, he had to send her to school. But that didn't mean he didn't want her. She was one of his possessions, and he liked to keep hold of them. And he certainly didn't want anyone else to have her, particularly a nobody like me. So he forbade the marriage, and when Fay went ahead and defied him, he told her she could stew in her own juice from then on, and cut her off without a penny. He was rolling in money, but he enjoyed watching us struggle. And it was a struggle at first, I can tell you. But we made it. I think it riled him that we showed him we didn't need him. I think that's why he offered to pay Marcus's school fees later on. But Marcus got a scholarship, so that wiped the old devil's eye for him.' He paused, perhaps listening to himself critically, for he went on, 'I felt almost sorry for him in the end. It must be sad to have to keep proving to yourself that people need you, and then finding out they don't.'

'Your son is how old now?'

'Twenty-one.'

'And what does he do?'

Coleraine frowned. 'What has all this got to do with Stefan's murder? Why are you asking about me and my family?'

'I'm just trying to get a picture of Sir Stefan's life,' Slider said innocently. 'You see, no-one seems to know of anyone who might want to kill him. So I have to collect every scrap of information I can, to put the whole jigsaw puzzle together. You never know which piece might prove crucial.'

'It all sounds a bit unscientific,' Coleraine said patronisingly. 'We aren't living in the nineteenth century, you know.'

'Oh, we've got people out doing all the high-tech things as well,' Slider said kindly. 'I have my own area of expertise.'

Coleraine, to do him justice, recognised fifteen-all when he saw it. 'Well, I don't know that I can tell you anything,' he said more helpfully. 'I can't think who might want to kill Stefan either.'

'When did you last see him?' Slider asked.

A slight hesitation. 'Actually, it was on Tuesday – Tuesday morning.' His voice had changed. He was trying to slip it out as lightly and unimportantly as possible, and his eyes were watchful. Presumably he thought it was a damaging admission, and that might mean something or nothing: people had the oddest ideas of what was damaging, and often lied about something of no importance at all. It was one of the major frustrations of police work.

'Where did you see him?' Slider asked.

'Oh, at home. At his home, I mean. I – just popped in.'

'Why?'

'No reason in particular. I was just passing, saw his place, wondered how he was.' He shrugged and smiled. 'Passing fancy, you might say.' Something visibly occurred to him. 'I think he'd been having a flaming row with Buster. They were glaring daggers at each other, so it was a good job I did turn up. Poor old Buster looked fit to burst into tears.'

Odd how everyone referred to Keaton as 'poor old Buster', Slider reflected. He seemed to have been very comfortably placed and quite content in his lot. 'What were they quarrelling about?'

'Oh, I don't know. They stopped when I arrived of course.

But I don't suppose it was important. They often had barnies. It didn't mean anything.'

Slider smiled. 'Like a married couple.'

Coleraine shook his head. 'It wasn't like that, if that's what you were thinking. And for God's sake, don't suggest anything of the sort to Fay. It makes her mad as hell. She hates the way people always assume that every friendship has to be that way.'

'I wasn't thinking that. I was only suggesting that people quarrelling doesn't mean they don't love each other or aren't happy together.'

'Yes, well, I'll pass over your use of the word love,' Coleraine said with a tight smile. 'Basically you're right.'

Slider switch-hit. 'Do you know how your father-in-law's estate was left?'

Coleraine opened his eyes wide and frank, to show this was not a problem question. 'The bulk of it goes to Fay. I think Buster was to have the house for his lifetime, which is only fair, considering the years he's put in with the old boy; but it did belong to Fay's grandfather, after all, so it's right it should go to her when Buster dies. He hasn't any family to worry about it anyway. But everything else goes to Fay.'

'It's a considerable fortune, I understand,' Slider said.

'Is it?' he said with enormous indifference. 'I don't know exactly how much. But Fay and I have all we need anyway.'

'Oh, a little extra money never comes amiss,' Slider said genially. 'Perhaps you could put it in trust for your son.'

That touched a nerve. Coleraine offered only a terse and forbidding, 'Perhaps.'

Slider changed direction again. 'Where were you on Wednesday afternoon?'

Something quickened in Coleraine's face. He was suddenly alert and wary. 'Why are you asking me that? Surely I'm not a suspect?'

Slider smiled. 'Telling me where you were doesn't make you a suspect.'

'Why else would you ask that?'

'I can think of lots of reasons. Supposing someone who was a suspect was naming you as their alibi? I'd need to check it out, wouldn't I?'

He had spoken more or less at random, but he seemed to have struck something. Coleraine's face was taut, his mouth ugly with tension. 'Has someone done that?'

'Have you some reason not to tell me where you were on Wednesday afternoon?' Slider countered smoothly.

'No. Not at all. I – er – I was at home,' Coleraine said with some reluctance. 'I was supposed to be lunching with a client that day, but I didn't feel well, so I cancelled it and went home. Mrs Goodwin, my secretary, will confirm that.'

'What time did you get home?'

'About a quarter to two, I suppose. I didn't go out again.'

'Were you alone?'

'Of course I was alone. What sort of question is that?'

'I meant, is there anyone who can confirm that you were there?'

He shook his head. 'Fay was at work. She came home about seven.'

'And your son?'

'He doesn't live with us. He has his own flat in Bayswater.' He tried a smile. 'I'm afraid it's not much of an alibi, is it?'

'Well,' Slider said innocently, 'as long as you don't need one, it doesn't matter, does it?'

'No, of course not,' Coleraine said, looking at Slider thoughtfully. 'You wouldn't, by any chance, be taking the piss, would you?'

'Not by any chance,' Slider said, returning the look. 'A man is dead, Mr Coleraine. What's dead can't come to life, I think.'

'Browning,' he said rather blankly. 'Not a very popular poet.'

'But then mine is not a very popular job. Except with the victims. We're the only ones who actually have to see the victims. The lawyers, the judges, the juries, the social workers, the journalists – they only see the accused, looking very small and put-upon in the dock, or being hustled into a police car.' He drained his whisky and stood up. 'I'm very grateful to you for your time. If I have any more questions, I'll be in touch, and I hope you'll be patient with me. We will find out who killed your father-in-law,' he promised.

'Yes,' said Coleraine, as if that was the only safe word he could think of for the moment.

* * *

In the outer office the secretary was rattling away on a word-processor. She looked up and smiled hesitantly at Slider, and he paused by her desk.

'Mrs Goodwin, isn't it?'

'Yes,' she said. 'Helena.' She was a striking-looking woman in her mid-thirties, with large brown eyes and high cheekbones, dark, fine hair escaping from an Edwardian cottage-loaf, the legal secretary's uniform garb of blue-and-white striped shirt and navy skirt. She looked as though she hadn't been getting much sleep lately: she was pale and there were dark shadows under her eyes, and the smile on her rather lovely mouth was troubled.

'You've been with Mr Coleraine for some time now, haven't you?'

'Four years, and two with Mr Antrobus before that. I don't know if you'd call that a long time.'

Slider nodded encouragingly. 'It's an upsetting business, this.' She watched him carefully, committing herself to nothing. 'A murder in the family,' he expanded, 'even if the victim wasn't particularly popular.'

'I didn't really know Sir Stefan,' she said. 'Only as an ordinary member of the public. He never came to this office.'

'Do you like classical music?'

'Some,' she said circumspectly.

'You've been to concerts when he's been conducting, I suppose?'

For some reason the question bothered her. A faint pinkness appeared. 'One or two. I – I don't really go out much. I have a little boy. Babysitters aren't always easy to find.'

'What does your husband do?'

'I'm divorced,' she said abruptly, the pink deepening. She stood up. 'May I show you out? I have rather a lot of work to catch up on.'

'I'm sorry, I don't want to put you behind,' he said with his most engaging smile, and she softened a little.

'No, it's all right, really,' she said, coming round the desk and crossing to the door. He waited until her hand was on the doorknob.

'Can you tell me what time Mr Coleraine left on Wednesday?'

The hand remained steady, but she said, 'I should have thought you could have asked him that.'

'What an evasive answer,' he said lightly. 'Is there something I ought to know about Wednesday?'

She turned and looked at him steadily. 'No, nothing at all. He left at twelve-thirty.' He waited in silence, looking pleasantly expectant, until she felt obliged to add more. 'He had a luncheon appointment for twelve forty-five, but he came out of his office at half past and said that he wasn't feeling well and was going home, and asked me to cancel it for him.'

'That was rather short notice, wasn't it?'

'Yes, but it wasn't a client, it was a colleague, Peter Gethers. His office is only round the corner in King Street, and they were going to a local restaurant, so I was able to catch him before he left. Mr Coleraine looked very unwell. I wasn't surprised he had to go home.'

She was defending him. Loyalty – or something to cover up?

'Did anything happen that morning to upset him? Anything out of the ordinary?'

'I don't think so.'

'Did he have any visitors?'

'Not that morning.'

'Phone calls.'

'Of course. Lots of them.'

'What was the last one you put through? Do you remember?'

'It was Marcus, his son,' she said with faint reluctance. 'He telephoned at about a quarter to twelve. Then Mr Coleraine buzzed me and asked me to hold all calls for half an hour. And at half past twelve he came out from his office and said he was going home.'

'Do you think those things had anything to do with each other?' Slider asked pleasantly, as though it were a matter of no importance.

She was not wooed. 'I don't know. How could I know that? You must ask Mr Coleraine.'

'Of course. I just thought he might have said something to you about it.'

'Well he didn't. Is there anything else now? Because I really do have a lot of work to catch up.'

'Nothing else at present. Thank you very much, Mrs Goodwin. You've been a great help.'

She opened the door for him, looking faintly puzzled about

what she could have said that was so helpful. There was never any harm in leaving people slightly off balance.

Slider walked in to his office and found Atherton lounging like a tame Viking against the cold radiator talking to WDC Kathleen Swilley – always called Norma for her sins which, since she led a social life of well-guarded privacy, had to be largely imagined by her colleagues, and were. She was blonde and bronzed and mighty like the heroine of a Halls of Valhalla SF mag, and she exuded a degree of sexual vitality you could light a campfire with if you only had a magnifying glass handy – the sort of woman who her colleagues told each other, with varying degrees of wistfulness, must be a lesbian.

'Oh don't be such a stiff,' she was saying sternly. 'You know exactly what I'm talking about. Your idea of safe sex is not telling the girl where you live.'

'Wearing a condom is avoiding the issue,' Atherton said, at his most maddening.

'It's not a joking matter, Jim, not any more. These days you—'

They both saw Slider at the same moment, and Norma sprang off the edge of his desk where she had been warming a neglected circulation file with her delectable and (Slider could only assume) peachlike bottom. She brushed her skirt down, turning to face him with a slight and extremely fetching blush; Atherton declined to be caught wrong-footed, and continued to decorate the radiator with a catlike smile, his weight on his hands and his legs crossed at the ankle, like a third-year student at a tutorial.

'Am I interrupting?' Slider enquired pleasantly. 'Don't stop on my account. I know my office is a public place within the meaning of the Act.'

'The ballistics report has come in, sir,' Norma said. She held out the sheaf of paper, trying to look like a civil servant and failing.

'Tell me,' he said, taking it and passing round his desk to sit down. 'I assume you've read it.'

'Yes, sir. The bullet was a .38, and it was fired from a Webley and Scott Mark IV revolver. Priest thinks given the range it was likely it was the model with the five-inch barrel.'

Chris Priest was the top firearms guru at the Home Office lab at Huntingdon. One glance at the striations on a spent bullet, and he could tell you the gunmaker's sock size. Nothing, unfortunately, about the gun owner.

'A .38 Webley?'

'It was a popular handgun for British officers during the Second World War,' Norma said, 'which would make it bad luck for us, because if it was a World War Two trophy it won't have been registered.'

'Why should you assume that?' Atherton said. He was looking faintly annoyed, perhaps at Swilley's display of expert knowledge in a subject in which he had no interest – or perhaps it was a residue from their interrupted conversation.

'Because, brain, all weapons issued during the Second World War are Government property and cannot lawfully be retained. Don't you know your firearms law?'

'All right, but it doesn't have to be a World War Two gun, does it?' Atherton objected. 'Presumably they've been used at other times.'

'Priest thinks the gun was pretty old; and besides,' she turned to Slider again, 'the actual bullet turns out to be quite interesting. It's marked DC 43, which stands for Dominion Cartridge 1943. It was a brand made in Canada and shipped over towards the end of the war. Apparently we couldn't make enough over here to keep up with demand.'

'Nice and specific,' Slider said, 'but unfortunately not much use to us unless we have a suspect.'

'I quite fancy the agent's boyfriend,' Atherton said. 'Stephen or Steve Murray. I've done a bit of work on him. He's a stage-hand at the Royal Opera House – sweat and singlet type – more brawn than brain. Apparently Kate Apwey likes a bit of rough trade.' He glanced at Norma but she refused to be provoked. 'I ran a make on him, and he's got a little bit of form: possession, a couple of cautions for drunk and disorderly – pub fights – and, here's the juicy one, a suspended for assault and ABH. Bloke on the management team of one of the big orchestras – Murray thought Kate was having an affair with him; waited for him outside the Festival Hall, caught him coming out of the artists' entrance and broke two of his ribs.'

'It's too much to hope that Murray's known for carrying weapons?' Slider asked.

'Much too much,' Atherton said. 'But he jumped this bloke in full daylight with people walking past, and then ran away – which is the same sort of MO as Radek's murderer – and also he had good reason to suppose Radek was humping Apwey – which is the same motive as the assault.'

Norma looked unimpressed. 'You think sex is at the bottom of everything.'

'Unfortunate turn of phrase, Norm.'

'But look,' she went on, ignoring him, 'the person who shot Radek was small, not a hulking great scenery-humper.'

'Ah, that's the beauty of it. I said Murray was brawny, not a hulk. He's more your small, wiry type. Kate Apwey reckons he's five-nine, but you can take an inch off for adoration. *And* he wasn't at work on Wednesday afternoon. He phoned in sick.' He looked appealingly at Slider.

'It sounds promising. You'd better check up on the alibi, and go round and have a look at his drum. Does he live with Apwey?'

'Surprisingly, not yet. She shares a flat with two other professional girls – sorry, Norma, women – and he has a flat in Covent Garden, handy for work. I don't get the impression he earns much.'

Slider nodded. 'That would tend to put him in a dilemma. On the one hand jealousy of his girlfriend's relationship with Radek, and on the other hand, knowing she needed both the job and the tips for them to be able to get a place together.'

'Jealousy, deep frustration, ambivalence of mind – boom!' said Atherton happily.

'On the other hand,' Slider said, 'we mustn't lose sight of the other possibles. It won't hurt to take a look at this sacked musician, what was his name? Preston, Bob Preston. At least find out where he was so we can eliminate him. And then there are the Coleraines.'

'Not Mrs, guv,' Swilley said. 'Polish checked her alibi and it's tight. She was at her shop until two o'clock, and then she drove to Peter Jones's to buy fabrics. They know her there, and the manageress of the department says she served her before she went off for her tea at three, and she was about fifteen to twenty minutes buying stuff. There's no way she could have been at Shepherd's Bush shooting Radek at two thirty-five and got to Sloane Square by two forty-five.'

'Good,' said Slider. 'I didn't really think it was her. Her husband, now, he's another matter. He struck me as nervous and evasive, and his alibi is unprovable. He says he was at home alone all afternoon.'

'Wait a minute, guv,' Norma said. 'He can't have been at home all afternoon, because we tried to phone Mrs Coleraine there and got no answer. That must have been about four-ish. We eventually caught her at the shop, after she got back from Peter Jones. That's when we told her about Radek being shot.'

'Coleraine says he got home at a quarter to two. Let's find out everything we can about him. Maybe his business was in trouble. Maybe his son's in trouble. He knew his wife would inherit Radek's estate, and a good dutiful wife wouldn't fail to share the loot with him.'

'It was quite a loot, too,' Atherton said. 'I checked with the solicitor that Parker, Pool and Law put me on to. Radek was worth about three million pounds.'

There was a brief silence. 'Just for waving your arms about,' Norma said wistfully.

'Now that's what I call a motive,' Slider said. 'I'm glad I didn't know how much before I talked to Mrs Coleraine.'

Slider put his head into the CID room, looking for Atherton, and Beevers looked up from his desk.

'Sir, over here,' he called.

'No, sir over here,' Slider corrected.

Beevers looked at him with grave Nonconformist reproof. 'Have you got a minute, guv? Only it's something a bit odd.'

Slider went meekly and looked over Beevers' shoulder at some printed lists. 'What's this, stolen property?'

'It's something that came in this morning, that I was working on before. You know that load of stolen antiques and stuff we found in that big house in Paddenswick Road?'

'We took Lenny Picket up for it.' Slider shook his head. 'I can never get over that name – Picket the Fence. What other line of work could he possibly have taken up?'

Beevers thought about it. 'I suppose he could have been a landscape gardener.'

Slider was thrown into confusion. Was the Pillar of the Chapel making a joke? Normally Beevers disapproved of humour, believing that lightness of mind was an infallible indicator of lightness of morals – and with the example of Atherton before them, who could argue with him? 'What about it, anyway?' Slider said hastily.

'Well, guv, there were some paintings in the haul, so we sent a description round all the dealers to see if they could place them. This letter came in this morning from Christie's. I was going to pass it on to one of the TDs when the name caught my eye. Look—' He squared the letter before Slider. 'They identify the three paintings as stuff they sold to Alec Coleraine only five months ago, paid for with a bank draft drawn on his personal account. Important paintings, too.'

Slider read, and let out a soundless whistle. 'You're not kidding.' A Turner, a minor Constable and an Italian painter Slider hadn't heard of – religious and Italian, sixteenth-century. The three together had been bought for a total of one million, two hundred and fifty thousand pounds. 'And Coleraine wasn't kidding when he said he was doing all right. One and a quarter million on piccies? I wonder if Lenny knew what he was getting into. Pictures like that are a bit out of his league.'

Beevers scratched his woolly head thoughtfully. 'The funny thing is, guv, Coleraine never reported 'em missing. You know McLaren used to be at Kensington, where Coleraine's gaff is? Well, he got a mate of his over there to look up the records. There was a break-in at the house on the fifth of June, three weeks after he bought the paintings. It looked like a professional job – burglar alarm bypassed and a window taken right out, nice as pie, not kid's stuff. This mate of McLaren's faxed us the report, and there's a list of stolen gear – small antiques, silver and some figurines – but no mention of these paintings. But,' he added the word weightily as he drew another sheet forward and turned it for Slider's scrutiny, tapping with his forefinger, 'if you look here, on this list of the gear we got from Lenny's, this occasional table sounds very like the one Coleraine says he lost; and these figurines, here, they've got to be the same, haven't they?'

Slider read. 'They sound like it,' he admitted.

'Staffordshire glazed figures, 1840s, Victoria and Albert, Admiral Nelson, Sir Robert Peel, George Washington, they're all on the list. George Hudson – who was he, anyway?'

'The Railway King. Pioneering railway builder. Didn't you want to drive a steam train when you were a kid?'

'I'm not old enough,' Beevers said with unconscious cruelty. 'Anyway, guv, here we've got gear from Coleraine's break-in turning up at Lenny's, plus paintings we know Coleraine bought, but he never reports 'em stolen.' He shook his head with dark reproof. 'It's a bit queer.'

After consulting with the duty sergeant, Paxman, whose specialist subject on *Mastermind* could have been Drinking Habits of Shepherd's Bush Lowlife, 1960 to 1990, Slider ran Lenny Picket to earth in The George in Hammersmith Broadway, a vast Edwardian pub of mahogany panels and acid-embossed glass screens, in whose womblike darkness the few daytime drinkers sat at a respectful distance from each other and politely never looked up when anyone came in or went out. As if out of a sense of artistic coherence, everything about Lenny was as narrow as his name – narrow face, narrow shoulders, narrow chest. He smoked very thin roll-ups and during the brief period they stayed alight narrowed his eyes against the rising smoke. He was a squirrel of a man, small, neat, quick and adaptable; a player of many rôles, who at the drop of a hat could switch speech modes from Parkhurst to Park Lane.

He was reading up the forthcoming antique sales in the *Telegraph*, and folded the paper hastily when Slider arrived alongside his table.

'Oh, Mr Slider, you gave me a start,' he said. He had a curiously husky voice which made him sound a bit like Lauren Bacall. Perhaps that was why Slider had always liked him.

'Hullo, Lenny. I wanted to have a word with you. Mind if I sit down?'

'Can I stop you?' Lenny shrugged. 'I'm on bail, my life isn't my own any more.'

'Drink?'

'Might as well take one off you. Gold watch – make it a double – no ice.'

When Slider returned with the drinks he settled down on the other side of the table, and Lenny abandoned the dismal remains of his last roll-up, brought out a packet of Rizla and a tin of Old Horrible, and started anew. 'What's the beef, then?'

'It's about that last haul we nicked you for.'

'Come on now, Mr Slider, I put me hand up for that like a good boy,' he protested. 'End of story. *Finito*.'

'All right, Len, it's not grief for you. I just want some information,' Slider reassured him. 'About those three oil paintings.'

Lenny looked gloomy. 'I wishter God I'd never touched 'em. I don't know what came over me. I've been in this business all my life, and rule number one is never touch nothing there's only one of. I mean, what the 'ell was I going to do with 'em? A nice bit of furniture, a nice garden stachoo, who's to say where it came from? But an oil painting, and a ruddy Gainsborough into the bargain—'

'It was a Constable, actually.'

'Don't say that word, please,' Lenny shuddered delicately. 'I'll never forget when that PC D'Arblay came bursting in. The irony was not lost on me, I promise you.'

'Does it never bother you that what you're doing is completely immoral?' Slider asked in wonder. 'You seem such a nice bloke otherwise.'

'Come on now, Mr Slider, be fair. I'm a businessman,' he said in wounded tones. 'I pay an honest price for what I buy, and sell it again at an honest profit. I've got thousands of satisfied customers who'd give me a testimony. I don't ask where the stuff comes from or where it goes to, but then who does? It's not my fault if other people break the law, is it?'

'A fascinating rationale,' Slider said. 'I like you, Lenny. It's such a pity you're bent.'

'Bent? Listen,' he leaned forward earnestly, 'I had a young bloke in my place a couple of weeks ago, posh accent, posh clothes, all the education money could buy: he comes in to look at some lead allegorical figures for his garden, argues about the price, finally writes me a cheque – and has it away with my fountain pen. Now *that*'s bent. Young people today! They got no standards.'

Slider smiled. 'Well, I'm not interested in statues. It's those oil paintings I want to know about. I want to know where they came from. D'you want to give me a name, Len, and save me a lot of trouble?'

Lenny lifted a hand. 'Now then, now then, you know me better than that. I may not be lily-white in your eyes, but I don't grass up a business associate. Where'd I be if I got meself a reputation? I'd be finished. No-one'd ever do business with me again if they knew I was going to put Plod on their tail.'

'And you know me well enough to know I wouldn't ask you unless it was important,' Slider said. 'I suppose I didn't really expect you to tell me, though I could make a fair guess – within three names.' He looked deep into Lenny's eyes, or as deep as you can look into the slit in a pillar box, but Lenny faced him out unmoved. 'Look,' Slider went on, 'at this stage you don't have to tell me who you got the pictures from, I just want to know where they were stolen from. The address, that's all.'

'What d'you mean, at this stage?' Lenny asked suspiciously.

'It may or it may not prove important. If it doesn't, you won't hear any more about it, my word on it. If it is important, I'll try to keep you out of it and establish the information from another direction.'

'Try?' Lenny sounded peevish. 'And I'll be inside *trying* not to get my boat altered during association period.'

'It's a murder case I'm investigating,' Slider said impatiently. 'Don't mess me about, Lenny. I'm asking you nicely now, and ten to one you'll hear nothing more about it. But we can do it the hard way if you like, and you can have all the publicity you want.'

'That's blackmail. I'm surprised at you, Mr Slider. I always thought you was a decent bloke.' He shook his head over the unreliability of humankind. 'Look, I tell you straight, I don't know where the pictures came from. That's not something I ever ask. I can go back to my supplier and ask him, but whether he'll tell me or not—' He shook his head again.

'He'll tell you. You'll make him. You'll find a way, Lenny. I have confidence in you.'

'It might take me a bit of time.'

Slider smiled. For such a kind-faced man he could look surprisingly menacing when he wanted to, Lenny thought.

'Oh, you'll have the information by Monday, I'm sure of it. An anonymous phone call is all I want. Just an address. Got me?'

'Got you,' Lenny sighed. He pushed his roll-up into the corner of his mouth and fumbled in his pocket for his lighter. 'Tell me, does anybody ever make the mistake of thinking you're soft?'

'Only my wife,' Slider said sadly.

CHAPTER SEVEN

Humming and Erring

On the whole Atherton liked what had happened to Covent Garden. Some of the shops might be a bit poncey, and it seemed to be impossible to cross the piazza without having to avoid someone in black tights and a striped jumper miming his way round a sheet of glass; but at least the place was vital now. Empty upstairs rooms were being turned into flats and bedsitters, the reversal of the usual trend in Central London, and it had the comfortingly Manhattan feeling of a place where people lived, shopped, ate and sat out on sunny evenings on their doorsteps and window-sills watching the world go by.

It had always been rich in restaurants, and he decided to fortify himself with lunch before seeking out Kate Apwey's lover. In a state of pleasant anticipation he strolled into what had been his favourite tatty tratt, a place of check tablecloths and heartwarming Italian vulgarity, only to find it had changed hands since his last visit. Atherton knew he was in trouble when he saw sun-dried tomatoes and balsamic vinegar on the menu: life at the Casa Angelo had suddenly got serious. Gone were the tight-trousered boys with priapic pepper mills, the vast mamma in black wedged behind the till, the clusters of strawed Chianti bottles hanging about in corners like evil funghi, the loop tape of *Volare* and *O Sole Mio*. Now there was rubber music played almost but not quite sub-aurally, the tablecloths were white and the light fittings chrome, and the pictures on the walls were numbingly abstract. Gone were the familiar comforts of avocado vinaigrette, spag bol and pollo sorpreso, the mountain of profiteroles on the sweet trolley overshadowing an untouched bowl of oranges in somethingorother. Now the food made sparse patterns on the oversize plates; olive oil seemed to get drizzled over most things, and the owner actually came out in a grey silk suit and supervised the drizzling. Atherton ate and left a sadder but not much wider man; nobody, in his opinion, ought ever to come out of an Italian restaurant still able to do up all their buttons.

Chastened, he sought Murray's address – a flat above a former warehouse – and found it with some difficulty, for the door was not where it might be expected to be, but round an apparently unrelated corner. He was prepared for there to be no answer to his ring, but after a few moments there was a thunder of feet and the door was opened by a young man, dark-haired and olive-skinned, small and powerful as an Etruscan warrior, standing on the bare wooden stairs onto which the door opened directly. He was wearing grey flannel trousers and braces over a bare chest, his bare feet were very dirty, his chin was unshaven, his eyes were bloodshot, and his hair looked as though he had slept in it. He looked about mid-twenties, though there were lines in his face which suggested a hard life – or perhaps merely chronic bad-temper. He looked at Atherton with an expression of suspicion if not hostility: this was not the man to give anyone the benefit of the doubt.

'Are you Steve Murray?' Atherton asked mildly.

'Who wants to know?' he barked.

Atherton showed his brief. 'Can I come in? I want to talk to you.'

'What about?'

The memory of the sad meal sapped Atherton's patience. 'Oh, don't get funny with me,' he said. 'What do you think I want to talk about? The Arts budget?'

'How the hell should I know?' Murray said. 'Have you got a warrant?'

Atherton sighed inwardly. They all watched too many tv cop shows these days. 'Should I need one?' he asked pointedly.

Murray stared a moment and then backed off, turning himself with some delicacy on the stairs, and Atherton followed him up. At the top was another door, letting onto a long dark corridor running the width of the building, fragrant with the ghost of a thousand cabbages and sounding hollow underfoot. At the far end a rectangle of light was the doorway into the main room: large, lofty and lit with a range of old-fashioned metal-framed windows all along one wall. An upstairs storeroom, he thought, and imagined it stacked with wooden crates of bananas from the Windward Isles, oranges from Cape Town, pineapples from the Gold Coast – ah, the romance of greengrocery! It had probably been a very good storeroom and was now, with the perverse fashion for housing humans in structures designed for inanimate objects, a comfortless living-room. It was bare-floored and sparsely furnished – some of the pieces giving the impression of having been made from those same crates – and one corner accommodated the kitchen, divided off by a breakfast bar. The air was heavy with the smell of joss-sticks not quite masking the smell of pot. Atherton was glad it was none of his business: he wouldn't have wagered a dead cat on there not being little plastic bags of forbidden substances lying about.

Without a glance at Atherton, Murray walked straight across the room, swung himself up onto a bar-stool at the kitchen counter, picked up the newspaper lying there and began to read it.

'Nice place,' Atherton said. 'Do you live here alone?' Murray continued to ignore him, turning a page with ostentatious concentration. 'I know you're not reading that,' Atherton said pleasantly, 'it's *The Sun*. You might as well talk to me and get it over with.'

Murray flung the paper down petulantly. 'You people never leave me alone, just because I got into a bit of trouble once. What do you want, anyway? I've got to go to work in half an hour, so you'll have to make it quick.'

'I want to talk to you about Radek – Sir Stefan Radek.'

Murray's face darkened. 'He's dead,' he said. 'Good thing too.'

'Did you kill him?'

The question didn't seem to surprise Murray. 'I wish I had. I hate his sort. They think money's everything. If you're poor you're nothing. Scumbag!'

'Did you know he was having your girlfriend?' Atherton enquired sympathetically.

Murray stared at him. 'What do you think, I'm stupid?'

'Is that a yes?'

'Of course I bloody knew. I'd have broken both his arms, but *she* wouldn't have it. Told me she was milking him. Huh! Piddling amounts he gave her; I knew who was screwing who.'

'How piddling were the amounts?'

'Couple of hundred. Tarts in Soho get that. Five hundred once, when she went to Hong Kong. For having that filthy old goat slobbering over her – I told her she was mad.'

'I'm amazed you let her do it.'

Murray's face darkened. 'What are you talking about, man, *let* her? A woman's got the right to do what she wants with her own body, right? She's entitled to her own space, rules her own destiny. What are you, one of these chauvinist scumbags, think you can own a woman?'

Ah, evidently a *Guardian* reader, Atherton thought. 'No, not at all,' he replied mildly. 'You seemed so angry about it I thought perhaps you were.'

'You didn't expect me to like it, did you, sharing her with that capitalist filth-bag? But it was her choice. No-one's got the right to tell her what to do and who to go with.'

'Very liberal of you,' Atherton said. It was a sound position for Murray to adopt: there must have been a few people urging Kate not to go with him, after all – Mr and Mrs Apwey, for a bet.

'She's too soft, Kate,' Murray said more reflectively. 'Lets people push her around. He blackmailed her, you know, told her she'd lose her job if she didn't do what he wanted. I told her to stuff the job, but she said no. It paid well, and she was saving up for us to get married and buy a house.' He sniffed and wiped his nose on the back of his hand.

Atherton was entranced by him. 'You were happy about marrying her and living in a house, were you?'

'Why not?' he said. 'Marriage is okay, and you gotta live somewhere. She doesn't like it here. I said, baby, you're paying for it, you got the right to live where you want. She wants furniture and stuff. Me, I can fuck on a bed or I can fuck on the floor, it's all the same to me.' He paused. 'What're you asking me all this shit for, anyway? Is this a bust?'

Far too much tv, Atherton thought. 'Does it look like a bust?'

'You people never leave me alone,' he muttered.

'You didn't go in to work on Wednesday,' Atherton said. 'Why was that?'

'Last Wednesday? I was sick. What's it to you?'

'What kinda sick? You see a doctor?' Atherton gave in and adopted the local style.

Murray glared at him. 'Sick like you get when you've had too much the night before, all right?' He jumped down off the stool and kicked at the newspaper, his voice rising. 'I had a few beers, did a few lines, I was canned, I felt lousy, so I didn't get up, okay? I called in and told them I was taking the day off. I stayed in bed all day. Okay?'

At that moment the door in the long wall opposite the windows opened, and a fair young man came out, tousled, gummy-eyed, wearing a grubby red towel over an expensive tan and a St Christopher on a gold chain round his neck. His nose was running, and if he was not now he had certainly recently been in an illegal state of mind. 'What's the matter, what's all the shouting?' he mumbled, and broke into a huge open-mouthed yawn revealing fine teeth and a regrettable tongue. Closing his mouth he looked at Atherton. 'Who's this bloke, Steve?'

The voice was blurred but the accent was unmistakably upper class. Steve Murray evidently believed in sinning above his station.

'Never mind. Just go back to sleep, dickhead,' Murray snarled.

'I'm Detective Sergeant Atherton,' Atherton said. 'Just having a chat with your friend. Who are you?'

The young man looked wary. 'Does it matter?'

Atherton smiled. 'I wouldn't have asked if I hadn't wanted to know, son. What's your name?'

The eyes flickered across to Murray and back, and he gave a tiny shrug. 'Marcus Coleraine, if it's any of your business,' he said sulkily.

'Oh, I think it is,' Atherton said smoothly, hiding the lift of his heart at the scent of a lead. 'I'm just asking your friend here what he knows about the death of your grandpa.'

Marcus's eyes widened. 'Oh shit!' he breathed.

Slider was just about to leave his office when the phone rang. He hesitated a moment, and then thought that it might possibly be Joanna and answered it.

'Bill!' Wrong. It was Irene, annoyed. 'Why didn't you call me back?'

'I didn't know you were trying to reach me,' he said stupidly.

'I rang you twice. Didn't you get the messages?'

Belatedly he identified Mrs Hislop-Ivory. He imagined the

exchange: 'Who's calling?' 'It's his wife, Irene.' McLaren must have been doing X-rays without his lead hat again. Or was he just deaf?

'Now I come to think of it, yes,' Slider said. 'Is something wrong?'

'Not wrong exactly, but we have to talk, you know. About the house, for one thing.'

'I can't talk now, I'm just going out.'

'Oh yes, it's lunchtime, isn't it? Don't let me spoil your pleasure!'

'It's not that. We've got a big case on. I've got a lot to do.'

'There's always some excuse. Well you can spare me a few minutes of your precious time. There are things we have to sort out.'

'Can't it wait until tonight?'

'Who's to say whether I'll be able to catch you tonight? You can't put it off for ever, Bill. I know you. You always think things will go away if you ignore them, but they won't.'

No he didn't. That annoyed him. He knew they wouldn't. 'Ernie Newman didn't go away. I tried ignoring him.'

'Maybe that was the trouble,' she said sharply. 'Any normal man would have felt jealous about another man hanging around his wife. Any normal man would have done something about it.'

'Like what?'

'Like taken a little interest in me.'

Ouch, that smarted. He turned the attack. 'No normal man could have felt jealous of Ernie Newman. You can't tell the size of his house and pension just from looking at him.'

'Do you really think I'm that shallow?' Irene asked, hurt.

Now Slider felt ashamed, and in his shame hit out again. 'Well, let's face it, you're not after him for his body, are you?'

'How dare you say that?' she retorted. 'Do you think because you don't please me that no-one can?'

Slider reeled, on the ropes. By God, that got him where he lived! On a scale of chauvinism he ranked pretty low amongst his peers, but still he had always assumed that Irene was not interested in sex. It was shocking to be told suddenly, after all these years, that *au contraire* she was simply not interested in him; the more so because of the unpleasant revelations it made about him to himself – not so much about his sexual technique, but about his conceit, of which he had believed he was fairly free. Perhaps the greatest conceit of all was to think you were not conceited? He'd have to run that one past Atherton's giant brain. In the meantime he wasn't doing too well, conversationally, and especially not in the office. He groped belatedly after a shred of dignity.

'I'm sorry,' he said. 'I shouldn't have said that. I didn't mean it.'

'It's all right. I know you didn't,' she said after a moment, but she still sounded hurt.

'What was it you wanted, anyway?' he asked, trying to be helpful. 'Something about the house, you said?'

'Yes. Well, it will have to be sold, you know, so that we can split the proceeds. Have you done anything about finding somewhere to live yet?'

'I haven't had time.'

'You must *make* time,' she said impatiently. 'Do you want me to sell it out from under you? I could, you know.'

'What are you in such a hurry about? You're comfortable, aren't you? It's not as if you're living on the street.'

'It's not the point,' she said, and something in her voice made him think that what *was* the point embarrassed her. Maybe Ernie was pressing her to get her share of the money. But no, not Ernie, he corrected himself. To be fair to old fart-face, Ernie wouldn't do that. More likely it was Irene's friend and mentor, Marilyn Cripps, in whose distressed pine kitchen he was pretty sure Irene would have poured out everything over the herb tea and rough-baked oat cookies. The she-Cripps had never liked him. She'd tell Irene exactly what she was entitled to and urge her to extract every last cent, if it meant squeezing him till his socks squeaked. And Irene, the cluck, was always fatally impressed by anyone with a detached house and a Labrador.

'The point is you're always prevaricating,' Irene went on. 'You've always been like it, and you're no better now. Look, I know what you're thinking,' she added more gently, 'but it's no good delaying things in the hope that I'll change my mind. I'm not coming back, and you might as well accept it, and get on and sort things out. You'll be happier in the long run. Start a new life of your own.'

'It's nice of you to care,' he said. There was a silence while she tried to work out if he was being ironic or not.

'Well, what are you going to do? Either we have to talk and agree a settlement between us, or my solicitor will have to talk to yours. You wouldn't want that, would you?'

This was such big talk from little Irene – 'my solicitor', forsooth! She was moving upmarket in a big way, leaving him far behind. 'How are the children?' he asked suddenly.

'Fine,' she said briefly; and there was a silence in which painful thoughts, memories and regrets surged about like bacterial activity. A great hopelessness swept over Slider. What had brought him to this pass, homeless, loveless, childless, and short of socks? As a punishment for sin it was pretty effective; the sin not so much of adultery but of vacillation.

'I'd like to see them,' he said, a statement of fact rather than a request, but she said cunningly, 'You'll see them if you make a date to come round here and talk things through.'

He panicked at the idea of going to Ernie's house and seeing his children nesting amongst the late Mavis Newman's furnishings. Too bizarre. He'd end up like Barrington. Anyway, there was the case – oh case, oh sweet oh lovely case! 'I just don't know what I'll be doing for the next few days,' he said desperately. 'I'll call you tomorrow about it.'

He could feel her doubting. 'Well, what about the house? Are you going to put it on the market?'

'You do it,' he said, 'I really haven't got time to talk to estate agents.'

'But what about the furniture?'

'I don't care about it. I don't want any of it. Get in a firm of house-clearers. Just let me know when they're coming so I can get my own things out.'

This clearly made Irene unhappy. 'But what are you going to *do*? You have to have somewhere to go.' He didn't volunteer anything, and she went on, 'You don't sound like yourself at all. I'm worried about you. Are you all right?'

'I'm deliriously happy, what do you think?' Then he regretted it. 'No, I'm all right, really. Just do whatever you want, and I'll make my own arrangements. Don't worry about me.'

'But are you sure you want me to sell the furniture? Won't you need it for wherever you go?'

'Quite sure,' he said firmly. He hated that three-piece suite, the reproduction mahogany dinette set, the Dreamland bed with the Dralon velvet headboard (which frankly he'd always thought rather unhygienic apart from anything else), the Jacobethan glazed oak corner cupboard in which were displayed the Birds of Britain limited edition decorative plates set. He'd always hated them. This was not life, it was a Home Shopping Experience.

'It'll be a load off my mind,' he said sincerely. 'Look, I must go. I'll call you tomorrow.'

'Well, see you do,' she said doubtfully, and rang off.

The Coleraines lived in one of those large Edwardian service flats at the back of Kensington High Street. Slider rang the bell, and the door was opened almost before his finger had left the button. Mrs Coleraine was standing there in the hall, half in and half out of her overcoat.

'Oh, Inspector,' she said with a smile and a hint of apology. 'Do come in. Did you want me? I was just going out.'

'No, as a matter of fact it was your husband I wanted a word with.'

The smile widened with relief. 'It's work, you see – well, half work, half pleasure. I'm doing up a little flat for Henry – Alec's godson Henry Russell. He's getting married and it's going to be my wedding-present to him. I want to have it all ready for them to move into straight away, but I've got so behind, and I expect – I imagine—' She paused, an anxious frown bending her fair brows. 'I was wondering about the funeral. I don't mean to sound callous, but I suppose I will lose some more time over it. Have you any idea when we're likely to be allowed to go ahead with it?'

'Well, we have to wait for the inquest, of course. In cases like this that's a brief formality. We tell the Coroner that an investigation is going on and ask for an adjournment, and unless there's any reason not to, he then issues a certificate allowing the body to be released for burial.'

'And is there,' she said carefully, 'any reason not to?'

'Not as far as I know,' Slider said. 'There was nothing mysterious about the death, except for who did it. I can't see any reason why the body shouldn't be released. The inquest will be on Monday, so I should say you could safely arrange the funeral for the middle of next week.'

'Thank you, Inspector. That's very helpful. I'll work on Wednesday, then, though the arrangements may be—' She sighed, and then straightened her shoulders. 'Well, I mustn't bother you with my worries. My husband is in the drawing-room. I'll take you to him, and then I shall have to go, if you'll forgive me.'

Slider got the impression Alec Coleraine had assumed his wife had gone, for he seemed startled when she appeared in the doorway, and was noticeably put out when he saw Slider behind her. He was sitting in an armchair with a book in his lap, a glass of whisky on the table beside him, and Barbra Streisand barely contained by the hi-fi. The room was large and almost aggressively comfortable, capacious chairs and sofas bloated with stuffing, a carpet so thick it looked as if it needed regular mowing, and heavy curtains at the window that would have muffled Armageddon. Every perching place had its little table to elbow, and there was a large drinks cabinet in one corner and a range of bookshelves along one wall filled with books in bright dust-jackets. This was not a room for impressing intellectuals, this was a room to slob out in, and Coleraine was slobbing out in leather house-slippers and the sort of cords and sweater Slider would have kept for best.

'Mr Slider's called in for a word with you, darling,' Fay was saying as she ushered him in. 'I must dash, though – you don't mind?'

Coleraine had stood up, courteously lowering Barbra's blood-pressure with the remote, but he hadn't time to assemble any words before his wife had disappeared again. Slider thought he was looking unwell, as though he was under considerable strain, which boded well for the investigation, though the human in Slider would have liked to hold back, even to leave well alone. These domestics were the devil, he thought. That nice woman would be the victim of anything that happened to Coleraine, and Radek had been an unpleasant man according to most sources, no loss to the world. If Coleraine had been driven by desperation to hurry him on his way, why should society care? It was not as if Coleraine was dangerous; he was unlikely ever to murder anyone else.

Ah, the comfort of sloppy thinking! But being an unpleasant old gink did not cancel your right to live, and every person's life was precious to them, whether they were universally sympatico or Noel Edmonds.

'Won't you sit down, Inspector,' Coleraine said with an obvious effort. 'Can I get you a drink?'

'No thank you, nothing for me,' Slider said. Coleraine resumed his seat and Slider perched on the edge of the sofa nearest him. The vast upholstered spaces behind him were clamouring for his body, but he was afraid he'd be sucked down and sink without trace if he leaned back. 'There's a little matter I wanted to talk to you about. I have here—' He produced from his inside pocket the paper Christie's had faxed through that afternoon. 'I have here a copy of a bill for three pictures you bought back in May from Christie's. Three oil paintings. I wonder if you could tell me what happened to them?'

Coleraine took the paper from him with a stringless hand. It was obviously something he hadn't expected to be asked, but there was a sick and confused look rather than honest puzzlement in his face. Whatever the story was, the pictures were part of it, Slider thought. Coleraine examined the bill for a long time, as though wondering whether he could doubt its authenticity.

'Why do you want to know about these?' he asked at last. 'Is there something wrong?'

'Just answer the question, please. Have you got the paintings here? Can I see them?'

'No. No. I – I don't keep them here,' Coleraine said. He put a hand up to his brow as though shielding his face, like a character in an old ham movie trying to get past the patrolman without being recognised.

'Oh? That's a pity. They must be lovely paintings,' Slider said warmly. 'I'm very fond of Turner myself. You didn't buy them for pleasure, then?'

Coleraine tried to smile and thought better of it. 'No, not really. They aren't my kind of art. I prefer something more modern, abstract.' There were pictures on the walls around them, all richly old-fashioned and representational. Seeing Slider looking, Coleraine hurried on, 'No, I bought them for an investment, actually.'

'A very sound investment, too,' Slider said approvingly. 'The chap I spoke to at Christie's said that you got them at a very good price on a rising market. He said that you could expect to sell them again in a year's time at quite a profit.'

'Yes. Yes, I hope so. Of course. But you haven't told me why you're asking about the paintings.'

'You haven't told me where they are,' Slider countered pleasantly. 'You don't keep them here, you said. So where?'

'At the office.' It sounded as if he'd spoken at random, and presumably hearing the same thing himself, he hurried to justify it. 'They're safer there. There's a better alarm system. I wouldn't want them to get stolen.'

'At the office? So if I come up tomorrow you can show them to me?'

Coleraine took a desperate gulp of whisky. 'Oh – er – no, I remember now. I sent them to be cleaned.'

'So, not at the office,' Slider said, like one questioning a very young child.

'No. They're still at the restorer's.'

'And which restorer's would that be?'

'I don't remember.'

'You don't remember?'

Coleraine flashed him a look of pure hatred, like a cornered cat. 'I didn't mean – of course I've got the address somewhere.'

'It would be on the receipt, I expect,' said Slider helpfully.

'Yes,' said Coleraine defiantly. He met Slider's eyes in the full knowledge that Slider knew he was lying.

'So perhaps you'd like to show me the receipt, then?'

'I – I'm not sure I still have it. I might have lost it.'

Slider stood up abruptly. 'Oh, come on, Mr Coleraine. This is getting silly. One and a quarter million pounds' worth of paintings, and you can't remember where you sent them and you're not sure if you still have the receipt?' He walked over to the mantelpiece and leaned an elbow on it, looking down at his wriggling victim. 'I may as well put you out of your misery and tell you that I know where those paintings are.'

'I doubt that you do,' Coleraine said, with a resurgence of spirit.

Slider smiled. 'I've got them.'

The whisky lapped up the side of his glass, and Coleraine put it down carefully. 'You've got them?'

'Yup.' Slider nodded. 'We recovered them as part of a burglary haul, including some other items stolen from your house, here, during a break-in in June. You reported the break-in to the police, but you didn't mention the pictures. Why?'

Coleraine looked as though he was not going to answer, but at last, licking his lips, he said, 'I had my reasons.'

'Well, do share them with me. Because if you didn't report the pictures stolen, you couldn't claim for them on the insurance, or hope to get them back. Now money may not be everything, but I've never met a man so willing to chuck away one and a quarter million for want of a few words to the police.'

'I don't have to tell you anything,' Coleraine said sulkily.

'Not yet you don't. This is just a friendly chat we're having. But I do advise you to confide in me now rather than later.'

Coleraine thought for some time, staring into the middle distance. He looked very unwell. At last he lifted his eyes to Slider and said with almost childish defiance, 'They weren't insured. The premiums would have been astronomical. So I couldn't have claimed on the insurance anyway.'

'Why didn't you tell the police they'd been stolen? How did you hope to get them back otherwise?' Coleraine didn't answer, only shook his head in a hopeless sort of way, looking down at the carpet. 'Where did you get the money to buy them in the first place? That's a lot of spare money to have lying around. Is there something you ought to be telling me about that?'

He glanced up. 'I've nothing more to say to you,' he said, setting his mouth into a hard line. 'My money is my private business.'

Prevarication is the thief of time. Slider looked at him wearily for a moment, and then looked away, fiddling idly with the things on the mantelpiece – an eclectic assemblage, fit for one of those Sunday supplement articles. *The View from My Mantelpiece*. 'Mr Coleraine, I'm bound to say that you haven't said anything to satisfy my curiosity about this business. In fact, rather the opposite. When people behave in an uncharacteristic way, there's usually a good reason, or perhaps I should say a bad reason, especially where large sums of money are involved—' He broke off. One of the things on the mantelpiece, which now came to his exploring fingers, was a length of black silk line wound around a brass spool. The presence beside it of a clear-plastic topped case of fishing-flies told him what it was doing there, but the interesting thing to Slider was that the brass spool was a spent .38 cartridge case. He picked it up.

'What's this?' he asked.

Coleraine looked up. 'It's fly-line.' He seemed surprised at the question. 'I go trout fishing. It's a hobby of mine.'

'No, I meant, what's this it's wound onto?' Slider asked.

Coleraine frowned. 'Well, what does it look like? It's a cartridge case. I've had it for years. I've always kept my spare line on it. I make my own flies, you see.'

'Where did you get it from?' Slider asked quietly. Why didn't detectives carry magnifying glasses? Come back, Lord Peter, all is forgiven! But there was a pair of reading glasses lying on the table by Coleraine's chair, and he stepped across and picked them up, and took them, with the cartridge, to the light.

'You do ask the most peculiar questions,' Coleraine was saying, sounding half peevish, half relieved. Evidently he liked this line of questioning better than the last, anyway. 'My father-in-law gave it to me, as a matter of fact, years and years ago. We were in his study talking about fishing, and the subject of making flies came up, and he took it out of his drawer and gave it to me. He said he always kept his line wound on one.'

'Did he have a gun, then?' Slider asked, angling the glasses to get the best magnification.

'Only his old war-time revolver. Souvenir. He fought on our side, you know. I don't know if he's still got it. The last time I saw it was when Marcus was a boy, and the old man showed it to him. That's got to be ten, twelve years ago.'

Ah yes, there it was, just above the rim: little stamped letters, DC 43. If it was a coincidence, it was going to make the *Guinness Book of Records.*

'Do you mind if I borrow this?' he asked politely.

CHAPTER EIGHT

I could have been a Judge, only I never had the Latin

'Hello, Bill?'

Slider's heart, and sundry adjacent organs, lifted at the sound of the voice. 'My dreams come true,' he said. 'How often I've picked up the phone hoping to hear those very words.'

'Stop messing around,' Joanna said sternly. 'You won't be so happy when you know what I've phoned about.'

'I'll get used to it,' he promised eagerly.

'Oh shut up. Look, I've had a phone call from Bob Preston. He was terribly upset. Apparently some of your blokes went round to his house, asking him and his family questions about Radek. Poor old Bob was in pieces, thinking you suspect him. He phoned me up to ask if I knew anything. What's going on?'

'It's just routine questioning,' Slider said warily. She sounded really annoyed. 'You know the form.'

'But you can't really be suspecting Bob,' she said wildly. 'He's a trumpet player, for God's sake!'

'That makes him immune from suspicion, does it?'

'Yes. And trombone players,' she said defiantly. 'You can't suspect the brass section. It's ridiculous.'

'Oh look, you know the form. We have to ask everyone, even if it's just to eliminate them.'

'You didn't ask me.'

'You didn't have a motive.'

'You think being sacked is a motive for murder?'

'Look, it's just routine—'

'It isn't routine to him or his wife or his daughters. They're really upset. And they're worried that it's going to get about to the neighbours and the other kids in their kids' school, and people are going to start saying there's no smoke without fire. Did you have to go trampling over his life like that? Haven't your people got anything better to do?'

He heard her hear herself say it, so he didn't follow it up. Instead he said, 'They won't be bothered any more. You know that we had nothing physical to go on. All we could do was look at motive. A man's been killed, you know. We have to be thorough.'

There was a pause, and when she spoke again her voice was defiant with contrition. 'Well I tell you one thing, Bill Slider, you were on the wrong track with Bob. No person who spends their entire life playing a musical instrument would ever commit murder – not even an oboist.'

It was an attempt at a joke, and he felt a surge of tenderness fit to melt his buttons. 'Jo—'

'I'm *telling* you,' she said as if he had argued the point, 'it wasn't a musician who killed Radek. You mark my words. You'll see I'm right.'

'I hope you are,' he said.

'You've definitely cleared Bob?' she asked after a pause.

'Yes. He won't be bothered again.'

'Because you don't realise how frightened ordinary people are by the law. Most ordinary people never open their door to find a copper standing there. It's like being invaded by aliens from Mars.'

'Of course I realise. Don't you think I know how I'm looked at? Do you think I like being a Martian?'

He spoke more warmly than he meant, and she said, 'I'm sorry.'

'No, it's all right.' There was an awkward silence. The real issue came thrusting upwards again. He had to say something. 'Jo, can we meet? I need to talk to you.'

'What about?'

'If I could answer that on the phone I wouldn't need to meet you, would I?'

'I suppose not. Oh, Bill, I don't know. It won't do any good, you know. It's over between us.'

'It isn't. If it were, you wouldn't be on the phone now, getting mad at me.'

'You were my friend once. I could get mad at you,' she said.

'I still am your friend. Whatever happens, you can't say there's nothing between us. Let me see you and talk to you, just that at least.'

There was a long silence, and he had no idea whether she was going to say yes or no. He thought probably she didn't know either. Then at last she said reluctantly, 'I'm off tomorrow night, as it happens.'

Relief rushed straight to his trousers. 'All right. Good. Wonderful. Look, I should be able to get away around six, half past six. I'll come round to your place, shall I?'

'Yes, all right,' she said, but on a dying cadence, as if the idea didn't exactly thrill her. But she'd said she'd see him. It was a start.

Slider was astonished by the change in Poor Old Buster. When he had first seen him he had been dapper, spry, with the alertness and movements of a man in his fifties; now, only a few days later, he had shuffled to answer the door like an octogenarian, and climbed the stairs ahead of Slider slowly, pulling himself up by the banisters. Here in the drawing-room he sat in the armchair with his hands in his lap, utterly immobile, like an old man in a home waiting to die, his eyes blank, his muscles slack, his clothes crumpled, his previously firm face seeming somehow untidy with grief. Here, if anywhere, was the justification for Radek's life. If even one person mourned him as deeply as Keaton, he could not have been without worth.

'Mr Keaton, I'm sorry to bother you again,' Slider began.

Keaton sighed and said with an obvious effort, 'It doesn't matter. I've nothing else to do.'

'Are you managing all right?' Slider enquired gently.

'Managing?'

'Cooking and shopping and so on.'

'Oh – that.' He shook his head. 'There's nothing I want. I have nothing to live for now.'

'Oh, you mustn't say that,' Slider protested, and Keaton lifted dull eyes to him.

'It's a statement of fact. How can I help you?'

'I understand from Mr Coleraine that Sir Stefan had a gun – a revolver, in fact.'

'Yes,' Keaton said, without any particular emphasis. 'It was the one he used during the war. He kept it as a souvenir.'

'Do you know where he kept it?'

'In the drawer of his desk, in his study.'

'May I see it, please?'

Keaton got up with an effort, pushing himself with his hands on the chair arms. The study was across the hall from the drawing-room, a large and handsome room furnished with desk, chair, map-table, a large leather sofa, and a handsome range of bookshelves, several shelves of which were dedicated to leather-bound music scores. There was also a baby-grand piano, and over by the window a magnificent mahogany and brass music stand. Seeing Slider notice it, Keaton said, 'He used to work here. People don't understand how many hours of preparation and practice went into his performances.'

Slider nodded sympathetically. Performances seemed an odd choice of word, until he noticed that opposite the music stand, fixed to the wall, was a full-length mirror. He actually practised his arm-waving then, Slider thought with wry amusement; watched himself in the mirror. He would love to tell Joanna that.

Keaton had shuffled over to the desk, and now opened the top left-hand drawer. 'He kept it in here,' he said.

Slider moved to his side. 'Wasn't the drawer usually kept locked?'

'Oh no. It wouldn't have been any use against burglars if he'd had to unlock a drawer to get at it,' Keaton said, as though it were obvious logic.

'Did he keep it loaded as well?'

'Of course. What use is an unloaded gun?' He pulled the drawer further out and bent to peer in. 'That's funny. He must have moved it.'

'The gun isn't there?'

'No. Here's the ammunition, all right, but—' He pulled out a box, old, softened, grimed with time, the lettering rubbed and faded: DC 43. Slowly, painstakingly, he searched every drawer. 'I can't find it. He must have put it somewhere else. I wonder why?' He straightened up, frowning at Slider. 'Is it important? Will we have to search the house?'

'No, I don't think so,' Slider said. 'Do you remember when you last saw it?'

A sort of bleak dawn suffused Buster's face, and his mouth sagged like a baby's who had just been given a spoonful of spinach. 'Oh my goodness, you don't mean—? Are you saying that it was his own gun? That someone shot him with his own gun?'

'I don't know for sure, but it looks that way.'

'Oh, but that's terrible!' He gaped with dismay. 'What a mean, awful thing to do! I had no idea! It never occurred to me that—' He shook his head agitated by the enormity of it. Humankind is so strange, Slider thought. Amid all the butchery of war, the fact that someone was shot on Christmas Day will be held up as the nadir of depravity. Forty-eight hours later it would be ho-hum just another body.

'If someone did steal Sir Stefan's revolver,' Slider prompted him, 'it would be useful if you could remember when you last saw it in its usual drawer.'

'To give you a *terminus a quo*, yes, I see,' Buster said helpfully. Blimey, the education you get on this job, Slider marvelled. Better than going to grammar school. 'But we haven't been burgled, you know. And Sir Stefan can't have missed it, or he'd certainly have mentioned it to me.'

'So it must have been taken by a visitor to the house – unless he lent it to someone?'

'Oh, I'm sure he wouldn't do that. He was very careful with it. He would never let Marcus touch it, for instance, however much he begged. You know how fascinated little boys are with guns.'

'Unfortunately, as it wasn't kept locked away, anyone who came to the house and was left alone for a few moments could have taken it. Do you remember when you last saw it?'

'Wait, wait, let me think. I'm sure it was—' Keaton folded one arm across his chest, rested the other elbow on it, and cradled his jaw in deep thought. At last his face brightened. 'Yes, of course, I knew there was something! It was on Sunday afternoon when I brought him his tea. He usually has it in here, and when I came in with the tray he was sitting at his desk cleaning it – the gun, I mean. I remember because I don't like the smell of the oil, and I was going to say something to him about being careful not to spill any on the carpet, but in the end I didn't because he'd been a bit on edge and I didn't want to start a quarrel.' He looked at Slider hopefully, as though for praise. 'Sunday afternoon, definitely.'

'Very good,' Slider said. 'Now if you could think very carefully and tell me everyone who called at the house between then and Wednesday.'

'Oh, but no-one came,' he said quickly. 'We don't have callers of that sort.'

'Of what sort?' Slider asked in private amusement. Was he visualising swarthy villains in masks ringing the doorbell and saying, 'Burglar, sir, come to nick your gun. All right if I go up?'

'Well, of any sort really. Nobody comes here – or at least, no-one gets let in, because we have people collecting and that sort of thing.'

'Mr Coleraine told me that he called on Tuesday to see his father-in-law.'

Enlightenment transformed Keaton's face. For a moment he looked almost happy. 'Oh, family, you mean? Naturally I didn't think you meant anyone we knew. Certainly Alec was here on Tuesday morning.'

'At what time?'

'It would be about half past nine. I was annoyed that he called so early, but he said he was on his way to work.'

'You let him in?'

'Of course.'

'And then what?'

'I don't understand.'

'Did you show him upstairs, or did he go up alone, what?'

'I accompanied him to the drawing-room, and then went to fetch Sir Stefan. He was still in his bedroom. He doesn't get up early unless he has an engagement.'

'So Mr Coleraine was left alone down here for some minutes?'

Buster's eyes widened. 'You surely aren't suggesting—!'

'I'm not suggesting anything. I have to make a note of every possibility, even if only to eliminate it.'

'But Alec wouldn't – you can't think he or Marcus—'

'Marcus? Was Marcus with him?'

'No, no, but he called on his grandfather on the Tuesday afternoon. It was inconvenient – we were just going out. But Sir Stefan saw him for a few moments in here.'

'Did he leave Marcus alone for any of the time?'

'I don't know. I was downstairs. I was really annoyed because it was making us late for rehearsal, and we dislike very much to be unpunctual. Young people are so thoughtless. I told him when he arrived we were on the point of leaving, but still he kept Sir Stefan a quarter of an hour, and put him in a temper.'

'In a temper? About what?'

'I don't know. I told you. I was downstairs. It was just some nonsense, I expect. Marcus can be very annoying.'

Slider nodded. 'And who else called between Sunday teatime and Wednesday lunchtime?'

'No-one else. No-one at all.'

'You're quite sure? Not friend or relative, however well trusted? Not meter-reader, plumber, double-glazing salesman, or wandering faith-healer?'

Keaton frowned. 'No-one. I'm quite sure. And I don't think this is a matter for levity.'

'I'm sorry. Do you know what Alec Coleraine called for? Did you hear his conversation with Sir Stefan?'

'I wasn't in the room. I went to make coffee. Sir Stefan wanted his coffee – Alec refused any. When I brought the tray in, things seemed rather heated. Sir Stefan was quite angry, and Alec was pleading with him.'

'Do you know what about?'

'I think he'd been asking for money.' Buster's lips folded in disapproval. 'It wasn't the first time. There's always some people willing to spend what they haven't earned.'

Money again, Slider thought. It was coming together nicely now. 'You think Sir Stefan refused?'

'Certainly. He believed people should stand on their own feet, as he always did.'

'I see. And you're quite sure no-one else came to see Sir Stefan?'

'Yes. But I'm also quite sure neither Alec nor Marcus had anything to do with his death. I know them, I've known them for many, many years. It is simply not in them to do such a thing. In fact—' He hesitated, something visibly working through his mind.

'Yes?' Slider prompted. 'You've thought of something else?'

'No,' he said, and then again, more surely, 'no. I was just going to say that in their own ways they were probably all very fond of each other. It doesn't do to judge by appearances. People often quarrel with those they love best.'

'Mr Coleraine said just the same thing to me the other day.'

'Yes, yes, so you see?' Keaton said eagerly.

Slider smiled comfortingly. 'I assure you I never judge by appearances. I always turn over every stone. It's astonishing what can be under them.'

'Quite so,' Keaton said. The animation drained from his face, and he returned abruptly to the listlessness of grief.

The drawback to being a human, Slider thought as he took his leave, was that pleasure tended to be over quite quickly, while unhappiness went on for great big indigestible lumps of time.

Nutty Nicholls was in the front shop when Slider went through. Nutty, a burly Scot from the rain-lashed shores of the far north west, had once at a fund-raising concert sung the *Queen of the Night* aria from *The Magic Flute*, and was known in consequence as the copper with the *coloratura*, or occasionally Noballs Nicholls. The latter was manifestly unjustified, but Nicholls only smiled and took it in his stride. It was a performance practised and polished to perfection, he told Slider, in a part of the world where there was nothing else to do, and no airborne pollution to damage the vocal chords.

He called to Slider as he passed through. 'I've got a message for you, Bill. An anonymous caller, no less, leaving you an address. I'd congratulate you on a secret assignation, but by the voice it was either a bloke or the bearded lady from the fairground on the Scrubs.'

'It was a bloke, and not my sort,' Slider said, coming across for the piece of paper. On it, in Paxman's bullish handwriting, was Coleraine's address.

'Is this to do with your murder?' Nicholls asked, rolling his r's superbly. 'Is that not the son-in-law's address?'

'How did you know that?' Slider asked in amusement. Not much got past Nicholls.

'I was at the fax machine when McLaren got his burglary report through. Is the son-in-law in the frame, then?'

'Like a Gainsborough,' Slider answered, and thought of Lenny Picket. But not like a Constable. 'Is Barrington in?'

Nutty shook his head. 'Not back yet. That man is developing a dangerously high tolerance of lunch.'

'Do you think it's lunch? It strikes me he's not firing on all cylinders these days.'

Nicholls cocked an eye at him. 'You think he's heading for a breakdown? I've been wondering myself. D'you know he was down here this morning looking through the waste-paper baskets?'

'Did he find what he was looking for?'

'He found a couple of paper clips in the charge room, and went straight into circuit overload. Paxman told me about it. Result is we've got a new ukase wet from the press.' He gestured towards a memo lying in the in-basket. 'To all departments: paper clips are not to be thrown away but must be kept and re-used. Department supervisors must make regular checks of the waste-paper baskets to see that this instruction is being followed.'

Slider shook his head sadly. 'He's just playing for popularity. Taking the easy course.'

'It doesn't surprise me,' Nutty went on. 'All that business over the chip-shop murders – Home Office, Foreign Office and everyone else asking him searching questions – and then you not taking your transfer. Every time he comes in to the office the sight of you rubs his face in it.'

'You think it's my fault, do you?' Slider protested.

'If you mean to sup with the devil, you need a long spoon,' Nicholls said with Highland inscrutability. 'You had troubles enough, but he'd four times as many. He'd yours times his.'

'That's what bosses are for.'

'Oh, I know,' said Nutty tranquilly. 'I'm just mentioning.'

The last thing in the world Slider wanted at the moment was to be induced to feel sorry for Mad Ivan Barrington: it came in even behind being trapped in a lift with a man who'd done his own conveyancing. He turned away, and then turned back to say, 'Oh, and I have got an assignation, as it happens. I'm having tea with a lady.'

Nutty grinned. 'You English!'

'The trouble with revolvers is that the cartridge cases are carried away in the chamber, so until we find the gun we can't be absolutely sure of a match,' said Swilley.

'This obsession with guns is just penis envy you know, Norma,' Atherton pointed out.

'Bollocks,' she replied.

'If you've got 'em, clang 'em,' said Anderson.

'You're all morons,' Norma said kindly.

She was perched on her desk resting her weight on her hands like a 1950s Coca-Cola girl. Normally this would have had Mackay dribbling at her feet, but in emulation of his old oppo, Hunt, he had recently bought a Golf GTI, and his lusts had all been diverted into motor-mechanical channels. Now all that passed through his mind was the extra pair of Bosch halogen superspots he'd set his heart on. 'It's a pretty fair bet we're onto the right gun, though,' he said. 'The same sort of ammo, and not your everyday brand either. Radek's shooter was kept loaded and in an unlocked drawer, where Coleraine knew where it was, and he was in the house and left alone for long enough to nick it.'

'It's a good start,' Slider said, 'but it's not proof. Norma's right, we've got to find that gun – and that means we've got to find where the killer went after the shooting. What's the latest on that?'

'We've got various reports to follow up,' Beevers said, referring to his papers. 'A woman saw a man in a duffel coat looking very nervous coming out of Queensway tube at about three o'clock. He turned left and went on up Queensway. She said he was youngish and medium height with light-coloured hair. But he didn't have a hat on.'

'All the better to recognise him without,' Atherton said, 'supposing it's our man.'

'Supposing,' said Beevers. 'Then there's a man with a hat and light brown coat who came running out of Bond Street tube at about twenty past three, but the witness doesn't know if it was a duffel coat or not. He ran across the road – almost getting himself knocked down, according to witness – and up James Street. And there was a fair-haired man acting suspiciously at White City outside the BBC centre—'

'Isn't there always?' Slider said.

'Probably Jimmy Saville,' said Anderson.

'—again at about three o'clock, but not wearing a coat or hat, though he was carrying a large carrier bag, so they could have been inside it. He was sweating and looked nervous. Hung around for a bit and then jumped on a seventy-two bus heading north when it stopped at the crossing.' He turned the pages back. 'The Anti-terrorist Squad got that report as well. Those three are the most promising. There's dozens of others, of course – men, women, hats, coats, parcels, and every tube station on the Underground.'

'Well, keep at it,' Slider said. 'Something will come up. Let's have videofits from those three to start with. And try them with a photograph of Coleraine, see if it tweaks any hairs.'

'But guv,' Anderson said, 'if Coleraine did want to off the old man, surely he wouldn't be so daft as to use Radek's own gun, when it could be proved he knew about it and had the opportunity to nick it? And when he's got a cartridge case from it stuck on his mantelpiece for all to see?'

'He probably never thought twice about the cartridge case,' Norma said. 'It'd been there so long it was—'

'Part of the furniture,' Atherton supplied.

'Well, it's not that easy for your average law-abiding citizen to get hold of a gun,' Slider said. 'He'd have to make do with what was to hand – and it must have been tempting, lying there loaded and ready and available.'

'Maybe he meant to put it back at some later stage,' Norma suggested, 'hoping no-one would make the connection. Not everybody knows that you can tell which gun a bullet's been fired from.'

'Let's not forget the son in all this,' Atherton said. 'He knew the gun was there as well, and had just as much opportunity to steal it.'

'You don't know that,' Norma objected. 'You don't know he was left alone.'

'You don't know he wasn't.'

'What's his motive then?' Mackay asked.

'The same – money,' said Atherton. 'From the little I know about Marcus so far, he's an immoral, selfish little tart who'd sell his granny for the gold in her teeth.'

'You've been looking into his background, haven't you?' Slider intervened to impose a bit of structure on the talk. 'Let's hear it.'

'Our Marcus is a naughty boy,' Atherton obliged. 'His prep school had him "could do better" – clever but lazy, not amenable to discipline and inclined to think too well of himself. The head I spoke to came over rather puzzled and a little wary: liked the boy in spite of everything but was afraid I was going to tell him he'd gone to the bad.'

'Prophetic,' Slider nodded.

'After prep school he went to Harrow by the skin of his teeth. They weren't too keen to take him, but he'd got a scholarship; and besides, Coleraine's mother was a Russell, and her family's men have gone there for a hundred and fifty years or something.'

'Coleraine's godson, Henry Russell—?' Slider remembered.

'Is a second cousin, yes. He was at Harrow at the same time and presented an unhappy contrast with Marcus, which probably helped to reinforce the bad behaviour. Anyway, Marcus got sent down in the end for running an adolescent version of long firm fraud: offering to get hold of tickets for popular events – student balls and pop concerts and the like – taking the money up front and then not delivering the tickets. One of the boys complained to his father, and the balloon went up. Coleraine managed to hush it up by paying back all the boys out of his own money – Marcus had spent the lot, of course – so the school didn't call in the police, but still insisted Marcus left. So he went to a crammer for two terms, got his A levels, just, and went to university.'

'What did he study?' Mackay asked.

'Economics. I spoke to his tutor, who said that the father had wanted Marcus to read Law, but he didn't have the grades – another source of friction. And from the first Marcus didn't make any attempt to do the work and obey the rules. It was all gigs and girls and drunken parties – the tutor thought he'd got interested in recreational drugs too – and he was frequently in minor trouble. Nobody was surprised when he dropped out. Since then he's set up to live in the flat in Bayswater and spend money – presumably his father's, since he's never done a day's work in his life.'

'Sounds like an absolute sweetie,' Norma said sourly.

'What's his connection with Steve Murray?' Anderson asked.

'Met him at a Radek concert at the Festival Hall. Marcus was hanging around backstage hoping to tap his grandad for a few bucks; Murray was hanging round hoping Kate Apwey wouldn't have to go off horizontal jogging with the old bugger. The two lonely lads took to each other and became friends. Reading between the lines, Murray had a supplier and Marcus was free with his money, so they were obviously made for each other.'

'Just a moment, are you saying that Marcus is an addict?' Slider asked.

'No, strictly a recreational user. You could almost like him better if he was – there'd be some excuse for him then. But he's just a self-indulgent little parasite.'

'I'm getting a sort of feeling here that you don't like him,' Slider said tentatively.

'He disgusts me,' Atherton said.

'He may be a spoiled brat but it doesn't make him a murderer. From what you've said his father keeps him supplied with money. Why should he take the risk of killing his grandfather when he can have anything he wants for the asking? Radek's money goes to Fay, anyway, not to Marcus.'

'Far more likely Coleraine's feeling the pinch, if he's funding his son's delightful habits,' Norma agreed.

'It'd come to the same thing, wouldn't it?' McLaren said as best he could. He had just finished eating a packet of McVitie's Chocolate Homewheat and was hooking squashy chocolatey bits from the corners of his gums with his little finger. 'I mean, if his old man was up the swannee, and his old lady came in for the wonga, it'd come to him anyway. She'd wedge him up all right.'

'English is such a beautiful language when spoken by an expert,' Atherton said admiringly. 'Why shouldn't Marcus and Murray have dreamed up the whole scheme in an idle moment – of which, let's face it, they have an unlimited supply – just for the fun of it? The idea of diverting the money from tight-fisted grandpa to soppily generous mamma would just be an added incentive.'

'You take a large size in assumptions,' Slider reproved. 'What about Marcus's movements that day?'

'Ah, now, there's the really interesting bit,' Atherton said. 'He says he was mooching about at home all morning, which rings true; left home at noon and went to see Murray, got there at half past one and stayed the rest of the evening. Murray confirms it all like a paid-up member. So for the crucial period they are each other's alibi.'

'How convenient,' Slider said wearily.

'Damnable, isn't it? Covent Garden being what it is, there must have been hundreds of people around, any one of whom might have seen Marcus arrive. The problem will be finding them.'

'But hang on,' Anderson said, 'how did Marcus know Murray would be there? Murray called in sick that morning. He should have been at work. Marcus would've known that, surely?'

'Right. But if Murray wasn't in, Marcus was going to pop into the Opera House and get his key to let himself in. Murray was a friendly soul, not above giving his mates the run of his gaff.' Atherton shrugged. 'As an alibi it's like a string vest – it fits all right, but it's full of holes.'

'It's a better alibi than Coleraine's got,' Norma pointed out.

'Which is not saying a whole hell of a lot,' Atherton retorted.

Slider cut through the witty badinage. 'Now here's something. Marcus left home at twelve and got to Murray's at one-thirty – an hour and a half for a half-hour journey. Coleraine left the office at twelve-thirty and says he got home at a quarter to two – an hour and a quarter for a half-hour journey. Where's the missing time? Suppose he met Marcus at twelve-thirty somewhere near the office?'

'You said Marcus phoned him at a quarter to twelve and rang off at about twelve,' Norma said. 'They could have arranged to meet. It fits all right. But what's it got to do with us?'

'Do you think they were both in on the job, guv?' Atherton said. 'That they met to arrange the murder?'

He shook his head. 'No, I can't see that. But suppose Marcus were in some worse than usual financial crisis, and after meeting him and hearing about it Coleraine went home in despair and decided the only way out was to kill Radek?'

'But he'd taken the gun the day before,' Mackay pointed out.

'There's no reason he couldn't have planned it earlier,' Atherton said. 'The meeting with Marcus might have been incidental.'

Norma said, 'If it was planned in advance why didn't Coleraine sort himself an alibi while he was at it?'

'Typical amateur. All right, maybe it wasn't planned. He might not have taken the gun for that: Radek might have lent it to him for some reason, and the fact that he had it gave him the idea of the murder.'

'At all events, there was something going on there, and it's a probable twelve to seven that it has something to do with the murder,' Slider said. 'And I'm sure the paintings are in it too. Christie's say they were a very good investment, likely to turn a good profit in as short a time as a year. Why did he buy them? Why didn't he insure them? Why didn't he report the theft?'

There was a generous silence in answer to all these questions.

'All right, action,' Slider said. 'I want to find out what state Coleraine's business was in. Norma, you've got a good head for figures. Find out who the auditors are, talk to them, and to the bank – the firm's and his own private one. Any irregularities, unusual transactions, change of pattern – you know the form.'

'Yes, sir.'

'Then I want to find out if Coleraine did meet Marcus that day. Restaurants, cafés, pubs in the area – probably they would have sat down somewhere to talk.'

'That sounds like a job for Superman,' Norma murmured, looking at Atherton.

'Yes, all right,' Slider nodded. 'But if you don't get a bite – sorry – try street traders, newspaper vendors, everything. If they walked about the streets talking, probably heatedly, someone must have seen them. Take Anderson with you. He'll help you resist temptation. And I want the home end of Coleraine's alibi checked out. Mackay, McLaren, try the tube station, try the neighbours, find if anyone saw him arrive or go out again.'

'And you, guv?' Atherton enquired.

'Following up an idea. I'm going to see a lady about a bit of a dog.'

CHAPTER NINE

It's a Game of Two Halves

It was quite obvious that Helena Goodwin had been crying over her keyboard: her eyelids were swollen and the wings of her nostrils were red, though she had repaired her make-up and seemed composed when she let Slider in.

'Alec – Mr Coleraine – isn't in today,' she said apologetically. 'I only came in to try to catch up with some work while it's quiet.'

'That's all right,' Slider said. 'It was really you I wanted to speak to.' He glanced at his watch, although he knew perfectly well what the time was. 'Look, I don't know what time you were thinking of knocking off, but would it be too early for me to buy you a drink? If you don't mind my saying so, you look as though you could do with one.'

She turned her head. 'I'm sorry. I must look a wreck.'

'Not at all, but my compassion circuits keep switching in and it plays havoc with my logic. How about a large gin and tonic? I've got a nice line in shoulders to cry on.'

She looked at him cautiously as if unsure how much of anything he was offering her, and then gave a slightly tremulous smile. 'You're very persuasive. All right, I'll give it up for today. Can you wait while I lock everything up?'

A little while later they were seated in a comfortable corner of a dimly lit pub in St Martin's Lane. Around them was the usual early evening clientele of a few anonymously tweedy men reading the papers, two reps with baggy suits and baggier eyes standing at the bar with two packs of Embassy, two gold lighters and two double Scotches in front of them, and some suburban couples done up regardless with time to kill before their pre-theatre meal. Mrs Goodwin had evidently been doing some thinking during Slider's lengthy absence at the bar trying to get served by a kohl-eyed blonde so laid back she was almost comatose; for when he had slid onto the plush banquette beside her, she said, 'I think there are some things you ought to know about Alec Coleraine and me.'

The sentence together with the red eyes told him everything in a nutshell, but he lifted his glass to her encouragingly, and while she took a therapeutic slug he said, 'I should be glad if you would tell me everything you can. I promise you I am very discreet.'

'Yes, you look as though you are,' she said, eyeing him judiciously. 'Tell me, do people often feel compelled to pour their hearts out to you? You look like the kind of man who has children who adore him.'

'Well, you're half right,' he said with a rueful smile. 'Policemen get home so little it's hard to sustain a home life without a great deal of patience from the rest of the family. Who's looking after your little boy today?'

'He's with my mother. She's always asking to have him, but she lives in Sussex so getting him to her is sometimes a problem.' She took another drink. 'She doesn't think I'm a very good mother. I sometimes think it might be better to leave him with her permanently. He seems to like her better than me anyway. "Grandma's more fun than you," he says.'

'You have the stresses of work to contend with,' Slider said. 'It's never a fair comparison.'

'No.'

'What does your ex-husband do?'

'He's a management consultant.' She met his eyes. 'So there were lots of opportunities for comparison, fair and otherwise, as he travelled around the country. My mother warned me not to marry him. Said he wasn't steady enough. Isn't it funny how it's only good advice no-one listens to? But when he left she said it was my fault for not staying at home and being a housewife.'

'Have you been on your own for long?'

'Almost four years,' she said. 'Nick left me just after Mr Antrobus retired and I transferred to Alec. I suppose that's why it all happened – with him and me. I was in a vulnerable state, you see.'

'And he was there. Nothing propinks like propinquity.'

She smiled. 'True. But he has a great deal of charm, you know. You probably haven't seen him at his best.'

'I wasn't criticising,' he said quickly. 'So how did it come about, exactly?'

'Oh, the usual corny way. Hackneyed as hell, only when it happens to you it all seems fresh and original, of course. We worked late together a few times, started going for drinks on the way home now and then. Then it was going for meals and working at weekends. Then one Saturday night we went for a meal and sat so long at the restaurant talking and laughing that the tubes had stopped, so he insisted on taking me home in a taxi. I invited him in. Ben was in Sussex and Fay was at some textile exhibition in Brussels—' She shrugged eloquently. 'Crescendo of music, soft-focus lens, montage of limbs, firelight and ecstatic expressions. It's been done to death on the screen.'

'But you loved him.'

'Madly. But why are you talking in the past tense?'

'I assumed from the fact that you'd been crying and having sleepless nights that it was over between you. Forgive me if I was wrong.'

'No, you're not wrong. It's been coming for a long time, but I've tried to pretend, even though it was only myself I was cheating. I've had to come to the conclusion that whatever he says, he's never going to leave his wife for me. In fact. I'm not even sure any more whether he ever meant it, or whether it was just what he said to string me along. I haven't said anything to him yet – I suppose that's cowardice, or hoping it will still come out right somehow.' She sighed and was silent a moment. 'Funny how you go on and on doing something you know is bad for you in the hope that it will turn out not to be. And most of the time it isn't even pleasurable – hanging around, pretending, being disappointed, feeling humiliated. The nice bit, being with him and actually enjoying it, works out at about ten per cent and the bad bit ninety per cent. Why do we do it?' She drained her glass and put it down. 'Do you think I could have another one of these?' Catching his very slight hesitation she met his eyes and said, 'Don't worry, I won't get drunk.'

'It wasn't that,' he said quickly. 'I just didn't want to interrupt your flow.'

'You're very frank, aren't you?' she said curiously.

'There wouldn't be any point in being anything else with a woman as intelligent as you.'

'You overestimate me.' Her eyes filled suddenly with tears which she tried to blink back. 'I want to be lied to as much as the next woman. It's more comfortable than the truth. But your professional interest is better than nothing.'

'My interest is both professional and personal,' Slider said, holding her gaze, 'and that's the truth. Otherwise I could have sent someone else to talk to you.'

'Thank you,' she said, a little unevenly. 'I believe you. Now if you'd be so very kind as to get me another gin. I'll blow my nose and pull myself together. Then I'll tell you the rest.'

Slider padded off to the bar feeling both hopeful and glum. A good secretary must know a great deal both about the business and the boss's private life, and a mistress gets told things that are kept from a wife. And if she had a beef against Coleraine, she'd be more likely to spill the beans. The glumness stemmed from her recital of the old, old story, and the recollection of his own ignoble part in the same play on a different stage. 'The nice bit works out at ten per cent and the bad bit ninety per cent.' Oh Joanna! Had she felt like that all that time? Surely not – he hoped not. He had really meant it – he hadn't been stringing her along. But the sad fact was that it must have felt just the same, whether he meant it or not. Without in the least meaning to he had treated her badly, and if she now made him suffer it was no more than he deserved, the bus fare to hell being paid with good intentions. Had Alec Coleraine been tortured by guilt while he romped, or had he merely felt like laddo-me-buck; rich and shameless, fingers stuck in the jelly bowl, getting his just desserts?

When he returned, she smiled at him more comfortably, as if they had long been friends. 'Thanks. I feel better now. You'd better ask me the questions you want, or I shall maunder on self-indulgently for hours.'

'I'm in no hurry. You talk. Tell me about when it was good between you. It can't always have been nine to one against.'

'No, of course not. For about the first two years it was wonderful. The only difficulty was how to see enough of each other. And then it was up and down for about a year, wonderful when I believed we had a future and terrible when I doubted it.

And this last year it's been getting worse all the time. He's been moody, depressed, irritable. I've seen he's had something on his mind, and sometimes I hoped it was us, but mostly I knew it wasn't, which made it worse when he took his tempers out on me. And finally I discovered—' She stopped and her expression hardened.

'Yes?' Slider prompted gently, though he'd guessed, of course.

'He's been seeing someone else,' she said, fixing her eyes on the stem of her glass as she revolved it in her fingers. 'I think it's only recent, but even so it's hard to believe. He still says he loves me, that he can't live without me; but for the last few weeks he's made excuses every time I've wanted to see him outside work. And I can't do a thing right any more, and he flares up at me over the least thing. I think he's been hoping to provoke me into breaking off with him, so as to save him the trouble. Bastard!' A silence. 'The difficulty now is what do I do about my job?' She flicked him a stormy glance. 'Oh, I know, I should have thought of that before getting involved with my boss. My own fault. Doesn't make it any easier though.'

'You've been worried about your job for other reasons lately, haven't you?'

The fingers stopped their restless twisting. 'Why do you ask that?'

'It wasn't just sexual infidelity that was making Alec tense and withdrawn. There's something else wrong – probably financial. You've had suspicions and they've made you feel disloyal, but you can't entirely suppress them. Am I right?'

'Quite a clairvoyant,' she said, trying to sound flippant and only managing nervous. 'Do you do this at parties?'

'You've no reason not to tell me now,' he went on. 'Apart from anything else, it may recently have got more serious, too serious for the ordinary rules of loyalty to apply – even if he hadn't already forfeited any right to your support.' She didn't agree or deny. He'd got to help her begin. 'Does it in some way involve Marcus?'

She took a deep breath, and then let it out slowly in a sigh. 'Yes, I think so. At least, I think that's what's at the bottom of it. Ever since he dropped out of college – oh!' She clenched her fist and thumped it softly on the tabletop. 'Selfish, ungrateful, self-centred little swine! He doesn't care who he hurts. Everything's me, me, me – and Alec gives in, every time, the idiot. He's just besotted with that boy. We argued about it sometimes. "I know you're right," he'd say, "but I can't help it. I love him." Only child, you see – I think Fay couldn't have any more – and he's such a good-looking boy, too, and charming when he wants to be. Have you met him?' Slider shook his head. 'Spoiled, I suppose. Unless it's something inherent. Alec's selfish, and Fay likes to have her own way. Maybe having it on both sides, it got concentrated. His grandfather, from what I heard, was an Olympic-class me-ist.'

'How did Marcus get on with his grandfather?'

'Oh, all right, I think. He liked anyone who flattered and spoiled him. And I think he found it useful to take sides and play one member of the family off against another. Sir Stefan wanted him to be a musician. Fay didn't mind what he was as long as it wasn't anything to do with music. Alec wanted him to go into the law. But Marcus couldn't see why he should have to work for a living at all, when everybody around him had loads of cash.'

'And had they?'

She frowned. 'I would have said so, yes. Sir Stefan wouldn't part with a penny of his, of course, but I thought Fay and Alec between them had plenty. But just lately I've begun to wonder. You were right about that.' She met Slider's eyes. She was plainly very worried.

'What does Marcus live on, now he's not at college?'

'That's it exactly, the same as he's always lived on: Alec. I don't know the details, but I gather a few years ago, when Marcus was still at school, there was a big scandal that it cost a lot of money to hush up. I don't know if he's been in trouble since then, but he's a constant drain, and he doesn't live cheaply. I don't know how he gets through it all, but I do know—' She hesitated. 'I overheard a bit of their conversation on Wednesday. I didn't mean to – I thought they'd finished and picked up the phone to make a call. But I'm afraid when I heard them I carried on listening. Marcus needed money for something – a lot of money – and he was threatening Alec, saying if he didn't give it to him, he'd just have to turn to theft. Breaking and entering, he said. Alec was horrified. The scandal would finish him, of course. He'd lose all his clients. Marcus knows that, the little swine. That's how he puts the bite on Alec every time.'

'So what did Alec say to the threat?'

'He said no, no, don't even think about it. He said to give him time and he'd come up with something.' She shook her head. 'I was so angry with Marcus I didn't listen after that. I put the phone down. Alec sounded so upset I couldn't bear it, even though – well, I suppose I still love him. I haven't quite had time to get over it.'

'And then half an hour later he came out and said he was ill and was going home.'

'Yes. He looked it too.'

'Did he go to meet Marcus before he went home?'

'No, not as far as I know. Why do you ask?' She seemed genuinely surprised.

'I just wondered. So tell me, how do you think he was going to get hold of money for Marcus?'

'Are you asking me in an official capacity, or is this still a friendly chat?' she asked, suddenly curious.

'I hope it's still friendly. But you know that Wednesday is a day I have to be particularly interested in.'

She stared, and he saw her scalp shift back as her eyes widened and her nostrils flared. 'Oh my God,' she whispered. 'Oh my God, you think Alec killed Sir Stefan!'

He looked at her with interest. 'Has it truly never occurred to you before that he might have?'

'No! No, I swear to you! But you're wrong, you must be wrong! He wouldn't do a thing like that, not Alec. He may be a swine in some ways, but he would never harm a soul. He's too soft if anything – that's why he spoils Marcus—'

'But if Marcus had got into some bad trouble and Alec was desperate for the cash—'

'No! Oh no, I promise you, he just wouldn't.' Her voice was stronger, more confident. 'He just isn't that kind of man.'

Slider well knew there was no kind of man, but that was not the discussion he wanted to have with Helena Goodwin. 'All right, then if you really hadn't considered that possibility, what was it about him that's been worrying you so much, that you wanted to tell me about?'

This was plainly difficult. She chewed her lip, staring at him rather blankly as she tried to make up her mind. 'If I tell you,' she said at last, 'it's going to make it look worse for him. And I'm positive he hasn't done – what you think.'

'Then what has he done? Really,' he added when she still hesitated, 'you'd much better tell me. We always find out in the end, and the sooner we can check it all out, the sooner we can eliminate him from suspicion, if he really is innocent. Keeping it from me isn't going to get anyone anywhere.'

'I just don't want it to be me who betrays him.'

'That suggests there's something to betray.'

She was silent a moment longer, and then seemed to decide to take the plunge. 'All right, look, I don't know if this is anything to do with it – it may be nothing at all, but it's been bothering me. Did you know that Alec is trustee for the estate of his godson Henry?'

'Henry Russell?'

'That's right. It's a family thing – Henry's also a sort of second cousin, I think. You know about it, then?'

'Not much more than the name. Is it a large estate?'

'Very. In the millions, I believe. Henry's father was Russell's Pies and Sausages.'

'Ah yes.' Russell's had always been a rather dignified, old-fashioned firm, whose products sported old-fashioned paper wrappers decorated with dull drawings of the various gold medals won in the days of Empire. They made steak and kidney pies and pork pies of the sort Celia Johnson might have bought at the station buffet while waiting for Trevor Howard (though never, of course, actually eaten). But just lately Russell's had suffered a belated panic and gone all trendy, with transparent cellophane packaging and a new range of synthetic fillings which McLaren adored: cheese 'n' potato, chick 'n' curry and crispy bacon bits. Whatever had happened, Slider wondered in parenthesis, to the word crisp? They were all ruled by nursery language these days. 'Yes, I know Russell's Pies,' he said. 'How old is Henry?'

'Twenty-three. And a half.'

'How come the money is still in trust, then?'

'Oh, the trust goes on until he's twenty-five. Apparently Henry's father was a bit of a wild thing in his youth, and expected Henry to be the same, so he wanted the money tied up until Henry had had a chance to sow his wild oats and grow sensible. But in fact he needn't have worried: Henry's never caused a moment's anxiety to anyone in his life. He's so sensible he doesn't even fret about not getting his money for another eighteen months. The only impulsive thing he's ever done is to get engaged rather suddenly, but the girl's perfectly unexceptionable. She's pretty and good, her parents have got a place in Berkshire, and she's called Camilla. Every mother's dream, in fact.'

Slider returned the smile. 'So what's bothering you about this trust?'

'It was something that happened a couple of months ago,' she said slowly. 'Quite a bit of the trust money is in shares in the family firm, as you'd expect, and about two months ago I happened to see a share transfer document, selling a block of them, on Alec's desk. I was surprised, because I hadn't seen it before, and usually I deal with all the routine paperwork. Alec was out of the room at the time, so I had a closer look at it. As trustee, he's quite entitled to buy or sell shares, of course, but share transfers have to have the signatures of both trustees.'

'Who is the other trustee?'

'David Fowles. He's another cousin of Henry's on his mother's side. The thing is, he's one of these lone yachtsmen and he's been sailing round the world for almost the last year. He keeps in touch, of course, but at that time, at that time I saw the transfer document, he was somewhere out in the middle of the Pacific, and had been for weeks. He could be contacted by radio, of course, but there was no way of getting a document to him for signature. But the share transfer had his signature on it all the same.'

'You think it was a forgery?'

'I think Alec forged it,' she said bravely. 'I've handled lots of documents for the trust, and I know David's signature. It didn't look quite right to me. Besides how could it be? And why hadn't Alec passed it through me in the usual way?'

'Because there was something wrong about it?'

'I think,' she said slowly, 'that he was so desperate for money he sold the shares and took the cash.'

Slider nodded gravely. Interesting that she didn't find this hard to suppose, though murder was unimaginable. 'How much cash?'

'I don't know exactly, because I don't know what he sold at, of course, but it wouldn't have been much under a hundred thousand pounds.' She looked at Slider like a puppy hoping not to be kicked. 'And it wasn't long before that that Marcus smashed Alec's car. A sixty-thousand-pound Mercedes. Marcus was drunk – or something worse – and climbed out without a scratch on him, but the car was a write-off. He lost his licence, of course, but there was a hefty fine as well, which Alec had to pay for him.'

'Have you said anything about this to anyone? To Alec?'

'No,' she said, almost in alarm. 'I couldn't be sure – I may have been quite mistaken. Maybe it was a perfectly normal transaction.'

'You didn't want to suspect him.'

'Of course not. I loved him. But I've never been able to put it quite out of my head. I keep – wondering.'

'Where would the money go, if he sold those shares?'

'There'd be a cheque to the trust's bank account. After that—' she shrugged uncomfortably – 'Alec could write a cheque to anyone he wanted. Even himself.'

'And who holds the cheque-book?'

'He does. He keeps it locked in his private filing cabinet in his office, with the other trust documents. Only he has the key to that.'

'Of course, sooner or later he'd have to account for the money,' Slider said thoughtfully.

'He had another eighteen months before Henry came of age. I'm sure he meant to replace it – only where would he get the money from? He'd have to sell something of his own, I suppose; or play the market. I suppose a hundred thousand isn't much to recoup in that time, if you play high enough. The big dealers make millions on a single transaction, don't they?'

Dream on, thought Slider, but he gave her a comforting nod, and she fell silent. Slider pursued his own thoughts. How did the paintings fit in with this? Had he bought them to make good losses to the trust? Christie's had said they would realise a good profit in a year; but he had bought them before the car-crash incident, so they couldn't have been intended to recoup that money. Maybe selling those shares had not been the first time he'd raided the piggy-bank. And if he had borrowed the trust's money to buy the paintings in the first place, he might well have fought shy of reporting their theft to the police. Rifling the fund, abuse of his powers as a trustee: he wouldn't want all that coming out. If that were the case, he had a bit more than a hundred thousand to find before Henry Russell came of age. But there was plenty of time – no need to be panicked into killing Radek for his fortune.

'Do you know what I think we ought to do?' he said at last. She looked up with faint, very faint, hope. 'I think we should go back to the office and see what we can find out.' The hope died. 'You'll feel better for knowing the truth, one way or the other.' And so will I, he added silently.

'I suppose so,' she said. 'But I've told you, all the trust documents are in his private filing cabinet, and I don't have the key.'

'With all that's been going on lately, he might possibly have left it unlocked,' Slider said. 'It's worth a look, anyway.'

Darkness had fallen while they were in the pub, lamplight had come, and the streets had filled with the evening crowds: theatre-goers, diners-out, and throngs of young people looking for the High Life without any clear idea of what it was going to look like when they bumped into it, except that it would probably be making a lot of noise and have an imported lager in its hand.

It was a pleasantly mild evening, so everyone was good-tempered, and already there were groups of sitters-out outside restaurants and bars. The biggest difference the last ten years had made to London, Slider thought as he and Mrs Goodwin picked their way through the backstreets, was in how much more people liked to stay out of doors, given half a chance. Being both naturally fond of company and a Libra, Slider liked the whole idea of sitting at a pavement café watching the world go by; and he enjoyed the lighted windows of the shops that stayed open late, and the smells of coffee and garlic and delicatessen produce that wafted out of the various open doors they passed. In his early childhood everything had stopped at night, there being in the fifties little to sell and no-one with money to buy it. He still remembered when the ban on illuminating shops at night had been lifted, and his parents had taken him up to London for a special treat, for the pleasure of walking along Oxford Street and looking in the brightly lit windows. Ah, simple pleasures! And they'd had fish and chips when they got home, bought at the chip shop opposite the station and hotted up when they got back to the cottage. Mum would never countenance eating in the street. Common, she called it.

Mrs Goodwin was plainly nervous when they reached the door of the office. 'I'm not sure this is right,' she said, turning to him appealingly.

'You're helping the police with their enquiries,' he said. He followed her upstairs, and she let him into the outer office, switched on the lights, and then unlocked the door to the inner office. The filing cabinets were ranged along one wall, rather prissily sheathed in veneered wood so that the sight of raw metal wouldn't offend the cultured client.

'This is his private one,' she said indicating the end cabinet, and reaching out a hand to test the drawer. Slider caught it gently.

'I think it might be an idea if you locked the outer doors, just to be on the safe side,' he said.

'Yes, of course, I should have thought of that,' she said, and hastened away. Slider examined the filing cabinet and smiled to himself. Piece of pie. By the time she returned, the top drawer was open.

'Look at this,' he said cheerfully. 'We're in luck – he did forget to lock it!'

She looked at it, and him, opened her mouth, and closed it again.

'Let's get busy,' he said.

Slider had meant to go straight to Joanna's, but at the last minute he had an attack of nerves, and decided to call in at the station first for a wash and brush-up and a clean pair of socks. He was sorry to see Barrington's car in the yard, and sorrier still to find a message on his desk summoning him to the presence as soon as he came in.

It struck him as he went in that Barrington was definitely showing signs of strain. There was something almost ragged about his movements, and though his face was still as inexpressive as tufa, his eyes were no longer steady, but moved and shifted all the time he spoke.

'You wanted to see me, sir? I was just going off.'

He expected to be asked about the progress of the case, but Barrington had other things of greater import on his mind.

'You've just driven into the car park, I assume?'

'Yes, sir.' This was an odd tack. Slider began to fear the worst.

'And did you notice anything?' Slider was silent. A man does not lime his own twig. 'Did you see my car there?'

'Yes, I did notice it,' Slider said cautiously. Should he add a word of praise? Jolly clean it looked too? I always wanted one of those myself?

'And what did you notice about it?'

Slider lost patience. 'Would you tell me what all this is about, sir?'

Barrington turned like a man goaded beyond endurance. 'What it's about, Slider, is parking! The cars in the yard are so badly parked that I was unable to get into my own space! I had to park half across the space next to it!'

Slider was still groping in the dark. The space next to Barrington's was his. 'That's all right, sir. I just put mine on the end. It doesn't matter.'

'It most emphatically does matter, Inspector,' Barrington said in cold rage. 'What do you think the lines are there for? Do you think they were put there for people to ignore? It only takes one person to park carelessly, and everyone in the yard is affected. Suppose your car had already been there? What would I have done then?'

Slider declined to answer, looking at Barrington with a stark disbelief he was afraid he was not managing to mask.

'Car parking space in the yard is at a premium. To be allotted a space is a privilege, and I won't have the men under my command abusing privilege through sheer carelessness, indiscipline and sloppy behaviour!' He began to walk up and down again. 'I've told you before that carelessness in small things leads to carelessness in larger things. That's where it all starts! Ignore the little faults, and where do you draw the line? The next thing you know, you have widespread corruption. I've seen it happen before. It only takes one rotten apple to contaminate the whole barrel.'

'Yes, sir,' Slider said. 'I understand.' Barrington stopped pacing and glared at him, as if waiting for further answer. 'I'll have the cars reparked,' he said soothingly.

The red seemed to dissipate slowly from Barrington's stare. He straightened slightly. 'Nonsense. There's no need for that,' he said, quite mildly for him. 'Just make sure that the men are told to park straight in future. It's pure inconsiderateness, and there's no excuse for it.'

Slider agreed, and escaped. What the hell was going on with the Demon King these days? These furious attacks on trivia were like little bursts of steam escaping from the safety valve of a pressure-cooker; Slider wondered at how many pounds per square foot he would finally blow, and how much of a mess there would be to clear up. He didn't fancy having Barrington all over the ceiling and down the walls. Maybe he ought to have taken the move to Pinner after all. And he hadn't even told him about the new developments in the case – though that may have been all to the good. Tomorrow was Sunday; perhaps Barrington would have a nice day out on the golf course and come back refreshed on Monday and ready to cope with the petty annoyances of a murder case.

Then Slider remembered that he was on his way to see Joanna, and already late, and it concentrated his mind wonderfully.

CHAPTER TEN

If you can't live without me, how come you aren't dead yet?

Joanna opened the door to him, and she looked so dear and familiar and had been so long longed-for that all he could say was, 'Aunty Em.'

'This ain't Kansas,' she said forbiddingly.

'Oh, don't say that. I've had such a strange dream, and unfortunately you weren't in it.' She stepped back to allow him in, and he walked as so often before into her living-room, where the fire had been kindled long enough to have reached a cheerful red glow. The curtains were drawn and there was one lamp on in the corner, so that the shabby furniture gleamed and winked like conspirators out of the friendly gloom. It was all so different from the neat brightness of the Ruislip house. Here there might be dust in the corners, but the baggy chesterfield opened its arms to you like a dear old mum, and the house rule was that it was pleasure that came next to godliness.

She followed him in and he turned to her. 'I'm sorry I'm so late. I didn't mean to get off to such a bad start.'

She raised an eyebrow at the word 'start', but said, 'It's all right. You don't need to explain – I'm an old hand at this game, remember.'

'Which game?' he asked nervously, thinking of Mrs Goodwin.

But she said, 'Waiting for policemen.'

'I'm not sure I like the use of the plural there, but still. I am sorry to have kept you waiting.'

'It's all right,' she said again, patiently. She reminded him of Irene.

'I wish you'd get angry with me. There's a thin line between tolerance and indifference.'

Her eyes widened. 'You want me to be waiting behind the door with a rolling pin? I think you've strayed into the wrong decade. And the wrong house.'

'And the wrong play. Oh dear. I'm sorry. Let's start again. Have you eaten already?' he asked in a brightly social voice. 'Do you want go to out somewhere?'

Wrong again. 'What d'you think, this is a date? You came to talk, that's all.' She cocked an eye at him. 'I suppose you're starving.'

'I seem not to have got round to lunch.'

'Just as I thought. Sit down, then, take your coat off, and I'll get you something.'

He watched her walk away from him. She was wearing her comfortable velvet Turkish trousers, which were so old the pile was all rubbed off the seams, and a loose, Indian-style crimped-cotton shirt of similar vintage. She was neither tall nor elegant; her feet were bare and her hair was untidy; and she seemed to him to contain every desirable quality. She was home, rest, sanctuary: the place where you were understood and welcomed, the place where you gave and received pleasure. He wanted to talk with her and eat with her and sleep with her and walk along all the sunset beaches in Hollywood with her – things he had never even considered wanting to do with any other woman. By their houses shall ye know them, he thought inconsequentially: designed for living in, his desired person, rather than for display. And desired, by golly – he was anxious to obey her hospitable parting instructions but wasn't sure that he ought to remove his coat yet. He had a promising young erection under there. Don't want to frighten the horses.

She was back very soon with a tray. 'This will keep you going.' She handed him a large malt whisky, and a plate on which reposed a pork pie cut into quarters. He had – as she knew of course – a passion for pork pies, especially proper ones like this with the dark, lean meat and the very crisp raised crust. And she then placed before him a jar of Taylor's English mustard and a knife, and everything was perfect.

'What a woman!' he said. 'How did you just happen to have a pork pie about your person?'

She sat down beside him. 'I'm a very wonderful person. Cut me a tiny piece just to taste.' He cut a piece, dabbed it in mustard, and held it out to her, suddenly doubtful. In the old days he'd have put it in her mouth, but it seemed too intimate a gesture to be attempted without permission. It was unnerving for his brain to be getting all these conflicting signals. That's how they gave laboratory monkeys ulcers.

She saw his difficulty. 'For goodness' sake,' she said, then ducked her head and took the morsel from his fingers. It was a strangely diffuse exclamation and he wasn't sure what she meant by it, but she seemed to know that too, because she said, 'Old dogs and new tricks. With anyone else it would be a deliberate ploy to disarm me by pretending nothing had happened, but with you it's just that you have no idea how to dissemble. Which is what makes you so dangerous.' She was looking at him as she spoke, actually meeting his eyes for the first time, which did nothing to divert the flow of blood back to his head from the eager part of him that was desperately trying to point at her like a game dog; and in fact an unexpectedly game dog he was turning out to be for a man who had been contemplating solitary old age only yesterday. It was on the tip of his tongue to ask her if they couldn't just go straight to bed and sort things out that way, but she caught that thought on its way up too. 'And this still ain't Kansas,' she added sternly, but she was trying to hold down a smile as she said it. She had never been very good at being angry, and positively pathetic at holding grudges.

'So what made you late?' she went on, turning sideways on and tucking her legs under her so as to face him. 'I bet you've been with a woman. I can smell scent on the air.'

'I've been comforting a very attractive divorcée who says she finds me very sympathetic. She's younger than you are, too.'

Joanna grinned. 'I'm younger than I am. This is something to do with the case, I assume?'

'It would be more flattering to me if you didn't immediately jump to that conclusion.'

'I wouldn't be interested in a man I thought even capable of entertaining the notion of a thought for another woman. Go on, tell me about the case.'

He would sooner have pursued the intriguing hint that she was interested in him, but he knew there was no help for it. He was not on safe ground yet.

'She's the secretary of Radek's son-in-law, Alec Coleraine.

She'd been having an affair with him and now discovers he's been two-timing her—'

'Three-timing her, presumably, counting his wife,' she said with horrible neutrality.

'As you say. Anyway, contemplation of her wrongs was enough to tip her into telling me about something that's been worrying her for some time. She suspected him of being less than a hundred per cent honest in his financial dealings, so I persuaded her to go back to the office and raid the filing cabinets.'

'You dog,' she said. 'And what did you find?'

He told her about the Henry Russell trust. 'All the papers were locked in Coleraine's private cabinet, to which he alone holds the key – and no wonder. There's been a steady sale of trust assets – shares, gilts, real estate – over the last two years, and no purchases, other than the three oil-paintings we know about, which he was careless enough to lose. I've taken down the share names and dates, and with a bit of research we'll be able to find out how much money has gone, but even at a conservative estimate it's got to be two million, given the paintings cost a million and a quarter.'

'And where's it all gone?'

'Where indeed. Unfortunately the cheque-stubs and bank statements weren't there, though Helena—'

'Helena?'

'You get friendly going through someone's drawers together. Helena assures me the bank statements at least ought to have been there, because she's seen him take them out on previous occasions. But we did find one dead cheque-book stuck in the crack at the back of the drawer, and it made interesting reading.'

'Hang on a minute. If he kept all this incriminating evidence firmly locked away, how did you manage to get at it?'

He met her eyes limpidly. 'I think in all his recent anxiety he must have left the filing cabinet unlocked. It's easily done.'

'Like fun he did. I suppose there was a coat-hanger lying about the office somewhere? Or had you brought your own?'

'I can't imagine what you're suggesting,' he said, shaking his head sadly.

'It's a good job I'm not wearing a wire. Anyway, tell me about this interesting cheque-book.'

'Most of the stubs were uncontroversial. But quite a few had the amount filled in – and large amounts they were – but no payee.'

'Sounds like belated caution. You think Coleraine paid the money to himself, then?'

'Don't you?'

'I'm not in the business of thinking,' she quoted him, and then slipped into Stan Freeberg. 'I just wanna get the facts, man.'

'The fact is that Coleraine's been under severe financial pressure because of his no-good son, who sucks at the parental wallet like a newborn calf—'

'I love your agricultural metaphors,' she marvelled.

'I'm a farm boy, remember. Also Helena told me that business has not been quite what it was because the old partner, Antrobus, had a lot of rich elderly clients who have now died, without being replaced by new ones. So his income was going down while his outgoings were going up.'

She had been thinking. 'But wait a minute, if Coleraine had been defrauding the trust, wouldn't it have been discovered? I mean, what about audits? Don't they have to have them done, by law?'

He shook his head. 'With family trusts, audits are carried out at the request of the trustee, whenever he thinks it's necessary. The last one was done three years ago, according to Mrs Goodwin, and presumably showed up nothing unusual. The other trustee is a sort of sleeping partner who leaves everything to Coleraine because he, the other trustee I mean, is a layman and only knows about boats. So he's not likely to ask for an audit, or want to look at the books.'

'But sooner or later Coleraine would have to come up with the money, wouldn't he? I mean, when the boy comes of age, he's going to ask where it is.'

'Ah yes, now that's the really interesting thing. Helena told me the trust went on until the boy was twenty-five, and Henry Russell is only twenty-three. Coleraine still had eighteen months to replace the cash – assuming for the moment he had taken it – and I think that's what the oil paintings were supposed to do, to turn enough profit to fill the piggy-bank again. When he lost them he must have been very, very worried; but he still had time, if he was clever. But then about six weeks ago, disaster struck. Henry Russell suddenly announced he was getting married.'

She grinned at him. 'Oh, you have a lovely way of telling a tale. I liked the artistic pause there. What's Our 'Enery's nuptials got to do with it?'

'While we were going through the filing cabinet, we found a photocopy of the actual trust deed. The trust ends when Henry is twenty-five, or on his marriage over the age of twenty-one, whichever is the sooner.'

'Ah, I see! Nice one. Suddenly he's got weeks instead of months.'

'If it's discovered he's misappropriated the trust funds, he'll be ruined. He'll never practise again. And it'll mean a gaol sentence, and gaol is not something people of his class can easily contemplate. He'd probably think his own death was preferable.'

'Or better still, someone else's death? You're thinking he murdered Radek?'

'Radek had millions, and it was all going to go to Fay anyway. He was an old man, it was only a matter of hastening him on his way. And it was generally believed Radek had a heart condition, and might pop off any time. I don't know whether Radek himself put the story about, but Buster certainly believed it, and would have been sure to tell Coleraine – though the post mortem showed up no evidence of heart disease.'

'What about the gun? Where would Coleraine get hold of a gun?'

'Haven't you heard that bit? I thought Atherton was keeping you up to date on all this.'

'I don't live in Jim's pocket,' she said with a sidelong look at him. 'Besides, he's got other fish to fry at the moment. Didn't you know about him and Sue Caversham – principal second violin in my orchestra? They've been at it like crazed ferrets ever since they met.'

He tried not to feel relieved. He never really thought Atherton and Joanna were – but with Atherton one never knew. He was said to have the social conscience of a dog in a room full of hot bitches, and he and Joanna liked each other very much and had so much in common and – well, Sue Caversham was a very nice person. 'Yes, I remember her. She's very nice.'

'Almost nice enough for Jim,' Joanna said disconcertingly. 'So what about the gun, anyway?'

'Radek's own gun is missing. A Second World War trophy, and the bullet that killed him was the same sort as the ammo we found in his house.'

'Poor old bugger. That's a nasty twist, shot with your own gun.'

'We haven't found it yet, but we know Coleraine had the opportunity to take it. And he has no proper alibi for the time of the murder; and he sure as hell had a motive.'

Joanna nodded. 'It looks pretty black. But what a silly way to murder anyone – in broad daylight in front of a hundred witnesses.'

'Yes,' he frowned. 'But then, Coleraine was an amateur in the business, and he was in a state of mental and emotional turmoil. There's a kind of loony theatricality to it that I can see might fit him. And it probably wasn't planned, you know. He probably thought about it as a tempting way out without really meaning anything serious by it. Then he found himself in the situation and just did it on the spur of the moment. And probably immediately regretted it.' He thought back over past cases. 'People who murder their nearest and dearest generally do it in a very silly and amateur way. The cunning criminal covering his steps, your domestic murderer is not.'

'So what's the next step?'

He shrugged. 'None of this is proof, of course. We have to grind on, verifying everything, and most of all looking for witnesses. That's the footslog of the job. And we have to find the gun, of course. No gun, no proof.'

'But you said the ammunition matched.'

'Yes, but it could have been fired from any compatible gun. The proof comes from the marks the gun leaves on the bullet and cartridge case when it's fired. Those are unique, like a fingerprint.'

'How so? I don't understand.'

He smiled. 'You should ask Norma about guns. Atherton thinks she's got a fetish. Penis envy, he calls it.'

'I'd sooner ask you. Norma hasn't got your looks.'

'It's jolly kind of you to say so. Well, you know what rifling means, don't you?'

'Going through someone's drawers?' He stirred in his seat. Had she spotted the dog trying to see the rabbit, then?

'Pay attention! A rifled gun barrel has spiral ridges all the way down the inside to guide the bullet. If you like, it's like a screwdriver turned inside out.'

'How graphic! Yes, I did understand that part.'

'All right. Now a bullet is slightly larger than the minimum width of the barrel, and the metal it's made of is slightly softer. So as it's forced down the barrel by the charge, the ridges make marks on the bullet – striations, they're called.'

'Gotcher.'

'And different makes of gun have different arrangements of ridges – the Webley automatic, for instance, has six right-hand thread grooves, while the Colt .45 has six left-hand grooves, and so on. So you can narrow down the type of gun a bullet was fired from. But in addition each individual gun has tiny variations in the rifling which are unique to that actual weapon. The same with the cartridge case – that will bear the marks of the breech-block and firing pin, which are never identical in two separate guns. So if we can find the gun, fire another bullet from it, then compare the marks on that bullet and on the one that killed Radek, we can prove that was the gun that was used.' He smiled ruefully. 'Then we only have to prove it was Coleraine who pulled the trigger.' He was silent a moment in thought. 'One thing, though: it does look as if you were right, that it wasn't a musician who murdered Radek.'

'Of course not. We couldn't do it. We're fools to ourselves, though. If anyone needed removing it was him.'

'Don't say that,' he said. 'I know it's only a joke, but don't say it.'

She looked at him quizzically. 'You really mind, don't you?'

'Someone has to care.'

'But nobody even liked him.'

'Buster did. Somebody has to avenge him.'

She shook her head. 'It isn't that, though, is it?' She studied his face for a moment. 'It's holding back the chaos, isn't it?'

He looked at her warily, like a cat eyeing a thermometer. He was about to have his soul probed, and after the events of the last four months it was already feeling delicate. Though she was right, of course. 'I suppose it is.'

'We all have our own ways of doing it. My mother bakes.' It was the first time she'd ever mentioned her mother to him. 'When I left home, for instance, she made a huge batch of shortbread and packed it in a tin in my suitcase, and it wasn't because she thought I might be hungry. Whenever she feels threatened she makes cakes and biscuits and buns – and she's terrific at it, they're always beautiful, symmetrical, really professional-looking. Of course there's only my father at home now to eat them, so mostly they end up feeding the birds, but still she bakes. When she lifts a steaming tray of perfect, golden fairy cakes out of the oven, she knows that she's in control and the Devil is still on the other side of the door with the bolt shot home.'

He thought of Irene, cleaning things that weren't dirty, plumping cushions no-one had leaned against. Why had he never thought of that before? Oh Irene! He felt a surge of sad, guilty compassion, fierce as canteen heartburn. But what could he ever have done, except what he did do?

'Yes,' he said comprehensively.

She went on, 'Do you know that poem by Auden? "The glacier knocks in the cupboard, the desert sighs in the bed, the crack in the teacup opens a lane to the land of the dead."'

'Nasty. There was a wardrobe in my bedroom when I was a kid—' He shuddered.

'For me it's always been music, of course. When I play, I know there's order, symmetry, the things of the light. I can believe the guys in the white hats are going to win and the floor under my feet isn't going to suddenly yawn and tip me into the pit – all common experience to the contrary.'

He smiled at her. 'My father always liked you, you know.'

'You are a master of the non sequitur,' she said. 'What's that supposed to mean?'

'You know what it means.' The moment seemed to have arrived unannounced. 'I love you. That's such an inadequate sentence, but there doesn't seem to be a word for the way I feel about you, which I think you know anyway.' He quickly forestalled whatever she might have said then. 'I know that I put you through two years of hell, though I never meant to hurt you, but please, now that we can be together properly and openly, without hurting anyone at all, won't you take me back?'

'You think it's as easy as that?'

'That wasn't easy,' he said, a little hurt.

She grew impatient. 'Oh don't pout at me! Tell me, do you really, *really* not understand why it's impossible?'

'No. It doesn't seem impossible to me. All the obstacles have been swept away. Now there's only us to please. Why shouldn't we?'

She looked at him broodingly for a while. But when she spoke it was quite gently, as though there was no point in being angry, which on the whole he thought rather a bad sign. 'In the beginning you fell in love with me – so you said. You said you couldn't live without me, but you kept on managing it. You had a wife and children and responsibilities, and I understood that, I honoured you for taking them seriously. But still in the end you didn't choose me. You chose to stay with them. And the fact that you're free now is still not because you chose me, but because you got thrown out. I'm not going to come second with you, because it's too important for that. You should have marched out for me with banners and trumpets and elephants. I'm not going to be your consolation prize.'

'It wasn't like that.' He looked at her despairingly with the recognition of an absolute gulf. Was this a man–woman thing? Or was it just him and her? It was like one of those stories in which someone goes and dies for a completely pointless principle, and you admire their courage and integrity, but you still think they're barmy. How could she want to throw away being together for the rest of their lives for the sake of hurt pride? 'It isn't like that,' he said. 'I don't want you *because* Irene's left me. And actually I did choose you—'

'You could have fooled me.'

'It was just a matter of timing. I mean,' as she looked about to interrupt, 'the way the end bit happened was an accident of timing. Please, listen to me. That last time we met, up in the city, when I was at the Old Bailey and you were at St Paul's—'

'Yes, I remember,' she said tonelessly.

'You said then that I must choose, and on the way home in the car I thought it all through and came to my decision. I realised I'd been procrastinating, and I decided I was going to speak to

Irene as soon as I got home, and sort it all out. I was going to tell her I was leaving. But when I got there *he* was there, Ernie, and she got her news in first.' He studied her face. 'You don't believe me?'

'Would you? It's a bit of a coincidence, isn't it?'

'But I was going to leave. I was going to tell her that very evening.'

'You said that to me before, on many occasions, and nothing came of it.'

'But I really *was* going to that time,' he said, his fists clenching with frustration.

She looked away. 'Well, we shall never know, shall we?'

'No,' he said. 'At least, you won't.' She looked at him again. 'Do you think that I don't remember how I felt that day? Or that I'm deliberately lying to you now? A cynical manipulation to get my own way? If you think that, then you don't really believe I love you, because you know I could never do that to you.'

She said awkwardly. 'No, I don't think that. But still, you didn't tell her.'

'Only because I was forestalled. History prevented me, that's all. I would have done it. And now that it can't be proved one way or the other, you have to give me the benefit of the doubt, because it would be unfair not to.'

She went on staring at him, completely at a loss.

'Jo, you must still want to be with me, or we wouldn't even be having this conversation.' He paused to let her deny it, but she didn't. 'And if it's the only thing that's holding you back, I swear to you, I swear that I did choose you, and that I was going to tell her that night.' Pause. Nothing. 'You either have to believe me, or tell me I'm lying.' He held her eyes. 'Am I lying?'

'I don't want to be unhappy any more,' she said in a low voice, and while he was still trying to work out what that meant, they were interrupted by the oven timer going off in the kitchen. 'Saved by the bell,' she said, jumping up.

He couldn't believe it. 'Leave it,' he said, annoyed.

'Leave it? Don't you know what that was?'

He stood up too. 'This is important, for God's sake!'

'So's that. That was our dinner in the oven, and it might burn. Don't you want to eat?'

'What the hell's the matter with you?' he scowled.

'I don't know. I think I may be hungry,' she said flippantly. Then she stepped up close to him and looked up into his face in a way that made the back of his knees ache, because she looked tired and beaten and he wanted to gather her up and make everything all right for her. 'Please, Bill, this is so hard for me. I've been living on my pride for a very long time and it's hard to give it up just like that.' She put her hands up round his neck in what seemed an automatic gesture, and that alone was like an electric shock to the gonads. 'Do one more thing for me, you good man. Have dinner with me before you ask me any more difficult questions.'

'You,' he said unsteadily, 'don't have to ask me for anything. I'm the one who's begging.' He wanted to put his arms round her but he didn't dare touch her at this point. Instead he managed to say, 'What's in the oven?'

'Cassoulet. It's Jim's recipe,' she added temptingly.

His saliva glands started up at the mere thought. Funny how the animal was always hanging around to debunk the spiritual man. 'With those spicy Portuguese sausages?' he asked. 'What are they called?'

'Chorus girls. Something like that. And bits of chicken. I've got a nice bottle of St Josèph too.'

'You must have been expecting company.'

'Nah, I eat like this all the time. Hungry, Inspector?'

'My stomach thinks my throat's been cut.'

'Come, then,' she said, backing off and holding out a hand to him. 'You can open the wine, and we'll eat in here by the fire.'

He took the hand, her fingers curled round his, and the juice of life started to flow again, strong as a river, strong enough to roll rocks away. He followed her towards the kitchen. 'What do you mean, elephants?' he said. 'What elephants?'

CHAPTER ELEVEN

A Stroll down Felony Lane

Secrets can make prickly bedfellows, and Slider had encountered more than once the villain who got to the point where he would sooner face the consequences than go on concealing the deed. So he was not entirely surprised to get a telephone call from Alec Coleraine, before he'd had a chance to call him. Coleraine sounded nervous and depressed.

'I'd like to talk to you, if that's possible.'

'Yes, by all means,' Slider said. 'Go ahead.'

'Not on the telephone. I mean, I want to talk to you privately. In confidence. Is that possible?'

'Do you want me to come to your house?'

'No, no, not here.' He lowered his already lowered voice. 'I don't want Fay to hear. I – it's rather delicate. Look, could you meet me somewhere? At a pub or something?'

'If you like. What about The Mitre?'

'No, they know me there.'

'All right, what about The Kensington? Do you know it, on the corner of Elsham Road? They have live jazz there on a Sunday morning, so it'll be good and crowded.'

'You think – oh, I suppose you're right. But you'll come on your own?'

When he had put down the phone Slider walked along to the CID room, where Atherton and Norma were poring over the lists of shares sold and the stock market prices, working out how much the Russell trust was down. Anderson and Jablowski were out trawling Covent Garden again, and the rest were going over statements and following up phone calls.

'I may be about to make you redundant,' Slider said. 'I've just had the prime suspect on the dog, wanting to arrange a meeting. He does not sound a happy man.'

'The hounds of hell are on his traces,' Atherton said.

'I think he wants to tell me All,' said Slider.

'Where? When?' Atherton asked. 'Do you want me to come with you?'

'Now. The Kensington. And no. He wants a private chat.'

'Be careful, sir,' Norma said. 'He might be desperate. If he knows you suspect him he might want to eliminate you as well.'

'In a crowded jazz pub? I don't think he's that irrational. But it's nice of you to care,' Slider said.

Atherton looked him over carefully. 'You're very jaunty this morning, guv. Have you won the pools?'

'Oh, better than that,' Slider said with a grin. 'Well, I must be off to the woods. I'll be back soon with fresh supplies. Be good, children, and don't tease the bears.'

Atherton remained staring at the closed door for some minutes, feeling hollow. Norma watched him sympathetically, and at last laid her hand on his arm. 'It's good for him. Be glad for him, at least.'

He looked at her. 'I am.'

'It would never really have worked out with you two, anyway,' Norma said sensibly. 'You're too alike.'

He pulled himself together. 'I'm sorry, who are we talking about?'

'That's right,' Norma smiled and patted him. 'You're a nice bloke. Fancy a cup of coffee? I'll get them.'

There are those whose sartorial standards never slip whatever the vicissitudes of life: they would not willingly meet the Grim Reaper himself without a tie on. Alec Coleraine was standing at the bar in The Kensington trying to get served – the social equivalent of trying to get a Council Tax office to acknowledge a change of address card – and looking as though the hounds of hell had actually got him by the shoelaces; but nothing could be more immaculate and correct for Sunday lunchtime drinkies than the cream turtleneck sweater, the tweed jacket with the leather elbows, the fawn cavalry twills, and the brown brogues polished so that the toecaps glowed like a bay horse's bum.

His flinching eyes sought Slider's and slid away again, and

he had to cough before he could ask, 'What would you like to drink?'

'I'll have a bottle of Bass, please.'

'Oh yes, jolly good. Good idea. I'll have the same. Make that two, will you?'

The band was on the small platform warming up, and Slider looked towards them, as he looked at all musicians now, with a sense of interested kinship, and thought briefly and gloriously of Joanna. They hadn't really talked, not to make plans or agree anything about the future. There hadn't really been time for that yet; they had been too busy catching up on lost opportunities. But there could be no doubt, not after last night, he thought – and short-circuited himself. Last night! Billowy, sensuous memories beckoned, and he caught his mind back hastily like a Labrador from the master bed, gave it a stern shake and sent it downstairs. Not now! He had a case to think about now.

And this poor devil, whatever he had done, was plainly suffering for it as he ought. He must help him get it off his chest. Nasty expression that, whichever way you took it.

'Shall we sit over there? It looks like about the quietest spot.'

'I didn't understand immediately why you suggested this place,' Coleraine said, following him, 'but I see now. If there's a lot of noise, we're not so likely to be overheard.'

'That's right.' Slider sat, wriggling round behind a table, and Coleraine hesitated and then came in beside him, so that they both had their backs to the wall, facing outwards. Slider turned a little sideways so that he was almost facing him. 'There is one thing I must get straight with you, however. You spoke on the phone about confidentiality. Anything I can keep secret I will, but you must understand that if what you tell me is material to any criminal case it will be my duty to report it.'

Coleraine put down his glass and looked at Slider, and drew a sort of shuddering breath. 'Oh God, what have I done? Why did I ever start on this – this – they call it a slippery slope, don't they?' He gave an unconvincing laugh. 'You go so far and you find you can't stop. But it wasn't for myself, I want you to understand that. I'm not as bad as you think. I didn't do it for myself.'

'It will be much better for you if you tell me everything,'

Slider said comfortingly. 'And if it helps you, you can assure yourself that I know most of it already. You won't really be giving yourself away.'

'I – I thought perhaps you did. That's why I – it's keeping the secret, you see. And wondering all the time what's going to happen next. It's got so I'd sooner know the worst than have to go on wondering from day to day when the blow's going to fall.'

'I'm sure I'd feel the same way.' There was a silence while Coleraine stared at nothing, absorbed in his own misery. Slider prompted him, 'So tell me about it, then. Where's the best place to start? With the Russell trust?'

Coleraine came back from his thoughts. 'Ah, you do know about that, then?'

'That you've been taking money from it over a period of years? Yes.'

He took the plunge. 'I didn't mean to defraud Henry, you know. In fact I meant to help him at first. It all started quite innocently with the Miniver fiasco – do you know about that?' Slider shook his head. 'Miniver was a mining company in South America – bauxite, cobalt, things like that. It was more or less exhausted and the shares had done nothing for years, but about three years ago I had a tip that they were going to rocket. Something to do with huge new deposits being found. Well, I like to do a bit on the market now and then, so I decided to have a flutter, but this friend of mine, the chap who gave me the tip, he persuaded me it was no use just dipping a toe in. With big profits to be made he said I ought to go the whole hog and, well, I was persuaded. I put all my spare cash into it; and then I thought of the trust. Why not do Henry a favour too? So I sold a large slice of his shares, and put that into Miniver too.' He took a mouthful of his drink, and stared at the glass as if he hadn't known what it was going to be. 'I suppose I don't have to tell you what happened next.'

'The shares didn't go up.'

'Oh, they went up all right,' he said bitterly. 'They shot up. It was very exciting. And then just as I was thinking I'd made a nice profit and perhaps I ought to get out with it, the whole thing collapsed like a pricked balloon. Up like the rocket, down like the stick. Overnight the shares were worthless. Firelighters.

Of course the whole thing had been contrived somewhere along the line to make somebody very rich, and a whole lot of us got our fingers badly burned – including my friend who gave me the tip, so I can't blame him. But it left me feeling—' He paused. 'It wasn't just the money, you see.'

'Wasn't it?'

Coleraine looked at him with a little flash of spirit. 'I know you think that's all I care about, but I wasn't born with a silver spoon in my mouth, you know.'

'I didn't think you were,' Slider said.

'I've had to struggle,' he said defiantly. 'I had nothing to begin with. In fact, I may as well tell you, since I'm telling you everything, that I was a Barnardo's boy. So you see, when I say I had nothing, I mean really nothing – not even parents who would own me. You can't imagine what that's like, can you, to know that right from the beginning no-one wanted you, not even your own mother?'

He seemed actually to want an answer to that, so Slider said 'No. It must be very hard.'

'And I was a shrimp of a kid, too, pale and puny, and you know what kids are like. I was bullied by almost everyone. It's no fun being the smallest. But it made me tough, and it made me determined. I had to think about what areas I could win in. I was never going to beat them on brawn, but I had good brains and I saw how if you had money in this world people had to give you respect. So I worked like a black at school to get on. I swore to myself I was going to be rich enough one day to cock a snook at everyone.'

Probably the other thing he learned, Slider thought, was that while he was never going to be able to beat the boys, he could win with the girls by playing on their sympathy and their motherly instincts. His defects would become virtues. Girls would be comfort and balm to him – and success with them would also be a means of getting one up on the members of his own sex he so hated. It was a syndrome he'd encountered before, the bullied boy becoming a successful ladies' man. Sadly, it was hardly ever because they actually like women. Manipulation is no basis for friendship.

'So you see,' Coleraine went in, 'everything I have, I got for myself with my own efforts. And losing like that in the Miniver crash – being taken for a ride – well, it hurt my pride. It was hard to bear.'

'You also had the loss to Henry Russell to make good.'

'Yes. Of course. Well, anyway, I started speculating. I took trust funds out of the safe stocks and started to make them really work, going into much more volatile areas where the big profits are to be made.'

'And the big losses,' Slider said.

'Yes.' He looked glum. 'It worked sometimes. I did make profits. But I reinvested them – and – well – bit by bit the fund was trickling away.'

'The fruit machine syndrome,' Slider said. 'Everyone always puts their winnings back in and goes on playing until it's all gone.'

'Yes. Yes, I suppose so,' he said rather blankly. 'The trouble was – I don't know how to say it. I don't quite know how it happened. But it seemed as if it wasn't just the money trickling away, it was my scruples. From taking the trust money to invest, and putting it on longer and longer shots, which was unethical if not illegal, it didn't seem such a very long step to taking it for myself. I don't mean stealing it,' he added quickly, looking at Slider. 'I only ever meant to borrow it, I swear to you. And it wasn't really for me, either. You see my son – my son—'

'Got into trouble,' Slider suggested helpfully.

'He isn't really a bad boy at heart. Just high-spirited. And he's been spoiled. His mother and his grandfather between them have spoiled him. I wanted him to go into the law, you know, and he would have followed me into my business and been a terrific success. He's got brains, you know. But they squabbled over him like two dogs over a bone, and the result is he hasn't done anything. I tried to push him, but it just made him defy me. He always knew he could appeal to them, you see,' he added bitterly, 'and they'd always side with him. Talk about spare the rod.' He seemed to feel he had painted the picture blacker than he meant. He looked at Slider quickly. 'But he's a good boy at heart. And when your boy gets into trouble and comes to you, you don't stop to read a lecture, you help him out, don't you? Have you got children?'

'Two. One of each.'

'Yes, well, you understand then. Marcus – he – I couldn't

refuse him, could I? I couldn't let them take him to court, maybe lock him up. It would have killed him. He's a free spirit. You can't put sensitive people like him behind bars.'

'So you borrowed from the trust, to pay for his – needs,' Slider said carefully. 'What about the oil paintings. Where did they fit in?'

Coleraine had the grace to blush a little. 'That was – oh, God, I mishandled everything so badly! I suppose you know all there is to know about the paintings. I met a chap, an art dealer, who told me the market was just right for investing in minor masters. The recession had brought prices down, but as interest rates fell everyone was going to look for a better home for their cash, and prices were all set to rocket. As long as you bought soundly, you couldn't fail. I was getting worried about the trust, and it seemed a way to get back on an even keel in one go. I went into it very carefully, you know. I didn't just take this bloke's word for it. But Christie's agreed with everything he'd said, and buying the paintings from them I knew they had to be good.'

Slider nodded sympathetically. 'But why didn't you insure them?'

'I know, I know. It sounds like madness. But at the time – you see, the premiums would have been astronomical, they would have cut into the profits; and besides that, the insurance company would have insisted on all sorts of modifications to the flat, which I could hardly have kept secret from Fay.'

'She didn't know about the paintings, then?'

'Of course not.' He looked aghast. 'How could I tell her where I'd got the money from, and why? Anyway, I thought it would be safe enough for a year or so. We'd never been burgled before. And the pictures were in the back of my wardrobe, all wrapped up. It wasn't as if they were hanging on the wall for all to see. It was just the most wretched bloody luck that we got turned over like that.'

An idea had been forming in Slider's mind, based on a general knowledge of Larry Picket's acquaintances. 'The art dealer who gave you the advice – was he a tall, thin, military-looking man with a sandy moustache? Well spoken – Guards' tie?'

Coleraine looked at him with awful reluctance. 'Bill Hanratty,' he said almost in a whisper. 'Do you know him?'

'I think so,' said Slider. 'I told you we'd got your paintings back, didn't I?'

'From him? He stole them?'

'We picked them up from a fence, but Ginger Bill's one of his known associates. Hanratty isn't his name, but it sounds like him. And the break-in at your place was a professional job.'

'He was so interested in what I'd bought, said I'd been very shrewd. I thought he was a nice guy.' Coleraine put his head in his hands. 'I've been such a fool. God, why was I born? I should have realised it was a bit of a coincidence, a bit odd that the burglars found the paintings. Oh, what have I done? What have I done?'

Slider let him alone for a moment or two, and then prompted him gently. 'All right, so the paintings were gone, and you were in a worse state than ever. So what happened next?'

'Next? I carried on. What else could I do? I thought at least I had a couple more years, I hoped something would turn up, I'd find some way to put the money back. I knew Stefan was filthy rich, and when he went all his money would go to Fay – that was understood. She'd give it to me, of course, to look after and invest for her, so that was no problem, as long as he died before Henry came of age, and there was a good chance of that because he had a heart problem—'

'He didn't, actually.'

'What? What are you talking about? Of course he did.'

Slider shook his head. 'The post mortem showed a perfectly normal heart for his age – no disease.'

'But – but Buster told me—'

'Possibly Sir Stefan made it up as a means to keep Buster in line. "Don't cross me or it might bring on an attack", that sort of thing.'

'Good God,' Coleraine said slowly. 'Yes, it's just the sort of thing he'd do. Poor old Buster. It was a good thing, then—'

'Yes?' A good thing I didn't wait for him to die naturally?

'Oh, nothing. I've forgotten where I was.'

'I think you'd just about reached Henry Russell announcing he was getting married.'

'Ah. Yes.' Coleraine looked suddenly very old and very weary. 'Well, you know, of course, that the trust winds up when Henry marries. Suddenly I was going to have to face the music. I can tell you I was worried sick. I didn't know which way to turn. And in the middle of it all, Marcus came to me again with more trouble, some—' He stopped, looking at Slider warily.

Slider shrugged. 'You may as well tell me everything. How much worse can it be?'

Coleraine sighed. 'I suppose you're right. It was some cocaine dealer who was into Marcus for big money. Threatening him if he didn't pay up. Marcus came to me – I gave him what I had – he said it wasn't enough. We had a bit of a row.' He stared sadly at the table. 'I was so worried already, I said some pretty harsh things to him, about how he'd bled me dry. He said his grandfather had plenty and why didn't I go and ask him. I couldn't bear the idea of that. I hated Stefan, you know, and his attitude towards us. I said I'd sooner die than ask him for money. So Marcus said that if I didn't, he was sure his mother would, especially if she knew what he needed the money for.' He looked at Slider appealingly. 'Fay – she doesn't know everything about Marcus. I mean, she knows about some of his – pranks, but – not the serious stuff. I try to keep it from her. He knows that, Marcus knows that. It would break her heart if she knew he takes drugs. So I said I'd go and see Stefan.'

'And that was the visit you paid him on Tuesday?'

He was very white now. 'Yes. It was useless. I knew it would be. He told me he wouldn't give me a penny, whatever I wanted it for. I went to work. I sat there all day going round and round like a rat in a cage, desperately trying to think of a way to raise the cash. I couldn't think of anything. Then on Wednesday morning Marcus phoned me to ask how I'd got on. I told him Stefan had refused. He said—' Coleraine swallowed. 'He said why didn't I kill the old boy then. Shoot him. Marcus knew he kept a loaded pistol in the house in case of burglars. "Go and get Grandpa's gun and shoot him, then you'll have all the money you want," he said. I thought he was joking, of course.' He stopped. 'Then he said if I didn't do something and get him the money, he'd take to crime. Breaking and entering was easy, he said, and no-one ever got caught. I lost my temper with him, told him to stop being stupid. I told him to come and meet me and we'd talk it out. He said he didn't mind taking a free lunch off me, and rang off.'

'You met him where?'

'Tottenham Court Road. There's a café in Hanway Place, somebody's Pantry. Kate's Pantry, I think. I'd have taken him somewhere better but I was afraid he was going to talk wild again and I didn't want to be overheard.'

'And did he?'

Coleraine nodded miserably. 'We had a row. He called me tight-fisted. He said he had to have the money and that didn't I care about him. He said he'd be maimed or killed by the dealer's gang if he didn't get the money.' He shook his head hopelessly. 'Terrible words. Words can hurt, you know, like a real, physical pain. Then he said if I was too much of a coward to kill Stefan, he'd do it, and once the old man was dead, perhaps I'd loosen up and give him what he wanted. And then he stormed out.'

'You really believed he was going to do it?'

'No! No, of course not! It was just talk. He was young and wild and he'd say anything when he was in a temper. But I felt terrible. My head was pounding, I felt sick, I couldn't think. I went straight home. Fay was out, thank God. I walked about the house, up and down, going over it in my mind. I even thought about what he'd said, about killing Stefan. It would be so easy, I thought, and then all my troubles would be over. I could put the money back into the trust, get Marcus out of trouble, maybe even set him up in some career that would keep him out of trouble in future. And Stefan was dying anyway – so I thought. It wasn't so much of a crime, was it?'

'Don't fool yourself. It was very much of a crime, and you know it. It's the worst crime there is. And the worst motive.'

Coleraine looked at him with a sick and beaten look. 'I know. Yes, I do know. I don't think I would really have done it. I mean, you don't know until you're face to face with it, do you? But I don't think I could have pulled the trigger. I've never handled a gun. It's different for Marcus – he's been out shooting, and though birds are different, of course, still it's shooting to kill, isn't it? But with me, even if I could have got hold of the revolver, I don't think when it came to it I could have shot him.'

Slider said, 'But you did, didn't you? You took the revolver out of his desk when you were left alone in his study on Tuesday. And you shot him in the church on Wednesday afternoon.'

Coleraine stared back with blank incomprehension. 'No,' he said. 'No, of course I didn't. That's what I've just been telling you.

Good God, did you really think—? But I've just been telling you I went home, and I didn't leave the house again that day. I felt so ill I went to lie on the bed, and I was so tired I fell asleep.'

'If you were at home, why didn't you answer the telephone? We tried to ring your wife there on Wednesday afternoon to tell her about the shooting, and there was no answer.'

'I didn't hear it ring. I turned off the phone in the bedroom, and I was so heavily asleep I didn't hear it ring downstairs. I slept until just before Fay came home at seven o'clock, and that's the first I heard about Stefan being shot.'

Slider studied his face, but it sounded true; he had sounded all along as if he was telling the truth. All around them the wall of noise had built up unnoticed; the band was playing, and people were listening, drinking, smoking, talking, tapping their feet, enjoying their Sunday morning socialisation, with no idea of the drama being run through in this unremarkable corner.

'You suspected me?' Coleraine said now in a dazed sort of way, as if it was beyond belief.

'I was just going to invite you to come back to the station and make a statement,' Slider said grimly. 'I shall still have to, of course, but a different sort of statement now. And the sixty-four-thousand-dollar question is, if you didn't kill Sir Stefan Radek, who did?'

But the answer was written large in Coleraine's sick and suffering face. 'I'm so afraid Marcus must have done it. It's a terrible thing to say, but – but—'

'It's a terrible thing to do,' Slider said.

'If he did it. I can't believe – but if he did, I can't shield him any more.' He looked a desperate appeal at Slider. 'I've got to know. I can't stand it any longer, suspecting him. Please—'

'We'll find out,' Slider said comfortingly. 'You come along with me now, and we'll get to the bottom of it.'

CHAPTER TWELVE

The Domino Effect

'So he came to you to grass up his own son, did he?' Norma asked with somewhat irrational indignation, considering their jobs depended on people giving information about each other. Coleraine was downstairs at this very moment, making a statement to Beevers and Mackay, and considering he was busy unpicking the best case they'd had so far, Slider was taking it very well.

'It all got too much for him. He hates himself even for suspecting Marcus, but he's got to the point where he can't bear the uncertainty any longer of not knowing,' Slider said. 'Of course, he says he's sure Marcus didn't do it—'

'Which is shorthand for he bets he did,' Norma said.

Atherton was jubilant. 'I said it was him, didn't I? Nasty little slime-bucket. Now we've only got to prove it.'

'You take a large size in onlies, my lad,' Slider said.

'Hang on, guv,' McLaren said untidily through a jumbo sausage roll he was eating out of a paper bag. 'Didn't I hear someone say Marcus Coleraine had a flat in Bayswater? We've got a possible sighting of chummy coming out of Queensway station, haven't we?' Flakes of greasy pastry fluttered down from his moving lips and stuck to his powder-blue and magenta striped jersey like terminal dandruff, but he had everyone's attention. 'Well, Queensway station serves Bayswater, dunnit? I mean, Bayswater tube station is in the same road. They're only about a hundred yards apart.'

Atherton looked at him almost with affection. 'I knew God must have had some purpose in creating you, Maurice. Of course, that's it! Marcus's flat's in Caroline Place, which is half way between Bayswater and Queensway stations. This is getting interesting.'

'And we know he had the opportunity to take the gun, because Buster said he'd called on Radek on Tuesday afternoon,' McLaren said.

'Opportunity is not proof. And what about his Murray alibi?' Norma said.

'I wouldn't value that above the paper it's written on,' Atherton said happily. 'If Marcus left his father in the café at a quarter past one, he had plenty of time to get back to Shepherd's Bush by half past two to be murdering his grandpa. He even had time to go home first and collect the gun, supposing he hadn't taken it with him for the meet with his dad. And he could have arranged the alibi with Murray either before or afterwards. My personal bet would be afterwards.'

'Tell us why, oh mighty one,' Norma said sourly.

'Well, I don't see him as the sort to plan anything in any detail. I imagine he went storming off in a frenzy of self-pity, shot his grandad, then ran home in a panic. He realised he had to fix himself an alibi, so he rushed off to land his old pal Murray in it; and incidentally indulge in a spot of the doings by way of calming his nerves after the horrid ordeal. That way he really would be at Murray's flat on the afternoon in question, and it would only be a matter of fudging the time he arrived.'

'And what did he do with the gun?' Norma asked.

'God knows. Maybe he stashed it at his flat, maybe he took it to Murray and asked him to get rid of it. But there's all of London on the way, or afterwards. It could be anywhere. It could be at the bottom of the Thames.'

'Not if he meant to put it back,' Slider said. 'Putting it back would still be the safest option, as long as no-one ever discovered it had been missing.'

'Does he know we know?' McLaren wondered.

'If he's been in touch with Buster he probably knows, but there's no reason he should have been. It's a good chance anyway that he doesn't. I think we ought to pay his flat a visit before he does find out. Even if we don't find the gun, we might find a duffel coat and a wide-brimmed hat.'

'I must say it's nice investigating a crime amongst the upper echelons for a change,' Atherton said. 'At least their houses and flats don't smell of urine and their cupboards aren't full of filthy rags.'

Slider was about to answer when Anderson and Jablowski came in. He looked at his watch. Three o'clock. 'You two are back early,' he said.

'We thought we'd get written up before end of shift,' Jablowski said.

'You've got something?'

'Nothing terribly exciting. Just a confirmation of the Marcus–Murray alibi.'

'What?'

'Another good theory destroyed by unnecessary facts,' Atherton said gloomily.

'What theory?' Anderson asked.

'We'd just got Marcus down for chummy,' McLaren said, and explained.

'Oh, bad luck,' Anderson said. 'But we've got a witness sighting of him going into Murray's flat at about half past one. There's a fruit and veg stall on the corner of Russell Street, just opposite the door to Murray's flat. The trader – Ray Tate's his name – knows Murray well. Reading between the lines, I think he gets certain illegal substances from him from time to time. Anyway, Tate says on Wednesday he'd been watching for Murray to come out because he wanted to "talk to him", inverted commas, and he saw a fair young man ring the doorbell at about half past one. He didn't know him, but he thinks he's seen him there before. Murray let the fair man in and shut the door. About half past three Tate takes a break and a cuppa tea, decides to ring Murray's door while he's got five minutes. No answer, which Tate thinks is odd because he's sure no-one's gone out in the last two hours. He rings again, and looks through the letter-box, sees Murray's feet half way down the stairs, just standing there. He shouts out "Steve, it's me, Ray," but the feet turn round and disappear, so he reckons Murray's got his reasons for not wanting company and gives it up. But he keeps an eye on the door all the same, hoping to catch Murray as he comes out. Only Murray never appears, not before Tate closes up at half-five.'

They digested this. 'Well, it's not conclusive,' Slider said. 'Someone could have slipped out while Tate was serving a customer or bending down picking up a box of apples. He can't have been watching every minute of the afternoon. But it's an indication.'

'Anyone slipping out wouldn't be able to tell before he opened the door that Tate wasn't watching,' Anderson said. 'The door panel's hammered glass, you can't see through it. So it would be quite a chance if someone managed to get out unseen.'

'In any case,' Atherton said, 'we're only interested in the time between half past one and, say, two o'clock. If Marcus didn't leave by about two, he couldn't have got back to Shepherd's Bush in time to do the murder.'

'Maybe it wasn't Marcus that Tate saw go in,' McLaren said hopefully.

'We showed Tate the mugshot, and he said he thought that was him,' Anderson said. 'It's as close as you'll get.'

'Never mind, I still think it's worth taking a look at Marcus's flat,' Slider said. 'It isn't what you'd call a water-tight alibi, and there's definitely a connection there somewhere. At the very least, instinct tells me that Marcus knows more about it than he's said.'

The house in Caroline Place had once been a handsome thing, but was showing the symptoms of being divided up into too many flats. The steps and rendering were cracked, the door and windows needed painting, and the heterogeny of curtains at the different windows gave it a shabby air. Still, it was central, close to a tube, and would probably be bringing in about a hundred pounds a body per week to the landlord.

The landlord came scuttling out from the basement like a crab out of its rock crevice as Slider and Atherton reached the foot of the steps up to the front door. He was stout and short, so that he looked almost spherical, a round head stuck onto a round body without benefit of a neck in between, like something a child had made out of Plasticine. He was dressed in a white shirt open at the throat and with the sleeves rolled up, black trousers and a black waistcoat with a gold chain across the extreme point of his circumference, which for some reason made Slider think of undertakers. His face was pudgily white, his head almost hairless, and yet he managed to give the impression of being exotically swarthy, perhaps because his eyes had the dark melancholy of an ancient race. He stuck his arms out, pumping his elbows and waving his thick fingers to help him up the steps out of his hole, puffing and calling, 'Yes, yes, I'm coming, vait, don't be so impatient!'

Slider stopped and looked at him with mild enquiry. He stood before them, looking them over with quick, suspicious eyes. 'Yes, yes, vot do you vont? I am Mr Rose, this is my house. Vot are you, police? Not customs, no, policemen, I think. Plain clothes. Vy you calling at my house?'

'We came to see one of your tenants, Mr Rose,' Slider said, somewhat amused at the quick identification. It spoke long experience.

'On a Sunday?' he protested, spreading his hands. 'It must be serious. Vich one you vont? I don't vont no trouble here. I keep a quiet house, I am honest landlord, trying to make honest living. Don't come here making trouble at my house.'

'No trouble, Mr Rose,' Slider said soothingly. 'We just want a little chat with Mr Coleraine. What number flat is he?'

The thick face sharpened, a quick intake of breath hissed between the teeth. 'Ah, so, number four. I knew it! Ven I see policemen coming, I knew it must be number four.' He gave the impression of leaning closer, though he could hardly have got closer than he already was. 'A bad boy that! I vood have got rid of him, but he pays, he pays, always on time, no trouble, and I am a businessman.' A shrug. 'I cannot turn away good money. But now he has someone sharing vid him, and this is forbidden. I say to him, Mr Coleraine, you know I let this rooms to you and you only, no others, no lodgers, and he denies. I cannot catch him, but I know there is another up there. If I can catch him, I get rid of him, I promise you. He's a bad boy. In a minute, he goes. Like this.' He made the gesture of snapping his fingers, but it was like trying to snap two grilled pork sausages.

'How do you know there's someone sharing with him?' Slider asked with interest.

Mr Rose shrugged again, and tapped his nose. 'This tells me. I let rooms all my life, and my mother before me. I know. I cannot catch him, but I know.' He slid his eyes sideways and up, glancing significantly at Slider's face and away again. 'I think he gives him key. This is forbidden, *absolutely* forbidden. I vont him out of my house.'

He folded his arms round his chest, a smouldering bonfire of ancient grudges, and watched broodingly as Slider and Atherton mounted the steps. The front door was on the latch, and Slider pushed it open. A communal hall, smelling of floor polish; institutional green lino, a large speckled mirror on the wall beside the door, a battered side table below it on which reposed a collection of leaflets which presumably had been pushed through the letter-box and picked up by some resident public spirited enough not to walk over them but too indifferent to dispose of them. Beyond the mirror was the door to the ground-floor flat with a plastic number 1 screwed to it; stairs leading up straight ahead; on the first floor doors numbered 2 and 3. Narrower stairs, and on the second floor a door numbered 4 and a very narrow, precipitous flight going on up to the attic.

Atherton laid his ear to the door and after a moment nodded to Slider. 'Music,' he murmured. 'Shall I knock?'

The door was opened after a few moments, just enough to reveal Marcus Coleraine in jeans, a purple singlet, bare feet and hayrick hair, blocking the view into the flat. At the sight of Atherton his face shut down. 'What do you want?'

'First of all, Mr Coleraine, we'd like to come in,' Atherton answered.

'What for?'

'We'd like to talk to you, son,' Slider said gently. 'I'm Detective Inspector Slider of Shepherd's Bush Police Station. Sergeant Atherton you know, of course. Your father's at the station at this very moment making a statement, and from what he's told us, we think there are some things you might be able to clear up for us.'

Marcus still didn't move, looking from face to face with an air of trying to calculate the incalculable. Finally Slider said, 'Can we come in? Or is there some reason you don't want us to see behind you?'

A moment's more resistance, and Marcus stepped back and opened the door. 'Come in if you must,' he said. Inside there was a sound of music playing very quietly – Dvořák, the *New World Symphony* – and an agreeable smell of bath soap. The short passage had two doors opposite each other, both open – one on the kitchen and the other on the sitting-room – and then bent round a right-angle up ahead, presumably to the bedroom and bathroom. All the walls were painted cream, the woodwork white, there was oatmeal Berber underfoot, and everything seemed clean and fairly new.

Marcus had backed up as far as the sitting-room door, but was not inviting them any further in. The assumption that they might be prepared to stand in the hall and talk annoyed Slider. What was the point in this time-wasting, unless it was simply meant to annoy for annoyance's sake?

'We'd like to look around, if you don't mind,' he said evenly.

'Have you got a warrant?' Marcus asked. Atherton gave Slider a look. Would they never learn?

'No,' said Slider patiently. 'I can get one if I have to. Is there some reason you don't want me to look around? Is there something you have to hide?'

Marcus hesitated. 'What are you looking for?' he asked, trying for a reasonable tone of voice. 'Maybe I can save you trouble.'

Slider held his eyes. 'For one thing, we're looking for your grandfather's revolver.' Marcus's eyes flinched slightly, and Slider felt a surge of triumph. The boy took an instinctive half-step backwards, and Atherton, adjusting his position accordingly, was able for the first time to see into the sitting-room.

'Guv?' he said, touching Slider's arm. Slider followed the direction of Atherton's nod. On a table just inside the sitting-room door was the telephone, and beside it a brown, broad-brimmed trilby-type hat. From where he stood, Marcus could not see what they were looking at, but there was alarm as well as enquiry in his eyes.

'What's the matter?' he asked quietly.

'What's the matter? You're in a world of grief, son, that's what's the matter,' Slider said gently. 'Why don't you tell me all about it, and get it off your chest? You know we'll find out in the end.'

'Yes, I suppose you will,' Marcus said rather blankly, his mind evidently working. And then suddenly, shockingly, he grinned. 'Oh well, it couldn't last for ever. I did my best, that's all.'

'Your best?'

'It wasn't me killed Grandpa,' he said cheerfully. 'You're barking up the wrong tree there. But I'm not going to get into trouble over it. I didn't mind helping as long as it didn't come back on me, but if Dad's fingered me, the simp, I'm getting out from under.' He turned his head and shouted towards the back of the flat. 'Lev? Lev! Come here, will you? It's all right, come on out!' Nothing happened, and Marcus turned back to

Atherton and Slider. 'He's hiding in the bedroom, the dumb bastard. Doesn't realise the game's up. Go in and sit down and I'll fetch him.'

But at that moment someone appeared at the turn of the passage, a small, slight young man, smaller than Marcus, with a narrow, pale, thin-skinned face, fine hair the colour of corn-silk, and over-large blue eyes set in delicate orbits of mauve shadow. His mouth was curious, wide and almost without a top lip, except for a small pink mark in the centre where there ought to have been a peak. His lower lip was soft and childlike and drooping, and when he saw the two men it began to tremble. He flung Marcus a look of mingled reproach and fear, to which Marcus merely shrugged with robust indifference.

'It's the police. Sorry, Lev old mate, it can't be helped.' He turned to Slider, completing the introduction in a parody of formality which he was obviously enjoying. 'Gentlemen, may I introduce Lev Polowski, who shot my grandfather?'

Transparent, unsullied tears slipped over Lev's lower eyelashes. 'I didn't mean to. Honest I didn't mean to,' he said in a husky voice.

Marcus grinned the wider, and slipped an arm round his shoulders. 'It's all right, don't worry, they don't hang you any more,' he said, and Lev broke into shuddering sobs.

Slider stepped in. He caught Atherton's eye and jerked his head towards the kitchen. 'Mr Coleraine, I wonder if you'd be so kind as to make some tea?'

He made a moue. 'Oh God, do I have to? I'm not a skivvy, you know.'

'And while you're in the kitchen, I'd like you to tell Sergeant Atherton your side of the story. Meanwhile, Mr Polowski, we'll go in here where it's quiet and you can tell me all about it.'

Lev Polowski sat on the sofa, his hands between his knees, his bony shoulders hunched up around his ears. He looked so fragile and innocent it was hard to think of him as a grown man.

'Stefan did everything for me. I owe him everything,' he said. He had a slight, attractive accent, but his English was excellent. 'I was a student at the Academy in Warsaw. I had a scholarship, which paid my fees, but things were very hard at home with me not earning and my brothers and sisters growing up. My father died, you see, when I was twelve, and Mamma found it harder and harder to make ends meet, and it was getting to look as though I must give up music and try to get a job. My father was a musician, and Mamma wanted me to be one too, but there are so few openings for a trumpet player, so little solo work, and a hundred good players after every orchestral place. And then – Stefan came.'

A rapt look crossed his face, and his hands clasped each other harder. They were large and strong compared with the rest of him, capable-looking, a man's hands grafted on to a boy's narrow wrists.

'You met him in Warsaw?' Slider asked.

He nodded. 'He came to conduct a public concert with the Philharmonic, and the next day to give a master class at the Academy. Everyone was so excited, for he is a great national hero to us – the poor Polish boy who fled into exile and became the greatest musician of our age. And also, we all knew he sponsored talented young musicians. Everyone hoped he had come to talent-spot, but how to catch his eye? He was going to walk about, look into classes, and so, and so; but also we were to give a concert for him in the lunch hour, we the senior orchestra. Everyone was practising as though their lives depended on it, and I—' He shrugged. 'I went over and over my part to make it perfect for him, but I had nothing to hope for. I was not a violinist, not even an oboist or clarinettist to attract his notice, to be taken up and polished as a soloist. We all thought that if it would be anyone, it would be Marta he noticed, our star pianist, who was going to play the Sans-Saens concerto for him, and we were glad, because Marta was so very, very good, and a lovely person too, worthy of being given her chance. No-one would have begrudged the luck to Marta.'

He lifted his head and his eyes were wide and distant. 'I did not dream – no-one dreamed – that he would notice me. It is a nice trumpet part in the Sans-Saens, very prominent, and pretty, echoing the piano and completing the tune. And I was good that day, I knew I was good, and I was glad to have made something fine for the great man. But afterwards, when we were walking from the platform, our Director of Music came to me and said, "Sir Stefan would like to speak to you."' He was reliving now what Slider could see had been the best moment of his life. His husky voice caressed the words like a lover. 'I was taken to the Director's office, and sent in alone. There was Stefan – so tall, so noble, his white hair, his fierce eyes, like a great eagle – and he was looking at me so piercingly, as if he could see into my soul. "You sent for me, maestro," I said. And he held out his hand to me, he took my hand in his—' His hands rehearsed the moment quite unconsciously in front of him. 'And he said, "You played today like an angel. Great trumpet players are very rare. I wish to help you become a soloist. Will you leave Poland and come with me?"'

He stopped. 'And you went with him?' Slider prompted after a while, and Lev sighed and looked at him as though he were waking from a deep sleep.

'Yes, of course,' he said with an effort. 'Since then he has done everything for me. He brought me to England, paid for me to have the best teachers, arranged my solo debut, took me with him on tours to play with him with some of the greatest orchestras in the world. And he gave Mamma money, too. He is a great, great man.'

'You must have been grateful to him.'

'Of course. Of course.'

'You admired him. It would not be too strong a word to say you loved him,' suggested Slider.

The boy's gaze grew troubled. 'Yes,' he said, his voice barely audible. 'I loved him.'

'And he loved you? He wanted you to show your love in a physical way, perhaps?'

Lev nodded, and then his eyes filled with tears again and he dropped his head, hiding them. 'I was—' He began and stopped, drew a shuddering breath, began again. 'I didn't want Mamma to know. She wouldn't understand. But I was not ashamed. I was proud to be his lover. Only—' He stopped again.

'How long did this go on? When did it begin?' Slider asked.

'Two years. It began almost as soon as I came to England. I was happy – I had my music, I had my career, I had Stefan. But then it seemed that I saw less of him. He changed towards me. He was still kind, but distant. He said I could stand on my own feet now, and I could, in a way, but I thought – I was afraid—'

'That he had someone else?' Slider suggested.

He nodded again, chewing his lower lip. After a moment he said, 'I tried to tell myself I could not expect – he was so much greater than me – I was nothing compared to him. I should not judge him. But when I remembered the things he'd said to me about love, I could not bear it. And then Marcus told me – he told me – that Stefan was – that he was having an affair with a woman. I thought he was lying at first, but when I faced Stefan with it, he admitted it. He said – *terrible* things to me.' He shook his head to shake away the memory.

'How did you meet Marcus?' Slider asked.

'At Stefan's house, of course. Stefan wanted us to be friends. I was pleased that he did. I thought he wanted it because I was important to him. But I think he hoped Marcus would distract me, keep me from finding out about the others.' He gave a short, humourless laugh. 'He never guessed Marcus would be the one to tell me.'

'How did he come to tell you?'

'It was on Tuesday – last Tuesday. We'd been out together, Marcus and I, just messing around and he asked me to go with him to visit his mother at her shop. I think he wanted to ask her for some money. I didn't want to go, because I was shy of her. Stefan had said she mustn't know about him and me, because she wouldn't approve, and I was afraid she might guess. But Marcus persuaded me. We went to her shop, and she was very nice, friendly to me, but I felt awkward. She told me about the concert Stefan was giving at the church for the charity she was interested in, and asked me if I would be going to it, and I said maybe. But really it was the first time I'd heard about it, and I wondered why Stefan hadn't said anything to me. And afterwards, when Marcus and I left, I said to him that I thought I would go along to the final rehearsal, because I hadn't seen Stefan for such a long time, he'd been so busy, and it would be a chance to catch up with him. Marcus said it would be a bad idea to go, and I asked him why, and that was when – when – he told me that Stefan was having an affair with a woman, his agent, and that she'd be there.'

'Kate Apwey,' said Slider.

'Yes, that's her.' He lifted his flamey eyes to Slider's face. 'I hate her name! I hate her! She could be with him all the time, any time! But how could he do it?'

'So what did you do when Marcus told you? You said you went to confront him with it?'

'Not straight away. I was too upset. I told Marcus I wanted to be on my own for a bit, and I left him and went for a walk.'

'Where?'

'On Hampstead Heath. That's where we were. His mother's shop is in Hampstead, you see. I walked about, thinking and thinking, and then in the end I decided I had to go and face Stefan, and ask him if it was true. I thought Marcus might be mistaken. Or that he might – be making mischief.' He bit his lip. 'Marcus likes to tease, you see. He likes making trouble. He doesn't mean any harm, really, it's just – it amuses him.'

Slider nodded. He remembered Marcus's glee when he called Lev out from the bedroom. 'What happened next?'

'I took the tube and went to Stefan's house. When I got there I saw Marcus coming out. I almost turned away, but he saw me and called to me. I went up to him, and he said, "Grandpa's at home. You'd better go in and have it out, hadn't you?" And he laughed. It made me angry. So I went in.'

'Wait a minute, you said this was Tuesday afternoon?'

'Yes.'

'Sir Stefan was alone?'

'Yes. Except for Buster, of course.'

'Did Buster see you?'

Lev looked puzzled. 'He let me in. Why?'

'No, nothing, it doesn't matter. Go on please.'

He resumed slowly. 'Buster showed me to Stefan's study, and in a minute Stefan came down. He was in a bad temper, I could see straight away. He said he was just going out to rehearsal, that he was in a hurry, and asked me what I wanted. I said that I would come with him, that I would like to watch the rehearsal, and we could talk afterwards, but he said he would be busy and that it wasn't convenient. He was so cold, I couldn't bear it. I said he was always too busy to see me these days, and so it began. We quarrelled. I accused him. He admitted it, and said it was none of my business, that I should be grateful to have been noticed by him. I asked how he could bear to touch a woman in that way, and we – he—'

'Yes, I understand. Things grew heated. You both said things you didn't mean.'

Lev shook his head. 'He meant them. That was the worst thing. He meant them. And then he told me to leave, and said he never wanted to see me again. I said he'd be sorry, and I ran out. I was crying, but I was angry too. I wanted to kill him, Just then, I wanted him dead.'

Slider nodded. 'You knew about the revolver?'

'I knew about it, but I didn't think of it then. He'd showed it to me once. He was very proud of it, and he liked to get it out and touch it. He made me hold it once and it – it – excited him.' The transparent cheeks showed a rush of blood. 'But I didn't think of it then. It was afterwards, when I went out into the street, Marcus was waiting for me. He asked how I got on. I told him everything. I was so hurt and angry, you see, and I said to Marcus I wanted to kill Stefan, forgetting it was his grandfather. But Marcus didn't care about that. When I said I wanted to kill him, Marcus took the gun out of his pocket and said, "You'll need this, then."'

'He had Sir Stefan's revolver in his pocket?'

Nod. 'I asked him where he'd got it, and he said he'd taken it just now in case I needed it. I didn't want to touch it, but he shoved it into my pocket, and when I tried to stop him he said to be careful, it might go off, and when I tried to take it out again he said not to be a fool because someone might see it. And then he patted me on the shoulder and said good luck and left me.'

'And what did you do?'

'I went home. I got the bus and went home, with the gun in my coat pocket, feeling huge and hot and as if it was burning a hole. I thought everyone looking at me must know. When I got home I took it out and put it on the table and I thought I could never touch it again. But when I remembered what Stefan had said and how he had treated me, I was so angry and miserable I wanted to die. I picked it up again, thinking I might shoot myself. Oh, I don't know what I was thinking! And then I remembered the time Stefan had first shown it to me, and then I really wanted to kill him. I decided I would go to the rehearsal the next day, and I would shoot him in front of everyone, shoot him down in public, and then shoot myself afterwards.' He nodded, his eyes dreamy again. 'It seemed so good, and I was quite calm then. We would be together for ever, and no-one else would be able to have him. I sat up all night, and I smoked – Marcus had given me a bit, along with the gun – and I thought about it, and in the morning it still seemed very good to me. So I had a shower and dressed myself and put the gun in my coat pocket and got the bus back to Shepherd's Bush. It was the forty-nine, the same bus I always took when I went to see him at his home, and that seemed right, too, like a pattern.'

Yes, Slider thought, that was the missing element. The theatricality of the act – shooting Radek down in front of witnesses – had always seemed ludicrous: it did not fit quite comfortably with the notion of Alec Coleraine killing for financial gain. But as the final, suicidal act of a jealous lover, particularly of one so young, ardent, idealistic, and half out of his peanut with illegal substances, it made perfect sense. Like a pattern.

'And so you went to St Augustine's church, and you shot him,' Slider said.

Polowski's eyes widened. 'No! I didn't! At least, I suppose I must have, but I didn't mean to. I swear I didn't mean to kill him.'

'All right, son,' Slider said. 'Just tell me about it.'

CHAPTER THIRTEEN

Some Enchanted Afternoon

In the kitchen Atherton had been hearing the story from the other side. It was an account to amaze but not much to delight.

'How did you know what the relationship was between your grandfather and Lev?' he asked, at the point in the narrative when it was evident Marcus knew.

Marcus, sitting on the kitchen table and swinging his legs with deliberate insouciance, said, 'Grandpa told me himself, of course. I think he saw it as part of my education to corrupt me – not that I saw it as corruption. I mean, who cares these days? I'd have guessed anyway. He didn't keep anything from me. God, if his adoring public only realised what a filthy old goat he was! He'd do anything, with anything, to anything, and he didn't care if we knew it. Well, apart from Mum, of course.' He screwed up his forehead in perplexity. 'For some reason he really minded what Mum thought of him – and she's so strait-laced, she'd have done her pieces if she'd ever discovered he was bi. I think she may have guessed that he had the occasional bonk with a female – I mean she's not totally naïve – but it would never cross her mind that he'd do it with a boy.'

'And you kept the secret from her too?'

He looked indignant. 'What d'you take me for? Do you think I'd deliberately upset her? I love my mother, I'll have you know.'

'I suppose everyone's got one weakness,' Atherton remarked.

'Besides, Grandpa would have killed me if I'd split on him. He had a filthy temper, you know – not something you'd provoke twice.'

'So if you knew about Lev and your grandfather, why did you tell Lev about Kate Apwey?' Atherton asked.

'Oh, just for fun,' Marcus said indifferently.

'Weren't you afraid your grandpa'd find out it was you who spilled the beans?'

'Even if he did he wouldn't have cared. He'd finished with Lev. He'd got bored with him, only Lev didn't realise it, of course. I was doing Grandpa a favour really, getting Lev off his back.'

'And Lev? Weren't you supposed to be his friend?'

'We knocked about together, but he was a bit of a geek really. I thought it'd be fun to stir him up. He had no idea what Grandpa was really like – he thought he was a genuine saint. So I painted him the real picture and watched him go green. Then I went round to Grandpa's and wound him up. It worked a treat – better than I'd expected, actually, because Lev arrived just as I left, so he came in for it all hot and steamy, before the old boy had had a chance to cool off.'

'God, you're a sweetheart, aren't you?' Atherton said, amazed.

'It was fun. You had to be there. I hung around outside and waited for Lev to come out, and when I saw the expression on his face! If looks could kill! So I gave him the gun and said if he—'

'You what?'

'Grandpa's revolver. He always kept it in his desk drawer, loaded. I took it when he wasn't looking and gave it to Lev.'

Atherton controlled himself. 'I suppose you had a reason for doing that?'

'Yeah, I told you, it was all a bit of fun. I thought Lev was so mad he'd go and wave it under Grandpa's nose and give the old boy a fright.' He slid his eyes sidelong at Atherton and, evidently feeling something less warm than total approval emanating from him, attempted justification. 'Well, he deserved it, stingy old bastard: all that money he had, doing nothing, and wouldn't give me a measly penny. Of course, Lev's such a wimp I didn't really think he'd actually shoot him—'

'But if he did it wouldn't matter?'

'Well, we've all got to go some time,' Marcus said virtuously. 'Grandpa's had a good innings anyway. And Dad says he's got – said he had a heart condition,' he corrected himself. 'He could have gone off any minute. It's not like he was young or anything.'

Youth was, of course, the only justification for being allowed to go on existing. Atherton had come across enough villains in his career to know that while they were all utterly self-serving, most were too stupid to be anything else. Marcus was a new phenomenon, and he stared at him with the professional detachment of a naturalist observing something particularly horrific in the insect world.

'I don't think you realise it,' he said gravely, 'but you are into serious naughties. By taking the gun and giving it to Lev you've made yourself an accessory.'

Marcus sniggered. 'You make me sound like a bloody handbag or something. Accessory!'

'It's no laughing matter, I can assure you. You could even be facing a charge of conspiracy to murder. That's twenty years in chokey.'

But it was impossible to frighten this appalling young man. 'Crap,' he said robustly. 'I didn't think for a minute Lev would do it. And in any case, he didn't mean to. It was an accident. He'll tell you.'

'We'll see,' Atherton said. 'In the meantime, you'd better tell me what happened on Wednesday.'

Marcus shrugged indifferently. 'Well, I got up, got dressed, went down to the shop and got some stuff for breakfast, messed around a bit – you don't want to hear all this, do you?'

'Not at this point. You can skip to the interesting bit.'

'All right, at about half-eleven I got a phone call from this bloke who said he had some gear to sell me, really good stuff, but expensive. Only I was brassic, of course, and he said he'd let it go to someone else if I didn't take it quick. So I telephoned my father and told him I owed some bloke and he was after my blood. Well, to tell you the truth, I'd already spun him that one a couple of days ago, to try to get him to cough up, and he hadn't, so I upped the stakes a bit: I said the bloke was threatening to carve me up if I didn't come up with the money. Poor old Dad believes all that stuff, you know. He thinks he's Philip Marlowe, poor old geezer! Anyway, he said come up and see him right away and he'd see what he could do.' Marcus's mouth turned down. 'That was a wasted journey. It turned out he was just playing me along. He dragged me all the way up to Tottenham Court Road and then said he couldn't give me anything. I was furious! We had a row, and I told him what a bastard he was:

he didn't even care if I got cut up. He said he just hadn't got it. I said in that case why didn't he kill Grandpa—' He stopped and smiled at Atherton. 'Which was amazing irony when you consider, wasn't it?'

'Amazing,' Atherton said hollowly.

'Well, eventually I saw there was nothing to be got out of Dad, so I left him and went off to see my mate Steve. I'd given my last bit of brown to Lev last night to cheer him up, you see – which I thought was pretty generous of me – so I went to see if Steve had got a bit in the house, which he usually did. I thought a smoke would calm me down. I mean, I don't like rowing with Dad, you know, only he's such a schmuck, I just lose patience with him. Anyway, I was still there, at Steve's, when Lev phoned me from my flat to tell me he'd killed Grandpa.'

'How did he get in to your flat?'

'Oh, I'd given him the key a couple of weeks before. We were mates, I told you.'

'Mates. I see. And how did he know you would be at Steve Murray's?'

'Good guess. I spent a lot of time with Steve. Anyway, Lev said he'd shot Grandpa and he didn't know what to do. So I told him to stay put, do nothing, speak to nobody.'

'In your flat? That was a bit risky, wasn't it?'

'Well, to tell you the truth,' Marcus said with a grin, 'we'd had a bit by then, so I probably wasn't thinking straight. All I know is, when I put the phone down and told Steve about it, we both thought it was terribly funny. We rolled about and laughed ourselves nearly sick. You know how it is when you're high.'

Atherton offered no response, and Marcus shrugged. 'Anyway, as it turned out no-one had seen Lev properly or recognised him, which was amazing when you think he goes about in that geeky duffel coat, which nobody but him would wear. And he'd worn that hat before, too. But no-one came looking for him, so I just let him stay. I thought eventually if he didn't get found out he could go back to Poland. I could probably get Mum to cough up enough for that, once she'd got Grandpa's money, and I thought it would be sort of appropriate really, for his money to pay to get Lev away. It was quite fun when you came round to Steve's and you obviously hadn't a clue what you were looking for. But when you turned up here, I knew the game was up. It's been a laugh, though.'

'You are, without exception, the most appalling animal I've ever met,' Atherton said with a mild, David Attenborough sort of interest.

Marcus looked sulky. 'Save that for Lev. He's the one who killed Grandpa, not me.'

Slider had found a box of tissues under the television, and Lev was now on his fourth. His eyes and nose were pink in his white face, so that he looked like an albino mouse; but he was talking freely, evidently glad of the chance to get it off his chest. Slider remembered Freddie Cameron saying, 'They like to tell the tale, old chum, they like to tell the tale.' Murder bestowed a kind of celebrity on both doer and done to. He had interviewed murderers in his time for whom it had been the one significant event between their birth and their death, and they had recounted it, not exactly with pride, but with a sense of occasion, like the Queen's Jubilee or When Gran Won the Premium Bonds. And when the murder was a *crime passionel*, of course, it was an integral part of the affaire, to be told along with the first sight, the first kiss, the first quarrel. Oh darling, they're playing our tune. 'When you shoot your true love, across a crowded room . . .'

'I don't know if I would have done it if I'd met him face to face when I first got there,' Lev said, hunching miserably over his soggy tissue like a bird in the rain. 'Maybe if it had been an ordinary hall . . . But that church – do you know it?'

'Yes.'

'Oh, of course, you must have been there. I was forgetting. Well, it is not like an English church, is it? It's very Russian in a way. We are Catholics in my family, but there are Orthodox churches in Poland too, and it made me think of home, and Mamma, and my brothers and sisters. When I first went in, the orchestra was there, but there was no sign of Stefan, so I had to stand and wait; and it was dark and smelled of incense, and there were the saints and the icons and the statue of Our Lady. And bit by bit all my anger and hate drained away and I felt very small and frightened, as if I was a little boy and God was watching me. And then Stefan came in. He stood at the side talking to some people, and when I saw him I remembered how much I owed him, how he had given me everything, brought me from Poland, given me the best teachers, arranged concerts for me. And then when I saw him walk across to the podium, as I had watched him so often, I knew I loved him, and I could never hurt him.'

'You were still standing at the back of the church?'

'Yes. I hadn't moved. I had planned to walk down right to the front and call his name, and when he turned round and saw me, then I would shoot him. I don't know if I would have. I don't know if I could ever really have pulled the trigger. It isn't a thing you can know ahead of time, is it?'

Slider shook his head. 'I've never been in that position.'

'No. No, I suppose most people haven't.' He blew his nose and continued, his drowned eyes staring at nothing. 'When he appeared I had taken the gun out of my pocket, but still I didn't move. And when he walked across the platform, all that filled me was love and care for him. He looked ill, and old, and frail, and I was suddenly afraid he might die – isn't that ridiculous? After planning to kill him, now I was afraid he might die.'

He stopped, and Slider had to prompt him. 'So what happened next?'

Lev looked at him with sudden blue. 'I don't know. Truly, truly I don't know. I must have been pointing the gun at him automatically, because I didn't know I was. I was tense and anxious, seeing how ill he looked – worried for him. Maybe I was squeezing the trigger, but I didn't mean to.' His hands were clenched with it now. 'He picked up the baton, and then he stopped. I know all his movements, I have watched him in life and on film a thousand, thousand times, and I knew something was wrong. I started forward, a step, one step only, and he collapsed and – and I heard the explosion.' He put his hands up to his face, flinching at his own touch as if he hadn't known he was going to do it. 'I didn't know what it was at first. I thought it was a bomb or a mortar or something. I thought of the IRA. It was so loud, you see, and close. I thought the roof would fall in on me. And then I smelled the smoke, and I looked down and saw the gun, and I realised I must have pulled the trigger. He was lying there, so still, and I was standing here with a revolver in my hand, and I almost died of horror. I realised I must have shot him, and I couldn't think of anything to do except run away. But truly I didn't mean to. You must believe me.'

The blue was desperate with appeal now. They like to tell the tale – and it matters how it is received.

'Yes, I believe you,' Slider said. 'What did you do next?'

'I ran. Just away, down the street, I wasn't capable of thinking. Then when I found myself at the tube station I thought of Marcus. He's so sophisticated, I thought he would know what to do. So I went to his flat. He wasn't in, but I had the key, so I went in and sat for a bit until I stopped shaking. Then I telephoned Steve Murray, to see if Marcus was there, and he was. He told me to stay put and he'd come to me, but he didn't, not till next day.' His face darkened with the memory. 'It was the worst night of my life. A hundred times I was going to telephone the police and give myself up. I wish I had. I didn't even know whether Stefan was dead or alive.'

'You could have watched the television news, or turned on the radio.'

'I didn't think of it. Not till the next day. I fell asleep eventually, you see – not having slept the night before I must have been tired. And when I woke in the morning I put the radio on and heard – heard he was dead.' Tears welled again in an amazing, easy flood. 'I was going to give myself up then, but Marcus came home and talked me out of it. He said to think of the scandal, and how upset his mother would be if she knew about Stefan and me. And how upset my mother would be to have a son a murderer. And when I thought of Mamma I just wanted to go home. So Marcus said I should lie low for a while, and that after a bit you – the police – would give up on the case, and then he would get me back to Poland somehow.'

Slider shook his head. 'You seem to take that young man's word for most things. But what would have happened when you were missed? You couldn't just disappear without anyone asking questions, and then the connection would have been made.'

'Did you make it? Is that why you're here?'

'We came here to search the flat for the revolver.'

'You suspected Marcus?' Lev seemed horrified. 'But how could you think he would kill his own grandfather?'

Slider passed on that one. 'Where is the gun, by the way? Have you still got it?'

'Yes,' he said, to Slider's deep relief. 'It's in the bedroom. Shall I get it?'

'No, it's all right, we'll get it in a minute.'

Lev looked at him cannily. 'Yes, there are five bullets left. You think I might shoot myself?' Close, son, close, Slider thought. 'No, not now. The moment has passed. Telling you all this has made me feel much better.' He thought a moment. 'What will happen to me now?'

'We'll take you back to the station and you'll make a statement, and then I'm afraid you'll have to be kept in custody until the powers that be decide what to charge you with.'

'Will they send me to prison? Will I be accused of murder?'

'That isn't for me to say, son.' Looking across the hall he could see Atherton just inside the kitchen, and gave him the nod to come in. 'Let's take one step at a time, shall we?'

Polowski nodded meekly. 'It's right that I should be punished. But I didn't mean to kill him, you know. In fact, I could almost swear he fell before I pulled the trigger.'

Barrington listened in silence, his massive face, pitted like lava, as mobile and expressive as a mountain side. Quinbus Flestrin, the Man Mountain, Slider thought suddenly, out of the far past and his education at the conscientious secondary modern in Timberlog Lane. All the things they used to force children to read that you hated at the time and were grateful for later. His mind was like the lumber-room of an old family house: comfortably crammed with odd and interesting stuff, most of which he'd forgotten he'd got, but which might come in useful one day. He thought of his own children and was sorely afraid that such rational, modern, purpose-built creatures would have nothing in their attics but triple-thick insulation: very useful, but not providing much amusement for a rainy Sunday.

'Right,' Barrington said, 'so what have we got besides the confession? The CPS won't go on a confession alone these days, and we don't want any mistakes over this one: Radek was a world celebrity. Let's tabulate.' He lifted his strong hands ready to count off on his fingers. 'You've got the gun?'

'Yes, and the ballistics report confirms the bullet taken from

Radek was fired from that revolver. It's the same make as the remaining bullets in the chamber. There's no doubt that was the gun used.'

'Fingerprints?'

'Messy,' Slider confessed. 'It's been well handled. We can identify some individual ones, but there are prints from both Polowski and Marcus Coleraine. The duffel coat and hat definitely belong to Polowski – we've got a witness who lives in the same house in Earl's Court to identify them – but we can't prove it was him wearing them at the time. And the coat originally belonged to Marcus.'

'What about the witnesses who saw him between Shepherd's Bush and Queensway?'

'It's the same as the witnesses at the church: none of them got a really good look at his face. The best is the women who saw him coming out of Queensway station, because he'd taken the hat off by then and had it stuffed inside his coat. Her description tallies, but I don't know whether she'd pick him out of an identity parade if Marcus was in it too. Superficially they are very similar – small, slight and fair. We'll try it, anyway. And there's Marcus's alibi, too. It isn't perfect, but as long as no-one wants to deny it, it'll just about stand up.'

Barrington frowned. 'You think there is some doubt as to which of them did it?'

'No, sir. I'm sure in my own mind it was Polowski at the church. And they're both telling the same story at the moment: as long as they continue to agree I think the external evidence is sufficient. I think the problem could arise when Coleraine realises how much trouble he's in. He may then want to back-pedal and deny any involvement at all, and defence would jump on that, of course.'

'Yes,' Barrington said judiciously. 'There's also the question of whether he can be allowed to incriminate himself. We mustn't forget his father's a solicitor.'

'Even if he is a bent one,' Slider added.

Barrington looked at him suddenly – at him, rather than in his direction. 'Yes,' he said thoughtfully. He drummed his fingers on his desk top, and Slider feared an outburst might be on its way, but in fact what he said was, 'This has been quite an unpleasant case. A lot of people have come out of it very badly.' Slider said nothing. 'Is there something particular about it that's bothering you?'

Slider was startled. Insight, sensitivity, sympathy – from Barrington? That would be an intriguing new sensation, though not necessarily pleasant – like having a hedgehog down your trousers. 'Sir?'

'You don't seem comfortable with the result.'

'Oh, I just don't like how much reliance we're having to place on Marcus Coleraine,' he lied.

'It's a good result, though,' Barrington said. 'And quick, too. It looks good for us. The Commander will want to give it publicity – and I want you to know that I shall make sure the credit goes where it's due.'

Slider was so surprised he only just managed to reply. 'It was a team effort, sir. Everyone's pulled their weight.'

'Good teams only exist because they have good leaders,' Barrington said. 'I've seen how your people work for you. You inspire loyalty, and that's the sign of a good officer.'

Wilder and wilder. Slider felt as though his head was rolling about the room like a bowling ball. He was so accustomed to taking the shinola shower that he never even took off his bath cap any more when entering the sanctum. Something strange seemed to be happening to Barrington, because he seemed to be suffering some mild spasms of the face. He looked at Slider and then down at his blotter and then at the portrait of the Queen on the wall to his right, and then at Slider again. And it was at that point that Slider realised the spasms were Barrington trying to smile. It was a ghastly sight and an even more ghastly notion.

'I think I've sometimes been too rigid in my ideas of what makes a good officer,' Barrington said at last. 'I took certain precepts and had them carved in stone, and when you're dealing with people, that can be a mistake.'

Oh shit, Slider thought, he's going to pour his heart out to me. He didn't think he could cope with that.

'Especially in civilian life. You can't apply battlefield rules to guerrilla fighting. What I'm trying to say is that I may tend at times to hold up an ideal, a template, and measure people against it, rather than valuing what they're good for in their own way.'

Slider could have translated for him: I worshipped my old boss, and anyone who wasn't like him was nothing; now I've found out that my old boss was nothing, I've been left all at sea. And looking more closely at the Man Mountain, Slider could see how far out on a Donald Duck lilo Barrington must have drifted in the past weeks. There was a strained expression in his eyes and his face looked thinner; his clothes seemed a little too big for him – even the ring on his wedding finger seemed loose. He had plainly been suffering, and Slider realised suddenly how little he knew about his chief's private life. Had he had someone at home to comfort him after a hard day making subordinates miserable? Was he married? Had he ever been? It was difficult to imagine him doing anything so normal as putting on striped pyjamas and going to bed with a wife. Slider knew that Norma, to her own annoyance, found him unaccountably sexy, and violent passions did not seem necessarily incompatible with that asteroid façade; but it was impossible to visualise him ever unbending far enough to pop the question to anyone. He'd probably have to send a memo.

No, that was unkind. If the poor old bean was trying to break the shell and emerge into humanity at last, it was only right to encourage the transmogrificaton. Thinking back to the last sentence, Slider decided he could hardly say yes sir or no sir, so he said, 'I understand, sir.'

'Do you,' Barrington said. And then as though the first had not been a question, 'Do you?' He paused, stood up, walked up and down the space between his desk and the window, looking as incongruous as a tiger in an estate agent's office. 'What I want,' he said slowly, 'if it's possible, is to start again. Clean slate. Do you think that's possible – Bill? Pretend these unfortunate – er – *tensions* have never existed between us. I want us to work together in future without prejudice. I promise you I'll back you all the way, and you'll find me a good man to have on your side.'

The smile finally broke the surface, and it was not a thing to dwell on. Slider wanted it over with as quickly as possible, before Barrington tried to shake his hand or something. 'Sounds good to me, sir,' he said, hating himself rather. But it was that or throw himself out of the window, and it was nearly teatime and they had Danish pastries in the canteen on Mondays.

'Fine. Good. Well, then – we start again from here, right?' Barrington stopped in the middle of his walk and thrust his hand out across the desk. Whimpering inwardly, Slider grasped it.

'I'd better be getting on with it, then,' he said, backing off. 'Getting this case together.'

He didn't manage to get very far before Barrington, with a great effort, said – or rather blurted out – 'I don't suppose you'd be free this evening, would you? To have dinner? We could talk over any problems you think I ought to know about. I'd like this to be a happy station.'

Come, Slider thought Alice-like, that's going too far. Enough is enough. 'I'm sorry,' he said, 'I've already got plans for this evening.' Which was true, actually and fortunately; and the conviction evidently carried.

Barrington looked for a fraction of an instant disappointed and Slider felt for an equivalent space of time rather mean. But then the fissures in the rock-face closed up, he barked, 'Some other time then,' and sat down and pulled some papers towards him; the silent dismissal.

Atherton stuck his head round the door. 'I wondered what you were doing tonight. Only Sue's coming round for dinner, and I thought you might like to join us. Little celebration, perhaps.'

Blimey, what it is to be popular, Slider thought. Suddenly I'm the Prom Queen. 'Thanks,' he said. 'Much as I hate to turn down anything you've cooked, I've already got a date for tonight.'

Atherton realigned his body vertically with his head, and leaned against the door jamb. 'Oh? Is it anyone I know?' he asked with elaborate unconcern.

Slider's grin would not have looked out of place on a Norman Rockwell paper-boy. 'Yup. She's forgiven me, and I think she's going to take me back. We're going to talk about it tonight – if we get round to it.'

Atherton felt as though his intestines had suddenly gone off without him. 'Oh, that's wonderful,' he said. 'That's really wonderful. I'm so glad for you.'

'Don't be too glad too far ahead of the game. You know how strong-minded she is, and how dumb I am. But it's a foot in the door. I'm going to depend on my hunky torso to argue the case for me.'

Atherton managed a smile. 'She's a gone goose, then.'

'What's this with you and Sue?' Slider asked. 'Is that serious?'

'When have you ever known me to be serious?'

'I thought perhaps it was a case of imitation being the sincerest form of flattery.'

'Oh well, you know how I feel about you, guv. Talking of cases, by the way—'

'Don't. It leaves a bad taste in the mouth.'

'I hate to think what a good defence counsel will make of it,' Atherton agreed. 'But I was just going to say that you should remember to tell Joanna she was wrong. You told me she said we'd discover it wasn't a musician who killed Radek.'

'She was wrong, and she was right, because he didn't mean to do it. I'll tell her that.' Slider stared away at nothing. 'I should think they'll let him off lightly, don't you?'

'Whether they do or not, he'll serve life in his own mind. What's done can't be undone.'

'And I still don't really know whether he was a great conductor or just a showman. How much has the world been robbed of?'

'You'd better ask Joanna,' Atherton said shortly.

CHAPTER FOURTEEN

There's no Police like Holmes

'I wonder if anyone has ever written about the rôle of spag bol in the process of seduction,' Slider said, stirring in the tomato paste. 'It does seem to me that once you've cooked and eaten it together, you're bound to each other for life.'

Joanna, wrapping the garlic bread in foil ready for the oven, said innocently, 'You never cooked it with Irene, then?'

'That,' Slider said, 'was well below the belt.'

She grinned quickly at him. 'Sorry. It just slipped out.'

'And actually, the answer is no. I've cooked it *for* her, years ago when we were first married and lived in a bedsitter with a gas ring, but never *with* her. So my case remains sound.'

'You really think,' she said, 'that once we've had dinner I won't be able to resist you? That I'll tumble into your arms like a ripe plum falling off a tree?'

'Counting on it,' he said, adding oregano like a man with palsy.

'Oh Bill, don't rush me.'

'Rush you?' he said indignantly. 'It was me that suggested we ate first.'

'What's this "first" business?' she objected. He put down the spoon, turned and put his arms round her waist, lifting her slightly off her feet and pressing her hard against him.

'Listen to me, woman,' he said. 'I've apologised for being such a complete and utter waste of space these last two years, and I'll apologise again as often as you like, but I'm not going to let you ruin the rest of both of our lives by making us live apart.'

She looked him straight in the eye, which given her position was all she could look him in. 'I suppose you think that being masterful is going to—' There was quite a long silence. 'My, you are strong,' she murmured at the end of it.

'I've always been strong in the arms and shoulders,' he said. 'It comes of shovelling muck all through my formative years.' He lowered her, still held against him, to the ground.

She looked up at him with a faintly troubled expression. 'It still hurts, you know.'

'I know.'

'I didn't want you to think it was just that easy.'

His smile faded. 'I had two children. I was married for fifteen years. No, I didn't think it was just that easy.'

'I'm sorry,' she said in a small voice.

'No,' he said. 'I'm not laying that on you. And I've no regrets. But I don't want to waste any of the time we've got. I—'

'Yes? You what?'

'No, it sounds pretentious.'

'So sound pretentious. You think someone's writing all this down for posterity?'

'I was just going to say, I deal so much with death and sadness in my job, I want everything we do to be a celebration of life.' He made a face. 'Yeuch, I can't believe I just said that.'

She smiled seductively. 'Your sauce is catching. I can smell it.'

He dropped her precipitately and grabbed the spoon. 'Just in time. How long is your bread going to take?'

'Ages. The oven isn't up to heat yet. We've time to sit down and have a glass of wine. And you haven't told me about the case yet. You must be pleased to have got it all sorted out so quickly.'

'The sorting out hasn't begun yet. Now we've got the real plod of putting all the documents together and trying to get it into a form that won't send the CPS into fits. Of course, I know in detective fiction it's all over once Sherlock fingers the villain and swans off for coke with Watson, but it's not like that in real life. In real life working out who dunnit is the least of our troubles – certainly in this case.'

'Well never mind, sit down here, take hold of this, and tell me the latest developments,' she said, handing him a generous glass of Dolcetto d'Alba, glowing liquid ruby in the firelight and smelling of the warm south. Ensconced in the depths of the chesterfield – it wasn't the sort of sofa you could apply a meagre verb like 'sit' to – with Joanna's thigh against his, he sipped and told her the tale.

'Atherton thought it was a nice change to investigate amongst people whose houses didn't smell of urine,' he finished, 'but I've found it depressing to see how badly all these people have behaved, people who ought to know better. Casual sin and casual lawbreaking – drugs, embezzlement, greed, adultery, murder – looting their way through life and dropping the litter behind them like tourists. Not one person's shown any compassion or had one thought to anyone else. It was just me, me, me.'

'All sin is selfishness. And selfishness is the root of all sin,' she said.

He gave her a tired smile. 'Oh, and by the way, Atherton told me to remind you you were wrong – about the murderer not being a musician.'

'He'd better not bank on collecting. Maybe Polowski didn't do it,' she said. 'Maybe it was Marcus all along, and he was only covering for him.'

'No, no, it was Lev Polowski who pulled the trigger all right.'

'But?'

'But what?'

'No, that's my line. You sounded as if you wanted to say "but". Is there something funny about it?'

'How well you know me.' He sighed. 'There's lots that's funny about it. I know we've got the right man and he's confessed of his own free will, but I just don't feel right with this case. There's something unsatisfying about it – like watching a film where the hero and heroine meet in a restaurant, and they keep loading the forks, but you never see the food go down. Nobody's actually chewing and swallowing.'

'All right.' She swivelled round to sit cross-legged facing him. 'Go through it with me, then, item by item. What doesn't feel right?'

'Well, to begin with, there's the question of why Buster didn't recognise Lev.'

'He was a long way away, and it was dark,' Joanna said. 'Remember we were sitting under the lights – you can't see out into darkness. And Buster had no reason even to look that way until after the shot was fired.'

'Oh, I know. I didn't mean that. But the description of the murderer included his small size, the duffel coat and the hat. Now wouldn't you have thought that would ring a bell?'

'Why should he know anything about Polowski's wardrobe?'

'He'd called on him just the day before. And duffel coats aren't that common any more.'

'Maybe he wouldn't know that. But probably he wouldn't even think of it. With the shock of the shooting itself, and then he's been devastated with grief ever since – he's hardly in a state to ponder sartorial niceties.'

'You sounded just like Atherton then. All right, I accept that – but then why didn't he tell me that Lev had called at the house on Tuesday? He mentioned Marcus and Alec Coleraine, and when I said was there anyone else, anyone at all of any description, he said no.'

'Forgot, maybe. People do.'

'Forgot? Marcus had, in his own words, "wound Radek up". They were about to go out and already late, and there's another interruption, and an emotional scene, and Keaton doesn't remember it, even when prompted?'

'Well then, why do you think he didn't mention it?' she asked Socratically.

'I don't know. I wish I did.' He sipped his wine thoughtfully, and she took the opportunity to go out to the kitchen and check on the oven. When she came back, he said, 'Polowski says Radek looked ill when he got up on the platform. Did you think so? Did you notice anything in particular?'

She frowned. 'Well, I told you he was sweating a lot, but he always did. Maybe it was more than usual. He wiped his face with his handkerchief before he began. I don't know. It all happened so quickly, and I wasn't really looking at him to notice him. He wasn't a man to gaze at.'

'Lev gazed at him. He said his behaviour was different from usual.'

'So what are you trying to suggest – that he knew he was going to be shot? But that wouldn't alter the fact that he was shot, would it? I mean, that is a fact, isn't it? You took a bullet out of him?'

'Not me personally. Jenkins the pathologist did, though. I wish it had been Freddie.'

'Why, don't you trust this new one?'

'He hasn't got so much experience. Maybe he missed something.'

'But I thought he had more firearms experience. Wasn't that his specialist area?'

'True.'

'Well, then. I don't understand what the problem is.'

'Nor do I really,' he said ruefully. 'Maybe I'm hungry.'

'There's always that,' she agreed. 'Combined with the fact that your life has been turned upside down recently, and you've been working long hours and probably not sleeping much.'

'And I haven't even told the worst yet. Mad Ivan wants to be friends with me.'

'What?'

'He asked me if we could start again with a clean slate, and then he invited me to dinner.'

She smiled slowly. 'And you chose me! Well, I need never doubt again.'

He reached out a hand for her. There was some extremely urgent unfinished business rushing about his bloodstream. 'We don't have to eat now, do we?'

'Yes, we definitely do. Try to be a little sophisticated. Anticipation is half the dish – didn't Sophocles say that?'

'I doubt it. He was Greek, wasn't he?'

Atherton lay on his back feeling – feeling – well, feeling like he'd never felt before, actually. 'I'm sorry,' he said.

Sue turned onto her elbow and looked at him over her plump shoulder like a partridge hiding behind a pink rock. 'Don't worry,' she said. 'There'll be plenty of other times.'

'It's never happened to me before,' he said with a voice driven by humiliation.

'It has to me,' she said. He glanced at her, unwilling to meet her eyes in case it was embarrassing.

'Has it?'

'Yes. But it's not a contest, you know.' She wriggled herself into a more comfortable position. 'The difficulty is knowing what to say. After all, if I say it doesn't matter it sounds as if I'm not disappointed, and if I say I'm disappointed, it sounds as if I'm blaming you. It's a bit like time travel, really. The danger is not that you might come face to face with yourself, but what on earth you'd find to talk about with someone who knows all your best lines.'

He grinned unwillingly. 'You really are a complete nut.'

'I know,' she said complacently. 'Did I dream it, or was there some of that pudding left?'

He sat up doubtfully. 'You want it now?'

She sat up too, the sheet miraculously continuing to cover her breasts just as if she was in a movie. 'Why not? It's the second most indecent thing I can think of to do at the moment. Can I have it in here, out of the serving bowl?'

'Yes, of course,' he said. He felt quite relieved. At least he knew he could cook. It was a mystery really, why he'd failed; and it wasn't because he hadn't really fancied Sue – after all, they'd been bouncing the springs every spare moment since they met.

He opened the bedroom door and Oedipus shot in and jumped up onto the bed, giving him an affronted look over his shoulder. He stalked up to Sue with his tail straight up like a broomstick and began rubbing himself against her, purring like a geiger counter. She laughed and looked up at Atherton. 'That'll learn you!'

'Nothing of the sort,' Atherton said. 'He's just showing his good taste.' Their eyes met and he felt better. He really, really liked her. More than anyone else he'd met in years.

He began to turn away to go to the kitchen and she said casually, as if quite at random, 'Did you ever sleep with Joanna?'

He stopped very still. His back was to her so she couldn't see his face, and the pause seemed to go on for a very long time.

'No,' he said at last.

'Well, that's okay then,' she said lightly. He forced himself to turn and look at her, to find out the worst, but she was smiling an all-embracing smile of perfect understanding. He felt comforted and comfortable, as if he'd been to confession and had all his sins cancelled.

'Bring two spoons,' she said.

Slider woke with a violent jerk. His head had fallen right back onto the arm of the chesterfield, and his neck hurt. He sat up, bewildered, met Joanna's eyes, and found the memory of a recent gigantic snore sculling about his brain. It must have been the noise of it that woke him.

'You fell asleep,' she said kindly.

'I'm sorry,' he said thickly. 'Bad manners.'

'It's all right. You're tired and full of good things, and it's warm in here.' She eyed him curiously. 'Were you having a dream? You were twitching and muttering.'

His absent brain cells started to ooze back into their usual crevices. 'Yes,' he said. 'It was – yes, I remember now! I was playing in your orchestra. We were doing a concert.'

'What were you playing?' she asked, amused.

'The trumpet.'

'You can't play the trumpet.'

'I can't play anything, but it was all right in the dream. I knew I could play it all right. That wasn't the problem. There I was sitting at the back with the others and—' He frowned. 'Oh yes, I remember, the problem was that I had the wrong music in front of me. Any minute the conductor was going to start waving his hands and I'd have to play, and I knew my bit wouldn't fit in with everybody else's.'

'That's what you were muttering, I think – "It won't fit, it won't fit."' She looked at him patiently, seeing by his frown that he was far away in thought. His hair was ruffled, his eyes bloodshot, the muscles of his face slack with tiredness. A fine stubble was just beginning to show at this distance from this morning's shave, and she could see that if he grew a beard now quite a bit of it would be grey. She had one of those infrequent moments of seeing him whole and separate, something complete and absolutely outside herself, as if he were rimmed with light; and she loved him so hugely she could only sigh, as one sighs sometimes with pain. That was why he'd gone on pursuing her in spite of her best efforts, she thought: because, being logical and clear-sighted, he saw that being apart wouldn't stop them feeling like that about each other, so there was no point to it. She was going to have to accept love with all its inconveniences, and she had a moment of panic, because she'd got used to living on her own and liked her independence, and the safety that came along with it. But on the other hand, there was a sort of reprehensibly girly excitement about the thought of setting up home together and doing the things ordinary people did, like choosing wallpaper and buying carpets and deciding where to go for their summer holidays. Doing things with Bill. Alice in Magazineland. Suddenly she felt like crying.

He came back from his long journey. 'Jo, I'm sorry, I'm going to have to go,' he said. He looked at her with such tentative apprehension, as though he thought it might be rolling-pin time again, that any indignation she might have felt expired in a puddle of amusement.

'Go where?'

'I've got to go back to the station. I need to have all the papers to hand.'

'It's the case, is it? Is there something wrong?'

'It doesn't fit,' he said. 'There's something that doesn't fit. I've just got to go over it again and—' He was away with his thoughts again. Joanna got up and went silently to fetch his coat. She thrust it into his arms and turned him towards the door.

'Go,' she said. 'And drive carefully.'

'I'm sorry to mess up your evening,' he began, trying to look over his shoulder at her.

'Your evening too. It's all right, I understand.'

'I'll make it up to you.'

'I know you will. Just promise me one thing? Phone me later – when you can, when you've something to tell me.' She reached past him to open the door, and he turned in the confined space and kissed her.

'I love you,' he said. And went.

Seven o'clock in the morning is usually a quiet time in a police station. The CID office is unmanned, night shift ending at six and early shift not coming on until eight. Slider lifted his head from the sea of papers and looked towards the windows, seeing the early sky pale and sunless, hearing the morning traffic getting into its stride along Uxbridge Road. He picked up the telephone and dialled.

'Freddie! I'm sorry to bother you so early. Oh good. Did you have a nice holiday? Well, it's something that happened while you were away. Oh, you heard about that? No, I don't know that there's anything wrong, exactly, but I wondered if you'd have a look at the PM report for me. I don't want to say until you've looked at it – I want your unbiased opinion. If I fax it to you now, could you look at it right away and ring me back? Yes, I know, but I do think it's important. All right. Thanks a lot. I'll go and do it right now. Thanks, Freddie. Bye.'

It was almost eight o'clock when Cameron called back. 'You were a long time,' Slider said.

'My dear old boy, you didn't expect me to sit and read your blasted report in my skivvies, did you? I had to bath and shave and dress, and then I read it while I had my breakfast.'

'Breakfast,' Slider said in a mixture of exasperation and longing. The spag bol of sacred memory was now a long way in the past.

'Certainly breakfast. Martha promised me kedgeree this morning. Only a certified madman passes up on Martha's kedgeree.' Even his voice was replete, Slider thought bitterly. 'Anyway, I'm here now. What's the problem with this PM?'

'Do you think the conclusion is all right. The cause of death?'

'I didn't examine the body, old chum. But it looks all right to me. Laddo James knows what he's doing. I don't know much about him personally, but his reputation is certainly sound.'

'But the bullet – it was hardly more than a flesh wound. It was at extreme range and it damaged no organs. Could it really have caused his death?'

'Let's be accurate: it was the shock that caused his death, and there's nothing surprising about that. He was an old man. Shock is a very individual thing. You can never be sure how it will affect people.'

'But Radek was very fit, and there was nothing wrong with his heart. Look, Freddie, you're a bit of a music buff. You know how healthy conductors usually are.'

'Yes, I know. They do tend to live for ever. I grant that on the surface it may seem surprising that such an unimportant wound should have led to his death, but as I said, shock acts very idiosyncratically.'

'All right,' Slider said, changing foot, 'but then there's something else. The cadaveric spasm. His left hand was clutching the neck of his jumper, his right hand was clenched on nothing.'

'That's right.'

'Just visualise it, will you, Freddie? He's standing there in front of the orchestra waiting to begin, with his baton in his right hand, his left hand poised in the air. There's a loud bang and he's struck in the lower back by a bullet, and in the emotion of the terrible shock he clutches at his sweater so violently that the spasm remains after death, but he *drops his stick.*'

There was a silence at the other end. 'Yes, I see what you mean. It is odd.'

'He must have dropped the stick before the death spasm. If it was the shot caused the spasm, why did he drop it?'

'I don't know, chum. Is this leading where I think it's leading?'

'Is it possible,' Slider said, 'that it wasn't the bullet that killed him?'

'I keep telling you, what killed him was the syncope.'

'All right, is it possible that something else caused the syncope? Could James have missed something?'

'It's possible, old boy, anything's possible. But are you suggesting the shooting was a belt-and-braces job, or just an accidental concurrence? For someone to have shot him at that precise moment would be a bit of a coincidence, wouldn't it?'

'Coincidences are coincidental. That's the thing about them. Anyway, the man who fired the shot says it was the surprise of seeing Radek fall that made him pull the trigger.'

'Sounds a bit thin to me.'

'But it's medically possible?'

'It's possible. So what are you thinking?'

'I don't know yet, only that I can't make it come out straight as it is. There's the cadaveric spasm. There's the fact that the gunman – and I admit he's not the most reliable witness – says Radek fell before he pulled the trigger. And there's the way he fell, too – he crumpled forward quite gently, didn't even knock over the music stand. If you'd been hit in the back by a bullet, wouldn't you arch backwards? Wouldn't you automatically clutch at it?'

'One would have thought so, yes. But I've never tried it, so I can't swear to it.'

'What else could have caused the syncope, Freddie?'

'Well, some other kind of shock or insult. Something that attacked the central nervous system. A virus or a bacterial invasion could do it. Or some kind of toxin. Did he drug?'

'Apparently, but not to excess. I don't think it's likely he took anything of that sort beforehand, though. It wasn't his way – he took stuff afterwards to wind down. But he might have taken something medicinal. He was a bit of a hypochondriac.'

'Accidental poisoning, then. Were there any symptoms?'

'No,' Slider said uncertainly. 'Not really. We've one witness says he looked unwell, another says he was sweating a lot, but nothing concrete. But even if they were symptoms, he was apparently all right up to about five minutes beforehand.'

'It could be a quick-acting toxin, with or without the added insult of the bullet – given his age, even though he was fit, the combination might bring on a syncope before any strong symptoms developed.'

'But if he was poisoned,' Slider said, 'wouldn't it leave post mortem signs?'

'Not necessarily to the naked eye. But all poisons are detectable in one way or another.'

Slider was silent a moment, thinking of the trouble it would cause, thinking of the resistance from the family, from his seniors, the ruckus in the press. But as it was, it didn't fit, it didn't fit. And Radek was still above ground. Just. It would make it much worse to have to get an exhumation order later. If he was going to go any further, he had to act today.

'Freddie, if I get the paperwork, could you do a re-examination? Could you test for poisoning?'

'Certainly, Bill, certainly. You just tell me which poison.'

Ah, yes, there was the rub. 'I don't know.'

'Can't test for that one, chum.'

'I'll find out,' Slider said, 'I've got to give it some more thought.'

'You certainly have,' said Cameron. Slider could hear in his voice the quizzical edge of a man who thinks his friend's got a chimera by the tail.

'But you'll hold yourself ready?'

'I'll have the bleeper with me, and I'll come running at the sound of your lovely voice,' Freddie promised.

Slider put the phone down dazedly. Which poison? Ah yes, and if there was a poison, who administered it, and how, and when, and why? It occurred to him that if Radek had been killed other than by shooting, it opened up the whole field of suspects again. It could be anyone. It could even be Fay Coleraine, and eliminating her from suspicion had been his only comfort from the beginning of the case.

CHAPTER FIFTEEN

Morning becomes Electric

Norma was the first in. Slider called her into his office and gave her a job to do. She listened gravely, nodded, and went away without comment or protest. Thank God for Norma, he thought, as he had so often thought before. Then he dialled Barrington's number, but there was no answer. Slider contemplated calling his bleep, but then decided he was probably on his way here anyway, so he might as well wait until he arrived before tackling the delicate problem.

As he put the telephone down, it rang again. He thought immediately of Joanna, whom he hadn't called yet; and then felt an absurd flush of guilt as it turned out to be Irene.

'I thought you'd have called me over the weekend.'

'I'm sorry. I didn't have time. The case broke, and I was working twenty-four hours a day.'

'You've got a result?' It was the most interested she'd sounded about his job in years.

'Yes. And a full voluntary confession.' No point in telling her his doubts.

'Oh good. I am pleased for you. And Matthew will be. He keeps badgering me for details.'

Slider thought briefly and painfully about the empty bedroom and the poster. 'How is he? And Kate?'

'They miss you,' Irene said, surprisingly generously. But then, he reminded himself, she thought she was the guilty party.

'They always did,' he said. 'Even when I was there.'

'Bill, don't. I don't want to revive old quarrels. I want us to be friends now. Can't we?'

'Yes,' he said. 'I want that too.' He made an effort. 'We must meet. I've got a lot of things to tell you.'

'We've got to talk about the house. And the divorce. I'm sorry, Bill, but we have to talk about that.'

'Yes, I know.'

'Have you got somewhere to stay yet?'

'Nearly. I'm working on it. I've got a bit of work to do on the case first, but I should be clear by the end of the week.'

'Then come and see us. All of us, I mean. Come on Saturday so you can see the children.'

'I don't – don't want to come to Ernie's house.'

'Oh *Bill*—!'

'I'm sorry. I don't want to hurt your feelings, but I don't want to see my children in his house.'

He surprised himself by the firmness with which he said it, and it seemed to surprise her, too. After a moment she said, almost respectfully, 'Whatever you say, darling. We'll meet you anywhere you like.'

'Thanks,' Slider said, and meant it. 'Look, I must go now. I'll ring you later in the week and arrange something for Saturday. We'll go out somewhere nice. Have a think meanwhile where the children would like to go.'

'I'll ask them.' A slight pause. 'Are you all right? Are you eating properly and everything?'

'I'm fine.'

'Only I know what you're like when you're in the middle of a case. You must take care of yourself.'

It was making him want to cry, all this tender concern. The sooner he confessed his guilt to her the better. 'I'm fine, really. I'll ring you on Friday.'

When she'd rung off, he pressed the rest for a dialling tone and called Joanna. The sound of her voice settled his ruffled feathers. 'Nothing's happened yet. I'm still working on my doubts. I'll let you know as soon as I've got somewhere.'

'All right. Have you had breakfast?'

'Not yet.'

'Have some. You must feed the inner man.'

He smiled. 'Not you as well! All this tender concern.'

'I love you more than Atherton does,' she said sternly.

'He's not in yet. I was talking to Irene.'

'Oh. Now you've made me jealous. You called her before me.'

'No, it's all right, she called me. But I'll have to go and see her next weekend. Her and the children.'

'That's all right. You don't have to ask my permission.'

'I'll have to tell her about us.'

'What about us?' She sounded suspicious.

'Well, everything.'

'Oh no you don't!'

'But I have to. It isn't fair. She thinks she's the guilty party,' Slider protested.

'Don't be such a gimboid! She probably enjoys it – all women like to feel dangerous, and precious little chance she's ever had before. If you tell her all our past history, just to ease your own conscience, you'll make her miserable and probably foul up the divorce into the bargain, and what good will that do? And the children will find out that you were unfaithful to their mother and they'll be miserable too. Then she'll probably try to stop you seeing them – and they'll probably agree with her.'

'You think so?' he said doubtfully.

'I know so. Leave well alone. Tell her nothing. You can pretend to meet me later on, and then she'll be able to feel good about being glad you've found someone.'

'That's so devious.'

'It's common sense.'

'But I'll feel bad about deceiving her.'

'So feel bad. That's the price you pay. But don't make her suffer for your sins.'

'You're a strange person. I should have thought most women would want to gloat.'

'I'm a very remarkable person. And you don't know anything about most women, whoever they are. Go and have some breakfast.'

The canteen was quiet, warm and steamy. Still glowing a little from being blessed by Joanna, Slider found himself with a huge appetite and wolfed down eggs, bacon, sausages, beans, double fried bread and two cups of tea as though everything in the garden was rosy. On the second cup, Atherton found him, looking worried.

'They said you were up here. And they said you'd been in all night. What's up, guv?'

Slider told him, and Atherton's frown deepened.

'There's nothing to go on, guv,' he said at last. 'Nothing at all.'

'It's the cadaveric spasm that bothers me most, I think,' Slider said, almost as if he hadn't heard him. 'And the way he fell. It was as if he didn't even notice he'd been shot. Look at the sequence of events: he drops his stick, clutches at his throat, collapses and dies with both hands clenched. Now what does that look like to you?'

'He was shot in the back. The shock caused a fatal syncope. Why look any further?'

'Why did Buster not mention Polowski's visit?'

'You want to make him the murderer? The only person who's actually mourning Radek?'

Slider shook his head, not in denial but exasperation. 'There's something not right about it.'

Atherton looked doubtfully at the top of Slider's head. 'Guv, you can't go to Mr Barrington with no more than this.'

'Can't go to him with anything. He's not here – still in transit, I suppose. I telephoned his house and there's no answer.'

That was a stopper, Atherton thought. If he'd tried to talk to Barrington, he must be serious about it.

'All right,' he said, sitting down opposite and putting his elbows on the table, 'let's have a look at it. If Radek was poisoned, because of the time factor he must have taken the poison in the dressing-room, otherwise he'd have developed symptoms sooner. So that narrows it down to Buster, who's got to be prime suspect because of his closeness to the victim, or Des Riley, who comes in at number two, or Tony Whittam. No-one else came near him.'

'Not Tony,' Slider said. 'He wasn't alone with Radek at any point.'

'Nor was Des, for that matter. But he might have gone into the dressing-room before Radek arrived and planted – whatever it was.'

'In that case,' Slider said, 'it could have been anyone. Anyone in the orchestra. The verger. Anyone who knew Radek would be there.'

'Ah, but what could they have planted? I went in there and clocked everything. There was nothing to eat or drink, not even a carafe of water. Only the water in the tap.'

'It would be hard to poison that intentionally,' Slider acknowledged. 'I wonder if Marcus could have spiked something the day before, something he knew Radek would take with him?'

'But what? Again, there was nothing in the dressing-room that he would have swallowed.'

'I know. I've been over the list and I can't work it out.'

'Unless Buster took it away with him. We looked in Radek's pockets but we didn't frisk him.'

Slider pondered. 'But look, if Buster – or anyone – deliberately poisoned Radek, they couldn't have known Polowski was going to shoot him and cover the trail. So they'd have had to do it in some way that wouldn't be found out, or at least that wouldn't be traced back to them. If Radek had collapsed with symptoms of poisoning, everything in the dressing-room would have been impounded and analysed, and questions would have been asked as to where it came from. And in that case Buster would certainly have had to empty his pockets—'

'Yes, if the symptoms had looked like poisoning,' Atherton said. 'But suppose it only looked like a heart attack? Everyone knew Radek had a bad heart—'

'Because Buster had told them so,' Slider finished triumphantly.

Atherton spread his hands. 'Brilliant. QED. Except that Buster's the only one without a motive to kill Radek.'

'Forget motive.'

'If you say so. But I repeat, you've still no real reason to think Radek didn't die as a result of the gunshot.'

Slider's face shut down. 'Go along with me on this,' he said tersely. 'Humour me. I've just got a feeling about it.' He got up, and walked towards the door.

Atherton shrugged and followed him. 'You're the guv'nor. And who am I to deny a man's hunch? What do you want me to do?'

'See if you can find anything in the records about Radek's wife's death. She's supposed to have OD'd on sleeping pills. It was brought in accidental death at the inquest, but Fay thought it was suicide.'

'I'll see what I can do.' He sounded puzzled, not seeing where that was leading.

'Look up the newspapers, local and national. See if there was any speculation. Maybe it wasn't what it seemed.'

'Right, guv. You think it was Buster, then?'

'I don't know. But he ought to have told me Lev called. I can't get over that.'

Back in his room, Slider picked up the phone and dialled Coleraine's office. It was answered by a new secretary.

'I'm temporary,' she replied to Slider's query. 'Mrs Goodwin's left.'

'That was sudden, wasn't it?'

'Yes, apparently,' she said with a determined lack of interest. 'Did you want to speak to Mr Coleraine?'

'Yes, please,' Slider said, rebuked.

Alec Coleraine was cool, and Slider wondered whether Helena had told him everything before she left. He didn't challenge Slider with it, however. 'I'm trying to catch up with things before tomorrow,' he said. 'It'll be another day off, for the funeral, and business doesn't look after itself. So I can't spare you much time.'

'I won't keep you long,' Slider said. 'I just wanted to ask you what you know about Lev Polowski.'

'What sort of thing do you want to know?' Coleraine asked cautiously.

'About his relationship with your father-in-law, particularly.'

'Just a minute,' Coleraine said sharply, and the phone went dead. Slider waited in the black felt embrace of Hold, his mind out of gear. At least there was no electronic 'music' here. It was quite cosy really, and he was very tired. Then Coleraine came back. 'Just sending the temp away. I didn't want her overhearing.'

'About Polowski? Was it a secret, then?'

'Look here, don't play games with me,' Coleraine said with something between anger and apprehension. 'I know Lev's been arrested, and I've worked the rest out for myself. He and Marcus have been hanging around together, and Lev's as poor as a church mouse. Marcus put him up to it, didn't he? Offered him a share of the loot. I should have realised—'

'Should you?'

'The duffel coat for one thing. How many people do you see nowadays wearing a duffel coat?'

'You knew Lev had one?'

'It was Marcus's. I bought it for him, and it was damned

expensive. From Burberry's. I was pretty annoyed when he casually gave it to Lev, just because Lev didn't have a coat. "Winter was coming on," he said. It was like something out of Tolstoy.'

'If you'd told us this before it would have saved a lot of trouble,' Slider said sternly.

'I didn't think about it,' Coleraine said, and there was a ring of truth to that. 'You don't think about overcoats when someone's been murdered.'

'All right,' Slider said, 'let's leave that. Tell me about Lev's relationship with Sir Stefan.'

'Well, Stefan found him in Poland, brought him back, gave him money for a time, promoted his career.'

'I know those things. I want to know about their personal relationship.'

'Look, Inspector, this mustn't go any further,' Coleraine said urgently.

'What mustn't?'

'About Lev being Stefan's – you know. About them having a – an affair.'

'You mean they were lovers?'

'Oh Christ, don't tell me you didn't know that? Isn't that what this is all about?'

'The question is not what I know, but what you know.'

'Well, they were – they went to bed together. But it's got to be kept secret. It mustn't get out.'

'I'm afraid it's bound to come out at the trial. It won't be up to me to prevent it.'

Coleraine almost groaned. 'Oh God, the scandal – the press – Fay mustn't know! It would kill her. Anything like that's anathema to her. She didn't really know what Stefan was like, and the idea that he could – that he did it with *boys*—'

'You really think she doesn't know? She is his daughter, after all.'

'You don't understand. Fay is very innocent. Such a thing would never occur to her. Look here, I'd do anything to keep it from her – pay anything. Surely there's something you can do? I mean, does it matter *why* Lev shot Stefan? Everyone saw him do it. There can't be any doubt about that, can there?'

Slider passed over the suggestion of bribery, and said, 'Did Mr Keaton know about Sir Stefan and Lev Polowski?'

'Know? Oh, you mean that they—? Well, I don't know, but I should think he must have. He never said anything to me, of course, but then he wouldn't. He's as particular as Fay, more so if that's possible. It's not a thing he'd ever talk about.'

'You think he'd mind?'

'Oh, he'd mind like hell. He's a real puritan, and he saw himself as guardian of Stefan's reputation, you know. I remember a time when one of the papers gave him a less than perfect review for a concert, and Buster nearly had a fit. He wanted to sue, then he wanted to go round and beat the editor up. In the end he only wrote letters, but he went on writing them for weeks, because the paper wouldn't publish a retraction. If he knew about Lev he'd want to kill him.'

'Thanks. You've been very helpful,' Slider said.

This seemed to strike Coleraine as ominous. 'Inspector, you have charged Lev, haven't you?'

'Yes. Yes, he has been charged.'

'And – and Marcus?'

'No decision has yet been made about whether to charge Marcus on any count.'

'Whose decision is it?' Coleraine asked eagerly. Slider could almost hear him fingering his wallet. Of course, he'd have all of Radek's money to spend now.

'The Crown Prosecution Service,' Slider said. Mentally he added, do you want me to give you their number?

Norma came in, looking quietly triumphant. 'There was something. I don't know if there's any connection, but you guessed right, guv.'

'Sit down. Tell me,' Slider said. He was so eager he hardly noticed her long, beautiful legs as she crossed them at him. Besides, her finding Barrington sexy rather took the shine off it. He couldn't relish coming a poor second to the Man Mountain.

She put her notebook on her knee. 'Keaton joined Fitzpayne School in September 1948. He married Doreen Scoggins in September 1949. I got hold of a man on the local paper, the *Uckfield Gazette*, who was very helpful, and he faxed me through the report on the wedding. It mentioned that Doreen had previously been engaged to a local boy, Peter Hepplewhite, who had died tragically in April that year, of food poisoning. The *Gazette* bloke sent me the report on that, too. There'd been quite a fuss about it. Hepplewhite fell ill after eating at the local newly-opened Chinese restaurant—'

'In 1949? It must have been one of the first in the country.'

'It didn't last long, anyway. No-one else was taken ill that night, and health inspectors couldn't find anything wrong with it, but it closed down all the same. I suppose no-one wanted to risk eating there after popular local builder Hepplewhite, twenty-three, popped off in lethal chop suey horror mystery.'

'Who was with him on the night? Did it say?'

'Not by name. A group of friends, including his finacée Doreen. The paper was too busy milking the bride-to-be tragedy to mention any other friends. We could try the local police for the names?'

'If it comes to anything we may have to, but not yet. Was there anything else? What about Keaton's reason for leaving the school?'

'He gave his notice in in December 1952. They have to give a term's notice, so it wasn't a sudden thing. I spoke to the principal, who knew nothing about it – it was before his time – but he put me on to a retired master, name of Harris, who was on the staff then. I spoke to him, and he said that Keaton didn't leave under a cloud or anything of the sort. He gave his notice in due form, and should have finished in July, but he got permission to leave a few weeks early because he'd found another job which couldn't wait. Harris says Keaton's given reason for leaving was that he wanted to write a novel. They all thought it was very dashing of him, but Harris wondered why he couldn't write a novel where he was. If he had to take a job to support him while he wrote, Harris thought teaching was better than chauffeuring, especially given the long holidays.'

'So, no quarrels, scandals, feuds at the school?'

'No, sir. But there was another death.'

Slider almost rubbed his hands. 'At the school?'

'One of the masters, Simon Phelps. During the previous summer hols. Fell to his death down a chalk quarry.'

'Accident?'

'Apparently. Just lost his balance and fell. The interesting thing from our point of view was that Harris said he was a close friend of the Keatons, went around with them, ate out with them, visited their quarters at all hours. And he was a bachelor.'

'Ah. And this accident?'

'He and the Keatons were out on a picnic together when it happened.'

Atherton tapped and entered. He looked at Norma's legs, but only just, and only out of aesthetic appreciation. He might have answered that morning, if asked, that Sue had grey-blue eyes and a wide, beautiful mouth, but he had no idea what her legs looked like.

'Do you want my report now, guv?'

'Yes, come in. No, stay, Norma,' Slider said. 'He's been looking into Radek's wife's death.'

'There's not much to say about it. She was found dead in the morning by Doreen Keaton – Radek and his wife had separate bedrooms. The bottle of pills was open on the bedside table and half full, and they calculated by the number left that she must have taken a double dose. She'd been taking the sleeping pills for about six months – prescribed by the doctor, nothing funny about it. Doreen said that she had been nervous and irritable, but not particularly depressed, though she'd been drinking heavily that night after a quarrel with her husband. The path report was unchallenged: she died of an overdose of narcotic. They brought it in accidental largely because there was no note and the dose, though lethal, was quite small. The thinking was if she'd meant to kill herself she'd have swallowed the whole bottle. As it was, they decided she'd been confused with drink and didn't know what she was doing.'

'And was there speculation?'

'Not in the press. It was very respectful – talked about Radek's genius and his war record, and what a terrible tragedy this was, and how it was to be hoped it wouldn't affect his work. Keaton was interviewed and gave them out a devoted couple, and Doreen said again that Lady Susan hadn't been depressed. The nearest thing to a hint was in a gossip column which said it was tragic when quarrels, which all married couples have, got out of hand, wondered why Lady Susan had been drinking so much, and mentioned apropos of nothing that Radek had recently conferred his patronage on a promising young female pianist who was as talented as she was beautiful.'

'So that makes three,' Norma said, looking at Slider.

'Three what?' Atherton asked.

'Bodies in Keaton's wake,' Norma said.

'Four,' Slider corrected. 'Don't forget Doreen, who died of gastroenteritis.'

'People do,' Atherton pointed out. 'And food poisoning. Hundreds every year.'

'Phelps fell down a quarry,' Norma said.

'Who's Phelps?' Atherton asked, and she told him. 'Staggered and fell?' he said when she'd finished. 'So you think he was poisoned at the picnic, do you?'

'I don't think anything,' Norma said. 'I leave that to my superiors. I'm just a humble footsoldier.'

Atherton, who had taken the other chair, leaned back in it, crossed his own long, lovely legs, and used his fingers to tick points off. 'So we have Buster wanting to marry Doreen and bumping off her fiancé to get him out of the way; then bumping off a master who – what was his crime? Hanging around Doreen? Was she that gorgeous?'

'Why not?' Slider asked. 'She looked pretty enough in the photo I saw, and in a closed community like that she wouldn't have too much competition.'

'In any case,' Norma said, 'a man can be jealous without having anything to be jealous of.'

'Or a woman. Quite: it's an intransitive sin,' Atherton acknowledged. 'So, why Lady Susan? And Doreen?'

'I don't know.' Slider sat for a moment longer, staring at nothing. Then he pushed himself to his feet. 'I think I'll go and ask him.'

'Ask Buster?'

'He's the only one who knows,' Slider said.

'Then I'd better come with you.' Atherton said, with a sideways glance at Norma.

'Sir,' she said, 'if Mr Barrington comes in, what shall I say?'

'If he asks, tell him where I am,' said Slider. 'Don't tell him about my speculations if you can help it. I'll explain everything to him personally when I get back.'

* * *

They waited a long time at the door, and Atherton had given up and was ready to go, but Slider stood as though planted. Atherton had seen him in this mood before. In the grip of an idea, he became dogged but also oddly confident. It was a comforting trait in one's superior, especially when he seemed to be sprouting a wild hair.

At last there was a movement behind the door, and it opened slowly, to reveal Keaton blinking like an owl. His chin was unshaven, his eyes baggy and bloodshot, his trousers liberally creased across the lap as though he'd been sitting in them for days, which he probably had: they looked to Atherton's searching eye like the pair they'd interviewed him in on Thursday.

Keaton looked at Slider, not even sparing Atherton a glance. 'I thought you'd be back,' he said wearily.

'There's something I wanted to ask you,' Slider said, not like a policeman but like someone familiar, an old acquaintance or long-term neighbour. 'Can I come in?' Even a paranoiac would have had trouble finding him threatening. It was beautifully done, Atherton thought. Buster had stepped back almost before thinking, and by the time suspicion caught up with him Slider was over the doorstep and wiping his feet carefully and absently on the doormat.

'Can't you leave me alone? I've already told you everything I know,' Buster said, turning a look of dull resentment on Atherton.

'Oh, I know,' Slider said vaguely. 'I just wanted a chat about something.' He was ahead of Keaton now, and moving towards the stairs. 'The drawing-room, is it? Shall I go up?'

Keaton hesitated, looking doubtfully at Atherton, but Slider had started up the stairs. 'After you,' Atherton said, smiling; and thus bracketed, Keaton could only go up. It was plainly an effort for him, and Atherton felt guilty for a moment at putting the old man through the mill again.

In the drawing-room Slider went and sat down on the chaise longue and gestured to Keaton to take the armchair nearest him. Keaton sat nervously, placing his arms along the arm-rests and his hands over the ends as though he were about to be strapped in and acquainted with the National Grid. Atherton sat to his other side so that Keaton couldn't look at them both at once; but his attention was still fixed on Slider. Whatever his apprehensions, they were focused on Slider: Atherton barely existed for him.

'You see,' Slider said, as though merely continuing a conversation, 'I think I understand most of it. There are just one or two details I haven't worked out.'

'Details? Details of what?'

'Peter Hepplewhite – that's obvious, of course. And Simon Phelps – a little nudge and over he went. But Lady Susan, that's the puzzle. Not so much how you got her to swallow the pills, but *why*? I know it doesn't matter in the long run, but do I like to understand. It nags at my mind otherwise.'

Atherton had thought Keaton looked bad before, but during this speech his face seemed to grey, and he thought Keaton would either pass out or throw up.

'I don't know what you're talking about,' he whispered at last.

'I think you do,' Slider said unemphatically. 'Your wife Doreen – she'd begun to suspect, hadn't she? Or perhaps she'd suspected all along but you'd begun to be afraid she'd talk. Easiest thing in the world to get rid of her, I do see that. Opportunity is everything, isn't it? And then you had Stefan all to yourself – once you'd got rid of little Fay.'

'I never hurt her,' Keaton said faintly. 'I would never have hurt Fay.'

'No, but you got her sent away to school,' Slider agreed. 'Was Stefan hard to persuade?'

'It was him that wanted her to go. He said she couldn't stay at home with no-one to look after her.' His voice grew a little stronger. He seemed not to have noticed that he had not denied any of the other premises. 'Well, that was true, wasn't it? We didn't tour so much in those days, but there were still all the evenings we wouldn't be at home. Who'd have stayed with her then? But *I* didn't want her to go. It was Stefan's idea. She wanted to go, anyway. She hated her father.'

'Did she like you?'

'Of course she did. She knew I loved her. She still does. Who do you think persuaded him to do the concert at the church? I did that, for her.'

'And was it for her that you killed him?'

Keaton stared, his jaw loose. It trembled, but no sound came out.

'You killed him so that she could have his money, is that it? You knew Alec was in financial trouble, and you didn't want her to suffer, so you killed Stefan so that she'd inherit his estate.'

'No!' He found his voice at last. 'No! You've got it all wrong!'

'All right,' Slider said placidly, 'then you tell me. Why did you kill him?'

'I didn't! You're mad! You know I didn't! Lev shot him. Everyone saw!'

'Oh yes, Lev shot him,' Slider agreed, 'but that wasn't what killed him. You and I know what killed him, don't we?'

Still Buster stared, as though unable to remove his gaze. Atherton was afraid he might have a stroke. The shock of all this, at his age – and the horror of being accused, if he hadn't done it – and Atherton still had doubts about the guv's whole theory—

'You know?' Buster said faintly.

'Of course,' Slider said comfortably. 'But if it wasn't for the money, then why?'

Atherton actually saw the blood return to Keaton's face. His voice rose with indignation.

'For the money? What do you take me for? A common, vulgar criminal? I wouldn't kill anyone for money.'

Slider caught Atherton's eye and silenced him with the minutest flicker of his own. 'Tell me then. It was something to do with Lev, wasn't it? Why didn't you tell me that Lev had visited the house on Tuesday?'

Keaton turned his head away, his mouth puckering as though over a bad taste. 'I don't want to talk about it.'

'About Lev and Stefan? You didn't like that little arrangement at all, did you?'

Goaded, Keaton showed a flash of heat. 'You have to have it all out, don't you? You can't keep things decently hidden, any of you! It was bad enough with the women – sluts every one of them – but *boys*? And it was all so blatant! Even Marcus knew all about it. The next thing it was going to be in the press, and then where would we be? I told him it had to stop – the boy was the worst sort, loose morals, loose mind, loose tongue! He told me he'd get rid of him, and I thought he had. I thought it was all over. And then Marcus came round and tried to blackmail him with it.'

'That was his visit on the Tuesday?'

'We were just about to go out. I told Stefan not to see him, but he was always contrary. Well, it was his own fault if he didn't like what he heard. Marcus said he'd take the story to the press if Stefan didn't give him money.'

'You heard it all, did you?'

'There's an intercom in there, to the kitchen, so that he can call me when he's working, if he wants something. I fixed it years ago so that I can turn it on to listen when I want,' Buster said casually. 'I had to be able to look after him. He never knew about it, of course.'

'And what did he say to Marcus, when Marcus threatened him?' Slider asked.

'He told him to go to the devil. You couldn't bully him – no-one could. Stefan may have been many things, but he was no coward.'

'And then Lev turned up.'

'He insisted on seeing him. I could have told him how it would be.' Buster's mouth turned down. 'The filth that flowed out of that creature's mouth! I wouldn't soil myself with repeating it. Afterwards, when he'd gone, I told Stefan he'd been too soft with the boy, that he should have threatened him with the law if he didn't go away and stay away. It was obviously a put-up job between him and Marcus, that's what I thought. And then Stefan said he'd changed his mind, he was going to take the boy back.' He paused, contemplating something black and yawning in his memory. 'I thought he was saying it just to upset me, but the next morning he said it again. He said Lev was talented and ought to be helped and that he was thinking – thinking of bringing him to live with him. In our house.' He stopped. He had reached the heart of the horror as far as he was concerned.

'What did you say to that?' Slider prompted him gently.

'I said I wouldn't have it. He said it was none of my business. We quarrelled – the worst quarrel of our lives. I told him I wouldn't stay under the same roof as that creature, and he said in that case I could pack my bags and get out.'

'Surely he didn't mean it? He must have said that sort of thing to you before, but he didn't mean it.'

'He meant it all right,' Buster mourned. 'He said he was fed up with me trying to run his life. He said I'd turned into a nagging old woman, and he wanted young people around him. He said he'd give me a month's wages and I could leave at the end of the week. But where could I go?' He raised his eyes to Slider's. 'I've no family. I've never had any other home. I've a little bit saved, but not enough to keep me. And besides – I've been with him for forty years. He's my life.'

'So you thought if you had to live without him, it would be better to kill him?'

'Everything seemed to be falling apart,' Buster said with a dazed look. 'We'd been so happy. And I'd been looking forward to his retirement, doing things together, a peaceful old age. Now he was sending me away and taking that – that catamite into his home. And Marcus was going to tell the press – oh, he'd do it, out of spite, you know, because Stefan would never give him any money. We'd be all over the papers, everything pawed over and sullied, his reputation ruined for ever, our lives destroyed. I couldn't let that happen. Better a quiet, dignified end. I knew his heart was bad; all it needed was a little push over the edge.' He shook his head. 'I had no idea Lev was going to do what he did. But then afterwards it seemed like a godsend. It was a way to get rid of him as well, and there'd be no more questions asked.'

'Yes,' Slider said sympathetically. 'You must have been afraid everything would come out – about Lady Susan and Doreen, and the others. It must have been a bad time for you.'

'I never thought about them. And I don't care about them now,' he said. 'How can you think it? It's Stefan: I gave my whole life to him, and he's gone. I just didn't realise before what it would be like to be without him. But there's nothing else I could have done. I couldn't let him destroy himself.'

'Why *did* you kill Lady Susan?' Slider asked.

'She was wearing him out. Her constant demands on him – physically, on his time, yes, but even more on his spirit. She wasted his vital forces. Music at his level takes everything a man has. I saw it every day. He was drained by her, and his music suffered. And she was jealous of me, of my influence with him. She was trying to turn him against me. He'd tired of her by then, anyway, but if they divorced he'd lose all her money, and he was terrified of poverty, after what he'd seen in Poland. So it was obvious what I had to do. She was an unhappy woman anyway, and I rid him of the burden of her, that's all.'

'How did you make her swallow the pills?'

He looked contemptuous. 'You can't make a person swallow pills – and if you could they'd throw them up again. It was in the brandy.'

'What was in the brandy?'

But the mood had been broken. Suddenly his focus sharpened. 'I thought you said you knew everything?' He remembered Atherton for the first time in ages and looked quickly at him, then back at Slider. 'You're trying to trick me, to make me tell you what you don't know.'

'No, no, not at all. I knew it all except that,' Slider said soothingly, but Keaton wasn't soothed. He seemed to shrink together on himself.

'I'll deny it,' he said. 'You can't prove I said anything to you – I know the law. You can't prove any of it.'

Slider looked at Atherton, and then stood up and walked across the room. 'There's a lot we can prove,' he said. 'For one thing, it was you who told everyone Stefan had a heart condition. But we know that wasn't true. His heart was as healthy as yours or mine.'

'What do you say?' Buster said faintly.

'Oh yes. That's a fact. The post mortem showed his heart was very strong. So why should you have put it about that he had heart disease, if not to pave the way for your plot to kill him?' He stood looking out of the window as he spoke, as though it were a matter so settled as to be unimportant. 'You thought that if he collapsed while he was actually conducting, everyone would assume it was heart and not look any further for a cause. That's why you gave him the stuff just before rehearsal, instead of letting him die at home, in bed.'

'But he told me! He told me he had a weak heart!' Buster seemed utterly bewildered.

'Well he was lying, I'm afraid. Which—' Slider stopped abruptly, his eyes fixed on the garden, things slotting into place with rapid, satisfying clicks. It was horrible, it was truly horrible, but it all fitted, and that was the only satisfaction one could ever have from investigating a murder – getting the answer right.

'Which makes you the prime suspect,' he finished. Atherton

heard the difference in his voice and looked at him sharply; and Slider nodded to him, just perceptibly. 'Lev's bullet, you see, didn't do enough damage to kill a man with a sound heart. But Stefan was already dying when Lev pulled the trigger, from something that attacked the central nervous system. Something you'd given him.'

'No-one will believe that,' Buster said, but his voice was faint.

'All poisons are detectable, if you know what to look for,' Slider said. 'The pathologist told me that only this morning. Things have advanced no end since 1959 – they didn't have gas chromatography or atomic absorption spectroscopy then, did they? And of course, no-one was looking for poison in Lady Susan's case anyway. No-one thought of testing the brandy, or looking in your little shed at the bottom of the garden where you do your botanical research.'

Buster jerked in his seat at the last words, and Atherton began slowly to smile as he began to follow Slider's path.

'One is nearer to God in a garden than anywhere else on earth,' Slider quoted softly. 'You made sure of that, didn't you, Mr Keaton? A very short route to God your pretty garden turned out to be. Tobacco plant, foxglove, deadly nightshade, henbane, laburnum – nature's a wonderfully deadly thing, if you know where to look. And you're a botanist. You'd know all about it.'

'I think,' Keaton said faintly but politely, 'I think I must ask you to excuse me for a moment. I have to go to the lavatory.'

He seemed hardly able to get out of the chair, but when Atherton made to help him, he shrank away. 'No, I can manage. Please – please don't touch me.'

Slider watched him walk to the door, and then flicked a nod at Atherton, who followed him out but came straight back in and said, 'It's just across the hall. We'll hear him come out.' Slider nodded and walked to the window again. 'At least it will get Lev Polowski off the hook,' Atherton said after a moment. 'Or will it? He'll have to be charged with something, I suppose. Attempted murder? Malicious wounding? But can you maliciously wound a dying man? And how close to dying was Radek, I wonder, when the bullet struck him? If it played any part in his death, if it only hastened it, Lev's guilty of something.'

'There's still Buster's little shed to examine,' Slider said, off on his own track. 'He may not have thought to clear it out yet, and even if he has, there might be enough traces to—' He stopped, frowning. 'What was that?' He listened, and then looked at Atherton.

'You don't think—?' Atherton said, and then they both ran.

The door was locked and there was no reply from within, but the hall was narrow there. Atherton hitched himself up onto the radiator, lifted both feet up against the door, and slammed it open. Buster was on the floor, his left sleeve pushed up. There was a medicine cabinet on the wall with its door open, and a hypodermic syringe on the floor by his right hand.

Slider crouched by the body. He wasn't dead yet. 'Call an ambulance,' he said.

Atherton hesitated. 'But they might save him.' Slider looked up. 'Just a little delay, guv,' he said urgently. 'He's killed five people, and they'll probably let him off.'

'Do it,' said Slider.

CHAPTER SIXTEEN

God wot?

The ambulance had been and gone, and the forensic team was taking the house and garden shed to pieces, and Slider and Atherton were standing in the drawing-room, waiting to go.

'I still think we should have let him die,' Atherton grumbled, but he didn't mean it now.

'You know we can't do that,' Slider said. 'And besides, we'll need his confession if we're going to get this one home.'

'It's going to be the devil to prove any of it.'

'I know. There's the trail of bodies following Keaton's career, and a few suspicious coincidences, but an awful lot of it's pure speculation. But Radek's still above ground, and Freddie said he'd find the poison if I could just tell him what to look for.'

'And can you?'

Slider grimaced. 'I think so. I think I know how he did it. It was the last thing left to work out, and I looked down from the window at his lovely border all full of blue flowers – including blue rocket, such a pretty, prolific plant. Also known as monkshood or wolfsbane.'

'Is it poisonous, then?' Atherton asked.

Slider rolled his eyes. 'Don't you know anything about plants?'

'I'm not a hayseed like you, guv,' Atherton protested. 'We didn't go about sucking hedges in Weybridge. None of this eye of newt business in the commuter belt.'

'The Latin name for blue rocket is aconite.'

'Oh, well, why didn't you say so?' Atherton said. 'Aconite is what Medea tried to poison Theseus with. The ancients called it the Queen of Poisons. So it comes from rocket, does it?'

'Aconitum to you. All parts of the plant are poisonous, and

you can make a stiff brew from stewing the root as well. It attacks the CNS and paralyses the heart muscle—'

'*Et voilà*, syncope!'

'—sometimes before any other symptoms have had a chance to develop. It's extremely toxic, and it can act very, very quickly – in as little as eight minutes.'

'Well, that sounds promising from our point of view,' Atherton conceded generously, 'except that we have to prove Buster gave it to the old man, and I still can't see how. If he gave him something to eat or drink, he obviously took the evidence away with him, and it will have been destroyed by now.'

'No, he wouldn't have given it that way, because if there was any suspicion, that's the first place we would have looked. If he was going to do it, he'd work out a way that gave him a chance of getting away with it.' Slider turned away and looked out of the window again. 'The other thing about aconite,' he said slowly, 'is that it can be absorbed through the skin. They used to use it externally to treat rheumatic pain – it sets up a sort of tingling numbness. I came across it years ago, when I was a rookie – a case of accidental death, where an ointment containing aconite had been used on broken skin.'

'I don't get it,' Atherton said. 'Am I missing something?'

'You made a list of everything in the dressing-room,' Slider said, 'and in the bathroom. I looked at it this morning, and I realised that there was something missing, but I assumed Keaton must have taken it away in his pocket, and it didn't seem important.'

'Taken what away?'

'A tube of ointment. I just didn't make the connection until I looked out of the window here.'

'A tube of ointment? Did Radek suffer from rheumatism?' Atherton said, still puzzled.

Slider turned to him with unwilling eyes. 'Not rheumatism, you clunk.'

Atherton stared, and then enlightenment came. 'Ouch,' he said, screwing up his eyes in genuine sympathy. 'What a way to go. The poor old bastard!'

'At least it was a quick death,' Slider said.

Slider was not looking forward to having to explain the new

developments to Barrington, even in his lately acquired pussy-cat mood. The shooting had at least been plain and unequivocal, a confession plus a gun plus a large assortment of witnesses, even if there had been unexplained and confusing shadows in the background. But this! As Atherton said on the way back to the station, in spite of anything Slider could do to stop him, this was just going to mean piles of work for everyone.

Barrington was still not in, however, when they got back, which meant a pleasant respite. Slider put the team to work on assembling the evidence of Keaton's past life, put Freddie on alert, and then went with one of the uniform boys to the hospital to see whether they were going to be able to drag Buster back from the brink. When at last it looked as though he was going to live, Slider left the constable there beside him and went back to the station. Barrington had not come in, nor called in, and was not answering the telephone at home. He was not responding to his bleep either.

'Gone out to play a nice round of golf and left it behind, I suppose,' McLaren grumbled. 'Bloody bosses. I know what kind of a row we'd get if we did something like that.'

The awkward thing as far as Slider was concerned was that he couldn't get Freddie onto the new autopsy until he had Barrington's cross on the dotted line.

'Necropsy, old thing,' Freddie said when he told him. 'Autopsy is an examination of oneself. Never mind, Radek isn't going anywhere. And Barrington will phone in before long feeling awfully silly about having left his bleep behind.'

'Well, if he's not back by close of play today, I'll have to get onto the Commander. We'll have to stop them taking the body away. You know they were going to bury him tomorrow.'

'Whoops,' said Cameron. 'I don't envy you that one. Grassing up your guv'nor to his guv'nor? Not very nice.'

'It's a bugger,' Slider said. 'And Wetherspoon thinks the sun shines out of Barrington's eyes, so the shower will be bound to fall on me.'

'From both directions,' Freddie agreed, with the relish even nice people usually display at the prospect of someone else facing an explosion.

'I wonder if there's anything wrong?' Slider said. 'It isn't like

Barrington to be so vague. Weird, yes, but always punctual. Maybe he's ill.'

'He'd have phoned in,' Cameron said comfortably. 'Or his wife would.'

At half past five Slider and Atherton went upstairs to the canteen for lunch, which they'd had no chance to have before. While they were there, Joanna came in, sporting a plastic visitor's badge.

'So this is where you're skulking,' she said.

'Oh God, I forgot,' Slider said. 'I was supposed to phone you, wasn't I?'

'When you had something to tell me. Apparently you've nothing to tell me.'

'You know,' he said examining her closely. 'Who told you?'

'Norma. I rang asking to speak to you and she spilled the beans. So I thought I'd pop round, since I hadn't anything better to do.'

'You don't fool me. You were just longing to see me.'

'Dream on, sonny,' she rebuked him firmly. 'So your funny feelings were right after all?'

'I don't know if that's a good thing or a bad thing. It's going to mean a lot of work, just when we thought we were nearly finished.'

'Never mind, at least you'll be able to feel satisfied at the end of it. How is Mad Ivan taking the disappointment?'

'Mr Barrington,' Slider corrected sternly, 'has disappeared.'

'God, the excitement of your job! What do you mean, disappeared?' Slider told her. 'That doesn't sound too good,' she said. 'Has someone been round there?'

'That would be the police equivalent of poking a stick with an 'orse's 'ead 'andle in his ear,' Atherton said. 'Who's going to volunteer for that?'

'But he might have fallen down the stairs or something, and be lying helpless,' she said indignantly.

Slider sighed. 'I was just giving him a chance to turn up or phone in, that's all, in case he'd accidentally taken the day off. I was on the point of ringing his local nick and asking them to send someone round to see.'

'So I should think. Are you going to get off this evening?

Because we've a lot to talk about and we still haven't got round to it yet.'

'I don't know when I'll be finished,' he said. 'Not until late, anyway.'

She smiled suddenly. Indeed, she positively grinned. 'Got anywhere else to sleep?'

He smiled slowly. 'Well, as it happens, I sort of haven't.'

As it happened, he didn't get to bed anywhere that night, because the local police, going round to Barrington's house and finding his car outside and no response from within, broke a pane in the front door and let themselves in. They found Barrington in the kitchen, sitting at the table, with the muzzle of his rifle in his mouth and his head – or quite a lot of it, anyway – on the wall behind him.

Joanna, in a brown furry sort of dressing-gown which made her look as if she ought to have a Stieff label sewn to the back of her neck, leaned her elbows to either side of her teacup and watched Slider eating a rather shapeless cheese omelette of her own hasty devising. It was a very late late breakfast and he felt as if he hadn't slept for years. Perhaps sleep was only a habit after all, and you could actually get out of it with practice.

'So it turns out he wasn't married?' she said.

'Never had been. It showed how little anyone knew about him. I feel so bad about him. He asked me to go and have dinner with him on Monday night. Think how lonely he must have been to unbend that far, and I turned him down.'

'It wasn't your fault. People don't commit suicide because of what other people do or don't do, but because of what they are to themselves.'

'I didn't say I felt guilty, I said I felt bad. You should have seen that place! Men have no talent for home-making.'

'Some men. Look at Jim's little bijou nest.'

'True. But Barrington's house was so comfortless. Lots of dark, depressing wood and leather – did you ever see Lawrence of Arabia's house in Dorset? You could tell the man was mentally ill. He had a whole room lined with grey aluminium – walls and ceiling, the whole thing.'

'What, Barrington?'

'No, Lawrence. What Barrington had was a great ugly shelving unit taking up half his sitting-room, that looked as if he'd made it up himself out of old wardrobes. And all his shooting trophies were displayed on it. He was quite a crackshot in the army, and afterwards in his shooting club. Rows and rows of silver cups and shields and framed certificates, and he ends up with his brains all over the washable vinyl.' He looked up at her. 'It was a horrible kitchen, too. The wallpaper had a pattern of red tomatoes and green peppers in squares all over it, and the units were old and painted bright yellow. It must have been like that when he bought it. He'd never done anything to it. What a place to die.'

'Oh don't,' she said.

'And do you know what was in the fridge? Two steaks and a bag of ready-mixed salad. That's what he was going to give me if I went to dinner with him. And a frozen blackcurrant cheesecake in the ice compartment. That was the dinner I didn't join him for. What a lonely man.'

He saw Barrington's rock-like, acne-scarred face in his mind's eye, and the feral eyes looking out from the impassive façade. Year by year the granite must have built up, layer upon layer, separating him more absolutely from any contact, beyond hope of reversal. It must have been like being walled up alive, watching the last bright seed of daylight grow smaller, knowing that when it was gone all that would be left was the darkness and the cold.

Seeing he needed to go on talking about it, Joanna said, 'Why do you think he did it? He didn't leave a note, did he?'

Slider thought of Freddie saying 'They like to tell the tale, old boy.' Not Barrington, though. Too proud. And no-one, in any case, to tell. 'I don't know. I suppose everything just got too much for him. The toughest on the outside are often the most fragile inside.' He shrugged. 'It's the job. We all go through it – but he had no-one's shoulder to cry on. Maybe that made the difference.'

She touched his hand. 'You couldn't have helped, if he'd gone that far.'

'I know. But I could have given him a few moments of human contact, even if it didn't make any difference afterwards.' He sighed and reached for his tea. 'Then I had to go and tell the Coleraines they couldn't bury their dead after all.'

'God, yes, old Radek. I'd almost forgotten him in all the excitement. He's made a hole in our schedules, you know. I've got dates into next year that were with him. I suppose we'll keep the concerts and get a new conductor for them, but we'll lose all the recording sessions. That's a lot of money, and even for us work isn't that thick on the ground.'

'That's a good enough reason to go to his memorial service, then. They're going to hold it next week, whatever happens about the burial.'

'Will you be going?'

'Yes. I'll be the official presence. Want to come with me?'

'If you like.'

'She cried, you know,' he said, remembering. 'Mrs Coleraine. Whatever she said, she did care for her father. She cried on her husband's shoulder, and he patted her and looked as if he wanted to cry himself. He looked as if someone had shoved a stick in his head and given his brains a good stir. He'd been suspecting Marcus, we'd been suspecting him, then it turned out to be Lev. Now he just couldn't grasp the idea that it was Buster who did it after all; and sooner or later Mrs Coleraine is going to put two and two together about her mother. It'll come out at the trial, if not before.'

'There'll be a trial, then?'

'If Buster survives. He's pretty old, and he's got no good reason to live. If he gets pneumonia it'll probably be the end of him. It might be better all round if he didn't make it – it'll be the devil of a case to put across, and it'll cause everyone misery. And how long's he going to survive in gaol anyway? Sometimes I don't like this job.' He hadn't told Joanna about Atherton's momentary lapse in Buster's bathroom. There were some things said that were better forgotten. 'Oh well, it won't be Barrington's problem anyway.'

'You'll have a new boss to get used to,' she said, pushing the toast-rack towards him. 'Won't that be fun?'

He gave her a tired smile. 'It couldn't be any worse than it was before.'

'Any idea who it might be?'

'None at all. I can think of some I'd like more than others, but in the long run it won't make much difference. The job is the job. Clearing up after other people's sin. The public refuse department.'

'In other words,' she said, 'everything's rotten. Life isn't worth living. Might as well end it all here and now.'

He smiled slowly. 'Oh no, I wouldn't say that.'

'I'm glad to hear it.'

'After all, I am going to be able to get rid of the house in Ruislip. The architect in me will rejoice at that.'

She grinned. 'If anyone will buy it.'

'Everyone isn't sensitive like me. And I'll have you know it's a much sought-after area.'

'That only means no-one can find it on the map.'

'There'll be a bit of money left over, after paying back the mortgage and giving Irene her half. Not much, but a bit. Enough for a deposit,' Slider said, and stopped. He felt too tired to start again. Lawyers, maintenance payments, removal men, custody agreements – a swarm of ants would have to pick over the bones of his old life before he could embark on a new one, and even then it would not be a clean start. You never shook free of your baggage, of course: failure and the consequences of it, responsibility, debt. That was why children could run up hills while adults always walked. Lucky Kate and Matthew. Lucky Joanna, for that matter, he thought, with nothing to be sorted out. She was just there, comfortably established, waiting for him to move in. And all he wanted to do now was curl up in her.

He had already forgotten his last sentence, but Joanna heard it echoing on the following silence. They still hadn't talked about future plans – not even the practicalities of where they was going to live, assuming they were going to live together. But she could see the time wasn't yet, and she wasn't sorry to put it off a bit longer. It was still a bit of a nervous notion. She was used to her little ground-floor flat and her independence, and the second toothbrush on the window-sill would take some adjustment on both sides. She looked at his heavy eyes and grey skin, and said, 'I'll tell you one piece of good news, though.'

'Hmm?'

'I haven't got to go to work until this afternoon, so you can go to bed and get some sleep, and I'll still be here when you wake up.'

He pulled himself back across the chasm and reached over the table to take her hand. 'Sleep? Who needs sleep?' he said.

She grinned. 'You're an ambitious man, Bill Slider. You'll go far.'

Blood Lines

CHAPTER ONE

A Scar is Born

In the canteen queue Detective Inspector Slider came up behind DI Carver.

'Hullo Ron. You look as if you've been up all night.'

Carver, a balding man with a perpetual grudge, grunted. 'Had a call-out last night.'

'Must have been something serious to get you out of bed,' Slider said blandly. The night shift in the Department consisted of one DC, who called up a DS in the case of something he couldn't handle. Only really serious crime warranted telephoning the Ops DI, who was likely to be just a teensy bit tetchy if disturbed for what he regarded as trivia. 'The big one, was it? Murder? Armed robbery?'

Carver looked a snarl. 'Attempted burglary. Big house in Stamford Brook.'

'Oh, bad luck,' Slider said with brimming sympathy. Ron Carver had sometimes said things about him behind his back. 'Open window, opportunist thief?'

'The window was shut, as a matter of fact,' Carver corrected loftily. 'Bloody sash window,' he added savagely. 'Child's play – two seconds with a five-bob penknife. It don't matter how often you tell 'em, they won't fit locks. And it's not as if this one couldn't afford it – she was loaded.'

'Much missing?'

'Nah, she frightened him off.' He glanced sideways at Slider and began to unbend. One couldn't waste a good story, after all. 'She didn't reckon he was after her Renwahs. Oh no. And she was ready to defend her honour to the hilt – literally. Gilbert says she come to the door brandishing a bloody great knife. Sacrificial dagger, apparently, real Abraham and Isaac job, souvenir of Tel Aviv.'

'Sharp?'

'As a lemon. Apparently, she's sat in the lounge in the dark thinking about going to bed when she's heard the window going up in her bedroom, so she's grabbed the knife off the coffee table, tiptoed in, and there's chummy on the drainpipe with his leg over the sill. Well, she reckons that's not all he wants the leg over – though to look at her you'd think it was more hope than fear – so she's only gone for him, hasn't she? Hacked him in the leg with this bloody pig-sticker, and he's gone. Near as damn it fell off the bloody drainpipe – first-floor window and a concrete strip at the bottom. But anyway, he shins down and has it away across the garden, and she's straight on the dog to us. Keeps the number on her phone pad – reckons it's quicker than nine-nine-nine.'

'A doughty female,' Slider commented.

'I haven't told you the best bit yet,' said Carver. 'Benny Cook feels it's his duty to warn her about the consequences, should chummy have broke his leg or his neck falling off her drainpipe. So he says, "You really mustn't go about hacking at people's legs like that, madam," and she comes back like the Queen Mum, "Young man, I was aiming for his genitals."' Carver's haughty falsetto was worth coming in early for, Slider thought.

Carver went off with his breakfast into the guv'nors' dining-room, but Slider preferred to mess with the ORs, and exchanging friendly nods with some of the sleepy night relief just coming off, who had stayed for a cuppa and a wad, he took his tray to a window table. A few moments later his bagman, Detective Sergeant Atherton, appeared beside him, dunking his teabag at an early morning andante. 'How long have you been here?' he asked.

Slider looked up. 'Who's Prime Minister? Pass the tomato sauce before you sit down,' he said.

'Dear God!' Atherton stared unwillingly at Slider's tray: two fried eggs, double fried bread, sausage, bacon and tomato, tea an' a slice. 'I see you've plumped for the Heartburn Special,' he said. 'Last train from St Pancreas.'

Slider chuckled. 'You're such a gastro-queen. How did you ever come to be a copper?'

'I was switched in the cradle by gypsies,' Atherton said, sitting down opposite him. 'Why are you breakfasting here? Oh, of course, Joanna's gone down to Glyndebourne.'

'She left early to miss the traffic. And she's got a couple of morning orchestra calls, so she's staying down tonight and tomorrow,' Slider said, trying to sound indifferent about it. But the fact was, sleeping in her bed in her flat when she wasn't there made him feel uneasy. He anticipated restless nights. 'What's your excuse?'

'I'm not early in, I'm late out,' Atherton said, extracting his teabag by the tail, like a drowned mouse, and laying it carefully in the ashtray where it would later infuriate the smokers.

'With?'

'One Nancy Gregg. A little blinder. Met her last week on that house-to-house in East Acton.'

'What about Sue?'

'Sue?' Atherton said as though it were a word in Urdu, of meaning unknown to him.

'Sue Caversham, violinist, friend of Joanna's,' Slider reminded him drily. 'I thought you and she were a big thing.'

Atherton sipped, at his most superb. 'No commitment has been made on either side.' And then, 'She's down at Glyndebourne as well, you know. You can't expect a healthy, red-blooded young male suddenly to become celibate. We 'as urges, guv.' He dropped into a whine. 'I dunno what came over me. It's all a blank. Summink must of snapped—'

'Yes, yes, I get the picture.' Slider folded a piece of wonder-bread and carefully mopped up tomato sauce. Atherton watched him in dilating horror. 'So, did you hear Mr Carver's firm had a sleepless night?'

'Yes, I was talking to Hewson about it,' Atherton said. Hewson was the DS on call. 'Modest bit of excitement. He quite took to the intended victim – told me she had balls.'

'Surely not?'

'She's one cool dame. You'll be able to meet her later on if you like. She's coming in to see if she can pick anyone out from the mugshots. Apparently she caught a glimpse of chummy's boat, though it was dark, of course, and it all happened quickly. Hewson isn't too hopeful, but it would be nice to nail one of our persistent offenders.'

'Did she actually wound him?'

'Apparently. There was blood on the blade of the knife,' Atherton said. 'Even if she can't pick anyone out, it might be worth tugging a few of our best customers and see if anyone's limping. A known section-nine-er with a matching cut on the thigh ought to be convincing enough even for the CPS.'

'And how would you propose discovering this cut? Ask them to take their trousers down?'

'That is one difficulty,' Atherton admitted. 'Not least because there's a few who'd agree to. Still, I understand Mr Carver intends putting the word out on the street that the villain ought to sue this woman for assault.' He shrugged. 'I can't believe anyone'd be daft enough to come forward. It means putting his hand up for burglary.'

'It never does to underestimate the stupidity of the criminal,' Slider said. 'I remember the time One-eyed Billy got nicked because he took a stolen Magimix back to Currys to complain one of the attachments was missing.'

'I never know whether to believe your stories,' Atherton complained. 'And I've never understood why he's called One-eyed Billy, when he's got two perfectly good ones.'

'Because his father was called One-eyed Harry,' Slider said, serene in the knowledge that he could only add to his own legend. 'It's like a family name. Harry's wife was always known as Mrs One-eye. It was perfectly respectful – everyone liked her. When she took her teeth out she could fold her lower lip right up over her nose. Broke the ice at parties.'

Atherton felt it was time to raise the tone. 'Reverting to the subject of that break-in last night, the lady in question, interestingly enough, is someone you'll have heard of quite recently: Christa Jimenez.' Seeing Slider's blank expression, he added, 'She sang in that *Don Giovanni* you went to at Glyndebourne.'

'Oh? Which one was she?'

'Donna Elvira. Don't you know? Don't tell me you slept through it all!'

'Of course I didn't,' Slider said indignantly. 'But I'm not an opera buff, the names don't mean much to me. She was the dame with the big maguffies, right? Looked like an advert for Cadbury's Dairy Milk?'

'Come again?'

'Low-cut dress.' Slider elucidated. 'A glass and a half of full-cream milk in every cup.'

'I'll take your word for it,' Atherton said drily. 'I haven't seen the production.'

'You haven't missed much,' Slider grumbled. Joanna was playing in two operas down at Glyndebourne this year, and orchestra members were allowed to bring two guests each to the pre-dress-rehearsal. Though there were many who'd have given their eye teeth for the privilege, and Slider was not unappreciative, it was still small compensation for the amount of time she had to spend away from him. Besides, though he didn't like to admit it in front of Atherton, he wasn't *all that* keen on opera – especially a modern, minimalist production which offered him nothing to look at while he listened. 'If I'd paid seventy-five pounds for a ticket,' he said in sudden wrath at the thought, 'I'd have expected at least some nice scenery and costumes, or my money back.'

Atherton didn't quite keep his smile under control. Slider gave him a suspicious look, and he straightened his face. 'It did have terrific reviews,' he mentioned, 'from some very serious critics.'

'You think I'm a philistine,' Slider said, a little ruffled. 'But I don't believe those critics really like all that modern stuff. They just pretend to so as to make themselves superior to the rest of us. Anyway, they get paid to sit through it. Something that's put on for the public, and paid for by the public, ought to aim at pleasing the public.'

'Ah, there you have the whole dilemma of arts funding in a nutshell,' Atherton said. 'Well, I'd better go and have a shave and change my shirt. Mustn't be late for work, must I, especially now we're short-handed. I wonder if we'll ever get a replacement for Beevers.'

Detective Sergeant Beevers had left three weeks ago. Slider said, 'Who ever would have thought of him entering the Church?'

'It's only a Baptist ministry,' Atherton said.

'Snob! A priest is a priest is a priest. But I'd have thought Beevers was in The Job for life. It isn't as if he had any outside interests—'

'Except the Church.'

'Well, yes, obviously. But if it had been one of the others, now – take Norma, for instance—'

'I've often taken Norma in my dreams,' Atherton said tenderly, 'but I'd never dare try it on in real life.'

There was a moment's reverent silence. Woman Detective Constable Kathleen Swilley was blonde, athletic and slim, with firm, pouting breasts and long, shapely legs – every man's erotic dream. She could also shoot the eyebrows off a fly at fifty paces and packed a punch like an army mule, and because of her machismo was generally known as Norma. She hated her given name so much she didn't even mind.

Atherton sighed, coming down to earth, and stood up. 'I suppose one of these days we'll get a new super, too. That'll be something to look forward to. Not that Mr Honeyman's any trouble.'

Since Detective Superintendent 'Mad Ivan' Barrington had committed suicide, they had only had a night watchman at the crease: Det Sup Honeyman, working out his time until retirement and hoping for a quiet life.

'I hear McLaren's started a book on who we'll get,' Slider said.

'He says that according to the grapevine – alias his mates at Kensington – nobody's very anxious for the job. With the last two supers dying in harness, they reckon Shepherd's Bush is a poisoned chalice. That's why we've had the night watchman so long.'

'They're a right bunch of Hans Andersens down at Kensington,' said Slider. 'Obviously now Mr Honeyman's here, they aren't going to replace him until he retires, and he won't have done his thirty years until next month.'

And a man on the brink of completing his thirty in an increasingly dangerous profession was not going to do anything to risk his life, health or reputation, which was why Eric Honeyman was 'no trouble' almost to the point of catatonia; but out of respect for the chain of command, Slider didn't say so aloud. 'I don't suppose it's possible ever to stop coppers gossiping,' he complained, pushing back his chair and standing up, 'but it'd be nice to break McLaren of the habit of phoning Kensington twice a day for fresh rumours. But he just doesn't seem to take to training.'

'Hit him with a rolled-up newspaper,' Atherton suggested, following him to the door.

Slider had stayed on at the end of the shift, clearing desultory bits of accumulated paperwork and trying to rearrange his 'pending' pile into stuff he was likely to do something about eventually, and stuff he was hoping would simply die of old age. Even as he tried to be conscientious about it, part of his brain knew that he was sitting at his desk because it was preferable to deciding what to do tonight. Ain't you got no home to go to? enquired a thread of song ironically. He had the key to Joanna's place, ten minutes away in Turnham Green, but despite his shaving gear in the bathroom it was still Joanna's place and not home, especially when she was not in it. When she was there it was a dear and familiar haven; without her it seemed as cosy as a 1950s seaside boarding-house.

The ex-marital home in Ruislip, from which his wife and children had decamped, he had never loved even when his family lived there. It was now fulfilling a secondary rôle as an albatross hanging round his neck. The idea was for him and Joanna to buy a place together once he had sold the albatross and paid Irene her half; but with the housing market suffering from clinical depression, even the estate agent had passed from cautiously jaunty to defensively evasive. All the same, a good number of his possessions were still stored there, and he supposed if he were stopped by the police, it would be the address he would give as his. It was where Irene thought he still lived: she didn't know about Joanna yet.

But he only went there when constrained; which left staying at work as the only alternative. It made him realise how few friends he had. Detective Inspector was a lonely sort of rank. Too much blokeing with the lads undermined authority; and in any case, he'd never been fond of football. Socialising above his station was even more out of the question: he was not ambitious enough either to ingratiate himself with his seniors, or to be welcomed by them as an aspirant. Besides, up there in the stratosphere internal politics and golf were the reigning interests, and he'd never really got the hang of intrigue. As to golf, he had met many golf-club members during his years of living in the suburbs. Most of them were dull, and many of them were called Derek.

Atherton was his only close friend. Atherton had no ambition and no nagging doubts about himself, so Slider had nothing to prove to him and nothing to fear from him. His intellectual curiosity made him the ideal partner at work, and his hedonism ditto at play. Moreover, Atherton liked Slider, and made it plain enough to reassure without embarrassing a solitary man with the usual difficulties of his age group in expressing his feelings.

In the feelings department, Joanna had been an earthquake to Slider. She had burst in on a lifetime's reserve and obedience to duty with revolutionary ideas about one's duty to oneself and the nature of happiness. She had turned his life upside down, and he had to admit he hadn't made a very good job of coping with it. Coming alive at his age was worse than pins and needles, and it was hardly surprising if he had periods of reaction, especially when she was not there to reassure him. But the boats were burned now, anyway. Irene had run off (well, sauntered off) with another man, taking the children with her, so there was no way back into his old life. A life with Joanna, some time in the future when everything had been sorted out, glittered like the distant prospect of the Emerald City. He told himself everything would be all right; it was the limbo of the present that was so uncomfortable.

'Sir? Mr Slider?'

Slider looked up, coming back from a great distance to find standing in his open doorway a man about whom much was familiar: a strong, fleshy, broad-bottomed man in a brown suit which original cheapness and subsequent hard wear had rendered shapeless, especially about the overworked pockets. He wore an off-white shirt with the sort of tie men choose for themselves, and thick-soled shoes scuffed at the toe and worn down at the heel. He wore a large, elaborate but cheap metal-braceleted watch on his right wrist, and a large, plain gold signet ring on the third finger of his right hand. The first and second fingers of his left hand were amber cigarette holders. He had detective written all over him.

He was in his mid-to-late thirties, dark-haired, dark-eyed and moley; his lower face had the bluish shading that went with really black hair and white skin.

'DS Mills, sir,' he said helpfully when Slider failed to respond.

'What does the DS stand for?' Slider asked. 'Dark Satanic?'

'Detective Sergeant, sir,' Mills corrected, deadpan.

'Are you being funny, lad?'

'No, sir. Would you like me to be?'

Both men broke into a grin, and Slider got up to stretch out his hand. 'Good to see you, Mills. How are you?'

'I thought for a minute you didn't remember me,' Mills said gratefully. 'It's a long time since the old Charing Cross days.'

'Ten years at least, I should think. So you made your stripes? Well done! And what are you doing here?'

'I've just transferred from Epsom.'

Slider raised his eyebrows. 'Nobody told me. I've been a sergeant short for three weeks. I thought I was never going to get a replacement.'

Mills looked embarrassed. 'Oh, no sir, I'm not for you. I'm joining Mr Carver's firm tomorrow, but when I heard you were here I thought I'd drop in as I was passing and see if you remembered me.'

Carver had been agitating for extra manpower for months, but he hadn't actually lost anyone. If anyone ought to have got Mills, it was Slider; but Ron Carver was on the square. Slider swallowed his disappointment and his paranoia. The ways of the Met were passing strange but there was no future in pissing into the wind.

'How are things in Epsom?' he asked instead.

Mills made a face. 'Quiet. Except on Saturday nights. You know what these outers are like, sir.'

'Ah well, you won't get bored here.'

'I'm from Shepherd's Bush originally,' Mills said. 'I mean, I was born here.'

'Were you? I suppose someone has to be.'

'We lived in Oaklands Grove,' Mills confided. 'I've been walking about the last couple of days, though, and the place has changed a good bit. I passed where the Congo Church used to be, and it's gone!' He sounded quite indignant. 'It's a block of flats now. I used to go to scouts in the church hall there when I was a kid.'

'Got any family here?'

'My mum, she's in sheltered in Hammersmith. And my auntie lives in Ormiston Grove.'

'Sir Robert Mark would have a fit,' Slider murmured. It had been that great man's contention that detectives should not get to know their ground too well, or corruption would inevitably set in, struggle how one might. 'Are you staying with her?'

'No, sir. I've got a temporary place just round the corner, Stanlake Road. I'll be looking for a flat a bit further out once I've got settled.'

'Well, I'm sure you'll be a great asset to Mr Carver, even if you do have to relearn the geography. I wish you were joining my firm. I've lost a DS, and the holiday season's always a problem. Have you had your holidays?'

'Yes, sir.'

'Where did you go?'

'Rhyl, sir.'

Slider was unable to think of a single thing to say about Rhyl. Possibly no-one ever had. 'You haven't taken up DIY, have you?' he asked suspiciously.

'No sir,' Mills said with faint surprise.

Slider was relieved. 'Better steer clear of DC Anderson, then,' he advised. 'He's just built his own sun-lounge extension.'

'Thanks for the warning, guv,' said Mills grinning.

The White Horse wasn't much of a pub, but it was open all day and the nearest to the police station, so it received more patronage than its efforts to please deserved. Slider pushed open the door of the saloon bar and a friendly fug embraced his head, an all-senses combination of cigarette smoke, cherry-coloured nylon carpeting, the smell of institutional gravy and the pinging and gurgling of a fruit-machine. Along the bar in front of him was a row of broad dark-blue serge behinds topped with a variety of anoraks and leather jackets: B Relief must have been on overtime. He imagined he could hear the steady sound of sucking, as when a team of plough horses just turned out nudges up to the water-trough.

One of them, alerted perhaps by the unnaturally fresh air that had wafted in with Slider, turned his head, and then smiled welcomingly. 'Hullo, sir. I'm up – can I get you one?' D'Arblay said. The others looked round as well, and their expressions were not wholly unwilling, but Slider felt shy of imposing himself upon them. They had been sucking in grateful silence, and if he joined them they'd have to make polite conversation.

'Oh, thanks, you're very kind, but I'm going to get something to eat,' he excused himself.

'You're a brave man, sir,' said Elkins, his moustache heavy

with froth like a hawthorn bush in May. Before them on the bar were four opened packets of Pork Scratchings. Courage is all relative, Slider thought as he made his way to the food counter.

Mein host was a tall, fat, cold-eyed man who resented the fact that the coppers from across the road didn't like his pub, and got his own back by making them feel as unwanted as possible. Slider's request for food pleased him because it gave him the chance to disappoint.

'At this time of day? You must be joking. I can't keep kitchen staff hanging about just on the off-chance.'

'A sandwich, then,' Slider said as firmly as he could on an empty stomach. The landlord's face registered a brief struggle. He hated customers, and especially policemen, but their constant presence on his premises meant he had very little trouble from drunks or vandals. Besides, policemen spent well. His overall aim was to make them feel miserable without actually driving them away; compromise was sometimes necessary.

'Only rolls,' he said at last.

'Two ham rolls, then,' said Slider.

'No ham. Only cheese.'

'I see you studied at the Hobson school of catering,' Slider said politely. 'Two cheese rolls, then; and a large scotch. And a packet of crisps,' he added, throwing caution to the winds. What the hell? You have to splurge sometimes.

'What flavour?' the landlord asked with the light of battle in his eye.

'Vanilla,' said Slider, staring him down; and after a moment he walked off, thwarted. The food, when it came, was as miserable as it could be rendered, the sort of rolls that were soft on the outside and hard on the inside instead of the other way round, scraped over with margarine instead of butter, with one thin square of processed cheese in each, whose four corners, poking outside the circumference, had gone hard and greasy from exposure. When Slider opened the rolls to inspect them, he found as a final insult a single wafer-thin circlet of tomato stuck to the marge in each, damp, anaemic and smelling of old knives.

And the crisps weren't. Slider ate and drank almost with a painful pleasure, a sense of supping life's dregs, after which things could not possibly get worse. As if to prove the point, the landlord approached, and said with offensive indignation, 'Phone call for you.' Slider made his way round the bar to the public telephone at the other end, and could only think it must be Irene; if it was business or Joanna they'd have used his bleeper.

It was Joanna. 'You forgot your bleeper again, didn't you?'

'I left it on my desk,' he discovered.

'So I've been told. Luckily someone saw you go across the road, or I'd have had a long search. What on earth are you doing there?'

'Making myself suffer. Nothing's any fun without you, anyway. Where are you?'

'At the Trevor,' she said through a blast of background hilarity. 'Can't you tell?'

He thought of the Trevor Arms, the nearest pub to Glyndebourne, the one the orchestra always patronised. He thought of a pint of Harvey's – mahogany nectar – and the house ham, egg and chips – the greatest trio since Schubert.

'What's the weather like?' he asked, hoping for relief.

'Terrible,' she said cheerfully. 'It's pissing down. I do feel sorry for the punters, all togged up and nowhere to go. If it doesn't stop by the interval, they'll all have to squeeze into the marquee for their picnics.'

'What you might call loitering within tents,' Slider said.

'What? I missed that, there's so much noise here. What's it like there?'

'Noisy.'

'The weather, I mean.'

'Oh – terrible. I don't know, really. Not raining, I don't think.'

'Darling, what's the matter?' she asked anxiously.

He searched for some succinct way to tell her, but the distance between them was too great, and the line wasn't good enough for delicate expositions. 'It's Thursday,' he said. 'I've never really got the hang of Thursdays.'

'Oh,' she said, wanting to get to the bottom of it, but feeling, like him, that the effort over the phone was too exhausting. 'Well, only another one and a half horrible *Dons*, and then it's lovely *Traviata*. You'll like that – frilly dresses and damask drawing-rooms. You will come to the pre-dress, won't you?'

'If I'm off, of course I will.' He thought of telling her about the singer whose house was broken into, but he couldn't remember her name. While he was hesitating she went on.

'I've got some good news.'

'Yes?'

'The BBC's going to do a television recording of the *Don*, and we're being booked for it. Best of all, they're not just taping a performance down here. It's going to be a studio recording. That means nine sessions.'

'That's wonderful.' He roused himself to enthuse: he knew what that meant to the finances. Then he frowned. 'Nine three-hour sessions? But the opera's only about three hours long, isn't it?'

'That's my detective, scenting the anomaly,' she said, and he heard her smile. 'The running time's about two hours fifty – depends a bit who's conducting. But you're only allowed to record twenty minutes of finished product per session.'

'Why?'

'Union rules, silly. We've got to eat. All the same, by the time you've run through, polished up, done a few takes, and hung around for the engineers to decide if it's good enough, you wouldn't get more than twenty minutes taped anyway.'

'Well, I'm glad for you,' he said. Work had been a bit thin on the ground lately.

'Be glad for yourself, too – the sessions are bound to be in London, maybe even at White City. We'll be able to have lunch together.'

She sounded so simply pleased at the idea that the words 'I miss you' were surprised out of him, with hardly a thought for the surroundings or the possibility of being overheard. 'When are you coming back?'

'Well,' she said, and he knew it was bad news. 'We've got two calls tomorrow for *Traviata*, morning and afternoon, and the last *Don* is on Saturday. So I thought tomorrow evening I might go and see my parents and stay over. It's my mother's birthday on Saturday.'

'Oh,' he said. Her parents lived in Eastbourne, which wasn't very far from Glyndebourne.

'Well, you see, I thought I could take them out for dinner tomorrow night, and then spend the day with her on Saturday, take her out for a drive somewhere maybe. I don't see them very often, and as I'm down here anyway—'

'It's all right, you don't have to ask my permission,' he said. He tried to say it neutrally, but he was afraid it sounded petulant all the same.

'You don't mind, then?' she asked doubtfully.

The question peeved him, because even if he said he did mind, she wouldn't change her plan. And why should she? It wasn't as if they were married. She could do as she liked – and did. 'It isn't for me to mind or not mind. You're a free agent,' he said.

There was a pause. It went on so long he thought she might change her mind, but at last she said, 'Well, as long as you'll be all right—'

Disappointment was mingled with a feeling of guilt for trying to spoil her evening, with resentment for being put in a situation where it was possible to feel guilty, with exasperation for his own feebleness in being so tied to her apron strings. She mustn't think he was going to be moping at home and waiting for her reproachfully. 'It's all right,' he said, and unthinkingly added what had just jumped into his mind, 'I've got to go and see Irene anyway.' Stupid, stupid! In the context that sounded like *sucks to you*.

But she only said, 'Of course you have,' and for the life of him he couldn't tell how she'd taken it. Then she said, 'Listen, I've got to go, there's a queue for this phone.'

'Have fun,' he said.

'And you.' She hung up, and he felt like forty-seven kinds of idiot. This love business was fraught with potholes. He hadn't even asked her if she was coming home on Saturday after the show. Surely she would? But if it was her mother's birthday and he had made her feel uncomfortable, maybe she'd spend the night in Eastbourne again rather than risk a chilly welcome. It was undignified to be cast in the rôle of reproachful, stay-at-home spouse, and ironic after all the years he had been failing to turn up in Irene's evenings. Boots and other legs didn't half alter your perspective on things.

He wandered back aimlessly to his end of the bar and tried to catch the landlord's eye for another large Bells. But, he thought, anomaly-spotting again, why hadn't she told him yesterday before she left that it was her mother's birthday and that she might go and visit? Come to think of it, she hardly ever spoke of her parents at all. So why this sudden flush of dutifulness? As far as he knew, she had never marked their birthdays with a visit before, not while he had known her.

Maybe she wasn't going to Eastbourne at all. Maybe there was someone else down there – another man.

At that point he actually made himself laugh. Someone else? She was playing in an orchestra of sixty musicians, the vast majority of them men; and male musicians were the most sexually irresponsible animals in the universe, next to policemen. It was the old unsocial hours syndrome, plus propinquity and being in a discrete group with its own esoteric language and experience. Just like policemen again. He reminded himself painfully how he had met her in the first place.

The monster of jealousy boggled at him round the corners of his mind, and like all monsters it was ludicrous and frightening in equal proportions. He took a pull on himself. If she was down there, out of his sight and unaccountable, he was up here equally unaccountable to her. You had to trust someone if you loved them; and jealousy was most unattractive behaviour. But of course there was still the old dichotomy between the mind and the balls. Even while his intellect was explaining everything to him rationally, his hormones were prowling up and down with a baseball bat, looking for a fight.

CHAPTER TWO

Knife Work

For once Slider beat Atherton to a call. In fact, he was so quick off the mark that when he reached the TV Centre at White City, there was only a single jam-sandwich parked in front of the main reception hall. Inside it was a forensic nightmare, with a milling crowd jostling around three tables set up along the left side, where they were apparently being checked in and badged, before moving slowly up the staircase at the far end. The main reception desk to the right was besieged only in a minor way by bored couriers, and as soon as Slider held up his ID a worried-looking young woman detached herself from a telephone conversation and hurried over to him.

'Detective Inspector Slider, Shepherd's Bush CID,' he said. 'There's been an incident – a body found?'

'Oh yes, it's on the fourth floor, in one of the gents' loos. I'll get someone to show you up.' She grew confidential. 'It's such a terrible thing – I mean, it isn't a *natural death*.' She pronounced the words in a voiceless whisper. 'No-one knows quite what to do – you see, it's a live programme, with an audience and everything. I do hope you can sort it all out. Do you think they'll have to cancel the show?' She raised hopeful eyes to his face.

'I expect so,' Slider said. 'What programme is it?'

'*Questions of Our Time*. Roger's one of the panellists. Well, was.'

'Roger who?'

'Oh gosh, didn't they tell you? Roger Greatrex. He's the one they found. Well, I don't know all the details, but apparently he's killed himself in some ghastly way. Poor Fiona's in a terrible state—'

'Is this the audience?' Slider cut her off, indicating the milling mob.

'The last of them. The rest are in the exec canteen, or on their way up to it. It takes ages getting them all in. We thought, as we didn't know what was to happen, that we'd better carry on as usual, rather than tell them to go home.'

'I'm sure that's right. Can someone show me upstairs now?'

'Oh, sorry, yes, of course. Kate, can you come here a minute?'

In a moment Slider was following a young woman who scurried like the White Rabbit up stairs, along a corridor, through some swing doors, up more stairs, along another corridor, without ever looking back to see if he was keeping up with her. At last she deposited him, completely disorientated, before a small worried knot of people standing before a closed door which bore the familiar straddling peg-man silhouette, the UN-approved International Idiot Icon for the gents' loo. A uniformed constable – Baker – was guarding the door and some bloody footmarks in front of it. To Slider's surprise, DS Mills was also there.

'What are you doing here?' Slider said.

'Oh, I just happened to be passing,' Mills said vaguely. 'I intercepted the call, and I thought I might be able to help.'

Slider said, 'I wouldn't be a bit surprised. What've we got?'

'He's in there, sir.' Baker gestured towards the closed door.

'He is dead?'

'As a fish,' Mills reassured him. 'I had a quick shufti. Looks like suicide.'

'You've got blood on you,' Slider noted with disapproval. Surely after all this time Mills hadn't forgotten the basics?

'It's off the bloke that found the body. He was hysterical, sort of threw himself at me,' Mills explained.

'Morley's taken him away, sir,' Baker intervened. Morley was his partner. 'Giving him a cup of tea.'

'Name?'

'Philip Somers. He's the assistant producer for this programme that apparently deceased was going to be on.'

Slider nodded, worked on a pair of gloves, and opened the door. It was a small, white-tiled room with off-white ceramic tiles on the floor. There were two stalls straight ahead, of the usual grey melamine and stainless steel construction, their doors open onto innocent untenanted sanitary ware. Three urinals occupied the far right hand wall, and a row of four washbasins with mirrors above the left-hand wall immediately inside the door. The door opened to the right, but in the mirrors Slider could see the reflection of the wall behind it, which supported an electric hand-drier and a condom slot machine.

That was the easy bit. The unpleasant bit was the blood, spattered across the mirrors, streaking the water in the washbasin, smeared over the washbasin rim, and puddled on the floor. The body was lying with its feet towards him, crumpled on its side. Even from here, he could see how Mills could be sure life was extinct: the neck had been severed so determinedly that the head was almost off. It lolled back at an unnatural angle, exposing the butchery aspect of severed vessels. Slider felt the familiar sense of pressure behind the eyes and had to look away for a moment and fix his gaze on something neutral; behind him Mills was breathing hard and swallowing rapidly. And then he heard Atherton's voice saying, 'If only blood were some nice unassertive colour, like grey or pale green, it wouldn't be half so bad. But red . . . !' Slider managed a smile, and the pressure behind his eyes evened itself out.

'Boss?' said Mills into his ear. 'Over there, on the floor, by the end stall.'

A knife with a bloodstained blade, an old-fashioned clasp-knife of the sort dreamed of by boy scouts in Slider's youth, with a leather-wrapped, steel-capped handle and a steel cross-guard, and a slightly curved blade about eight inches long.

'Suicide, you think?' Mills prompted.

'Mmm,' Slider said non-committally. He stared around a few moments longer, memorising the layout, and then closed the door. Atherton was a little way off, chatting to a young woman, his hands in his pockets, the curve of his back at its most languid. Slider knew that pose, and left him to it.

He said to Mills, 'This man, Somers, who found the body – he raised the alarm?'

'Apparently he stayed on guard here while he sent someone else – a female, Dorothy Hammond, one of the assistants – to tell the producer – that's the top bod in this set-up. Somers said once he knew this bloke was dead, he realised he had to stop anyone else going in there and touching anything.'

'An intelligent member of the public,' Slider commented. 'How rare, Who's the producer?'

'Fiona Parsons – female over there in the suit.' The one Atherton was chatting up. No, had been chatting up – he had left her now. Slider met him halfway.

'It seems there's a bunch of celebs in a room along there,' Atherton said, gesturing with his head, 'who will be growing restive. Miss Parsons wants to know what to do with them. I suppose we'll have to interview them?'

'Even if it is suicide,' Slider agreed.

'If?' Atherton said.

'Better safe than sorry. You can go and pacify them in a minute. You've a light hand with demigods.'

'Years of practice in the CID.'

'But fill me in first on this programme.'

'*Questions of Our Time*. Haven't you ever seen it?'

'Of course I've heard of it, but I've never watched it.'

'You haven't missed much. Well, you know the formula – panel of experts, studio audience, chosen topic, audience put questions, panel exercise egos. They put it out live, in an attempt to inject some excitement into it. It's cheap telly, of course, because the audience isn't paid, and as long as they pick publicity-junkies, the panel do it for nothing as well.'

'And what was today's question?'

'Right up your street, guv. Funding of the arts – elitist, or essential? Bringing culture within reach of the masses, or subsidising middle-class taste with working-class money? A question that is no question, really,' Atherton added provocatively, but Slider wouldn't be drawn.

'So who are these celebrity guests, then?'

'Well, Roger Greatrex, music critic and opera aficionado, alias the deceased, you know. Then there's Sir John Foster, Director of the Royal Opera House; Jack Mallet—'

'The Heritage Minister, yes.'

'Dame Barbara Frankauer – novelist, Islingtonite and token woman,' Atherton went on. 'And Sandal Palliser. You know who he is?'

'Of course I do.'

It would be hard to categorise Sandal Palliser, except to call him a Media Star. He had done crits, written columns, presented programmes on television; he was frequently to be seen at awards dinners making speeches, and at film premières escorting the nubile and famous under the barrage of flashing lights. His opinion was sought on discussion programmes, his *bonhomie* on game shows, and his showbiz anecdotes on chat shows. He had recently even written a novel, a surprisingly slushy love story set in his native Derbyshire Peaks, which had reached best-sellerdom – partly, so Atherton said, on the strength of Palliser's famous name, but mostly on account of a much-talked-about sex scene in chapter eight, in which the heroine encountered the hero after hours in a porcelain factory and did quite surprising things to his person with china clay before being bonked to within an inch of her life on a heap of packing straw. Since the book was assumed to be autobiographical, That Chapter had been the talk of the dinner-party circuit for weeks, while the Groucho seethed with speculation as to who the heroine really was.

'I should have thought with Sandal Palliser and Roger Greatrex on the panel, they'd hardly need anyone else,' Slider said.

'They're a debate on their own,' Atherton agreed.

Recently Palliser, who liked to pose as a champion of the people, had conducted a printed slanging match with Roger Greatrex on the subject of the unacceptably esoteric nature of the modern arts. Palliser had cited in particular the latest Booker prize novel that no-one would ever want to read, the Turner prize winner that only a regurgitation fan would want to look at, and the Glyndebourne *Don Giovanni*. It was the latter which had actually sparked it all off, for they had happened to be at the same performance and got into an attention-grabbing row in the foyer during the interval. The following day Greatrex had praised the production in his review column in the *Guardian* as 'daring, innovative and thought-provoking', while Palliser, in his commentary page in the *Mail*, had castigated it as 'pretentious adolescent clever-dickery'.

Greatrex had responded in *The Sunday Times*' Arts Supplement by accusing Palliser of 'pseudo-blokeism', and Palliser, perhaps a little unfairly, had brought out the big guns by devoting a whole edition of his *Arts and Minds* programme on ITV to the proposition that the whole modern arts machine was an exclusive back-scratching club paid for out of tax-payers' money.

All this had stirred up quite a lively ongoing debate in the letters columns of the national dailies. Slider had followed it at first because he had seen the *Don Giovanni* production which had started off the row – with Joanna playing in it, it was almost a family concern. But the argument had become blurred by a number of letters complaining that the DG production was blasphemous, on account of the Act Two supper-room scene taking place, for no adequately explained reason, in a church, where the Don had done a number of sacrilegious things around and on the altar. Even at the pre-dress which Slider had attended, there had been disturbed murmurings from the audience, and though Slider had merely thought it silly, it had obviously upset some people. After a couple of days the correspondence in the papers had wandered off into the byways of what constituted blasphemy and whether it should still be a criminal offence in the nineteen-nineties, and Slider had lost interest.

But he could quite see why any discussion programme about the arts at this moment in time would have to include Sandal Palliser and Roger Greatrex if it wanted to be topical.

'All right,' he said to Atherton, 'you go and pacify the great and famous. As soon as reinforcements arrive they can give their statements and go home.'

'What about the audience, guv? There's a couple of hundred bods penned up in a canteen upstairs with nothing but sandwiches, tea and the daily papers to keep them quiet.'

'Someone had better go up and talk to them. Mills, find Morley and send him up. He's to tell them as little as possible, but keep them quiet.'

'Right, guv.'

'Aren't we going to let them go?' Atherton said in surprise.

'Not yet. I might want statements, and you know what people are like once you let them get away. I want their names and addresses, anyway.'

'All of them?'

'All of them. You'd better contact the factory and ask the Super politely for some more uniforms. We'll need a few just to keep this area clear of sightseers, let alone all the interviewing. This is going to mean a bit of overtime, I'm afraid. What are you smirking about, Baker?'

The duty police surgeon had been sent for, but it was the forensic pathologist who arrived first – Freddie Cameron, the man for whom the adjective 'dapper' might have been invented. Slider had been distributing his troops when he arrived, and hurried back to the scene of the crime to meet him. Cameron was engaged in putting on a set of overalls to cover his light grey Prince of Wales check suiting; Atherton was with him, holding a plastic cup of something that steamed, Cameron's clipboard under his arm.

'Hullo-ullo-ullo,' Freddie said jauntily. 'The hounds of law on felon's traces, eh?'

'Come again?' said Slider.

'My words exactly,' Atherton said.

'Which, mine or his?' Slider asked. 'No, don't answer that. How did you get here so fast, Freddie?'

'I was only down the road at Hammersmith Hospital. Just finished a post when the call came, so here I am.'

'You've beaten the surgeon to it.'

'Where's he coming from?'

'It's Prawalha. From Fulham.'

'Oh well you can forget that,' Freddie said effortfully as he hairpinned his foot up within reach and tugged on a plastic overshoe. 'Fulham Palace Road's solid – accident at the junction of Lillie Road. I'll do the necessary, if you like.' He met enquiring stares over his arm and said simply, 'Heard it on the car radio. On Classic FM Roadwatch. Don't you coppers know anything?'

Atherton grinned at Slider. 'I'd better see if I can turn Dr Prawalha back. He won't like coming all this way for nothing.'

'Right, all togged up,' Cameron said. 'Let's have a look.' He opened the door, stepped carefully over to the body and examined it in silence for a moment. He looked at his watch. 'I pronounce life extinct at – eight-oh-six p.m. Forehead still warm; warmth in the axilla. Death within the last three hours, probably two.'

'We know he was alive within the hour,' Slider said.

'Good. That's a help. I hate doing all that mental arithmetic with temperature readings. Well, not much doubt about the cause of death.' He examined the wound. 'Single clean incision from under the left ear across and downwards to the right. All the structures through to the anterior spinal ligament completely severed. Death due to anoxia caused by severing of the windpipe – more or less instantaneous.'

'More or less?'

'Depends on your point of view. Who can say how long an instant of terror lasts, subjectively?'

'You're a great comfort,' Slider complained. 'Anything else?'

'No superficial cuts or haggling around the wound – a sign of great determination or great strength, or both. No apparent bruising or other wounds. Clothing a little rumpled, but no signs of a struggle.'

He stood up and looked at the basins and mirrors. 'Now you see there, across the mirror, the typical spread pattern of droplets from the arterial pumper? He went straight through the left external carotid with the first cut. Lovely work.'

'So he was facing the mirror,' Slider said.

'Yes, or had his head slightly turned to the right, as you'd expect if it was a suicidal cut. And the blood in the basin and the smears on the rim suggest that he collapsed slightly forward and then hit the rim, or brushed against it, as he fell. Blood on the hands, under the nails, on the cuffs and sleeves, as you'd expect. Both hands. Two-handed action for extra penetration, perhaps. Blood on the cheek, too, but that's from resting in it on the floor.' He pondered.

'So it looks like suicide, then,' Atherton said from the doorway.

'The wound is consistent with a right-handed suicidal cut,' Freddie said. 'And he was right-handed, by the look of it. See the writer's bump on his right middle finger? Don't see so many of those in this world of the word-processor, but in my day every school-kid had a whopper of a one. He must have been a nice old-fashioned sort who liked to write longhand,' he finished regretfully, as though one fewer of those in the world was a real loss. 'On the other hand, it could have been a homicidal cut by someone standing behind him. No way of saying.'

'Doesn't the lack of other superficial cuts suggest homicide?' Atherton asked.

'Not necessarily. I've known a homicide case where the

murderer slashed away like a mad salami-slicer before he got through to the business parts. You never can tell. Deceased's quite a tall man, though, by the looks. If it was a homicidal cut, you want a tallish murderer. Or a short one with his own set of steps.'

'What about the weapon? There's a knife over there,' Slider said.

Freddie turned and looked. 'Yes. I'll have a closer look when it's been photographed, but from a cursory glance it's certainly consistent with the wound, and there's plenty of blood on it.'

'Yes,' said Slider, frowning thoughtfully. Freddie looked up and met his eyes, and an intelligence passed between them.

'There's something else,' Freddie said quietly, and reached for the corpse's jacket. 'Look here.' Slider looked. 'And here. You see what this is? Might be nothing, but—'

'As you say,' said Slider, 'but. Well, if that's all you can tell me for now,' he went on, straightening, 'I'd better strike while the iron's hot.'

Reinforcements were arriving all the time, and over Slider's shoulder Freddie saw the photographer shoving his way to the front. 'Ah, there you are, Sid. About time. I can't do anything until you've recorded this little lot for posterity.'

'Traffic's bloody terrible,' Sid grumbled. It was his usual mode of communication. 'And no wonder, with every bloody copper in West London hanging around in here. Why don't some of you lot go and do something useful for a change, and sort the bloody traffic out?'

'That's a new one,' Atherton said mildly. 'We generally get asked why we don't solve murders instead of harassing motorists.'

'Well come on, come on, let the dog see the rabbit,' Sid hustled his way into the doorway. 'Oh, bloody hell, it's a wet one! If I'd known I was going to go bloody paddling, I'd have brought me bloody wellies. I suppose you want this lot in bloody colour? Who's got the plastic shoes?'

Slider left them to it, and eased himself away from the door of the gents.

'What next, guv?' Atherton asked.

'I want to talk to Miss Parsons,' Slider said.

'I don't think you have any choice in the matter,' Atherton

murmured. 'She's determined to talk to you.' He gestured with his head to where Fiona Parsons was lingering just to one side with her eyes fixed on Slider.

'I'll do her first, and then Philip Somers. And I want someone to talk to this Dorothy person, see if she can pin down some times. Oh, and see if you can get me a drink, will you?'

'A drink drink?'

'Some hope. What's the coffee like in the machine?'

'All right, if you don't swallow,' Atherton said.

Atherton moved away, and Slider allowed himself to be waylaid by Fiona Parsons. 'Do you have to leave him lying in there like that?' she asked indignantly, looking towards the rest-room door. 'I mean, in that place of all places. It seems so – unfeeling. Can't he at least be put somewhere more, well, dignified?'

'I'm afraid we can't move him for the time being,' Slider said gently. 'It's a matter of collecting evidence, you see. I really would like to have a word with you. Is there somewhere quiet nearby we can go and talk?'

'There's a dressing-room just along here,' she said. 'Will that do?'

The dressing-room was small, windowless and bare, containing a padded bench fixed to the wall, a broad shelf with a mirror over it for a dressing-table, and a small table and hard chair. Fiona Parsons sat down on the bench, so Slider pulled out the chair and sat down facing her. It was no hardship to look at her. She was tall, athletic, and tanned, with a clear, freckled face and short, heavy fair hair cut in a bob and held off her face with a black velvet Alice band. She was wearing a severely cut, but very short-skirted pinstripe suit with three-quarter sleeves, over a plain white shirt with an open neck, from which her throat rose somehow fragile and vulnerable, encircled by a fine gold chain. Legs to rival Princess Di's in the sheerest of hose and plain, flat-heeled shoes; the manly cuffs on her jacket contrasted with a delicate gold watch on one wrist and a narrow gold bracelet on the other. Everything about her was a mixture of the businesslike and the feminine, which Slider assumed was deliberate, but was nonetheless intriguing.

There was no doubt that she had been shaken by the event. She was pale under her tan, her face wore the numb look of shock, her eyes were pink-rimmed, and she fiddled constantly with a handkerchief crumpled in her strong fingers. But she was determinedly under control, and looked straight into Slider's face with a directness that rather disturbed him. It reminded him of Joanna.

'This must have been a shock for you,' he began. 'I won't keep you too long, but I want to get an overall picture of the events of the evening, and I believe you are in charge of the programme. Am I right?'

'Except for Martin Fletcher – the editor. But he's more of a policy-maker. The day-to-day, hands-on running of things is down to me.'

Slider smiled. 'I've never been quite sure what a producer does.'

'The short answer is everything. But a programme like this is pretty easy compared to, say, drama, where you've got studio sets, outside shots, VT, actors, costumes, all the hoo-ha to keep track of. Properties alone can give you grey hairs – practicals, for instance, always go wrong. I started off as a properties buyer, so I know a bit about it. And actors are the very devil. But with *Question* you've got one set and five guests and that's that.'

'Yes, I see. So, then, can you tell me what time Mr Greatrex arrived?'

'Half past six. I went down to meet him at reception and took him up to green.'

'Green?'

'Sorry, the greenroom. Sometimes called the hospitality room.'

'Ah. For drinks?'

'And briefing,' she corrected with a faint smile. 'Not that Roger needed briefing, really, he's been on the show so often.'

'Has he?'

'Well, yes.' The question seemed to embarrass her for some reason. A slight pinkness appeared in her cheeks. 'He's one of our leading critics and columnists,' she said as if justifying herself. 'And besides that, he's such an all-round man, with so many interests, we've had him for several different topics. He's a great communicator, too. We always get a lively discussion going when we have him, that's why we—' Her voice faded and her face drained as she remembered. 'I can't believe he's dead.

I can't believe he would do a thing like that. He was laughing with me only—' She stopped and shut her lips tight.

'He was quite happy when he arrived? Relaxed, nothing apparently on his mind?'

She nodded, as if speaking was too risky.

'Was he the first to arrive?' She nodded again. 'And you met all the guests in the same way?'

She took a deep breath. 'No, my assistant, Phil, went down for the others.'

'And they were all taken to the greenroom?'

'Except for Jack Mallet. Martin took him away for a private drink – politics, you know. Martin always has to be thinking about budgets. The others had drinks and sandwiches in the greenroom. Dame Barbara was the last to arrive. I didn't actually see her because I had to go back to the studio while Phil was fetching her.'

'Leaving them alone?'

'Gosh no, Dorothy – one of the production assistants – was there all the time, and Phil was in and out. It's an absolute rule that the guests mustn't be left alone at any time. It is a live show, you see.'

'So just before Dame Barbara arrived, you went to the studio. What time was that?'

'Oh, about sevenish I suppose,' she said vaguely. 'I don't know exactly.'

'And at that point Mr Greatrex was in the greenroom having drinks and sandwiches, and seemed quite happy and relaxed?' She nodded; her eyes shone suddenly, and she blinked hard. 'Did you go back to the greenroom?'

'No, I was busy in and around the studio then, until Dorothy came and told me—'

'Yes?' he prompted gently. 'What did she tell you?'

'It was awful. She was white as a sheet, and shaking. I couldn't understand what she was saying at first. I told her to calm down and speak slowly. Then she told me she met Phil in the corridor. She said he was covered in blood, and he just said to her, "Roger's dead. He's killed himself," and told her to run and fetch me.'

'And what did you do?'

'I said to her, "Are you sure?" or something like that. And

then I told her to telephone for the police while I went back to Phil.'

'You didn't tell her to call for an ambulance?'

'No.' She stared at him as though the question made no sense.

'You were quite sure he was dead, then?'

'Oh! But I—' She frowned, and shook her head, looking confused. 'Phil said he – Dorothy said he was covered in blood. Phil was, I mean. I didn't think—' She paused. 'It never occurred to me that he might still be alive. Phil's terribly sensible. I suppose I just took his word for it.'

Slider left it. 'So where was Phil when you found him?'

'Where Dorothy said, at the door of the men's room. He looked dreadful. He said, "Roger's in there. He's killed himself. He's c—" She stopped, swallowed with a dry click, and tried again. 'He said, "He's cut his throat."' Her eyes filled again, and she shook her head slowly from side to side, staring sightlessly at the floor.

Slider saw she needed steadying, and gave her a practical question to answer. 'What time was it when Dorothy came to fetch you?'

She breathed deeply and managed to answer. 'I'm not sure to the minute. Twenty, twenty-five past seven, something like that. I didn't look at my watch.'

'And did you go into the men's room?'

'No. Phil said he'd been guarding the door, and no-one had been in except him, and no-one else must go in until the police came.'

Slider didn't comment on that. He asked, 'So you didn't actually know that it was Mr Greatrex in there?'

She licked her lips. 'I just – just looked in. For a second. Phil didn't want me to, but I had to.'

Bluebeard's Castle, Slider thought, not without sympathy. Of course she had to. Wouldn't anyone? And this was her punishment, that she would never be able to erase from her memory the picture of what she saw.

'Can I go now?' she asked. 'I've still got a lot of sorting out to do for the programme.'

'What do you do about that?' Slider asked out of interest. 'It was supposed to be live, wasn't it?'

She put her hands to her cheeks in a curious, unfinished gesture, and then said almost absently, 'Oh, we have one in the can for emergencies.'

'Here's one I prepared earlier?' Slider said, trying to lighten the atmosphere.

'Yes.' She pulled herself together. 'Of course, it puts the schedule out. This *Question* was announced last week. But I suppose it will be all over the papers by tomorrow morning, and everyone will know why it was changed.' She looked into his face, bravely. 'Will someone have told his wife?'

'That will be dealt with by the local police. Someone will go round from the nearest station.'

'I see,' she said. 'Poor Caroline.' It was the most natural thing for anyone to say, but there was something about the way Miss Parsons said it that puzzled Slider a little, though he could not immediately decide what.

CHAPTER THREE

Brief Encounter

Philip Somers was a tall, gangling man in his twenties, dressed, as the fashion was, in clothes of various shades of beige that looked too big for him, and with floppy, toffee-coloured hair which kept slipping forward to hang like a pony's forelock over his brow, giving him a somewhat daft look. His cheeks were lardy with shock, which seemed with him to be taking the form of anger: his indeterminate-coloured eyes were glazed and shiny with it. Beyond that, or underneath it, Slider thought he looked drawn, as though from a long illness or constant pain: there were those deep, fine creases like hairline cuts under his eyes that you see in people who have been sick unto death in their recent past.

He was sitting on the bench in another of those spartan dressing-rooms, a red blanket draped over his shoulders, and his stockinged feet set one on top of the other, as if they felt vulnerable without their coverings.

'When am I going to get my shoes back?' he demanded as soon as he saw Slider. 'It's ridiculous, taking them away.'

'I've told him, sir, that we didn't want him to make bloody footmarks which might confuse the investigation,' Morley said over his head.

'Well, when can I have them back?'

'I've brought you a cup of coffee,' Atherton intervened, holding it out. 'I hope you take sugar – I had to guess.'

'Yes – thanks – but—'

'I'm Detective Inspector Slider, and this is Detective Sergeant Atherton. I'd just like to talk to you about finding Mr Greatrex.' Even a cursory inspection showed that Somers had a great deal of blood about him. There was blood on his hands, under his fingernails, in his ears and around the edge of his face, flecks of it in his front hair, a smear under his jaw, and stains on his sleeves, on the lapels of his jacket, and on the front of his trousers. 'You seem to have got yourself into a bit of a mess.'

'That was lifting him up to see if he was dead. And I must have wiped my hands down my front.'

'You seem to have blood on your face, too.'

'I suppose I must have put my hands to my face – the shock, or something.' He imitated the gesture. 'I tried to wipe my face on my hanky. They wouldn't let me wash. You try to do the right thing, and this is all the thanks you get!'

'I won't keep you very long. There's just a few things I want to ask you while it's all fresh in your mind. I'm trying to build up a picture of Mr Greatrex's exact movements this evening.'

'Well, it's no good asking me,' Somers said petulantly. 'I don't know where he went. I was the one who went to look for him.'

'He was lost? Missing?'

'Not really lost, of course, but he wasn't where he was supposed to be. You see, everyone was asked to come at six forty-five, but they all arrived at different times, and Dame Barbara was late. Typical! I mean, the only woman, so naturally I wanted to get her to make-up first, but I couldn't hoosh her off the moment she arrived, so I asked Roger if he'd go first, since he was the first to arrive – for a wonder – and he never has more than just the shine taken off. He said okay, and I said I'd take him in a sec, as soon as Fiona came back, because I couldn't leave Dame Barbara alone, not when she'd just arrived, and bloody Dorothy had disappeared again. But Roger said not to bother, he knew the way all right, and he'd go on his own, so I said okay, and he went.'

'What time was that?'

'Just after seven, I suppose. Well, anyway, about ten past he hadn't come back and I thought I'd better go and fetch him, because if he got chatting to Sylvia – the make-up designer – he'd be there all night – she talks like a train – and time was getting on. So I went up to make-up—'

'Up?'

'Oh, yes, didn't I say? There's been a burst pipe and our make-up room can't be used because the electrics aren't safe, so we were using number five upstairs. It's all right, I had told

Roger, he knew where to go. The layout's exactly the same on five as down here, he understood that, he only had to go up one floor.'

'I see. So you went upstairs to make-up,' Slider prompted.

'Yes, and Sylvia said he'd never turned up. Then I got worried.'

'Worried? Why worried? What were you afraid had happened?'

'Nothing, I don't mean that,' he said irritably. 'But he was one of our panellists. You can't go mislaying your panellists like that, not on a live show. And I shouldn't have let him go alone. So I went looking for him.' His mouth pulled down. 'If I'd known–! Well, I didn't really know where to look. I popped my head round a few doors, and then I thought of the loo. We had one guest once who was so nervous he got sick and I showed him to the loo and then I couldn't get him out, he just kept throwing up. Of course, I didn't think Roger was nervous like that. But anyway, I went and looked and just pushed the door open on the off-chance and – and there he was.'

'That was the nearest lavatory to the greenroom, was it?'

'Yes – well, on this floor, anyway.'

'What does that mean?'

'The gents and ladies are alternate, on alternate floors,' Somers said, and seeing he had not explained himself sufficiently, began again. 'On this floor, if you turn right out of green and go to staircase four, there's a ladies by the lift, and immediately above it, on the fifth floor, there's a gents. But if you turn left out of green and go to staircase five, there's a gents on this floor and a ladies above. D'you follow me?'

As far as I'd like to, Slider thought. 'And which way is the make-up room?'

'From the greenroom? You turn right, and it's past staircase four and on the right.'

'So if Mr Greatrex had been going up to the make-up room, he would have passed a men's room upstairs, on the next floor.'

'Yes, I suppose so.' Somers did not seem to see where that was leading. 'But I told you, Sylvia said he never arrived at make-up.'

'Quite so. But considering where he ended up, perhaps he never actually meant to go there.'

'Oh,' said Somers. 'Well, I don't know. Maybe he just had to *go*, you know,' he added delicately, 'and decided to go first.'

Slider moved on. 'What time was it when you found Mr Greatrex?'

'About twenty past, I suppose. I didn't look at my watch, but I'd been looking for him for about ten minutes.'

'You opened the door, and saw him – what, lying down?'

'Yes, of course. What do you think, he was dancing a jig?'

'Lying down how?'

'He was crumpled up, more or less face down.'

'And what did you do?'

'There was blood everywhere. I knew he was dead straightaway, but I had to be sure.' His voice was toneless. 'So I went and lifted him up. I thought at first maybe he'd slashed his wrists, but when I took him by the shoulders to turn him over, his head – his head sort of flopped and – and rolled backwards—' He put his hands to his face, dragging at his cheeks with his knuckles. 'It was horrible. Like a mouth opening. I dropped him and got out as fast as I could. I thought I was going to be sick. I wanted to run and run, but as soon as I was outside I realised I had to stay there and stop anyone else going in. But I had to get help. I didn't know what to do. And then Dorothy came round the corner, and I told her to run and find Fiona and tell her that Roger Greatrex had killed himself, and to call the police.' He seemed suddenly exhausted now, and looked greyly at Slider as though asking for mercy.

Slider pressed on. 'So you stayed there outside the door until the police arrived? You didn't go back in?' He shook his head. 'And no-one else went in?'

'No-one. When Fiona came, she wanted to see him. I tried to stop her, but she insisted, so I made her just look from the door. One quick look was enough.'

'Just one more thing, Mr Somers,' Slider said, leaning forward confidentially, letting his hands dangle between his knees. 'It's rather important. When you first went in, where was the knife?'

'The knife?' Somers said blankly. Exhaustion or prevarication?

'Yes, the knife. Whereabouts was it? Under the body, beside it, where?'

'I don't know. I didn't see it. I didn't see any knife.'

'You must have seen it, Mr Somers,' Slider said, giving him a chance, 'because you threw it across the room. Or did you kick it out of the way? An automatic gesture of revulsion, perhaps – quite understandable in the circumstances.'

Somers looked frightened. 'I didn't touch it. I tell you I didn't see any knife!'

Slider straightened up. 'Very well, Mr Somers, thank you. I'll leave you in peace for a bit. But I will want to talk to you again later.'

Outside, Atherton said, 'What was all that about?'

'I had my doubts from the beginning about suicide, but I wasn't sure.'

'And now you are?'

'Somers says he didn't touch the knife. He's quite forceful about it. So what was it doing on the other side of the room?'

Atherton thought it out. 'Greatrex didn't cut his throat over there, because the blood's all by the basins.'

'Right.'

'Maybe he threw the knife away after he made the cut?'

Slider shook his head. 'With a cut like that, he'd have collapsed instantly. He'd have dropped the knife where he stood.'

'Well, let's say it's likely. So – either someone else went in there and moved the knife – or Somers is lying and he moved it—'

'Or the murderer threw the knife aside after making the fatal cut,' Slider concluded.

'That sounds logical, captain. But you said you had doubts from the beginning?'

'The basin was full of soapy water. If Greatrex was standing facing the mirror with a bowl of soapy water before him, what do you suppose he was doing?'

'You think he was disturbed while washing his hands?'

'Only an obsessive would wash his hands before killing himself; and someone that obsessive would surely empty the basin first. I think someone came up behind him, yes.'

'I wonder why the murderer didn't pull the plug out? It would have made it look more like suicide.'

'I don't suppose he even thought about it. I think he had other things on his mind,' Slider said.

'Specifically?'

'There was something else that Freddie pointed out to me – there was blood on the *inside* of Greatrex's top inside pocket, and a corresponding smear on his shirt. Someone with bloody hands was looking for something in that pocket. I wonder if they found it?'

Atherton was thinking. 'Well, if it was murder, there'll be no shortage of suspects.'

'You mean all that lot upstairs?'

'No, I mean everyone he's ever given a bad review. He was a critic, don't forget – the most hated creature on the planet, after the housefly.'

WDC Swilley had never been self-conscious about her height, feeling it was an unalloyed advantage to be able to see over the heads of a crowd and get things down off shelves without needing a chair. There were occasions when close encounters with members of her own sex made her wonder how they coped with life way down there, and this was one of them. Being shut in a dressing-room with Dorothy Hammond, Production Assistant, made her afraid to move too quickly for fear of crushing her.

Dorothy Hammond was a tiny person with a neat, sharp face behind large gold-wire-rimmed glasses. Her dark hair was cut short and layered so that it looked like soft feathers; her mouth was curving and tender; her little pointed fingers were tipped with pale-pink nails that looked as unused as a baby's.

She didn't seem particularly upset by the events of the evening – more cheeringly stimulated by the novelty. 'Well, I'm sorry to have to say it,' she said briskly, 'but I didn't like Roger, and as far as I'm concerned he'll be no great loss. Not that I'd wish him ill, of course, but—' She let it hang. 'I couldn't be more surprised that he's killed himself, though. I wouldn't have thought he was the type.'

'Is there a type?' Norma asked.

'Oh, I suppose that sounds a stupid thing to say,' she said, not as if she believed it. 'But he wasn't a bit depressed, from what I saw – quite his usual chirpy self. And I'd have thought he liked himself too much to want to deprive the world of his wonderful presence.'

'Conceited, was he?'

'Oh, one of those who think that anyone who isn't a celebrity is dirt. Calls you darling all the time, but can't be bothered to remember your name or say please or thank you. Always arrives late, never mind who he's inconveniencing – leaves his rubbish around for other people to clear up. I had no time for him. I don't like Sandal much either, but at least he knows his manners. I mean, I don't expect them to fawn over me, but I do expect common courtesy. I could never understand what—' She stopped herself abruptly, and as Norma looked enquiringly at her, she blushed a little, and said hurriedly, 'I suppose it was suicide? I mean, I didn't see the body, but they say he cut his throat, is that right?'

'His throat was cut, yes,' Norma said.

'That's a rotten way to go,' Dorothy said. 'No wonder Phil was in such a state. I've never seen so much blood. I thought he'd cut himself. It was on his face and everything.'

'There was an awful lot of blood around,' Norma said. 'His throat was cut right through.'

Dorothy looked away. 'Well, I'm sorry. I wouldn't wish that on anyone,' she said. 'But really, I would never have thought he was suicidal. Everyone else on the programme, maybe.'

'What d'you mean?'

'Oh, I knew it was going to be a bad evening before we started. Everyone was in a rotten temper. Having Roger Greatrex and Sandal Palliser on the same panel was a big mistake in my opinion. I suppose Martin – Martin Fletcher, the editor – was hoping for a verbal punch-up to boost the ratings, but to my mind you don't take that kind of risk on a live programme. I think that's why Fiona was in such a state.'

'What do you mean, a state?'

'She was like a cat on hot bricks all day. Speak to her and she wouldn't hear you the first three times, or else she'd jump like a kangaroo. And she couldn't speak a civil word to Phil. *He* didn't want Roger on the show at all. It was his job to book the guests, and when it came up I heard him saying to her something about, if she wanted Roger she should phone him herself because he didn't want it on his head, and she said don't be stupid, all you've got to do is pass the message, it isn't up to you, and he said if it was up to him he wouldn't have that man on the same planet, let alone the same programme, and they'd all live to regret it.'

'What do you suppose he meant by that?'

'Well, Roger and Sandal hated each other. Everyone knows that.'

'Because of this debate in the newspapers?'

'What, that thing about the arts?' Dorothy laughed derisively. 'God, no! That's a put-up job to boost circulation. They're both on the same side, really. Sandal might pretend to be Essex Man, but he's as middle-class and elitist as Roger. You couldn't put a fag-paper between them. They'd both be horrified at the idea of the Royal Opera House losing its subsidy.'

'Their livelihood depends on that sort of thing?' Norma suggested blandly. 'It's a gravy train, the whole arts bit, isn't it?'

'You're telling me! Well, not Glyndebourne, because that's private, but the rest of it's a disgrace. The Opera House soaks up millions in subsidies every year, but let some inner-city school ask for a couple of hundred to mend the roof, and they're told there's no money in the kitty.'

Norma took a tug at the reins, before she was galloped away with. 'So what is the trouble between them, then, if it isn't that?'

Dorothy looked blank for a moment. 'Oh. I don't know exactly. Something personal, I don't know what. All I do know is they can't be trusted not to go for each other. I mean, they even had a row tonight while I was out of the room for a second.'

'What about?'

'I didn't really hear anything, only the raised voices, and of course they stopped as soon as I came in. All I heard was as I opened the door, Roger was saying something like, "He doesn't even know what day it is," and then Sandal said something I didn't hear, and Roger said, "It's none of your bloody business anyway," and then they saw me and stopped. But Roger's face was really red, and Sandal looked like thunder.'

'Who else was there at the time?'

'No-one,' she said. 'You see, Fiona brought Roger up and left him with me, and then Phil brought Sandal in, and we four were there for about ten minutes, chatting, until reception rang to say Sir John had arrived. So Phil went down to meet him, and I – well, I just popped out for a minute to the loo, and when I came back, I heard them at it.'

'Do you think Roger Greatrex was really upset by the quarrel?'

'What, enough to want to kill himself?' she asked. 'No, I'd have said he was more mad than upset. Like I said, I couldn't have been more surprised that he did it. The last time I saw him, he was looking really cheerful – like the cat that got the cream, really, which was his usual expression.'

'What time was that?'

'About seven, I suppose. I was just going back to green, and he must have just come out. I asked if I could get him anything – we're not supposed to let them wander about on their own, really, in case they get lost – but he said he was going up to make-up and he knew the way, and he made it quite plain he didn't want me around so I left it at that and went back to green.'

'And he went up the stairs?'

'I suppose so. I didn't watch him go. He was heading in the right direction.'

Norma nodded. 'And what about Sandal Palliser? Do you think he was upset by the quarrel?'

'It's hard to say. He doesn't show his feelings really – always polite on the outside, whatever's happening. You can't really fathom him.' Something obviously struck her. 'Oh, but he—'

'But he what?' Norma prompted when she didn't go on.

Dorothy blushed again. 'It's nothing really. But after I passed Roger in the corridor, after I went back to the greenroom, Sandal said he had to go out and make a phone call. I said he could use the phone in there, but he said he needed a bit of privacy, and he had his mobile with him, and he'd only be a minute. Well, I couldn't stop him, could I? And he said he'd only be a minute. And after five minutes I went out to look for him – and that's when I met Phil, all covered with blood.'

'You didn't see Sandal, then?'

'Well, no. But he was there with the rest when I went back up after phoning the police.'

It was, Norma thought, like one of those tiresome farces where the characters keep going in and out of different doors and just missing each other, for no apparent reason except to further the misunderstandings of the plot.

Though the post mortem did not promise any great surprises, there was the usual crowd of onlookers with their hands in their pockets and the Trebor's Extra Strong Mints energetically a-suck, just in case. Lying on its back, the corpse didn't look quite so bad. Slider looked into the face, and examined the hands. Roger Greatrex had been tall, lean, blue-eyed, and with artfully tousled, possibly streaked fair hair. He had a long, rather melancholy face, prominent nose, high cheekbones, a wide, thin-lipped mouth, a strong chin. His hands were long, large-jointed and veined – that's where the age always showed, Slider thought – his nails were well-kept, and he wore no rings.

'Would you call him good-looking? Attractive to women?' Slider asked generally.

'Except the mouth,' Atherton answered him. 'That's a bad mouth. From what I can see of the teeth, they weren't too good either. Didn't take care of them when he was a lad.'

'His clothes are expensive,' Slider said. And stylish: a light-biscuit-coloured double-breaster, hanging fashionably loose from the bony shoulders, trousers with pleats and turn-ups, brown moccasins – expensive but not well-polished. All of course were now spoiled with blood – the tie was so stained he had to turn it over to see the design: a blue and lilac Matisse, very 'in'. Along with the streaked hair, it spoke a man for whom appearance was important, a man who wanted to be younger than his age.

Freddie was preparing to undress the body, and Mackay was standing by with the evidence bags, having tossed Anderson for it and lost. 'I say, guv,' Mackay said suddenly, 'the dirty bugger's left his flies undone.'

'Fly,' said Atherton automatically. 'Flies are what you have in theatres or on dead meat.'

'Well, what d'you call him?' Mackay protested.

'Was that how he was found?' Slider asked Freddie.

'No-one here's touched it, if that's what you mean,' Freddie said.

'Probably doesn't mean anything,' Slider said. 'He wouldn't be the first man to forget.'

'Those pleat-fronted trousers hang better anyway, so you don't notice so much,' Atherton said.

Freddie drew open the inside top pocket with forceps. 'See what I mean about the bloodstains?' he said to Slider. 'I'll cut some pieces of the fabric for the lab.'

'If someone's had a hand in there, it's just possible we may get a fingerprint,' Slider said. 'Can you cut the whole outside of the pocket away?'

Freddie grunted and complied, and removed from the exposed pocket a very battered leather wallet. It contained a number of credit and other cards, two hundred and fifteen pounds in cash, and three wrapped condoms.

'Not robbery from the person, then,' Slider said. 'What's that?' A piece of card, about four inches by five, had fallen out from behind the wallet onto the corpse's chest. Freddie passed it over.

It was blank on one side; on the other side a plain black cross was embossed at the top in the centre, and below it was printed in Letraset:

> When the righteous turneth away from his righteousness, shall he live? In his trespass that he hath trespassed and in his sin that he hath sinned, in them shall he die. Ezek. 18:24.

'Very nice,' said Atherton.

'Ezekiel,' Slider said. 'Nice warlike book – lots of smiting and swords and wrath-of-the-Lord.'

'You wouldn't have thought he'd be religious,' Mackay commented. 'Not dressed like that.'

'What's dress got to do with it?' Anderson asked.

'Well, he's not got sandals on, or a beard.'

'He doesn't have to be religious, anyway,' Anderson said.

'Then why's he carrying that card?' Mackay said with triumphant logic.

'Hasn't it occurred to you,' Atherton said kindly, 'that perhaps the murderer put it there?'

'If he was murdered,' Mackay returned. 'There's no blood on it, anyway.'

'Maybe he had gloves on. Or it could have been sent to him earlier as a threat.'

'So, but why would he carry it around in his pocket?'

Atherton rolled his eyes and left Mackay to his triumph.

'Send the wallet and the card for fingerprinting too,' Slider said. There was nothing else in the inside pocket. The other pockets revealed nothing of more interest than a used handkerchief, a handful of change, a stick of lip salve, a key-ring with car and house keys on it, a two-week-old tube ticket from South Kensington, and a very crumpled small paper bag containing five Pontefract cakes, two of which had stuck to the paper.

'There aren't many places you can still get sweets weighed out and put in a bag,' Slider said. 'I wonder how long he's had these?'

'Probably prophylactic,' Atherton said. 'He looks the type. Muddy complexion – dead giveaway. No personal things, you notice. No letters, photographs, anything like that.'

'Not everyone carries them,' Slider said.

'But if they do, they often carry them in the wallet or the inside pocket. Maybe that's what the pocket-fumbler was after.'

'It's possible,' Slider said. The rest of the clothes were of no particular interest, except that the socks had holes in them, and the toenails were long and not over-clean.

'I'm liking this man less as we go along,' Atherton complained.

'Maybe he had a touch of arthritis and couldn't bend down that far,' Slider suggested kindly. Atherton snorted derision.

There was a moment's respectful silence, however, as the underpants were taken off. 'Well, that accounts for his popularity with women,' Anderson said at last, rather wistfully.

'No wonder he wore pleated trousers,' said Mackay.

'You'd have thought he'd have trouble balancing,' Anderson said. 'I mean, with all that forward drag—'

Freddie was examining the equipment in question with rather closer attention than might be thought necessary. 'Look at this, Bill.'

'It's not easy to look anywhere else,' Slider complained.

'No, but look – here, and here. Smears of blood.'

'That's more than I need to know.'

Freddie snatched back the purple bikini briefs which Mackay was in the act of bagging. 'Yes, look, and here, on the waistband. Now what do you make of that?'

'I'd rather not make anything of it,' Slider said. 'But if you force me to, I'd say somebody with bloody hands has handled it. Please don't ask me why.' To Mackay, 'Bag the pants and the trousers separately. We might get a lift off one or other of them.'

'It's more evidence that it was murder and not suicide,

though,' Atherton commented. 'Unless Philip Somers – or somebody else – found him dead and interfered with the body.'

'Yes, I'm afraid there's always that possibility,' Slider said.

'If somebody was looking for something in his inside pocket and didn't find it,' said Atherton, 'maybe he went on to look in his underpants as well. No, scrub that, it's stupid. What would a man keep in his underpants instead of his pocket?'

'Maybe he wanted to check if he's Jewish,' Mackay said. There was a short silence. 'He was circumcised.'

'So are lots of people,' Atherton said. 'Anyway, he's a blue-eyed blond. What's to check?'

'Here's another little problem to add to the collection,' said Freddie, who had been re-examining the trousers through a magnifying glass. 'There doesn't seem to be any blood on the tag of the zipper.'

'So maybe he had just forgotten to close it,' Atherton said.

'And chummy just couldn't resist a peek?' Mackay suggested. 'If he was famous for the size of his salami—'

'I'll make it the first thing I ask everyone who knew him,' Atherton promised.

CHAPTER FOUR

Definition of Character

Detective Superintendent Honeyman was a small, tidy man with a pale face and a repressed expression, which always made Slider think of Richmal Crompton's William scrubbed clean and pressed into his Eton suit for a party he didn't want to go to. Honeyman parted what was left of his hair low down just above his right ear and drew it carefully over the bald top of his head in a Robert Robinson to meet up with the side-linings on the left. Did he really believe it would convince onlookers that there was a full head of hair all present and correct? Slider pondered. Or was it a more complex form of self-delusion, or even self-hypnosis carried out in front of the looking-glass? It was very dark, shiny hair, and Honeyman oiled it into place, so that from the front it looked rather as though he was wearing a crash helmet. The worst thing about it was trying not to look at it; concentrating on the effort meant Slider frequently missed things that Honeyman said.

'Ah, Slider, there you are,' he said. He had a small, high, rather fluting voice, which must have been a terrible handicap to him when he was a uniformed PC out on the wicked streets of London – even if villains were more polite in those days. 'This Greatrex business.'

'Yes, sir,' Slider said, fixing his eyes on the point between Honeyman's eyes. This meant looking down rather, since Honeyman standing up was shorter than him; and perhaps subconsciously Honeyman compensated by tilting his head back so that he could look at his subordinate from under his eyelids, like a small mistress of the house trying to subdue a tall housemaid by the power of personality.

'I suppose it's suicide,' Honeyman said hopefully.

'I don't think so, sir,' Slider said, and an expression of dissatisfaction overspread the little features.

'Oh dear. And why not, pray?' Slider told him about the knife, and Honeyman's suffering lightened a little. 'I can't see your difficulty. It is possible deceased threw the knife away himself, isn't it?'

'Possible but unlikely, sir. The pathologist says death would have been instantaneous.'

'Ah, the pathologist. Expert witness and all that. Well, personally, I wouldn't hang a dog on scientific evidence. I think we need more than that, don't you?'

'There's the religious text card, which sounds rather like a threat.'

'No reason to think it wasn't his.'

'And the bloodmarks on the inside of the pocket—'

'Well, deceased could have made those too – fumbling for something in the confusion of the moment.'

'—and on the underpants.'

'Oh dear, I don't like what you're suggesting. You think the body has been interfered with?'

'It certainly does seem so to me, sir.'

'Still, even if someone else did go through the pockets and – et cetera – it doesn't rule out suicide.'

'He was remarkably cheerful that evening, apparently.'

'Ah well, they often are, you know. And in any case, a mood can change in a moment.'

'But appearances are more on the side of homicide than suicide. There are too many anomalies for me to be happy with writing it down.'

'Oh dear,' Honeyman said again, and lapsed into silence like an overstretched personal computer. Slider waited. At last the screen flickered again. 'It's a tricky one. I don't know that we would be justified in setting a full-scale investigation in train on the strength of your not feeling happy about it.'

He made it sound like PMT, Slider thought. 'Well, sir, it's still a suspicious death. There has to be some sort of investigation.'

Honeyman looked at him sharply. 'I'm quite well aware of that, thank you.' It was like being savaged by a goldfish. 'But I can't let you monopolise all this manpower indefinitely. There's a crime wave out there on the streets, you know, and I am responsible to the public for the way we use our resources.'

'There are an awful lot of people to interview, sir,' Slider said. 'It's important that we find some witnesses before memories cloud.'

'Oh, yes, yes, yes,' Honeyman said testily, 'but it's ten to one that it *was* suicide, and the press will be following every detail of this one, and the BBC. We can't afford to look foolish, and be accused of throwing money about recklessly.'

'If it turns out later that it wasn't suicide, we'll look even worse,' Slider pointed out. Honeyman gave him a goaded look. 'Greatrex must have been somewhere in the building during those ten minutes, sir, and somebody must have seen him. There were hundreds of people wandering about. And he was a striking-looking man.'

'Oh, very well,' Honeyman said disagreeably. 'I'll let you have the extra men for a week, but if you haven't come up with something by then, I shall have to cut you down to just your own squad. I'm perfectly certain in my own mind,' he added pathetically, 'that it was suicide, so do make it your first priority to look for a note. There's bound to be one somewhere – he wouldn't have missed the chance to tell his public all about his state of mind. These media-types are notoriously self-obsessed, they like nothing better than to talk about themselves. And,' he added severely, 'they blow their own little problems up out of all proportion. Can't see the wood for the trees. I can't waste my budget on that sort of thing. I'm answerable to the Commissioner, you know.'

Talk about pots and kettles, Slider thought glumly, trudging dutifully out.

'Things always look better in daylight,' Atherton said, sitting on his desk and contemplating the shine on his shoes. 'There was something almost surreal about the TVC. I began to think I was in something by Stendhal.'

The CID room was crowded with the extra personnel so begrudged by Honeyman. Mills, on loan with other members of Carver's team, was clipping his nails into the wastepaper basket. 'What about the post mortem, then, eh? Is that right, they found bloody fingermarks on his old man?'

'Why do you men always have to bring everything down to the lowest level?' Norma said, busy writing.

'I could explain it to you, if you'd like to meet me after,' Mills offered.

'Oi! There's a queue, you know,' Atherton said. 'Get thee behind me.'

'In your dreams,' Norma said, going on calmly writing. 'Anyway, what about that nice woman you were going out with, Jim? I thought you might be going to settle down at last.'

'I do settle down,' Atherton protested. 'Just not in the same place every time.'

McLaren, who was reading the *Sun* and eating a bacon roll, called across, 'Eh, Atherton, have you ever had two women at the same time?'

'At the same time as what?' Atherton enquired.

Unfortunately, McLaren didn't know a rhetorical question when he heard one and answered, which made Norma look up at last, severely. 'You disgust me, Maurice,' she said.

'Oh he has,' Atherton agreed. 'Certainly with everyone here.'

Mills finished snipping, put down the bin and dusted off his hands. 'Does the guv'nor really think it's murder?' he asked Atherton. 'I can't see it myself.'

'He has a feeling about it,' Atherton said. He remembered the Radek case, when it all looked sewn up, except that Slider felt something was wrong about it. 'When he's got one of those, it's best to go along with it.'

'If the guv'nor says it's Christmas, we all sing carols,' said Hewson, another of Carver's team.

'He's not like that,' said Norma, beating Mills to it.

'They're all like that,' Cook, Hewson's partner, contradicted. 'It's just some show it sooner than others. You'll find out.'

'I've been with him for six years,' Norma said firmly. 'He's the least dogmatic man I've ever worked with.'

'It's there underneath all the same,' Hewson said, unconcernedly, looking over McLaren's shoulder at the page three tits. 'Stands to reason. A guv'nor's a guv'nor, spelt gee-oh-dee. You can't get away from it.'

'I've met a lot of people in my life,' Norma said icily. 'You two are not amongst them.'

Cook looked annoyed. 'Don't give me that. Are you telling me—'

'Brass at twelve o'clock,' Mills warned as Slider appeared in the doorway, and a sudden silence fell.

Slider looked round curiously, caught Atherton's minute shrug, and strode front and centre. 'Right, the Greatrex case. Suspicious death. Let's have some views. I know you're for suicide,' he added to Mills, 'in which you have the great and good on your side. Mr Honeyman sees no reason to suppose it's anything else. But if it was suicide, someone at least interfered with the body. Either it was Philip Somers, and he's not admitting it; or someone was there before him, and is keeping quiet about it.'

'To me, it's murder,' Norma said. 'There was definitely something funny going on. I had all sorts of hints from Dorothy Hammond—'

'Oh, women are always gossiping, trying to stir up trouble,' Mackay said easily.

Norma sailed straight over him, '—about a row between Fiona Parsons and Philip Somers over whether Greatrex should even be on the show or not; and then about a row between Greatrex and Palliser. And Palliser left the greenroom just after Greatrex, on a flimsy excuse.'

'My money's on Somers,' Atherton said. 'If you're covered in blood, what better way to explain it than to be the one to discover the corpse?'

'I can't see it,' Mills said. 'You'd have to be pretty cool to think of that, and carry it off, and the last thing he was when I arrived was cool. He was nearly hysterical.'

'He struck me as such a wet ponce, he'd never have the balls to cut someone's throat,' Mackay said.

'He's still got to be favourite,' Anderson put in. 'He's the only one with blood on him. And he was out of sight for the crucial ten minutes, by his own admission looking for Greatrex.'

'But Dorothy Hammond said he didn't want Greatrex on the show at all,' Norma said.

'Because he hated him, maybe.'

'But if he wanted the chance to kill him, he'd have argued to have him on, not the other way,' Norma said.

'If it was planned ahead,' Anderson said. 'Maybe he just hated him so much it came over him on an impulse, and he was left trying to cover up the best way he knew.'

'That sounds very nice,' Slider said, 'except for the knife. If it was impulse, why did he bring the knife with him?'

'We've got to try to tie the knife in with someone,' Mackay said.

'Oh, did you think of that all by yourself?' Atherton murmured.

'It could have been Somers, it could have been Palliser, it could have been Fiona Parsons for that matter,' McLaren said. 'It could have been anybody at all – if it was anybody.'

'McLaren's right,' Slider said into the stunned silence. 'The difficulty is that we don't know where Greatrex went or what he did in the missing fifteen or twenty minutes. We've got a situation where an unknown number of people are wandering around a large building, and nobody knows where anybody is at any given moment. Nobody's accountable, nobody can be pinned down to exact times. Our particular problem is that until we can find some witnesses, we can't prove it was murder and not suicide, and we can't get the manpower to do the sort of investigation we need to find witnesses until we can show that it was murder.'

'Catch twenty-two,' Mackay said triumphantly.

'So we're going to have to start at the other end,' Slider said, 'with motive. We've got to find out all about this man Greatrex, who loved him and who hated him, who wanted him dead – and if it turns out that he hated himself most of all, well, so be it.' He gazed round them at his blandest. 'I'm not dogmatic.'

Norma and Atherton exchanged a look. Was it possible he had heard?

'And in the meantime, we've got to talk to everyone who was in the building at the time, and that includes all the members of the audience of the show – telephone work there for everyone with bad feet or a poor excuse. And I want two teams to comb the immediate area around the exits from the building for anything that might have been dumped, because if it wasn't Somers, somebody must have had some bloodstained clothing to account for. Start outside and work your way back in. Mills, as you were in at the beginning, I'm going to make you office manager. Right, there's a lot to organise, so let's get busy.'

The room broke into a buzz of talk and movement, amongst which one voice came out clearly saying, 'Overtime all round, then.' That was Honeyman's concern, of course; but Slider had a moment of doubt as he looked at the pleased faces following the remark. For when all was said and done, the fact that the body had been interfered with did not mean it wasn't suicide, and if that's what it turned out to be, Honeyman was not going to be happy with Slider. Slider liked to keep Det Sups happy – that was the route to a long and untroubled life.

Slider had long wanted to see the inside of one of those houses in Pelham Place, and Roger Greatrex turned out to have lived in one of them.

'Ah, I know where he got the liquorice,' Atherton said in sudden enlightenment as they approached the wedge of South Kensington Station along Harrington Road. 'There's an old-fashioned sweet shop just outside the station, by the Thurloe Street exit. They do sherbet lemons and acid drops and toasted teacakes and all that sort of tackle.'

'I'm so glad we've cleared up that point,' Slider said. 'What's the wife's name?'

'Caroline, formerly – and I ask you to believe this – a Miss Fiennes-Marjoribanks, daughter of Viscount Chirnside.'

'Money?'

'Dunno. Somebody has, though, to live in Pelham Place. I suppose a media honey like Greatrex must have been pulling down big biccies, but I'd be surprised if it was enough for a house like that. Be sure to wipe your boots before entering. And curtsey while you're thinking. It saves time.'

The house – white, elegant, shapely – smiled in the sunshine across its railings and semi-basement with a century and a half of assured beauty. Slider sighed with satisfaction. The terrace led the eye away kindly and then bent to the supple curve of Pelham Crescent, in all the loveliness of perfect proportion. Ah, they didn't write 'em like that any more. 'Didn't they use one of these for the outside of the house in *Upstairs Downstairs*?' Slider asked.

'Before my time,' Atherton said cruelly. They trod up the steps, and he ostentatiously wiped his hand down his trousers before pulling the bell. Caroline Greatrex received them in the drawing-room, which was chilly with the spaciousness and quiet of real wealth. Atherton, disposing himself elegantly on a brocaded settle, took a quick inventory of the age and value of the appurtenances. It reminded him of that line from the *Goon Show* – the curtains were drawn, but the furniture was real. Though in this case, it was the widow who was drawn – and pale, even through her perfectly applied make-up. Her hair, ash-blonde over natural ash, was arranged as carefully as if she had been to the salon that morning, in the rather bouffant page-boy bob that a certain section of Society favours, drawn back in a curve to show the ears, decorated with large pearl studs. Three rows of pearls around the neck, and if they weren't real, Atherton thought, he was a monkey's uncle. A black roll-neck sweater showed off the pearls; below that she wore a grey-and-white-fleck tweed skirt and black court shoes. All very plain and suitable; and no other jewellery except a rather ugly collection of rings on the wedding finger: a broad gold band, a three-stone diamond engagement hoop, a diamond-studded eternity ring, and a keeper of thin gold with clasped hands filled all the space between knuckle and first joint. She had ugly hands, Atherton thought, stubby and pale with fleshy joints, and the sort of nails that shouldn't be drawn attention to, and were painted bright scarlet.

'May I offer you sherry?' she asked. 'Or are you not allowed? I never know whether that's pure fiction or not.'

'Thank you,' Slider said. He liked to give them something to do if they were likely to be ill at ease, and she ought to be, though she was outwardly completely composed. The English upper classes in adversity, Slider thought: there's no-one like 'em. As a farmer's son in a wealthy county he had had more experience of them than Atherton, for all the latter's urbanity. Town gentry are not like the old county families.

When she had brought their glasses and sat down opposite them, Atherton could see what Slider had already noted, that her composure was only outward, and liked her better for it. Death should never be a matter of no moment, he felt. She turned her sherry glass round slowly in her fingers, and at rest her mouth trembled. She looked much older than the corpse of Roger Greatrex had done – sixty, perhaps, to his fifty – but then death smoothes away lines while bereavement adds them.

'I'm sorry to have to trouble you at such a time,' Slider said, 'and I'm very grateful to you for seeing me.'

'That's quite all right,' she said bleakly. 'You have to do your job, I understand that.'

'I have to ask you first if you know of any reason why your husband might have wanted to do away with himself? Was he depressed? Unhappy? Worried about anything?'

'No, not at all,' she said firmly. 'I can't believe that he would do such a thing. He was at the height of his career, he had no financial worries. In fact just lately he has been particularly cheerful.'

'Why is that?'

She looked chilly. 'I have no idea. He did not discuss it with me.'

She paused reflectively. Her eyes wanted to take a look at Atherton, but Slider held her glance and said, 'I can assure you that anything you tell me will be held in confidence if it possibly can be.' Atherton noted with faint surprise that his boss's usually regionless voice had taken on a very slight country softness – hardly an accent, more a cadence. But something in Mrs Greatrex seemed to respond to it. Atherton saw her begin to relax, as a nervous dog does with assured handling, and could only admire. He could not have done that, he knew.

'I think I should tell you, then, that my husband and I have for a long time gone our separate ways. Our marriage is more a formality than a union of any intimacy. We have separate suites upstairs, we each follow our own activities – though we keep up appearances for the sake of the family, and there are still occasions when we appear as a couple. *Appeared*, I should say.'

'You were on friendly terms?'

'Oh yes, it was not a rancorous arrangement. But I didn't care for some of Roger's media friends, and he was utterly bored by mine.'

'Did he have any enemies?'

She raised an eyebrow. 'He was a critic, and not generally a benign one. I should say he had many enemies – but I can't believe anyone would kill over a bad review. That *is* what you're asking me? Did anyone hate Roger enough to kill him?'

'Did anyone?'

'I don't know. I can only say, not that I know of. But I can't say what would be enough, can I?'

Slider let the question slip past his ear. 'Did he have any relatives?'

'His parents are both dead now. He has a sister, Ruth. They were always very fond of each other, but she's married and lives in America. They write to each other once or twice a year, but we haven't seen her since – oh – it must be four years, if not five.'

'What about your family? Did he get on with them?'

Her mouth made a wry movement. 'Oh yes, we all got on with each other. He didn't like them and they didn't like him, but on family occasions we would all turn up and be polite. That's what happens in civilised society. I shudder to think how much time we all waste being polite to people we don't much care for.'

'Why didn't they like him?'

'*Not good enough.*' She sipped her sherry, scanning Slider's face for comprehension. 'My parents thought I made a disappointing marriage. Roger wasn't one of us. But they tried to make the best of it. The trouble was that Roger resented being made the best of. He wanted to be judged on his own merits. I'm afraid Daddy's generation wasn't very good at that.'

Slider nodded gently, the quiet stream into which she might slip her painful confessions. 'Have you any children?'

Her eyes hurt. 'Just one. Our son, Jamie.' She looked for his benefit towards a framed photograph on the sofa end-table, of a smiling, gap-toothed, very ordinary-looking boy with tousled hair, in an open-necked shirt. 'That was taken when he was nine.'

'How old is he now?'

'Mentally he's still nine. Chronologically he's twenty-five.' She held Slider's gaze, as though for support; Atherton she had clearly forgotten. 'He's in a home, in Sussex – near Petworth. He's very happy there. It's a very nice old house, large grounds, even a lake. We go down three times a year to see him – at Christmas, Easter, and on his birthday.' She seemed on the point of adding something else, and then didn't.

Was that part of the not being good enough? Slider wondered. He looked into her naked face and could only be silent in the face of the world of hurt revealed there. If her husband had been murdered, life had already dealt her a worse blow. He moved a foot, scuffing against the floor, and she drew back into herself a little, enough for him to be able to put the next question.

'Do you know Sandal Palliser?'

Her expression grew veiled. 'Yes, of course I know him. He's one of Roger's friends.'

'Friends? I was told he and your husband didn't like each other.'

'Who told you that?' she asked, but warily.

'They had a violent quarrel at the television centre the night he died. I was told it was not unusual. And they did have a long running dispute in the newspapers.'

'That had nothing to do with it. That was merely a professional debate,' she said unwarily.

'So, what was the cause of the enmity?'

She hesitated, as though she contemplated not answering. Then she answered in a voice which was suddenly harsh, 'I don't know what, specifically, they quarrelled about the other night. But I imagine it had something to do with a woman. My husband – well, you'll find out sooner or later, I suppose – my husband had other women. At one time he and Sandal used to go out together and get drunk and pick up – women, girls, call them what you will. There was rivalry between them as to who could do best at it, but it was friendly rivalry at first. Then I believe Roger "stole" one from Sandal, and after that it became hostile. They would do each other down if they could. I thought it was all very silly at first, but then it seemed to get nastier. I don't know why – except that Sandal was always jealous of Roger, because he'd done so much better in his career. And financially, of course,' she added. 'Sandal is a great believer in money. He would love to be rich, and failing that, he likes to be with the rich. And old money, of course, is more desirable than new. He hated the fact that Roger had the entrée into that sort of society, while he didn't.'

'Through you.'

'Through me, yes. But Sandal would have married well if he could.'

Slider glanced across at Atherton, and Mrs Greatrex, seeing

the eye movement, remembered where she was and drew the perfect composure back over her face. Slider stood up.

'May we see his room?'

There was a bedroom, dressing-room, bathroom and sitting-room, all interconnecting, on the second floor. The maid who showed them up explained that Mrs Greatrex had a bedroom and bathroom on this floor, but used the morning-room downstairs as her sitting-room. All the rooms were expensively carpeted and furnished with antiques, and also expensively cleaned. The wastepaper basket in the sitting-room was empty, and all the surfaces were clear. The fireplace contained only a log-effect electric fire in an elaborate iron basket, almost comical in its inappropriateness. It went to show, Slider thought, that everyone has their blind spots.

The room had been done yesterday morning when Mr Greatrex left, the maid said. He had returned in the late afternoon to shower and change before going to the BBC, and the room had then been tidied again, and the towels changed. If there had been a note, it would have been found and given to madam, but there was no note. He seemed, the maid said, very cock-a-hoop when he came back to the house for the last time; not at all depressed or sad.

But there was a small bureau in the sitting-room, and a lowboy in the bedroom, both stuffed with personal effects. 'We'll have to go through them all,' Slider said, opening drawers without enthusiasm. 'We'd better get someone sympathetic on the job. Anderson's a nice, clean-living lad.'

'Pity the maid's so efficient. These rooms are as unrevealing as a hotel.'

'Oh, I don't know,' Slider said. 'There's negative evidence: if his clothes are taken away to be washed when he takes them off, the only way he could get holes in his socks would be by not changing them.'

'Dirty boy, eh?'

Slider opened another drawer, lifted up some neatly folded shirts, and found under the lining-paper, two pornographic magazines. 'You might say.'

'What's that? Oh, hygiene publications. I'm beginning to build up a picture of this man in all his loveliness.'

Slider was now in the sweater drawer, and found, similarly

hidden, a black-and-white photograph in a very old leather frame, of a girl of about fifteen, with short fair hair pulled back at one side by a slide, and a cheerful grin. On the back the photographer's name was stamped in curly Gothic print, and an address in Pulborough.

Atherton looked over his shoulder. 'The sister, do you think?'

'Could be. But why is it hidden? Mrs G said he was fond of his sister.'

'Maybe it didn't go with the decor.'

Slider stared at the photograph, frowning, and then slipped it into his pocket. Atherton noted the action and forbore to comment. His boss, as he knew, often had trouble with photographs. They upset him, in the same sort of way that dead people's shoes upset Atherton.

On their way out, they approached Mrs Greatrex again to ask permission for someone to come and go through the papers. Then Slider produced the knife. 'Have you ever seen this before?'

She looked at it, and her face seemed to turn a shade paler, almost yellowing. 'Was that – ? No. No, I haven't seen it before. It's not Roger's.'

'To your knowledge.'

'Why would he have such a thing?' she countered.

'Was he ever in the Boy Scouts?'

'Really, what odd questions you – oh. I see. No, I don't think so. It wouldn't have been in his family's tradition. And Roger was never a joiner. He liked to be different from everyone else. He wouldn't have cared for the uniform.'

'One other thing,' Slider said, remembering, 'was your husband religious?'

She raised her eyebrows. 'Not particularly.'

'He wasn't a churchgoer? Fond of the Bible?'

'Good heavens, no!'

Slider explained about the card.

'I don't know where that would have come from,' Mrs Greatrex said, 'but I knew very little of what he did day by day. But he wasn't a Christian. His father's name was Grossvater. They changed it when they came over, when Roger was a little boy.' She looked quizzically from one to the other. 'I thought you realised, that was what I was saying earlier. I come from an Old Catholic family. It was largely why my father thought Roger unsuitable.'

Front wheel skid, Slider thought. Well, who'd a thunk it?

'But he was fair-haired and blue-eyed,' Atherton said, unable to withhold a faint protest.

She looked at him blankly, as though the table lamp had spoken. 'Sephardic Jews often are,' she said after a moment, as if he ought to have jolly well known that.

CHAPTER FIVE

Who Dragged Whom?

Sandal Palliser's house on Addison Road had been a semi-rural villa when it was built in the eighteen-forties, but the countryside had retreated like the tide fifteen miles further west and left it stranded. Now it stood on the one-way system which was the southbound extension of the West Cross Route, and traffic thundered or coughed past it all day, wreathing it in noxious fumes and making its walls shake. Flats and houses pressed up close on every side; but it slept in its secret, unkempt garden behind the high brick wall as though entranced, and amongst the overgrown shrubs and trees city birds found a green haven which must have surprised the socks off them.

Slider's practised eye took in the signs of neglect. 'Either Palliser's not doing well enough to pay for the upkeep,' he said as they walked up the path, with twigs tugging at them like fractious children seeking attention.

'Or he doesn't care,' Atherton finished for him, 'and spends his money on something else.'

'That roof wants looking at. And the guttering. I hate to see a lovely house let go.'

Inside, it was as different as it could be from Greatrex's pampered surroundings. The walls had a long time ago been painted magnolia, and then left to get on with it. The furniture was old, some of it antique, some merely ancient, and there was an awful lot of it, which at least helped to hide the deficiencies of the decor. There was clutter everywhere, books, sheet-music, toys, bicycles, china, clothes, plant pots, an art-deco naked lady lampstand with a broken flex, a footstool only half re-covered with a petit-point of pansies in a vase, a Royal Standard typewriter, an ancient record-player and a tottering heap of 78s, a scooter with the front wheel missing, a pair of leather riding-boots on wooden trees, a headless teddy bear, a wooden high-chair with the reddish paint worn off in patches so it resembled brawn – it was as though the house had been visited in the fifties by a huge family of cousins, and never tidied since.

Easing his way past a battered Utility sideboard loaded with vases and jam-jars, which was almost blocking the passage, and tripping on a hole in the carpet, which seemed to be made of off-cuts, Slider was led into the kitchen where he was able to take stock of Mrs Palliser. She was a surprise, too, after the steely glamour of Mrs Greatrex. She was a comfortable, motherly-looking woman with a kind face, iron-grey hair pulled back into an unfashionable and rather unsuccessful bun at the nape of her neck, and unexpectedly dark eyes. She was wearing a flowered smock over a shapeless brown skirt, and the sides of her forefingers were deeply ingrained with the sort of stain that comes from a lifetime of peeling vegetables. She seemed to have been making soup, and there was a complex smell of food in the air.

She scanned the faces of both men while Slider introduced them. 'You've come about Roger, I suppose. That's a terrible thing, isn't it?' She had the hint of a Scottish accent. 'It said in the paper this morning that he committed suicide, is that right?'

'It looks as if it could be suicide,' Slider said cautiously.

'I can't believe that,' she said firmly. 'He wasn't the sort. Sandy doesn't believe it either, I know that for a fact. Roger had everything to live for. I suppose you want to talk to Sandy, don't you?'

'Yes, please.'

'He's up in his study, working. He doesn't like to be disturbed when he's writing, but of course this is an emergency, isn't it? I'll just show you up. Can you wait a moment, I was making his coffee, and you can take it up with you. I dare say you'd like a cup of coffee? How do you take it?'

Shortly afterwards they were following her upstairs, Atherton in the rear carrying a tray with coffee and a plate of shortbread and trying to keep watch round it for hazards: the stair carpet was as full of holes as the hall, and there was in addition the problem of the books stacked on both sides of each stair, leaving only a narrow space in the middle. Mrs Palliser climbed like a stayer, using her hands to push down on her thighs to boost her upwards, talking breathlessly the while.

'We've been here since nineteen sixty-five, bought the house with the money Sandy got for his first book. It cost two thousand pounds, can you imagine that? Of course, it was in a terrible state.' Behind Slider, Atherton snorted and changed it to a cough. 'We'd to do it up ourselves, bit by bit, for we hadn't a bean in those days. Years it took us. It's worth half a million now if we wanted to sell it. When we first moved in, there weren't even any floorboards in the hall. It had been empty for years. The garden was like a jungle. Well, we've been happy here. It's a good house, a happy house. Oh, mind the step-ladder on the landing. We keep it there for changing the light bulbs, the ceiling's so high, and they seem to pop every five minutes. They don't make them to last the way they used to. Sandy says we ought to get the wiring looked at. I dare say it might be that.'

Slider dared say, too. The light switch he was just passing, skirting the step-ladder and a standard lamp with a split shade and a trailing flex, was a round, dark brown bakelite one with the little nipple-like protrusion in the middle, the sort he remembered from his childhood. Hitler still wanted to be an engine-driver when this house was last wired.

'I suppose it's a bit cluttered, the house,' Mrs Palliser said without apology as she embarked on a second flight, 'but you tend not to notice your own messes, do you? And you never know when something might come in. Sandy! Here's visitors.'

She had reached a door on the half-landing and pushed it open. It opened only part way, stopped by some further foothill of gubbins concealed behind it. Through the doorway Slider saw a man sitting at a vast desk which bore a personal computer at the centre with piles of books and notepads all around. The rest of the room contained nothing but a side table, a red leatherette-covered armchair with curved wooden arms, and some bookshelves on metal supports fixed to the wall; but almost every inch of surface was covered in heaps of books and papers. The large, beautiful sash window looked out over the avian paradise of the garden; and the naked light bulb dangling before it on a pre-war plaited fabric cord had been hitched across by a piece of string tied to a nail in the bookshelf so that it would hang over the desk.

'This is the police,' Mrs Palliser announced. 'And here's your coffee. I'll leave you the while, then.'

Sandal Palliser swung round to look, and then got up and came to take the tray from Atherton. Slider had not expected him to be so tall, or so old. He had thick white hair which sprouted upwards from his head and only bent over at the ends from its own weight. His face was deeply lined, his eyebrows bushy, his large nose spread and coarsened with age and hard living, his neck chicken-skinned. He wore old-fashioned glasses with brown plastic rims, and behind them his eyes were an unexpectedly bright blue, which made them somehow look completely round and rather blind. But his movements were vigorous and his voice powerful; probably, Slider thought, he was not as old as he looked – late fifties, perhaps.

'You've come about Roger, I suppose,' he said. He put the tray down on top of the papers on the side table. 'Chairs, now. You'd better have the armchair,' to Slider. 'Shove all that stuff on the floor. It's all right, it won't hurt. And if you,' to Atherton, 'go into the next room, you'll see a kitchen chair just behind the door. Bring that in.'

When the arrangements were complete he took up his coffee and sipped it, and passed the shortbread around. 'Phyllis makes it herself. She's a wonderful cook. No bloody use at anything else, and eccentric as a parrot, but she can cook. I've been married to her for thirty years, and she gets more like Princess Fred every day.' He looked from Slider to Atherton and back with a quick, appraising glance. 'Are you an historian?'

'Architecture's my interest,' Slider answered. 'But there are overlaps.'

The round blue eyes reappraised in the light of that information, but he only said, 'Perhaps you'll know who Princess Fred was, then. So, Roger Greatrex. I didn't kill him, if that's what you're thinking.'

'It says in the paper it was suicide,' Slider said blandly.

Palliser grinned without humour. 'Oh no, you don't catch me with that little game! I know perfectly well it wasn't. Roger loved himself much too much to want to deprive the world of his presence. And since you can't cut your throat by accident, he must have been murdered. No big surprise, really. There must have been a waiting-list of people wanting to kill him.'

'Who was at the head of the queue?' Slider asked.

'Don't ask me. That's for you to find out. I should look amongst the women, if I were you – there were a few with grievances. God knows what they saw in him, though. He was a dirty little bastard. I don't mean sexy, I mean dirty.' He caught Atherton's eye and grinned again as he looked around the room. 'Oh yes, it's untidy here, all right. I have a theory, that there are people in the world who are untidy but clean, and people who are dirty but tidy. Roger was immaculate on the outside, but it was all a façade. Whereas me – you could eat your dinner off me. And many a woman has done so, but that's another story.'

Atherton gave a tight smile, and seeing Slider's dreamy expression, gathered he was to ask the questions this time. Briskness, he thought, was the order of the day. 'You had a quarrel with Mr Greatrex in the greenroom. Would you mind telling me what about?'

'Oho, that's it, is it? Amazing how predictable you people are. *Ay* quarrel, followed by *ay* murder, ergo – not that you'd know what ergo means – the quarreller must be the murderer. Ha! Well, not this time, chaps, sorry. *Cherchez la femme*, that's my advice to you.'

'Mrs Greatrex says you and he used to compete over how many women you could pick up,' Atherton said, obligingly changing tack.

'Dear Caroline! Serves her right for marrying Roger. If she'd married *me* instead – but that's yet another story. Oh yes, Roger and I used to haunt the streets together. You wouldn't think we were the same age, would you? He had the body of a twenty-year-old – several times a week if he could get it.' He laughed at his own joke. 'Phyllis says he must have had a picture in his attic.'

'Would that be a reference to the novel by Oscar Wilde, sir?' Atherton asked ponderously, making pretence to lick a pencil.

Palliser laughed, more naturally. 'All right, one up to you! Very well, I'll grant you so much, that I disliked Roger cordially, even though we were once friends, and no, I am not going to tell you why. I admit we had words on Thursday night, but I'm not going to tell you what about, because it's none of your bloody business.

I didn't kill him, though I half wish I had – there would have been an artistic symmetry to it. Trouble is, he probably would have enjoyed it, and it wasn't my business to pleasure him, thank God. It's not my business to sort out your problems, either. In short, I have nothing to say to you about myself – but I will tell you one or two things about Roger that you may not know, and that probably no-one else will tell you. That's my bargain. How about it?'

The narrative was long, made longer by the evident fact that Sandal Palliser liked the sound of his own voice. He was a gifted narrator, and though the story was not an edifying one, it at least cleared up one question: the identity of the hidden photographee of the sweater drawer. According to Palliser, Greatrex had had two sisters – Ruth, five years older, and Rachel, two years younger than him. He was fond of them both, but being closer to Rachel in age, was particularly attached to her. As they grew up together, they became inseparable, so much so that when Greatrex was seventeen and due to go up to university, the parents had difficulty in persuading him to leave her. He went unwillingly; and shortly before the end of his third term Rachel became ill with leukaemia. Greatrex came home, missing his exams, and through the summer holidays watched his sister die slowly and in agony. When she was gone, he refused to go back and resit his first-year exams, without which he could not continue at university – for this was St Andrews and the Scottish system – and instead left home and went to London – as far away as he could get, according to Palliser – to seek his fortune. After drifting through the various jobs the unqualified could get in 1960, he found himself in Fleet Street and was lucky enough to catch the eye of the editor of the *Daily Express*. Thus started his apprenticeship to journalism and his ultimate stardom – and, for reasons yet to be discovered, his bloody death in a loo in the TVC.

That was also when he first met Palliser, who was working for a publisher and freelancing for the papers when he could get the work; and drawn together by their both having been brought up in Scotland, they became friends.

'I don't think Roger ever really got over Rachel's death,'

Palliser said, lighting a Gitane. 'My mid-morning indulgence.' He proffered the pack. 'Do you—?'

Atherton shook his head, and Slider said, 'No thanks, not while I'm breathing.'

Palliser gave a tight smile. 'A policeman with sense of humour. I thought that wasn't allowed.'

'Some of us slip through the net. Do go on.'

'Where was I? Oh yes, Rachel's death and Roger's obsession.'

'Why do you suppose he hid her picture, if he was so fond of her?'

'He never spoke of her. It was all too painful, I think. It forced its way out in his obsession with young women. Well, that's what it amounted to – always markedly younger than him, though fortunately they got a bit older as he did. I suppose he was maintaining the differential – the latest one probably seemed to him at fifty the way Rachel had seemed to him at eighteen.'

'You aren't suggesting his relationship with Rachel was incestuous?'

'Not physically – good God, no – but mentally, isn't it always? If you love your siblings at all, that is?'

'I'm an only child,' Slider mentioned.

'Ah, then you'll have had the Oedipus bit instead,' Palliser said easily. 'Roger spent his life trying to find his lost sister in other girls. He couldn't keep his hands off them. Luckily, most of them didn't want him to. He was a good-looking sod, sort of like a young Peter Cook. You know, fair, clean-cut, terribly English – if only they knew! He went especially for suburban dollies, "up west" for the evening with stars in their eyes. They had no resistance, and Roger was always one to go with his best stroke. They took him for public school, and he didn't bother to disillusion them. It was a great pulling line. And then of course the sixties started in earnest, and he couldn't go wrong. Dear God, what a picnic that was! I remember my father saying the same thing about the Great War – a holiday from the normal rules of decency and decorum. Every now and then, civilisation needs to be let off the leash for a run—'

Palliser paused at that point, and his face went blank for a space. Writing his next article, Atherton thought, not without envy – a nice little quasi-historical, cod-psycho-social analysis for those who like their thinking done for them. And he'll get a couple of thousand for it.

Then the animation faded back in, and Palliser said, less flippantly than hitherto, 'Except that it was all wrong for Roger. Underneath it all there was a streak of suburban prude, a longing for lace-curtain propriety. He could never be a whole-hearted hedonist – he was too middle-class for that. I think what he really wanted from the dollies was just to be with them, talk to them, maybe pet them a bit. He wanted someone to be a big brother to. But he was a healthy lad, and they were looking for excitement, so it never stopped there. And after a bit I think he forgot why he was doing it – not that he ever knew, not consciously. The ambivalence, the conflict, resolved itself in that streak of dirtiness – not washing his feet, not changing his underpants. He was punishing himself for his inner loathsomeness, you see – and he did like punishment. That was another manifestation of his bourgeois soul. Yes, now I come to think of it,' his round blue eye, satirical as a parrot's, roved from Slider to Atherton and back, 'he was just the sort to commit suicide after all. Gentlemen, I have solved your case for you.'

Slider let all this pass him by with a policeman's patience. 'What happened when he married?'

'Oh, it didn't make any difference to his habits. Caroline would never make a fuss. That's the advantage of marrying into the aristocracy.' An expression of displeasure crossed his face. 'The Honourable Caroline Fiennes-Marjoribanks – Christ, what a name! Do you know Chirnside? The old boy's still hanging on to life, God knows how, he must be ninety-something. Sheer stubbornness, I wouldn't wonder. Stiff upper lip – stiff upper everything, solid wood from the neck up. You know these old Lowland titled families, more English than the English.'

Slider nodded as if he did. 'Mrs Greatrex said that they were married in the face of family opposition.'

Palliser's expression hardened. 'Oh, you've spoken to her, have you? Well, yes, I suppose you'd have to. Not that she'll have told you much. Never complain, never explain, that's the motto of these old families. That's why they decided in the end to make the best of it and accept Roger. Worst thing they could have done all round, as it turned out.'

'How did it turn out?' Slider prompted, at his most inscrutable.

'The union wasn't blest,' Palliser said harshly, 'and it turned out to be Roger's fault – chronically low sperm count. The Chirnsides were devastated – they were longing for grandchildren. I knew the family – grew up in the same part of the country. And then when Caroline did sprog down at last, the kid turned out to be mental.' Palliser looked away for the first time, turning a blank gaze onto the garden, where a blackbird was ducking and running along the line of the bushes, pausing to rummage with those familiar, abrupt movements, amongst last year's dead leaves. His voice became strained. 'Fact of the matter is, it wasn't Roger's kid. We all knew that. The whole thing broke him up. And Caroline – you can imagine what a strain it was on her. After that he and Caroline came to an *accommodation*' – he made a moue to show he knew the word, though old-fashioned, was nonetheless necessary – 'and he went back to his old pursuits. I think you probably met his latest conquest. Nice-looking girl, but horribly earnest. I think he was getting in over his head there. I believe the dreaded M-word had been mentioned. Of course, Roger would never leave Caroline in a million years, even if he could – she's his security blanket – but I doubt whether he will have told *her* that.'

'Her?'

'The female in question.' Palliser grinned mirthlessly. 'And no, I'm not going to tell you her name. You can work it out for yourself or go hang. I don't kiss and tell, even when it's someone else doing the kissing.'

Slider reverted to the question of the quarrel with Greatrex, hoping that with the better atmosphere generated by Palliser's self-satisfaction, the cause of their enmity might be forthcoming. But Palliser was quite determined, though also quite cheerful, about refusing.

'I don't have to tell you anything, and I'm not going to. My private life is none of your bloody business.' He said it with a grin, but Slider felt there was a tenseness under it, and that the eyes were wary behind the shielding glass.

Even the old 'by the way' ploy chalked up a big fat zero. 'By the way, I understand you left the greenroom alone shortly after Roger Greatrex left it for the last time. Would you mind telling me where you went?'

'I went to make a telephone call,' he said, and cocked his

head consideringly. 'Now who told you I left the room? One of those daffy girls the Beeb is infested with, I suppose. That's where our licence money goes – from our pockets straight to Monsoon and The Body Shop, merely filtered by all the Emmas and Katys and Sarahs. It's social work, pure and simple. No-one else'd give them a job.'

Slider refused the enticing flicker of the lure. 'There was a telephone in the greenroom,' he said. 'You could have used that.'

'Ah, but I wanted privacy,' Palliser grinned. 'And no, it's no use looking like that, I'm not going to tell you who I telephoned.'

'If you won't tell me, I may draw my own conclusions from your refusal,' Slider warned.

'You can do what you like – I can't stop you,' Palliser said almost gleefully. 'I've told you I didn't kill Roger, and unless you want to charge me with it, that's all I am going to tell you.'

The inner man needed fortifying after that, notwithstanding the coffee and shortbread.

'Do you fancy a pint?' Atherton asked tentatively.

'Does Carmen Miranda wear fruit?' Slider responded; so they drove back to the Crown and Sceptre in Melina Road to collate the information over a pint of Fullers and a plate of pasta.

'So what do you think of all that, guv?' Atherton asked. 'Likes listening to himself, doesn't he?'

'A practised performer,' Slider said. 'He was putting up smokescreens, watching himself do it, and watching us watching him.' Too many layers of overlapping consciousness for the truth to be obvious, which was the purpose of the exercise. 'He was hiding something, but what, and why?'

'Maybe just for the hell of it,' said Atherton. 'Another one of those clever dicks who think it's amusing to mislead coppers by concealing perfectly innocent information.'

'Maybe.'

Atherton looked at him. 'You liked him,' he discovered.

Slider looked up. 'That doesn't mean I don't think he was capable of doing it. He's a clever man, a thinking man, and if he did kill Greatrex he'll be one step ahead of us all the way.' He sipped his pint. 'And if he did kill him, he'll have had a very good reason.'

'He's got to be up there with the star suspects,' Atherton said, and told off on his fingers. 'There's the acknowledged enmity between them, the quarrel on the night itself, his being missing at the appropriate time, and the fact that he's concealing things from us. And,' he remembered, 'he's tall enough, and he looks strong enough.'

'There's one big objection,' Slider said.

'How did he manage to cut Greatrex's throat and return to the greenroom without a speck of blood on him?'

Slider nodded. 'Protective clothing, perhaps, which he concealed somewhere before going back to the greenroom.'

'And probably meant to collect afterwards, but which might still be hidden somewhere?'

'Maybe,' Slider said.

'After all,' Atherton reasoned with himself, 'whoever killed Greatrex had the same problem. He'd have had to have protective clothing, or wander about the Centre covered in blood and have someone notice it. How would he explain it away?'

'By saying he got it all over him when he examined the corpse,' Slider said. 'It's good psychology to be the first to find the body. If you raise the alarm, no-one's going to think it was you that did it – everyone expects a murderer to make very long tracks – and if you're bloodstained, you've got the perfect excuse.'

Atherton thought about it unwillingly. 'But you'd have to be a very cool customer to brass that out. Your average person, even if they meant beforehand to kill, would instinctively want to run away and try to conceal everything afterwards. You're talking about a cold, ruthless cunning, calculating the odds. Did Philip Somers strike you that way?'

'No,' Slider admitted. 'And there was the mistake about the knife. If he was a calculator, he'd have taken my hint about the knife.'

Atherton grinned. 'I love the way you always see both sides.'

'But a man doesn't have to be completely consistent. You can have a degree of calculation intermingled with unforeseen panic. He could have planned it all beforehand, but not have reckoned on how upset he'd be afterwards; clung to his original plan without being able to adapt as he went. And certainly he stuck to his post, guarding the door and preventing anyone else from going in. Don't you think that was an odd thing to do?'

'Unusually self-controlled, anyway,' Atherton granted. 'Well,

Somers certainly had the opportunity – and he is the one person who didn't have to explain the blood away. But what would his motive be? Did he know Greatrex?'

'We have Dorothy Hammond's story that he said he didn't want Greatrex on the show. For reason or reasons unknown.'

'And then there's Palliser's hints about a woman in the case,' Atherton said. 'If Greatrex was a womaniser, there could have been any number of jilted lovers and cuckolded husbands after his blood.' He sighed. 'Let's face it, it could be absolutely anyone.'

'Yes. We have so little to go on.'

'Who dragged whom at the wheels of what, how many times round the walls of where?' Atherton said. 'Ah well, it's early days yet.'

'Quite. We have lines to follow up, so let's follow them. Palliser, to begin with, I think. His wife may have some interesting information, if she can be got to open up.'

'Me for that,' Atherton said. 'I'm good with old ladies. It's my old-fashioned courtesy mixed with my boyish good looks. They always want to pet me and give me toffees.'

'And we might trace the knife, or find witnesses, or more forensic evidence. If it wasn't Somers, there must be more blood somewhere.'

'Blood will out,' said Atherton. 'I'd settle for a nice thumbmark somewhere – Palliser's print and Greatrex's blood-group.'

Slider ignored the taunt. 'If only it had happened somewhere more private and confined. I hate to think of all those hundreds of people coming and going and trampling about. A nice little domestic where you can seal it all off would be a piece of cake compared with this.'

'That's why we get the big money,' Atherton said cheerfully. 'Want any pud?'

CHAPTER SIX

The Bridgers of Kensington County

Norma was looking for him when he got back to the factory. 'The Lab phoned, guv. Mr Arceneaux. Wants you to phone him back.'

'Right, thanks.'

She followed him into his room. 'Any luck?'

'Lots of interesting stuff about Greatrex. He and Palliser were friends from thirty years ago, but there was a lot of rivalry between them. Palliser won't say what their quarrel was about, but all the indications are that Greatrex was an inveterate womaniser, and Palliser reckons we should be looking for a woman. But if it was a woman that killed him, she'd have to have been tall and strong – like you, in fact. Any offers?'

'As a matter of fact,' she said, 'I have. It struck me as odd that the only guest Fiona Parsons went downstairs to meet in person was Greatrex. And, after what Dorothy Hammond said about her quarrel with Somers, I checked with the editor, and it was actually Parsons who suggested Greatrex for the show. Martin Fletcher, the editor, was doubtful about having Greatrex and Palliser at the same time, but she persuaded him.'

'It was a topical choice,' Slider pointed out. 'After all, they had been having a newspaper argument about the very subject of the show. It might have been no more than that.'

'Yes, guv, but it was Parsons who suggested the subject as well. Maybe she was having an affair with Greatrex, and wanted the chance to be with him – what d'you think?'

'If she was having an affair with him, surely she'd have wanted to be alone with him, not see him in a public place like that? After all, how much time could she hope to spend with him in those circumstances?'

'But he was married,' Norma said, and then, seeing he hadn't followed the point, elaborated. 'A woman who's having a secret affair with a married man jumps at any chance to be with him, whether alone or in public, for however short a time. Those are the crumbs from the table she lives off.'

Slider felt uncomfortable to be reminded of this, and said, 'Even if she was having an affair with him, why should you think she murdered him?'

'I don't think it,' she said, offering him his own customary words back, 'I'm only looking for anomalies.'

'And have you found any?'

'I think so. Parsons says she was in the studio at the time of the murder, and that that's where Hammond found her to tell her of the death, but after I spoke to Hammond I went and talked to some of the people in the studio, and there's not one who can say exactly where Parsons was at any particular time. And when I checked with Hammond again, she said she had to look all over the studio before she found Parsons.'

'Go on,' Slider said.

Encouraged, she perched on the edge of his desk. 'Well, guv, you saw the studio: it's not as if it was a brightly lit open space. There's the set in the middle, with the panellists' table and a sort of backdrop screen behind it. A person could be standing behind the screen and not be seen by the rest of the studio. And all the lighting is focused on the set, so everywhere else is dim and shadowy. Then there's the tiers of audience seating, set up on scaffolding – you can walk right under that. And then there's the control box and the lighting gallery, and all sorts of little rooms off the studio floor – props and make-up and dressing-rooms. What I'm saying is that there's any number of places someone could be in the studio without anyone seeing them. So what better excuse, if you actually *weren't* there at the time? Parsons can't prove she was there—'

'But no-one can prove she wasn't,' Slider said.

'Exactly. And she was dodging about all evening, which could have been her way of making sure everybody remembered seeing her around, but nobody knew where she was at any given moment.'

'Is that all?'

Norma made a face, which meant it was. 'She's tall and

strong. She plays basketball for the BBC team. And she insisted on having a look at the body, even though Somers tried to discourage her. Maybe she was making sure the scene looked right for the police.'

'If he was her lover, why would she want to kill him?'

'Any number of reasons. Love and hate, jealousy, frustration—'

Slider smiled at her. 'You know you've got nothing, don't you?'

'All we've got is nothing,' she pointed out boldly.

'However, on your side, Sandal Palliser said that we had already met Greatrex's latest female fancy, which suggests it was someone at the BBC. So it's quite possible it was Fiona Parsons. While that doesn't make her the murderer, it can't do any harm to find out a bit more about it. She might have some light to throw on the situation. So you can go and talk to her—'

Norma jumped up. 'Thanks, guv!'

'—carefully.'

'I'm always careful,' she said indignantly.

'I've heard that.'

When she had gone, he picked up the phone and dialled. Tufnell Arceneaux was a scientist at the Met Lab, whose specialist field was forensic haematology; a life-loving man with whom Slider had spent some memorably Byzantine nights when they were both younger and his head was harder.

The handset roared, and Slider held it back hastily. Tufty's voice was as large as his appetites. 'Hello, Tufty, it's Bill.'

'Hello, old fruit! How's it hanging?'

'Symmetrically, thank you. How are you?'

'Bloody awful, thanks for asking. I haven't been to bed for two days – feel as if some bastard's borrowed my body and been careless in it.'

'What was the celebration?'

'Burns night.'

'I thought that was in January?'

'I'm talking about that fire at the fertilizer factory in Cricklewood,' Tufty roared triumphantly. 'I've just spent the last thirty-six hours tissue-typing the victims. Identified all but one, though – had to send that one off to the tooth fairy. However, all that aside, I've got some good news for you. Your culture vulture who cut himself shaving—'

'You've managed to look at that, with all you've had to do? I'm touched.'

'Had a sleepless moment to spare. Couldn't let my favourite dick down – does that all by itself these days!' Tufty chuckled massively at his own humour. 'Anyway, I managed to get a lift off the wallet – quite a nice one – a thumb. Good enough to identify, I should have thought. I'll send the print off to you.'

'That's terrific. Thanks, Tufty. Oh—'

'No, no it's all right, I thought of that. It isn't the corpse's. But I've got something else for you as well. I got a whole forefinger and thumb off that holy card jobbie you sent over—'

'The Bible text?'

'That's the chap. There are all sorts of marks on it, but one finger and thumb – ordinary greasers, not bloody – have come out a treat. And in my humble op, the thumb's not the same as the one on the wallet. Here's the thing, though – it's not the corpse's either.'

Slider was silent for a moment. 'Just one finger and thumb?'

'Just one identifiable.' Slider was silent, thinking. 'Does that help?' Tufty howled anxiously.

'Like a hernia,' Slider said. 'I've no idea what it all means.'

'You mean, before you hadn't a clue, and now you haven't a clue?'

'Nutshell.'

'Life's a bugger, isn't it?' Tufty sympathised. 'Tell you what, I'm just off in ten minutes or so. Handling flame-grilled factory workers doesn't half give you an appetite. Why not join me somewhere and we'll have a meal and a drink or two, make a night of it. You need the oils wheeling, old horse.'

'I've still got the hangover from the last time we did that,' Slider said, 'and that was two years ago.'

'Time you let go again, then. You introverted types get your pipes clogged up – too much thinking and not enough drinking. What say?'

'I'd love to, really, but I've got to go and see Irene this evening. I promised. She wants to talk about the divorce and everything.'

'Christ,' Tufty said, awed. 'Well, best of luck, old chum. If you survive it, give me a bell, and we'll get together some time.'

Atherton was lucky – quite a short vigil rewarded him with the sight of Sandal Palliser leaving the house alone. He watched him walk up to the main road and turn left, and a few moments later was ringing the doorbell in hope. He had armed himself with an excuse, but it wasn't needed. Mrs Palliser expressed no surprise or curiosity on seeing him, but simply bid him come in, and padded before him towards the kitchen.

'Sandy's away out, you just missed him,' she said over her shoulder. 'He'll not be back until late. It's his night for bridge with the Frasers – they live in Kensington Court, just a step up the road. D'you know them? She writes the society column in one o' those glossy magazines, and he writes plays no-one can make head or tail of.'

Atherton knew who she meant. 'Too rich for my blood,' he said. 'I'm just a humble copper. Don't you play bridge?'

She turned to him, and her eyes crinkled with amusement. 'I do not. There's nothing so daft as a card game – except those who play them. But Sandy likes being with his own sort of people now and then; and I like an evening doing what I like.'

'And what do you like?' Atherton asked, obediently taking his cue.

'Being left alone in the house with a handsome young man can't be bad at my age. What's it to be, now? Tea, coffee, or a drop of something?'

She sounded positively roguish. Atherton plumped for safety and tea.

'We'll stay in here, if you've no objection,' she said, pulling out a chair from the kitchen table. 'It's the only warm room. When Sandy's out, the central heating goes off.'

Atherton didn't know whether she meant he turned it off, or she did, whether he was supposed to sympathise or approve of the thrift. However, the kitchen was cosy, with a four-oven Aga sitting fatly under the chimney throwing out heat, and the smell of recent baking in the air. There was an ancient bakelite wireless with an illuminated dial half-hidden in the clutter on the dresser making conversational sounds just below the level of comprehension; and an enormous black cat, which had been curled up looking like a fake-fur cushion on a high-backed wooden chair by the range, unfurled itself and hopped lightly down to come and wipe its nose politely on Atherton's trouser, purring like a food-mixer. It was no hardship to sit in here amongst the amiable clutter. Atherton lolled at his ease at the table, the cat now heavy on his lap, and watched while Mrs Palliser made a pot of tea, and buttered a plateful of oatcakes and decorated each with a slice of cheese. He had a sense of absolute comfort and safety, and he wondered if Palliser knew how lucky he was.

Mrs Palliser brought everything to the table, sat down catty-corner to him, and put the plate between them. 'Help yourself,' she said. 'I see Gordon's taken to you. You like cats.'

'I have one myself,' he said, and told her about Oedipus as he watched her put milk into two enormous teacups and fill them with strong orange-brown tea from the fat black earthenware pot. Then she reached for the bottle of Teacher's she had put down nearby, unscrewed the cap, and poised it over his cup. 'You'll take a nip,' she said, and it was hardly a question. 'Or do you like it separate?'

'I'll have it your way,' he said, fascinated.

She poured a good slug into each cup, screwed the cap back on the bottle, and drew a hearty sigh. 'Ah,' she said, as though he had passed some test, 'you're a good boy. Here's how!'

'Good health,' he found himself replying. It didn't taste half bad, actually, almost perfumed; and since he was ravenous, he followed her example and took an oatcake, and found the combination faultless. Soon, elbows on table, they were talking cosily. Mrs Palliser would have been happy to indulge his curiosity on any subject – 'Chatting's my best thing,' she told him at one point – but it was easy to bring her to the subject of Roger Greatrex, which must have been on her mind in any case.

'Of course, Sandy and Caroline were goan out together at one time, did you know that?' she said. 'Before she married Roger, of course. As a matter of fact, it was through Sandy that Roger met her. It's queer to think about that now,' she added reflectively. 'How things happen, and you can't see the end of them. That's how it's meant to be, I suppose.'

'It seems that way sometimes,' Atherton said encouragingly.

'Sandy'd known the family from boyhood, you see – Caroline's,

I mean. His father was a solicitor, and he did some work for the old lord, and that's how Sandy met the young folk. They lived nearby, and Sandy used to get invited to make up the numbers.' She gave a wicked little smile. 'That's where he got his taste for the high life and the County Set. Of course, it's different there in the lowlands.' She poked her chin up. 'Me, I'm from Deeside. We don't bow the knee to anyone.'

'I can't imagine you ever needed to,' Atherton said gallantly, and she rewarded him by pouring him more tea. 'You must have had the world at your feet.'

She didn't deny it, only looked at him with a wry smile and crinkled eyes. 'Well, Sandy was a handsome young man, and as clever as a knife,' she resumed, 'and he was popular with the younger ones, and the old lord quite approved of him too. Anyway, after Sandy came to London, Caroline came down too – not for his sake, you understand, but for a bit of excitement and change, to see life and so on. But of course, knowing Sandy was there, and maybe feeling a bit lonely, she got in touch, and he offered to show her the sights, and one thing led to another, and so they started to walk out. I don't know how serious it was on her part – it was before my time of course – but I know Sandy wanted to marry her. But then he got friendly with Roger, and introduced him to Caroline, and before he knew where he was, Roger'd taken her away from him.'

'How did he take it?' Atherton asked.

'Oh, well, Sandy would always put a good face on it. He'd not let Roger know he minded – that'd be letting him win. But to my mind there was always a tension between them. A rivalry, you might say. They were friends, right up to the end, but underneath they watched each other like two cats. Maybe that's why the friendship lasted so long,' she added with a little nod. 'It mattered too much to the pair of them, d'you see, ever to drift apart. And Sandy was always devoted to Caroline. Devoted.'

'Didn't you mind?' Atherton asked, intrigued by the lack of rancour in her voice as she said it.

'Mind? Why should I mind? It was me he married. I've half an idea the old lord asked Sandy to keep an eye on her. Poor Caroline hasn't had an easy row to hoe. Married to Roger was no picnic – and then the child being not just right in the head, and there was never another. I dare say they were afraid to risk it. No, I wouldn't have swapped places with her for anything. But Sandy would always do her a good turn if he could. Not that she ever said anything. It wasn't in her to complain, and I liked her better for that, I can tell you. Except just the once—' She paused, though it may only have been to concentrate on pouring. 'Will you have a piece of my Dundee cake?'

Atherton accepted, since she obviously wanted him to, and watched her in silence as she pottered about the kitchen fetching the huge, nut-studded cake, the cheese, a knife and two small plates. She cut him a dark cliff of cake, laid a matching wedge of cheese against its side, and passed it over, and waited while he sampled and pronounced. It was excellent, and she smiled at his praise as though it genuinely pleased her.

When at last she was settled again, he prompted her. 'So what happened, that one time that Caroline complained?'

She looked at him quickly and then away. 'Oh, it was a long time ago. Before the baby was born. The marriage was in trouble, and for a while there Sandy thought they might be going to split up. Caroline wanted a baby, you see, her family was pressing her about it, and Roger – in defiance, maybe, I don't know – was flaunting this young woman at her. He'd always had a roving eye, but this time it was blatant. Anyway, Caroline broke down for once in her life and ran out on him, she actually moved out, to a bedsitter in Earl's Court. Shocking it must have been for her to do that, and her a Catholic. Sandy went and saw her, of course. He said she was in a desperate mood. I think he thought she might do something silly. But he talked to her and he talked to Roger, and finally they got back together and it was all hushed up.' She paused, just a breath, but Atherton felt he could hear the wings of the Kindly Ones beating the air around them in the moment of silence. 'And then she found she was pregnant.'

She looked at Atherton, and he nodded very slightly as encouragement to go on. She sighed, as though he had given her the wrong answer, and looked down at her hands again. 'Well, that sorted things out. Roger dropped the young woman, and it all looked set fair. Then the baby was born.'

'And that was the—?'

'The poor simple boy, yes. Jamie, they called him. After that, I don't think it ever really worked between Roger and Caroline, but they always kept a good shop-front, as they had to, really, since they couldn't divorce. I think it suited them, really, to have their separate lives. But Sandy always thought Roger treated her badly.'

'Do you have any children?'

'No. We've none. We'd have liked them but – Sandy can't.' The last words were almost swallowed, as if she felt she shouldn't tell him, but wanted to too much to stop. And then she looked up suddenly into Atherton's eyes, and he stared down into thirty years of silent disappointment. 'But I've plenty nephews and nieces. And we've had a good marriage, Sandy and me,' she said defiantly. 'We understand each other. He has his little ways to put up with – but then, so have I. And he'll never leave me. I've always known that.'

And that was what she had to be grateful for, what she settled for? he wondered. He felt hugely, horribly sad. The ramshackle, cluttered house suddenly became a gigantic metaphor, a neglected opportunity, at the heart of which this shapeless woman cooked huge vats of nourishing, tasty food – for whom? He wanted to ask her but didn't dare. He didn't think he could bear the sadness of her answer, whatever it was.

He met Slider in the White Horse for a quick one before going off. 'So there you are,' he said at last, when he had told everything.

'Where am I?'

'There's our suspect. No alibi, suspicious behaviour, won't answer questions, is obviously hiding something – and has the cast-iron motive. The Big Green One. As the Southern planter said about the bougainvillaea, it's all over my jalousie.'

'Because Greatrex pinched Palliser's bird?' Slider said discouragingly.

Atherton was hurt. 'Why not? A lifetime of dissembling, hiding his hurt and jealousy, pretending to be friends with this despicable nerk, just so as not to let him get the better of him. Seeing Greatrex swanning around making a bigger and better name for himself, succeeding everywhere just that bit more than Palliser can manage. They have a long debate in the newspapers about modern art, and Greatrex even wins that one—'

'Does he?'

Atherton was confused. 'Does he what?'

'Does Greatrex win the debate?'

'Well of course,' Atherton said impatiently. 'No-one could take Palliser's position seriously – all that guff about art being elitist, and the arts subsidies ought to be spent on welfare instead. It's hackneyed – the wealthy liberal's guilt-trip. No-one really believes it. He probably only took up the argument to be on the opposite side from Greatrex.'

'You think so?'

'He earns his living from it,' Atherton pointed out. 'And all he achieves by being contrary is to make himself look like a plonker, while Greatrex, who is still a handsome son-of-a-gun, gets the pole position, the praise and the totty. Then he comes face to face with him at the TVC, and it all becomes too much. Thirty years of resentment boils over, and he tops him.'

'With a knife he's brought with him for the purpose?'

'All right, it may not have been absolutely spontaneous. But he knew he was going to be on the same panel with Greatrex.'

'Did he?'

'Oh yes. Anyone in the country could have known, because they announce on the programme the week before who's going to be on next week, and it was in all the TV listings. But anyway, Palliser knows. He arrives early, hoping for a moment alone with Greatrex, and when the opportunity finally presents itself – when Greatrex leaves the room alone to go to make-up, Palliser follows him.'

'Lures him into the gents – with the offer of sweeties, perhaps?'

'Greatrex probably went of his own accord. After all, it wasn't essential to Palliser's plan to kill him in that particular place, was it? Whoever killed him,' he added, seeing Slider about to object, 'it's hardly likely to have been the chosen spot.'

'Fair enough. But then we're back to the problem of the bloodstained clothes, or lack of,' Slider said, sighing. 'Did you try Mrs P with the knife?'

'Yes – no go.'

'Still, it's better than Norma's theory,' he said, 'and worth following up. Since the motive for the murder wasn't robbery from the person, it must have been someone who knew him, and Palliser seems to be the one who knew him best. We'll have to get him to volunteer some fingerprints. Somers too. Even if only for the purpose of elimination.'

'As long as you can keep Mr Honeyman sweet. He still wants it to be suicide.'

'Ah, on that subject – I had a telephone call from Freddie. Good news from our point of view – he's found subcutaneous bruising on the chin and jaw, including one very fine fingermark on the right side just below the ear.' He watched Atherton visualising it. 'So that gives us the murderer coming up behind him, grabbing him with the left hand under the chin—'

'To force his head back,' Atherton supplied, 'and pull the neck taut.'

'Right. Freddie says he thinks it was inflicted immediately prior to death, which accounts for it not spreading to the upper layers.'

'Well, Mr Honeyman can hardly argue with that. Congratulations, guv.' Atherton looked at his watch. 'I'd better go. I've got a hot date.'

'Oh?'

Atherton grinned. 'Sue isn't playing in *Traviata*, remember.'

'Lucky you.'

'Where are you eating tonight? Why don't you come round later, have some supper?'

'I've got to go and see Irene.'

'Will she be feeding you?'

'Absolutely not.' Slider shuddered at the thought.

'Well, then, come round. Look, you don't have to commit yourself. I don't suppose you know how long you'll be. Just come round if you want to. I'll be cooking something that doesn't spoil, just in case.'

Slider was tired and his mind was full of little jumping bits of information, like a dog with fleas, which was not the best state to be in for an interview with his future ex-wife. Not only that, but he had to go and see her in the house of the man she had ambled off with, which made him feel awkward and see red. The place was large and overstuffed and dull, like Ernie Newman himself, and it had a funny smell about it, which he couldn't pin down, but which reminded him depressingly of visiting aunties when he was a child – in particular Aunty Celia, who was ferocious about children being seen but not heard, and who always made him kiss her, instead of contenting herself, like other relatives, with kissing him. The texture and taste of her Coty face powder was all woven into the nightmare which began when Dad rang her doorbell. Ernie Newman's house had the same door chimes as Aunty Celia's.

The children had been allowed to stay up to see him, but he was so late that they had been scrubbed and pyjama'd and were waiting for him in brand new dressing-gowns and slippers which they wore with the air of lamb chops wearing paper frills. Matthew in particular was pale with shock, and after staring at Slider with his lower lip under his teeth for an agonising moment flung himself into Slider's arms to whisper passionately, 'Oh Dad, can't we go home? He bought us these slippers, and he calls them *house shoes*.'

Slider's heart lurched with sympathy. In such small things does true horror reside. When he was Matthew's age, there had been a teacher at school who had filled him with crawling dread because she pronounced the name Susan as Syusan. There was no arguing with that kind of aversion. The person concerned might be the paradigm of every kindly virtue – it was still garlic flowers and stake-through-the-heart time.

Kate was not stricken, but even her bounce was less ballistic. 'They don't do Nature Study in my new school,' she complained, 'they do Eartha Wareness. And Melanie took the gerbils home, even though it was my turn. It's not fair.'

'Didn't you say anything to the teacher?' Slider asked.

Kate's tiny chest swelled with indignation. 'I *couldn't*. Because Mummy said I couldn't have my *turn*. Because *he* gets *assama*.'

Irene caught Slider's eyes and looked flustered. 'Don't call Uncle Ernie *him*, it's rude,' she rebuked her daughter.

'He's not my uncle,' Kate returned smartly, and forestalled further rebuke by grabbing Slider's hand. 'Come and see my room, Daddy. I've got four new horses in my c'lection, and I'm going to have a shelf over my bed to put them all.'

Matthew reddened and glared at her. 'Shut up,' he hissed. 'Dad doesn't want to see your bedroom.'

'Shut up yourself,' she retorted, clearly getting out of hand. 'Daddy, don't you think I'm old enough to wear a bra? Stephanie at school's got one, and Melanie's getting one next week.'

'You'll have to ask your mother. How are you getting on at school?' Slider asked Matthew hastily. 'Settling in?'

His son regarded him with troubled eyes. 'All right,' he said guardedly. 'I wish I didn't have to go on the bus, though. If I had a bike I could cycle there. It's only six miles.'

'Not on that main road, Matthew,' Irene said, plainly treading a path that had been trod before. 'I've told you.' She appealed to Slider. 'He'd have to go part of the way on the A412. You know how the cars zip along there. It's too dangerous.'

'What's wrong with the bus?' Slider asked, trying not to get sucked in.

Matthew blushed again and chewed his lip before admitting, 'The others get at me.'

'What for?'

Even more reluctantly, Matthew said, 'They say the police are the fascist lackeys of state repression.'

Slider was impressed. 'They use longer words than the boys you used to mix with. There's something to be said for private education after all.'

'Don't joke, Dad,' Matthew said. 'Can't we—' He flicked a glance at his mother, which proved he had been going to say, *can't we go home*, and changed it to, 'Can't I go back to my old school?'

'No you can't, Matthew,' Irene said angrily, 'and I wish you'd stop asking that.'

I wish I could help you, Slider thought sadly, but I can't. Sometimes you just have to bear things. 'You'll get used to it,' he said instead, uselessly. 'Everything seems strange at the moment. Just give it time.' And Matthew looked at him in silent reproach, just as he would have done in the same situation.

After such soul-searing, it was quite a relief to be left alone with Irene, even if it was in Ernie Newman's best parlour. The three-piece suite was covered in white and gold brocade, the shagpile carpet was off-white, and the occasional tables had green onyx tops with gold rims. He looked to see what Irene had been doing before he arrived, and saw on the table nearest the dented cushions Irene's reading glasses lying on top of a book called *The Acol Method and After* and next to it a shorthand pad on which notes had been made in Irene's small and careful hand.

'What's the Acol method?' he asked, and refrained from adding a joke about birth control, which would have gone too near too many sensitivities.

'It's bridge,' she said, almost irritably. She knew what he thought about the game. 'As you know very well. I'm brushing up on my bidding.'

'Is he giving you a hard time?'

'Of course not,' she said. 'Everyone gets frustrated sometimes when their partner misses a signal. In fact, Marilyn says husbands and wives shouldn't partner each other – but she's only joking, of course,' she added hastily, perhaps fearing Slider might say something about her not being Ernie Newman's wife.

He felt an enormous sympathy for her welling up, and said instead, 'How's your mother? Did she have her operation?'

She looked at him with relief and gratitude. 'No, they think she might not have to now. She's much better since they've put her on the new pills.'

'Good,' Slider said, nodding encouragingly.

'She asks after you,' Irene offered him, kindness for kindness.

'Well, give her my love next time you speak to her. If you think it's appropriate.'

'Of course. She'll be pleased I've seen you.' And now she was looking at him almost wistfully. 'I'm glad to see you, too,' she said in a small voice.

He met her eyes for an agonising moment, and saw in them the same look of bewilderment as in the children's. She was out of her place too; for two pins, Slider thought, she would ask him if they couldn't all go home again. And it was a tempting scenario, that was the damnable thing. It was always easier to settle for the familiar, however disappointing, than to get through the pain of change in the hope of something better. That weight of inertia was marriage's best friend. The words hung unspoken on the air – couldn't we forget everything that's happened in the past year and go back – sink back into our cosy frowst – it wasn't so very bad, was it?

Slider stiffened his sinews. Having got this far, he thought – and that reminded him that he ought to help things along a little, in case, apart from anything else, the ratepayer returned. Seeing his wife in Ernie's house was bad enough, but with Ernie present it would have been intolerable. There was a peculiar –

given the circumstances – seed of possessive fury somewhere in him which he did not want to confront. He hardened his heart against her loneliness. She looked so little against Ernie's overstuffed furniture. 'So, you wanted to talk to me about the divorce?'

She chewed her lower lip, for a moment looking absurdly like Matthew, another thing he didn't want to think about. 'I wish I didn't have to, but things have to be sorted out. The thing is, I have to ask you if you're going to contest it. You see, we could arrange everything between us and then instruct a solicitor just to do the paperwork, and that way it could all be done as friendly as possible. I think what none of us want is for things to get nasty – I mean, especially with the children and everything, it would be so awful for them if we quarrelled.'

'Quarrelled?' He was almost amused at the inappropriateness of her nursery language.

'Over – well – money and things. I mean, you've been so good about all this – I just can't tell you how grateful I am that you've taken it so well – and I feel so guilty as well, all I want is for it all to be as easy as possible for everyone concerned.'

He had to put her at her ease. Her guilt reminded him too pointedly of his own. 'That's what I want too,' he said soothingly. 'And of course I won't contest it, as long as we can come to an agreement that satisfies us both.'

'Oh, I won't ask you for anything for myself,' she promised hastily. 'I mean, I want to be fair. And you can see the children whenever you want. There's absolutely no trouble about that. Ernie agrees with me. It's just a question of settling about maintenance for the children.'

'I'm sure we can come to an agreement without anyone getting angry,' he said. 'After all, there are always faults on both sides,' he said. 'A marriage doesn't break up through just one person's fault.'

She allowed her shoulders to drop in an exaggerated gesture of relief which was designed to conceal her very real relief that he was not out to seek vengeance. 'You always were a fair person, Bill. It's one of the things about you,' she said. 'Sometimes it used to annoy me, that you always saw both sides of every argument, but now—'

She was looking at him more meltingly every minute, and the

hedgehog of guilt on which he was sitting was growing longer and longer spikes. He didn't want to meet her eyes, for fear of what he might be tempted to blurt out. She was the mother of his children, he had woken up beside her every morning for fourteen years, and even now he could have gone into the strange bedroom she was at present inhabiting and known exactly where she had put every item of her clothing. It was a huge dry bath-bun of knowledge to be swallowed down in one gulp.

'I've got a murder case on at the moment,' he said.

'You look as if you're not getting enough to eat,' she said.

As fine and evasive a pair of *non sequiturs* as you were likely to meet in a twelvemonth, Slider thought. He wondered what Joanna was doing at that very instant.

CHAPTER SEVEN

Sleepless on the Settle

Fiona Parsons lived in Chiswick, in that strange tangle of little streets between Chiswick High Road and the river, where Georgian country villas, Victorian workmen's cottages, and Edwardian clerks' semis jostle for proximity to the fabled real-estate values of the Strand on the Green. Miss Parsons lived on the top floor of a two-storey Victorian house which had been almost converted by the owner, who lived downstairs. The almost-conversion had made two separate dwellings within the house without separating them, which meant that when Norma rang the doorbell, the owner – a tall, vague, gangling, bushy-haired, media intellectual inevitably called John – opened the door onto the vista and smell of new buttermilk emulsion, and when asked for Miss Parsons called up the bare and polished staircase like a husband, 'Fee, darling, it's for you!'

Fiona Parsons' voice floated back unintelligibly from somewhere above, upon which John smiled in a daffy, well-meaning way and said, 'She's upstairs. You'd better go on up.' Norma thought she had better, too, but had only got as far as the first step when John caught up with his thought processes sufficiently to say, 'Isn't that an awful, awful thing about poor Roger! Did you know him? Oh, I just couldn't believe it when she told me. Poor, poor Fiona. And she was actually *there*, poor thing! I can't believe anyone would do such a terrible thing. Such a sweet man!'

'Yes,' said Norma comprehensively, escaping up the stairs.

'She hasn't been to work since,' he called after her. 'It's totally *wrecked* her life.'

Upstairs the conversion had been carried out in the unengaggingly dotty manner of the amateur, which meant that while the paint-clogged plaster of the elaborate vine-swag cornices had been painstakingly scraped, cleaned and restored to its full, crisp glory, there were bare wires hanging from the ceiling and the electric sockets were lying on the floor waiting to be chased into the walls; the handsome panelled doors had been stripped to the wood, but their hardware had not been replaced, so that presumably they could not be closed; all the floors had been filled, sanded and varnished, but the kitchen door was leaning against the wall out in the hallway and the hall window was broken.

While Norma was taking a quick peek in at the rooms, Fiona Parsons appeared from the bathroom handsomely wrapped in a fluffy dressing-gown and with her hair turbaned in a towel. She looked, Norma thought irritably, sensational, despite – or perhaps because of – the dark shadows under her eyes. She was the kind of woman who, rising from her bath, always looked like Aphrodite instead of a turbot like the rest of humanity; who naked and smeared with whipped cream would look like a sex goddess rather than just a mucky herbert.

Her mouth took on a downward curve when she saw Norma. 'Oh—!'

'I'm sorry, I was told to come up.'

'It's John – he's hopeless! My doorbell's never worked. D'you know, I've been here nearly a year and I've *still* only got a single ring to cook on. The trouble is he won't get anyone in. He insists on doing everything himself, in between writing his stupid scripts. I wish I'd never agreed to come here. I mean, the house will be lovely when it's finished, and he charges me hardly any rent, but I'd sometimes sooner pay the rent and have a bit of privacy. D'you want some coffee?'

'Will it be any trouble?'

'Oh no, I've got an electric kettle. I was going to make some for myself.' She turned towards the kitchen, and Norma followed. 'I don't do much cooking, I have to say. I take most of my meals out. I'd like to be able to entertain sometimes – or rather—' She stopped in confusion, and busied herself with her back to Norma making coffee with much clattering.

'Your landlord seems to have known Roger Greatrex,' Norma said.

'John?' she said with unnecessary insouciance. 'Well, everyone knew him, didn't they. John was a producer at the Beeb before he started freelance scriptwriting.'

'I think it was a rather more personal knowledge than that,' Norma said kindly. 'He's been here, hasn't he?'

Fiona turned with nervous eyes, and her voice came out rather high. 'Why d'you say that?'

It was so pathetic it was touching. 'You've got his picture on your bedside table.'

The eyes filled alarmingly with tears. 'Oh God – oh God—!'

In the end, Norma made the coffee, and by the time she carried in the two mugs to the sitting-room, Fiona Parsons had regained control, and was sitting on the sofa with her legs curled under her, a small alp of wet tissues beside her, ready to talk.

'How did you guess? I thought I was being so discreet.'

'I didn't really, I just thought it might be the case. It was you who asked for him to be on the show; and you went down to meet him in person.'

'But I did that with most of the guests. Phil and I shared the duty between us.'

'Not that night. You only met him, none of the others. And he was early. According to what I've heard, that was very unusual.'

She sighed. 'Yes. I did persuade Martin we ought to have Roger on the show – not that he needed much persuading, Roger's always good value – but Martin wanted to approach the question more from the government side. And he objected that we'd only had Roger a few weeks ago – although it was actually eight weeks, but it was still quite soon – so I pointed out that Roger and Sandal had both been in the news recently, and that we ought to have both of them. I said we could hardly have an arts-funding debate without them and in the end he agreed, and so that was that.'

'Why did you want him on the programme, though?'

'It was a chance to see him,' she said, and sighed again. 'I hadn't had a moment with him for weeks, and I'd hardly even spoken to him for days. It was so difficult to find time to be together, with both of us so busy, so it seemed too good a chance to miss.'

'You arranged the whole programme just to spend a few minutes with him?'

She blushed. 'Oh, I know that sounds awful and teenagery, but I just needed to be with him. Haven't you ever been in love?'

'Yes.'

Fiona studied her face as if to test how likely that was to be true, and then, apparently satisfied, said, 'Well, then, you'll know.'

'How long had you been seeing each other?'

'A year,' she said with faint pride, as though the length of time added legitimacy. 'Well, I've known him for ages, but it was just a year since we first – since we fell in love.' She looked defiantly at Norma as though she might challenge the phrase.

Obligingly, Norma did. 'Was he in love with you?'

'We were going to be married.'

Norma felt sad. She had heard this bilious tale before. 'But he was already married.'

'Yes, but he didn't love her. It was all over between them, really – had been for years. Just a marriage of form. They didn't sleep together or anything.'

'So she knew about you?'

'Well – no. He had to keep it secret from her. I mean, he was going to tell her, but he had to wait for the right moment. You see, everything was in her name – the house and everything – and if she wanted to be vindictive, she could have made it very difficult for him.'

So could you, Norma thought, marvelling yet again at the unquenchable silliness of even the most intelligent women in the quest for *lerve*. 'And in the meantime, you and he slept together, when he could spare the time.' When it was said, she wished she hadn't, for she didn't want to alienate her.

'I suppose it's your job to put the worst gloss on everything,' Miss Parsons said with dignity, 'but I can assure you that Roger and I were in love and were going to be married. It's just—'

'Yes?'

Fiona hesitated, evidently unwilling to spoil the picture she'd painted. 'It was difficult for us to get time together,' she said as if it were the beginning of a sentence.

Norma finished it for her. 'And just lately it had got more difficult?'

'Yes.'

'You began to wonder whether he was avoiding you?'

'Yes. No! Well, yes, all right. I did wonder if he was cooling off a bit.'

'Seeing other women.'

'He wouldn't have done that. He loved me. But – but I did wonder if he was trying to back out of marrying me. He didn't like discussing it. Sometimes he got angry if I brought the subject up. We had rows. He said it spoilt our time together, arguing about it, and I suppose it did, but somehow when I thought he was trying to avoid the subject it seemed to be the one thing I couldn't get out of my mind.' Norma nodded encouragingly. 'It was wonderful at first. He used to come here – John was sweet about it – and it was bliss, he's a wonderful lover, and then we'd go to a restaurant – there are lots of really great ones in Chiswick – and we'd talk about where we'd live when we were married and what we'd do, and then we'd come back here and he stayed quite late, sometimes all night.' She sighed. 'We had a terrible row about three weeks ago. I wanted us to go on holiday together. I'd been talking about it for ages, and he'd sort of not said yes or no, so I assumed it was all right, and I got the brochures and everything, and when I showed him and tried to get him to agree on a date, he told me it was absolutely out of the question. And I flared up, and all the old stuff came up again, and we quarrelled – and—'

'And after that you didn't see him and he was offhand on the phone and you were afraid he was going to drop you. So you thought if he was invited on the show he'd have to come and you'd have a chance to talk to him,' Norma finished for her. Fiona, looking shamefaced and much younger than her years, nodded.

'It sounds awful, doesn't it?' she said in a small voice.

'We've all been there, love,' Norma said sadly. 'So tell me what happened on the night.'

'I'd asked him to come early, and I was so pleased when he did. I went down to meet him, and I could see straightaway he was in a good mood. We went up to green, and as soon as we were inside with the door closed he started kissing me. I tried to talk to him, but he kept stopping me by kissing me, and in between he said, "No talking tonight, all right? Let's just be happy like we used to be." And then he said, "I've missed you, darling Fee. Let's have tonight to remember."'

'What do you think he meant by that?'

'I don't know. I didn't want to think. It sounded so final, I thought maybe he meant to drop me.' She raised appalled eyes to Norma's. 'You don't think he meant that he was going to kill himself, and that it would be our last time?'

'No, I don't think he meant that.'

The appalled voice was down to a thread. 'It wasn't suicide?'

'I don't think so. Do you?'

'I didn't want it to be,' she said voicelessly. 'But if it wasn't – who could have killed him?'

'I was hoping you might tell me,' Norma said with grim humour.

'You don't think – *I* did it?' Fiona stared. 'You can't! I didn't. I wouldn't! Why would I?'

'It was one way of stopping him leaving you. After all, this way he'll never belong to another woman. If you weren't his first love, at least you're his last.'

Fiona Parsons did not burst into tears, for which Norma liked her better. She seemed, rather, puzzled by the accusation.

'But I could never have done that. Not however angry I was with him.'

'And were you angry?'

'I suppose – yes, I was underneath. It was treating me like an object. I mean, I loved our lovemaking, but he kept stopping me from talking. He wouldn't discuss things with me. It wasn't treating me like an adult.'

'So where were you between seven o'clock and twenty past? Where were you during the time Roger Greatrex was out of the greenroom, supposed to be going to make-up but never arriving there?'

She was still staring, her brain evidently working behind her stationary eyes. 'You think—? Oh but that's absurd!'

'Where were you?' Norma insisted.

'Well, with him, of course.'

Norma was wrong-footed, but caught herself up quickly. 'Naturally you were. But where with him?'

Now Fiona blushed richly. 'In the properties room on four. I had the key, and there was a chaise-longue in there. I said I'd meet him in there. He said he'd make sure he went up to make-up alone, and instead of going up he'd come to me.'

'So you were making love with him on a chaise-longue in the properties room while Philip Somers was scouring the building for him, and you never thought to tell us?'

'I – I couldn't – I didn't like to—'

'Where is this properties room?'

'It's on the left just past stairway five. That's left out of the greenroom and past the stairs. Past—'

'Past the gents where he was found.' She nodded painfully. 'Let's have some times, then. You met him when? And left him when?'

'I don't know exactly. I went to the props room when I left green, and he arrived a few minutes later. And we made love, and then straightaway he went. I wanted to talk, but he just smiled and put his finger on my lips – like this – to stop me – and he went. And that's the last time I saw him.' She was fighting tears now.

'So how long were you making love? Ten minutes? Fifteen?'

'*I* don't know. How long does it take?'

Norma was afraid any minute something gagworthy about eternity might be said, and let it go. Clearly Miss Parsons was not going to put her lover against the clock, but Norma betted it was on the shy side of a lingering experience, to judge from the peripheral mood that had been described. 'When you came out of the props room, was he anywhere in sight?'

'No. The corridor was empty.'

'And you went—?'

'Down stairway five to the ladies on three, and then to the studio.' She bit her lip to keep it from trembling. 'I dodged around a good bit in the studio, so that no-one would know where I'd been. And also because I didn't want to speak to anyone. I was too upset.'

'I should think you were,' said Norma. Then, remembering Slider's last minute instruction to her before she left the station, she asked, 'What form of contraception did you use?'

She blushed furiously. 'What business is it of yours?'

'Believe me, it's important. I'm not asking for thrills. What did you and Roger use?'

'I'm on the Pill,' she said.

'Despite the fact that he was sterile?'

'He wasn't,' Fiona said, indignantly, as though it was a slight.

'One of his closest friends says he was sterile, that he and his wife couldn't have children.'

'They *didn't* have any,' Fiona said – evidently she didn't know about Jamie – or didn't know Norma did – 'but that's because he didn't want them. He told me so. He said his wife had always wanted a family, but he hated the idea, so he took precautions.'

'He told you that – but you don't know it for a fact?'

'Why would he lie?' she asked simply. 'In fact, we used condoms at first, but he hated them so much he made me go on the Pill. If he was sterile, why wouldn't he have told me so?'

Pride, Norma thought; but Fiona had a point. Maybe he hadn't been lying. Maybe Palliser had got it wrong. Maybe it wasn't all that important anyway – except that the guv'nor wanted it asked, and he usually had his reasons.

'Well,' Norma said at last, 'my guv'nor won't be happy with the fact that you've been withholding information. You've wasted a lot of our time.'

'I couldn't talk about it. It's too important to me to have you people picking over it like ghouls. I knew you would make it sound sordid.' The eyes were filling again.

Quickly Norma asked, 'Were you ever in the Girl Guides?'

'Yes, I was. Why?' The surprise of the question had the effect of stopping the tears in their tracks.

'Oh, I just thought you might have been,' Norma said shortly. She'd taken quite a dislike to Miss Starry-eyed Parsons.

McLaren put his head round the door. 'Did you call me, guv?'

Slider looked up. 'Why would I call you guv? I'm the boss.' McLaren didn't quite roll his eyes, but it was close. 'What's this note on my desk? I can't read it. I wish you people would learn to write clearly.'

'Victim of child-centred teaching methods, guv,' McLaren said smartly, in the manner of one asking for two bob for a cup of tea. He studied his note for a moment with frowning concentration. 'Oh, yeah, it's about the audience lists. It might be nothing, but there's a discrepancy between the names the tickets were sent to, and the names we took up in the hospitality room.'

'I imagine there'd be some no shows.'

'There were eight. But this is something else. There was a ticket sent to a Mr James Davies, spelt "ies", but the name he gave in the hospitality room was John Davis, and spelt with an "is".'

'Could be a mistake. Who actually took it down?'

'I haven't worked that out yet. I don't recognise the handwriting, and there were a lot of them up there. But it's SOP to check spellings, so I thought I'd better mensh.'

'Whoever it was might have misheard, or even heard it right and written it wrong. These things happen.'

'Yeah. All the same—' McLaren said hopefully.

'Of course, check it out. It's the unturned stone that gathers the moss,' Slider said. 'No luck from the search parties, I suppose?'

'No, guv. But they've still got the big outside bins to check.'

'Joy to the world. And no witnesses?'

'It's hard to find out who was actually in the building at the time. I'm glad I'm not their security chief.'

'We really need some more general appeal.'

'TV? *Crimewatch*?'

'I think it's early days for that. Anyway, I didn't mean that general. I'd like to leaflet every BBC employee but that's out of the question, both from the time and the expense point of view.'

'Sandwich board, then, in reception?'

'Yes,' Slider said. 'That might be best.' The difficulty would be to persuade Honeyman to it. Once you went public, the stopwatch started ticking, and your performance was under scrutiny. 'Check out this Davis, anyway. Clear as you go along. On the subject of which, Somers and Palliser are both supposed to be coming in to give their fingerprints. Ask the counter to let me know as soon as they arrive.'

'Rightyoh.'

'She obviously thought telling me was letting herself out,' Norma said in the canteen, hunching forward over her cup of tea with the urgency of persuading him, 'but she could still have done it. Reading between the lines, what Greatrex was after that night was a quick dip, not extending of the frontiers of sensuality. I reckon a few minutes, ten at the outside. There was still time for her to kill him afterwards and tidy herself up.'

'Whoever killed him,' Slider pointed out fairly, 'did it after he left her, so there must have been time.'

'Right, guv. And, you see, I was thinking: what's the first thing a man does when he's finished making love?'

Slider pondered. 'Goes home to the wife?'

'Very funny,' Norma said loftily. 'He goes for a pee, doesn't he? It's the most natural thing in the world. Greatrex bonks her, says goodbye, then heads for the make-up room, popping into the loo on the way. It's the first one he'd pass. It explains why he went there, and not the one upstairs nearest to make-up. And Parsons, furious with being treated like a substitute Mrs Palmer, follows him straight in there and whacks him. It makes sense, doesn't it?'

'So far.'

'And she admits she deliberately foiled her own trail in the studio. So she's got no alibi, and she had the motive, and we know she was in the vicinity. A big, strong, baseball-playing girl,' she reminded him.

'Yes,' Slider said. 'But you're talking spur of the moment, not slow burn—'

'Both. She'd been building up a fury for weeks.'

'But she'd have had to bring the knife with her. That means planning.'

Norma leaned towards him so eagerly that one or two others in the canteen ostentatiously didn't look at them, in case it was an assignation. 'I had a thought about that, and it makes her very attractive for the frame. The knife could have been lying about in the properties room where they had their hump. Or she could have got it from any of the props stores. She started at the Beeb as a properties buyer – who better than her would know? And those places are full of junk – you just never know what's in 'em. And they're not locked – anyone can walk through.'

'I wish you hadn't said that,' Slider complained. 'Now someone will have to check whether such a knife is missing.'

Norma's face fell a little as she realised the work involved. 'I doubt whether you could ever say conclusively it wasn't,' she said. 'Even if anyone knows what should be there, they wouldn't be able to say what never had been.'

'I get your drift. But what about the blood?'

'I've been thinking about that, too – need there have been that much? Standing behind him, reaching round, and making one quick, hard slash – I wonder if there'd have been more than a bit of blood on the hands? Remember she was wearing three-quarter sleeves. And she says herself she went to the ladies before going back to the studio – she could have washed and checked she was all right there.'

Slider sighed. 'It's all very plausible, but you know that's not enough, don't you? We've got to have evidence.'

'Yes, guv. I'll check out the properties to start with for the knife. And we could ask for her watch and bracelet – even if she's washed 'em, there might be traces of blood in the links.'

'It's possible. All right, you can ask her.'

'Thanks, guv.' She jumped up energetically, and then thought of something. 'By the way, why did you ask me to ask her about Greatrex being sterile?'

'Oh, just a little stream I was meandering along. Probably leading nowhere.'

'Never mind,' she said comfortingly, 'we might still find a witness.'

Palliser did not show up, but Somers came in, looking more ill than ever, and allowed his fingerprints to be taken, looking down at the operation as though it were happening to someone else. Slider took the opportunity to question him more closely about exactly where he had been to look for Greatrex, and whether he had passed anyone on the way, but he was of little help, seeming to have slipped into a deeper state of shock than he was in on the night in question.

Slider showed him out. Nicholls, the sergeant on duty in the front shop, let Slider back in behind the counter and said, 'That bloke – I know him from somewhere. What's his name?'

'Somers,' Slider said, pausing to look at Nicholls with interest. Nutty had a capacious memory for detail. 'Philip Somers. One of the witnesses in the Greatrex case. He found the body, in fact.'

'Somers. That name rings a bell. I'm sure I've seen him before.' Nicholls pondered.

'I've checked his record. He's got no previous,' Slider said. 'I had 'em all checked. Greatrex himself was nicked a couple of times for possession of cannabis in his young and heady days, which is just what you'd expect, but everyone else is as clean as a whistle.'

'Och, don't worry, it'll come to me. Somers – Greatrex.' He tapped his forehead. 'It's all in here somewhere. The mind's a computer, Bill – a computer of fabulous power.'

'I know that. But remember, the first rule of computers is rubbish in, rubbish out.'

'And we get to deal with all the rubbish,' Nutty said in an undertone as the shop door opened and a lean man in a stained fawn mackintosh came in. He had the sort of hair that looked as though he'd been playing with live wires, and carried a plastic bag ominously full of documents. His face wore the monomaniac intensity of the intellectually disrupted, and Slider beat a hasty retreat, hearing Nicholls behind him say with massive patience, 'Yes, sir, can I help you? It's not the CIA tapping your phone again, is it?'

Slider was woken from a heavy sleep by a kiss on the cheek, and struggled up through layers of black flannel to find Joanna hunkered beside him, smiling. She was still in her coat, which was over her long black dress; she smelled of outdoors, with a faint whiff of cigarette smoke from her hair.

'What are you doing, sleeping on the sofa?' she said.

'I wasn't sleeping, I was thinking.'

'You're an awful liar,' she said kindly. 'Why didn't you go to bed?'

'I don't like that bed when you're not in it,' he said feeling foolish.

'You don't mean you've slept on the sofa ever since I went away?'

'Not at all. I just haven't slept,' he said with dignity, struggling into a sitting position. 'What are you doing home so early?'

'I couldn't wait to be with you, so I didn't even go to the pub.'

'You smell of the pub.'

'That was the interval. Don't you want me? Shall I go away again?'

'I wasn't sure you were coming back tonight. I thought you might stay with your parents again,' he said.

She eyed him cannily, resting her elbows on his knees and her chin on her hands. 'What's the matter?' she asked.

'Nothing,' he protested. He expected her to wheedle it out of him, but instead she got up and went out of the room, and he was afraid she had taken offence – afraid and annoyed. He could hear her moving about, and after a bit got up and followed her. She was in the kitchen. She'd taken off her coat and was making cheese sandwiches by the simple method of cutting wedges of cheese and folding a slice of unbuttered bread round each. He sniffed the air for her mood, but she said in a normal voice, though without turning round, 'I'm starving. Have you eaten? D'you want one of these?'

'No thanks.'

She flicked a look at him over her shoulder, and said, 'I want a whisky. Have one with me? I wish you'd lit the fire – I've been looking forward to a Laphroaig in front of the fire all the way up the M23.'

'It didn't seem cold enough,' he said, hoping his voice sounded natural to her, because it didn't to him. He collected the bottle and two glasses and led the way back into the sitting-room. He sat on the chesterfield, and she got into the opposite corner with her legs tucked under her so that she was facing him, what he thought of as her interrogation position. The thought that he knew so many of her gestures made him smile inwardly, and she saw it.

'So, what's the matter?' she asked again. 'Did seeing Irene upset you?'

He was surprised. 'No! Well, yes, it did, I suppose, but I'd forgotten all about that. There's nothing wrong, really. I've missed you, that's all. I don't like it here without you, but I've got nowhere else to go.'

'And?'

He gave an embarrassed sort of smirk. 'If you must know, I was jealous.'

'Jealous?' She sounded incredulous.

'There you were, in the Trevor, drinking pints, having fun—'

'I was working.'

'—with all your friends around you.'

'You had nothing to be jealous of. On the other hand, I've had a hellish time thinking of you going to see Irene.'

'You can't be jealous of Irene,' he protested.

'But I am. She had you for all those years. Her interest in you was legitimate. You shared your life with her, she knew everything about you.'

'It was never the way it is with you, with her,' he said.

She grinned. 'I'm glad to hear it. But even knowing that doesn't help. I'm not talking rationality here.'

'I'm glad to know you do get jealous. I find that comforting. When I think of you surrounded by all those men – and musicians at that! What are you laughing about?'

'I've spent all my spare time for the last two days in the company of Clive Barrow, principal cello, and his friend John. They're wonderful company.' Slider raised an enquiring eyebrow. 'We call them the Botty Celli. You had nothing to worry about.'

'If lack of opportunity is the only assurance I've got—'

She put her plate down, reached for his neck, and pulled him to her to kiss him. 'There's no pleasing some people. And when I came home early especially to give you something.'

'I've got something for you, too,' he said.

'Oh? Oh, so you have.'

Fortunately it was not until about fifteen minutes later that the telephone rang. 'It's bound to be for you,' Joanna said, struggling into a sitting position and pushing the hair out of her eyes.

It was. 'Ah, Bill – did I get you out of bed?' It was Tufty.

'No, I'm still up.'

'Lucky pup. Wish I was.'

'What are you doing still on duty?'

'Looking after your interests. I had a swiftie with Bob Lamont earlier, and I bullied him into having a look at your fingerprints. He's just come through to tell me he thinks the thumb on the wallet is the same as the set you sent through today – Philip Somers. He's got to go over it again in the morning in more detail, but he mentioned in passing he's pretty sure it's the man, so I thought I'd mention it to you, in case you wanted to go and surprise a confession out of him.'

'At this time of night?'

'Best time – catch him unawares. A few sharpened matches under the fingernails—'

'We don't do that in the CID.'

'No? Oh well, suit yourself. At least it'll give you something to chew over in the stilly watches.'

'There's plenty to chew,' Slider said.

'Mastication is the thief of time,' Arceneaux warned.

'I wish you hadn't said that.'

'Said what?' Joanna asked as he returned to her.

'My prime suspect's just been and got primer,' he said, gathering her into his arms. 'God, you feel nice! I'm tired. Let's go to bed.'

'Not one of those sentences goes with another,' she complained.

CHAPTER EIGHT

Relative Values

They arranged to meet Atherton for breakfast at the Dôme down by the river at Kew Bridge.

'How's it going between him and Sue?' Slider asked on the way there.

'How does he say it's going?'

'Don't you start getting evasive,' Slider complained.

'Like that, is it? Well, as far as I can see, they're very interested in each other, and each is trying to advance their relationship by pretending not to be.'

'That's helpful,' Slider said.

'It's a problem,' Joanna said seriously. 'Sue's had a couple of lousy relationships, so she's not going to be the first one to show her hand. And from what I can gather, he seems to want her to make the running. It isn't fair.'

'He has more to lose than her,' Slider said absently, and drew down a storm on his head. 'I only meant that he's quite happy being single, whereas she—'

'Happy? Much you know. And I tell you something else – if Jim doesn't sort himself out soon, he's going to end up a very sad case. If you're his friend you should tell him so. Sue's the most generous person in the world, and she'd give him everything, but she's not going to parade herself like a concubine while he lies back on a divan and plays the sultan. It's for the man to make the first move, always has been and always will be.'

'I love it when you play the traditional woman,' Slider smiled. 'Can't you see my chest swelling?'

Joanna looked sideways at him. 'I know how to handle men,' she said modestly. 'Flatter their egos and they're putty in your hands.'

'I don't like those plurals,' Slider objected.

'That's exactly what Sue says.'

They found Atherton sitting alone in a patch of sunlight like a contented cat, reading *The Observer*.

'Make you go blind,' Slider warned, pulling out a chair for Joanna. 'No Sue?'

'She's got a rehearsal. She's doing a concert tonight – Verdi's Requiem at Woburn Parish Church.'

'Bad luck,' Slider sympathised.

Atherton shrugged. 'Her family lives in Woburn Sands, so it's a chance to see them.'

'At least it's the Verdi,' Joanna said. 'It's the only choral piece anyone really likes doing. We call it the Okay Chorale.'

'Anyway, she needs the money,' Atherton added repressingly.

'Who doesn't?'

'In the midst of life we are in debt,' said Slider. The waitress arrived and they ordered, and the conversation wandered off on the trail of breakfast generally, and where you could get the best hash browns in New York – a subject on which Slider had little to say, since he'd never been there. So it was not long before they reverted to the case, some of the details of which were new to Joanna.

'From a professional viewpoint I can't be sorry he's dead,' she said. 'Critics like him do nothing but harm. They know nothing about music – often their crits are the purest bunkum. I've read a crit in a serious paper that said the playing was "off-key". What the hell does that mean, "off-key"? And they perpetuate all sorts of ghastly snobberies and one-uppishness about which composer's "better" than another, just because it's this year's fad. And they never give *us* credit, even though we do all the work. It's because of them soloists and conductors can get such humungous fees.'

'Don't sugar-coat it,' Slider advised. 'Tell us what you really think.'

'How can you say they know nothing about music?' Atherton said indignantly, from the vantage point of an arts page reader.

'Because I've read what they've said about concerts I've played in.'

'You just don't like criticism.'

'*Informed* criticism I can take. But look at what Roger Greatrex said about the *Don*, for instance – praising Lupton's "incisive conducting", for a start, without mentioning the fact that every single evening he follows us for the first sixteen bars because he hasn't the faintest idea how to cope with that opening.'

Slider listened indulgently, having trodden these paths before in Joanna's wake. 'Well, perhaps whoever murdered him was a music lover,' he suggested lightly.

'You said you had a prime suspect?' Joanna veered obediently.

'We've several,' Slider said. He told Atherton about Tufty's telephone call.

'I'm not sure where that gets us,' Atherton said, 'except that it proves Somers interfered with the body. Which means he's lied to us. But what did he want from the wallet? He didn't take money or credit cards.'

'Whatever it was he wanted, it suggests he may have had a motive for the killing.'

'Anyone *may* have had.'

'He was the only person covered in blood, the only person we actually know had contact with Greatrex's essential fluids,' Slider said; but his tone was dissatisfied.

'What?' Atherton asked. 'You prefer Palliser or Parsons?'

'Or Person or Persons Unknown,' Slider said. 'The trouble is we haven't found an explanation that fits all the circumstances yet. All we're doing is eliminating this and that. What about that religious tract card, for instance? How does that fit in?'

'Maybe it doesn't,' Joanna said. 'Maybe he picked it up somewhere out of curiosity, or did it for a joke to give to someone. Or maybe some nut shoved it at him in the street and he put it in his pocket absent-mindedly and forgot about it. There could be any number of explanations that've got nothing to do with his death. I wouldn't like to take bets on the odd stuff you'd find in my pockets after a day on the tubes or in the streets. I was given a flyer for an evangelist meeting at St Martin-in-the-Fields last week, and just stuck it in my pocket. If I'd been killed next minute you'd be hanging around the Crypt looking for a killer in Jesus boots.'

'True, if unhelpful.'

'Which takes you straight back to your prime suspect.'

'Of course, we don't *know* that Somers had a motive, just

because he messed with the body,' Atherton said. 'He might just have been exercising an unpleasant curiosity.'

'But he did say something to Fiona Parsons about not wanting to have anything to do with Greatrex,' Slider said. 'According to Dorothy Hammond he said he wouldn't share the same planet with him if he could help it.'

'It doesn't mean he had the drive – or the balls – to kill him,' Atherton said. 'Now Sandal Palliser, he's a different class of a man, as O'Flaherty would say. He's mean and he's tough, and we know he's concealing something from us. That's suspicious behaviour.'

Slider sipped his coffee. 'Sandal Palliser said *cherchez la femme*.'

'That alone should be enough to condemn him,' Atherton said. 'Anyone who uses cliché like that—'

'French cliché, which is even worse,' Joanna added.

'I should like you to follow up Somers,' Slider said. 'See what frightening him with the fingerprints will do.'

'Whatever you say, captain,' Atherton said. 'What about you?'

'I'm going to see Palliser again – after I've made a couple of phone calls.'

'I thought you didn't think it was Palliser?'

'That's why I'm bringing an unbiased mind to it.'

'Clear as you go, that's what you always say,' said Atherton, getting up.

'Are you staying here?' Slider asked Joanna.

'Might as well,' she said, and to Atherton, 'Leave me the paper?'

'I'll phone you later,' Slider said. 'I don't expect I'll be late today.' It still seemed odd to be saying that to Joanna instead of Irene. Odd, but nice.

Sandal Palliser seemed resigned rather than surprised to see Slider. 'Can't I even have my Sundays to myself?' He was looking tired, and some of the steel had gone out of his frame. Age had crept up a bit closer to him over the weekend.

'I'm sorry,' Slider said without regret. 'There are some things I want to ask you about your movements on Thursday. There are still some gaps to be filled.'

'Dogged type, aren't you?' Palliser sneered. 'I've told you all I intend to tell you. Unless you want to charge me.'

'Oh, I don't want to do that,' Slider said calmly. 'Not yet, anyway.' Palliser was still blocking the door, and Slider glanced past him and said, 'Can I come in?'

Palliser had looked at him carefully after the penultimate words, and said at last, more soberly, 'Oh, very well. You can talk to me all you like. I don't promise to answer you, that's all.'

'Is Mrs Palliser in?' Slider asked, following him into the passage and closing the door behind him – there was not room for him to pass and let Palliser do it.

'No, she's gone to church.'

'You don't accompany her?'

'I'm not of her persuasion,' Palliser said coldly. 'You'd better come up to my study.'

Upstairs, Palliser turned his chair from his desk so that he was facing the window, and gestured Slider to the other. The room was chilly with the sun off it, but outside the garden romped and burgeoned and seeded itself as nature intended, and Palliser fixed his gaze on it, as though it comforted.

'Very well,' he said. 'Talk away.'

'I've been trying to get to the bottom of the relationship between you and Greatrex and Mrs Greatrex,' Slider began.

'What the hell business is it of yours anyway?'

'A man's been murdered. I'm afraid that means a lot of things become my business, whether I want them to or not. Frankly, I'd just as soon not delve into your private life' – Palliser gave a grim little smile in acknowledgement of the touch – 'but you haven't been very forthcoming, Mr Palliser. You've refused to answer some questions. And you've told me lies.'

Palliser stared at the garden. 'Oh really?' he said indifferently.

'For one thing, you told me that Roger Greatrex was infertile. Now that just wasn't true.' Palliser did not move or answer. 'I checked with his mistress. I checked with his GP. And this morning I checked with his wife.'

Now Palliser shot him an angry look. 'You can leave Caroline out of it.'

'Well, no, I can't do that,' Slider said gently. 'But she confirmed what I had already been told by someone else – that their lack of children was because he wouldn't, rather than because he couldn't. Now, I can't help wondering why you would tell me such a thing – unsolicited – when it wasn't true.'

'It's what he told me. I can't help it if he lied to me.'

'Oh, but I don't think he did. It just isn't a lie a man would tell without a good reason, and he had no good reason. And if you and he went woman-hunting together in earlier days, it's something that would have been on your minds – the fear of unwanted pregnancies. No, I don't think Greatrex would have lied to you on that score; so I come back to the question, why would you tell me such a thing? And more importantly, why would you want to believe it?'

Palliser's face looked yellow, but it might have been the cold northerly light from the window. 'For God's sake—' he muttered, and stopped.

'The other thing you told me that relates to the subject is that Greatrex's son Jamie is not really his son,' Slider went on, watching him closely. 'If that was the case, whose son is he? You don't answer. Well, it was meant to be a rhetorical question. Because unless you're suggesting that Mrs Greatrex was inclined to run around with other men, you must be wanting me to think that you were the father.'

Palliser jumped up angrily. 'Oh shut up!' he said, fists clenched by his side. 'Shut up! Shut up!' But he didn't move, either to threaten Slider or leave the room. Slider had seen that rage before in his own son – the ineffectual rage of helplessness – of pain and guilt that can't be escaped.

'It all begins to make sense,' Slider went on, 'when a few other facts are added. The fact that you and Mrs Greatrex were fond of each other before her marriage, and that you went on being "devoted to her" – according to my source. You were always ready, even longing, to help her. You felt she demeaned herself by marrying Greatrex. You hated him for being unfaithful to her. When she ran away from him that one time, you went to her to comfort her; and it was after she returned to him that she announced she was pregnant—'

'Shut your mouth! If you say one more word—!'

Slider ignored him. 'I'm not sure whether you really thought you were the father of the child, or if you only wished you were, and gradually convinced yourself. But at all events, you liked to keep an eye on the child, and on Mrs Greatrex. Letters, phone calls, little presents. And any slight to either the boy or Mrs Greatrex from Roger Greatrex you regarded as a cause for anger on your part.'

Palliser was trying to regain control of himself. He sat down, facing Slider but not meeting his eyes. 'You seem to have quite a talent for fiction. Well, as long as you're enjoying yourself—' he said, trying for lightness and managing only to sound brittle. The muscles of his mouth were trembling. 'Though I can't imagine where you think it will get you, or what you think your fairy tale has got to do with Roger's death—'

'Well, you see, I had to account to myself for two things in particular,' Slider said helpfully. 'Your quarrel with Greatrex on Thursday, and the telephone call you said you made. They were the two things you wouldn't tell me about, so I couldn't help wondering whether they were connected. Fortunately, you used your mobile phone, and all calls on mobile phones are logged by the phone company. It was quite simple for me to find out what number you called.' Palliser was definitely yellow now. 'Didn't you realise that? Oh dear. Well, it turned out to be a Petworth number – the number of a home for retarded children.'

Palliser said nothing. He looked at his clenched hands which rested on his knees, and he looked very, very old. Slider felt almost sorry for him.

'One other telephone call I made added the last bit of information. It was to St Catherine's House – that's where they keep the register of births and marriages nowadays, what used to be Somerset House when we were younger. Doesn't have quite the same ring to it, does it? Anyway, it turns out that Thursday was Jamie Greatrex's birthday, one of the three occasions during the year when Roger always went to visit his son. Went rather reluctantly, according to Caroline, but still, he did his duty. Only last Thursday he didn't go. He called it off. Told the lad he was too busy. But he wasn't, was he?'

Slider had hoped for but not expected an answer, but Palliser gave him one. 'No, he wasn't busy,' he spat. 'He was with a woman. His new one – not that pathetic Parsons cow – even she didn't know about her. He boasted to me about it – boasted! He—'

Palliser stopped abruptly, and Slider said, 'Oh, it's all right, you haven't told me anything I didn't know. That's what you quarrelled about, wasn't it? You were furious that he'd let the boy down. He told you to mind your own business. You asked how he would make amends. He laughed and said one day was like another to Jamie, that the boy wouldn't notice whether he visited him or not. You were interrupted before the argument could go further. Later you went out of the room to get a little privacy to telephone Jamie, though you'd already phoned him earlier in the day, your usual birthday call – oh yes, the lady I spoke to at the home was most helpful. And you discovered that Jamie was very upset about the missed visit – she told me that, too.'

Palliser put his hands to his face and rubbed his eyes. He seemed almost dazed. 'You've been busy,' he said. 'You don't really need me to tell you anything. What did Caroline say?'

'That Jamie was Roger's child,' Slider said. 'That you had no reason to think otherwise.'

His face sharpened. 'There was reason,' he said quickly. Then he sighed. 'It was only the once. She was desperately unhappy and turned to me for comfort; but she never forgave herself, or me. It was the only time she was ever unfaithful to Roger. She's of the old school, and very strict with herself. Ironic, really, when you think what she married. But Jamie was the only child she ever had, and he was born nine months after our – our one time. What would you think?' Slider declined to answer. 'I don't care what Caroline says, Jamie's mine – and she knows it, though it doesn't suit her ideas to admit it, not even to me – perhaps not even to herself. He's mine – but for her sake I'd never say anything, or let the boy guess – of course I wouldn't. I'm just his Uncle Sandy,' he said bitterly, 'and that bastard Roger was Daddy. I'd have given him a home – Phyllis would have accepted him for my sake – but bastard Roger shut him up in an institution, and only spared him three visits a year – and even then only if it didn't interfere with his *pleasures*. I hope he rots in Hell!'

'Yes,' Slider said. 'It's no wonder you were angry. Especially after you found out how upset the boy was. I expect you wanted to kill him, didn't you?'

Palliser looked at him, and bared his teeth in what might have passed for a smile in a different culture. 'Oh no you don't! I'm not simple-minded. I can see where you're going, but it won't wash. Besides, I've got my alibi now, conveniently ferreted out by yourself: I was on the telephone. You've established that.'

Slider shook his head. 'The call was logged from seven-oh-three to seven-fifteen. That still left you time to find Greatrex and kill him, I'm afraid. Unless you want to tell me where you were after you rang off?'

'I – don't know. Not exactly. I walked about a bit. I was very upset, I needed time to compose myself.' He seemed suddenly to have come to a realisation of danger.

'Where did you walk?'

'Just – around. Along the corridors. I don't know exactly.'

'And did you see anyone? Did anyone see you?'

'I don't know. I don't remember.' The game had been abandoned, the pretences put aside. He looked at Slider helplessly. 'Are you going to arrest me?'

Slider let him wait for a long minute. Outside, the birds shouted in the tangled garden. He thought of Mrs Palliser's complex web of pain, of how much she must know and how much guess about her husband's obsessions; and he made it a good long minute. Then he said, 'No. But don't leave the country, will you?'

Palliser saw him out in a rather depressed silence. At the door, Slider said, 'When you told me you were not of your wife's religion – you're a Catholic, aren't you?'

'Why should you think that?'

'Oh, a guess. If Lord Chirnside is a devout Catholic but found you an acceptable companion for his children, it seems likely that you were one too.'

Palliser studied Slider's face, seeming almost puzzled. 'You're oddly perceptive for a policeman,' he said.

'We're not all Mr Plod, sir,' Slider said, parodying. Palliser was silent. 'Well, are you?'

'Lapsed,' he said tersely.

Philip Somers still lived with his parents, a little to Atherton's surprise, in a house in The Fairway in East Acton. The door was opened to him by a smart, pretty young thing of around twenty, framed by a narrow hallway with unforgivable wallpaper and a carpet which was obviously new and must therefore, hard though it was to believe, have been intentional. There was the sound of a wireless in the background and a level of voices and clashing crockery which suggested a large number of people somewhere inside; and the air was heavy with a complex of roast beef, roast potatoes, Bisto gravy and cabbage.

Atherton showed his ID and introduced himself. The girl smiled brightly, like a well-trained receptionist. 'Hakkun a hip yey?'

'I would like to speak to Philip Somers, if he's in. Would he be your brother?'

'That's right. I'm Mandy. I s'pose you'd better come in.' She turned her head to yell, 'Mu-u-um!' on three cadences, and then stepped back from the door and almost bowed. 'Do come in.'

Atherton advanced far enough to see through the first door a sitting-room crammed with furniture and knick-knacks, a brown cut moquette suite of early seventies vintage, another new carpet with swirls of brown and cream on a coffee background, and a television the size of a Fiat Uno dominating the corner beside the imitation York stone fireplace. A second door just beyond presumably led to the dining-room, for it was from there that the sounds of voices and clashing came, and straight ahead was a narrow kitchen, filled with steam and women.

One of them detached herself – a grey-haired woman in an apron, worn over a tight Sunday dress Atherton recognised as quintessentially Marks and Spencer – and approached him with polite enquiry. The fingers of her hands were thick as sausages and shiny with years of food preparation and housework; the features of her face were blunted and blurred with years of wife – and motherhood. Atherton adored her on sight.

'Mrs Somers?'

'That's right,' she said, the faintest hint of Irish in her voice almost eroded by time.

Atherton introduced himself. 'I'm awfully sorry, I'm afraid I've come at a bad time. You're just about to have dinner.'

'It'll be a half an hour yet,' she said. She scanned his face anxiously. 'Is it Phil you've come to see? He's not in trouble, is he?'

'I just want to ask him a few questions,' Atherton said soothingly.

She seemed reassured. 'Ah, well he's not back yet. He plays

football on a Sunday morning. He should be here any time, though. You're welcome to wait.'

'If I won't be in your way,' Atherton said humbly.

'Not at all. Come on in. Will you have a glass of sherry? Mandy, get that bottle of sherry out o' the sideboard, and one o' the best glasses. Come on in, Mr Attenborough. Everyone's in the back, now.'

The second room, to the rear of the house, was evidently not only the dining-room but the gathering place. There were french windows giving a glimpse of a tiny garden and the backs of all the houses round about, a large table in process of being laid, and a massive oak sideboard almost invisible under a drift of framed photographs and ornaments. On the wall above it was a highly-coloured framed print of a revoltingly anatomical Sacred Heart of Mary which might have come straight out of *Pathologist Weekly*. On the far side from the door a pair of splay-legged Contemp'ry armchairs flanked an electric fire. In one of them a small man in a clean shirt with no tie, and a shinily shaved chin, sat in his braces reading the *News of the World*. Two large young men with thick hair still damp from bathing and a thin one with glasses were crouched before a Roberts radio on the other side of the fire, and two handsome young women and a sulky girl of fifteen were laying what looked like a vast number of places at the table. It reminded Atherton of a scene out of *Bread*.

The one called Mandy reappeared with a tot-glass decorated with flamenco dancers, filled with brown syrup. 'There you go,' she informed him brightly. 'Would you like a bag of crisps, atawl?'

'Oh, no thanks,' Atherton said, and seeing many eyes on him, he bravely sipped the sherry and smiled and said, 'Very nice. Thank you.' The faces all beamed with accomplished hospitality and the eyes were removed.

'So, you'll have come about that dreadful business at the BBC, I suppose?' Mrs Somers said. 'Poor Phil's been in a narful state, though what he thinks he could have done about it I don't know. The man was already dead when he found him. And his clothes were ruined.' She folded her lips in disapproval. 'I threw the shirt and the undies away, though it was a wicked waste, but the trousers were nearly new. I've washed them three times, but I don't suppose they'll ever be good enough for best again. And all for that wicked man!'

'Mum,' Mandy said warningly.

'God rest his soul,' Mrs Somers added perfunctorily. 'I must get back to the kitchen, if you'll excuse me, Mr Attenborough. Make yourself at home, now.'

She hurried away, and Atherton turned to Mandy, who was idly picking at the edge of a raffia table mat, her eyes down either in boredom or discomfiture.

'Why does your mum think Roger Greatrex was a wicked man?'

'Oh, Mum thinks everyone outside the fam'ly's wicked. Permissive society and all that, you know. We're never allowed to do anything. Dad's as bad. They never even let me wear make-up until I was fifteen.'

'But you don't need it anyway,' Atherton said, and she brightened visibly at the compliment. For Atherton it was rather pleasant to be in a household that didn't view him as the enemy, that gave him sherry rather than spitting at him.

Mandy had evidently decided that tall and handsome was tall and handsome, whatever trousers it came in. 'It must be exciting being a detective?' she cooed, almost batting her eyelashes at him in her eagerness to please.

'Sometimes,' he said, and since he had to wait, he spent the next few minutes being agreeable to Mandy and playing her game. Only when he had downed the last of the execrable sherry and was trying to convince Mandy that he couldn't have any more because he was on duty did he hear the welcome sound of a key in the front door.

'Oh, that'll be Phil,' Mandy said brightly, and darted into the hall. Atherton followed her quickly, wanting the first look at the face when Somers saw him. He was looking thin and worn, though still red in the face from the game and the subsequent shower; he was carrying an Adidas bag, and listening distractedly to his sister as he tried to shut the door when, evidently before he had understood her words, he caught sight of Atherton standing in the passage. His face drained so suddenly that Atherton found he had moved instinctively forward to catch him in case he fell. Even Mandy noticed, and looked from her brother to the policeman in sudden apprehension.

'I just want to ask you a few questions,' Atherton said. 'In private, if that's all right.'

Somers seemed to pull himself together. 'You'd better come in the lounge,' he said; and seeing his sister's questioning look, added, 'It's all right, Mandy. Give this to Mum, will you,' pushing his bag at her. 'I won't be long.'

The part of the sitting-room Atherton had not seen from the door was a wall covered in framed family photographs; and in the far left-hand corner beside the window, on a little table, the largest photo of all, in a silver frame, of a pretty girl of about seventeen, with a vase of flowers beside it. Somers sat down on the edge of the seat of the large brown sofa, so Atherton sat at the other end, facing him.

'I'm afraid I've crashed in on a special occasion,' Atherton began. 'You seem to have all your family here.'

'It's just Sunday dinner,' Somers answered automatically. He seemed a little dazed.

'It must be lovely to be part of a big family. How many of you are there?' Atherton asked pleasantly.

'Well, there's me and Kevin, Eileen, Denise, Mandy and Katy at home, and Patrick and Sheila are married, but they come every Sunday with their husband and wife.' The line of questioning seemed to soothe him, and he volunteered, 'Mum moans a bit that she hasn't got any grandchildren, and she goes on at us to get married, but she likes having us at home really. She'd hate it if we all left and she didn't have anyone to fuss over and cook for.'

Eight people living in this tiny house, Atherton thought, which could hardly have more than three bedrooms. For an instant he tried to imagine the bathroom rota in the morning, and then desisted.

'It must be a lot of work for her,' he said. 'Nice to have company, of course, but I suppose you must all get on each other's nerves sometimes.'

'Not really,' Somers said, looking wary now. 'We're used to it.'

'Still, tensions build up, don't they, even in the happiest families?'

'Look, what is it you want to ask me?' Somers said abruptly. 'Mum'll be dishing up soon.'

'Yes, I wouldn't like to keep your mum waiting,' Atherton said. 'All this must have been a shock for her.'

'All what?'

'Roger Greatrex being murdered. She knew him, didn't she?'

'Of course she didn't. Why should she?' But the eyes were watchful.

'Well, she just described him to me as "that wicked man", which doesn't sound like the judgement of a complete stranger.'

'Everyone knew about his reputation as a womaniser,' Somers said, fairly fluently. 'She doesn't approve of that sort of thing.'

'Is that what you had against him? That he was a womaniser?'

Somers almost answered and then caught himself back. 'Why should you think I had anything against him?'

Atherton felt it was time to lean a little. 'Oh, come on, Mr Somers, don't waste my time. You hated him. You were violently against having him on the show. You told Fiona Parsons you wouldn't have him on the same planet if you could help it – and now your wish has come true. I'd just like to know why you hated him. It's hard for me to believe it was just a general dislike of a man who slept around a bit.'

Somer's lips were compressed with fury. 'A bit!' escaped him before he could clamp them down.

'So why didn't you want him on the show?' Atherton pushed when no more was forthcoming.

'I didn't think it was a good idea. He and Sandal didn't get on. I didn't want there to be a row. We are a live show, you know.'

'But controversy is the life breath of a live show, surely? What better than to have a genuine argument on air? Lift your ratings no end.'

'You don't know what you're talking about,' Somers said scornfully.

'All right, then,' Atherton said, 'tell me instead why you went through Roger Greatrex's pockets – once he was dead, that is.' Somers stared, as if trying to gauge how much he knew. Atherton smiled unlovingly. 'It might save time all round if I tell you that we've found your fingerprints on Roger's wallet, so it would be a waste of breath to deny it. Fingerprints in his blood, I should add. Now I'm sure you weren't after his money, so what did you take out of there?'

'Nothing. I didn't. I don't know what you're talking about,' Somers gabbled.

'Whatever it was you took out of his wallet, I think it was something you knew was there. You didn't go through his other pockets, after all. And whatever it was, if it was important enough for you to take it from his dead body, it was probably what you killed him for.'

Somers groaned and leaned forward, clutching his stomach, his face so white that Atherton moved his feet back sharply.

'Come on, Mr Somers, much better get it off your chest,' he said, though it wasn't his chest that looked the likeliest candidate at the moment. 'Tell me everything, clear your conscience. You know we'll find out in the end. Why did you kill him? By all accounts he was a bit of a bastard anyway, no great loss to humanity. Why did you do it?'

'I didn't,' Somers moaned. 'I didn't kill him. I wish to God I had, but I didn't.'

'What had he done?' Atherton coaxed. But Somers shook his head, still hugging himself and rocking. 'You'd better tell me. You're only making it worse for yourself.'

The door opened at that moment, and Mandy looked in. 'Mum says—' She broke off, staring at her brother in concern, and then at Atherton. 'What's going on? What've you done to him? Did you hit him?'

Atherton stood up, exasperated. He'd get nothing out of him now. 'I'm afraid your brother doesn't feel very well. I think I'd better go. I'll call again some other time and talk to you, Mr Somers,' he added, 'unless you change your mind and want to talk to me. You know where to reach me if you do.'

Mandy saw him to the door in a half-resentful silence. As Atherton stepped out into the open air, she said, 'I don't know what all this is about, but Phil hasn't done anything. He wouldn't. He'd never do anything that might upset Mum.'

'Say goodbye to your mother for me, will you? And thank you,' said Atherton.

CHAPTER NINE

The Wife of Acton's Tale

'Hello! What are you doing here?'

'There's a nice greeting. Aren't you glad to see me?'

'I didn't say I wasn't.'

'That's all right then,' Joanna said. 'I got bored on my own, that's all. I thought I'd come and see if you were going to have lunch. How did it go this morning?'

Slider told her. 'What a sad story,' she said. 'Do you think he really believes it's his kid?'

'I'm sure he does, at least on one level,' Slider said. 'But people can easily believe several conflicting things at the same time – though you can't say that in court. In court you've got to present a nice, simple world where everything's black or white and people behave consistently. Fortunately,' he backed out from the cave of gloom opening before him, 'juries are amazingly sensible on the whole. They generally get it right, whatever antics counsel get up to. It's the one great argument for the jury system.'

'And do you think Sandal Palliser is your man?'

'I'm not sure,' Slider frowned. 'I hoped when I got on the trail of the telephone call that I'd be able to put him out of the frame, but I can't, entirely. He still had time to do it, and a better motive you couldn't want. Real, world-class resentment—'

He was interrupted by Atherton's arrival. 'I've just been comprehensively tortured by the smell of the Traditional English Sunday Lunch. Anybody ready for a bite?'

'We can get a sandwich upstairs if you like,' Slider suggested, more to Joanna than his partner. 'How did you get on with Somers? Get anything?'

'*Nada*. But he's definitely on the run now – gasping at the surface like a holed fish. I think he'll break soon. And there was an atmosphere of tension in the house. I think the mother knows something, or suspects something, at least. She mentioned Greatrex in uncomplimentary terms and then frightened herself and ran away. But what a household,' he added happily, and described it to them. 'In other circumstances it would give you renewed faith in society – a whole family living together and keeping up the traditions.'

Slider told him about his morning, and Atherton brightened. 'Maybe Palliser's our man after all. I'd sooner it was him than Somers. Somehow I can't see Somers cutting Greatrex's throat in that determined way. He'd have hacked about and made a mess of it.'

'Those quiet ones can be the most determined when they screw themselves to the sticking point,' Slider said.

'He couldn't screw himself to the wall. No, it's Palliser for me,' Atherton said cheerfully. 'Mystic Meg has spoken. I see a tall man with a warped mind – oh no, that's the mirror.'

Slider wasn't listening. 'But what did Somers go into Greatrex's pocket for?' he said with a dissatisfied frown. 'I wish you'd found that out. All we can do in a case like this is—'

'Clear as we go,' Atherton finished in chorus with him, and grinned at Joanna.

'Do I really say that a lot?' Slider asked.

'It's just a phrase you're going through,' Atherton said soothingly. 'What about that sandwich?'

But the phone rang from the front shop. 'Excuse me, sir, there's someone here who wants to talk to whoever's in charge of the Greatrex case. Says she's got some information, won't give it to anyone but the top man.'

Slider relayed this to Atherton. 'Don't tell me we've got a witness at last?'

'We can but pray,' said Atherton.

Joanna stood up. 'I'll go and leave you to it. Where are we eating tonight?'

'You notice she doesn't ask when,' Atherton said. 'You've got her trained.'

'I'll give you a ring before I leave,' Slider promised, and she stepped aside and let him pass, seeing his mind had already gone ahead of him, and she was forgotten.

* * *

As they passed through the charge room Nicholls, who had just come on and was still in his anorak, making tea, put out a hand to stop him.

'Oh, Bill, just a minute. That guy we were talking about – it's just come to me, where I knew him from.'

'Philip Somers?'

'That's right. Though strictly speaking, it wasn't him I remembered, it was his sister.'

'You'll have to do better than that,' Atherton said with a grin. 'I was round his house this morning, and they come in six-packs.'

'Is that a fact? Well, her name'll come to me in a minute. Anyway, the Somers business – it was about eight, nine years ago – you can check it out with the Thames Valley records. It was while I was at Maidenhead. Oh yes, Madeleine! That was her name. Madeleine Somers. She was about seventeen, bright, pretty girl.'

'I asked Somers about his family, and he didn't mention a sister Madeleine,' Atherton said.

'I imagine not,' Nicholls said. 'Sister Madeleine was going out with Roger Greatrex.'

'What!'

'S'right,' Nicholls nodded. 'I don't know all the details of the affair, but one night Greatrex was driving her back from a hotel in Bray where they'd been making the beast with two backs, and they were involved in an RTA. He wasn't hurt, just cuts and bruises, but she went into the windscreen, suffered head injuries, and died a couple of hours later in hospital.'

'The photograph!' Atherton said. 'I should have realised the significance: there was one photograph on its own on a table with flowers. Pretty girl of about seventeen.'

'The memorial corner,' Nicholls nodded. 'Nice old-fashioned custom. They do it in my part of the world.'

'The mother's Irish,' said Atherton.

'But what about Philip Somers?' Slider said impatiently. 'What was your contact with him?'

'I remember him from the inquest,' Nicholls said. 'I had to give evidence, seeing I was on traffic patrol at the time and I was one of the first on the scene. Anyway, your man Somers maintained Greatrex was to blame for the accident, made quite a scene in the coroner's court. Said he'd been drinking – well, he undoubtedly had been, but we breathalysed him on the spot and he was below the limit, and there was a lot of black ice about that night, so nothing came of it. It went down as accidental death and that was that.'

'Was it, indeed?' Slider mused.

'So it seemed. But it occurs to me that people are much less forgiving these days than they used to be. There's no such thing as an accident any more. We're all encouraged to think someone must be to blame.'

'And some of us don't need much encouraging,' Atherton said. 'There's the motive, hot and strong! And we know Somers still resented Greatrex, because he tried to keep him off the programme.'

Nicholls watched the two of them with intelligent interest. 'Well, make of it what you will. It'll be in the records, as I said, though there wasn't a big splash in the papers as you'd expect. I think Greatrex must have had friends in high journalistic places, and used his influence to play it down.'

'Did the rest of the family share Somers's view?'

'I dunno, Bill. I only saw the mother in court, and she kept quiet. It was Somers who did the shouting. I think they'd been particularly close, as I remember.'

'Well, thanks, Nutty. That's a great help,' Slider said.

'N't'all. By the way, you did know there's a customer in the shop for you?'

'That's where I was going. Better not keep her waiting any longer.'

The customer was a stout, motherly woman in a cheap coat and even cheaper perfume, whose fantastically wrinkled face was explained by the equally fantastic nicotine stains on her fingers and the yellow streak across the front of her grey hair. She was sitting with a suffering expression under one of the No Smoking signs, and stood up as Slider approached.

'You the boss?' Slider introduced himself and Atherton. 'Gor blimey, you don't half make it hard for us smokers these days. I'm gasping for a fag. Can we go somewhere I can get one on, 'fore I passes out? You a smoker, dear?'

'I'm afraid not. But there's an interview room over here we can use. You've got something to tell me, I understand.'

'About that murder at the BBC,' she said. 'Well, I did see something, dunno if it's important.' She slid her eyes about. 'Don't want to make a song and dance about it, dear. Walls have ears, y'know.'

Slider nodded wisely and led the way to the small interview room. The woman fumbled in her bulging handbag, lit up, and sucked on the burning stick with an almost sexual ecstasy. 'Aaah, that's better!' she sighed like a genial dragon, smoke billowing from her nose and mouth and, Atherton fantasised, her ears too. 'Gor, I thought I'd had it, waiting all that time without so much as a puff. I dunno what the times are coming to, when a respectable woman can't even light up in her own local p'lice station.'

'I'm afraid it's all to do with the insurance company,' Slider lied gently, 'Mrs—?'

'Dorothy Edna Reynolds, 19D Mandela House, South Acton,' she supplied smartly. 'But that's between you, me, him, and the furnicher, all right? I didn't like the look of that bloke, and I don't want him coming round my house, supposing he *is* the one.'

Slider's soul thrilled to her words. An orchestra entirely composed of strings struck up somewhere. 'You saw somebody you think was connected with the murder?'

'Blimey, yes, what d'you think I come here for?' She sucked again, wriggled herself comfortable, and began. 'Thursday night, right? I come on six o'clock – six till eight, I do.'

'Do?'

'Cleaning. Just the offices and the lavs. Corridors is done by a contract firm during the night. Don't ask me what happens to the stoojos. Anyway,' she gathered her audience's attention in a thoroughly professional way, ''bout quarter past seven time, going on har past, I finish floor five and come down the stairs with me box to do four.'

'What staircase?'

She looked approval at the question. 'Well, it was number five, wannit?' she answered rhetorically. 'That's the one right next door to where it all happened, which is what made me think. Not at the time, see, because I didn't know nothing about it at the time, but after.'

'Quite,' Slider said encouragingly.

'All right, so I come out the swing doors on four, and there's this bloke just come out the gents next door and stood in front of the lift.'

'Did you actually see him come out of the gents?' Atherton asked.

'Well,' she looked bothered and fortified herself with another suck of smoke, 'I been thinking about that, and I can't honestly say if I axshully *seen* him come out, but I know in me mind that's where he come from.' Her brow furrowed, sending fault lines of wrinkles racing in all directions. She seemed genuinely puzzled by her own inability to be sure on the point.

Slider said, 'Maybe you saw the door just closing. Those doors with the hydraulic hinge on the back do close very slowly.'

He expected her to leap at the explanation, but she didn't, only went on puzzling and puffing. 'I dunno,' she said at last. 'I dunno why I know, but if you'd asked me right then where he come from, I'd've said the gents, certain as I live.'

'All right,' Slider said, 'never mind that now. What did the man do?'

'Well, he stopped at the lift and pressed the button.'

'Up or down?' Atherton put in.

She shook her head. 'I dunno. I think, down, but I can't be sure. I mean, it was on'y just a second I looked at him as I come out through the swing doors, because I turned the other way, see, to start with the offices down that end—'

'You turned right out of the swing doors?'

'Yeah, that's right. But I looked at him and he looked at me, and that's what sort of burned on me memory, otherwise I wun't have thought twice about it. Because he looked at me, right into me eyes, and he looked—' she paused again, rummaging through her memory or her vocabulary, or both, for the right description.

'Afraid? Anxious? Startled?' Atherton offered when the pause lengthened. She made a distracted movement of her hand and Slider stilled Atherton with a glance. This was a good witness. She knew what she knew.

At last she shook her head. 'I can't describe it. But it wasn't a nordin'ry look. That's what took me attention, see?'

'So he rang for the lift, and looked at you, and then you turned and went away – and that's the last time you saw him?' She nodded. 'Can you describe him to me?'

She fixed her eyes on the wall, the better to rifle her memory. 'He was medium height,' she said at last. Atherton converted a snort into a slight cough, and she glanced at him. 'Not so tall as *you*, and not so short as *you*,' she said indignantly. 'What would you call that, if it's not medium?'

'Thin? Fat?' Slider prompted.

'He was what I'd call a big man,' she said thoughtfully. 'Not fat, really, but, like, well-fed. Meaty. He looked strong. And he was really dark, with one o' them blue chins, and black hair and dark eyes. Sinister, I'd call 'em. And a beauty spot on his cheek, here.' She pressed the inner curve of her cheek just beside and below the corner of her left nostril.

Slider could feel Atherton seething with disbelief beside him as this Boy's Own description reeled out, but he knew a good witness when he met one. 'Age?' he asked.

''Bout fortyish. Give or take.' She grinned lasciviously at Slider. ''Bout your age. My fav'rite.'

'How was he dressed?'

'Oh, just in a suit an' tie. But he was carrying a bag, one o' them nylon bags, what d'you call 'em, flight bags, is it? Like with a shoulder strap, only he was holding it by the handles. Blue, it was, just plain blue.'

'Did it look full? Did he carry it as if it was heavy?'

She seemed distracted by the question. 'I dunno. He was just holding it, down by his side. I didn't notice it, except it was there.'

Slider could feel that Atherton was longing to ask questions, but was too good a subordinate to ignore the silencing look he had been given. 'Did you see anyone else in the corridor at the time?' Slider asked.

'No, there was no-one around. I never see anyone going either way. I went straight down to the office at the end of the corridor and went in and started cleaning, and I never see anyone at all until about a half-hour later when I got nearly up to stairway six and found the whole place roped off and a copper standing there like he was stopping the traffic. So I says what's going on, and he says never you mind, there's nothing to see, and you can't come this way, so I says, it don't matter to me, I can go the other way, and I do, and that's that, because it was my time to knock off anyway. Six till eight I do.'

'Can you pin down the time any closer for me, the time you saw the man by the lift?'

'Well,' she said regretfully, 'I didn't look at me watch right after, but it's got to've been between quarter and twenty past, 'cause it was coming up to quarter past when I finished the gents next to stairway six on five, and I'd only just walked along to stairway five and down two flights.'

'Why didn't you use stairway six?' Atherton asked, unable to restrain himself any longer. 'Why walk back?'

'Because stairway six and seven was full of the aujence for *Questions of Our Time* going up to the canteen,' she said with just a hint of triumph. 'I wasn't up to pushing me way through that little lot.'

There was a pause while Slider digested all this; and then he said at last, 'So, this man you saw rang for the lift and looked at you, and you went away. Now what made you think he had anything to do with the murder?'

'Well, because of coming out of the gents where the poor bloke was topped,' she said.

'But you didn't actually *see* him come out of there?'

'Not to say, *see* him,' she said reluctantly, 'but I'm sure in me own mind that's where he come from.'

'And that's all?'

'And the look he give me. I wouldn't want to meet *him* again in a dark alley.'

'And that's all?'

'And the blood,' she said, as though affirming something already agreed.

'Blood?' Atherton exploded, unable to prevent himself.

She looked reproachful. 'I was just coming to that, if you'd a give me half a chance. See, when he put his hand out to press the button, his sleeve like kind of pulled back and I see his hairy wrist an' his wristwatch and the end of his cuff, and he had blood on it, on his cuff. Not a lot, but it was red, so it must've been fresh, mustn't it? And I thought at the time he'd cut himself shaving—'

'At that time of night?' Atherton protested.

'With his sort of beard he'd have to shave more'n once a day,' she told him scornfully. 'You thank your lucky stars you're nice an fair, my lad. My first 'usband had that sort of beard – wicked on the razors, it was. Three I've had, counting this present one – buried two of 'em – and five sons, one of which was a sailor, so I know a bit about beards. And my first – he was one o' them blue-chin ones. If we went out of an evening, up west dancing or down the dogs or anything, he had to shave again afore we went, and by the time we got home and went to bed he was like a coconut mat again. You could've sanded down doors with his chin. Now my boy Reggie—'

'Did you see blood anywhere else?' Slider asked, drawing her back from this primrose path.

'No-o,' she said reluctantly. 'That's all I see. I didn't see no cuts on his face, anyway.'

'So why has it taken you so long to come forward?' Slider asked, but still gently. He didn't want to rouse her resentment.

'Well, I never thought of it,' she said. 'It went straight out of me head, and it was only yesterday when I went in to work I found out it was *that* lav that the poor gent was killed in. So that was what made me think of it then, and the blood an all.' She looked at Slider wide-eyed for once. 'D'you think that was him, the murderer?'

'It's possible,' he said cautiously.

She gave a shudder. 'Fancy, I was that close to him,' she said. 'I lived in St Mark's Road when the Christie murders was going on, and my mother reckoned she'd stood at the same bus stop with him. She said he had 'orrible eyes, like a dead cod. And now I've met another one. It's like fate, innit?'

'The most important thing, Mrs Reynolds, is, do you think you could recognise him again?'

'What?' she said derisively. 'Printed on my brain, he is! I'd know him anywhere.'

'And you'd be willing to come in again and look at an identity parade for me, if necessary?'

'Oh, I'd do that all right,' she said, 'but I want your word that my name'll be kept private. I don't want it all in the papers that I'm the key witness or nothing. Because you haven't caught him yet, have you?' She looked from one to the other and did not require an answer. 'That's what I thought. See, I don't want my life being at risk, if this bloke finds out

I'm the only person what can pick him out. I want witness protection.'

The effects of watching too much television, Slider thought. 'I can assure you that if protection is needed, you'll get it,' he said. 'And for the moment, there's no need for anyone but us to know your name. But you mustn't tell anyone about this either, you know. That's the way these things usually get about. A witness tells a friend in confidence, and the friend tells another friend, and so on.'

'I'm not a fool,' she said briskly. 'I haven't told no-one any of this – not even your bloke at the desk,' she added with a flick of her head. 'I know how to keep my mouth shut. Careless talk costs lives – and it's my life we're talking about.'

'It won't come to that,' Slider said. 'I'm sure you won't be in any danger, even if this does turn out to be the man we're looking for.'

'You didn't see him,' she snorted. 'He looked capable of anythink to me.'

'Well, what do you think?' Slider asked Atherton.

'I think it's a load of old Tottenham,' he said robustly. 'You heard what she said about her mum standing at the bus stop with Reg Christie. She's a sensation-seeker, wants to be important, so she invents a sinister-looking man at the scene of the murder covered in blood and giving her threatening looks.'

'Hmm,' said Slider. 'Well, she didn't say covered in blood, did she? Just a little bit on his cuff.'

'You believed her,' Atherton discovered.

Slider paused. What he thought was that sometimes in this game all you had to go on to decide between what mattered and what didn't was a policeman's instinct; and something in his scalp had prickled when Mrs Reynolds started talking. If she was genuine, even following what he had come to think of as the Honeyman theory, the Man by the Lift, if he had come out of the gents, might at least be able to help pin down the time a bit more accurately and would therefore qualify for following up and tracking down.

What he said was, 'If she had been attention-seeking, she might well have said he was covered in blood. And if she was attention-seeking she'd have surely said that she *saw* him come out of the gents loo.'

'And that's what convinces you? That she hasn't told us anything useful?'

'I think she's telling the truth, and I think she's an observant person and not given to embroidery. It doesn't mean to say the man she saw was our man, of course.'

'Her description doesn't sound like Somers,' Atherton complained. 'And we'd just got him the perfect, hand-cut crystal motive.'

'It doesn't sound like Palliser either.'

'Maybe it was Parsons,' Atherton said recovering his sense of proportion.

'She didn't see anyone else in the corridor, so she must have come down the stairs before Somers discovered the body, or he'd have been standing at the door. So if the man she saw *had* come out of the loo, either he was the murderer, or—'

'Or he wasn't,' Atherton finished with grim humour. 'The trouble has always been that we haven't any exact times.'

'What we have got now,' Slider said, 'is the bag to look for.'

'You think the bag's important?'

Slider grinned suddenly. 'Me? Think? In this case? I think either the bag's been dumped somewhere near the scene—'

'Or it hasn't. God help us, what a case! When this is over it'll be hols all round at the Latex Hilton. Still, we've got something to work on with Somers, at least. Shall I go back and confront him, guv, see if he breaks down and confesses?'

'No, not today,' Slider said. 'I want to get the full report on his sister and Greatrex before we go any further with him. It's always best to lead from strength.'

'I thought you didn't know anything about bridge.'

'I can't help knowing the language, can I? Anyway, it won't do any harm to let Somers stew for a bit. You can go and roust him tomorrow morning, if the report's come through.'

'Thanks. So what now?'

'What now? Food, rest, recreation. Remember those?'

'All right for you, you've got a woman to go back to,' Atherton complained.

'You can come too.'

'Thanks, but won't you want to be alone?'

'Oh, no, it's all right. We did all that last night – the reunion, the heartsearching, the confessions, the forgiveness—'

'Stop it, you're getting me excited. What confessions?'

'I had a fit of jealousy to explain and get over,' Slider said.

'Oh,' said Atherton wisely, 'she told you about it, then? Sue seemed to think she wouldn't. We had quite a discussion about whether it was best to tell or keep silent.'

'Tell? Told me what?' Slider said.

'About this old flame of hers turning up.' Atherton looked at him. 'Wasn't that what you meant? Oh, sorry, I don't mean to pry.'

'What old flame?'

'Oh, blimey, guv, me and my big mouth! Have I gone and put my foot in it?'

'Stop clowning. What old flame?'

Atherton looked serious. 'Look, there's nothing to tell. It's some bloke she had a do with years and years ago turned up at the orchestra as a substitute for someone who was sick. That's all. End of story. She didn't know he was coming. Hasn't had any contact with him in years. Sue was just debating with me whether it would be better for Joanna to tell you he'd been there, and risk your feeling jealous over nothing, or not tell you and risk your finding out later and thinking there was something to be jealous about simply because she hadn't told you. And now,' he added, striking his brow, 'I've gone and given her the worst of both worlds.'

Slider pulled himself together. 'No you haven't. Don't be so dramatic. There's nothing to tell, as you so rightly said. So are you coming back with me to Joanna's?'

Atherton hesitated, wondering whether he would really be welcome. 'I'm not finished,' he said.

'Then I'll disregard the rumours,' Slider said kindly. 'Come on, make your mind up, I've got to phone her.'

'Well, if I really won't be *de trop*.'

CHAPTER TEN

Into Each Wine, a Little Leaf Must Fall

'By the way, did you hear the news?' Joanna said. 'Laurence Jepp was attacked in his home last night and killed.'

'Laurence Jepp?' Slider said. The name sounded vaguely familiar.

'Singer,' Atherton supplied, dabbling his last chip in the salty vinegar which had accumulated at the bottom of the bag. A sudden longing had overcome Joanna for fish and chips, and Slider had gone along with it on condition that they ate them out of the paper, anything else being a spineless compromise.

'He sang Leporello in our *Don Giovanni,*' said Joanna. 'It's terrible. I can't believe he's dead – I was standing just behind him in the coffee queue in the Courtyard only last week.'

This sounded uncomfortably like Mrs Reynolds. Slider said, 'It's always a shock when it's someone you know.'

'Well, I knew him to say hello to, that's all,' Joanna said, reaching for a sense of proportion. 'Its a good job the *Don*'s finished now. He was a terrific Leporello, and the understudy was very weak.'

'I saw his *Pagliacci,*' Atherton said. 'It's a sad loss to music.'

'Was he married?' Slider asked.

'Apparently not. He lived alone, anyway – in Ealing. They showed it on the news – one of those big houses on the Green. Really enormous. I expect he only had a flat in it, though. I can't believe he was that rich – I mean, not in the Pavarotti class. None of the English singers are.'

'What happened?' Atherton asked.

'They didn't say much. Someone broke into his house while he was asleep. A burglar, I suppose. Apparently he had a panic button beside his bed and he must have pressed it before he got clobbered, because the alarm went off and the police were there within minutes, but it was too late.' She leaned over to top up the glasses with hock. 'It's a bummer, isn't it? Poor old Larry.'

'As you say, it's a good job the *Don* is finished,' Atherton said lightly. 'Jepp wasn't in anything else, was he?'

'Not that I know of, but I'm only in *Traviata* now.'

'Who's singing Violetta?'

'Sonia Morgenstern,' Joanna said, and Atherton made a face. 'Well, all right, she's a bit ripe and fruity—'

'I wouldn't mind that, but she's got so much vibrato she never gets within a tone of the note she's aiming at. And her coloratura—'

'I thought that was wallpaper,' Slider complained.

'No, that's Coloroll,' Atherton corrected. 'But you weren't far off. They're both decoration—'

'Yes, thank you, I don't want a music lesson,' Slider interrupted. 'Can we talk about something else? I'm up to my navel in culture these days.'

'You're the boss,' Atherton shrugged. 'Who d'you fancy for the cup, then, sir? Booked anywhere for your holidays?'

'Did you read that story in the newspaper the other day,' Joanna said, 'about the girl who worked in the unisex hairdressers? She was clipping round the back of this middle-aged bloke's neck when she saw his hand going up and down under the cape, so she thought that's enough of that nonsense and whacked him quite hard on the head with the clippers. And it turned out he had his glasses under there and was cleaning them on his tie.'

They sat late in Joanna's garden, drinking wine under the terminally blighted oak tree that took up most of the space, listening to the sounds of the evening and talking. When the wine was finished and Atherton had gone, ranging out into the night like a lean cat with the flattest of eyes and demurest of goodbyes, Joanna returned to Slider and gave him a brooding and not entirely friendly look.

'What was all that about, then?' she asked.

'What was *what* about?'

'Don't be tiresome. I'm talking about your performance tonight.'

'My performance?'

'Snapping at everyone. Making sarky remarks about opera and music. Playing the poor beleaguered Essex Man surrounded by pretentious Islingtonites.'

Slider stared in amazement. 'I didn't. I wasn't. I was a bit surprised by your performance, though – since you coined the word.'

'I didn't coin it, I only used it. Please try to be accurate. I thought it was part of your job.'

'You're doing it again, you see.'

'Doing what again?'

'Making pointed remarks about my job. It doesn't matter so much about sneering at me, but Atherton's a policeman too, you know.'

'Leave Atherton out of this—'

'I'd love to, but it was me who was being left out by you two, yakking on and on about music. It was perfectly obvious which of us you found the better company—'

'And I was right, wasn't I? The way you've been behaving tonight, you weren't fit company for anyone.'

'You should have stuck with him while you had the chance, then.'

'And what's that supposed to mean?'

'Work it out for yourself!'

'Oh, we're back to that are we? I thought we'd come to it sooner or later. It never fails – as soon as a man thinks he's got you, he starts throwing your past in your face, complaining that you weren't a virgin when he met you. You're such hypocrites, all of you!'

Slider opened his mouth to snap at her, and then shut it again as the echoes of the last few exchanges came back to him. 'What are we doing?' he said at last, appalled. 'This isn't us.'

'Why should we be different from anyone else?' she said grimly, but the heat had gone out of her, too. She looked at him for a long moment, while the grimness slowly gave way to wryness. 'You want to tell me about it?'

'About what?' he said defiantly.

'About what's wrong,' she said, and seeing the denial in his face said, 'I take back everything I said up to this point. But there is something wrong, isn't there?'

'Not with you, with me,' he said unwillingly.

'Is it the case?'

'Oh—! No, not directly.'

'What, then?'

He sat down abruptly, and she sat too, facing him across a little strip of carpet that seemed suddenly as daunting as the Mojave Desert. He licked his lips nervously. As an until-recently married man, he wasn't used to this talking to each other business. Better, though, as he was always telling reluctant criminals, to have it out in the open. 'Atherton told me that – that there was an old flame of yours down at Glyndebourne.'

A faint smile. 'What lovely language. An old flame.' But that was all she said.

'Well, was there?' Slider asked after a minute, feeling foolish, truculent and insecure in about equal proportions.

'Little tattle-tail, isn't he?' she said without affection. 'What business is it of his, I'd like to know? Well, since you ask, a person I knew a long time ago and haven't seen for years turned up, called in as a sub in the orchestra, that's all.'

'A person you knew,' he repeated. 'More than knew, surely?'

She looked at him with some deep unwillingness, but what it related to he couldn't be quite sure. 'I used to live with him.'

Damn, Slider thought; though he had feared as much. 'And?'

'And what?'

'Why didn't you tell me about him before?'

'I don't have to discuss my past with you. I don't ask you about yours.'

'I haven't got any,' he said bitterly.

'That's beside the point—'

'It is the point. You aren't going to spend your life tripping over people I've been to bed with.'

'Oh—!' She got to her feet in a movement of frustration and suppressed rage, walked a few steps, and turned back to him, her fists clenched with the effort of keeping her temper and being reasonable. 'The past is past. It's gone and dead and over, and it's none of your business anyway. What happened to me before I met you is *mine* and you can't have it – not because I won't give it to you,' she hurried on, 'but because there's no way you can possess it. So just leave it alone, or you'll destroy what we have.'

'What about when it isn't over and dead? When it gets up and walks back in?'

'I'll tell you when it does.'

'You didn't tell me about this bloke being at Glyndebourne.'

'There wasn't anything to tell. I can't control who gets booked to play at the same dates as me.' She met his eyes steadily. 'You've got to trust me, Bill. We're going nowhere if you don't trust me.'

He knew that was true, but he had been stinging for days. 'It isn't a matter of trust. I do trust you – but I can't help feeling jealous.'

'You've *got* to help it. Do I spend all day fretting over what you might be up to? Do I worry about the gorgeous women you might be meeting every day who are just cra-a-azy over policemen, in or out of uniform, and who'd do anything for a little squint at your truncheon?'

'What about Irene?' he said.

'That's different,' she said after a moment. 'She's not out of your life.'

He stood up and stepped towards her, but something in her face stopped him touching her. 'Why didn't you tell me about this bloke?'

'There's nothing to tell,' she said wearily. 'He turned up, that's all.'

'But you went for a drink with him. He was there in the Trevor when you phoned me.' This was a guess, but an easy one.

'Everybody goes to the Trevor,' she said. His heart sank at this confirmation. He'd rather hoped the bloke went somewhere else.

'What's his name?' he asked, almost against his will.

'You don't want to know his name,' she said, and her eyes were suddenly humorous.

He resisted her. 'I do. What's his name?'

'Andrew,' she said.

She was right. He didn't want to know it. He felt a bit sick. He began to turn away, and now she moved, grabbed his hand, pulled him back.

'Nothing happened,' she said. She lifted his hand, kissed it, put it to her head. 'Not even in here.'

By its own will his hand cupped round the side of her skull, fingers in her short, rough hair.

'I love you,' she said. She was always generous, always made the first move. He drew her against him, held her head against his cheek. It was like coming home, the touch of her body. It was something he couldn't do without. He sighed. 'Into each life a little rain must fall,' she said. 'It's hell, isn't it – jealousy?'

'Now I know how Irene used to feel,' he said. He was aware immediately he said it that he should not have introduced another name at that particular moment, but he couldn't take it back once it was out, so instead he said, 'I love you, too.'

'Let's go to bed, then,' she said, and it seemed to him like an excellent idea.

There was nothing like an emotional scene before bedtime for making you wake up early. Slider woke feeling unrested to the sound of the dawn chorus. Joanna's bed, in any case, had been old when he met her, and was beginning to sport the scars of vigorous usage. There was a spring which caught him just under one hip. They ought to buy a new one, but he didn't know how to approach the subject, given that they had never actually discussed their future together, and he had never officially moved in to her flat. It had been merely diffidence on his part – or so he had thought until last night. Now he realised that however much they loved each other, they were both nervous about making so serious a commitment as to mention aloud what Palliser had called the M-word. In these post-feminist, modern times, it had become the love that dared not speak its name. Suppose he asked her and she refused? It was one thing to live with her like this, unmarried and undeclared, face not merely saved but never even staked; but to live with her unmarried after they had spoken of a permanent attachment would not do. He would always wonder what her reservations were, whether he had failed to measure up in some way, or whether she was holding back in the hope that someone better might come along. Besides, there were his children to think of, and the example he set them. Sooner or later, if he and Joanna stayed together, they would have to meet her, and he didn't want them thinking of her as 'Daddy's girlfriend', with all the tacky connotations of the phrase.

If they stayed together? What was he thinking? There could not be a question about it – could there? He pushed himself up on one elbow to look down at her, still sleeping and curled on her side with her hands under her cheek Shirley Temple-style. She looked so complete, as people sleeping often do, that he felt shut out from her. After all, she had managed without him all these years – without anyone. She had her own career, money, establishment, interests and friends: what could she need him for? He thought back to their first weeks together, and the time he had taken her to visit his father. She had said that a woman on her own for long enough became a sort of stray dog – a man might play with it in the park, but would never think of taking it home. And he saw that it was true. That completeness of hers might not be something she liked or enjoyed, might not be what she wanted, but it existed none the less. He had no idea what either of them could do about it.

To avoid thinking about these imponderables, he thought about the case, and immediately experienced a rush of blood to the head that had him out of bed. He went into the sitting-room to use the phone there so as not to wake her.

The leather of the chesterfield was chilly to his bare behind. He rested his elbows on his knees and looked down with detached curiosity at his own feet, legs and dangly bits. God's supreme joke; His way of cutting Man down to size. There was nothing laughable about the back end of a horse or even a dog, but the human male's wedding tackle was essentially ridiculous.

Fergus answered. 'What are you doing up so early?'

'Contemplating my navel,' Slider said. 'The feminists are right, y'know. If God was a man, He'd never have put the balls on the outside.'

'Izzat what you woke me up for, to tell me that?'

'I thought you'd like to know.'

'You're tryin' to think on an empty stomach, that's what's wrong wit you. A plate o' bacon an' eggs'll get your brain functioning right,' O'Flaherty said wisely. 'What *do* you want, anyway?'

'Is anyone from my team in?'

'I got Mackay standing beside me this very minute. Will he do?'

'Perfectly,' said Slider. When Mackay came on he said, 'I've got a job for you. I want you to go to the TVC for me. Go to the lift right next to the loo where Greatrex was killed. Inside it there must be an inspection hatch in the ceiling – get up there and see if there's anything hidden on the roof of the lift.'

'Now, guv?'

'Yes, now. You'll need someone with you to give you a boost.'

'Am I looking for anything in particular?'

'Well, I hope you may find a bag there containing bloodstained clothing. That would be my favourite result.'

Mackay was enlightened at last. 'Oh! Right! Nice one, guv. Why didn't we think of that before?'

We? Slider thought. 'Get on with it,' he said. 'I'll be in in about twenty minutes.'

When he returned to the bedroom, Joanna was awake and watching the door.

'I didn't mean to disturb you,' he said.

'This phone pings when you pick the other one up,' she said. 'Who were you calling?'

Was there something cautious about the question? 'Just the factory,' he said. 'I had an idea about where the bag might be hidden. I don't expect anything will come of it, but a man can dream.'

'Are you going in now?'

'Yes,' he said. He sat down on the bed beside her and stroked the hair back from her brow. Touching her head brought a rush of feelings through him, as though he had plugged in to something. 'About last night—'

She rolled onto her back to free her arms to reach up to him. 'Let's forget it. We wouldn't quarrel like that if we didn't love each other.'

He bent and kissed her. 'Could we find some other way of showing it in future, do you think?'

Her hand ran up and down his flank. 'You don't want to fight? What sort of a man are you, anyway?'

If he showered and dressed like lightning afterwards, he thought, there was just time to show her.

Half the force seemed to be gathered around a single desk in the CID room when Slider arrived, and it parted in a Red Sea of smiling faces before him to lead him to a rather dusty blue nylon flight bag sitting on Atherton's desk.

'Just where you said it'd be, guv,' Mackay gloated.

So his instinct about Mrs Reynolds had been right after all.

'I had inside information,' Slider said modestly. He didn't yet quite understand his own thought processes, but something was going on in the back of his mind. 'Let's have a look at it.'

Or more importantly, in it. The outside yielded nothing but a quantity of dust and an oil stain which probably came from the lift cable, but inside the bag was a pair of bloody surgical gloves and an elderly mackintosh with blood-soaked sleeves, bloody smears down both front coats, and an almost round bloodstain further down where, Slider surmised, the wearer had gone down on one knee.

'Oh Tufty,' Slider murmured, 'you lucky, lucky lad.'

The one person not pleased with the discovery of the bag was Mr Honeyman, whose doll face did not quite manage to express disapproval, but whose unchuffedness was evinced by the silence with which he received the news, a long silence during which he searched his mind for a budget-friendly reason for the bag to be found where it was. He had managed to believe that the bruising to the chin was not convincing evidence of foul play, coming up with the alternative – in both senses – theory that Greatrex might have bruised himself shaving, but this was harder going. He did not go so far as to suggest Greatrex might somehow have managed to conceal the bag in the lift after cutting his own throat but before collapsing, but he did say, 'You will check that the blood group is the same as that of Greatrex, won't you?' – as though it might be that of a clumsy, DIY-loving lift maintenance engineer with a strict wife.

'Of course, sir,' Slider said patiently – so patiently that Honeyman was recalled reluctantly to reality.

'Well, I suppose this changes things quite considerably,' he said. 'I suppose I must tell Mr Wetherspoon that we have a murder investigation on our hands.'

Slider had no mercy. 'Yes, sir.'

'You realise what this means, don't you?' Honeyman said irritably. 'If the murderer wore protective clothing, it could be anyone, anyone at all. There were hundreds of people in that building.'

Yes, there were, Slider thought as he walked back to his room;

but whoever murdered Roger Greatrex must have planned it beforehand, to have brought the gloves with him, and must therefore have had a grudge against him. So it could not have been just anyone amongst the hundreds. The prime suspects were still the same three people who had had good reason to want to kill him; or someone else with a beef they hadn't unearthed yet.

But why didn't the murderer carry the bag away out of the building and dump it somewhere far from the scene? Because he couldn't leave the building just yet? Because he had to go back and join a group of people – like those in the greenroom, for instance – who would notice his absence?

And where had the bag been before – or rather, where had the mack been? Those nylon bags hadn't much bulk to them – it could have been stuffed into an overcoat pocket, for instance – but the mack couldn't have been concealed. It must either have been worn or carried over the arm – unless it was already in the building somewhere. Damn! There were going to have to be a lot of questions asked about that mack.

And why had the murderer hidden the bag in the lift? It was a good hiding place, provided you could get it up there in the first place. You'd need to be athletic to jump up, hold onto the ledge round the top of the lift, and hang there by one hand while you used the other to push the inspection hatch aside and swing the bag up into place. Athletic and tall. Well, all three of their suspects were tallish, and even Sandal Palliser was skinny and strong-looking.

The big drawback to the lift was that even if you happened to find it empty in the first place, you were just as likely as not to be interrupted by someone getting in or out, whereupon you might find it hard to explain why you were dangling about from the ceiling like an ape on whacky baccy. The lift couldn't have been essential to the plan, must surely have been a spur-of-the-moment thing. Perhaps being surprised by Mrs Reynolds, he had decided it was safer to hide the bag than go on carrying it about.

But Mrs Reynolds' description of the man at the lift didn't match any of the best suspects. If he wasn't the murderer, how did the bag get onto the lift roof? And if he was the murderer, then it wasn't Palliser, Somers or Parsons.

No, Slider sighed, he'd have to face the fact that they had been barking up the wrong street and pursuing red herrings down blind alleys all this time. His whole pack had been cur-dog hunting, and the fox must be two valleys away by now.

Still, clear as you go, that was the thing. A piece of the bloodsoaked raincoat material must be sent off to Tufty, Mrs Reynolds must be called in to identify the bag, and the forensic team must be dispatched to see if there was any trace of anything useful left in the lift. And the ground team would have to go back in and start asking everyone whether they'd seen anyone answering the description entering or leaving the lift, or entering the building wearing or carrying the mack.

The only good thing was that now he would not have to fight Honeyman for the manpower.

Atherton seemed as little pleased as Honeyman when he arrived and heard the news about the bag.

'It could still be Somers,' he said doggedly. 'He had every opportunity to plan the murder, bring the bag in at any time beforehand, and hide it again afterwards. He was only next door, and he's the only one who can say exactly when and how the body was discovered.'

'And why would he go to the trouble of putting on protective clothing and hiding it, and then go and dabble in the blood?' Slider said patiently.

'Well, we know he went into Greatrex's pocket for something. Suppose he did the murder in the protective gear, stowed it away, and then remembered whatever it was in the pocket. He had to go back for it, and then, seeing he'd got blood on him after all, he had to make the best of it by being the one who found the body. That would account for the state he's been in ever since – his perfect plan went astray, and now he's terrified he's going to get caught.'

'But—'

'And he was the one who had longest to brood over his wrongs and plan the thing. All those years of resentment, and then a couple of weeks of knowing Greatrex was going to be on the show and available to him.'

'But he doesn't answer the description of the man by the lift,' Slider managed to get in at last.

'We don't know he was anything to do with it. There could be a thousand reasons he had blood on his cuff.'

'He was carrying the bag,' Slider pointed out.

Atherton fought a noble rearguard action. 'It might not be the same bag. They're as common as blackberries. Or maybe Mrs Thing was mistaken. Or maybe she's confused the man she saw with somebody else.'

'You know you're beaten. Why don't you just admit defeat gracefully?'

'Show me the man who laughs at defeat and I'll show you a chiropodist with a warped sense of humour.'

'That's no answer.'

'Can I at least ask Somers about the mack?' Atherton pleaded.

'Of course you can, dear,' Slider said soothingly. 'In any case, you've got to clear up what he went into the pocket for. When you tell him he's out of the frame for the murder he'll probably come across. But the mack—' he shook his head. 'That's not a young man's mack. It's old, but it was once very expensive and very conservative. It's a stuffy mack. It's a wealthy, middle-aged, establishment sort of a mack.'

'It could have been bought second-hand,' Atherton pointed out.

'So it could, of course.'

'Or borrowed.'

'Quite. It's going to be no help at all.'

Mrs Somers opened the door to Atherton and drew a quick little breath. Her eyes searched his face for information, and, liking her, he said at once to relieve her, 'I know about Greatrex and your daughter.'

Her expression hardened, but there was still fear in her eyes. 'Phil didn't kill him. He deserved to die, but Phil would never do a thing like that.'

'I know,' Atherton said gently. 'Can I talk to him? There are some details he hasn't told us that are getting in the way of finding out who really did do it.'

She hesitated only a moment, and then stood aside to let him in. 'He's having a lie in. He's not been well since this happened, so I told him to stop in bed. I'll go and get him up.'

'No need, I can talk to him in his room.'

She bristled. 'You can not! You'll sit down in the front room, and when I've called Philly, I'll make you a cup o' coffee. D'you take sugar?'

Philip Somers appeared at last in trousers, shirt and bedroom slippers, pale, unshaven, seedy about the eyes, and definitely apprehensive. His fingernails, Atherton noticed with distaste, were bitten to the nub.

'Mum says you want to talk to me,' he said, though from the sulky tone Atherton reckoned it was rather Mum says I've got to talk to you.

Atherton, who had been standing by the window, took a step and picked up the photograph from the corner table. 'Is this Madeleine?'

'Put that down,' Somers said sharply. Atherton took his time about complying.

'She was very pretty,' he said. 'Why did you hold Greatrex responsible? The inquest said it was an accident.'

'I didn't kill him,' Somers said sickly.

'I know,' Atherton said, and saw relief register so strongly on Somers's face that he wondered for an instant whether his own beloved theory was right after all. Somers sat down with involuntary abruptness. 'So tell me,' Atherton said again, 'why did you hold Greatrex to blame for your sister's death?'

'He was to blame, even if it was an accident,' Somers said fiercely. 'She was there because of him, she was in the car in that place at that time because of him. If he hadn't seduced her, she wouldn't have died. She'd be alive now, properly married, to a decent bloke, probably with children of her own. Mum would be a grandmother, like she always wanted. Now – maybe she'll never be.'

'There's plenty of time, isn't there? And she has plenty of children.'

Somers shook his head. 'It affected us all. You don't understand. Maddy was the life of the family. She was the bright one, the funny one, always on the go. She was the one who made us do things. She was the one who made Mum and Dad buy this house when the council put it up for sale. She introduced Patrick to his wife. Without her—' He lapsed into a trembling silence.

'How did she meet Greatrex?'

'She was a voluntary steward at the Festival Hall, and he was always there, of course, being a music critic. He just saw her and decided he had to have her.'

'She was pretty,' Atherton commented.

'She was beautiful!' Somers cried. 'He had to have her, to spoil her. Whatever was fresh and good and clean he had to spoil. He seduced her and ruined her, taking her to cheap hotels—'

'That one in Bray wasn't exactly cheap,' Atherton said mildly.

Somers glared at him. 'Are you condoning what he did?'

'Well, you know, she was over age – what he did was no crime. She could presumably choose for herself, and most people don't regard having a sexual relationship with someone as disgraceful any more.'

'Most people! What do you know about most people? Maddy would never have gone to bed with him if he hadn't forced her – telling her lies, making her promises. I begged her to give him up, but she wouldn't. She said he meant to marry her. Marry her! He was degrading her! She was getting worse and worse, doing things she'd never have dreamed of doing before. But I could still have got her back, if only I'd had the chance. Now she's dead, and lost to us for ever. He did that.'

Crackers, Atherton thought. He's as mad as a fish in a privet hedge. 'You wished he was dead,' he suggested lightly.

'Yes,' Somers said fiercely. 'But I didn't kill him.'

'All right, tell me about it.'

'When I found him there like that, I thought he'd killed himself. First of all I was glad. Then I was angry that he'd escaped so easily, without ever realising what he'd done to us. I'd wanted him to feel remorse, and now he never would. I was furious. I took him by the shoulders and shook him, I was so angry. That's how I got blood on me. And I kicked the knife across the floor, sort of in temper.' Atherton nodded encouragingly. 'And then – then I realised that it might look bad that I'd got blood on me. I'd been out looking for him, and here I was alone with him, and it might look as though—' He stopped, staring at his fearful memories. 'I – I suppose that's how I got it on my face. I must have put my hands up to it, like this.'

He cupped his face in his hands, and his long fingers reached into the hair at the edges of his ears.

'So I lay him down again, to try to make him look natural. I would have fetched the knife back, but I had blood on my shoes, and I knew I'd make a mark if I went to pick it up. I thought if I raised the alarm, I could explain the blood on me by saying I'd examined him to see if he was dead. Anyway, I reckoned no-one would think I had any reason to kill him. And then I remembered—'

'Yes,' said Atherton. 'You remembered what he kept in his pocket.'

Somers nodded slowly, seeming relieved that Atherton knew about it. Atherton waited, hoping for enlightenment. At last he was forced to ask, 'How did you know it was there?'

'He'd showed it to me once. Years afterwards, when he was on a programme I was working on. He recognised me, and came up to talk to me, showed it to me, said that it proved he'd really loved her. I wanted to kill him then,' he said, trembling. 'I wanted to. It wasn't only Maddy, you see. There were others. They were all there, all the girls he'd seduced.'

Oh, I doubt it, Atherton thought – unless his boasts had far outstripped reality.

'I couldn't leave her there – part of his *harem*,' Somers said bitterly. 'Degraded into just one of his conquests. So I took it.'

'And where is it now?' Atherton asked, still flying by the seat of his pants.

Somers put a slow and reluctant hand into his trouser pocket. 'I thought you'd ask to see it,' he said unhappily, drawing out and handing over what looked like a leather wallet. Atherton took it and opened it. Inside transparent pockets on both sides were photographs. Photographs! Why didn't he think of that? 'That's Maddy,' Somers said, pointing.

'Yes, I recognise her,' Atherton said. The smiling face of Madeleine Somers gazed back through the plastic from the far side of death.

'Will I be able to have it back?' Somers asked in a small, defeated voice.

'Yes, of course, when we've completed our investigation,' Atherton said.

'I couldn't leave her there,' Somers said again. 'There's no knowing who those others were. And besides—'

'If the picture had been found, people might have thought you killed him,' Atherton said. 'Quite. But why did you put the card in his pocket?'

'Card?'

'The religious card. The tract – a Bible quotation.'

Somers shook his head, puzzled. 'I don't know what you're talking about.'

'You didn't put anything into his pocket?'

'No. I took out this wallet, that's all. I got the wrong one first – his money wallet. He had – you-know-what's – in it,' he added in disgust. 'I put that back and took this one. I'd have taken Maddy's picture out and left the rest, but I was getting nervous, I thought someone might come in and find me. So I took the whole thing and went outside to raise the alarm. Luckily Dorothy was coming along the passage.'

'And you stood guard to stop anyone else going in until the police arrived. Why did you do that?'

'Well, that's what you do. I've seen it on the television. You're not supposed to disturb anything.'

'But you already had disturbed things. Wouldn't it have been better from your point of view if a few other people had done it too?'

'But I hadn't done anything wrong. I thought he'd committed suicide. I wanted to make sure the police would see that.' He looked at Atherton pleadingly. 'Don't you think he did? It could be suicide, couldn't it? I mean, now you don't think I killed him.' Atherton didn't immediately answer and Somers plunged on in alarm. 'You don't think I did, do you? You do believe me, what I've told you? It's the truth, I promise you. He was dead when I found him, and all I did was take the photos.'

'Yes, I believe you,' Atherton said, and only he knew how disappointed he was to be saying that. 'But you've given us a lot of trouble by not being honest with us from the beginning. You've wasted a lot of our time, and my guv'nor's not going to be pleased about that.' Somers looked suitably cowed, and Atherton went on, 'I shall have to ask you to come down to the station and make another statement. And this time, please don't leave anything out.'

'Will it have to come out – about Roger and Maddy?' Somers asked pathetically. 'We kept it from the younger ones at the time. Kevin and Mandy and Katy don't know – what Maddy did. They think she was working with Roger the night she was killed.'

Like fun they do, Atherton thought. This man was a dreamer. 'I don't see why it should,' he said aloud. 'Provided you've now told us everything, I don't see why the matter of the photograph need be raised again.'

'Thank you,' Somers said. 'Mum'll be so glad. The shame of it nearly killed her at the time.'

Atherton would have thought rather that the grief nearly killed her; or the shame of having a son as spaced out as Silly Philly might do it.

CHAPTER ELEVEN

Deliver us from Ealing

'Well, I'm not going to blow any sunshine up your skirts,' Slider concluded. 'We've now got a very long haul ahead of us, but you can comfort yourselves that this is what police work is really all about.'

With a sad smile in response to the irony, the troops dispersed. Slider called McLaren over. 'How have you got on with that discrepancy over the names on the lists? Davis or whatever it was?'

'Well, guv, the address Davis gave doesn't exist – Bishop's Road, SW11, which is Battersea of course. There isn't a Bishop's Road in Battersea. There's a Bishop's Park Road in Fulham and one in Mitcham, but he doesn't live in either of them. There's a Bishop's Terrace in *SE*11, but he doesn't live there. And there's four other Bishop's Roads in various places, five Bishop's Avenues, four Bishop's Closes, one Bishop's Court, and one Bishop Road without the "s". I haven't got round to checking them yet.' He looked up from his list. 'Doesn't the word "Bishop" start to look funny when you stare at it a long time?'

'What about the other name, the one that was on the ticket list?'

'Oh, that address is all right – Oakley Square, that's round the back of Mornington Crescent. Flats and bedsits, a lot of students and singles. But we knew that address must be all right anyway, because that's where they posted the ticket to.'

'And have you checked to see if Davis lives there?'

'Not yet. I was doing the other one first.'

'Well get onto it now,' Slider said, restraining himself nobly. 'Find out what the score is, whether he went to the BBC that night and if not, who did. And have you checked the no-shows?'

'All but one, and he's apparently abroad. His firm says that's pukka. The others seem genuine enough, but only one of them still had the ticket – the rest threw them away.'

'I don't think that's going to be important.' He turned to Norma. 'We need to get Mrs Reynolds in to identify the bag. Liaise with Atherton, see if you can get her here at the same time as Somers comes in to do his statement, and let them pass each other, just to see if she recognises him. I don't think it was him, now, but he was always our best chance. No harm in running him past her.'

'Yes, boss.'

'And then take Mrs Reynolds along to do a photofit.'

'Are you going public?' she asked with interest.

'That's up to Mr Honeyman, not me, thank God. He's having a press conference this afternoon, by the way, so he'll want as many things cleared up as possible before then. Let's snap to it.'

The later edition of the paper had a report of the Laurence Jepp incident. Slider was surprised to read that Jepp had not been beaten to death, as he had been imagining, but had had his throat cut. Any mention of throat-cutting immediately caught Slider's attention these days – like seeing your own name on a page, it was the thing that jumped out at you. It was not usually the preferred method for a surprised burglar, in his experience, and not a particularly common method of homicide overall. It was a long shot, but could there possibly be any connection between the Jepp case and the Greatrex murder? Greatrex was a music critic, after all, and he had reported on the *Don Giovanni* in which Jepp had been performing.

It was worth checking up on, at any rate, he thought. For want of a nail, and all that sort of thing. Probably there was nothing in it, but—

McLaren looked round the door. 'I think I got a result, guv,' he said.

'Davis?'

'Yeah. The one with the "e".'

'Come in.'

McLaren sidled in with his notebook in one hand and the stump of a Mars bar in the other. 'Well, guv—'

'Leave the chocolate outside, please. Last time you got it on my telephone, God knows how.'

McLaren looked at his left hand in surprise, as if he hadn't known the confectionery was there. 'I forgot I was eating that,' he said, and shoved it whole into his mouth. Slider averted his gaze. McLaren screwed up the paper and lobbed it accurately into the bin. 'Well, guv,' he resumed, bubbling a little, 'I got hold of this Davies guy. It turns out he's got an interesting story.'

Slider gestured McLaren to sit down. 'Did he go to the show on Thursday?'

'He went to White City, but he never went into the building. While he was queuing up outside with the rest of 'em, this bloke comes up to him and asks if he's there on his own. Davies says yes, and this bloke spins him a story, says he and his wife always come to these things together, only this time this bloke thinks he's working so his wife gets a ticket to come on her own, then at the last minute it turns out he's not working but by then there's no tickets left. So he says to Davies he really wants to go to this thing with his wife, and asks if Davies will sell him his ticket. Well, you don't pay for these tickets in the first place, and Davies isn't that struck on the show, really – he only goes 'cause he hopes to meet somebody—'

'Somebody?'

'He's a bit of a sad-act, this Davies guy. Unemployed, no money, no bird – no friends either. So he goes to a lot of these free shows at the BBC. It's a way of passing the time, which he's got a lot of, and he reckons it's his best chance of meeting birds, though they'd have to be desperate to fancy a legover with a pathetic nerk like him. Still, you get a lot of left-wing birds at the political ones like *Questions of Our Time* and they might see it as social work. The BBC's like a free dating agency to him.'

'I see.'

'So anyway, he asks this geezer how much and the geezer says a score, and Davies reckons for twenty quid he can go to the pub for the night and pick up a tart there, so he says okay and hands it over and the bloke gives him a twenty note, nice as pie. He's just walking off when the bloke asks him his name – says he'll need to know it at the door for the security check, which is true, which Davies knows it is – and Davies tells him Jim Davies, and off he goes.' McLaren leaned back in the chair with satisfaction. 'Geezer must have misheard the Jim for John; and not knowing the spelling went for the simplest version.'

'The man didn't tell Davies his name, I suppose? No, we couldn't be that lucky.' Slider thought a moment. 'Did Davies believe his story?'

McLaren shrugged. 'He didn't say he didn't. He told it to me as if it made sense to him.'

'Did he see the man's wife?'

'He says he didn't notice him at all until the bloke spoke to him. And when he'd got his score in his hand he shoved off fast, case the bloke changed his mind. Saw a bus coming and ran across the road and jumped on, and never looked back.'

'Did you ask him for a description of the man?'

'Yeah. He wasn't very helpful. He says he never really noticed. I s'pose he's standing there miles away and it's all over before he's on the ball. Probably more interested in the twenty than the bloke.'

'Well, what *did* he give you?'

'Middle age, middle height, clean-shaven, short hair but not bald. Brown or dark – not fair. Thinks the bloke may have worn glasses.'

'Clothes?'

McLaren shrugged again. 'A suit, he thinks, or possibly an overcoat. Not jeans, anyway.' He anticipated the next question. 'He doesn't remember if he was carrying a bag.'

Slider sighed. Davies had taken in merely an impression of a conventional grown-up rather than a shaggy youth. He could probably have told you the number on the bank note, though.

'All right, get him in, get a statement.'

'I've arranged that, guv. He's coming in today some time. D'you think it's the murderer?'

'It could be. Whoever it was was pretty determined to get in. I wonder why he picked on Davies, though?'

'He was right at the back of the queue, and on his own,' McLaren said. 'And he sounds like a dozy git. Maybe he looks like he sounds. At least he probably looked as if he needed the money.'

'Fair enough. Well, see if you can get a better description out of him – maybe a photofit. Then we can compare it with Mrs Reynolds's efforts.'

'Rightyoh.' McLaren stood up. 'D'you think it's anything?'

'Anything could be anything. There could be any number of reasons why he wanted to go to this show, but—' He let it hang.

'Yeah,' said McLaren sympathetically. 'You gotta clear as you go.'

Slider determined never to say that again. He had always despised bosses who fell into tricks of speech and catchphrases. Mental laziness. That was one of the things he relied on Atherton for – to keep his mind perpetually on the hop.

DS Phil Hunt had been one of Slider's team, until he had got his stripes and gone to Ealing. He'd always been a bit of a pill. His one great passion in life was his customised red Escort XR3 on which he hung, screwed or stuck every new gadget that came out, like a crazed automotive Cophetua. No trouble was too great where his car was concerned. Slider vividly recollected a week during which his sole topic of conversation was a set of imported tyres he had ordered from a specialist dealer on the North Circular – how they brought the good pneus from Brent to Hayes, as Atherton had wearily put it.

The good thing about Hunt was that he did not realise what a dickhead he was, and had such an unshakeable sense of his own superiority that he never held grudges and was gracious to everyone. So when Slider rang to say he was in the area and asked if Hunt would like to slip out for a drink, he saw nothing suspicious in it, and met his former boss ten minutes later in one of the pubs in Madeley Road.

It was not difficult to get him to talk about the Laurence Jepp case. 'Ground-floor flat, conversion,' he said in his familiar, episodic style. 'One of those old Victorian piles down the side of the Common. Sash windows, no locks, of course – just the original catches. Child's play. Straightforward burglary, it looked like. Probably the bloke panicked when Jepp woke up and hit the alarm.'

'Anything missing?'

'Nothing obvious, but it's hard to say, with Jepp being dead, and living alone. He had a lot of nice stuff, if you like that sort of thing – antiques and pictures – but not what you'd expect a break-in for, not unless it was a proper daylight, front-door job with a van.'

'Opportunist thief, then?'

Hunt drew long and satisfyingly on his pint. 'Hard to say,' he said, wiping his foamy moustache with the back of his hand. 'It was a bit on the late side for a real kid, and a bit neat and tidy for a junkie. I thought maybe there was some really rare thing that someone was stealing to order. The way the catch had been slipped looked professional. But then, some of these addicts are virtually pros these days. My guv'nor reckons chummy was looking for something to sell, chose a big house in the hope, and then whacked Jepp when he woke up and hit the alarm.'

'So how was Jepp killed? Blunt instrument?' Slider asked casually.

'Throat cut,' Hunt said. 'Right through – hell of a mess in the bed. Amazing how far eight pints will spread.'

'Hard to cut someone's throat lying down,' Slider said.

Hunt gave a mirthless grin. 'Evidently that's what chummy thought. Jepp was lying face down with his knees under him. Pathologist reckons the perp dragged him out of bed, turned him round, knelt him down on the bed, and cut his throat from behind. Knew what he was doing – you don't get so much blood on you that way.'

'He must have been strong.'

'Right. Though Jepp's only a little shorthouse – five foot five or six. But he cut his throat right through first cut – no haggling – so he must have been strong.'

Slider picked up his own pint so as to continue to look casual, but had to put it down again. He was afraid he'd spill it on the way to his mouth. He tried a wild shot. 'Was there a religious tract left on the body, or by the bed? A card with a verse from the Bible on it?'

Hunt looked surprised. 'How'd you know that, guv?' Slider jumped inside, but managed to keep still, as though it was matter-of-fact. 'Bloody hell, has somebody leaked? My guv'nor'll be right pissed off if anyone's been talking.' He evidently did not see the irony of that comment.

'What did it say on the card?' Slider asked casually. 'What was the verse?'

'Some bollocks about blood.' Belated caution visited Hunt. He narrowed his eyes. 'I don't remember exactly. Probably not important. Here, is that the time? I'd better be getting back.'

But Slider stood too. 'I think I'd better come and have a talk with your guv'nor,' he said.

Hunt stared in alarm mingled with resentment. 'What's all this about, guv? I thought you just wanted a social drink.'

'Don't worry, son, I won't get you in dutch,' Slider said.

'I never told you anything,' Hunt insisted.

'Of course you didn't. It's just that I've got a special interest in the late Mr Jepp.'

DI Gordon Arundel – known behind his back as Gorgeous Gordon or sometimes Glorious Goodwood – was a large and handsome man who left a trail of broken hearts and fractured marriages behind him wherever he served the forces of law and order. He had two ex-wives and seven children that he knew about and his maintenance payments were such that he could now afford to pursue only women who were independently wealthy, which had forced him dangerously high up the social scale. Stories about him were legion; he had now passed almost into legend. 'Did you hear DI Arundel had a nasty accident? He pulled out quick to avoid a child and fell off the bed.' 'Did you hear the Super's wife's up the club? It's a grudge pregnancy – DI Arundel had it in for him.' And so on.

He was also extremely jealous of his intellectual property, and Slider had much to do to allay his suspicion. Arundel would hardly admit the Jepp case existed, and would divulge nothing about what evidence they might have, though Slider gathered from the tone of his talk that it was not much. It took ten minutes of hard talking to persuade Goodwood even to let him see the Bible card. It was spattered with blood, which was appropriate to its text:

> All things are by the law purged with blood; and without shedding of blood is no remission. Hebrews 9: 22.

'It was on the bedside table,' Arundel said. 'It's a misquotation, in any case. I looked it up. It should say "*almost* all things".'

'Not as punchy as this version,' Slider said, passing back the plastic bag in which the card resided. It was a disturbing quotation either way, especially taken in conjunction with the one found on Greatrex. 'I think,' Slider said cautiously, 'that it's just possible we may be looking for the same man. There seem to be similarities in the MO.'

'Well?' Arundel said impatiently. 'What are you saying, we've got a serial killer on the loose?'

'Not exactly.' Slider told him quickly about Greatrex. 'I don't know if there was any connection between them, anything specific, I mean, apart from music and opera generally. But it's possible someone had a grudge against them both.'

Arundel looked askance at him. 'It sounds like cobblers to me,' he said. 'Just because they both had a card with a Bible text on it. They could both have been given them by the same person. Or your bloke could have given it to my bloke, or vice versa, if they knew each other. Anyway, your man was done in a public place. Mine was done by an intruder. People's houses get burgled every minute of the day – especially old houses with sash windows.'

'And the MO?'

'A throat-cutting's a throat-cutting. Granted it was done professional, but they all know how to use a knife these days. They're tooled up by nine years old. If I was to be given a fiver for every kid walking about my ground who had a blade on him, I could retire a rich man. No, take my word, it was a burglary, plain and simple, some coke-head looking for something to sell.' He looked sidelong at Slider. 'I wouldn't like any of your lads trampling over my ground, Bill. Friendly advice. If anything comes up that might be of interest to you, I'll make sure it gets passed on.'

'Thanks Gordon.' Slider stood up. 'I know I can count on you.'

'Naturally,' Arundel said. 'And you'll help me in exactly the same way, of course.' It was meant to be ironic, Slider saw. It was a pity there were so many coppers who saw other coppers as opponents rather than oppos.

Norma brought Mrs Reynolds to Slider's office door on her way out.

'Mrs Reynolds has identified the bag, boss.'

'That's right, dear,' Mrs Reynolds said, not one to let someone else speak for her. 'It was that one, or one just like it.' Slider had stood up for her, and she gave a little nod of approval for the courtesy. 'But there's plenty around, aren't there? I mean they're not expensive.'

'That's true. But it's a help anyway, and we're grateful to you for coming in.'

'Oh, that's all right. Got to 'elp each other, haven't we? And I've enjoyed meself. Your young lady here has looked after me beautiful.' Behind her back Norma rolled her eyes.

'And you've made up a photofit for us of the man, have you?' Slider asked, more of Norma than Mrs Reynolds, but it was she who answered.

'Oh yes, I've done that. It was a queer feeling, seeing his face come together like that in front of me. I'll never forget him, nor the look he give me.'

Norma said, 'It looks faintly familiar, guv, but I can't place him. Not one of our front-row villains, though I've got a strange feeling I've seen him somewhere quite recently.'

Slider nodded. 'When you've got a minute, sit down with it quietly and go through your recent cases; and try it against the files. Perhaps you'd like to see Mrs Reynolds out now.' He gave his best boyish smile to the old lady. 'Thank you very much for coming in. We really do appreciate your help.'

He flicked a glance at Norma, who ushered the woman out, then asked her to wait in the corridor just a moment and popped back into Slider's office. 'No go, guv,' she said quietly, so that Mrs Reynolds wouldn't hear. 'I trundled her right past Somers in the front shop, and she didn't even glance. And the photofit she's done doesn't look anything like him.'

'Never mind, I didn't really think—'

He was interrupted by a breathless ejaculation from Mrs Reynolds – 'Oh, my good Gawd!' – followed by her hasty re-entrance from the corridor, clutching her bosom in alarm, her eyes wide with urgency. 'It's 'im! 'E's out there! Oh my Gawd, it give me such a fright!'

'Who?' Slider said and 'Where?' Norma said simultaneously.

'The bloke I seen by the lift!' Mrs Reynolds hissed. 'Go on, quick, 'fore he gets away!'

Slider gestured Norma tersely with his head and she crossed to the door and looked out. 'There's no-one there,' she said.

Mrs Reynolds extended her neck tortoise-like and peered round the door. 'You bleedin' blind? Down the end by the coffee machine!'

Norma looked at Slider, shrugged, and stepped out into the corridor. 'Mills!' she called. 'Can you come here a minute?'

Mills appeared opposite the doorway, plastic cup in hand, an enquiring expression on his face. Mrs Reynolds backed, clutching her coat to her neck in an instinctive gesture of alarm. 'That's 'im! Keep 'im off me!'

Slider stood up and went to her, laid a soothing hand on her arm. 'This is Detective Sergeant Mills, one of my team.'

Mrs Reynolds didn't take her fascinated eyes off Mills. 'I don't care. It's 'im all the same, the bloke I seen by the lift, with the bag.'

'Are you sure?' Slider said gently, with a glance at Mills. Mills was still looking at them with the mild enquiry of incomprehension.

'Course I'm sure,' she said scornfully. 'Look at 'im! You couldn't mistake that face, could you? That's 'im all right, sure as I stand here.'

'I suppose you haven't got a twin brother?' Slider asked hopelessly. 'Or a brother who looks a lot like you?'

Mills, sitting glumly on the other side of his desk, looked up from the contemplation of his hands dangling between his knees. 'I haven't got a brother of any sort. I'm adopted.'

'Oh yes, so you are. I'd forgotten.'

Norma smacked her forehead with a reproving hand. 'And there was I saying I thought the photofit looked familiar and I was sure I'd seen him recently.'

Slider was worried. 'That photofit is a real problem. She picked that out before she identified him in the corridor, which means she didn't just point a random finger.'

'Sir,' Norma said, 'Mills was there on the night on duty and she could quite easily have seen him. His face stuck in her memory for some reason, and she's confused him with the man she saw by the lift. If she actually did see a man by the lift at all. It could all be a figment of her imagination.'

'It could,' Slider agreed, 'but unfortunately she's a good witness – very sure and very circumstantial. She'll take some getting past. And she identified the bag.'

'She might have said yes to any bag we showed her.'

'She said beforehand it was a blue nylon flight bag. She could have said any colour. I'm afraid I have to take the bag as fact.'

Mills gave a tight smile. 'Nice try, Norma.' He looked at Slider. 'Am I in the clarts, sir?'

'Do you remember seeing Mrs Reynolds at all? Did you pass her in the corridor or speak to her or anything?' Slider asked.

'No sir, not that I remember. But she could have seen me, all the same. I didn't hide the bag in the lift. I've never owned a bag like that. And I didn't kill Greatrex.'

Slider sighed. 'I'm afraid it doesn't look very good, clartwise. I shall have to take you off the case. And I shall have to tell Mr Honeyman. Whether he decides to go further is up to him.'

'Sir,' said Mills. He bit his lip, but did not look overpoweringly anxious, which was a comfort. Slider nodded to Norma to go. When they were alone, Mills said, 'You don't think I did it, do you, sir?'

'When I knew you at Charing Cross, I'd have bet my life on you. I suppose I actually did a few times. But I haven't seen you for ten years. And as I said, in all fairness Mrs Reynolds is a very good witness. She described you moles and all. It speaks volumes about my opinion of you, though, that I didn't identify you from her description.'

Mills seemed disconcerted by Slider's less than wholehearted endorsement of him; but he said, 'Thank you for being frank, anyway, sir. At least I know where I stand.'

Slider leaned forward. 'Off the record, Mills, I'd still trust you with my life. But I've got to keep an open mind, even if it is against my will. Did you have any connection with Greatrex?'

'No, sir.'

'Are you sure?'

'I'd never seen him before in my life, as far as I can remember. Well, not in the flesh, I mean. Of course I'd seen him on television.' He gave a strained laugh. 'It's fantastic. It's like asking me if I'd murdered Melvyn Bragg or Jeremy Paxman.'

'Ah, now we're talking wish-fulfilment. Well, I take your word for it. But you know we're going to have to investigate this, don't you? Go into your past life. Go through your drum.'

'I've got nothing to hide, sir,' Mills said, meeting his eyes steadily.

'Examine your movements,' Slider added on a more worried note. 'For instance, I have to ask you again what you were doing at the TVC at all on Thursday night. You weren't on duty.'

'Ah!' It was a barely articulated sound of – enlightenment? Realisation of danger? Mills's dark eyes were full of understanding for an instant, and then he looked away from Slider, and answered neutrally, 'Like I've already told you, guv, I just happened to be passing and saw the mobile go in. So I followed out of curiosity, to see if I could help.'

'And what were you doing to be just happening to pass?'

'I'd been to see my auntie earlier. I didn't want to go home, it not really being much like home yet, so I was walking round the ground, getting my bearings again.'

Slider watched him for a moment, but he didn't waver. 'You're going with that, are you?'

'It's the truth.'

The trouble with the truth was that it was so often entirely unconvincing. A good, well-woven, colour-co-ordinated suit of fiction could always outclass it; but Slider could hardly say that to his subordinate.

'I'm very, very unhappy about this, Slider,' Honeyman said, like an enraged cairn terrier. No, strike that simile – it made Slider immediately envisage a small pink bow on the top of his boss's head, which wouldn't do at all.

'I'm not very pleased myself, sir,' he murmured, fixing his eyes on the bridge of Honeyman's nose, about which there was nothing risible, except its being part of Honeyman.

'It was bad enough having to announce that we don't think it was suicide after all, after four days of investigation—' He glared at Slider as though daring him to say he had favoured murder from the beginning. Kamikaze was not high on Slider's list of hobbies, and he kept a respectful silence. 'I was anticipating some upsetting analyses in the papers, though I did hope for sympathy from the BBC. At least they would understand the difficulties we were labouring under. But now this – this—!'

He slapped his hand down on the copy of the *Evening Standard* whose front page was half obscured by the thick black headline OWN GOAL and the only slightly smaller subhead MEDIA-STAR MURDER – COPS NAB ONE OF THEIR OWN. Slider didn't like to mention the later edition which had just come out, which Honeyman hadn't seen yet. It was on Slider's desk at that moment, and two-thirds of the page was now occupied by only three words: BILL THE RIPPER?

'At least they haven't got a picture,' Slider said comfortingly. 'In fact, they haven't even named Mills – just "a detective investigating the case".'

In fact, of course, in tabloids the size of the headline was always inversely proportionate to the amount of actual substance to the text. If there'd been enough story to fill the front page, they wouldn't have needed the heavyweight, scandal-sized, 144-point scream.

'It can only be a matter of time,' Honeyman said. 'But in any case that isn't the point. The point is that someone has leaked, and on this of all issues, the most sensitive, embarrassing subject of all. It's going to make us look complete fools!'

For 'us', read 'me', Slider thought.

'I want to know who it was who gave the story to the papers! I want a full investigation, and when the culprit is found, I warn you, Slider, I shall have no mercy! This sort of thing has got to be stopped. I shall come down on him as heavily as I possibly can!' He stamped away a few steps and back again in uncontainable rage. 'What is Mr Wetherspoon going to think? What do you think the Divisional Commander's going to think? It'll be all over the dailies tomorrow, and there's no knowing how far it may go.' Honeyman's eyes bulged at the awful prospect. 'Imagine what the ADC's going to be reading over his breakfast marmalade!'

'I think it much more likely the leak came from the witness, sir,' Slider said. 'The fact that there's no name mentioned suggests that. She probably just said something to a neighbour and the neighbour's phoned the local paper with it, and it's gone on from there. But it hardly matters—'

'Oh, I'm glad you think that! I'm very glad indeed you think it doesn't matter that we're marked with sending a man out to investigate his own murder!' Honeyman moaned as the whole of his pension flashed before his eyes. 'We'll never live this down!'

'What I meant, sir, was that the important thing is to sort out what this accusation means. Recriminations can wait until later, but Mills's whole life and career are on the line here.'

'Career!' Honeyman ejaculated helplessly; but then he pulled himself together. 'Carver tells me you worked with Mills some time ago.'

'Yes, sir, for three years at Charing Cross.'

'And what sort of officer was he?'

'The best, sir. Quiet, efficient, conscientious.'

'You had no doubts about his honesty?'

'He was my bagman on several cases. I had complete faith in him.'

'I've pulled his record, and that's clean,' Honeyman said regretfully. 'And Colin Washbrook over at Epsom speaks highly of him. But that's his duty life. His private life is less satisfactory. He isn't married, you know. I don't like the idea of policemen who aren't married. And he's a loner. I prefer a policeman to be the sociable type. That way we all check up on each other.' He looked up. 'He had blood on his clothes, you say?'

'He said Somers had clutched hold of him, and the blood came off on him. That's a reasonable explanation. And Baker confirms that Somers was hysterical and that Mills had a job calming him.'

'He might have grabbed hold of Somers deliberately to hide bloodstains he had got earlier.'

'But Mrs Reynolds doesn't say the man at the lift had blood on his clothes, only a little on his cuff.'

'Even that would be enough for him to want to hide. He wasn't to know that the woman had noticed, if they only saw each other for a second – or that she would come forward.' Honeyman's fingers drummed absently on the newspaper on his desk. 'The fingerprint on the religious tract card doesn't match, you say?'

'Bob Lamont says they are very similar, but there are certain distinct features which differ in Mills's.'

'Well, fingerprinting's not an exact science. You can always argue it either way. It's negative evidence at best. And that print could have got onto the card at any time, as we always knew. The most damning thing is the fact that he was there in the first place. It's going to be hard to get round that.'

Slider was silent. He knew that was true. It was the bit, on the whole, he didn't like; yet putting himself in Mills's shoes, he wondered if natural curiosity might not have made him act the same. Walking your new ground trying to get a feel of things, trying to assemble the knowledge on which your future success, possibly even life, would depend . . . Well, it was arguable, at the outside.

'You've checked with the mobile team – what were their names?'

'Baker and Morley, sir. They say Mills just appeared soon after they got to the scene of the murder.'

'Ah. And what about reception?'

'Mills says he didn't go to the desk, he just followed the uniformed lads. No-one tried to stop him because the reception area was crowded with people – the audience going up to the show.'

Honeyman looked seriously at him. 'This could be crucial. If you can find anyone who saw him arriving, and pin down the time, we might have a defence.'

'Yes, sir,' Slider said patiently. 'We're on it.' The team was already re-contacting all the people who might have been in the reception area at the time to ask, rather hopelessly, if they had noticed the uniforms arriving and the dark-haired man following. It was not necessary to tell them how urgent the matter was; Mills might be new, but he was one of their own, and, loner or not, he was instantly likeable.

'For the time being, I have no alternative but to suspend Mills,' Honeyman said, and to his credit he sounded regretful; Slider hoped on Mills's behalf and not his own. 'On your recommendation I shan't take any further action yet, but of course Mills must be very, very careful and very circumspect. I've told Carver, and he thinks that as Mills has been working on your case, you should be the one to tell him.'

Oh joy, Slider thought. Thank you, Ron.

'One other thing, Slider – nothing's been said yet to the Complaints Investigation Bureau. I want to give you a chance to justify your faith in Mills. But I have to warn you, if he is named in the press, or if you fail to progress within the next two days, I shall have no alternative. And once Mills has been turned over to the CIB, it will be out of my hands.'

'I understand, sir,' Slider said. Forty-eight hours to get old Dark Satanic out of the brown and viscous. And to rescue dainty Eric Honeyman's career from an ignominious end. On the whole, he thought, I'd rather be in Philadelphia.

CHAPTER TWELVE

Close to Home

'You never got married, then?' Slider asked, sitting at one side of the table in the tiny kitchen while Mills sat at the other. Through the open door they could hear the soft sounds of Atherton searching the bedroom. Mills had a tiny flat on the top floor of a house on the bend of Stanlake Road, where it bumped into the edge of the New Park and swung away again. From the little window behind the sink you could see through the trees a bit of the park and the BBC building on the other side of it. It was much too close to the nick for a policeman to settle in permanently, but it had often been let for short periods to newcomers while they looked for a place – having the advantage that it was almost impossible to be late for work while living there. As Atherton said, you could almost smell the canteen from the door.

'Never,' Mills answered Slider's question, with a quirk of his lips at the word, as though it amused him in some way. He took a sip from his mug of coffee. Slider's sat untouched before him. He didn't like instant coffee anyway, and this was edging towards record-breaking awfulness. It was the colour of ditch water and smelt like a stale face-flannel, and those were only its good points. Odd that 'a coffee' had always been the accepted precursor to – and even euphemism for – a sexual encounter. But then, like sexual encounters, instant coffee was usually disappointing and often left a funny taste in your mouth.

'What happened to that nice girl you were seeing when we were both at Charing Cross? Dark-haired girl. What was her name?'

'Ruth.'

'That's the one. Scottish, wasn't she? She was a nice girl.'

'She married a nice man,' Mills said. 'With a nice job, nine to five and a company car and no hassle.'

'Ah. I'm sorry.'

'So was I.' Mills looked at him with a gleam of humour. 'There have been others. I'm not queer.'

'I didn't think you were.'

'For the record, then. But the longer you're on your own, the harder it is to get it together with someone. You know the problems – the only people who understand are policewomen, and if you date a plonk from your own ground, it's like having it off in a goldfish bowl. No romance could survive that.' He shrugged. 'So I keep it outside and I keep it casual. Or it keeps itself casual. Women don't like taking second place to the Job.'

'Are you seeing someone at the moment?'

'There was someone in Epsom.'

'The girl you left behind?' Slider suggested.

Mills didn't smile. 'She was married. He was a sales director for an ice cream company. He didn't know. She didn't want him to. It suited her that way. Having her Arctic Roll and eating it.'

'And you? Did it suit you?'

He shrugged. 'She wasn't the one great love of my life.'

'So who was?' He didn't answer. 'Ruth?'

'I suppose – if it was anyone. But if I'd married her we'd probably be divorced by now. Statistics. Are you divorced, sir?'

'Not yet,' Slider said. He wasn't going to let Mills turn the point. 'So tell me about your family.'

'My Dad's dead – ten, eleven years ago. He was a lot older than Mum. Mum's getting a bit—' He rocked his hand. 'Well, she's pushing seventy. It's not Alzheimer's, apparently – something to be grateful for. But she doesn't always remember things. Gets confused.'

'She's in a home, you said?'

'Not a home. Sheltered accommodation. St Melitus's in Brook Green.'

'And you go and visit her?'

'That was mainly why I got myself transferred here, so I could get to see her more often. When I was in Epsom I couldn't just "drop in". It was too far. And when they get old like that, you don't know how long you'll have them. After Dad died – well, when it's too late, then you realise how often you missed the chance to visit them because you were tired or couldn't be bothered or whatever.'

Slider thought of his own father, and thought away again. 'Any other family?'

'Only Auntie Betty. When I was a kid there were some ancient uncles and aunts on my Dad's side that we saw occasionally, but they're all dead now, and I never kept up with the cousins. My mum just had the one sister. Like I said, she lives in Ormiston Grove.'

'And you visit her too.'

'I always called on her when I came to see Mum. But she was a bit cross about me transferring to Shepherd's Bush. Told me she didn't want me hanging around bothering her.' He smiled to show it was a joke. 'She was always very fond of me. I loved going round her house when I was a kid. She used to take me out places, tried to widen my horizons. She took me to Covent Garden, the museums, the zoo – to the Oval to watch Surrey—'

'You had an aunt who liked cricket?' Slider said in envious tones.

'She was a very unusual aunt – an education in herself. She really made me what I am. She and Mum never really got on, but I will say Mum never tried to stop me seeing her. I think she disapproved because Auntie Betty had a career instead of getting married and having children, like a proper woman. But it was nice for me. It meant I got all the attention and all the presents. It was Auntie Betty bought me my first bike.'

'That's quite a present from an aunt,' Slider said.

'It caused a bit of a fuss at home,' Mills said with a rueful grin. 'Mum and Dad didn't have a lot of money, they couldn't afford to buy me stuff. I remember some pretty sharp comments about that bike. I think Dad had half a mind to send it back, but it would've broken my heart. I'd wanted one for years. I suppose it was a bit tactless of Auntie, but she had a good job in the Civil Service and no-one else to spend the money on, and she was very fond of me.'

'She wasn't married?'

'Married to her career.'

'Like you.'

Mills shrugged. 'I'll be a bachelor like my father – that's what I used to say. It used to drive Mum mad.'

'Did you know anything about your natural parents?'

'No,' Mills said firmly but indifferently. 'I never asked.'

'Weren't you curious?'

'Why should I be? I was happy as I was. My mum and dad were good to me, and as far as I was concerned they were my parents.'

'You must have heard something about the circumstances, though, over the years. How you came to be born.'

'I gathered my natural mother was unmarried and the bloke didn't want to know, that's all. The usual story. Of course in those days it was a serious thing, getting pregnant. A girl couldn't just keep the kid and live on the State like she can now. I mean, she needn't have been a bad lot. But she was nothing to do with me. How could she be? I was taken away from her at birth and adopted when I was a couple of weeks old. My parents didn't talk about it, and like I said, I didn't ask.'

'You grew up around here, you said?'

'You could hardly get a more local boy than me. Went to Ellerslie Road primary and Christopher Wren secondary. Supported QPR. Went dancing at the Hammersmith Palais. Got drunk for the first time at the General Smuts and fumbled my first girl in Wormholt Park.'

'Impressive credentials,' Slider smiled. 'And what made you become a policeman?'

'I suppose that was down to Auntie Betty in a way. Mum and Dad wanted me to go in for something like banking or accountancy, something respectable and secure in a suit. But Auntie used to talk about public service. She really believed that being a civil servant was doing something for your country, bless her. And she used to say, "You can't just live your life as if you were the only person on the planet." She was quite scathing on the subject of doing a job just to earn money. I think that was another reason she and Dad didn't get on. He must have thought she was criticising him all the time. I don't think she was – I think she was just tactless. But everything she said and did must have looked as if she was saying the way Mum and Dad lived wasn't good enough.'

'Weren't you afraid joining the police would look like siding with her against them?'

'I never thought about it. Once the idea of the police took root in my brain, it was all I wanted. And anyway, there was never any open hostility between Auntie and Mum and Dad. It was just little things that, looking back, I can see now must have annoyed them. But they were always polite. And I don't think in the end they minded me being a policeman. Mum nearly died of pride at the passing-out parade – any time she saw me in uniform, really; and Dad was always trying to get me to come and talk to his Sunday school class.'

'Were they churchgoers, your parents?'

'Oh yes. In the Pillars Of class – though of course it wasn't so unusual in those days. If you were respectable people you went to church, and that was that. But they were quite religious. I was adopted through the Church. I suppose they might have been grateful on that account as well – it was quite hard even in those days for a couple with such a big age difference to adopt. Dad was twenty years older than Mum.'

Slider nodded. 'Was your aunt religious, too?'

Mills made an amused face. 'I don't know. I was never allowed to visit her on Sundays. But I rather doubt it. She was always a bit of a rebel, my Auntie.'

'Nothing,' said Atherton. 'Normality encapsulated. You couldn't get anything less Dark and Satanic. The only iffy thing in the house was a large collection of Barbra Streisand records; but I suppose it is possible for a Barbra Streisand fan to be a good man,' he added doubtfully.

'I once knew a thoroughly decent person who quite liked Barry Manilow,' Slider admitted.

'You just never can tell,' Atherton said wisely. 'So what about Mills?'

'I don't know,' Slider said. 'I don't believe he's a murderer, but you don't necessarily have to be a murderer to kill someone, do you? The question is, if it was him, why Roger Greatrex? There's got to be some connection. I can't believe Greatrex was dispatched completely at random, and if it wasn't robbery from the person, it was because of something he did, or was.'

'Or even everything he did and was,' Atherton said.

'Yes, perhaps,' Slider said absently.

'Well, what do we do now?' Atherton asked after a moment. 'Keep looking for some connection between Mills and Greatrex? Or accept that the old bird was confused?'

'We haven't got a lot of options. We'll have to do a full investigation into Mills, because if we don't the CIB will. That means someone will have to go to Epsom and try to find out who his friends were, what he did in his spare time, whether he had any cases that bear on the situation. And we'll have to try to trace his movements on Thursday night and since he's been back in the Bush.'

'This aunt might throw some light, I suppose?'

'We can only hope so. And meanwhile, we continue to act on the assumption that it wasn't him Mrs Reynolds saw by the lift. We keep asking questions, look for witnesses, show people the photofit and see if they recognise it, try and trace the bag—'

'Ha ha.'

'And the coat.'

'And the knife?'

Slider frowned. 'Mills said he was in the Scouts as a lad. And the knife is the sort of old-fashioned clasp-knife that Scouts used in those days. But it could have been anyone's, and come from anywhere. I think the most likely thing is that Mrs Reynolds saw someone by the lift who was superficially like Mills; she'd seen Mills at the TVC without realising it, and compounded them in her mind when she saw him again at the station.'

'Sounds good to me,' Atherton said. 'And we've still got the spare Mr Davis to follow up. No need to despair yet.'

'How do you follow up someone you know doesn't exist?' Slider said rhetorically.

Miss Elizabeth Giles, Mills's Auntie Betty, turned out to be a tall, vigorous, chain-smoking lady in her sixties, whose intelligent dark eyes made her face look younger than her white hair suggested. Though thick and bushy, it was cut very short.

'Unseemly, I know,' she said, having made an apology for her 'skinhead crop' the opening gambit in their conversation, 'but I've let it grow out since I retired – I used to dye it, you see, sad effort to look younger than my years – and with the ends dark and the roots growing out white, I looked such a sight, like a skewbald pony. So I keep having them cut off. The last of it's gone, now, as you see, so I can start to resume the dignity due to my vast age. Except that I rather like the freedom.' She shook her head about. 'Like Jo, you know, in *Little Women*? No, delete that. *Silly* thing to say. What would a chap like you be doing reading *Little Women*? Even if you have a daughter, I'm sure the PC brigade will have banned books like that from sale.'

She occupied the ground floor of a tall terraced house in Ormiston Grove which showed, by its paper bell-signs, to have other occupants upstairs and in the semi-basement. 'I bought it years ago for an investment, in case I ever got married and had a lot of children, but what sort of man would marry a woman who owned a house large enough to have ten children in?' she said cheerfully. 'Don't attempt to answer that. In case you wonder, I've had plenty of offers of marriage over the years, but never from anyone I'd have dreamed of accepting. I suppose my trouble is I could never respect any man who'd want to be married to a woman like me. So here I am, all alone, except for the students in the basement and the bats in the belfry. I like to keep some young people about me, keeps me on my toes.'

'Bats in the belfry?' Slider managed to slip a question in.

'Oh, God love them, they're not really bats, of course, but one can't resist, can one? *Le mot juste* and all that. CICs they call them now, bless them – Care in the Community. I've got two upstairs, and you couldn't want better lodgers. Besides, it makes the tax position so much more favourable. God knows I've paid enough in all these years – not that I begrudge it. You have to do your bit, don't you? No man is an island. Would you like tea? Excuse the mess, I'm not one of nature's Little Housewives, and now I'm at home all the time, I seem to make ten times the mess. But it's all clean dirt, as my mother used to say. Do you mind dogs? Do you mind if I let mine out? I shut them in the scullery when I came to the door because they're off out into the street if they get the slightest chance. Can you switch the kettle on while I let them out? It is full.'

Slider obeyed, while Miss Giles picked her way through the cluttered kitchen and opened a coat-infested door at the other side, whereupon two small, hairy projectiles shot out between her feet and hurled themselves round the room like wall-of-death riders, making frantic love to each pair of legs as they passed them. After a moment they slowed down enough to resolve themselves into two grey schnauzers with very short haircuts and muscle-packed bodies who, for some reason, seemed to Slider to reinforce the view that people choose dogs that look like themselves.

'Loonies,' Miss Giles said affectionately, shoving the nearest one with her foot. 'You'd think they'd been locked in there for days instead of minutes. Now, tea. Where did I put the teapot? Oh, wait, I remember, it's got flowers in it, in the other room.' She smiled engagingly. 'I was sent rather a large bunch a few days ago, and had to press every vessel into service. Never mind, it's teabags anyway. Do you mind my being terribly vulgar and making it in the cup?'

'Not at all,' Slider said. 'Was it your birthday?'

'Good lord, how did you—? Oh, the flowers, you mean! Yes, my birthday, though at my age it would be more seemly to stop having them. But Steve always remembers, bless him. He's a good boy.'

'Have you—?'

'Do you want a cup or a mug?' she overrode him. 'The cups are rather twincey, you get more if you don't mind a mug. And how do you take it? Milk, sugar?'

'No sugar, thanks.'

'Right. We'll stay in here, if you don't mind. The other room is such a tip. Sit down, boys. No, no, we're not going out. Go and sit down. Basket!' She smiled through the steam. 'It always made me laugh when people shouted "Basket" at their dog. I started doing it as a joke, but of course they don't know any better. It works, though – a nice, sharp-edged, distinguishable word.' The two little dogs had certainly obeyed her, and were sitting side by side in the large, old-fashioned wicker basket by the back door. The kitchen was unreconstructed fifties, with a wooden table and chairs, a grey enamel gas stove, a porcelain sink, and a wooden cupboard with an enamel top for a work surface. The only modern thing in the room was a gleamingly large portable radio/tape recorder – what they used to call a Brixton Briefcase because the West Indian boys always carried them – in the corner from which music and voices were issuing quietly. After a moment Slider identified it as probably a Mozart opera, and felt proud of himself. Apart from the books, clothes, newspapers and personal clutter washing about the room like a landlocked tide, everything was in pristine condition. Slider wondered if it had been like this when Mills visited as a child.

'Have you lived here very long?' he asked while she paused for breath.

'Thirty years. I must have been one of the first single women on earth to get a mortgage on my own salary, and even then I had to get a special recommendation from my boss to the building society. They assumed all women were going to marry and get pregnant, as night follows day. I've often wondered what he told them,' she grinned. 'Maybe that no-one would have me on a bet.'

'So it was here that Mills – Steve – used to visit you as a child?'

'Yes. Well, they lived just round the corner in Oaklands Grove.'

'Is that why you bought the house? I mean, bought it here rather than somewhere else?'

'Property was cheap here at the time,' she answered, and he thought there was something about that which was slightly less straightforward than her previous deliveries. She dealt with the teabags before she spoke again. 'I didn't mind living nearby. I didn't see much of Maggie and her husband, but it was nice to have Steve popping in. I suppose he's told you I was very fond of him as a boy?'

'He spoke very warmly of you,' Slider said. 'He said you took him to cricket matches and the opera.'

She laughed, and he saw that she must have been attractive in her youth, though probably overpowering even then. 'I had to do something to counteract the football culture. Arthur – his dad – used to take him to see QPR play most Saturdays in winter. His idea was to make Steve as ordinary as possible, as much like himself and everybody else as he could. Whereas I wanted him to be as individual as possible. I could see the boy had great potential. I introduced him to a wider set of horizons. I hoped he might be musical – my mother played the piano very well, and Father sang apparently. I didn't want Steve growing up thinking football and the Methodist Church was all there was in life.'

'How did his father like that?'

She looked at him sharply, and set his tea down with rather

more of a bang than was strictly necessary. 'You mean his dad? You don't expect people like Arthur to appreciate other people's points of view. Their minds run on rails. Anything at all different from their experience is automatically suspect, and a criticism of themselves.'

'You didn't get on with him?'

The expression became veiled. 'Oh, I wouldn't say that. Arthur was a good, decent, Godfearing man. I dare say he found me irritating. And of course he hated the fact that I had a career. In his eyes, a woman's place was in the home. But he was a good dad to Stevie, according to his lights. I just felt I could offer him something he wouldn't get with Maggie and Arthur – but I tried to do it discreetly.' She met Slider's eyes, and gave a hearty laugh. 'Yes, I know! You don't need to look at me like that. And of course, I'm not the most tactful person in the world. But we all tried to put a good face on it and get along, for the boy's sake.'

'Your sister's older than you?'

'Eight years.'

'And there were just the two of you?'

'There were two brothers in between, twins, but they died at birth. Poor Maggie was always very much the elder sister, running after me, trying to keep me out of trouble and getting the blame when she didn't. And then Father died untimely, and Mother went to pieces rather, and Maggie had to mother me. It made her old before her time, poor darling, whereas I could go on being disgraceful all my life, safe in the knowledge that I was the baby of the family. Wicked!'

'Were you? Wicked, I mean?'

'Oh – no, not really. It's just the mores of the time were against me. I mean, Arthur was a perfect example of the normality of those days. He thought it was disgraceful to see a woman smoking. And as for having my own bank account and cheque book – slippery slope! I often wondered why Maggie married him.'

'Why do you think she did?'

'Father replacement, I suppose. Move over Sigmund. But he was twenty years older than her – thirty in spirit. I suppose she was fed up with being Mother and wanted to become somebody's daughter again. Well, that's what we all want really, isn't it – someone to take responsibility for us? Some more than others.' The last words were muffled by the cigarette on which she pulled hard, blinking her eyes rapidly in the smoke.

'Were they very religious – your sister and her husband?'

'Well, quite, I suppose. Very, compared with me. But they weren't weird about it or anything like that. Straightforward Methodist. They went to church every Sunday, Arthur taught the Sunday school, Maggie did teas at various church dos, that sort of thing. Arthur was a bit old-fashioned about keeping the Sabbath, but then he was old-fashioned about a lot of things. Wouldn't let Steve eat in the street, for instance – not even an ice cream. Imagine, if the boy wanted a threepenny cornet, he had to bring it indoors and eat it sitting down at the table. Where's the fun in that?'

Slider smiled. 'My mother was the same. She wouldn't let us eat fish and chips out of the paper. We had to take it home and have it off plates. She said it was common to eat in the street.'

Miss Giles smiled broadly. 'I call that sheer cruelty! Was she a Methodist?'

'No, just the normal C of E.'

'Well, anyway, you can see why I felt I had to do my bit to introduce a little leaven into Steve's life. Thank heaven Arthur never had a daughter, that's all I can say.'

'They never had any children of their own?'

She shook her head. 'They wanted them, but nothing happened. I rather fancy Arthur couldn't, but it wasn't something that was discussed in those days – and in any case, Maggie would never have discussed it with me. Loyalty, you know. So they adopted.'

'Through the Church, I understand?'

'Yes.'

He waited for more, but she said nothing, sipping at her cigarette, her eyes fixed on the rising smoke.

'Was anything known about the baby's parents?'

'It was a private adoption, arranged by their minister,' she said. 'Because of Arthur's age they couldn't go through the usual routes. But it was all legal and above-board.'

She sounded defensive, and he said soothingly, 'I'm sure it was. I just wondered if anything—'

'Joshua Green was his name. I always think that sounds like a village in a children's book. Not that there was anything pastoral about him – he was a real, eye-flashing, fire-and-brimstone preacher. Had a terrific following in the flock. And he was a great organiser. Maggie used to say he could organise a cat into having puppies.' She puffed again. 'It wasn't the only adoption he arranged – Green. He was attached to a mother-and-baby home, financed by the Church. It was his pet charity, I believe. I suppose it was natural for Maggie to turn to him when she found she couldn't have a child.'

'But you think she knew nothing about the natural mother?'

'How should I know what she knew?' She sounded irritable. 'All I know is that they kept those things very discreet in those days. Once the woman had given the kid away, she was supposed to bow out for ever. Nobody in those days thought adopted children would ever be allowed to look up their past, as they can now. The Children Act, or whatever it was called. Retrospective law is bad law, that's what I've always been told. Fortunately most of them don't bother. In any case, what has it got to do with anything? Maggie was the one who brought Steve up. She's the one who moulded his character, if that's what you're enquiring about.'

'According to him, you had quite a lot to do with it,' Slider said smilingly.

She got up abruptly from her seat and went over to the sink, emptied the dregs of her cup and ran the tap noisily into it.

'I'm sorry, I didn't catch what you said,' Slider said when she turned it off.

'I said, what did you want to know specifically about Steve? What's he supposed to have done – or aren't I allowed to know?'

'There seem to be some irregularities in the conduct of a case in which he's involved,' Slider said carefully. 'I'm just trying to clear things up. I worked with Mills some years ago and I'd prefer to get it straight myself than to see it passed to an outsider.'

'You worked with him?' she asked, her gaze sharpening. 'Yes, wait a minute now, I remember your name. I thought there was something familiar about it. It was when he was at Charing Cross, wasn't it? He used to talk about you sometimes – thought you were a good 'un and destined for high places.'

'They don't always go together, I'm afraid,' Slider said. She was looking at him with interest and more friendliness now.

'Well, what's he supposed to have done? How can I help? What is this case?'

Slider told her; and explained how Mills had been seen at the scene of the crime at the wrong moment. 'I don't believe there's anything in it myself,' he said casually, 'but the witness seems a very steady sort of person, and she described him very well. She compiled a photofit picture for us, and it does look very like.'

She sat down slowly in her vacated chair. She stared at him as though she had thought of something. 'But he—' She tried to lick her lips, and then went into a coughing fit. At the end of it, drumming her fist briskly against her chest she said, 'Got to give these damned things up. You were saying – you don't think there's anything in it.'

'I think the most likely thing is that the witness saw him somewhere else, and simply remembered him in the wrong place. After all, he was there during the evening. But with such a positive identification, I have to follow it up.'

'Positive, yes,' she said, and she laughed strangely, as if at a private joke. 'Well, obviously, Steve isn't a murderer – if you've worked with him, you know that anyway. He did come to see me on Thursday afternoon, and he left about – oh, I don't know – half past six. Ish. I wasn't checking, but it would be somewhere around there.'

'Yes,' Slider said. That tallied with what Mills had said. 'Is he religious at all?'

'Religious? What a horrible expression! If you mean, like his mum and dad, no he isn't. But I'm sure he has an inner belief and an inner code, as most of us do. I don't think he could be a good policeman if he didn't believe in anything, do you? And he is a good policeman, isn't he?'

'I think so,' Slider said. 'But he isn't a regular churchgoer? Doesn't belong to any special groups?'

'Not that I'm aware of.'

Slider nodded, and went on chatting to her while his thoughts roamed. They hadn't found anything of a religious nature in Mills's flat, not even a Bible – though with an upbringing like his, Mills was likely to be *au fait* with the Bible, perhaps enough to be able to quote from it from memory. And as he was living in temporary accommodation, he might not have all his things with him. He must make a mental note to check that out.

He rose to leave. 'By the way, why didn't you want Mills to come back to Shepherd's Bush? I'd have thought you'd like to have him a bit nearer than Epsom, fond of him as you are.'

She was ready for that one. 'I didn't like to think of him tied to the apron strings of two old biddies like me and his mum. Especially now Maggie's going gaga. We could be a real drag on him, especially given his kind heart, and that's not what I ever wanted for him. He's got his own life to lead. I told him when he came round on Thursday that I didn't want him popping in to see me every five minutes. That's not the way to get ahead.'

'And you want him to get ahead?'

She looked at Slider with slightly narrowed eyes, though it might only have been because of the smoke rising from the freshly lit cigarette. 'He's the nearest thing I ever had to a son,' she said. 'Of course I want him to get ahead.'

CHAPTER THIRTEEN

Private Lives

Atherton knew that look. When Slider returned, he wore the expression of internal preoccupation, like a man who has just eaten rather too large a curry along with several pints of the Anglabangla's Super Mistral lager.

'What it is, guv?' he asked, but without much hope. At this stage his guv'nor often didn't know himself. It was just that something was trying to connect up inside his mind.

Slider merely shook his head and headed for his office. Atherton followed. 'No luck so far with the photofit, but it's slow work, of course, everyone being so scattered. Thirteen staff and about twenty of the audience have been shown it and so far only one has said it looks familiar, and even she's pretty vague – thinks she saw someone like that at some point but can't be sure. People are so unobservant,' he complained.

'Yes,' said Slider.

Atherton looked at him enquiringly. 'I can't quite work out whether we want people to recognise this mug or not. I mean, if people saw Mills knocking around the building – is that good or bad?'

'Has the photofit been shown to the man who sold his ticket?'

'Jim Davies? Yes, and he thinks it might have been the same man, but he's not sure. Still, at least he hasn't said absolutely not, which gives us the possibility that the ticket-buyer looks enough like Mills to have confused Mrs Reynolds, and that makes him the murderer and then we only have to find him.'

'Have you found out yet who actually wrote down the Davis name and address up in the canteen?' Slider said abruptly.

'Oh, yes, it was Coffey. D'you want to talk to him?'

Coffey, a young officer lent by the uniform side, came in looking shamefaced.

'Your handwriting's so bad you could have been a doctor,' Slider said. 'Did you think you were writing Dav*is* or Dav*ies*?'

'It's Dav*is*, sir, definitely. And I always check spellings like that. I know I did,' he added earnestly, 'because I'm a bit sensitive about names. Nearly everyone spells mine wrong.'

'So you remember this man?'

'Well, sir, no, not really.' Slider looked up sharply, and Coffey lifted his hands slightly in a gesture of surrender. 'There were so many people there, all milling about this sort of canteen, and we were sitting at tables writing while they came up one by one and sat down and gave their names and addresses. It was like a sausage machine. I just kept writing.'

'You've had a look at the photofit?'

'Yes, sir. Well, I suppose it could have been him, but I honestly can't say I remember. I suppose I must have looked up at the people when they sat down, but I didn't really take in any faces. I wasn't looking to recognise them, I was just trying to hear what they said. There was so much noise in there, you could hardly hear yourself think, and—' The sentence trailed off, and Slider could easily add the rest for himself – we were all cursing the guv'nor downstairs who thought we had nothing better to do than take the names and addresses of a couple of hundred punters. 'But the photofit is supposed to be Mills, isn't it, sir? I mean, I'd have noticed if he sat down in front of me, or someone like him.'

Slider wouldn't have bet on it, especially as Coffey could only have seen him for an instant downstairs. And as Atherton said, people were so unobservant.

He was about to go home when Norma put her head round the door and said, 'Mr Honeyman wants you, boss.'

'What's he still doing here?' Slider said wearily.

'It looked like the Maori Haka,' she said. 'Have you seen the paper?'

'Oh, don't tell me!'

'They've named Mills.'

'How the hell did that get out?' Slider cursed. 'Well, I suppose I'd better go and face it.'

Honeyman was very upset. 'This couldn't have come from your witness,' he said accusingly, rapping the paper with an admonitory finger. 'Someone in your team has leaked.'

Slider took the paper in silence and read.

> The police officer in the Roger Greatrex murder case, who has been suspended over alleged irregularities of conduct, has been named as Detective Sergeant Steven Mills, 38. Mills, recently transferred to Shepherd's Bush, lives locally and has no previous disciplinary record. The Police declined to comment on the specific reasons for Mills's suspension.

Then it went on to rehash the details of the Greatrex murder. There was nothing else about Mills. But there was a picture – rather a bad one, but recognisable if you knew him.

'They don't really know anything,' Slider said, handing the paper back.

'It won't be long,' Honeyman grumbled. 'God knows how they got hold of the photograph, but now they have, some neighbour will recognise him and then they'll find out where he lives and it will be all over the six o'clock news. I'm very, very unhappy about this, Slider. I looked to you to keep your team in order. This is very unprofessional conduct, quite unacceptable.'

'It could have come from anywhere, sir,' Slider began, but Honeyman interrupted.

'The point is, it came from somewhere,' he said, silencing Slider with admiration. 'This alters the situation. I shall have to inform Mr Wetherspoon. I imagine he will take it out of my hands.'

'Sir,' Slider said urgently, but Honeyman held up his hand.

'I know, I know. I will do my best to get you some time, but I can't promise anything. Have you made any progress?'

Slider looked frustrated. 'Only negatively, sir.' For an instant something flickered in his mind at the sound of the word, but he had no time to lay hold of it then. 'There's nothing to indicate any connection between Mills and Greatrex,' he went on. 'But—'

'It's not enough,' Honeyman said with vast regret. 'Well, as I said, I'll try and buy you some time. But my advice to you is to try to come up with something a bit more positive, and as soon as possible.'

Now what the Sun Hill does he think I've been trying to do? Slider asked himself glumly as he trod away.

Joanna knew that look, too. 'Are you on to something?' she asked as he leaned against the kitchen door, watching her with unseeing eyes.

'Mmm,' he said vaguely.

'A line on the case?'

'I don't know. Nothing makes any sense yet. I think I'm about to understand what I'm thinking, but I'm so far out to the side I can't see the play. What are you cooking?'

'Minestrone soup. Thick enough to trot a mouse on. It's nearly ready. Do you want any bread with it?'

'Umm,' he said unhelpfully.

'Was that a yes?' Joanna asked, but he had wandered away. She sighed, and then thought of Irene, and restrained herself. This is what it must have been like to be married to him all those years, and in Irene's case she didn't even have the comfort of knowing herself deeply loved and fancied rotten by him. The bread was a bit stale so she decided to toast it, and then thought it would be nice to make it garlic bread, so she took her time peeling and crushing two cloves of garlic and mixing them with salt and butter to spread on the warm toast. But for all Bill noticed she might as well have given him the table mats to dip in his soup.

Between mouthfuls she looked at the blank face opposite her and felt her brief peeve dissolve to be replaced by a rather wistful affection. The difficulty always was that you loved a person as they were, and you couldn't get rid of the annoying factors without changing who they were. Bill's job got in the way, but separate him from his job and what you had left was not Bill. She supposed he must feel the same way about her job – or would if he was given to introspection. He had been pretty annoyed and upset that she had not been around over the weekend, though she doubted if he would have got right to the bottom of his own feelings. Apart from anything else, he hadn't had time to think about much but the case.

She wasn't at all surprised when after the meal he said

apologetically, 'Look, I'm sorry, but I think I've got to go out again.'

She protested only because she felt he expected it, and might think she was indifferent if she didn't. 'It's my only evening at home this week. Does it have to be now?'

'I'm sorry,' he said again, helplessly. 'I'm up against the clock, and there's one of my own men in trouble as well.'

'Yes, I know – Mills. Do you think he did it?'

'It isn't my business to think anything. I'm supposed to collect evidence, whichever way it goes.'

'Yes, but do you think he did it?' she insisted, knowing him.

'I'm hoping to prove he didn't,' he admitted. 'You remember that attempted burglary of Christa Jimenez that I mentioned to you?'

'You think that's part of it?'

'It did occur to me to wonder, in the light of Laurence Jepp being murdered, whether there was a connection, whether it really was a burglary.'

'Because they were both in *Giovanni*? You think there's a curse on the production?'

'I haven't got as far as that. I just wondered if it was intended as an attack rather than a burglary; if so, it might have been by the same man. So I've asked Mills for a blood sample, and I've persuaded Ron Carver to let me compare it with the blood on the knife that Jimenez attacked her intruder with – because it's his case, of course. I'm waiting to hear from Tufty. Of course, it's negative evidence at best. There's no certainty that incident was any part of it. And there's still the identification to be got over.' He lapsed again into his thoughts.

She studied his face. 'Is that what you've been thinking about since you came home?'

'Not entirely,' he said. 'There's something else I've got by the tail, but even if I'm right, I don't see where it gets me. But you've got to do the next thing. It's the only way forward. The next step. Maybe I'll see more clearly when I've taken it.'

'Go,' she said. 'With my blessing.'

A slightly lightened look was her reward. 'Really?'

'A man's gotta do what a man's gotta do. You're no use to me anyway, in this mood.' She saw the doubt, and reached across to pat his hand kindly. 'I mean it. Really. Go on, I ought to practise anyway, and I'll never do it if you're here looking provocatively sexy all evening.'

He even managed a grin. 'Thanks.'

She came with him to the door, and kissed him so that the bit of his mother in him worried about what the neighbours might think.

'Anyone might be looking.'

'Poor things,' she said, and did it again, but this time he reached behind her and switched off the hall light. He didn't like feeling exposed in the spotlight like that – but then, unlike her, his life had been threatened more than once. Looking over your shoulder got to be second nature.

There were lights on in Miss Giles's flat and faint music, but no answer when he rang the doorbell. He thought of trying the top bell, but then remembering who she had said was living there, decided to try the basement instead. There was a noise of pop music inside, and after a while the door opened and a young girl with a towel wrapped round her head looked out.

'Oh, have you been ringing long? I had my head under the tap,' she said, looking at him with such an open and trusting expression that he thought of his daughter, Kate, and a fatherly sternness came over him. He could have been anyone, and there she was in a dressing-gown and completely defenceless.

'I'm a police officer,' he said quickly, though she evidently had no apprehension about him. He showed his brief, but she barely looked at it. 'You ought always to check when someone shows you an ID like that,' he admonished her, but she only grinned at him.

'Oh, I had a look at you through the glass before I opened the door. I could see you were all right,' she said.

'You can't tell from appearance,' he objected.

'I can,' she said simply. 'What's the matter, is there something wrong?'

'I hope not,' he said. 'I've been ringing Miss Giles's doorbell and there's no answer.'

'Oh, that's all right, she never answers the door at night.'

'Unlike you.'

'I might miss out on something,' she pointed out with unconscious cruelty. 'Did you want me to get her for you?'

'Can you?'

'There's an inside door to her flat. She always hears if I knock on that. Come in.'

He followed her, but said, 'You shouldn't let me in when you haven't checked my ID.'

'Why are you so worried about me?' she asked gaily over her shoulder.

'I've got a daughter myself. These are dangerous times.'

'You're sweet,' she said, looking back at him for an instant. He gave it up. Maybe he shouldn't try to spoil that wonderful confidence of youth. Statistics were on her side; it was just the caution that was built in to the job.

The house had originally been all one, of course, and the stairs down from the first floor had not been removed when it was made into three. The young tenant used them as display shelves, but there was passage through the middle to the door at the top. Slider stood at the bottom while the young woman rapped briskly, held a brief conversation through it, and then crouched down to field the schnauzers as the door was opened.

'It's all right, come up,' she said.

Miss Giles looked very different from when he had first seen her. She was dressed in an ancient red felt dressing-gown with a striped cord tied tightly about her waist, which probably didn't help, but she looked old, and very much less vigorous. Her face without make-up looked pale and lined, her lips without lipstick thin and blue. Even her silky white hair looked limp, and her freckled hands shook a little as she lit a cigarette from the stump of the previous one and put the pack back in the pocket.

'I don't answer the door at night,' she said. 'You hear such terrible things.'

'Very wise,' he said. She led him, as before, into the kitchen, where a one-bar electric fire was set up near the table, on which stood a bottle of Famous Grouse, a tumbler, and an ashtray already overflowing with stubs. He looked quickly round to see what she had been doing when disturbed, but there was no book, paper, letter. Perhaps she had just been listening to the music and turned it off when she heard the knock on the door. Or perhaps she had been sitting and thinking.

She sat down on the side of the table nearest the fire.

'D'you want a drink?' she asked, unscrewing the cap from the bottle.

'No, thanks, not just now.'

'Well I'm having one. Let me know if you change your mind. One advantage to retirement is that it doesn't matter what you look like the next morning.' She looked up and met his eyes; hers seemed apprehensive. 'Oh yes, I've had a few already. And I mean to have a few more.'

'Is there something on your mind?'

'Is there something on yours?' she countered. 'It must be something urgent to warrant a visit at night. Or do they pay you overtime?'

'Sometimes.'

'So what do you want? I've told you everything I know.'

He smiled. 'It would take a great deal longer than one short visit to learn everything you know.'

'You flatter me,' she said. 'But I've worked in many parts of the world in my time, and I wouldn't have lasted long unless I knew how to keep my counsel.'

'Every life has secrets,' he said. 'They're harder to keep at the beginning than at the end, though. They have a sort of energy when they're first born, and they wriggle and wriggle to get out. But once that's exhausted, they tend to give up and lie quietly. If you can keep a secret for the critical period, you can keep it for ever.'

'Very poetic,' she said.

'Unless it becomes important for some reason to let it out.'

'And what possible reason could there be?'

'Oh, if someone was in danger of some sort, for instance.'

She shook her head, puffing busily. 'I can't see it, myself. A secret kept absolutely and for ever couldn't hurt anyone. A secret no-one knows effectively doesn't exist.'

'Maybe you're right,' he said. One of the dogs came up and sniffed his leg, and then stood up with its front paws up on his knee, and he caressed its ears absently. 'It's probably the half-known things that are more dangerous,' he went on. 'They're certainly an irritant. They nag at your mind until you can't rest. Things you can't quite understand. Things that don't quite add up.'

She looked at him unhelpfully. Whatever he guessed at, it

would be less than she knew, and he still didn't know where what he guessed at might get him.

'For instance,' he said, 'I made a phone call this afternoon to a very helpful friend of mine at St Catherine's House, who never minds looking things up for me. She told me that Margaret Rose Giles married Arthur Mills in September 1955.'

Miss Giles shrugged. 'I could have told you that, if you'd asked. It isn't a secret.'

'I didn't want to bother you,' Slider said. 'But the thing is, you see, that Steve Mills's date of birth in his records is May 1957, and he told me that he was adopted when he was just a couple of weeks old. That means your sister had been married less than two years when she adopted him.'

'What of it?' Miss Giles said with massive indifference.

'Well, it struck me, you see, that it was rather early days to decide you're never going to be able to have a child naturally and that the only course is adoption. Most couples wait five, six – even ten years before giving up hope.'

'You're forgetting Arthur's age. He didn't have ten years to wait,' she said, and Slider smiled inwardly. Once they start giving explanations, you've got them on the run. 'Maybe he'd had tests.'

'In 1957? It wasn't that easy on the National Health, and I gather there wasn't much money in the case. No, I think if you'd gone to a doctor in 1957 and said you hadn't become pregnant after less than two years of marriage, he'd have just told you to go away and try again.'

'Perhaps,' said Miss Giles. 'I've never been married, so I don't know.'

'It struck me as odd,' Slider continued, 'both that they should leap to that conclusion so early, and that they should have settled for adoption so quickly. Even after a couple despairs of pregnancy, it's usually a long time before they've talked enough about adoption to decide on it.'

'Well, it doesn't strike me as odd, but everyone to their own,' she said briskly. 'I don't see what it's got to do with me, anyway. They didn't confide their thought processes to me, however fascinating you may find the subject.'

'I'll come to that,' Slider said. 'I thought, you see, that if they didn't decide to adopt when they did because they'd exhausted all hope and all other channels, maybe the timing depended on the baby being available just at that moment. And if that was the case, then perhaps it was because they wanted to adopt not just any baby, but that particular one. That it was special to them in some way.'

She said nothing, but she kept on looking at him, in the manner of one who must know the worst.

'You were very fond of Steve when he was a boy,' Slider said gently. 'Unusually fond, perhaps, given that you and your sister didn't get on.'

'The boy wasn't to blame for that. And besides, he was very lovable.'

'Yes, I imagine so. But you loved the boy so much you even bought a house one street away to be near him—'

'That wasn't why—'

'Please. Bear with me. I'm just describing my thought processes. You bought this house, one street away, and the boy came to visit you, and you took him out places, interested yourself in his education, in the broader sense, encouraged him to make something of himself. And all this for the adopted child of a sister you didn't get on with married to a man you despised. And what was odder still, even though the sister and her husband disapproved of you, they let you take a hand in the upbringing of their son.'

She was silent.

'I also noticed that while you referred to your own father as "Father", you referred to Arthur as Steve's "dad". You even corrected me when I used the word "father" in respect of Arthur. And you're a woman, I've noticed, who uses words with skill.'

'You notice a lot,' she said acerbically.

'I noticed quite a few things you said. For instance, when you spoke of adopted children being able to trace their natural parents these days, you said, "Fortunately, most of them don't bother." That "fortunately" struck me as odd – as if it had personal relevance for you.' She didn't respond to that. 'And although you are not a churchgoer and seem rather contemptuous of your sister and brother-in-law's religion, you seemed to know an awful lot about the minister who arranged the adoption. Well,' he sat back from the table and put his hands down on it with a completing gesture, 'I thought everything over, and eventually I came to the conclusion that when you said Steve was the nearest thing you ever had to a son, you were having a little private joke at my expense.' He looked up from his hands. 'I'm right, aren't I? Steve is your son. He was your baby. Your knowledge of Minister Green and his mother-and-baby home came from first-hand experience.'

He wasn't sure what reaction he had expected from her – stubborn silence or even furious denial, perhaps – but he had not expected her to cry. It was painful and horrible for both of them, and there was nothing he could do to comfort her. He knew well enough that to touch her or offer her sympathy would compound his crime. After a moment of struggle she put her hands over her face and cried without grace, with the clumsiness of the unaccustomed, and with the tearing anguish of a lifetime of constraint and concealment. The dogs ran to her, looking up and wagging their tails curiously at the noise, and then began to grow distressed in their turn, running round her and trying to jump up. They finally settled for sitting at her feet crying in sympathy, occasionally pawing at her unresponsive leg.

'You can have no idea,' she said. Red-eyed, blotchy, and old, so old, she sat hunched at the table, smoking slowly. 'None of you men has any idea. Well, I can't blame you – I didn't have any idea either. I thought you could just have it and walk away. A baby you'd never seen – how could it mean anything to you? But it isn't like that. It's a part of you, you see. Oh, not your flesh, you can part with that. People don't hanker to know what happened to their amputated leg or whatever. But a part of who you are. And there's a bit of you that can't let go. However sensible and pragmatic you think you are. You can't – let – go.'

She smoked again, and he was silent. Now that she was talking, he must let her take her time.

'They took the babies away at birth. That was supposed to be the best thing for the mother. Kinder – the clean break. I don't know.' She shook her head. 'It seemed sensible to me at the time – beforehand. Maybe it is best for some people. A few months in the home, then into hospital, whisk the thing away like an appendix – that is a joke, you know, of a sort – and six weeks later you're back to normal and ready to take up your life again. That's the theory. But it wasn't that simple. Those girls in the home—' She was silent, looking at memory. 'They were so pathetic. All they wanted was to be able to keep their babies, but it wasn't allowed. Society didn't allow. You can't imagine how impossible it was then.' She looked at him for an instant. 'Nowadays nobody thinks twice about it. People even do it intentionally, when they don't have to, people who have the choice. "Starlet's love-child" and all that sort of thing. And if you haven't any money, the State pays. But not then. You simply couldn't. It was impossible, and those girls knew it. But oh, how they cried! The matron said it was just their condition – hormones all shaken up – but it wasn't. God damn it, she didn't hear them at night! They cried from their souls upwards. It was a river, an unstaunchable flood of tears. Have you ever heard a cow calling for its calf? They cried like animals for their stolen children, those poor, ignorant girls! But they were trapped. Even if society had let them, Green and his Church wouldn't. That's why they took the babies at birth, you see, to give us no chance to change our minds. The Church had put down good money for those babies. Those babies were *capital*.'

'You mean they took money for arranging the adoptions?' Slider asked.

'Good God, no,' she said contemptuously. 'Green wasn't interested in money. His vanity was purely religious. It was souls he wanted. He placed the babies with good, churchgoing couples, in return for which the couples kept on being churchgoing, and brought up the kid to be, too. It was God's work – evangelism in its most practical form. Give me a child at an impressionable age – and so on.' She sucked on her cigarette and then snorted with unamused laughter. 'He used to preach to us, too. Not content with the babies, he wanted our souls as well. A lot of the girls were swayed – that *was* hormones. You feel quite sexy at a certain stage of pregnancy, and your mind is rather loose in the haft as well, easily unbalanced. And he was quite a man. They yearned for him, and thought it was religion. Poor saps!'

'What about the father of your child?'

'What about him? He doesn't come into it. He's dead now, long since. That's one mercy.'

'How did it happen?'

'How d'you think?' she said, and then relented. 'He was my boss. Married, of course. I was just starting out on my career. I fell for his status and he fell for my earnestness. I have to say he behaved decently according to his lights. He was horrified when I told him I was pregnant – it would have been the end of him in those days, if it had got out – but he tried to do the decent thing. He arranged for me to have a sabbatical, and gave me money to keep me going. He was so glad when I said I was going to have it adopted. I think ideally he'd have liked me to have an abortion, but of course it cost the earth to have it done properly in Switzerland, and even he wouldn't have expected me to take the risk of an illegal in England. So Joshua Green's salvation plan for fallen women filled the bill perfectly.'

'How did your sister come into it?'

'Oh, she introduced me to Green, of course. It was her I turned to first of all, even before I told the father. She'd been like a mother to me, after all, so I naturally thought she could sort me out. But Arthur was horrified. His first worry was what would the neighbours think and what would the Sunday school think. He'd have thrown me out into the snow if he could, but Maggie talked him round. I think she must have suspected by then that he wasn't going to be able to give her a baby, and she wanted one so badly. And at least mine would share her genes – not that she thought in those terms, but the idea was there. And it was common cant that a woman who adopted often got pregnant soon afterwards, so she had nothing to lose. I don't know how she persuaded Arthur, but I think religion came into it. I was a fallen woman and past redemption, but the child could be rescued from sin and brought up by Arthur in the paths of righteousness, and wouldn't that be a good thing to do? Worth a gold star, ten points towards his halo at least.'

'And the minister, Green, arranged all the legal side, did he?'

'Yes. He wasn't too keen on the arrangement, really – didn't like the idea that an unmarried mother would know where her baby had gone. There was supposed to be an absolute cut-off and no contact ever after. He only agreed to it – and Arthur only agreed to it – on the condition that I kept out of the way while I was pregnant, and went right away afterwards and didn't come near Maggie and Arthur ever again.' She shrugged. 'I was happy enough with the arrangement. I wanted my career, I thought babies were revolting, I wanted to be a free-wheeling, hard-headed power-woman in a suit, get to the top of the Civil

Service, and have no ties, and retire with a small gong and a large pension.'

'But it didn't work out that way.'

'Not entirely. I went away to begin with. I went back to work, kept my mouth shut and my head down and started to climb the ladder. But there was always the question mark. And Green was right in one way. Knowing where they were made it difficult not to go and take a look at them. So finally I gave in to the voices and bought this house and—' She shrugged again.

'I imagine Maggie and Arthur weren't too happy about it.'

'You imagine right. But there I was, like a mountain, and it was easier to work round me than try and remove me. I promised I would never tell Steve, or even hint at it, and I kept my word. Maggie knew I would, and I suppose she persuaded Arthur. Besides, I was the only one in the family who was ever going to have money, and he'd have thought by rights it ought to come to Stevie. But it galled him, I think, that he had the expense of keeping the child while I had the fun of taking him to the zoo. Like a weekend father.' She looked at him quickly. 'It isn't all roses being a weekend father.'

Slider nodded. Had she guessed? Statistically, it was a fair bet.

'But I'd made my bed, and I wasn't going to whine about it. And nobody has ever guessed until today, until you – damn you.' But she said it without heat.

'Are you sure?' he asked.

She searched his face. 'You mean, does Steve guess? No, I don't think so. Have you reason to think so?'

'No. Not really. I just thought—' He studied her. 'There is a resemblance, when you look for it.'

'But people don't,' she said. 'People never do. Those gothic romances where the heroine looks at a family portrait and realises it's her mother – it just would never happen in real life. Steve – Steve looks like his father. But even if he'd ever come face to face with his father, I doubt if he'd have noticed.'

Slider sat silent. Much more made sense now, question marks had been exploded and swept away. But it didn't get him any further on. He hadn't known where he was going with his doubts, and he still couldn't see daylight ahead. All he had done was to upset this woman and rip a secret out of her that she had taken a lifetime to bury under the foundations.

As if she heard his thought, she said, 'You were right about secrets losing their energy. If I was going to blurt it out to Steve, it would have been when he was about eight years old. I loved him so much then, and he was so fond of me, I used to think sometimes I'd done the wrong thing, that I should have kept him and tried to bring him up myself. But it would have been hell for all of us. The way it turned out was the best for him, and for me in every way but one.' She paused a moment, staring at the middle air. 'But after that, there was never any danger I'd tell, or let anything slip.' She changed her focus. 'You guessed because you were looking for something. Or maybe – maybe because you're unusually perceptive.' She sounded puzzled by the notion.

'I don't think I am,' he said. 'If I were I'd know what the hell was going on in this case, and I don't. I'm trying to clear your – your *nephew*, and the only way I can think of to do it is to solve the case, find who really did it. But I don't even know where to look.'

'Find out who did *what*?' she asked. 'What is he supposed to have done?'

'He's been identified by a witness.' He looked at her thoughtfully, wondering if the gravity of the situation would make her more or less forthcoming. 'It's a case of murder. A man carrying a bag which turned out to contain clothes stained with the victim's blood was seen and described by a witness, and she's picked out Mills as being the man.'

She was silent, but her face was drawn, her eyes seemed to have gone back in her head. After a moment she said, 'I saw – in the paper it said – it was a murder case. But I didn't know he was suspected. Oh my God.' He half wished he hadn't told her now. She seemed not just distressed, but terrified. After a moment she said, '*You* don't think – do you?'

'No. No, on the whole I don't.'

'But how can you have *any* doubt? He just isn't capable of murder!'

'I always maintain you can't say that about anyone. Anyone is capable of murder, if the circumstances are right. But I don't happen to think that Steve is capable of this particular murder.'

She said nothing more, though her eyes scanned his face urgently as if she was trying to glean more information from him without having to ask the questions. Or as if she was wondering if she ought to tell him something. He wasn't sure which. There was something on her mind, that was a fact. Did she suspect Mills of something, or know something about him she wasn't telling? Possibly, even probably on both counts. But she did not divulge it, though it looked as though it was making her sick – by the time he left her, she was looking as crook as rookwood, so much that he felt constrained to ask if he ought to call someone for her, or ask the girls downstairs to come and sit with her a while. That suggestion at least aroused her to scorn, but it was on the surface, and didn't touch the undercurrent of preoccupation. He went away feeling vaguely anxious for her and vaguely hopeful for himself, for whatever was preying on her mind, he felt it could not prey there long, and that if he came back the next day she would surely let it out. She liked him, and if she was going to tell anyone, it would be him.

CHAPTER FOURTEEN

Death at Auntie's

Slider drove slowly and on automatic, running his mental fingers idly through the mass of facts, searching for inspiration. Something somewhere needed to connect up, was wanting quite urgently to connect up. When you were stuck, you looked for patterns and you looked for anomalies. Roger Greatrex – media star, chronic womaniser, neglecter of his wife and child, accidental killer of Madeleine Somers – was dead. Someone had reason enough to kill him; specifically, to cut his throat. There was something about that, something calculated, perhaps, or professional. It was not the enraged bash on the head with the nearest implement to hand. Someone had brought the knife to him. A swift and silent death, that – but you had to be determined. You had to be single-minded. Not every person could cut a throat like that.

Assuming it wasn't Mills, for the moment – what about Sandal Palliser? Slider thought he had the intelligence to plan it, and the determination to do it, and would be unlikely to be squeamish – but that left the question of the clothes in the bag. Yes, Palliser might well think of the lift roof as a good hiding-place, and he of all suspects would have had to hide them on the premises, since he had to get back to the greenroom. But surely if Mrs Reynolds had seen a striking-looking man like him, even supposing she did not recognise him as the television star, she would have remembered him, and not confused him with Dark Satanic.

On a sudden impulse he did a series of left turns to reverse direction and drove towards Kensington. There were lights on in the house in Addison Road, but there was also a sense of emptiness, and it was so long before there was any response to his ringing that Slider thought he was not going to be answered.

But at last the door was opened, by Palliser himself. He looked gaunt and grey and wild-haired, and somehow insubstantial, like a scarecrow with the stuffing removed. Slider had the impression that if he joggled the wrong bit, Palliser would collapse in an empty heap at his feet.

A look of dislike came over Palliser's face as he saw Slider. 'You again! Can't you leave me alone? Haven't you done enough damage?'

'What have I done?' Slider asked.

'My wife has left me,' Palliser said – blurted, rather. 'Phyllis has walked out on me, after thirty-two years. I mean, now, after all this time! It's unbelievable.'

Seeing how shocked Palliser was, Slider inserted himself into the house and closed the door behind him, and Palliser allowed the movement, obeyed the body language instruction and led the way into the kitchen. It was warm from the Aga, and as chaotic as ever, but lacking the smell of food which had given it its homeliness and purpose. Palliser sat down at the table and leaned on his folded arms in an attitude of helpless despair.

'She went yesterday, after church,' he said dazedly. 'She just came home, packed a bag, and went. Didn't even take her hat off.'

'Where did she go?' Slider asked. He hefted the kettle, judged there to be enough water in it, and pushed it onto the hot ring. Tea was in order, he thought. Always tea in a house of bereavement.

'I asked her that. I said where can you go on a Sunday, and she said there were plenty of hotels around, and they all had rooms on Sunday nights. I said, that's crazy, and she just shrugged. I said stay, talk about it, but she said she wanted to go, it had taken her two days to make up her mind and she wasn't going to unmake it again. She phoned later to say where she was, but I couldn't persuade her to come back.'

'But do you know why?'

'It's this business over Roger.' Palliser looked up resentfully. 'Murder is so commonplace to you, you never think how it affects ordinary people. She'd known Roger almost as long as she knew me. It's hard enough coping with someone dying naturally, but when someone's murdered, especially in that brutal way—'

'Is that what she said? That that was why she was going?'

'Yes. No. Not exactly. She said it had made her think a lot about things. She said – she's suspected about Jamie for a long time, but then when you and that other one came here asking questions and obviously thinking I'd killed Roger, it confirmed it in her mind. All those questions made her think – about everything, her and me and Caroline and—' He rubbed his face with his hands as though trying to rub normality back into his life. 'She said she'd just decided she'd had enough. After all these years. I mean, she was always happy enough. I gave her everything. She knew I'd never leave her.'

Slider made the tea. 'She'll come back,' he said comfortingly.

'You think so?' Palliser was eager for comfort, whatever the source.

'She probably needs a bit of time alone to think things out, that's all. She'll get her mind settled, and then she'll come back.'

'It's been unsettling for her. For all of us.'

'That's right. Your patterns have been disrupted – hers most of all, because she doesn't have a career, like you, to take her out of herself.' He brought the tea to the table, milked two cups, and poured. Even as he did it he realised he'd forgotten the tea-strainer, and cursed inwardly as the dark rush of leaves sprang into the first cup. Oh well. Important not to break the flow now, of tea or talk. He took the leafy cup himself and pushed the other towards Palliser. Making the tea had made him unthreatening. Palliser took it unprotesting, and looked at Slider without hostility.

'I didn't kill him, you know.'

'Didn't you?'

'I wanted to – that night most of all. But often. For what he did to us. But I didn't kill him. It isn't in me to kill another human being.'

'It's in all of us,' Slider said for the second time in one evening. 'That particular murder just wasn't your murder. But whose was it?'

'Don't you know yet?'

Slider shook his head. 'I was hoping talking to you might help me get there. You were the person who knew Roger best – better than his wife, probably. You were almost the last person to see him alive – probably the last to have a quarrel with him.'

A bitter expression crossed Palliser's face. 'Oh, that! I wish to God – you'd never have come here asking questions, but for that.'

'Yes I would, for the same reason I'm here now. What did Roger Greatrex do that made someone want him dead?' He asked it seriously, and saw that Palliser was thinking about it seriously. He sipped his tea. Slider sipped his, incautiously, and got a mouthful of tea leaves, which he nobly swallowed rather than make a fuss and disturb the other man.

'What he did most of was writing and fucking,' Palliser said at last. 'I can't see anything in that to drive anyone crazy. Caroline was the person with most to object to about the fucking, and I'm sure she didn't do it. As to the writing – well, that brings it back to me, doesn't it? We had a well-publicised difference of opinion over his critical acuity.'

'I have it on good authority that that was manufactured for publicity purposes, to advance the careers of both of you.'

'I don't know whose authority you think carries weight,' Palliser said scornfully, 'but I can tell you it was a genuine disagreement. It wasn't manufactured – although, of course, we argued intellectually and not personally, if that's what you mean.'

'But you actually quarrelled in public, at Glyndebourne, over the *Don Giovanni*, didn't you?'

'Oh yes, but that didn't mean anything. I get heated over my opinions – so does Roger – but that's an intellectual exercise. An opinion isn't worth holding unless you're vehement about it. It doesn't mean I'd kill anyone for disagreeing with me. Only an intellectual pygmy would do that. Or a religious fanatic.'

A stillness fell in Slider's mind, a sensation like a great lump of white silence in the middle of his head, into which after a moment small, crystal-clear words were spoken very quietly. A religious fanatic. The *Don Giovanni* row: Greatrex had praised the production, had identified himself closely with it as his idea of a fine example of opera production. There had been a lot of talk in the papers about the production being blasphemous. And Greatrex had been murdered. Far-fetched?

But Palliser had condemned the blasphemous aspect of it in print – and Palliser had not been harmed.

Laurence Jepp and Christa Jimenez – but then, why those two singers and not any of the others? Or, if other victims were intended, why those first? Because they appeared in the blasphemous scene? But Lassiter, the man who sang the Don himself, had not been attacked. Mere geography, perhaps, because the other two lived not too far apart? Or accessibility – maybe Frederick Lassiter was abroad, or had family or minions around him all the time, or had a terrific security system. The other two had lived alone, and in old houses with easy windows. Would a religious fanatic worry about such things? Well, why not? Maybe he had to. If he was working up to slaughter everyone connected with the blasphemy, maybe he would start with the easy ones. In which case—

'You've thought of something,' Palliser said. Slider realised he had been looking at him curiously for some time.

'Yes,' said Slider with an effort. 'It was something you said, reminded me of something.' A religious fanatic. It didn't do to underestimate the power of religion – especially these days, when there was so little of any other sort of power. But there was Mrs Reynolds to be got over, and her description of the man at the lift. Damn it, he'd got to get Mills out of the frame – or, reluctantly, into it. Because everyone was capable of some murder, and Mills was an unmarried man living alone, and Slider couldn't really swear on his soul that this was not Mills's. He had been brought up by deeply religious people, though he showed no symptoms of it himself. And all three attacks – if they were connected – had happened since Mills came to Shepherd's Bush. 'Tell me,' he said, reaching into his pocket, 'have you ever seen this man before?'

He handed over a copy of the photofit, and Palliser looked at it, turning it first for better light, and then taking a pair of half-glasses out of his pocket. 'Yes, I have,' he said. 'Now, let me think, where do I know him from?'

He stared for some time, and Slider waited, wondering whether he hoped more than he feared, or vice versa. At last Palliser flipped the paper with the backs of his fingers. 'Well, of course! Why didn't I place him at once, considering we were only just talking about it? It was down at Glyndebourne, when Roger and

I were having our famous disagreement in the foyer. Of course we gathered quite a crowd – and I won't say,' he added with a faint smile, 'that we weren't conscious of it, and that it would make good publicity. But he was saying his usual fatuous things about modernity and innovation and exciting new interpretation, and I must admit I got a bit heated, especially considering the exciting new interpretation he was so thrilled about had run to that completely gratuitous defiling of the altar, for which there's no textual authority, and which of course had only been put in to shock a few reviews out of people who might otherwise ignore the production, and to tempt the sillier element of the population to buy tickets out of mere prurience—'

'It worked,' Slider remarked.

'It always does,' Palliser snorted. 'Mainly thanks to reviewers like Roger who are so ready to be thrilled by the meretricious – but however,' he recalled himself to the task in hand, 'this man was at the front of the crowd and listening to every word. I noticed him because he really looked as though he was listening to the argument, as opposed to merely gawping with open mouth at the sight of two celebrities sparring, like the rest of the dinner-suited dross that infests opera audiences these days. Of course, Roger's reviews were addressed to just those people, which is why he made so much money. You can count the real music lovers in the average audience on the fingers of one foot.'

He ought to get together with Joanna, Slider thought. 'Are you quite sure this is the same man?'

'Oh yes,' said Palliser, quite surely. 'He tried to accost me afterwards, I suppose to carry on the argument, but I avoided him. It's a thing one gets quite good at.' Then, looking again at the picture, 'There is something different. Maybe he had his hair differently. But certainly this looks like the man I saw. I particularly remember this mole on his cheek.'

'Have you seen him anywhere else?'

'No, I don't think so. Not that I remember. When I noticed him at Glyndebourne, it wasn't as someone I had ever seen before, and I'm not aware of having seen him anywhere since.'

'Well, thank you. You've been a great help,' Slider said. There was no reason Mills shouldn't have been to Glyndebourne. His "aunt" had said she tried to interest him in opera and Mills himself had said she took him to Covent Garden. When he said it, Slider had registered it as the jolly place full of shops and jugglers it had now become, but of course in earlier days the name was synonymous with the Royal Opera House – and still was in some circles. Silly him. And if Mills had been at Glyndebourne that night, why shouldn't he have listened with more than average intelligence to the critics' row? Slider didn't know whether it helped the case or hindered it. He only knew that he had to get away somewhere and think, because the idea that had been struggling to be born an hour ago was still struggling. Something he had seen or heard somewhere had impinged itself on the pattern in his mind as out of place, and he needed peace and quiet to ferret it out.

'You're going?' Palliser said as Slider stood up, and he sounded quite disappointed. Perhaps he'd hoped Slider would cook his dinner for him as well as make his tea.

'I'm sorry, I have to,' Slider said. 'I've still got a lot of work to get through tonight.'

'I was going to offer you a spot of supper,' Palliser said. 'I – I'm not used to being in the house alone.'

He sounded so pathetic, compared with his former arrogant self, that Slider felt sorry for him. 'Why don't you phone her up? She's probably lonely too – especially if she's in a hotel. They're dismal places to be alone in.'

'Do you think I should?'

'I think you can hardly ever make something worse by talking about it,' Slider said, and Palliser nodded at these words of wisdom.

'Thanks,' he said.

And Slider thought of Phyllis Palliser, and reckoned that, sad as her life had been, it would be better to be sad at home in her own kitchen than in a cheap Kensington hotel; and that, being a sensible woman, she'd probably realise it for herself soon enough.

He drove back to the factory, for no other reason than that he wanted to be alone to think, and walked in from the yard to a warm reception.

'There you are! Christ, Billy, you got to start carryin' your little tinkler wit' you,' O'Flaherty cried expansively. 'Everyone's goin' mad tryin' to find you, and worryin' the bejasus out of your woman, phonin' there when she thought all the time you were here.'

'I left it on my desk,' Slider discovered again. 'Psychological. I hate that thing. What's happened, anyway?'

'A very nasty murder,' O'Flaherty said, and for once he was quite serious. Slider felt a chill in the middle of his back, because Fergus hardly ever spoke in that tone of voice. 'You were round the house o' Mills's anty earlier on, weren't you?'

'About an hour and a half back.'

'Yes, the girls downstairs said it was you. Ah sure God, it's a bad business.'

'You don't mean it's her?'

'Hacked to death. A frenzied attack.'

'For Chris' sake, Fergus—!

'The girls saw a man goin' in. Described him, said he'd visited there before.' He shook his head, partly in wonder and partly in pity at Slider's frantic look. 'Don't take it to heart, Billy.'

'Where else am I to take it?' Slider said wildly.

The girls – the pretty one he had met before and her plain friend who had come in from a late library session shortly before the incident – had heard the thumps from upstairs, and a bit later the dogs howling and barking like mad.

'When they didn't stop, we thought something must have happened to her,' said Valerie, the prettier one, her eyes red with weeping. 'We thought she must have fallen over and hurt herself, so we went and knocked on the inside door, and shouted really loud. She always answered when we shouted at the door. But there was no answer.'

'We couldn't open it because we hadn't got a key,' said Sue, the plainer one, briskly. She was dry-eyed but very pale, determined to do the right thing and not let the side down. 'So I climbed up from the area to the back garden. There's some wooden steps down from her back door, and if you lean right over you can just about see into the kitchen. I could hear the dogs locked in the scullery, barking like mad. I could hear them scratching the door. And I could see—' She swallowed. 'I could see a chair was knocked over from the kitchen table, and what looked like a bundle of clothes on the floor. Except

I knew Miss Giles's dressing-gown. So I told Val to call the police.'

Slider turned to Valerie. 'You say she had a visitor, after I left?'

'I didn't see him,' she hiccupped. 'It was Sue.'

'When I was just coming in,' Sue said. 'I was standing at our door getting my key out and I saw him pass the railings, coming from the Uxbridge Road direction.'

'Wearing?'

She frowned in thought. 'Trousers – not jeans – dark-coloured. An anorak, I think – dark blue maybe.'

'Shoes? His feet must have been more or less at eye-level.'

'I don't remember,' she said after a moment.

'Trainers?'

'I don't think so. I think it was shoes. But I'm not honestly sure. He just walked past. Oh – I think he was carrying a bag.'

'A carrier bag? Briefcase? Suitcase?'

'No, just a bag – like a sports bag or an airline bag, something that size.'

Slider nodded. The *modus operandi*. It was deliberate, then – can't walk back through the streets covered in blood. And where was the bag now? 'Did you see him go in?'

'No, I just saw him pass, but I heard his feet on the steps before I went in.'

'Didn't you say she never let anyone in at night?' Slider asked Valerie.

'That's right. She never even answered the door after about six o'clock,' Valerie said.

'So,' to Sue, 'why didn't you warn him he was wasting his time?'

'It was none of my business,' she said indignantly. 'I'm not her guardian. Anyway, she must have let him in, mustn't she?'

'Did you hear her doorbell?'

'No,' Sue said. 'Val didn't either. But we might not have noticed, if he only rang once. Or he might have had a key?'

'You'd seen him visit her before? But you said you only caught a glimpse.'

'Enough to recognise his face. Yes, I've seen him come to the house before, though I don't know that he was visiting her

– he could have been for the upstairs people, it's the same door, though a different bell. I had an idea, actually, that he was a social worker.'

'Why do you think that?'

'I don't know really.' She seemed genuinely puzzled at her own perception. 'I suppose maybe – there was just something about him. I honestly don't know.'

'But he did visit her last week, one afternoon,' Val said, 'because I saw her at the door with him. I thought he might be a relative of some sort,' she added with an apologetic glance at Sue.

'Why a relative?' Slider asked.

'The way she was talking to him. And I can't think who else would visit her, anyway. She never had friends round. She didn't entertain.'

'That's right,' Sue agreed. 'She said to me once she lived too much like a pig to want anyone to see her house.'

'Do you remember which afternoon it was last week?'

Valerie screwed up her face with effort. 'It might have been Wednesday. Or Tuesday? No, I'm not sure. I think it was the middle of the week. Not Friday, anyway, because I wasn't in Friday afternoon.'

'So it could have been Thursday?' She assented. With a sense of inner weariness, Slider drew out the photofit print and offered it to the girls. 'Is that the man?'

'Yes, that's him,' Valerie said eagerly. 'I'm sure it is.'

Sue didn't answer at once. She looked at the picture very carefully, and said at last, hesitantly, 'I *think* so. It's so hard to tell from a picture, isn't it, unless you actually know someone very well. I mean, pictures never really look like people.'

'Oh Sue,' Valerie said reproachfully.

'Well, I can't help it,' Sue said irritably. 'I can't swear it's the same man, all I can say is he does look quite like this.'

'You're right to be cautious,' Slider said. 'Identity is a tricky thing.'

Sue looked at him eagerly. 'I always think it's an interesting word – identity.' She obviously had a theory and was glad of the chance to expound it. 'I mean, we use it carelessly, but what it means is saying something is identical with something else, saying it is exactly the same thing, and therefore unique. And

I can't say a picture is identical with a human being. I can't say that someone I've only just seen is exactly the same person as someone else I've seen, not unless I know them personally.'

'Oh, you always quibble,' Valerie objected. 'How you can talk about words when poor Miss Giles is lying up there—' and she burst into tears.

'*That's* no answer,' Sue said unkindly. Slider agreed, though it was not for him to say so.

'I didn't do it,' Mills said, with the calmness of desperation. 'How can you even think it? I loved her. She was like a mother to me. For God's sake—'

Slider remained impassive. It was hard to get out of his mind what he had seen in that now-familiar kitchen. Miss Giles had been lying on her back, half under the kitchen table, her eyes open. Her throat had been cut, severing the carotid artery, which had probably been the fatal blow, but she had been stabbed in the upper torso another seven times. From the blood distribution it looked as though she had been standing near the stove, facing the wall – perhaps putting the kettle on – when the first blow had been struck; had then been whirled around, struck in the back, which had made her fall forwards, knocking over the chair and hitting her head on the edge of the table; and then rolled over or been turned over to receive the other wounds from the front. One blow had been so forceful it had gone right through her torso and nicked the lino underneath. It was indeed, in the words beloved of police reports, a frenzied attack: as if the throat-cutting had been calmly planned, the rest of the blows the result of a rage of hatred.

A terrible wave of sickness and despair had overwhelmed him as he looked at the pathetic bundle of old clothes which only a few hours ago had been a vigorous and intelligent woman. The appalling waste – the stupid vandalism which could destroy in seconds a personality which had taken more than sixty years to create, a unique and fascinating personality that could never be restored – made him angry. And he felt a personal loss, as for a friend, for in the short time he had learned a lot about her; he felt she had given him more of herself than she had given to anyone for a long time. When someone gives you something of themself like that, you become guardian of it, and responsible.

He was responsible. He ought to have foreseen this. He had seen that she was worried, even afraid, and he had virtually assured her that Mills was not the man, instead of putting her on her guard against him.

But he would not have thought it of Mills. He would not have thought it. He had been badly wrong, and Miss Giles had paid the price of his arrogance, which had led him to do what he was always warning against. He should have paid attention to the evidence, not tried to explain it away. Mills had put up a convincing show of bewilderment when he was brought in, so convincing that Slider was toying with the idea that he had shut the murder out of his mind completely, and genuinely had no recollection of it. He had to force himself to be calm, and to ask the questions in the sort of matter-of-fact tone that eases out information that might otherwise be held on to.

'So, tell me, you let yourself in with the key, didn't you? You have a key to her flat.'

'No, I haven't,' Mills said, almost indignantly. 'Auntie Betty would never give anyone a key. She was a very private person. She wouldn't have liked anyone to be able to go there when she wasn't in.'

'But you were – her nephew. Very close to her. Probably the person she loved most in the world.'

'She still didn't give me a key.'

'So how did you get in, then? According to her tenants, she never answered the door at night.'

'No, that's right. If I wanted to visit her at night I always rang her from the nearest telephone box and said I was on my way, so she knew it was me.'

Slider nodded. 'And that's what you did tonight?'

'No! I didn't go there tonight.' Oh he was good, very good. Slider looked at the man he had once known so well, and his conviction faltered. Surely a man could not be so psychotic without something showing? 'I didn't kill her,' Mills said. He sounded bewildered now. 'I don't know what's going on here, boss, but you've got to believe me. I loved her. I wouldn't hurt her. And I was home all evening. I never left my flat.'

'Doing what?'

'Watching telly.'

'What programme?' Mills hesitated and Slider hardened. 'Come on, what programme?'

'I don't know. I can't remember,' Mills cried in a panicky voice. 'I dozed off while I was watching. Some investigation programme – *Panorama* or something. About computers. I dozed off and when I woke up it was a film. I didn't fancy it so I turned it off.'

'Look, Steve, why don't you tell me about it?' Slider asked. 'We know it was you. You were seen going to the house. She wouldn't have opened the door to someone she didn't know. She was killed by someone she offered tea to, someone she trusted enough to turn her back on.'

He shook his head slowly, like an animal in pain. 'Why would I kill her? Tell me that. Why on earth would I do such a thing?'

'Well, I don't know,' Slider said wearily. 'I wish I did. I hoped you might be able to tell me.'

'I don't understand any of this. Ever since I came back, everything's been weird. You've got to help me, guv. They want to stick this on me. And the other business, at the Centre. But you know I didn't do it. You *know* I didn't.'

'I wish I did.' Slider closed his eyes for a moment. 'Just imagine you did set out from your place tonight to walk to your aunt's house. Which way would you go? Describe your route.'

'I turn right out of the house, round the corner into Abdale Road,' Mills said, rather surprised, 'down Ellerslie Road, across into Halsbury, and then right into Ormiston Grove.'

'You wouldn't walk along Uxbridge Road, then, at any point?'

'Well, no,' Mills said, 'because she lives nearer the other end, the Dunraven Road end. There'd be no need to touch Uxbridge Road. It'd be a longer way round.'

'That's what I thought,' Slider said. 'I just wanted to be sure.'

'I'm holding you personally responsible for this, Slider. It was on your recommendation that I didn't act earlier. You were so sure your former colleague was innocent – and now look what's happened.'

'I'm not absolutely sure it was him,' Slider said hesitantly, and against his will.

Honeyman's eyes bulged. 'Not sure? He was seen going into the house. What more do you want?'

'Being seen at the house doesn't mean he was the murderer, sir.'

'Then why does he deny it? If he was there for an innocent purpose, he'd say so.' Honeyman shook his head. 'I'm sorry, Slider, I know how hard this is for you – a colleague, and particularly a close colleague from many years ago. I can see you're genuinely confused, and I would be the same. It's hard for all of us when one of our own goes astray. But that's the more reason to have no mercy. If he did kill his aunt, he's a very dangerous man. It was a frenzied attack, you know.'

'He seems genuinely to believe what he says, sir—'

'But that only makes it worse,' Honeyman interrupted heatedly. 'If he killed without remembering it, he might be subject to psychotic episodes. He could kill again. We can't take the risk. Can't you see the headlines, if we let him go and he struck again?'

'Sir, if we charge him, it'll be all over the papers, and he'll never live it down. He may be innocent. All we've got is one witness who admits herself she only caught a glimpse of a man passing. Can't we wait until we've got something more? He's not trying to run away. He's co-operating. He's given intimate samples.'

'For God's sake, man, I've already given you time to clear him of one murder, and now I've got another on my hands. Do you want a bloodbath, is that what you want?'

'His flat's been searched – not a drop of blood anywhere, nothing on his clothes. And nobody saw him leave his house or re-enter it this evening.'

'Negative evidence is no evidence,' Honeyman said impatiently. 'I agree with you we haven't got a case against him yet, but the witness identification is enough to charge him. It's up to you to get the rest. Someone will have seen him at some point on the double journey. The bag will turn up, the knife, the stained clothing. Until then, we can't take any chances.' He looked at Slider's mute and puzzled defiance. 'You've been up all night,' he said quite kindly. 'You'd better go home. Things will look clearer when you've had something to eat. Get a couple of hours' rest, have a hot bath and a change of clothes. It's going to be a long day.'

'Yes, sir,' Slider said. 'Thank you.'

Nice advice from one to whom the length of the day would be voluntary. He was tired, but not ready for sleep. He had far too much to do, anyway.

Tufty telephoned. 'I've got some news for you, my old banana. Are you ready for this? I don't know if it's good or bad, but those last blood samples you sent – I think I've got a match for you.'

That was the Jimenez knife sample, and Mills's blood. Slider had been expecting no match – hoping for no match? He sat down heavily. 'Tell me the worst.'

'Oh, didn't you want it to be the same? Well, not to worry. The sample from the knife wasn't good enough for me to go the whole way. There was a variant in the lysate EAP of both samples which is fairly rare – only five and a half per cent of the population – but even that gives you a pretty big leeway.'

'Five per cent?'

'Well, old boy, Tufty said cheerfully, 'statistics is what you make 'em. If you *wanted* the match, you could say *only* five per cent and call it a practical certainty. If you don't want it to be the same you can point out that five per cent of the population still gives you going on two and a half million bods to play with.'

'What I wanted,' Slider said, 'was certainty one way or the other.'

'Ah! Well, you'll have to talk to God about that.'

'What about genetic fingerprinting?'

'I've sent the samples off for you already. You should have a result in about a week. But as I said, the sample from the knife wasn't too hot. Don't pin your hopes on it.'

Slider went down to see Mills again. Now he didn't know what to think. 'Have you got a cut on your left thigh?' he asked.

'A cut? No sir,' Mills said, too weary now to be much surprised by any question. He surveyed Slider's face. 'Do you want to see?' He stood up and lowered his pants.

'All right,' said Slider. 'Cover up and sit down.' When Mills had complied, Slider said, 'I've just got a few more questions for you.' He looked at him carefully for a long time, and Mills did not look away. Though tired, he seemed eager to answer anything that was asked him. Eager to explain. 'How did you like *Don Giovanni*?' Slider asked suddenly.

'What, Mozart? It's not one I know very well,' Mills said, and seemed a little embarrassed at admitting it. 'I like the lighter stuff, really. Puccini – the Three Tenors – you know, something with good tunes. But I like some Mozart. I saw *The Magic Flute* once—'

Slider interrupted. 'I meant the production of *Don Giovanni* at Glyndebourne,' he said.

'I haven't seen it,' Mills said, looking puzzled.

'You were there. You were seen.'

'Sir, I've never been to Glyndebourne,' he said. When Slider didn't respond he went on, 'I've always wanted to. But it's one of those things you plan for when you're retired, isn't it, like going on the QE2. I mean, you'd have to be rich and idle.' Slider went on looking at him thoughtfully, a slight frown between his brows. Eventually, Mills said, 'Would you mind if I had a smoke, guv?'

'No. Go ahead.' He watched absently as Mills dragged his cigarettes towards him, extracted one and lit up. Then he asked in a neutral voice, 'You're left-handed, aren't you, Mills?'

'Yes, sir. You know I am. Well,' looking down at his own hands, 'I suppose I'm ambidextrous really, but I write with my left hand.'

'You perform delicate tasks with which hand?'

'My left, probably, for preference.'

'What about tasks needing strength? Right or left?'

Mills shrugged. 'It could be either. It would depend how I was standing, I suppose.'

'So you could, physically, cut someone's throat holding the knife in your right hand?'

Mills looked sick. 'Sir, I swear to you—'

'Answer me!'

'Yes, I *could*,' Mills said with deep reluctance. 'But then,' he added defiantly, 'you could do it with your left hand.'

'True,' Slider said. 'The question is, would I?'

'No more than I would.' Slider was silent. Mills studied his face and experienced a slight dawning of hope. 'Sir? Have you thought of something?'

'I don't know.' Slider said quickly. He got up. 'Mr Honeyman wants you charged with the murder of your aunt. Is there anything you want to tell me, anything at all? Think, man!'

'I've been thinking,' Mills said despairingly. 'I didn't do it. I was in all evening. What more can I say?'

Slider nodded briskly and turned away.

CHAPTER FIFTEEN

On a Clear Day You Can See Fulham

He went back with Atherton to his house for breakfast. Atherton had a gentrified Victorian workman's cottage on the Kilburn/Hampstead border, two up, two down, and a tiny garden about ten foot square at the back which generally smelled of privet and cats, but today, in the early morning, had that airy, ozony smell of young days that are going to grow up to be hot. Slider sat by the open window with Oedipus kneading bread on his knees and purring like a JCB. Somewhere outside a sparrow was doing its best to be a skylark, and from somewhere inside the heartbreaking perfumes of fresh coffee and frying tomatoes came wafting sweetly over him. Slider felt his mind ticking like the metal of a cooling car, and knew he was in danger of drifting off, but he had promises to keep, and miles to go before he slept, and miles to go before he slept . . .

The phone had rung, Atherton had answered, and was now saying, 'It's for you,' over his shoulder as he hurried back to his kitchen. Slider removed fourteen stone of cat from his knee and staggered over to the phone.

'Slider.'

'So where were you all night?'

Oh shit, Joanna. He'd forgotten her. 'I should have phoned you, shouldn't I?'

'Well, I think you should.'

'But they told you where I was?'

'Nobody told me anything. They rang me to find out where you were. And of course, I didn't know.' Her tone was reasonable, but he couldn't help knowing she was batey.

'There was another murder last night—'

'It's a bit late to tell me that now. I was worried about you. For all I knew, you could have been dead in a ditch.'

He groaned. 'Why do wives always say things like that?'

'I don't know about wives. I've never been one,' she said tautly.

'Sorry. But you know how it is. Don't make a big thing out of it.'

'I'm not making a big thing out of it.' Now she was really trying to be reasonable. Probably the wives taunt, though tactless, had struck home. 'I just think you could have let me know at some point that you weren't coming home, or asked someone else to let me know. What do you have all those minions for?'

'Yes, I'm sorry, you're quite right. I just forgot. I had a lot to think about.'

'So I understand.'

'Oh, come on, Jo, it's my job. I always thought you could cope with my job.'

'I do. I am.' A pause. 'After all, you have to cope with my job.'

'That sounds ominous.'

'Only that I've got to go now, and I'd hoped to see you again before I leave. I won't be back tonight.'

'Oh, Christ. Glyndebourne. I'd forgotten. Why can't you come home tonight?'

'It isn't worth it. There's an orchestra call tonight, and a rehearsal tomorrow morning. By the time I got home it'd be time to leave again.' That was not strictly true, but as if she heard him think that, she added, 'Besides, you don't even know if you'll be home.'

'I probably will be. Well, at some point.'

'You might be back, or you might not,' she corrected. 'I'm not doing all that driving just to spend the evening alone.'

'Who are you going to spend it with, then?'

'What's that supposed to mean?' she said irritably. He hadn't meant anything in particular by it, he'd just been being smart, but her reaction immediately made him think of the Old Flame.

'Will he be there? This Andrew person?'

'Oh, for God's sake. Yes, of course he will. He's doing *Traviata*.'

'The whole thing? So you'll be seeing a lot of him.'

'Not really. He sits behind me. Look, Bill, this is stupid, I'm not going on with this. I've got to go, anyway. I'll see you tomorrow – if you're home.'

'All right.' He didn't want them to part on a sour note. 'Drive carefully.'

'In Sussex? You betcha. Good luck with your case, Inspector.'

'Good luck with your rehearsal.' He was going to add, 'I love you,' but she had put the phone down. He stared at the receiver for a moment, wondering what the hell had got into him recently, why he was feeling so peculiar and suspicious. But was it all him? She seemed tense and irritable. Maybe something *was* wrong, and he was picking up subliminal signals.

Atherton came through with plates. 'Sit,' he said, putting them on the table. He cocked an eyebrow at his boss. 'Trouble at t'mill?'

Slider gave him a weak smile. 'I wish you hadn't told me about the Other Man. Now I keep wondering.'

'I wish I hadn't told you, too. Honestly, Bill, the woman's nuts about you. She has eyes for no-one else. I should know.'

'What does that mean?' Slider asked indignantly of his retreating back.

In a moment Atherton came back with the coffee. 'It's just first-night nerves, that's all,' he said. 'It's a big step – for both of you. It'll take time to get used to it.' He nudged the plate in front of Slider. 'Eat. You're tired, your sugar levels are down, and you're not thinking straight.'

'My sugar levels can't have been down continuously since Sunday.'

'No, that's just hormones,' Atherton smiled. 'If I were you I should just relax and revel in it. Feeling jealous is a luxury commodity, you know. You have to have someone, and be in love with them, to feel jealousy. When you live hand to mouth like me, you'd be grateful for a bit of it.'

'You do talk such bollocks,' Slider said, sitting down, but he felt comforted all the same. And the food revived him, so that he felt the renewed sensation of blood flowing about him, and the thoughts began to bubble up in his mind, like coffee percolating.

With the plates pushed back and the second cups before

them, they went over the case notes, the photographs and the transcriptions.

'We've got to keep a grip on this,' Slider said. 'Try to look at it logically. Mills looks like a good suspect for Miss Giles, because of the witness ID and because he was the closest person to her. He doesn't look quite such a good suspect for Greatrex, because we can't find that he ever knew him, but there was still the witness ID, and Palliser says he saw him down at Glyndebourne, which Mills denies.'

'As he would.'

'Indeed. But I think whoever killed Miss Giles also killed Roger Greatrex.'

'Because the MO is similar?' Atherton said.

'And because of the timing. Why else should she be killed, if it wasn't something to do with the investigation?'

'Beats the hell out of me. But it's a short walk if that's where you're going.'

'Bear with me. Greatrex was killed. Laurence Jepp was killed by the same method. Both had a Bible tract card on or near them, though Greatrex was lapsed Jewish and Jepp was a lapsed atheist. The fingerprint from the card was similar to Mills's, although as Mr Honeyman pointed out, fingerprinting is not an exact science. There was also a query attempted attack on Christa Jimenez. These three had in common that they all had to do with the *Don G* production at Glyndebourne. Tufty says the blood on the knife with which Jimenez attacked her intruder is not incompatible with Mills's. And Mills has no satisfactory alibi for any of the three times in question.'

'Nor had I, for that matter. That's the trouble with living alone,' said Atherton. 'Did Mills have a cut on his leg?'

'I looked—'

'Lucky you.'

'—but I couldn't see anything. But the Jimenez incident was almost a week ago, and we don't know how deep the cut was. It could have healed in that time.'

'Without a trace?'

'It's possible. We might know more when the genetic test comes back.'

'But meanwhile we've got to get on with what we've got. Why would Mills kill or attack all those people?'

'I don't know. The only connection I can come up with is the Glyndebourne one.'

'Religious fanaticism, you mean?'

'There is something very biblical about the throat-cutting. The one strong cut from behind – like a sacrifice at an altar. And a religious fanatic would be cold-blooded enough, or at least single-minded enough, to do it first time like that.'

'Then why Miss Giles?'

'Because I'd been talking to her, and she knew something that might be dangerous to him.'

'Is Mills religious?'

'Not that I know of,' Slider said. 'But of course he could be. I haven't seen him for years. And they say at Epsom he was a bit of a loner. I thought I knew him, but how much do you ever know people?' They were both silent for a while. 'It seems to me that Mrs Reynolds's evidence is the real hair in the custard,' Slider sighed at last.

'The what?'

'The thumb in the gravy – the unpleasant detail that can't be ignored. It was such a definite identification. Without that, we wouldn't be looking at Mills at all.'

'But as you say, you can't ignore it. And what about the girl who identified him going to his aunt's house?'

Slider tapped his notes. 'She didn't identify him. She only says he looked quite like the photofit.'

'A distinction without a difference. Anyway, nobody ever really looks like a photofit unless they've got a bolt through their neck,' Atherton grumbled. He looked at Slider. 'What is it?'

Slider was staring hard at the empty air, evidently in labour. Then he rummaged through the papers and brought out Mrs Reynolds's statement and a copy of the photofit. He read the former, and then tapped the latter with a forefinger. 'Look, look at this. She's put the mole on the wrong side.'

'You'll have to do better than that,' Atherton said. 'Mills has got more moles than M.I.5.'

'This one,' Slider pointed to the large mole on the curve of the cheek, half an inch below and to the side of the nostril. 'His most distinguishing one. She's put it on his left cheek; but it's on his right.'

'Are you sure?' Atherton frowned, trying to visualise. 'No, it's on his left, surely.'

'Trust me. I know Mills's face very well.'

'Let's see her statement.' Atherton read it through. 'She says left cheek. Well, if you're right then she's wrong. So what?'

'So what? What d'you mean, so what?'

'She just made a mistake. Left, right, what does it matter? The rest of the description fits, and he's *got* a mole. Who cares which side?'

Slider shook his head slightly, thinking rapidly. 'Damn it, I can't remember. I think it was on the left, but I'm not sure.'

'You just said right,' Atherton complained, but Slider wasn't hearing him, rummaging through the photographs.

'The one thing we haven't got a photograph of! I'll have to go and check.'

'Check what?'

'The lift. No, wait, maybe you remember.' He focused belatedly on Atherton. 'The lift next to the men's room where Greatrex was killed – the lift where Mrs Reynolds says she saw the man – do you remember it?'

'What's to remember? A lift is a lift.'

'Visualise it! Which side was the control panel? The buttons? On the outside, I mean – out in the corridor.'

'On the left.'

'Are you sure?'

'Yes.' Atherton, good subordinate, didn't ask again what did it matter. He waited. Slider went on thinking.

'And Auntie Betty's dead, damn it,' he said at last. 'The one person—' He hit his palm softly with his fist. 'Maybe that's why! God, I hope so! That poor woman.'

'Guv, can I know what it is?'

Slider looked at him for a moment. 'Not yet. I'm so far out on the branch on this, it won't take the weight of two. You'll have to trust me for a bit.'

'*I* trust you,' Atherton said with delicate emphasis. 'Can I do anything to help?'

Slider thought for a moment. 'Not yet. Just cover for me – I'm going to stay out of reach of the office for a bit. I'll ring you the moment I've got something to work on.'

'All right.' Slider was already on his feet. 'Keep your mobile with you, then.'

'Yes.' A brief smile, like sunshine between fast-moving clouds. 'Thanks.'

First things first. Clear as you go. He went in search of Mrs Reynolds, who lived in one of those high-rise flats in Bollo Bridge Road. A complex community of streets and little houses had been erased to create the windy veldt on which the towers were erected, which accommodated slightly fewer people than had lived in the same space before; but, by golly, the ones on the top floor had a terrific view.

The door was opened by a tiny, wizened man whose trousers had obviously been bought to last before age had shrunk him. He wore them now hauled up so high by his braces that the waistband came under his armpits. He also wore a white shirt, buttoned up but without a collar or tie, tartan bedroom slippers and a tweed cap. The saddest looking roll-up Slider had ever seen was stuck magically to his lower lip, and he breathed so badly and his nose was so blue that Slider feared the slightest extra exertion would see him off. Perhaps he ought to tell him to answer by blinking his eyes – one blink for yes, two for no.

But Mr Reynolds Mark Three seemed quite cheered by the visit and impressed by Slider's official status. He actually took the ID from him and caressed it with an orange thumb before returning it. 'Dolly's in the front room, having a lie-down,' he wheezed. 'She's not too clever s'morning. Jwanna come in?'

There were few things Slider wanted less, but in the line of duty he had sometimes to risk life and limb. There was no air inside the little flat, not a cubic centimetre: it had all been displaced by cigarette smoke. In the 'front room' an electric fire was on, heating up the smoke to rival the atmosphere of Los Angeles on a summer afternoon. The television was on, tuned to a breakfast show on which people with the air of having been up all night and knowing their mental agility to be impaired by the experience sat on a hideous sofa and desperately tried to keep talking until the adverts came on. On an equally hideous sofa in real life, Mrs Reynolds reclined, her sparse hair in small, tight curlers. She was covered from the waist down by a tea-stained 'honeycomb' blanket evidently stolen from a hospital, with an ashtray in her lap, a cigarette in her fingers, and a depressed-looking dachshund on her feet.

'Oh my good Gawd!' she said as Slider came in, and clapped her hand to her bosom. 'You arf give me a fright – I thought it was the council!'

'Not allowed to keep dogs,' whistled her husband sadly. 'She's always afraid they'll find out. I told her—'

'He says they don't care slongs we pay the rent,' she took over for him. 'But I told him – I've told you,' she swivelled her head to her husband, 'they'd dearly like us out of here, and put darkies in. They want to make it all darkies, this 'ole estate.'

'No they don't. Thass cobblers.'

'The social lady said.'

'She never. She said they'd move us if we ast to, on *account* o' the darkies.'

'It's the same thing.'

Slider knew a single-track line when he saw one. 'Mrs Reynolds, there's something I'd like to ask you,' he said. Before my breath runs out, he added silently.

'Course there is, dear. I didn't think you come 'ere for the pleasure o' my company,' she said archly. 'Not but what—'

'Concerning that night at the BBC Television Centre. I want you to think back to the moment when you saw the man at the lift.'

'Yes, dear.'

'You came through the swing doors, he was there by the lift, and you said in your statement you saw him press the button to call the lift.'

'Thass right.'

'Picture it in your mind. The lift buttons are on the left side as you face the lift. The man puts his hand out and presses the buttons—'

Her face was screwed up in the smoke as obediently she visualised the scene. 'Yeah, I got it.'

'Which hand is he using?'

'His left,' she said promptly.

'So he's holding the bag in his right hand?'

'Thass right.'

'Now, you said in your statement that you saw blood on his cuff – that's on his left cuff, correct?'

'That's right, dear.'

'You saw his hairy wrist, his watch, and the end of his cuff sticking out beyond his jacket sleeve.' She nodded. 'You're quite sure about that?'

'Why shouldn't I be?' she sounded slightly annoyed now.

'It's just that the detail is very important on this point – I can't explain to you why, but it matters very much. You definitely saw his left wrist, with a watch, and blood on the cuff, reaching for the lift buttons?'

'I said it, and I meant it,' she said firmly. 'And if you want me in court, I'll swear Bible-oath to it.'

'Thank you. That's very satisfactory.' She smirked through her cigarette. Slider was getting black spots before his eyes from lack of oxygen. Oh no, that was just the pattern on the carpet. 'One other thing, now. Can you visualise the man's face? You said in your statement he had a mole on his left cheek, here.' He tapped his own face. 'Now are you sure it was his left cheek and not his right?'

She thought for a moment, and his heart misgave, but then she said, 'Yes, o' course I'm sure. Because that's the way he was facing. That's the side of his face I could see, wannit? His head wasn't turned right round towards me, it was more, like, three-quarters, and it was his left side nearest me, see?'

'Thank you,' said Slider. 'You've been very helpful.'

'Will you ave a cuppa tea, sir?' Mr Reynolds asked courteously.

'Oh my Gawd, ain't you put the kettle on yet, Bert?' Mrs R exclaimed, struggling to extricate herself from her blanket. The movement stirred the comatose dog, which lifted its head mournfully for a moment and emitted a just-audible hiss from the other end. 'I'd a made you one meself first off if I hadn't been feeling a bit iffy this morning. Only *e's* not been so clever either, with his chubes—'

'No, really, thanks, no tea for me. I must go,' Slider said, backing hastily. 'I've got an awful lot to do today.' He was almost sure a bit of the pattern on the carpet had moved, and he really didn't want the chance to find out for certain.

The next part would be harder. He could not ask Mills without revealing the true nature of his relationship with his Auntie Betty, which, if he was innocent of the murders, Slider was almost certain he did not know. And Auntie Betty was now silenced – an image of her face, bloodied, staring, slid out from his memory. He imagined a stumbling step, the jolt of a knife in the back, and just time enough to know betrayal, to the background clamour of hysterical dogs, before the darkness came up. He shook the thought away violently. Whatever it took, he had a duty to her now. He got into the car and drove towards Brook Green.

St Melitus's was a low, two-storeyed block in yellow brick, with picture windows over a rather severe patch of garden which sported grass with a military haircut and two oblong flowerbeds in which bedding geraniums, salvias and begonias kept rank or else. An utterly lovely seventy-foot London plane grew up from the pavement near the front gate, with languid limbs trailing scarves of leaves like Isadora Duncan, but it was evidently out of the gardener's jurisdiction, or it would surely have been pollarded to within an inch of its life to make it smarten its ideas up.

Inside there was a central sitting-room – regrettably called an 'association area' – with high-backed, high-seated armchairs ranged round the walls as in a hospital waiting-room, where old people, women to men in a ratio of about eight to one, sat facing forwards and waiting for something to happen – the tea trolley or death, whichever came first. A rosy-cheeked, black-haired woman in a blue nurse's dress fielded Slider as he came through the door.

'Come to visit someone, have we?' she enquired cheerfully with a hint of Irish. 'I don't think we've seen you before. Now, which one did you want?'

'Are you the – er – matron? Head person?'

'Superintendent,' she helped him out. 'No, that's Mrs Maitland. Is it about a vacancy? We haven't any at present—'

Slider didn't like the idea of that 'at present'. Some of the old people were dozing with their mouths open, and looked too close to supplying a vacancy for Slider's comfort.

'No, not that. I'd like to speak to Mrs Maitland about one of your residents, if I may. I'm a police officer. Detective Inspector Bill Slider, Shepherd's Bush.' He spoke quietly and made a discreet gesture towards his ID, in case the police presence alarmed any of the frail folk, but the cheery one laughed aloud.

'Oh my God, have you come to arrest one of them?' she cried in extremely audible amusement. 'What've they been up to now? I'll bet it's our Cyril looking up ladies' skirts again – you wicked old divil!' The only man in the direction she threw the witticism was one of the fast-asleep ones, but the ladies on either side of him seemed to appreciate the jest. One broke into whispery laughter, and the other made a riposte so broad that Slider realised even twenty years in the police force had not prepared him for communal old age.

'Come along, Inspector,' said the nurse, noting his embarrassment with amused sympathy. 'This is no place for you. I'll take you to the office.'

Mrs Maitland turned out to be disconcertingly young, very smart, and wearing a bright yellow suit, presumably to make her easily visible. It had a very short skirt and she didn't quite have the legs for it, but it certainly made her a more cheering sight for a matron than Hattie Jacques in NHS blue and a lamb chop frill on her head.

'Mrs Mills – Margaret – we like to use first names here,' she confided unsurprisingly. 'Yes, she's in flat 5. She's been here for years – quite able-bodied, spry really, but she gets a bit confused sometimes.'

'Is she aware of what's going on? Her son's name has appeared in the newspapers.'

'I don't know about that. They do get various papers here – the *Mail* and the *Mirror* and the *Evening Standard*. They're put out in the association area – but whether she will have read about it I can't say. Of course, some of them buy their own papers too, but Margaret doesn't go out very much. Hardly at all, really, except to church sometimes, when one of the others takes her. We don't encourage her to leave the premises alone. She spends a lot of time in her own room, in fact. A bit solitary. Sometimes we have to positively chase her out. It isn't good for them to sit alone too long, especially the confused ones.'

'Does she know about her sister?'

'Not as far as I know. I didn't know about it myself until you told me. Murdered, you say?' She shook her head. 'I'd rather you didn't say anything about that. It's a bit too upsetting. Can't you ask her what you want without mentioning that?'

'She'll have to know sooner or later that her sister's dead,' Slider pointed out.

'Yes, but I'd sooner one of us told her. We know them, you see, and we're trained to deal with these things. You never know how the shock might affect them.'

Slider was beginning to take a dislike to Mrs Maitland, and was forced to restrain himself from pointing out that all of these old people had lived through one war, some of them two, and had probably experienced worse things than Mrs Maitland could imagine without the aid of a video. He didn't like the idea that this pert young thing called the old people by their Christian names – probably without asking permission – and referred to them as if they were a species, like starfish or algae, with generic attributes. But he reminded himself that he did not take care of even one old person full time, let alone thirty or forty, let further alone not related to him, and bit his tongue.

'Can I talk to Mrs Mills, then?'

'Yes, of course. I'll get someone to take you up, and stay with you while you have a chat, if you like.'

A middle-aged woman in a white overall dress and surprisingly peroxide hair took him up to the flat. She rang the doorbell, simultaneously putting the key hanging by a chain from her belt into the lock, and called out, 'Maggie, it's Joyce. Can I come in, dear?' as she opened the door. She looked in and then nodded to Slider, preceding him into a tiny room, furnished in early MFI, of which every surface was covered in china ornaments and plaster knick-knacks whose only virtue was that they were small, and therefore of limited individual horribleness. Cumulatively, they were like an infestation. Little vases, ashtrays, animals, shepherdesses, tramps, boots, tobys, ruined castles, civic shields of seaside towns, thimbles, bambis, pink goggle-eyed puppies sitting up and begging, scooped-out swans plainly meant to double as soap-dishes, donkeys with empty panniers which ought to have held pin-cushions or perhaps bunches of violets – all jostled together in a sad visual cacophony of bad taste and birthday presents and fading holiday memories, too many to be loved, justifying themselves by their sheer weight of numbers as 'collections' do. Maggie's collection of china ornaments. What can we get for Maggie? Oh, get her one of those Chinese horses – she collects things like that. That thimble with the arms of

Bexhill-on-Sea – that ashtray with the Spanish dancer painted on it – that bulldog with the Union Jack waistcoat – they'd never be looked at again, they were just there, swelling the numbers, like the forgotten sleeping oldies downstairs. And when Maggie died, they'd be shovelled into a cardboard box and sent off to a misnamed Antiques Fair in a scout hall somewhere to be the things left on the stall at the end of the day.

Mrs Mills was sitting in one of the high-backed chairs by the window, her hands resting on the arms, looking out, away from the ugliness and confinement and clutter, out at the beautiful tree. She turned her head as they came in and said, 'Go away.'

'Now then, Maggie, don't be like that,' Joyce said coaxingly. 'I've got a visitor for you. This gentleman's a policeman, dear, come all this way to talk to you.'

Mrs Mills looked at Slider, and said, 'He can stay. I don't want you, though. Go away.'

'Ooh, we can be rude when we try,' Joyce said archly. She turned to Slider. 'She's a bit – you know,' she whispered perfectly audibly, tapping her temple. 'And a bit unsociable. Unsociable,' she added loudly, 'aren't you, Maggie? All right, I'll leave you alone with your boyfriend.' She lowered her voice again. 'There's a button over there by the fireplace if you have any trouble. Let Mrs Maitland know when you leave again, won't you.'

When they were alone, Mrs Mills looked at Slider, and then poked her tongue out at the closed door. 'I was rude, wasn't I? Can't stand them, stupid bitches. Think if you're old, you're daft. Wait till they're seventy, then they'll see. What did you say your name was?'

'Slider. Bill Slider.'

'Well, sit down then. There's a pouffe over there. They only give you one chair – afraid you might have company in your room, enjoy yourself or something. Bitches.'

Slider fetched the pouffe and sat on it in front of Mrs Mills. She looked down at him with a gleam of malicious pleasure, presumably at his reduced elevation. 'Can't see out from down there, can you? I like to look out. Sit here and look at the tree. You get birds in that tree. You'd be surprised how many. Watch 'em for hours. Did they tell you I'm gaga?' She didn't wait for him to answer. 'Well I'm not. But I let them think it – saves me having to listen to their rabbiting.

What do you want, anyway? What did you say your name was?'

'Inspector Slider,' he said, with less confidence.

'What, police are you?'

'That's right.'

'My boy Steve's a policeman. Well, a detective.'

'I know. I used to work with him years ago. That's what I've come to talk to you about.'

She looked at him sharply. 'He's in trouble. I saw it in the newspaper. They think I don't know, just because I don't talk about it. I wouldn't talk to *them*.'

'I think your boy's innocent, Mrs Mills, and I want to prove it,' Slider said.

'Course he's innocent. He's a good boy, my Steve. Always been a good son to me.'

'That's why I've come to see you. I want to talk to you about your sister.'

'He's in the police. Out in Epsom. I never see him now. Too far to visit. But he's always been a good son to me.'

Slider leaned forward a little and tried to catch her eye. 'I want to talk to you about your sister – about Betty.'

She sharpened. 'Betty? What about Betty? Is she dead? Is that it?'

Alarmingly prompt – but at her age, you must hear a lot about death. Slider hesitated only a moment. 'Yes, I'm afraid so.'

Mrs Mills seemed to think about it. 'Comes to us all. But she was younger than me, you know. Still, she didn't lead a pure life. She smoked, drank – had affairs. Men!' She snorted. 'I could tell you a thing or two! She was always a wild one, even as a girl. I had to be mother to her, after Father died and Mother went a bit gaga. I always said she'd get herself into trouble one day – and she did! But she'd never listen to me. Oh no, I was just boring old Maggie, good enough to come to when she wanted something, but take advice – huh!'

'When she got into trouble,' Slider inserted, gently but urgently, 'she went into a home, didn't she? A mother-and-baby home.'

'I'd have had her with me,' Mrs Mills said, not as if she was answering, but as if following her own thoughts. She was not looking at him. 'I mean, blood is thicker than water, and I was fond of her in a way. But Arthur wouldn't have it. He was a good man, mind,' she added sharply, as though Slider had argued, 'but she made fun of him. I told her, the Devil laughs at the virtuous, and you'll laugh on the other side of your face when you go Downstairs. I told her that. But she liked to make fun of him – until she wanted his help. Then it was a different story, oh yes! Well, he was a good man and he helped her, but as to having her in the house – never, and I couldn't blame him. He was right, too,' she added with a wise nod, 'because she broke her word. She promised to go right away afterwards, but she came back.'

'Why do you think she did that?'

'To show off, of course, because she had money and we didn't. Always buying him things, taking him places, trying to set him against his own parents with her money and her outings and I don't know what. Arthur couldn't stand her – painted hussy, he called her. They had some set-tos! But then just when you thought she'd gone too far, she'd come round and apologise, really handsome, and bring Arthur something, a book or a present, something he really wanted, and talk to him so nicely about church and the Scouts and Sunday school and everything, it made you wonder why she couldn't be sensible like that all the time. He had to forgive her. She had charm, you see, when she wanted to use it. She wasn't really a *bad* woman – just wild.'

'Was that why you let the boy see her?'

'Well, he was a fair man, was Arthur. She never appreciated him, really, because he had his funny little ways and he could be a bit ridiculous sometimes, I have to admit, but he loved the boy and he'd have done anything for him. And Steve really loved *her*, and Arthur said, he said, after all – you know.' She nodded wisely. 'And he said the boy must come first, we can't put our pride before his happiness.'

'That was very noble of him,' Slider said, but she took it the wrong way and looked at him suspiciously.

'What's it to you, anyway? Who are you?'

Slider didn't bother with the introductions. 'The mother-and-baby home your sister went into – do you remember where it was?'

'She's not in a home. She works for the Civil Service – did very well for herself,' Mrs Mills said. But she seemed to be tiring, and he knew he had to get on.

'When she was a girl, when she got into trouble, she went into a special place. It was run by your minister, Mr Green, wasn't it?'

'Mr Green? Mr Green? He was here the other day.' She looked rather dazed. 'He keeps a friendly eye on the boy. Always did. I think he's afraid she might steer him wrong. She was never one for religion. But she'll think on the other side of her face when she goes Downstairs.'

'Mrs Mills, I really need to know,' Slider said urgently. 'What was the name of Mr Green's home for girls in trouble? What was the address?'

'Out in the country, that was, to keep 'em out of harm's way. Talk about hate it! She never liked the country. Nothing but mud, as far as the eye could see – mud and potatoes, she said afterwards. That's all the country is – mud and potatoes. Five miles even to get a packet of cigarettes. Essex, I think it was. Or Kent. Some village.'

Wonderful, Slider thought. Only two counties to search. He could see she was tired now, and thought he had failed, but suddenly she spoke again out of her thoughts, quite sharply and lucidly.

'*He* lived in East Acton, though. Shaa Road. House on the corner. Just up the road from the church. They've pulled that church down now, building a block of flats instead, sacrilege I call it. He was a great big man, great big hands and a deep voice. Joshua Green,' she said, shaking her head. 'Betty always said it sounded like someone off *The Archers*.' She looked at him, seeing him suddenly, and frowned. 'She's dead, isn't she? That's why you came. Policeman, aren't you? Betty's dead.'

'Yes, I'm afraid so.'

She sighed. 'I always knew I'd see her out. She was younger than me, but she led a wild life. I expect my boy will see about it, the funeral and that. My boy Steve. He'll see to everything. He's a policeman. Well, detective really. What did you say your name was?'

CHAPTER SIXTEEN

Negative Evidence

In the nature of things, there were likely to be four corner houses to Shaa Road, and even if he found the right one, he didn't expect Green would still live there, if he still lived at all. But Slider hoped to catch hold of the end of a chain which might lead him to the information he wanted. This was something he could hand over to the team, but he wanted at least to find the right house to begin with, to see it with his own eyes.

As it happened, he hit the right one first shot. A neat, thirties-style urban villa with a red-tiled bay window and stained glass in the front door yielded to his ring at the doorbell a neat, small woman in her late fifties, wearing a nylon overall. Just behind her on the hall table a pair of rubber gloves, a duster and a tin of Mr Sheen stood where she had put them down; the smell of the polish mingled on the air with a slight threat of oxtail soup and that particular odour that some boarding houses and small hotels have – something of cheap carpets and institutional food gently ripened in a centrally-heated, double-glazed airlock.

'Good morning. I'm looking for a Mr Green,' Slider began. 'He—'

'If it's about a wedding, I'm afraid he's retired now,' the woman interrupted with a sweet smile.

'Oh – no,' Slider said, beguiled. Did he look as though he wanted marrying? 'He does live here then, Joshua Green? I have got the right house?'

'Yes, that's right.' The woman waited patiently. Clergy wives were first filters, had to cope with all the nuts.

Slider reached for his ID. 'Would you be Mrs Green?'

'Not for all the tea in China,' she said with unexpected wit. 'I'm the housekeeper. Mrs Hoare.'

Slider blinked, and stopped himself asking why she had never thought of changing her name. 'Detective Inspector Slider,' he said steadily. 'Is Mr Green at home? Could I have a word with him?'

'I expect you could. Come in. He'll be *reading* in his study at the moment.' One of her eyelids dropped and rose again with oiled smoothness. 'I generally wake him up for lunch, but it won't hurt him to be disturbed for once. Just wait here.'

She went off round the corner and Slider waited, listening to the sound of a clock ticking, looking at the row of cacti on a shelf along the hall window, the neat piles of pamphlets and tracts on the hall table, the capacious umbrella-stand, the carpet chosen for its ability to take wear and hide marks. The walls were decorated with framed reproductions of Canaletto views of Venice, and there was a hideous Edwardian mahogany hallstand, complete with mirror and numerous tiny what-not shelves, which sprouted coat-hooks upon branched coat-hooks like a ten-point stag. It was a home that was a public place, and vice versa. It must be a rotten life being a priest, he thought – especially these days when you couldn't even enjoy the satisfaction of a hearty malison when provoked. On the subject of which, he drifted closer to look at the tracts, but they were pre-printed on shiny paper with coloured colophons, and their messages had the kick of a pair of suede sandals. No more swords, wrath and vengeance for the Church, no blood, wine, betrayal and agony in the garden – just little homilies about being more understanding, helping Oxfam, and loving your brother regardless of race, colour, creed or sexual orientation. Slider wondered what the prophets of old would have made of that – what Joshua Green, if he was really a fiery preacher in his youth, made of it. It was all very restful, though. Maybe the Church Militant had been an aberration, and this was what God had wanted all along.

Mrs Hoare reappeared and beckoned to him. 'He'll see you,' she said, leading him where she had gone before. 'He's just a little deaf, but if you talk clearly and straight at him he hears all right. You don't need to shout.' She opened a door. 'Here's Inspector Slider, now,' she announced, and stood back to let Slider pass, saying to him, 'Do you prefer tea or coffee?'

'Oh, tea please. Thank you.'

The small room had french windows onto a very dull garden, and one whole wall was covered in bookshelves. The rest of the available space was taken up with a large old-fashioned desk with a much-buttoned leather wing chair on one side of it, and a depressed-looking row of wooden upright chairs on the other. Green was seated on the master's side of this arrangement, and gestured Slider towards the supplicants' position. He made a gesture of standing up, but did not actually rise, and seeing how upright he sat and the large-knuckled deformity of his big hands on the chair arms, Slider suspected arthritis and did not blame him.

'It's good of you to see me, Mr Green. I do call you Mr?'

'Yes, yes, that's all I am now – a retired soldier in God's army – or perhaps I should say a reservist? Ha!' He gave a single shout of laughter which Slider guessed had become a mannerism over many years, a jocularity designed to show that a man could be a devout Christian and yet *not at all dull.* 'One never knows when one might be "called up" again.' He marked the waggish inverted commas in his speech by speaking the words more slowly and in an even deeper voice. 'And what do I call you? Inspector, is it?'

'Mr will do,' Slider said, taking the middle seat in Penitent's Row.

'Very well. "Mr" Slider. Puts us on equal footing, eh? Ha! Now, what can I do for you?'

He made a curious movement of his hands across his midriff and back to the arms of the chair, which Slider recognised as an attempt to steeple his fingers, thwarted by their crookedness. He had not yet grown used to his disabilities. Slider could see how he must have been 'a great, big man', and he was tall still, though age had shrunk him somewhat. He still had a fine head of hair, worn brushed back so that it framed his head like a lion's mane; his bushy eyebrows had stayed black, and jutted out like rock formations over his dark eyes, hinting at the charismatic figure he must once have cut. Slider would have put his age at around eighty, but it was a vigorous eighty which might just as easily have been ninety or seventy. His features still had strength and firmness, though there was something rather ugly, Slider thought, about his mouth – very wide and very thin, with an unexpectedly red lower lip and no upper lip at all.

'I've come to raid your memory,' Slider said. 'I am here concerning the case of Elizabeth, or Betty, Giles—'

'The case? Is she dead, then?' Green interrupted sharply.

'She was found dead at her home last night,' Slider said carefully, looking at the man with interest. 'You were very quick on the uptake.'

'You'd hardly have called her a case otherwise. I doubt she was "drug smuggling" or organising "a rave" at her age. She must be—' He paused as if to work it out, but in fact left it to Slider. When Slider didn't help, he concluded, 'An elderly woman.'

'You do remember her, then. Even though it was such a long time ago.'

'Her sister was one of my flock, and her brother-in-law ran my Sunday school most competently for very many years. Naturally I remember her.'

'And her son?'

The eyes were cautious under the bushes. 'Her son? I was not aware that she ever married.'

'She didn't. Come, Mr Green, let's not waste time fencing. Miss Giles herself told me the story only yesterday. Steven Mills, who was adopted by her sister Margaret, was her illegitimate child.'

'Well, you astound me,' Green said emphatically.

'Surely not. It was you who arranged the adoption – amongst many others.'

'If you know that, then you must know that I am not at liberty to disclose the circumstances surrounding any adoption. The children I placed are entitled to my absolute discretion – as are the adopting parents.'

'I appreciate that,' Slider said. 'But in this case, Miss Giles herself told me half the story, and would have told me the other half today if she had not been silenced. She was murdered last night, Mr Green, brutally murdered, and her son Steven, whom she loved, is under suspicion.' Green's face was impassive, but he was listening hard. 'Now I worked with Steve for some time a few years back, we were friends, and I was pretty close to him. I think I know him, and he's a decent, good man, and he loved his Auntie Betty and would never have harmed a hair of her head. I need your help to prove that.'

'There is nothing I can tell you,' Green said, but Slider could hear that he was weakening. He attempted to steeple his fingers again, and instead raised them to his lips. It wasn't quite the magisterial gesture it ought to have been. It looked more as if he was sucking both thumbs at once.

Slider went at it again. 'Nothing you tell me can harm Miss Giles any more. Arthur Mills is dead and Margaret Mills is in a home and, I'm afraid, mentally confused. Steve Mills, whom you helped once as an infant by placing him with good, loving parents, needs your help again. In those circumstances, it would be quite wrong of you to refuse information. It's your duty as a citizen, but I think also as a Christian, to answer my questions.'

Green was silent for a few moments. Then he removed his hands from his mouth and said, 'You are very persuasive, Mr Slider. You should have been a minister.'

'I suppose I'm a fisher of men in my own way,' Slider said, with a smile to show he was joking. 'But my job is to go after the sharks.'

'Ha! A useful occupation all the same. Well, then, well then—' He paused a moment. 'I suppose you are right. Betty Giles. You want to know about Betty Giles.'

'You obviously remember the whole family very well. Did they stick in your mind for any particular reason?'

'I remember all the adoption cases I handled. I've kept in touch with many of them: the children are like my own children, in a spiritual sense. I like to keep a distant but fatherly eye on them – and their adoptive parents. Not the unfortunate girls, of course – they would not wish to be reminded by me of what they once were. In those days, you know, society punished them very severely, condemned them for ever on the grounds of one sin – which sometimes they were too ignorant to realise was a sin. It's quite different now. I think we have gone rather too far in the other direction these days. We are supposed to hate the sin and love the sinner. Nowadays we don't even hate the sin.'

'I'm sure you're right,' Slider said anodynely. 'Please go on.'

'Of course. Well, my idea in those far-off days was to offer a safe, clean, Christian home to these girls during their pregnancy, and afterwards to place the babies with Christian couples of my acquaintance, and to help the girls find respectable employment. But for them to begin a new life free of the taint of their error, everything had to be conducted with the most complete discretion. No-one must be able to point a finger at the girls afterwards; and for the sake of the babies and their new parents, the girls must never know their identity. So we rented a house in a village called Cooksmill, near Chelmsford – it was real countryside in those days, very remote and out of temptation's way for the girls, but also out of the public eye. The girls could "disappear" there, and it was unlikely they would ever meet anyone afterwards who had seen them there. When the time came they went into the hospital in Chelmsford, and the baby was taken away at once, usually without their ever seeing it, certainly before they had any opportunity of forming a fondness for it. Afterwards they spent six weeks recuperating at the house, and then they were placed in suitable work.'

'What happened if they wanted to keep the baby?' Slider asked.

Green looked as though he had said something mildly offensive. 'That was not possible. The social climate in those days made it impossible for an unmarried girl to bring up a child alone.'

'But if they were determined?'

Green looked his loftiest. 'It was a condition of our helping them that the child was given up. We could not have operated on any other basis.'

Slider thought he understood. 'How did you choose the couples who adopted the babies?'

'On the grounds of their Christian commitment and moral probity. We were very thorough – otherwise it would have been "out of the frying pan and into the fire" as far as the poor infants were concerned.'

'But how did *they* find out about *you*?'

'Through the Church, or by word of mouth, usually. Sometimes couples were referred to us by doctors or almoners. But there was never a shortage. Childless couples are very determined about seeking what they want.'

'Did they pay you?' Slider thought the bluntness of the question might shock something out of Green, but he had evidently faced this ball before, and played it straight down the wicket.

'There were expenses involved, and the applicants made a

contribution to that. It was not a fee. Some paid more and some less, according to their resources.'

'What if they were really poor?'

'If they were unable to afford any contribution, it is unlikely they could have afforded to bring up a child in the proper manner. We did not,' he added, lowering the brows sternly, 'consider couples where the woman went out to work. A woman's place is in the home, nurturing her child and caring for her husband.'

Slider thought of Joanna's version of that adage: A woman's place is in the wrong. He was getting quite a clear picture of the frying pan and fire the 'unfortunate girls' alternated between. At that point the housekeeper brought in a tray, with a cup of tea, a cup of milky coffee, a sugar bowl, and a plate on which reposed two Nice biscuits, two garibaldis, and two bourbons. She placed everything within reach, looked the two men over carefully, as if gauging whether they were likely to come to blows if left alone again, and went.

Slider took up his teacup and said, 'Tell me about the case of Miss Giles. That was rather different, wasn't it?'

'It was,' Green admitted, as though seeing now it had been a mistake. 'The identities of all the parties were known to each other, which was dangerous.'

'And Miss Giles was not a common, ignorant girl. She was bright, ambitious, career-minded.'

'She was very difficult, from beginning to end,' Green said gloomily. 'It was her sister who brought her situation to my attention. I had met her once or twice at the Mills's home, and did not like her. She struck me as what we used to call in those days "fast". It did not come as a surprise to me when Margaret came to say that her sister had got into trouble.'

'Did Mrs Mills know about your activities in that field?'

'She knew I had arranged adoptions for other couples, and I think she had a vague idea that I was connected with some kind of home. What she asked, that day she came to see me, was simply whether I could help Elizabeth. I asked in what way, and she said, "Betty doesn't want the baby. I'm afraid she might try and get rid of it."'

'By that you understood abortion?'

'Some girls found it preferable in those days to the shame of being an outcast,' he said sorrowfully. 'It was another reason for our operation.'

'So it became not just a matter of saving Elizabeth from her predicament but of saving the baby too?'

'Its life as well as its soul,' he nodded. 'I told Margaret that I could only help Betty if she placed herself entirely in my hands, and did exactly as I said. She said she would talk to her. But by the time they both came to see me on the next occasion, the plot had been hatched between them. Margaret had some fear that she could not have a child of her own, and would rather adopt her sister's baby than a stranger's. Elizabeth would sooner know what sort of a home her infant was going to. I said in that case they had no need of my services and could arrange matters between them. But they insisted,' he finished gloomily.

'What did they want you to do?'

'It was a matter of maintaining secrecy. Elizabeth had a career which would be damaged by her shameful condition. She needed to be able to go somewhere discreet where she would be looked after. On their side Margaret and Arthur wanted an arrangement which safeguarded them, a proper, legal adoption, and no chance that Elizabeth would go back on it at the last moment.' He sighed. 'I warned them of the hazards, I told them it was not an arrangement I could recommend, and suggested alternatives, but they were adamant. Margaret had set her heart on having the baby, and Elizabeth wanted to be rid of it as conveniently as possible, and Arthur was in the middle hoping to keep everything respectable. So I helped them.'

Slider said encouragingly, 'I expect you did the right thing. It might have turned out much worse if you hadn't.'

Green inspected him for irony, and then nodded. 'I think you are right. I did my best to build in safeguards. Any breach of the rules by Elizabeth while she was at Coldharbour House would terminate the agreement. The baby was to be taken from her immediately as with the other girls and she was to sign the adoption papers before leaving the hospital. And after her convalescence she was not to contact her sister again or go anywhere near the house. But of course she broke the agreement on every count. She was a troublesome inmate at Coldharbour, flouting the rules and disturbing the other girls. And she not only contacted her sister, she returned to live almost next door and to insist on contact with the child.'

'She never told him she was his mother, though,' Slider said, feeling driven to Miss Giles's defence. He remembered what she'd said about the weeping girls in the home, and the 'kindness' of having the baby taken away at birth. Green, he thought, must have been a Mr Brocklehurst to them. 'Steve doesn't know even now what their relationship really was.'

'I'm glad to know she had even so much decency,' Green said stiffly. 'I hardly think she was a good influence on the boy. And she made Margaret and Arthur very unhappy – good, decent, Christian people.'

'It was a difficult situation,' Slider said, needing to placate him as they approached the tricky part. 'I'm sure on reflection you must be satisfied that without your help it would have been much worse.'

'Perhaps,' he said, unwilling to be seduced. 'So, Mr Slider, have you the information you required?'

'Not quite,' Slider said. 'I need to know what happened to the other one.'

'The other one?' The words came out naturally enough, but the body had suddenly become still, watchful.

'The other baby. There were two, weren't there?' Green did not answer. 'Twins,' Slider said helpfully. 'Miss Giles had twin boys, didn't she?'

'You are mistaken,' Green said stiffly. 'I can't think where you have your information, but you are quite mistaken.'

'Come, now, Mr Green, it's pointless denying something that can so easily be proved. The hospital records will show it. I would sooner not have to go to the trouble, but I can get the documentary evidence and bring it to you if you insist. Don't make me waste my time.'

Green looked almost dazed. 'Nobody knew. It was the most absolute secret. Of course, there were no scans in those days, and the girls were all as ignorant of these things as each other. The matron was under my instructions, and even Elizabeth herself knew nothing until she actually gave birth. If it could have been done by Caesarean section, as I wished,' he added bitterly, 'she wouldn't have known even then. But the hospital wouldn't play ball. They said the decision must be made by the doctor, and for medical reasons only.'

Slider looked at him in amazement. 'Why? Why did you want to keep it a secret?'

There was a flash of the power that must have once made him a formidable man. 'To save something from the wreck! I knew the arrangement could never work, that Elizabeth would not keep her word. The child the Millses took would be in constant jeopardy. But I thought that if I could place the other as it ought to be placed, with neither side knowing the other's identity, something good would have come out of it. It would not all have been in vain.'

'And so what happened to the other baby?'

Green was silent a moment, seeking escape. 'It died.'

'No, I don't think so,' Slider said gently. 'You see, I've been puzzled by a number of things recently that didn't make sense; someone I kept crossing the path of, someone who was so like Steve Mills people were willing to swear to his identity. But as someone pointed out to me, identity means actually being the same person, not just looking like them. And I found myself wondering about a person who looked like Steve; whose fingerprint was similar to Steve's but not exactly the same; who had the same blood-group; but who was right-handed where he is left-handed. My Steve Mills, like other left-handed people, wears his watch on his right wrist. The Steve Mills I was looking for wears his watch on his left wrist, like the majority of the population. And there was the matter of the moving mole – a mole on Steve's right cheek that suddenly wandered over to the left cheek.'

Green was watching him warily, but following everything with an air of waiting for the inevitable blow to fall. Perhaps he had known what was coming. Perhaps he had been waiting for this blow for years.

'It does happen sometimes,' Slider went on almost conversationally, 'that zygotic twins are mirror images of each other, like left hand and right hand.' He lifted his hands and put them together to demonstrate. 'And unless you see them side by side, you are not likely to notice the differences. It also happens that a tendency to have twins runs in families, and I knew there had been twin brothers in Miss Giles's family.

So when a friend of mine at St Catherine's House told me that Miss Giles's mother was also one of a pair of twins, I started to put two and two together, if you'll pardon my little joke.'

Green didn't look as if he would. He said, 'What exactly is it that you suspect?'

'I think that you placed the other baby with a couple, that the adult that child became now lives somewhere not too far from here, that he has committed a crime, and that he knows, because he read it in the newspaper, that his twin brother is suspected of the crime and is happy enough to let that ride. I know a few things about him. He is very religious, fond of music, probably interested in scouting or something of that sort – an athletic, outdoor type. Probably unmarried. He is intelligent, too, a planner, not easily flustered. But a man of strong feelings and strong convictions.'

Green looked shaken. 'You seem to know a good deal.'

'Am I right, then?'

'How should I know? You are telling your own story.'

'You haven't corrected any of it. Where is the twin now?'

'I placed an infant for adoption almost forty years ago,' Green said loftily. 'How should I know where it is now?'

'But you said yourself that you liked to keep a distant, fatherly eye on them. Your children – in the spiritual sense. And you must have been particularly proud of this one – your success story, snatched out of disaster.'

'Leave me alone,' Green said suddenly in a weak voice, the last thing Slider would have expected. 'Don't mock me.'

'I'm not mocking. Just give me what I want, and I will leave you alone.'

'What do you want?'

'I want to know what happened to Elizabeth's other baby.'

Green gripped the arms of the chair and breathed hard, as though he had been running and was distressed for breath. 'I placed him with a couple – a very good, pious couple, churchgoers, total abstainers, very strict. The best start he could have had.'

'And did Elizabeth know? Did she ever find out?'

'Not from me. But I think – I suspect – *he* may have found *her*. There was a break-in – some of my papers, records, were taken from my files. They were returned later. The details of that adoption were amongst them.'

'You suspect he was the one who took the papers?'

'He had asked me several times who his natural mother was. I had always refused to tell him, and he got very angry.' He swallowed. 'He wasn't a bad boy, but very determined. Very – single-minded. He felt it was his *right* to know.'

'So he broke into your house and stole the papers.'

'He returned them later. And he would not have done anything like that unless he felt he had good reason.'

'How old was he when this happened?'

'Eighteen – nineteen perhaps.'

'You had kept in touch with him all that time?'

'I – he – I looked upon him as my special trust. I felt almost like a father towards him. I watched him grow up, and took a delight in seeing how he developed.' He stopped abruptly, frowning, as though some memory did not please him.

'So he found out who his mother was, and went to see her?' Slider prompted.

'I don't know,' Green said forcefully, looking at Slider now. 'I think he may have, but I don't know. I never spoke to him about it, and Elizabeth certainly never said anything on the few occasions after that when I met her. But he was not the sort of boy *not* to act. He liked to be *doing* – a very practical Christian. He was a leading light of the Boys' Brigade, loved camping and mountaineering. Later he ran adventure holidays for disadvantaged boys and young offenders. He's a *good* man. Whatever you suspect him of, you are quite wrong.'

'What's his name?'

'I won't tell you,' Green said heatedly. 'You want to persecute this good man to try to get your friend off the hook.'

'He can't be persecuted, or even prosecuted, if he's done nothing wrong. If he is a good man as you say he is, he has nothing to fear.' Green said nothing, his thin mouth pressed shut. 'Mr Green, Betty Giles has been savagely murdered. It's very important that we get the right man into custody, in case he attacks again.' Silence. 'I believe she was killed because she was in a position to tell me the secret of the existence of a twin brother to Steve. How many other people know that secret? How many others are at risk?'

'You don't know,' Green cried, 'that he has done anything! You are only guessing! For all you know it could be someone else entirely!'

'All the more reason, then, for me to find him and ask him some questions, so that the shadow of suspicion can be lifted from him. What has an innocent man to fear?'

'Nothing.' Green swallowed. He looked shaken. 'Nothing, of course. Very well, his name is Gilbert, Geoffrey Gilbert.'

'And his address?'

'I don't know.' He set his jaw stubbornly. 'That's the truth. He used to live in Acton, but he moved about ten years ago, and I haven't seen him since. We had a – a disagreement at about that time and I haven't had any contact with him for years. I've no idea where he is now.'

The door opened again at that point, and Mrs Hoare came in. She gave Slider a stern and significant look, and then said to Green, 'I'm going to have to disturb your little talk now, because you know the doctor said you hadn't to sit still all morning, so if you're going to have your walk before lunch—'

Green seemed happy to take the excuse of dismissing Slider. He became almost courtly in his relief. 'You'll excuse me seeing you out, I hope. The weight of years, you know. I hope I've been of some help. It was pleasant meeting you, though it was sad news indeed to hear of poor Miss Giles.'

'I'll just see the gentleman out, and then I'll come back and get you ready for your walk,' Mrs Hoare said, and hustled Slider away. Alone with him in the hall she said, 'You'll forgive me disturbing you, but I knew you'd get nothing more from him after that. He's as stubborn as a donkey, and I don't want him upset for nothing.'

'You were listening?' Slider said, half-shocked, half-amused.

'At the door.' She bridled a little. 'I always listen. He's an old man, and we get some very funny customers in here. I have to protect him.' She looked at Slider with grudging approval. 'You did all right with him. You're good at handling people. But when I heard that tone of voice, I knew you'd not shift him any further. You've got your job to do of course,' she added sympathetically. 'You might get more out of him another time, but you'd have to wear him down. Isn't there some other way you can find out what you want to know? Surely an address shouldn't to be too hard, with all your computers and everything?'

'When all you have is a name,' Slider said, 'and the whole country to search – the whole world, for all I know.'

She made an impatient movement of her head. 'Whole country, nothing! When he moved from Acton, he went to Askew Road. If he's not there still, you can trace him from there, can't you?'

'Does Mr Green really not have any contact with him now?'

'Not for many years. They quarrelled. Too much alike, you know, each thinking he knew best. And between you, me, and the bedpost, the Gilberts had done too good a job with the boy. If ever there was a pair of smug, self-righteous bigots! Well, I thank God I'm only a housekeeper, so I don't have to forgive everybody. Hard, that's what they were, holy and hard, and they made him hard too. I heard him once telling Mr Green what they'd done to punish him for having a – well, not to put too fine a point on it, a wet dream – and I tell you, even Mr Green was shaken, though he's heard some things in his life. That was why he tried to keep contact with the lad, if you ask me, to be a bit of a softer influence on him, though God knows he was a firebrand himself in his younger days, though you wouldn't think it to see him now. But Geoffrey was beyond softening, and I wasn't sorry when he stopped coming here. I didn't like him upsetting Mr Green. And he had funny eyes. I didn't like the way he looked at *me* sometimes. I've had plenty of comments in the years I've been housekeeper here, and they're water off a duck's back to me, but Geoffrey looked as if he wasn't going to say anything, he was going to do it.'

'What number Askew Road?' Slider asked.

'Ah—' She thought, and shook her head. 'I don't remember. It was a high number. Seventy-six? Sixty-seven? No, I don't remember.'

'Wouldn't he have it written down somewhere?'

She opened her eyes wide. 'How should I know that? You aren't suggesting I should look through his things, I hope?'

Slider felt he had nothing to lose. 'Yes.'

'I couldn't do that,' she said firmly. 'No, if you can't find out any other way, you'll have to come back and ask him again. But I'd sooner he wasn't upset. He's an old man, and his heart's not too good any more. I'm sure you'll think of something.'

Slider allowed himself to be thrust out into the day, and walked back to his car, feeling that unreal sense of not quite touching the ground that comes from having missed a night's sleep. So he had been right! It had seemed so improbable before, that it was only because it had also seemed so obvious he had had the courage to pursue it. Now he felt as if he had been struck rather hard on the head with a padded bludgeon. He had been right. Steve Mills had a brother. A doppelgänger. And maybe, just maybe, he was within smelling distance of the fox.

CHAPTER SEVENTEEN

Bishop's Move

After driving rather hopelessly up and down Askew Road, Slider parked down a side street and went into a corner newsagents. A tall and chubby Asian man stood behind the loaded counter, adding further evidence to Slider's contention that it must be part of God's great plan for gentlemen from the subcontinent to own corner shops. What was that line in the hymn about every corner Singh? Further in, a short, stout white woman was serving sweets and gossiping to a bosom pal, and neither looked round as Slider came in to a tinkling of the doorbell.

Mindful of the niceties, he bought a newspaper and a chocolate bar from the man, who bemused him rather because he had parted his hair straight down the middle and oiled it, in a style Slider had not seen outside of nineteen-thirties' photographs, and also wore a Fair Isle pullover. The effect, combined with the dark, overstocked chaos of the shop, made him feel he was time-travelling. Pocketing his change, Slider drew out the photofit print, which was becoming rather dog-eared. 'Do you know this man?' he asked.

The man took it and looked at it briefly before scrutinising Slider rather more thoroughly and asking, 'Are you police?'

Slider produced his ID. 'I've reason to believe he lives somewhere near here. Have you seen him before?'

'Yeah. I know him,' the man said, still searching Slider's face for information. 'What's he done?'

'I can't tell you that,' Slider said. 'Does he live near here?'

'He's one of my customers. Binden Road, is it? Or Bassein Park Road?'

'I was hoping you'd tell me.'

'Oh, d'you want me to look him up? Half a mo, then.' He

dragged out a large black ledger from under the counter and began to turn the pages, which were covered with elaborately loopy handwriting and many crossings-out and insertions. 'Oh yeah, here we are. Bassein Park Road – d'you know it? It's just up there on the left. He has the *Guardian* every day, plus the *News of the World* and the *People* on Sunday, plus he has *Opera* monthly, *Music* magazine which is also monthly, and *Scouts and Scouting*, which is quarterly.' The bosom friend departed, passing behind Slider's back, and the stout woman turned her face in their direction. 'Very good customer. Mr Gilbert, his name is. I call him the Bishop.'

'Who's that, Mr Gilbert?' the woman chimed in, sidling nearer. 'He's a very good customer. Very nice man.'

'Been coming in years.'

'My husband knows him very well.' She slipped her hand through the man's arm, seeming eager for a share of any kudos forthcoming from the acquaintance.

'Why do you call him the Bishop?' Slider asked.

'Oh, that's just his silly joke,' the woman said anxiously. 'He doesn't mean anything.'

'He's very holy, is Mr Gilbert. Always talking about God and religion. Says he wanted to be a reverent once, only it didn't work out for some reason. He talks like a bishop an' all. Posh and snooty.'

'He does not,' the woman urged.

'If he'd been a reverent, he'd've been a bishop by now. Never comes in without having a chat to me about the state of the world and what he'd do if he was in charge.' He grinned. 'Tried to get me to give out religious stuff to my customers once – I mean, me!'

'What sort of religious stuff?'

'Cards with religious stuff printed on them – from the Bible and that. Wanted to leave a stack by the till for me to give out.'

'It does seem to suggest a lack of touch with reality,' Slider said.

'I said no. But still—' The man shook his head in wonder at the idea. 'Anyway, he reckons to be holy and everything, but he buys *Knave* and *Fiesta* when he thinks I'm not looking.'

'He does not!' the woman said, removing her hand to signify her complete detachment from this judgement.

'Yes he does, Reet,' the man insisted. 'When Barry's at the till on a Saturday and I'm up the other end doing the bills. He waits till he thinks I'm not looking and he slips them under a *Dalton's Weekly* and takes them to Barry. I've seen him do it.'

'Oh, you!' the woman said, furiously.

'What's up? Nothing wrong with that. It's all good clean fun. Mind you,' he turned to Slider, 'he looks a bit funny to me sometimes. He comes in in shorts, which isn't natural in a man his age. And he has a funny look sometimes. Barry says he's queer.' The woman tutted vigorously and moved away, to distance herself further from the views being aired. 'I wouldn't be surprised if that wasn't why he didn't become a vicar or whatever you call it. Got himself into trouble. With a boy scout, eh?' He gave Slider a grin and moved his elbow in a rib-jabbing gesture.

'Do you know what he does for a living?' Slider asked.

'I think he's a social worker or something, isn't he? Rita?'

The woman, appealed to, stopped pretending not to be listening and said, 'He's a counsellor, I think they call it. Down the advice centre in Acton High Street.'

'Have you seen him around lately?'

The man frowned. 'Now you come to mention it, no. And I didn't see him in here Saturday. He always comes in Saturday morning. Reet?'

'I never saw him. But I was in and out.'

'It was pretty busy,' the man added apologetically. 'Maybe he's been ill. He's not been in for a day or two, anyway.'

'So I might catch him at home now, then?'

The man assented, and watched him with shining eyes, evidently longing to know what the Bishop had done. Slider extricated himself, seeing out of the corner of his eye how the couple flew together as soon as the door was closed to engage in eager speculation, and went back to the car. He radioed in to ask for Geoffrey Gilbert's police record to be looked up. He expected a negative, but after a lengthy wait Norma came on.

'Guv? There's quite a bit of it. Nothing for the last twelve years, but the seventies and early eighties there's all sorts of things. Do you want me to read it out to you?'

'Summarise a bit.'

'All right. There's a whole scad of burglaries and thefts, small stuff, some affrays and resistings – oh, here's one, early on, riding a bicycle without lights, that's what probably turned him into a wrong'un. Who is this guy?'

'More recently?'

'June 1979 fined for behaviour liable. Another in December 1979 for assault and resisting arrest. January 1982, three months' suspended for conspiracy to wound—'

'Is that the most recent?'

'No, there's December 1982, two years for ABH. I looked that one up. It was a youth who was disrupting a scout meeting he was holding. He went for him like a madman and did him over a treat. Served nine months, came out in January 1984. After that he's been clean.'

Slider was silent. That would be about the time he moved away and severed relations with Green. Probably lost his scout troop over it. Fines and suspended sentences he could have hidden from the authorities, but an actual spell in the pokey would have obliged them to make an example of him. Whatever fires raged in him must have gone underground.

'Is Atherton there?' he asked.

A pause while presumably she looked around. 'He was here a minute ago. Must have just popped out.'

'When he gets back tell him to meet me at this address.' He gave the address the shopkeeper had given him.

'Right, boss. Anything else?' Even over the telephone he could hear her curiosity.

'No. Is everything all right there?'

'Everyone's upset about Mills. Mr Carver's been doing his pieces. I think he thinks you ought to have warned him.'

'Warned him of what?'

Norma heard the chill. 'I don't think Mills is guilty either,' she said hastily. 'Is that what you're working on?'

'I'll let you know when I know. Get that message to Atherton.'

'Okay, guv. Be careful.'

'I always am,' Slider said, and signed off. He drove the short distance to Bassein Park Road and parked across from the house. He watched for a while, but there was no movement at any of the windows. The house had an unkempt look, with paint peeling from the window frames, a chunk of stucco fallen from the façade, the front gate missing, the brown paint of the front door old and dirty. Unlike its neighbours it had no nets at the windows, and in the gap between the dark red curtains at the front ground-floor bay a large clear-plastic cross was stuck to the pane on the inside with one of those transparent sucker-caps. Nothing like nailing your colours to the mast, he thought. He got out of the car and walked over, and after a brief internal debate, rang the doorbell. He couldn't hear it inside, so in case it was broken he knocked long and loudly. There was no sound of movement within. Gilbert was probably at work, establishing his alibi. When Atherton arrived they could pursue him there.

He moved across and looked in at the front window. The room was empty except for a wooden kitchen table on the far side on which was a pile of books and several of what looked like pamphlets, and two wooden chairs against the left-hand wall. The floorboards were bare and dusty and the wallpaper pale brown with age; there was an open fireplace with a spotted mirror above the mantelpiece, but the hearth and grate were littered with waste paper, sweet wrappers and apple cores.

Still no sign of Atherton. Slider was feeling light-headed with fatigue now. He went on round to the side gate, which was falling to pieces as side gates so often are, hanging by one hinge and a rusty nail, and propped half-open. There was a damp, mossy passage down the side of the house, leading to a square of unkempt grass littered with bits of broken furniture and metal of unimaginable purpose, and a large, stout and fairly new garden shed. The back door, presumably the kitchen door, had frosted glass at the top. The kitchen window was high up and had extremely dirty brown check curtains, and what had once been french windows from the back room onto the garden had, oddly, been bricked in and reduced to an ordinary-sized window, which had dark red curtains drawn across it.

It was all horribly drab and depressing, not the sort of thing you would associate with a Christian or a scoutmaster. Slider knocked at the back door, and then idly tried the handle and found to his surprise that the door was unlocked. He opened it cautiously and stepped in.

'Hello! Is anyone at home? Hello, Mr Gilbert?'

The house was silent. Slider looked around the kitchen. It was furnished with cheap units in dark brown melamine, the electric stove was encrusted with burnt fat, and there was fawn and brown chequered lino on the floor, though little of the pattern showed through the ancient spillages and general dirt. The air smelled of mould and boiled fish. The sink was an old, chipped earthenware one, brown with years of having tea leaves emptied down it, and a heap of used enamelled tin plates and mugs sat in an inch of greasy water, awaiting the day of reckoning. The cupboard door under the sink was half-open, forced out by an overflowing waste bin, from which an eggshell, some toast crusts and an empty packet which had once held Bachelors Savoury Rice had already escaped onto the floor. Other used saucepans and more plates lay about the worktops, remembrances mostly of meals featuring toast toppers, baked beans, fried things, and one of boil-in-the-bag cod and bottled sauce which had added its perfume to the stale air. This was not the scouting way, Slider thought. Even if he had nothing but a running stream and a piece of twig, a scout cleared as he went. Gilbert had certainly let standards slip.

By the door into the rest of the house was a cork notice-board, and Slider padded over to it, each footstep sticking slightly to the gunky floor and coming up with a little sucking sound. To the notice-board were pinned a number of newspaper cuttings, mostly just headlines from the sensational Sundays. MAN SHOT WIFE AND LOVER CAUGHT IN ACT. BISHOP'S SECRET LOVE-CHILD. 'QUIET' MAN GOES BERSERK WITH AXE – FIVE DEAD. PC'S HAND SEVERED IN MACHETE ATTACK. ROCKER VICAR'S KNICKER SHOCKER. REVENGE KILLER BLOODBATH HORROR. There was also the cutting about the Greatrex murder with the picture of Mills and the news that he was being questioned about irregularities, and a cutting from a shiny magazine which was a review of a recording of *The Damnation of Faust* with Lupton conducting the RLP – Joanna's orchestra – with the CD serial numbers marked with shocking pink highlighter.

This was one disturbed dude, Slider thought – but the cutting about Mills was real evidence. It was too good an opportunity to miss. He opened the door and stepped out into the hall. The floorboards were bare, and a bicycle stood between the stairs and the front door, an ancient sit-up-and-beg bike with black paint and chrome mudguards which, unlike everything else he had seen so far, was clean and shinily well-kept. He walked past the open door to the front room he had seen through the window, and went lightly up the naked stairs. There was a bathroom on the mezzanine which he looked into and quickly out of, and three small bedrooms which were all empty – unfurnished and with no floor coverings. Puzzled, he went downstairs again. Gilbert must live and sleep in the only other room left, the ground-floor back.

He opened the door cautiously. The room was in half-darkness because of the curtains drawn across the window, but he could see well enough. It had a frowzy smell of feet and stale bedding and sweat and dust and general uncleanness that made Slider want to gag; certainly, this was where the man lived and moved and had his being. It was horribly ugly and comfortless – underfoot a variety of dirty old rugs of different sizes and colours almost concealed the original carpet, and a naked light bulb dangled from the centre of the ceiling. The room was almost square. Along the left-hand wall was a narrow divan bed, the bedclothes thrown back and rumpled, the linen grey with use and the blankets old and stained, and on the floor beside it were further used plates and mugs. Beyond it was an old armchair littered with clothes, and in the corner a hand basin, with a shelf bearing a clutter of half-used toiletries and a mirror above it.

Under the window was a table covered in papers and books, amongst which Slider could see some London telephone directories, a *London A–Z*, and a couple of foolscap student's pads closely written.

Behind the door on the right was a paraffin stove standing on a tin tray, and next to it a wicker chair, on which he noted coats and jackets were piled. On the right-hand wall was an enormous old-fashioned wardrobe with a mass of boxes and bulging bags on the top, and next to that, between it and the window wall, ran a wooden bench. It looked handmade, a plank seat, thick, stout square legs, and a tongue-and-groove back screwed to the wall with heavy coach bolts. Slider looked at it reluctantly, for it had plainly been customised for some purpose he did not want to imagine. A semi-circular piece had been cut out of the front edge of the seat in the middle, and two thick iron rings – the sort you might tether horses to in an old-fashioned stable – had been screwed into the seat, one at either end. A piece of dirty rope lay on the bench and a crumpled piece of cloth which might have been a pillowcase; underneath it was stacked an impressive collection of soft-porn magazines. Slider swallowed saliva and moved his gaze elsewhere. The wardrobe. What was in the wardrobe?

The door hung half-open, and he pushed it a little wider. The hanging section was stuffed with clothes, suits, trousers, jackets, shirts, coats, some newish, even tolerable, others old, scruffy, smelling dirty. In the bottom a jumble of shoes gave out a strong but cold smell of feet – oddly enough not a pair of trainers amongst them, but two pairs of black plimsoles, one with holes where the big toes had worn through. There was also, significantly, a shoebox which proved to contain several packets of surgical gloves. The shelved section was stuffed with pullovers and underwear, all but the bottom three shelves, which contained scouting clothes – shorts, shirts, a Baden-Powell hat which must be an antique – and insignia, all clean, pressed, and neatly folded. It might have been poignant in other circumstances.

God, this was a hellish place! Slider was beginning to feel sick, though whether from fatigue or the smell he was not sure. He had no doubt now that he had found his man; in his mind he compared this dismal, grim den and the normality of Mills's rooms. If ever there was an example of nurture versus nature, this was it. Gilbert was obviously an abnormal and possibly dangerous man, and coming home to these surroundings night after night would be like marinading meat to increase the flavour. Slider wondered how he managed to keep up a normal life outside at all, which he must do if he gave advice at the centre, unless his customers were even further spaced out than him.

Slider knew he must get out of here to wait in a safer and pleasanter place for reinforcements and the return of the householder; but he had one more small hunch to play. He crossed to the table and flicked through the London telephone directories. Yes, it was as he thought: both Jimenez and Jepp were listed. Not only that, but, joy of joys, their addresses had been marked with highlighter. Gotcha, you bastard, Slider thought. And Greatrex was not listed, nor was Lassiter, nor Lupton; rifling his memory Slider came up with the name of one other singer, Connie Malcolm, and the producer Ben Edgerton, and they were not listed either. The answer, then, to why those particular people had been chosen was one of simple access. How the campaign would have progressed he could guess from some of the things lying on the desk – the Musician's Union directory, a list of what seemed to be agents' addresses and telephone numbers, and a copy of the programme from Glyndebourne for *Don Giovanni*, carefully dissected, with the cast list and the stars' profiles laid out separately. He had meant to get them all, given time and reasonable luck.

The thing now was to get a search warrant. There was plenty of stuff here that he could see, and probably more that he couldn't, maybe even bloodstained clothing – for Gilbert must be believing himself quite safe, knowing that Mills was under suspicion and that Mills had no idea he had a twin. Presumably that's why he had killed Miss Giles, because she was the only one who was likely to give away the secret to Slider. He felt miserably guilty for her death. The thing now was to get the evidence before Gilbert had a chance to destroy it.

Slider left the room, closing the door carefully behind him, and retraced his steps, feeling an enormous weight of oppression lift as he breathed the comparatively fresh air outside. He walked back down the side of the house, reaching for his mobile to ring Atherton and find out where the hell he was, why he wasn't here yet. He had to stop for a moment still short of the side gate to disentangle the clip from the torn edge of his trouser pocket (would Joanna mend that if asked, or would that be tactless?) thinking that it was odd that there had been no religious stuff in the house, nothing except that cross in the front room, which given that he—

The smell of sweat – sharp, rank as nettles in a ditch but much less reassuring – warned him an instant before the single footfall he actually heard. He swung round, his hand holding the mobile going up instinctively as though to defend himself, to see a man wearing Mills's face but certainly not Mills's expression, holding a piece of lead piping – how traditional! – in a surgically-gloved hand – how odd! – but not just holding it, swinging it. Too late to dodge. Slider heard the smack of the blow, felt the sickening thud of it at a level that was beyond or at least outside pain, felt his stomach rise up nauseously, and saw a brief confusion of ground coming up to meet him and old-fashioned black plimsoles (quiet) (*another* pair?) before he fell through the ground and surprisingly and completely out of the world altogether.

He came to himself to the awareness of a headache – mother, father and both grandparents of a headache which precluded any other sort of thinking just at first. It was a smashing, sickening sort of pain; as he adjusted to it, other, lesser pains faded in, a deep ache in his neck and shoulders, a stinging, raw pain in his cheek, sharp bands of it round his arms and legs. He had no idea what had happened to him, and was aware that the first priority was to open his eyes, but this he was deeply reluctant to do, from a sharp certainty that it would hurt, and from a duller suspicion that he would not like what he saw.

It was at that point that someone grabbed his hair at the back of his skull and dragged his head up. It seemed an unkind thing to do. Simultaneously he smelled rank, horrible sweat and surprisingly the sweet perfume of wood shavings. A voice above him said, 'You're awake. Come on, stop pretending.'

Memory flooded back, his muscles tensed to leap for escape, and he realised he was tied up and couldn't move. Now he opened his eyes. He was inside the garden shed, which accounted for the smell of wood, and he inwardly cursed himself for not having thought of looking in the shed which was so anomalously new and smart. Now he was in deep, deep shit.

The sweat factory released his hair and came round from behind him to sit on a wooden stool between him and the door. The man with Mills's face (yes, there was the mole on the wrong side) wore his hair without a parting, brushed straight back, but otherwise looked startlingly like Mills, in general size and shape as well as features. He was wearing a khaki short-sleeved shirt with large dark rings under the armpits and down the middle, tucked into khaki shorts, and his thick muscular legs (there was a very fine red mark on one thigh, the last trace of a healed cut) bulged out from below them to disappear into olive green socks and the black plimsoles. These things Slider was sure Mills would never wear. The other really serious difference from Mills was that this man was holding in his right hand a large and glittering combat knife.

The true depth of the trouble he was in caught up with Slider's dazed mind and for a moment pushed the headache into the background. He was sitting in a very heavy wooden chair, like a one-seater garden bench except that there seemed to be a hole cut out of the seat, commode-style, the edges of which were cutting into his buttocks and upper thighs. The size and squareness of the chair made it very stable. His ankles were tied to the front legs, his arms behind the seat back, and there was a cord round his thighs and the chair seat, all of which accounted for the bands of pain he had registered. The cords were tight and a covert wriggle convinced him that the knots were good.

As though he heard the thought, Gilbert smiled. 'Don't waste your energy, I know how to tie a rope. They used to teach you knots in the Scouts, you know. Not any more. It's all environmental awareness and cultural sensitivity.'

Slider said nothing. The shorts, the knife and the smile added up to bad, bad news; he was frantically searching the situation for some escape, but the headache made it hard to think. Gilbert had hit him on the temple, possibly fractured his skull. He could feel the stickiness of blood on his left cheek where presumably it had trickled down. His right cheek was also painful, stingingly so, and after a second he realised he must have been dragged to the shed, scraping his face on the ground. That also accounted for the pain in his shoulders and neck.

Gilbert must have been in here, in the shed, all the time – that was why the back door was unlocked – saw Slider come out and crept up on him. What had he been doing in here? Slider now realised that the shed contained some odd things. Under the window, to his left as he sat facing the door, was a wooden workbench, on which was an old manual typewriter, some Letraset sheets and a stack of white cards printed with a cross at the top, a very large Bible and various other religious books – one a luridly coloured children's picture storybook called *Bible Stories for Children*. There were various woodworking tools, and a set of brass weights of the sort used with old-fashioned kitchen scales; the largest, the 2lb weight, had a thin piece of cord knotted through its ring with a thick elastic band on the other end. There was also a set of powder-paints ready mixed up in jars, and another jar full of brushes. On the wall to either side of the window could be seen the fruits of the brushes, a series of paintings pinned up, of simple, highly coloured Bible scenes, presumably copied from the children's book. Abraham about to sacrifice Isaac, Moses and the Burning Bush, Absalom caught up in the thicket. How innocent and sweet, except that they had been painted by a man of thirty-eight.

On the blank wall to his right was a less beguiling collection, of ropes and cords of different thicknesses, textures and materials, all carefully rolled up and tied, and hung from nails. The ropes were interspersed with various ceremonial knives and swords, many of them with decorative sheaths, and the whole was arranged in a pattern, as sometimes old shields and battle-axes are hung up in stately homes.

And there were crosses everywhere – wood, plastic, raffia, metal, ivory – all different sizes, probably a dozen of them at least, with the largest on the back of the door straight ahead. What had Gilbert been doing in here? Not painting – nothing was wet. Reading? Praying?

'So, what were you doing here,' Gilbert asked suddenly, 'snooping around my house? Up to no good, that's obvious, or you'd have called at the front door like an honest man.'

'I did call at the front door,' Slider said – his voice came out in a croak and he had to adjust it. 'I rang and knocked but there was no answer.'

'So you came round the back.' Gilbert was not looking at him. He was looking at the knife which he was turning back and forth softly against his bare thigh, almost as if he was stropping it.

'Yes,' Slider said. 'To knock at the back door.'

'To ask the time? Or did you want a drink of water?'

'I wanted to speak to Mr Gilbert. Is that you?'

'And what did you want to see me about?' Gilbert cooed, smiling.

Slider was watching the knife. That dreamy, preparatory movement terrified him. In his imagination it had already flashed out to open a slit in him. If he said the wrong thing – but what was the right thing the say to a five-star nutter? I'm sorry, Mr Gilbert, I'm not very good at pain. Can we skip this bit? This isn't what I joined the police for. 'I heard you were an expert on opera,' he heard himself say, and immediately regretted it as he saw Gilbert begin to move. Oh shit, oh shit—

But Gilbert stood up and laid the knife down on the workbench. Slider's relief was so intense he'd have slumped if the ropes allowed. 'Opera?' Gilbert said. 'You're fond of opera, are you?'

'Well, I don't know much about it, but I'd like to learn,' Slider said, trying to sound conversational.

'Would you like to hear some?' said Gilbert, crossing behind him. 'I've got just about everything here. Oh, of course, I beg your pardon, you can't see, can you? I've a very nice sound system, and everything on CD.' Slider heard various small sounds and clicks interspersed with Gilbert's breathing which he could easily follow in his mind's eye as a CD was selected and put into the machine. In a moment a chorus roared out from speakers just behind him, and was immediately turned down, though not by much. It was still loud, and Slider recognised it without welcome as a bit of *Don Giovanni*.

'I come out here to listen because I can have it on as loud as I like without the neighbours complaining,' Gilbert said, still behind him. His mouth approached Slider's ear as at the same time his arm came out past Slider and picked up the knife again. 'It will also do nicely to cover any noises you might make,' he said, warm, wet and close. He put an arm round Slider's neck and laid the blade delicately against his throat. 'And now suppose you stop playing silly games and tell me what you really came here for, Detective Inspector Slider. I've been through your pockets, you see. I know who you are.'

Slider felt the tickle of the cold metal on his skin, and had a vivid image of exactly what the inside of his neck would look like. He had seen the inside of Roger Greatrex's and Elizabeth Giles's recently enough to remember. 'If you know who I am, you must know what I'm here for,' Slider said. Oddly enough, though, it wasn't so bad now as when he could see the knife at a distance. At least now he knew where it was aiming. Maybe throat-cutting wasn't too painful. Freddie said death was almost instantaneous when done by an expert. And this man was *good*.

'Not quite,' said Gilbert. 'I want to know how much you know.'

'I know everything,' Slider said, 'so if anything happens to me, someone else will come after me, and someone else. You'll never get away. So it won't do you any good to kill me.'

'It won't do *you* much good, either,' Gilbert said logically. Out of sight, he even sounded quite a bit like Mills. 'So if you know everything, why are you here alone, snooping around?'

'I'm only the scouting party,' Slider said. 'The others are on their way.' Atherton! he thought suddenly. Praise be, of course someone *was* on the way, and would be here any minute. Why the hell wasn't he here already? 'The others will be arriving any time now,' he went on, and something in the changed tone of his voice must have carried conviction because the knife was removed from his throat and Gilbert came back round, first to look out of the window, and then to sit down again facing Slider and looking at him thoughtfully.

'I don't believe you,' Gilbert said at last. He began that evil stroking of the blade again. 'Tell me what you know, and then I'll decide what to do to you.'

Slider didn't like that preposition. *With* you would have been kinder. He decided to be bold. 'I know about the three people you killed and the one you didn't manage to, and I know why you did it.' Gilbert watched him quizzically. 'You were shocked and outraged by the blasphemy you witnessed – and by society's calm acceptance of it. Why, Roger Greatrex even praised it! He was symptomatic of the whole sickness of the modern world – slick, clever, evil. And his private life was as bad as his professional one – everyone knew what sort of a man he was. That's why you decided to start with him.'

'Go on,' Gilbert said. He sounded pleasantly interested, and the knife now lay still on his knee. Everyone likes hearing about themselves, Slider thought. If he could keep the talking going until Atherton got here—

'The difficulty was getting near him. You didn't even know where he lived. Then you saw in the paper that he was going to be on the television programme, *Questions of Our Time*, which goes out live from White City. You went along there on the evening and picked out somebody scruffy-looking at the back of the queue who'd be glad to give you his ticket for twenty pounds. Once inside, it was easy enough to slip away from the rest – it's always chaotic in there.'

'My, you do know everything, don't you?' Gilbert said ironically, but he didn't seem angry, only fascinated.

Slider went on, trying to sound conversational. 'The one thing I don't know is how you managed to find Roger Greatrex – or was that just luck?'

'Not entirely. I'd been to that programme before – when they had religious or ethical questions – so I knew the routine. And I went on a guided tour of the centre years ago with my school, so I knew the layout. The difficulty was going to be getting him on his own. I hid on the staircase and watched the greenroom through the glass. I couldn't believe my luck when he came out alone. But then he went into another room.'

The knife was now being tapped briskly against the kneecap. Slider swore if he got out of this alive no-one over whom he had any influence would ever wear shorts again.

'I went to the door,' Gilbert said, 'and listened. I thought if he was on his own—' He stopped.

'But he wasn't. He was with a woman,' Slider said.

Gilbert glared. 'I heard them – the filthy animals! I heard him slaking his filthy lust – just wherever it took him, like a dog. Oh, I knew then I was right to kill him. He came out at last and went into the men's room. I was going to follow when the female came out and I had to dodge back. I thought about putting her down, too, but I wanted Greatrex. She could wait. When she'd gone I went into the men's and there he was. Do you know what the filthy creature was doing?'

'Yes, I think I do,' Slider said. 'He was washing himself.'

'As if water alone could cleanse him of that!' Gilbert paused a moment and looked at Slider thoughtfully. 'Are you a Christian?'

'Yes,' Slider said, grateful he could say it with some conviction.

'Churchgoer?'

'When I can. When I'm not working.'

'You shouldn't let work interfere with your duty to God,' Gilbert said sternly. 'That's no excuse.'

'Go on about Greatrex,' Slider said weakly. He licked his lips and tasted blood. His head was bleeding again. 'When you found him in the men's room—?'

'I went up behind him, held him, read him his sentence. Ezekiel, chapter 18, verse 24. "*When the righteous turneth away from his righteousness, shall he live? In his trespass that he hath trespassed and in his sin that he hath sinned, in them shall he die.*" He didn't struggle. Unlike the dumb beast, he knew what was coming to him, and he knew what for. I saw the understanding in his eyes as I looked at them in the mirror. Then I put the card into his pocket, caught him by the chin, and *cut*.'

Slider had never known there could be so much emotion

in such a small word. It was a sharp-edged, lip-smacking, blood-filled word. The music behind him boomed, sounding distorted, he felt very sick and there were specks before his eyes. Concussion, he thought. He struggled to keep hold of his consciousness.

'Afterwards,' he said. 'Tell me what you did afterwards.'

'I thought you knew everything,' Gilbert said, sharply suspicious.

'You went up in the lift – to the canteen – mix with the others,' Slider said with difficulty. 'Hid – hid the bag – on the roof of the lift.'

Gilbert relaxed. 'I was sorry to part with that raincoat, but the blood would never have come out.'

'But the knife,' Slider said. 'Why did you leave the knife?'

'He knocked it out of my hand as he fell, and landed on top of it. I didn't want to move him. It always shows, doesn't it, when someone's been moved?' Slider nodded and then wished he hadn't as lumps of pain went rolling about his head like rocks. 'The only thing I did was to put his *thing* away. I couldn't leave him like that. The knife – well, that didn't matter. I've got plenty of others. I collect knives,' he added, looking dreamily at the display wall. 'There's something beautiful and pure and simple about a blade – that's why they talk so much about them in the Bible. Especially as an instrument of God's vengeance. Draw the blade across the taut flesh, and let the soul out in a great gushing fountain of redness. That redness which is man's animal nature, his sin. The thirsty earth drinks the sacrifice, and is quenched. And his soul goes to God for judgement. So simple, so easy.'

Slider blinked as a trickle of blood stung his eyes. He was losing his grip on things. 'Why,' he croaked, 'did you kill your mother?'

Gilbert's dreaminess disappeared, his expression sharpened. 'My mother died ten years ago, of cancer. The good woman who brought me up, she was my mother. The whore who bore me was nothing to me. She was lewdness and filth, she was Babylon—'

'She was the only person who knew about you and your brother. She knew you were going to let your twin brother take the blame for what you'd done. She reproached you, didn't she? And you couldn't stand it. She said you ought to take your punishment—'

Gilbert moved with astonishing swiftness for such a large man, and the knife was against Slider's throat again, his head being pulled back agonisingly by the hair, the stink of sweat almost overpowering. 'Punishment? Don't you think I know about punishment? I learnt about it at my mother's knee. Scourge thou the flesh that the soul may be made clean. In suffering is salvation. Scourge the back with rods and flails – as my father did for me, out of his love for me. Beat the devil out and let God in!' He flung Slider's head down and walked away, marching about the confined space to the beating music. 'The flesh is just an envelope for the soul, an envelope with no address. The flesh is a snare and delusion. But the temptations of the flesh are strong, oh yes. So strong! You have to punish, punish every day, crush out the lewdness and the evilness. When the Devil stands up, you have to force him down again.'

Through the waves of nausea, Slider suddenly realised what Gilbert had been doing in here, what the kitchen weights were for, and the hole in the chair seat. He groaned, unable to help himself. This man, he thought dimly, is seriously bonkers. He is probably also going to kill me – but it was getting harder to care. He wished Mozart would shut up. How long can you hang out a death scene? His head hurt so much. But he thought the end was very near.

And suddenly Gilbert stood still, frozen in mid-stride and mid-rant. He would have looked ridiculous in those shorts and socks if it hadn't been for the knife. Slider couldn't see the knife any more. Was it somewhere in him? No, surely he'd remember that. What was up with Gilbert? Slider's chin was sunk on his chest, and with a great effort he lifted it up, raised the throbbing football and peered through the blood and sweat that blurred his vision. Gilbert was standing by the door, listening, every line of his body taut. Then suddenly he flung it open. A breath of heavenly fresh air came in, and Slider saw Atherton standing there – elegant, fragrant Atherton. The cavalry.

Atherton said, 'What the—' and his eyes widened with surprise for an instant as he recognised the face in front of him. 'How did you get here?'

Slider tried to warn him, but he couldn't make a sound. It was all he could do to keep his head up. He saw an instant's struggle as Gilbert thrust Atherton violently aside and ran. Atherton reeled sideways, briefly out of sight against the side fence, and Slider saw beyond Gilbert, oh blessed sight, the dark blue-black of uniformed police coming up the side passage. Atherton had thought to call out the infantry too, probably when Slider didn't answer his mobile. The lads didn't need telling to catch Gilbert – to bring down a running man is the most basic of a copper's instincts. They were on him like the hounds of Hell on winter's traces – hounds of fell – felon—

Atherton reappeared in the doorway, a puzzled expression on his face, his hands clasped over his stomach like a post-prandial bishop. Slider desperately wanted to say something – he'd thought of a really wonderful bishop joke, about long time no see – but all the talk had gone out of his tongue. Atherton unfolded his hands and looked at them, and the palms were red, and there was red all over his shirt. While Slider was trying to puzzle it out, Atherton said, quite conversationally, 'Oh shit,' went down on both knees like a shot ox, and fell gracefully sideways.

Killing Time

With special thanks to Laurence Cohen for his generous help with the background, not forgetting tea and biscuits.

CHAPTER ONE

Second Class Male

Early on Monday morning, DI Carver, about to head downstairs, saw a familiar figure walking away from him along the corridor. 'Bill!'

Slider stopped and turned. 'Hello, Ron.'

'I didn't know you were back.' Carver looked him over keenly. 'Shouldn't you still be on sick-leave? You look terrible.'

'Thanks,' Slider said. 'I feel a bit under the weather, but Honeyman asked me to come in. We're short-handed, with Atherton in the cot.'

'How is he?' Carver's face pursed with a moment's sympathy.

'Still very poorly.' Slider marvelled for a moment at the word. It was how the hospital had described him yesterday. They had a box of these strange shorthand terms for the varying degrees of human distress – critical, comfortable, stable, poorly – which they used like flashcards. It was kinder than describing reality. Reality was Atherton with a hole in him; Atherton a white face and fragile blue eyelids above a sheet, drips and drains and bags, and a cradle to keep the bedclothes off the wound, so that he looked like Tutankhamun without the gilding.

It was hard to think of clearing up the Gilbert case as a success, though Gilbert was under wraps and the CPS was as chuffed about it as the CPS ever was about anything. But Slider had stupidly allowed himself to be ambushed by Gilbert, coshed, trussed up and, for a harrowing period, kept prisoner and threatened with a knife. When Atherton had come looking for him, Gilbert had jumped him, and the same knife had ended up where Atherton normally kept *quenelles de veau* or designer sausages with red onion marmalade. Slider had narrowly escaped a fractured skull, but Atherton had nearly died, and was not out of the woods yet.

'You've been to see him?' Carver asked.

'More tubes through him than King's Cross,' Slider said.

'It's a bastard,' Carver said in omnibus disapprobation. 'He'll be off a while then.'

It was not a question. Slider shifted uncomfortably away from the subject, and said instead, 'I hear Mills is leaving the Job?' DS Mills, alias Dark Satanic, an old colleague of Slider's, had been a suspect for a time in the Gilbert case.

'Yeah. Well, I can't blame him. It'd be tough after what he's been through. But I'd only just got the extra manpower,' he complained. 'I don't suppose Honeyman'll roll for it again – not with you being short.' He gave Slider a resentful stare as if it was his fault.

'Where's he going?'

'What, Mills? Wales, I gather. What's that place he went on holiday every year?'

'Rhyl?'

'That's it. This bloke he met there, owns his own business, offered Mills a billet. Salesman. Computerised security systems. Thought it'd be a boost to have an ex-dick toting the brochures round.'

Poor old Dark Satanic, Slider thought. Going on the knocker was a bit of a come-down from the CID. Or was it? 'I suppose it's a job,' he said doubtfully.

'I don't think he minds,' Carver shrugged. 'I think he wants to see a bit of life before it's too late.'

'In *Wales*?'

'He's taking his mum with him,' Carver said – one of his better non-sequiturs. 'I dunno but what he hasn't got the right idea,' he went on, his face settling into familiar creases of gloom. 'The Job's changing, Bill. Every day coppers are getting shot and knifed, bashed on the head and dumped, and for what? We work our balls off catching the villains, and the courts let 'em off with a slap on the wrist, because some social worker says they had a rotten mum and a no-good dad. Yeah, but if one of us makes some pissy little mistake in procedure, it's wrongful arrest and the tabloids start screaming about fit-ups. It makes you wonder why you go on.'

Slider, accustomed to Carver's style, deduced his heart was not bleeding for Slider's bashed head or Atherton's knifed stomach. 'Has someone else got hurt, then?'

'You haven't heard about Andy Cosgrove?'

'No. What about him?' Cosgrove was the very popular 'community beat' copper for the White City Estate, a PC of the Neo-Dixon school, calm, authoritative, patient, knowledgeable; worth his considerable weight in gold to the Department for the background information he could give on any case arising on his beat.

'He was attacked last night. Beaten up and left for dead.'

'Shit,' Slider said, appalled. 'How is he?'

'Not too clever. He's in a coma, on life-support in St Stephen's.'

'Who did it? What have you got?'

'Sod all,' Carver grunted. 'He was found on that piece of waste ground round the back of the railway arches down the end of Sulgrave Road, but that's not where it happened. He got smacked somewhere else, driven there and dumped.'

'Professional? What was he working on?'

'Nothing in particular – nothing I know about, anyway. Just routine stuff. Like I said, there's nothing to go on.' He was silent a moment, sucking his upper lip. He'd had a moustache once that he used to suck, and though he'd shaved it off ten years ago, the habit remained. A bloke and his face-fur, Slider reflected, could be as close as man and wife. 'Honeyman's shitting himself. It was the last straw for him,' Carver went on. 'You going to see him? Reporting back?'

'That's where I was heading.'

'He's like a flea in a frying pan. Wants a bodyguard to cross the parking lot.'

I don't blame him, Slider thought when he left Carver. Honeyman was only a temp in the post of Detective Superintendent, having been put in as a night watchman when the last Det Sup had died at the crease. Recent events were enough to make anyone nervous, but Honeyman was only a few months short of his pension, and sudden death or grave injury could seriously upset a man's retirement plans.

Through the open door Slider could see Honeyman at his desk, writing. Slider tapped politely and noted how the little chap started. 'Oh, Slider – come in, come in. Good to see you back.' Honeyman stood and came round the desk and held out his hand, all evidence of unusual emotion. Slider stood patiently while Honeyman looked him up and down – mostly up, because Eric Honeyman was built on a daintier scale than most policemen. 'And how are you feeling now? Quite recovered? I must say we can use you. We seem to be terribly accident-prone recently. You've heard about Cosgrove?'

'Yes sir, just this minute.'

'Terrible business.' Honeyman shook his head hopelessly.

'Ron Carver's firm is on it, I gather.'

'Yes,' Honeyman said, rather absently. He seemed to be hesitating on the brink of a confidence. 'I've not been feeling quite on top form myself, lately.' Slider made a sympathetic noise. 'The fact is,' Honeyman plunged, 'I've asked to have my retirement brought forward. On medical grounds.' His eyes flickered guiltily to Slider and away again. 'This sort of thing – involving your own men – it takes it out of you. I suppose that must sound to you—'

'You've done your time, sir,' Slider filled in obligingly.

'Nearly thirty years,' Honeyman agreed eagerly. 'It was so different when I joined the service. Policemen were respected. Even the villains called you "sir". Now you have respectable, middle-class people calling you "pig". And breaking the law so casually, as if it was just a matter of personal choice.'

Slider had no wish to stroll down this lane in this company. 'Have you got a date for leaving, sir?'

'The end of next week. I haven't announced it yet, but I asked them to relieve me as soon as they could find a replacement.'

Honeyman chatted a bit, something about his retirement plans and his wife, and Slider drifted off. A silence roused him, and coming to guiltily he asked, 'Is this still confidential, sir? About you going?'

'I don't see any reason to keep it a secret. No, I shall send round a memo later today, but you can spread the word to the troops, if you like.'

Start the collection for my leaving present, Slider translated. 'Very well, sir.'

McLaren was at his desk, eating a fried egg sandwich from Sid's coffee-stall at the end of Shepherd's Bush Market. Slider knew that was where it came from, because it was the only place nearby you could get them with the yolk in the correctly runny state. You had to be in the right mood to be on either side of a fried egg sandwich, Slider thought. It helped also not to be just out of hospital after a whack on the head.

'Hello, guv,' McLaren said indistinctly. 'I didn't know you were back. You're looking double well.'

'For Chrissake, McLaren, not over your reports,' Slider said.

McLaren swivelled in his chair and dripped over his waste paper basket instead.

'How're you feeling, boss?' Mackay came forward, tin tray in hand. 'Can I get you a coffee?'

Slider sat down on the nearest desk – Atherton's, as it happened. 'A few days away, and I'm forgotten. You know I don't drink instant.'

'Tea, I meant,' Mackay said hastily.

'Thanks. No sugar, in case you've forgotten that as well.'

Mackay apologised in kind. 'We've got some doughnuts.'

'From Sid's? Now you're talking.'

His eye found a stranger, a tall man in his late thirties, with sparse, sandy hair, plentiful freckles, and that thick, pale skin that went with them. He wore large gold-rimmed glasses and a bristly moustache, and he gangled forwards, slightly drooping, with an air of practised melancholy, as though expecting to be ridiculed.

'We haven't met, guv. I'm your new DS,' he said, holding out his hand. He had a strange, semi-castrato, counter-tenor voice and a Mancunian accent. His eyes behind the glass were bulgingly soft, greyish-green like part-cooked gooseberries, but held a gleam of humour. With a voice like that, you had to have a sense of humour to survive.

'Ah, yes, Beevers' replacement,' Slider said. 'You came last week, didn't you?'

'That's right. Colin Hollis,' he offered. Slider immediately felt more comfortable. A CID department without a Colin in it never seemed quite natural, somehow. 'From Manchester Stolen Cars Squad.'

'Ah. This'll seem like a bit of a holiday for you, then,' Slider said.

'Talking of holidays.' Anderson sidled up, a menacing photo-envelope in his hand. 'Would you like to see these, guv? My loft conversion. I've done a lot while you've been away.'

This was Anderson's latest project – a Useful Games Room Stroke Extra Bedroom. He had decided, unsurprisingly, to line the whole room with pine stripping. 'I've got before and after shots,' he added beguilingly.

Slider was deeply grateful to be interrupted by the arrival of WDC 'Norma' Swilley. Tall, athletic, blonde, gorgeous, and yet with a strangely unmemorable set of features, small-nosed and large-mouthed in the manner of a Baywatch Beauty, she was, according to Atherton, the living proof that Barbie and Ken had sex. She was a good policeman, but she had a low fool-suffering threshold – which probably accounted for why she was still a DC – and she swept Anderson aside with the authority of a staff nurse.

'The boss doesn't want to see those. How are you, guv? And how's Jim? All we get is the official report.'

'Progressing slowly. I saw him yesterday. He's sleeping a lot of the time, though.'

'Drugged, I suppose. It must still be pretty painful.'

Slider nodded. 'Haven't you seen him?'

'Just once. They're restricting visitors. I suppose you know that. Just one from the firm, they said, so I tossed Mackay for it.'

'Doesn't he wish,' McLaren muttered.

'Of all people,' Norma said, ignoring him, 'for Jim Atherton to get it in the stomach!'

Slider nodded. He'd thought of that. 'It's like a pianist getting his fingers broken.'

'Him and food,' Norma said, 'it's one of the great love affairs. Paris and Helen, Antony and Cleopatra—'

'Marks and Spencer?' Anderson suggested absently.

McLaren licked the last of the yolk and grease from his fingers. 'They say he's not coming back. Lost his bottle.'

'You've got the most hyperactive *They* I've ever come across,' Slider said. 'All I know is he's still very sick and he'll be in hospital a while yet, and after that he'll have to convalesce. We're going to be without him a good few weeks. What he'll decide after that no-one knows – least of all him, I should think.'

There was a buzz of conversation about what Atherton might or might not be feeling, and to break it up, Slider told them about Honeyman leaving. The news was met with a storm of equanimity.

'I know he hasn't been with us long,' Slider concluded, 'but I think we ought to organise a whip-round. At least buy him a book or something. And a card. Get everyone to sign it.'

'I'll do it,' McLaren offered, preparing to engage a doughnut in mortal combat.

'Fair enough,' Slider said doubtfully. 'But try not to get fingermarks on it.'

McLaren looked wounded. 'I won't let you down, guv.'

'There's no way you can,' Slider assured him.

He had lunch in the canteen. Chicken curry, which they made halfway decently except that they would put sultanas in it which to his mind belonged in pudding not dinner, and raspberries with *crème aux fraises*, which was cateringspeak for pink blancmange. Slider didn't mind because he actually liked blancmange. He was spooning it up when a shadow fell over him and he looked up to see Sergeant Nicholls bearing a tray. Nicholls' handsome face lit in a flattering smile. 'You're back. That was quick.'

'Honeyman begged me. I couldn't stand seeing a strong man weep, so—' He shrugged.

Nicholls obeyed his tacit invitation to sit down. 'But are you able for it?' he asked, unloading his tray.

'Such tender concern. Yes, thanks. I still get the odd headache, but on the whole I'd sooner be working. Takes the mind off.'

'Bad dreams?' Nicholls asked perceptively. 'Yes, I'm not surprised. It has to come out somewhere after a shock like that. But I'd feel the same in your shoes: get back on the horse as soon as possible.' He reached over the table and laid a hand on Slider's forearm. 'Gilbert's banged up tight as a trull,' he said, 'and there's enough evidence to send him down for ever. He's not getting out, Bill. Keep that in mind.'

'Thanks, Nutty.' They had a bit of a manly cough and shuffle. 'I expect I'll be kept busy, anyway, being two men down.'

'Och, well, I've some better news for you on that front,' Nicholls said. 'They're sending you a DC as a temporary replacement for Atherton. Someone called Tony Hart, from Lambeth. D'ye know him?'

'Never met him,' Slider shook his head. 'Ah well, that's better than nothing. But I wonder Honeyman didn't tell me. I was in there this morning.'

'Honeyman'd mebbe not know yet. He hasn't got my sources. Did you know he was leaving next week?'

'Yes, he told me that.'

'I shall miss him, in a way, you know,' Nutty said, thoughtfully loading his fork with Pasta Bake. 'He's a real lady.'

Colin Hollis stuck his head round Slider's door. 'There's some bloke downstairs asking for you, guv. Won't take no.'

'Won't what?'

Hollis inserted his body after his head. 'Well, I say bloke. Bit of a debatable point, now I've had a look at him. Ey, guv, if a bloke wears woman's underwear, is that what you'd call a Freudian slip?'

'Wipe the foam from your chin and start again,' Slider suggested.

'Bloke,' Hollis said helpfully. 'Come in asking for you, so I went down to see what he wanted, but he says he knows you, and you're the only one he can talk to now that PC Cosgrove is gone.' He eyed Slider with undisguised interest.

'What does he want?'

'He wouldn't say. But he's nervous as hell. Maybe he's got some gen on the Cosgrove case.'

'Name?'

'Paloma. Jay Paloma.' Hollis gave an indescribable grimace. 'I bet that's not his real name, though. Una Paloma Blanca – what's that song? D'you know him, guv?'

Slider frowned a moment, and then placed him. 'Not really. I know his flatmate, Busty Parnell.' He sighed. 'I suppose I'd better come.'

Hollis followed him through the CID room. 'He's got some gear on him. Making a bit, one way or the other. Probably the other. Funny old world, en't it, guv, when the Game makes more than the Job?'

Slider paused at the door. 'Every man makes his choice.'

'Oh, I've no regrets,' Hollis said, stroking his terrible

moustache. 'I'd bend over backwards to help my fellow man.'

Slider trudged downstairs, feeling a little comforted. It was early days yet, but it looked as though Hollis was going to be an asset to the Department.

Slider had become acquainted with Busty Parnell in his Central days. She described herself as a show dancer, and indeed she wasn't a bad hoofer, but a small but insidious snow habit had led her into trouble, and she had slipped down the social scale to stripper and part-time prostitute. Slider had busted her once or twice and helped her out on other occasions, when a customer turned nasty or a boss was bothering her. Sometimes she had given him a spot of good information, and in return he had turned a blind eye to a spot of victimless crime on her part. And sometimes, in the lonely dogwatches which are so hard on the unmarried copper, he had taken a cup of tea with her at her flat and discussed business in general and the world in particular. She had made it plain that she would be glad to offer him more substantial comforts, but Slider had never been one to mix business with pleasure. Besides, he knew enough about Busty's body and far too much about her past life to find her tempting.

Her name was Valerie, but she had always been referred to as Busty in showbiz circles to distinguish her from the other Val Parnell, the impresario, for whom she had once auditioned. Slider had lost sight of her when he left Central, but she had turned up again a year or so ago on the White City Estate, sharing a flat with Jay Paloma. The last Slider had heard Busty had given up the stage and was working as a barmaid at a pub, The British Queen. Her flatmate was employed as an 'artiste' at the Pomona Club, a rather dubious night club whose advertised 'cabaret' consisted mainly of striptease and simulated sex acts, and which distributed more drugs than the all-night pharmacy in Shaftesbury Avenue.

Jay Paloma was waiting for Slider in one of the interview rooms. He was beautifully, not to say androgynously, dressed in a white silk shirt with cossack sleeves, and loose beige flannel slacks tucked into chocolate-coloured suede ankle boots, with a matching beige jacket hanging casually over his shoulders.

There was a heavy gold chain round his throat, a gold lapel pin in the shape of a treble clef on the jacket, and discreet gold studs in his ears. A handbag and nail polish would have tilted the ensemble irrevocably over the gender balance point; as it was, a casual glance suggested *artistic* rather than *transvestite*.

Jay Paloma was tall and slenderly built, and sat with the disjointed grace of a dancer, his heels together and his knees fallen apart, his arms resting on his thighs and his hands dangling, loosely clasped, between them. The hands were well-kept, with short nails and no rings. His thick, streaked-blond hair was cut short, full and spiky like a model's; his face was long and large-nosed, and given the dark eyeliner on the underlids and his way of tilting his face down and looking up under his eyebrows, he bore an uncanny resemblance to Princess Di, which Slider supposed was purely intentional.

He was a very nervous, tremulous Princess Di today, quivering of lip and brimming of eye. He started to his feet as Slider came in, thought about shaking hands, fidgeted, looked this way and that; and obeyed Slider's injunction to sit down again with a boneless, graceful collapse. He put a thumb to his mouth and gnawed the side of it – not the nail or even the cuticle but the loose flesh of the first joint. Probably he had been a nail-biter and had cured himself that way. Nails would be important to him; appearance important generally. Given that he shared an unglamorous flat with Busty and worked at the Pomona, his expensive outfit suggested that he exploited his body in a more lucrative way out of club hours.

'So what can I do for you?' Slider asked, pulling out a chair and sitting facing him. 'Jay, isn't it? Do I call you Jay?'

'It's my professional name,' he said. He had a soft, husky voice with the expected slightly camp intonation. It was funny, Slider reflected from his experience, how many performers adopted it, even if they weren't TWI. It was a great class-leveller. It was hard to guess his origins – or, indeed, his age. Slider would have put him at thirty-five, but he looked superficially much younger and could have been quite a bit older. He had makeup on, Slider saw: foundation, mascara and probably blusher, but discreetly done. It was only the angle of the light throwing into relief the fine stubble coming through the foundation that gave it away.

'It's nice of you to see me,' Jay said, with the obligatory

upward intonation at the end of the sentence; the phantom question mark which had haunted Estuary English ever since Australian soaps took over from the home-grown variety. It made it sound as though he wasn't sure that it was nice, and gave Slider the spurious feeling of having a hidden agenda, of being persecutor to Jay's victim.

'Any friend of Busty's is a friend of mine,' he said. 'How do you come to know her, by the way?'

'Val and me go way back. We were in a show together – do you remember *Hanging Out in the Jungle*? That musical about the ENSA troupe?'

'Yes, of course I do. It caused quite a stir at the time.'

Slider remembered it very well. It had hit the headlines not only because it was high camp – still daring in those days – and full of suggestive jokes; not only because of the implication, offensive to some, that ENSA had been riddled with homosexuality; but because before *Hanging Out*, the star, Jeremy Haviland – who had also directed and part-written the show – had been a respected, heavyweight actor of Shakespearian gravitas. Seeing him frolicking so incongruously in satin frocks and outrageous makeup had been one of the main draws which kept packing them in through its short but momentous run. But the gradually-emerging realisation that Haviland had merely type-cast himself had caused secondary shock-waves which had destroyed his career. This was some years before homosexuality had become popular and acceptable. Six months after *Hanging Out* closed, Haviland committed suicide.

'Val was in the chorus, singing and dancing, but I had a proper part,' Jay went on. 'It was a terrific break for me.'

'Which were you?'

'I played Lance Corporal Fender – the shy young lad who had to play all the young girls' parts, and got all those parcels of knitted things from his mother?'

'Yes, I remember. You did that song with Jeremy Haviland, the Beverley Sisters number, what was it?'

'"Sisters, sisters, there were never such devoted sisters",' Jay Paloma sang obediently, in a sweet, husky voice. 'It was Jeremy got me the part. I really could dance – I'd been to a stage-and-dance school and everything – but all I'd done before was a student review at UCL. I was sharing a flat at the time with the president of Dramsoc, and he wangled me into it, because frankly, none of the rest of them could sing or dance worth spit. Anyway, Jeremy saw me in it, liked me, and took a chance. He was so kind to me! I owed him everything. I got fave reviews for *Hanging Out* and everyone reckoned I was headed for stardom. But then all the fuss broke out over poor Jeremy, and the show folded, and we were all sort of dragged down with him. Tarnished with the same brush, you might say. It was hard for any of us to get work after that, and, well, Jeremy and I had been – you know—'

'Close,' Slider suggested.

Jay seemed grateful for the tact. 'He tried to help me, but everyone was avoiding him. And then he—' He gulped and made a terminal gesture with both hands. 'It was terrible. He was such a kind, kind man.'

'I didn't know Busty was in that show. It must have been before I met her.'

'She and I shared lodgings. She was like a big sister to me.'

'She was at the Windmill when I first knew her.'

'Yes, that's where she went when *Hanging Out* closed. It was always easier for women dancers to get work. Well, we sort of lost sight of each other for a long time. And then about eighteen months ago we bumped into each other again in Earl's Court.'

By then both had drifted down out of the realms of legitimate theatre and into the shadowy fringe world where entertainment and sex were more or less synonymous. Busty was doing a bit of this and a bit of that – stripping, promotional work, topless waitressing. Jay was dancing when he could get it, filling in with drag routines, modelling, and working for a gay escort agency.

'Val was doing the Motor Show – dressed in a flesh suit handing out leaflets about some new sports car. She was supposed to be Eve in the Garden of Eden, the leaflets were apple-shaped. The car was the New Temptation – d'you get it?' He sniffed derisively. 'She hated promo work – we all do. Being a Sunflower Girl or a Fiat Bunny or whatever. Humiliating. And the hours are shocking and the pay's peanuts, unless you sleep with the agent, which you often have to to get the job at all. Well, you have to take what you can get. And we're neither of us teenagers any more. There just isn't the work for troupers like us. Everyone specialises, and the kids coming out of the dancing schools now can do things – well, they're more like acrobats to my mind. It's not what I'd call dancing.'

'And what about you? What were you doing?'

'I had a spot at a night club in Earl's Court – a sort of striptease.'

Slider had a fair idea which club. 'Striptease?'

Jay Paloma looked haughty. 'It wasn't what you think. In fact, it was my best gig after *Hanging Out* closed. I came on in this evening gown and white fur and diamonds and everything, and did this wonderful routine. Like Gypsy Rose Lee, you know – all I ever took off was the long gloves. Absolutely classical. It brought the house down! Well, anyway, Val and I bumped into each other in the street, and we were so glad to see each other, we decided to share again. We had this place in Warwick Road to start with, and then we moved out here.'

Fascinating though this was, Slider had a lot to do. 'So what did you want to talk to me about?' he asked, with a suggestion of glancing at his wrist.

Jay hesitated. 'I say, look, d'you mind if I smoke?'

'Go ahead.' Paloma reached for the pocket of the jacket. The cigarettes were in their original packet, but the lighter looked expensive, a gold Dunhill, Slider thought. 'It always amazes me,' he added as he watched the lighting-up process, 'how many of you dancers smoke. I'd have thought you'd need all your breath.'

Jay Paloma looked up from under his brows and smiled in a fluttery, pleased way – because Slider had called him a dancer, perhaps. 'It keeps the weight down. You don't—?'

'No, thanks.' Slider pushed the ashtray across the table and prompted him again. 'Well, now, what can I do for you?'

'I've got a problem,' Jay said. He puffed at his cigarette. 'I think – well, I suppose you won't believe me, but I think someone's trying to kill me.' The big blue eyes turned up appealingly at Slider. He was certainly nervous. He was sweating – Slider could smell it, even through what his daughter Kate would have called his anti-shave. Light and lemony: *Eau Sauvage*. Slider recognised it, because it was the one O'Flaherty favoured – though O'Flaherty, the patriot, pronounced it O'Savvidge.

'What makes you think so?' Slider asked encouragingly.

The tense shoulders dropped a little. 'Well, there've been, you know, funny phone calls.'

'Heavy breathing?'

'Not exactly. No. I mean, it rings and I pick it up, and there's just silence. I know there's someone there, but they won't speak. And then, ten minutes or so, it rings again. Sometimes it goes on for hours. I take the phone off the hook, but as soon as I put it back on, it rings again. I can't leave it off all the time because of work. I mean, you never know when someone might want to get hold of you.'

'It could be kids.'

'Kids wouldn't go on and on like that, would they? I mean, they'd get bored and go off and do something else.'

That was a point. This man had obviously thought about his predicament, which made Slider more inclined to believe him.

'Has Busty picked up these calls too?'

'No, that's another thing. It never happens when she's home. It's as if,' he shivered subconsciously, 'as if he's watching the house, and knows when I'm home alone.'

'Have you seen anyone hanging around? Anyone suspicious?'

He shook his head. 'But it's a block of flats. There are always people around, coming and going. And plenty of places to hide, if you wanted to watch someone.'

'How long has this been going on?'

'Oh, months now. Six months maybe – but I didn't think much of it at first. I mean everyone gets those dead calls, don't they? But about three months ago, the letters started coming.'

'Letters?'

Jay nodded, almost reluctantly, 'At first they weren't really letters, just empty envelopes. Like the phone calls. Sort of unnerving. You tear open an envelope and there's a piece of blank paper in it. But then the messages started to appear.'

'Written? Typed?'

'Cut out of newspapers and stuck on, you know the sort of thing.'

Slider knew. He sighed inwardly. It was so hackneyed. A hoax, he thought. A spiteful hoax by someone who had taken a dislike to Jay Paloma. A homophobe perhaps, or a purity-nut with a personal campaign to rid the world of sleazy entertainers.

'And what did they say?' he asked.

'It started with one word – "You". Then the next had two words – "You are." By the end of the week it said "You are going to die."'

'A new letter each day for a week?' This was unpleasant. It was beginning to sound obsessional. Poison pens could be obsessional, of course, without ever meaning to carry out their threats. But there was always the risk that they might convince themselves, steep themselves in their own culture to the point when the unthinkable last step became the inevitable next one.

'Every week.' The head drooped. 'They got worse – about what he was going to do to me. Cut my throat. And – other things.'

'I suppose you haven't brought them to show me?' Slider said, in the tone that expects the answer no.

'I didn't keep them. I destroyed them,' Jay said, still looking at the floor.

'That's a pity,' Slider said mildly.

'I couldn't bear to have them in the house. And I didn't want Val to see them. I didn't want to worry her.'

'You didn't notice the postcode, I suppose?'

'All over the place,' he said. 'London postcodes, West End, Earl's Court, Clapham – Heathrow once. All different.'

'What sort of paper? What sort of envelopes?'

'Just plain white notepaper. Basildon Bond or something. And white envelopes, the long sort, self-sealing. The name and address was printed – you know, like on a printer, on a label. And the words inside, like I said, cut out of newspaper and stuck on.'

'Well, if you get another one,' Slider said, 'perhaps you'd keep it and bring it in to me.'

'You don't believe me,' Paloma concluded flatly.

'I didn't say that.'

'But you're not going to do anything?'

'It's difficult to do anything without having an actual letter to work on.' Paloma continued to look at him with a half-defiant, half-angry look – Princess Di at bay, badgered by a *Sun* reporter. 'Look, I believe you're frightened,' Slider went on, 'and that's evidently what the letter merchant wants. It doesn't follow they'll actually do what they threaten.' Paloma said nothing. 'You haven't told me everything yet,' Slider said after a moment. 'Something else has happened to trigger your coming here.' No answer. 'I don't think it was an easy step for you to take.'

'You're right,' Paloma said, softening at this evidence of Slider's percipience. 'I don't like police stations. I don't like police – most of them anyway. But Val said – she said you were different. So I thought—' Slider waited in insistent silence. Paloma swallowed and took the plunge. 'A photograph. This morning. Cut out of a book or something. Of a dead body, all beaten up, with its throat cut.' He reached out and stubbed out his cigarette with a violently trembling hand, and then quite suddenly turned corpse-white. Slider had been vomited over many times in the course of a long career. It taught you quick reactions. He shot out of his chair, grabbed the back of Jay's neck and pushed his head down between his legs. Jay moaned and dry-retched a couple of times, but didn't actually throw up.

'Breathe deeply. In, and out. In, and out,' Slider commanded.

After a bit Jay sat up again, still pale but not quite so green.

'D'you want some water, or a cup of tea?' Slider asked.

'No. No, I'm all right, thanks. Thanks,' he added more particularly, eyeing Slider consideringly. He lit another cigarette, and Slider sat down again, keeping a wary eye on him.

'I suppose,' Slider said at last, 'that you didn't keep this latest mail-shot either?'

Paloma shook his head. 'I burned it. In the ashtray.' He gestured tremblingly with his lighter. 'I couldn't bear it hanging around.'

Slider sighed. 'It would have helped if you'd brought it to me.'

'I didn't know I was going to come in,' Paloma said. 'I only decided at the last minute. And I felt – I don't know – that if I didn't get rid of it, it might, you know, happen.'

Superstitious, Slider thought. Understandable, but not helpful. He said, 'If anything else comes, any more of these letters, or anything you're suspicious of, bring it to me unopened, will you?' Paloma assented. 'So, now, who do you think is doing this?'

'That's what I've come to you for.'

'Quite. But you know more about your life than I possibly

can. It has to be someone you know, someone who knows you.' He surveyed Paloma's face. 'And in my experience, the victim usually has a pretty good idea who.'

'But I don't,' Paloma said, his chin quivering with suppressed tears. 'I don't have the slightest idea.'

'Who have you upset? Who has a grudge against you?'

'No-one. I don't know.' He drew a long, trembling drag on his cigarette. 'I don't know anyone who would do such a horrible thing. The phone calls maybe, but not the letters. Not the – not the picture.'

'If you're working at the Pomona, I should have thought you must have rubbed shoulders with plenty of people capable of that sort of thing,' Slider said.

Unexpectedly, Jay flared. 'Oh, now it comes out! Val was wrong – you're just like all the rest! You despise people like us. You think we deserve whatever happens to us!'

'I'm not in the despising business,' Slider said. 'Look here, son—' This was chronologically generous, but the blush of anger made him look more than ever like a beleaguered Princess Di, and who would not feel fatherly towards her? '—as long as what you do isn't against the law, it's none of my business. Sending threatening letters is. So why don't you tell me who's behind it?'

'I don't know!' Jay Paloma cried. 'I tell you I don't know!' He ground out another cigarette with shaking hands. There were tears on his eyelashes. Slider studied him. He was plainly in trouble, but there was a limit to what sympathy could achieve.

'Well, that's that, then,' Slider said, standing up.

Paloma looked up. 'Aren't you going to do anything about it?'

'What would you like me to do?'

'Just stop it. Stop him sending things.'

'Stop who?' Silence. 'If you won't help me, I can't help you.'

'I've told you everything I know,' Paloma said sulkily. And then he was overcome with his grievance. 'I should have known you wouldn't do anything. Who cares if something happens to someone like me? If I was a film star or a famous actor, if I was—' He named a couple of big stars who were prominent homosexual campaigners '—it'd be different then, wouldn't it?'

'I'd say the same to them as I've said to you,' Slider said patiently. 'Unless you give me something to go on—'

'I've *told* you about the phone calls and the letters. I want protection.'

Slider's head was aching. He grew just a touch short. 'A policeman on guard at your door, perhaps?'

'You'd do it for them, all right,' Paloma snapped. 'But I'm just a nobody. What I do is sordid, but when they do the same thing it's smart and fashionable. Just because they're rich and famous. Some Hollywood bimbo gets her kit off and humps on screen, and she gets an Oscar. If I do it, it's pornography.'

'If anything else happens,' Slider said, 'come and tell me about it. And if you get any more of these letters bring them in.' He walked to the door. 'Give my regards to Busty.'

He left behind a seething discontent and a chip rapidly swelling to the size of a musical-comedy epaulette, but there was nothing else to do. When Paloma overcame his reticence enough to disclose who he was afraid of, a discreet visit of disencouragement could be made, and things could go on from there. He was already on the edge; another postal delivery would probably be enough to unseal his lips.

CHAPTER TWO

Cruel as the Grave

A smart rap at Slider's open door on Tuesday morning recalled him from the sea of reports through which he was swimming: the whole of Monday had been spent on paperwork without making any appreciable inroad into it. A young, slight, very pretty black woman stood in the doorway. She had short-bobbed, straightened hair held back by a black Alice-band of plaited cotton, small plain rings in her ears and a gold stud in her left nostril. She was wearing a green two-piece suit and an enquiring look.

'Scuse me, sir, Mr Slider?'

'Yes?'

'I fink you were expecting me. Tony Hart?' The information failed to connect up across the spaces of Slider's brain, and he merely stared stupidly. She smiled a 150-watt smile. 'Don't worry, guv, I'm used to it. It's always 'appening. You were expecting a bloke, right?'

'I – er – yes, I suppose so,' Slider managed, remembering Nutty's information at last.

'Well, look at it this way,' she said chattily, 'you're fillin' two quotas at one go wiv me, right? They call me the PC DC. Pity I ain't a lesbian, or I'd be well in demand.'

Slider stood up and extended his hand. 'I'm sorry, you took me by surprise. I'm very glad to have you here.' They shook. Despite her look of slenderness she had a strong hand, and was as tall as Slider. 'Is it Toni with an "i"?'

'No, guv. Would you like it to be?'

'Short for Antonia?'

'No, actually it's just Tony on me birth stificate. I was named after me dad. Me mum's a bit of a weirdo. She called me sister

Billy after her baby bruvver. Her older bruvver was called Bernard, so I s'pose me sister had a lucky escape.'

Slider suppressed a smile, suspecting that this genial patter served the same purpose as a conjurer's. Major television drama series notwithstanding, women still had a toughish time surviving in the Department, and a joke or two and a bit of camouflage was probably the best defence. 'I'd better take you through and introduce you to the firm,' he said.

'Rightyoh,' she said chirpily. 'Is there much on at the moment?'

'Routine. Nothing very exciting. But we're always busy, and at the moment we're short-staffed.'

'Yes, guv, I heard about DS Atherton. That was a bastard.' Slider looked at her, surprised, and she gave him a sidelong look. 'Yeah, all right, Lambeth is south of the river, but the newspapers come in once a week on the flyin' boat. How is he, sir, DS Atherton?'

'Improving slowly. It'll be a long job.'

'And you, sir? You took a bit of a bashing an' all, didn't you?'

Dotty charm was all very well, but Slider was still the boss. 'If I think I'm going to faint, I'll let you know,' he said, and wheeled her into the CID room. He raised his voice over McLaren's whistle and Mackay's 'Babe alert!' and said, 'Listen, everybody! This is DC Hart come to join us temporarily.' He went quickly through the names and then passed her over to Anderson's care before retreating to the haven of his own room. Why Anderson, he wondered mildly as he walked back. Because he was safe? Less sexist than Mackay and less sticky than McLaren? The least likely to tease the girl on her quota-bility quotient? No, on analysis, it was because he hoped Anderson would try and show her his latest photos. Slider had no doubt she would sort him out.

He could have sworn when he got back to his desk, the pile had grown. What Atherton would have called bullshit on an Augean scale. He missed Atherton. How was he going to find a *mot juste* for every situation without him? By lunchtime, after a busy morning's shovelling, the heap was larger, word having gone round that he was back. And as if that wasn't enough, Irene had telephoned. She had been mightily peeved that no-one had told her he was in hospital until he wasn't any more, and was still harping on about it.

'After all these years, you'd have thought *someone* would have let me know.'

'I suppose they didn't know how things stood between us,' Slider temporised. Lumps of headache were falling off the inside of his skull like rotting plaster.

'One of the sergeants at least might have thought to tell me,' she grumbled. 'I mean, I've known them for years. And I *know* Sergeant O'Flaherty has got my new telephone number, because I made a point of giving it to him just in case.'

'In case of what?'

She sidestepped that one. 'If I'd only known, I'd have visited you in hospital. It's not right. I mean, I am your—' She stopped herself, and her voice fell an octave or two. 'I can't bear to think of you being hurt,' she said, 'and lying there in a hospital bed all alone.'

They didn't usually allow sharing beds in hospitals, he thought; but he didn't say it. He felt rather tender about Irene. And of course Atherton would normally have coped with a tactful briefing of his future-ex-spouse, but Atherton too was out of commission. 'Well,' he said soothingly, 'it doesn't matter now.'

But it did matter to Irene, and nothing would satisfy her but to see him, so he arranged to meet her for lunch at the Crown and Sceptre. He telephoned the flat to tell Joanna he wouldn't be about – she sometimes dropped in to lunch with him if she was in the area – but the answering machine was on the blink and he wasn't sure the message had taken. So he told Nicholls as well, in case she phoned while he was out.

He was at the Crown before Irene, and stood at the bar opposite the door where she'd see him as soon as she came in. She wasn't really a pub person, having been brought up genteel, and still felt awkward about entering them alone. She arrived punctually, looking both familiar and strange. Familiar because – well, he had been married to her for most of his adult life. Strange because she was wearing a new suit in a style not normally her own, camel-coloured with chocolate accessories and the sort of costume jewellery that you see in the windows of high street beauty salons: twirly over-bright gold and enormous fake pearls, set round with tiny things that weren't diamonds; patently false and patently very expensive. To Slider the existence of such stuff had always been a mystery on a par with ceramic fruit. Obviously someone must buy it, but *why*?

Her resentment seemed to have dissipated. She smiled uncertainly.

'Hello.'

'Hello. Go and sit down over there, and I'll bring the menu. What d'you want to drink?'

She was no fun in a pub – she always had orange juice. But today she said, almost naturally, 'Oh, a gin and tonic, please.' Gin and tonic, eh? Imbibing at lunchtime? This could spell bad news. He got her drink and took it with his pint over to the banquette where she sat deportmentally, knees and ankles together, hands folded over her handbag in her lap. She was ill at ease and trying womanfully to carry it off. He felt a tug of sympathy for her.

She looked up and smiled uncertainly as he put down her drink on the low table in front of her. 'Thanks. You don't look as bad as I expected. I thought you'd be really traumatised after what that terrible man did to you. Thank God they got him.'

Traumatised? That was a new word. New vocab, new drink, new outfit. She was not entirely – and he noted it with an odd small pang – his Irene any more, not the same woman he had been married to for so long, the woman who'd read the *Sunday Times Magazine* adverts with wistful envy. She was wearing a different scent as well, heavy and gardenia-ish, where she'd always preferred the light and flowery before. What was that one the children used to buy her? *Je Reviens*, that was it. Kate used to call it Jerry Vines. 'You look nice,' he said, sitting down beside her. 'New suit?'

She looked down at herself, as though she needed to check what she had on. 'Yes,' she said distractedly. 'Marilyn made me buy it. I'm not sure it's me, really, but she said I ought to—'

Ought to move up a class, Slider suspected. Marilyn Cripps, her new Best Friend, seemed determined to do a pygmalion on her. It was the she-Cripps who had introduced Irene to Ernie Newman, the man with whom she had run away from the marital semi in Ruislip to a five-bedroom detached house in

Chalfont. The Crippses lived in Dorney and had a son at Eton. Say no more.

'You look very nice,' he said firmly.

'I didn't come here to talk about clothes,' she replied, just a little reproachfully. He waited, and she went on at last, 'It's getting more dangerous, isn't it? I mean, it seems no time since you were in hospital with those burns after that dreadful Austin case. And this time you were nearly killed. And Atherton—'

'Yes, I know.'

'I suppose he is going to be all right, isn't he?'

'I hope so.'

She bit her lip. 'I worry about you all the time, you know. Madmen with knives, drug addicts, guns. I thought I could stop when I – when we split up. But it doesn't seem to make any difference. I still worry.'

'You shouldn't.' He tried to say it kindly, not snubbingly – though it would probably be kinder in the long run to snub. He began to see where this might be leading. 'You've got Ernie to think about now.'

She looked at him doubtfully, wondering if he was being ironic. It was hard not to be, about Ernie. 'I don't need to worry about him,' she said.

He didn't know how to take that. After a silence he said, 'How are the kids?'

'All right. Matthew was really upset when he knew you were hurt. He saw it in the paper – one of the boys at school showed him before I had a chance to talk to him about it. He was more worried than me, even. He thought you were going to die.'

That hurt. 'He watches too much television.' He said it lightly, but he meant it. 'Too many cop shows.'

'It's hard to stop him.' She sighed. 'He's got a television in his bedroom now. Ernie bought it for him.'

'You shouldn't have let him. You know I don't approve of kids having their own TVs.'

'I know. I don't either, really. It means I can't stop him watching unsuitable programmes – violent ones, that give him bad dreams. But Ernie wanted to buy it for him, and Matthew wanted it, and what could I do? I was stuck in the middle.'

Slider saw the scenario quite clearly: Ernie wanted to bribe Matthew to like him – and was probably also quite keen to get the children to stay in their own rooms and not clutter up his lounge; and Matthew was being opportunist after the manner of children throughout the realms of time and space. And Irene – Irene wanted to please everyone. Well, that was a new Irene, too. She must be feeling very unsure of herself if she was not insisting on having her own way. He felt a huge and unwelcome surge of pity for her, and thrust it away. 'I'll have a word with him, if you like.'

'Ernie?' she said in alarm.

'No, Matthew.'

She looked at him hesitantly, opened and closed her mouth, and then took the plunge. 'He wants to go home. Matthew, I mean. He doesn't take to Ernie. And he doesn't like the house. It's all so strange to him. He keeps asking me, why can't you and Dad get together again?' She swallowed. 'He says, you haven't sold the house yet, why can't we just all go home?' Slider could find nothing to say, and into his unready silence Irene said in a small voice, 'I've wondered the same thing myself, sometimes.'

Slider didn't want to hear this. It was too inexpressibly painful. He saw quite clearly that she felt lost, out of her place, living in Ernie's home, which was not her own, according to his style and manners, which were not what she was used to. The familiar sight of Slider rekindled whatever affection she had once had for him, and blotted out the memory of his inadequacies as a husband, the years of unhappiness she had suffered as a copper's neglected wife. With the slightest encouragement she would ask if they couldn't 'try again'; and standing on the brink of that question, he realised with a new clarity that he didn't want to go back. Definitely. Even if he and Joanna didn't make it, his marriage to Irene was definitely over.

But Irene didn't know about Joanna, of course, and this was not the time to tell her, so he changed the subject with a desperate lunge. 'How's Kate?' he asked, as if there had been no implied question in her last words.

She reassembled herself with an effort, and said brightly, 'Oh, you know Kate. She's agitating for piano lessons now, because her new friend at school, Flora, has them.'

'Fancy naming a child after margarine, poor kid,' Slider said to amuse her.

She wasn't. 'It was one of the names we considered for Kate, if you remember.'

Actually, it was she who had considered. He'd expected another boy, for some reason, and had got as far as Michael and no further. When the baby turned out to be a girl, he went blank. Irene had kindly suggested Michaela and he'd roared with laughter and she'd got into a huff, and he'd placated her by saying she should choose, she was better with names than him, and she'd produced a list with Kate at the top, which he'd grasped enthusiastically for fear of what might be lurking further down.

'I always wish I'd learnt the piano,' he said, to distract her. 'It'd be nice for her to learn. I seem to remember seeing a piano in Ernie's lounge, so there'd be no problem about an instrument, would there?'

'But you know what would happen,' Irene said crossly. 'She'd be all enthusiasm for a week, then she'd slack off, and I'd be the one who'd have to make her practise, and it would be nothing but row, row, row. It was the same with those gerbils. I always ended up cleaning them out – and then you talked about getting a cat or a dog!'

'I only—'

'You got the children all excited about it, without thinking that it would be me who ended up with the responsibility, because you just wouldn't be there when there was a row about it. And then it was down to me to tell them they couldn't have one. I always ended up with the dirty jobs.'

Ah, this was better, this was more like it. Slider almost smiled at her, seeing the steel return to her face, so much easier to bear than wistfulness; but also oddly poignant, because it meant she was *his* Irene again, the disapproving Irene he knew and – well, almost – loved. Best to keep her annoyed, he thought. 'You don't have to clean out a piano,' he said. 'I can't see what harm there'd be in—'

The door opened, and Joanna came in. Perhaps it was because he was in the middle of a familiar-feeling argument with Irene; perhaps it was simply long habit – fourteen years of faithful marriage and two of bowel-churning deception. Perhaps it was Fate sending down a googly. At all events, he panicked.

'Ah, there you are,' Joanna said, heading straight for him. 'They said I'd find you here.'

Nicholls, you die for this, he thought, stuttering to his feet. 'Oh, hello, Joanna. Er, this is Irene. Irene, this is Joanna, a friend of Jim Atherton's.'

Joanna's smile solidified, and he saw her nostrils flare. Irene said, 'How do you do?' nicely, and Joanna repeated her words and even her intonation, while her mind plainly worked furiously behind her mask. Slider's head felt as concrete as her expression; he couldn't think, he couldn't cope. He looked from Joanna, in white jeans, a Greek cotton tunic and sandals, her rough hair held off her face with a pair of sunglasses, to Irene, neat and polished in a suit with matching accessories and a proprietorial smile, and wanted to be anywhere but here, the further away the better.

It was Joanna who spoke at last – it seemed like several suspicious hours later, but it must have been almost instantly, because Irene was still looking social and pleasant. 'Yes, they told me you'd be here and that you could tell me the latest on Jim. How is he?'

'Pretty much the same. I saw him yesterday. They say he's improving slowly.'

'Is he allowed visitors yet?'

'I'm not sure. He's asleep most of the time, but if you telephoned the hospital I'm sure they'd let you know. Have you got the number?'

He thought he was doing pretty well but she shot him a look of fierce impatience and said, 'Yes, of course. Well, I won't interrupt your lunch any longer. I was just passing. Goodbye,' to Irene, and with a whip-flick glance at Slider, 'it was nice neeting you.'

When she was gone, Irene said, 'Is that Atherton's latest girlfriend? She doesn't seem his usual type – not glamorous enough. And she's a bit old for him, isn't she?' She chattered on for a bit, until she realised he was too quiet, and said, 'Are you all right? You look a bit pale.'

'A bit of a headache, that's all,' he said.

She was all concern. 'Do you want to go? Shall we forget lunch? You must be careful, after a crack on the head like that. Look, shall I get you a taxi to take you home? Where are you staying at the moment, anyway?'

That was one question to head her away from. He pulled himself together. 'No, no, I'm fine. Let's have a look at the menu. They do quite good grub here. No, really, I'm all right. I wouldn't drag you all this way and not give you lunch.'

He couldn't wait to get back to the shop and talk to Nicholls; but Nicholls wasn't there. Paxman was on duty, a broad, solid man with a congested face and slow eyes, whose tight curly hair gave him more than a passing resemblance to a Hereford bull.

'Oh, hello,' he said. 'Did your friend find you?'

'Yes, thank you,' Slider said with tight irony. 'Where the hell is Nicholls?'

'He's gone to court. He left a message where you were, if your friend asked.' Paxman always referred to Joanna as 'your friend'. He disapproved of extra-curricular activities, but there was no malice or guile in his face. Plainly he thought he had done what was required. Slider thanked him and went away with an inward whimper. Some days were like this, with a high likelihood of precipitation, dark brown variety; and it wasn't over yet.

Joanna's car was there when he got home, but she had only just arrived: it was still warm and ticking. Her bag and fiddle were dumped on the hall floor, and she was in the kitchen, still in her coat, reading her mail while waiting for the kettle to boil. Oedipus was on tiptoe, his tail straight up, winding himself back and forth around her lower legs. When Slider appeared he started towards him, but got sidetracked by the kitchen table, whose legs he caressed in lieu. He had settled in very well, but they still didn't dare let him out, for fear that he'd try to find his way back to Atherton's flat across ten miles of London traffic. It meant a good deal of dirt-tray cleaning-out, of course, but they shared the burden between them. Slider was a New Man.

Joanna turned and raised an eyebrow at him. Enigmatic, he thought. Could go either way. The fact that she had fallen in with his deception at the pub had puzzled him all day. Did it mean she loved him so much she would spare him any embarrassment, even at the cost of her own dignity; or that she had given up on him and cared so little it was no longer important?

'Are you going to throw plates?' he asked meekly.

'Nah. Too expensive.'

She was not going to be angry. A tidal surge of relief. 'I'm sorry,' he said abjectly. 'It was so stupid. I just don't know what came over me. I panicked, I think.' She was regarding him with suppressed humour; a sort of exasperated, what-am-I-going-to-do-about-you expression. He could never prejudge what would tickle her sense of the ridiculous. It made life interesting, at least. 'I'm really sorry,' he said again for good measure.

'Well, it was me who told you not to tell her in the first place,' she said. 'I suppose I've only got myself to blame. Though I didn't expect you to go on denying me for ever. And so automatically, the moment I appeared – like Simon Peter on speed.' And then she laughed. 'Oh, your face, though, when I came up and spoke to you!'

He didn't think it was terribly funny, though he managed a polite smile. 'Well at least you and Irene have met now. It gets the first time over with.'

'What d'you mean, first time?' she said suspiciously.

'Well, you're bound to have to get to know each other in the long run. It would be nice if you could be friends—'

'Oh my God, no!' she shuddered. 'Don't say that. There's something very weird about men who want to get their wives and their mistresses together.'

'You've known many such?' he asked coolly.

'By association. In the nature of things, my female friends have mostly been musicians. And equally in the nature of things, female musicians tend to have to go out with married men, because that's all there is. All that'll put up with their lifestyle, anyway. Inevitably comes the day when the bloke arranges accidentally-on-purpose for the completely unexpected, surprise-surprise, what-else-could-I-do meeting between the two women he's poking. And then the self-satisfied dingbat stands back and gets some creepy thrill out of seeing them talking to each other.'

'It wasn't my idea,' he said, hurt.

She put an arm round his neck and kissed him casually. 'I know. I absolve you of malice aforethought. You're a gent, really. Just don't ever talk about Irene and me becoming friends.' She released him and turned to reach for the teapot as the kettle switched off. With her back to him she said, 'And if there is another accidental meeting, don't deny me again, will you?'

That was the important bit, the bit she couldn't look at him for. 'Definitely not,' he said. 'Scout's honour.' He watched her making tea, knowing there was more to come.

'I was jealous,' she said at last. 'And I don't like myself when I feel like that.'

'I suppose it's quite flattering really,' he said lightly. 'To think you love me that much.'

She gave him a quick glance. 'It didn't feel much like love. I wanted to kill her. And then, when she was mashed to a pulp, to kill you.'

'Me?'

'For having been married to her. It drives me crazy that whatever happens in the future, I can't change that. She's had you for all those years, and I can't wipe that out, run the film back and erase it. It's a horrible thing to feel that sort of possessive fury. It makes you understand axe murderers. Only obliterating you would have given me relief. Of course, *I* wouldn't do anything about it, but that only makes it worse, because I know I wouldn't, and that just adds frustration to all the other seething acids.'

She was serious, and he had to be careful not to say the wrong thing and offend her. But he couldn't help feeling all the same that it *was* flattering. It might not have felt much like love to her, but he was glad to know, after some of the things that had happened, that she cared that much about him, when he had sometimes wondered whether she couldn't take him or leave him. He touched her on the shoulder, and she turned into his arms. He held her, and felt her relax against him. Then at last he kissed the top of her head, and put his lips against her ear, and murmured tenderly, 'I want to obliterate you, too.'

It was not until much later, when they were in bed together, that she brought the subject up again. 'What was she doing there, anyway? Irene.'

'She wanted to see me, to check I was in one piece. She was upset that no-one had told her I was in hospital.'

'So you asked her to lunch?'

'She more or less asked herself.'

After a silence, Joanna said, 'What did she really want to see you about?'

'Why should there be another reason?'

'I'll put it another way: what did she really want to see you about?'

'I think she wants us to get back together,' he admitted. There was no way round that.

'Oh,' she said.

He waited for more, and then said, 'She feels guilty and uncomfortable, and the children are unsettled, and since she knows the house hasn't been sold, she thinks it would all be so much easier if we just let bygones be bygones and slid back into the furrow.'

'Rut.'

'That's what I told her.'

'I bet you didn't. I know you, Bill Slider. I bet you avoided the whole issue.'

'It wasn't really an issue. She didn't ask outright, only hinted at it. I didn't take up the hint, just changed the subject. So that's that. She'll know it's not on.'

'She won't. Women will always believe what they want unless you tell them otherwise in words of one syllable. Have you never heard of being cruel to be kind?'

'I feel sorry for her. And guilty. She thinks the whole break-up is her fault.'

'You aren't thinking of it?' she asked warily out of the dark. 'Going back to her?'

'Not in these trousers.'

'Are you sure?'

He thought honesty might reassure her. 'It was realising that she wanted us to get back together that finally convinced me I could never do it.'

'Finally? So you had been considering it?'

'Well, obviously it had crossed my mind on the odd occasion.'

'Which occasion?'

'When you're being unreasonable and cruel. When you're away and I think of you frolicking in seaside towns with abandoned musicians.'

'I'm never unreasonable.'

'I notice you don't say you never frolic,' he said suspiciously.

'I have to keep some mystery. How else can I allure you?'

'Allure isn't a verb,' he objected.

He felt her smile against his neck. 'I miss Atherton, don't you?'

'Of course.'

'He is going to get better?' she asked like a child wanting reassurance. Are there bears under the bed? But Atherton was real. The best he could manage was, 'It'll be a long job.'

There was a long silence. He thought she had gone to sleep, but then she said, 'Did Irene recognise me?'

'Recognise you?' He searched the files. 'Oh, you mean from that concert?'

'You practically introduced me then.'

'No, I'm sure she didn't.' He re-ran Irene's words and expressions. 'She said you weren't Atherton's usual type. Not glamorous enough.'

'Cheeky mare,' Joanna said sleepily. A little while later she was asleep. Slider lay wakeful for some time, his mind jumpy with the unaccustomed stimulation of being back to work. He slept at last, but fell into a nightmare in which he was stalked through the White City Estate by a sweating, knife-wielding Gilbert. If only he could get back to the station he'd be safe, but the blocks of flats proliferated all around him, identical, confusing, every door and corner a possible ambush point, and he couldn't find his way out.

CHAPTER THREE

A Fit of Peaks

The shout came on Wednesday, at a time when Slider, who wasn't going in early, was still in bed.

'A nice murder for you,' said Nicholls, who was on earlies. He pronounced it *murr-durr.*

It was a dead body in a flat on the White City Estate. Listening to Nicholls' sealskin-soft Atlantic coast accent, Slider was reminded that the Anne-Marie Austin case had begun just this way, with all its consequences to his private life. Only then, of course, it had been Irene asleep beside him, and she hadn't woken, as Joanna just had, sitting up to look at the clock.

But the flat in question was Busty Parnell's, and the dead body was Jay Paloma's. Busty had arrived home from spending the night away to find the front door open, the keeper of the Yale lock hanging loose from one screw; and inside, Jay Paloma dead in a welter of blood.

Slider's guilt chip had already been overworked with regard to Atherton, and now threatened to go into overload. The poor little bastard knew what he was talking about after all. He had been frightened with a cause. Slider should have done something: his guilt nagged him as he listened to Nicholls with another part of his brain. But what could he have done? Blimey, it had happened so quickly, he could hardly have got him an armed guard for his door even had he wanted to. In the time available, there was nothing he could have done, nothing the system would have let him do, to prevent this. But it didn't change the fact that Paloma had come to tell him he was afraid for his life, and now he was dead. It was breast-beating time, whichever way you sliced it.

'Are you there, Bill?' Nicholls asked into the silence.

'Oh – yes – I was just thinking. I saw him on Monday, you know. The victim. He knew it was coming.'

'Chrise, no. That's a bugger,' Nicholls commiserated. 'And you with your overactive glands.'

'My what?'

'Your compulsion to be responsible for everyone's troubles. Global Mammy Syndrome. Ah well,' Nicholls comforted him, 'this'll keep you busy for a while. Nothing like being run off your feet for keeping your mind off things.'

'Thanks,' said Slider shortly.

'What is it?' Joanna asked as he put the phone down.

'A corpus,' Slider said, pushing Oedipus off his legs and getting out of bed. He turned back to kiss her. 'I shan't be back before you go to work. Have a good day.'

'You remember I'm on at the Festival Hall tonight?'

'So you are. Well, I'll see you when I see you, then.'

'Good luck,' she called as he headed for the bathroom.

By the time Slider got there, Busty had been taken away in hysterics, with WPC Asher to lean on, which was one comfort. Hollis was waiting for him.

'I suppose he is dead?' Slider asked, without hope.

'In spades,' Hollis said. 'Hart's inside.'

The flats on the White City Estate had all now been modernised to within an inch of their lives, with double glazing, central heating and solid wood doors – the glass panels in the originals having been a gift for felons. But of course no-one locks their door on the mortice when they are at home, and judging by the size and singularity of the footmark on the door, the murderer had been a very large and powerful man, strong enough to kick the door open at the first blow.

The flat seemed tidy and clean. In the kitchen everything was put away, except for two coffee mugs, a saucepan and a plate with a knife and fork lying on it, which were sitting in the sink. Slider examined the evidence. Scrambled eggs, he concluded. On toast. The bathroom was likewise tidy with hand towels neatly folded and bath towels stretched to dry along the shower rail. The bedrooms were tidy with the duvets straightened on the beds. He could tell which was Busty's by the collection of cosmetics spread out on the dressing-table, which was larger than the collection in Jay's room; and by the brown-and-red silk Noël Coward dressing-gown flung across his bed and the leather mules on the floor by its hem.

Only in the sitting-room did disorder reign, and even there only in one small area. The television was on with the sound turned low. On screen a bunch of people with demented expressions were talking non-stop over the top of one another, mugging at the camera, and prancing about a set done out with huge cut-outs in primary, not to say dayglo, colours. Someone at TV headquarters had evidently decided that only the brain-damaged and the under-fives watched television at that time of day, and for all Slider knew they could be right.

An armchair near the television had been turned over backwards, and Jay Paloma lay sprawled half out of it, cruelly illuminated by the bright sunshine from the window. His head had been beaten to crunchy red-and-yellow breakfast cereal. He was wearing a chambray shirt, jeans and moccasin slippers. The front of the shirt was liberally soaked in blood, which was not surprising because his face had been stoved in by a mighty blow across the bridge of the nose. There were no apparent other injuries, and his clothing was not torn or disordered, his shirt still tucked into his trousers and his slippers still on his feet.

Hart, at Slider's side, turned her head away quickly, swallowing with a clicking sound.

'Feeling sick?' Slider asked. She made an affirmative sound. 'Is this your first time?'

'No, sir, I've felt sick before.'

He gave her points for trying. 'First murder?'

'Not the first, but the messiest,' she said.

'You never get used to it,' he told her from the depth of his own present misery. 'You just have to learn to keep your stomach detached from your eyes. Now, using your eyes, what do you think happened here?'

She looked around, grateful to have her attention taken from the corpse. 'He doesn't seem to have put up much of a fight. None of the furniture's out of place, apart from the one chair.' There was another armchair, placed opposite the first, both of them facing the television on a slant, and between the two, but set back so that only the end of it was within reach, was a coffee table on which stood a whisky bottle – White Horse, almost empty – and an empty glass, an ashtray with five cigarette ends in it, and an untidy pile of papers and magazines. Back against the wall was an elderly sofa of the armless couch type, covered with what was nowadays known as a 'throw' in a vaguely Polynesian pattern of mutually hostile colours – not so much a throw as a throw-up, Slider thought. Against the wall nearest the door was a large and ugly sideboard in pale highly-varnished oak with bulbous legs, dating, judging by its style, from the nineteen-fifties. On it was a collection of framed photographs, mostly black and white, of Busty and Jay in their separate high moments: Jay with Jeremy Haviland in a dinner suit; Busty with a celebrity so blurred it could have been David Nixon or Richard Nixon for all Slider knew; Busty in a lineup of Windmill girls; Jay in an Arran sweater against a wild sea from a knitwear catalogue – and so on. Some of the frames were as old as the photos. Slider touched one gently and its wonky foot slithered on the highly polished surface and collapsed.

'If anyone had bumped against that, the pictures would have fallen over,' Hart said.

'So?' Slider encouraged.

'So no fight. The villain must have took him by surprise. Crept up on him and whacked him from behind.'

'But the villain kicked the door in. Wouldn't you think he'd have heard that?'

'He might've been asleep. People do drift off in front of the telly.'

Slider grunted non-committally. 'Does anything strike you as odd about that ashtray?' he asked her. She looked, bent close to peer, and shook her head. 'There are five dog ends in it,' he said, 'but no ash. How did he manage that?'

'He didn't. Look here,' Hollis said. Between the coffee table and the couch there were traces of cigarette ash on the carpet, and an area where it had apparently been rubbed in, with a hand or a foot. 'And there's whisky been spilled here too,' he added, sniffing. It was a damp patch which smelled strongly. 'Chummy's had the table over.'

'Hang about, what's that?' Hart said. It was another glass, on the floor beside the other armchair, but standing upright, as though it had been placed there by someone sitting in the chair. 'Maybe the whisky come from this glass.'

'But you can see table's been knocked over,' Hollis said impatiently. 'Look at the impressions in the carpet where it stood before. It wasn't put back in exactly the same spot.'

Hart said, 'The table could have been knocked over any time. It didn't have to be the murderer.'

'True,' Slider said. 'But it strikes me that everything is very neat and tidy here. Clean, dusted and polished. Would such a houseproud person knock the table over and then just rub the ash into the carpet? Wouldn't he clean it up properly?'

'All right,' Hart conceded, 'but if it was the murderer done it, why would he pick everything up again, put the dimps back in the ashtray and all that?'

'No offers,' Hollis said with a shrug.

'Well,' Slider went on at last, 'there's a few things to think about, anyway. Bag up the whisky bottle and the glasses. And we'll take the ashtray and contents as well.'

Certainly, Slider thought, further pondering the room, Jay Paloma was killed there, in that spot, and probably in that chair. Apart from no signs of a struggle, there were no bloodmarks anywhere else. No reeling about locked in mortal combat à la Reichenbach Falls. There was blood on the chair, and on the carpet around it, some smears on the end of the coffee table, and a few specks on the TV screen. But why had Paloma sat there and let himself be killed? Asleep, maybe – but wouldn't the kicking in have stirred him, wouldn't he at least have been struggling to his feet?

The worse possibility was trying to suggest itself to him. If Paloma had been pursued to the edge of breaking by a campaign of poison pen letters, it might have bred in him such a conviction of hopelessness that he had simply given up. Believing there was no escape, he had just been killing time here, waiting for the inevitable moment when he would hear the executioner's approaching footsteps. To such a mentality, the crash of the door being kicked in would be almost welcome, signalling an end to the hideous anticipation.

He didn't want to think like that. His global-mammy circuits couldn't take it. Perhaps Paloma had been drunk, and dead to the world. That might do it. Or doped. Leave that, have a wonder about motive, for light relief. It was pretty obviously not robbery. Slider wished the murderer had even made a pretence of ransacking the place. Whoever had killed Jay Paloma had gone straight in and come straight out again – apart from the brief pause to put the coffee table straight. They knew what they wanted all right, and it wasn't loose change or a video recorder.

Busty was waiting for him in one of the interview rooms, WPC Asher in attendance, a cup of tea steaming on the table in front of her. She was dressed in a smart coat with an imitation lucca-lamb collar, which was hanging open over a pink twin-set and a regulation barmaid's black straight skirt. The eponymous udders were discreetly corseted now, but still peaks of splendour; in the first fine braless rapture of their acquaintance, the sight of Busty stepping out down Wardour Street had always set Slider to thinking about Barnes Wallis.

She was not a bad-looking woman still, even in the harsh strip-lighting of an interview room. Asher had escorted her to the ladies where she had had a wash to remove her ruined makeup, and without it she looked surprisingly young, despite her recent bout of hysterical weeping. She was calm now, but looked up at Slider with swollen, brimming eyes and pale and shaking cheeks.

'Busty, I'm so sorry,' he said. She nodded, keeping her lips closed. 'I have to ask you some questions. You understand?'

She nodded again, and then unlocked enough to say, 'You do your job. I want you to get the bastard that did this to my poor—' She lost it a moment. 'I want you to get the bastard, and then I want you to let me have five minutes alone with him.'

'You've no idea, I suppose, who it might be? Who hated him that much?'

'No,' she said. 'He was a good, kind soul. He never hurt anyone in his life. He looked after me, Mr Slider. He was like my big brother. It was him got me the barmaid job, because he didn't like me stripping and such at my age. I haven't turned a trick since we started sharing again, d'you know that? He said to me, Val, he said, you'll never have to do that again as long as I live. *That*'s the sort of person he was. Always thinking of others.'

'I'm sorry,' Slider said again. He was going to be sorrier when he had to tell her about the poison pen letters, but that was for later. 'Tell me what you know. You'd been away for the night, you said?'

Busty had been visiting her sister who lived in Harlesden. She had set off at about half past eleven on Tuesday morning, taking an overnight bag with her, intending to return at about the same time the next day. 'It was my day off. I wasn't due on again at the pub until this evening. And my sister's not been too clever lately – you know, women's stuff,' she explained delicately, 'so I went over to give her a bit of a break, let her have a day in bed and an evening out.'

'I didn't know you had a sister.'

'Why should you?' Busty shrugged. 'We were close when we were kids, but then we weren't all that much for a long time. Actually, I think when I first knew you was when we weren't talking. Well, Mum and Dad didn't approve of my way of life, and Shirley sided with them. It's only since Dad died that we've sort of started liking each other again. She married a real bastard, so I suppose it made her realise there wasn't much to choose between us.'

'Come again?'

She gave him a wan smile. 'Between her and me. Doing it for one man you don't like isn't much different from doing it for several men you don't like.'

'I see. So, you came back from your sister's early. What happened to change your plan?'

'The bastard came back. Her Trevor. He's a lorry-driver. He wasn't due back till this afternoon, but he fiddled his tacho and cut his breaks to get through early, and there he was. Lucky I'm a light sleeper, I heard him parking his lorry outside, so it give me a chance to get out of bed, grab me stuff and lock meself in the bathroom while I got dressed. Only if Trevor had come upstairs and found me asleep in his bed—' She shrugged eloquently.

'In his bed?'

'Shirley's not got a spare room. I was sleeping in with her.'

'What time was that, when he got home?'

'It must've been about six-ish, a bit before. Anyway, by the time I get downstairs, Shirl's got the tea on the go, and Trevor's mellowed out enough to let me phone for me taxi, otherwise

I'd've been stuck. I mean, you try finding a phone box that works in Harlesden.'

'And you got home about half past six?' Slider said, checking his notes. The shout was timed at six thirty-five.

'I s'pose so. About then,' she said, the animation draining from her face. 'I didn't realise at first. The door looked as if it was shut. It was only when I went to put my key in the lock that I felt it move, and then I realised it was only pushed to. I went in, and—' She stopped, shutting her mouth hard.

'Yes,' Slider said helpfully. 'I'm sorry, but I have to take you through it. Did you expect Jay to be home?'

'Well, yes – at least, he hadn't said he wouldn't. Normally he'd be asleep at that time, with working late and everything. Well, he doesn't get back from the club till around four, so he never usually got up till half-twelve-ish. The only reason he wouldn't be home would be if he went somewhere with someone, straight from the club – like, a pick-up, you know. But he hadn't been doing that lately. He'd hardly been out at all, not socially, and he hadn't had any casuals in months.'

'So you thought he was at home and asleep? Did you call out to him?'

'No. I'm always quiet if I'm up early, not to wake him.'

'So what did you do next?'

'Well, I heard the telly was on, so I went in to the front room to see. And there he was.'

'You didn't touch anything or move anything?'

'No. I didn't really go in the room. I could see straight away, from the door, that he was – that he must be—' She shook her head. 'I just went straight and dialled 999.'

'From your telephone? Which is where?'

'In the hall. Opposite the front door. And then I just stayed by the telephone until the police come. I didn't want to go back in there. I was in a state of shock. I didn't even cry. It wasn't until they came and started talking to me that I broke down.' She took out a handkerchief and blew briskly.

Slider waited for her. 'Would you like some more tea?' Busty made a sound of assent through her hanky, and he looked at Asher, who nodded and slipped out. 'Did he often watch television when he got back from the club?'

'Well, no,' she said thoughtfully, 'I've never actually knew him to do that. But I suppose if he was upset or something and couldn't sleep he might have.'

'And the whisky? Was it his habit to have a nightcap before he went to bed?'

'I wouldn't say habit,' she said carefully, 'but he has done on occasions. Whisky is his drink, but he doesn't have it any special time. I've known him pop down the pub lunchtime and have one, or at home in the afternoon, if there's a good film on. He liked all them old black and white ones, especially if they were about the war. Richard Attenborough and that. Or with his supper, before he went to work. He'd have a pie or a bit of cheese or something, and a Scotch with that.'

'When you last saw him – when was that, exactly?'

'When I left for my sister's yesterday. He got up to see me off. He came out in his dressing-gown and made us a cup of coffee and sat with me and drank it while I did my makeup.'

'And how did he seem? Was he in his normal spirits?'

'Yes.' She hesitated. 'Well, he's not been all that bright recently. A bit quiet and off it.'

'Did he give you any reason?'

'He was worried about something.' She hesitated again. 'I think it had to do with his friend.'

'What friend is that?'

'His gentleman friend,' she said rather primly.

'Name?'

'He never told me. He always just called him his friend. All I know is, he was very rich. Someone important and famous – that's why Maurice was extra discreet.'

'Maurice?'

'That's his real name, Jay's – Maurice McElhinney. Didn't you know? Well, I suppose it's only me that calls him that now. His parents were Irish – from Dublin. I think they were quite well off and that. Anyway, they wanted him to be a lawyer or a doctor or something, and they were really disappointed when all he wanted to do was be a dancer. He persuaded them to let him go to stage school, but when it came out that he was bent as well – well, all he could do was leave home and come to London. I mean, in those days it was hard enough being One Of Them over here, let alone in bleeding Dublin with Catholic parents and everything. And he's never went back. I don't think he's ever even written to them. He said to me only last week, I was all the family he had.' She began to cry again. Slider left her alone until Asher came in with the tea, and then he gave her handkerchiefs and jollied her along until she was back in control.

'So tell me what you know about this friend of his,' Slider resumed. 'Have you any idea who it was? Any clues at all – where he lived or what he did for a living or anything like that?'

She shook her head. 'Usually he talked about his friends a bit to me – not the intimate stuff, just that he'd been to see them and where they'd gone and what they'd done. But this one was different. All I gathered was, if it had got out about Maurice, it could have caused this man trouble.'

'Was Jay – Maurice – in love with him?'

'Oh, I don't think so,' she said consideringly. 'He was generous, this man – gave Maurice presents and money. It was because of that I was able to give up turning tricks – though that was a lot easier on the feet than barmaiding, I can tell you!'

'How long had he known him?'

'About a year.'

'And relations were normally smooth between them?'

'Oh, I think so – except I think the secrecy got on Maurice's nerves a bit. But just recently – well, the last few weeks, I suppose – he hasn't been his usual self. Always very cheerful, he was, and sort of – brisk. Always cleaning the house, singing to himself, nagging me about my appearance. Try this lipstick, Val; have your hair cut, Val; get yourself a new dress, Val. All good-natured, you know. He wanted me to make the most of myself. But lately there hasn't been much of that. He's been sort of quiet and – off it. And then yesterday morning, while he was sitting fiddling with my makeup, I said to him, "What's up, Mo darling, you look as if you've got the blues," and he said, "Oh," he said, "my friend and I had a bit of a disagreement yesterday, that's all."'

'He'd been to see him, then, on Monday?'

'Monday lunchtime. He was spending the afternoon with him, but I'd gone to work before he got back. That's why he got up, I suppose, to see me off.' Her eyes filled. 'To say goodbye. If only I'd known. If only we'd both known.'

'Did he say what the quarrel was about?'

'He didn't say quarrel, he said disagreement. He didn't say what about, but they had argued before, so I suppose it was about the same thing. I gather his friend has been objecting to Maurice working at the Pomona.'

That made sense to Slider. 'Well, it isn't exactly Rules, is it?'

'Isn't what, pardon?'

Slider waved that away. 'Did you know that Jay had been receiving threatening letters?'

'No, I didn't.' She scanned his face keenly, and then let out her breath in a slow hiss. 'So that was it! I knew he'd been keeping something from me. No, I didn't know that, but I knew there was something wrong. I thought at first it was one of those summer colds, you know, that sort of hang on and never come out properly. But no wonder, with that hanging over him, poor lamb! Why didn't he tell me?'

'He didn't want to worry you.'

'So you knew about it? He reported it to you, did he?'

'He came to see me on Monday afternoon. Unfortunately, he hadn't kept any of the letters, so there wasn't much I could do. And I had the feeling he was hiding something. I thought he knew who was doing it, but wasn't willing to tell me. I told him to come back if anything else happened.'

She looked at him, her eyes widening. 'Do you think – this friend of Maurice's – do you think he killed him?'

'It's possible, at any rate, that whoever sent him the poison pen letters may have killed him.'

'You knew about the letters,' she said. 'You could have saved him.'

'I don't know how,' Slider said abjectly. 'Busty, I'm sorry, believe me. I feel terrible about it. But what could I have done? I had nothing to go on, and short of posting a bodyguard on him—'

But she turned her face away, grieved, and rocked herself. 'If only he'd told me, I'd never have left him. I'd have stayed with him every minute.' She wiped at her nose and eyes, but they went on leaking, like a slow bleed. She turned back to Slider. 'It's funny, isn't it? He was always so careful – went everywhere by taxi, made me go everywhere by taxi, 'cause he said public transport wasn't safe, especially late at night, and with the kind of places we worked. And always a proper taxi, never a minicab, because he said you never knew who you'd get. There was that time, d'you remember, when I was working at the Nitey Nite Club, what was it, back in 'seventy-eight, when Sandra Hodson got abducted by a minicab driver? D'you remember her? She did that act with the python. Madame Ranee she called herself.'

'Yes, I remember.'

'And she got driven out into the sticks and raped and dumped naked somewhere—'

'Beaconsfield.'

'That's it. Miles out in the country. And poor Sange always hated fields and cows and that. Wouldn't even walk through St James's Park if she could help it. So ever since then I've never had anything but a proper black cab, and Maurice was the same. That careful, he was. And then they come and get him in his own home – sitting in his own front room, Mr Slider, watching his own telly. It's not fair. It's—' She struggled for a word. 'It's like *cheating*.'

'Yes,' said Slider. 'I know.'

'And I'll tell you another thing,' she said, flame-eyed with tears and outrage now. 'Just Sunday, he was talking about chucking the whole thing up. He said he was fed up of it, the whole set-up, the club, show-business, working all night and sleeping in the day, being treated like dirt, being slobbered over by drunks. And he said to me Sunday, he said, "Val," he said, "let's chuck it up and get out of London while we've still got a bit of life in front of us." Well, he'd got this plan, you see, for us to retire and get a place in the country, in Ireland, and do bed and breakfast for holiday-makers. He'd been saving up ages to buy a little place. It was his dream, but now he said, "Val, let's really do it."' The animation faded. 'He meant it an' all. It's not fair. He deserved a bit of luck, poor Maurice.'

He'd had his bit of luck, Slider reflected. It's just that it wasn't good.

CHAPTER FOUR

Fissure of Men

Busty's next-door neighbour was torn between the obligatory reluctance to 'get involved', and the temptation of being a star, for if she became a witness for the police, she might get herself on the telly. She havered and wavered, but finally the glamour of potential fame overcame her to the point of inviting Hart in for a cup of tea – a courtesy Hart would have dispensed with. The flat smelled of urine, babies and chip fat. Why didn't humans have those useful nostrils that closed flat, Hart wondered. When her hostess left the room to put on the kettle, Hart sneaked her Amarige out of her handbag and dabbed a bit on her upper lip for protection.

Charmian, was the woman's name, God only knew why. Charmian Hogg. She sat on the sofa opposite Hart, a pasty female, spots at the corners of her mouth and a crop of blackheads on her cheeks like an aerial view of black cattle grazing across a parched plain. Her hair was dirty, her teeshirt much stained, her short skirt straining into corrugated creases across her belly, her bare legs blotched red and mauve, her feet in broken-down slippers. She pulled a pack of cigarettes out from behind the sofa-cushion and lit one, and a dirty child of about three, in sagging, nappy-bulging shorts, wandered in and climbed up next to her, clutching her arm and staring at Hart as if she were Sigourney Weaver. In another room a baby cried monotonously. In a corner of this one, in a playpen, another child of about eighteen months picked listlessly at the tacky bits of trodden-in food on the carpet, and stared out through the bars with its mouth open.

'Them next door,' said Mrs Hogg, 'I never had nothing to do with 'em. I told the Council, I don't want the likes of them living next door to me. Disgusting. Well, I don't mind blacks,' she said generously, for Hart's sake, 'but that lot—! And him! Filthy, I call it. I mean, I suppose some of 'em can't help being that way, which you don't mind when they're nice, like that actor, what's his name, he's very funny, you know the one I mean, the big fat one. But to do it like him next door – just selling himself for money. Just like animals. Not but what he wasn't polite, always looked smart, and said hello nice as you like when I met him on the stairs or anything. Offered to help me up the stairs with the pushchair once, but I wouldn't let him anywhere near my Jason – would I, Jase?' she addressed the odoriferous child beside her, which was now absently exploring its nose with a forefinger, never taking its eyes from Hart's alien face. 'You never know what you might catch off someone like that. Riddled with diseases they are – AIDS and that – and I wouldn't have him touching none of my kids.'

Hart moved further towards the edge of the armchair she was sitting on, which she had a horrible suspicion was damp. 'So you didn't know 'em very well?'

'I never even knew his name until you told me.'

'What about your husband?'

'He ain't here. He's got his own flat over Fulham. He don't come here much now. He's got this girlfriend. Right little slapper *she* is!'

'All right, tell me what you heard last night,' Hart said, anxious to get her to the point.

'Last night?'

'You said you heard something?'

'Oh. Yeah. Well, there was a noise. Like someone was having a barney. It woke my Jade up, so I wasn't best pleased, I can tell you.'

'Woke your what?'

'Jade. Over there.' She indicated the child in the playpen. 'My little girl.'

Blimey, thought Hart. 'What time was that?'

'Oh, middle of the night. I dunno exactly.'

'After midnight?'

'Well, maybe not. I didn't notice.'

'Were you in bed?'

'No, I was in here, watching telly. I might of just dropped off, though,' she admitted reluctantly.

'What exactly did you hear?'

'I heard this crash, like the door was being kicked in, and then a load of shoutin' an' crashin' about, like someone was havin' a real barney.' She waxed enthusiastic. 'All furnicher bein' knocked over and glass broken and that. And then someone shouted, "I'm going to kill you, you dirty bastard." And then there was a kind of thud, like a body falling over. And then it all went quiet.' She shuddered. ''Orrible it was!'

In your dreams, Hart thought, making notes with an inward sigh. 'What direction did these noises come from?'

'Are you taking the piss?' Mrs Hogg asked with a derisive look. 'Them next door, o' course. That's what you was asking about, isn't it?'

'Yeah, right. But you see, there's no sign of anyone having a fight in there, no furniture turned over or broken glass. So I thought it might be some other barney you heard.'

Mrs Hogg grew sulky. 'I know what I heard. You callin' me a liar?'

'I just want you to think carefully about what you really heard. It's not going to help us if you exaggerate.'

'I did hear the door bein' kicked in,' she said defiantly. '*And* I heard some furnicher crashin'.' A pause. 'Maybe that was all,' she added reluctantly.

'What about the shouting?'

'Well, maybe, maybe not. I can't say for sure.'

'And can you help me some more about the time?'

'Like I say, I must of dropped off in front of the telly,' she said, eyeing Hart as though she saw her chance of stardom dissolving.

'And it was the noise that woke you up? Do you remember what was on the telly then?'

Further probing brought the admission that Mrs Hogg had been hitting the Cinzano earlier in the evening, which had caused her to drop off, and the noise next door had only partly woken her. She had dozed again, and it was only when Jade's howling had started off baby Pearse that the combined racket had penetrated her cobwebs. By then all was quiet next door. It was then ten past midnight, so the door-kicking-in could have happened at any time before that.

The neighbours on the other side were harder to coax out, and less forthcoming, but probably more reliable. The elderly couple glared at Hart suspiciously round the chain on the door, and would only open it when she had got PC Baker to come and flash his uniform, and both sets of ID had been carefully scrutinised.

'Can't be too careful,' the oldster grunted begrudgingly as he opened the door a little wider. He wore a very sporty home-knitted cardigan of grey wool with a white reindeer-motif border, whose pockets sagged hopelessly under the burden of handkerchiefs, tobacco tin and matches.

'Only you see stuff on the telly all the time,' the oldstress added over his shoulder. She was inclined to be apologetic, and would have asked them in, had her husband not blocked the way as robustly as his trembling frame could manage. Hart was quite happy to interview them on the doorstep. Over their diminutive shoulders she could smell the house aroma of liniment, cold roll-ups and dirty bodies, and had no wish to pitch her Amarige against this new Everest.

The old man said their name was Mr and Mrs Maplesyrup, but the old lady, whose teeth fitted better, corrected this to Maplesthorp as Hart wrote it down. They had heard the door being kicked in all right. It was just before half past eleven, because the film was just finishing, which was *Assassination* with Charles Bronson, very loud and lots of banging, guns and that, and Mr Maplesyrup had thought at first the noise was just part of the film, but Mrs Maplesyrup had said turn the sound down a minute, Charlie, I think it was next door. So he had done, because it was just the whajjercallums, the titles by then, and they'd listened, and they'd heard a sort of bang next door, or it might have been a thud, maybe, like something heavy being dropped or knocked over. And then nothing, just quiet, so Mr Fudgefrosting had turned the sound back up because there was that advert he liked, the supermarket one with the little boy and the shopping, he was a laugh that kid, and Mrs Hotjamsundae had gone to put the kettle on for their cuppa, which they always had before they went to bed. And while she was in the kitchen it was all quiet next door, and no-one had come along the communal balcony past her window. And this morning when she went out to go down for the paper she had just looked next door, just a quick peek, and she'd seen that the door wasn't closed properly and a big footmark on it and sort of splintery-looking at the edge where the Yale was, so she'd known they hadn't imagined it after all.

'I suppose you didn't think of calling the police?' Hart said. Mr Maplesthorp looked witheringly at her, and said they couldn't go phoning the police every time they heard a thump or a raised voice, or they'd never be off the phone. And the police wouldn't thank them neither, they never did nothing if you did phone them. Anyway, you didn't stick your nose in on this estate, you left well alone as long as *you* were left alone. It wasn't like it used to be in the old days, when you could leave your front door open all day and no bother, and neighbours were neighbours. They were only waiting to be rehoused, but they'd been on the waiting list five years now, so unless they won the lottery—

Mrs Maplesthorp interrupted to add apologetically that they hadn't thought anything about it really, the noise next door, though they'd always been quiet people, no trouble, and not usually given to fights or kicking doors in, but you didn't get thanked for interfering between man and wife, she'd learnt that lesson the hard way when she'd tried to make peace between her brother and his wife, and got an earful from both of them, and they'd never spoken since, except at family funerals and things, though they always sent a Christmas card, which was a bit hypocritical when you thought of it . . .

Satisfactory, Hart thought when she finally made her escape. Three witnesses giving a similar story – you couldn't ask for more than that in an imperfect world.

'Has there been any trouble at the Pomona recently?' Slider asked Sergeant O'Flaherty on his way out to the yard. Fergus was one of his oldest friends, a man of sharp, sidelong wit and vast experience, who lurked, like a birdwatcher in a hide, behind the persona of a joke Irishman, a pantomime Thick Mick. Sometimes Slider suspected that he had slipped so far into self-parody that he had started to believe it.

'Not more than usual,' O'Flaherty said. He was on his break and eating a sausage sandwich, washing it down with gulps of tea. 'There was a bit of a frackarse Saturday night, but it didn't amount to much – more of a comedy turn in the end. Some animal rights nutters tried to storm the place, but the doormen dusted 'em off.'

'Animal rights?' Slider was puzzled. 'What were they protesting about?'

'One o' the cabaret acts. Simulated sex with a sheep,' Fergus explained with a curled lip.

Slider frowned. 'But that's—'

'Asherjaysus, it wasn't a real sheep, it was paper mashy an' a bit o' woolly stuff stuck on; but the animal libbers didn't work that one out until they got in and chucked some paint at the performers. It missed them and hit the sheep, at which point the truth dawned. They was so gobsmacked it give the doormen a chance to grab. They gave 'em no resistance and the doormen chucked 'em out with just a bunch o' bruises. They thought about suing, but when I pointed out what the headlines'd be, sense prevailed and they thought they'd better keep quiet about it, for the sake o' pride.' He finished his tea. 'D'you know what the Pomona called the act, anyway?' Slider shook his head. '*A Pair o' Sheepskin Slippers*.' He gave a snort of mixed disgust and amusement.

'So how come it wasn't all over the papers?'

'The Pomona's owned by Billy Yates, and he didn't want the publicity any more than the animal libbers.'

'Ah, of course,' said Slider, understanding. Billy Yates was a local businessman with his fingers in almost every pie, and an inordinate influence in the local community.

'He squashed the locals, and they didn't dare syndicate. There was a paragraph in Monday's *Evening Standard*, but it didn't have the interesting details, so nobody else picked it up. Yates was fed up, mind you, having to take off the act, but he couldn't have his *artistes* shagging a green sheep, now could he? O' carse, he'd a' had to take it off anyway, One o' the slippers in question was your man Jay Paloma.'

'Was it indeed?'

'Didn't you know that? I thought that was why you was asking.' He looked at Slider keenly. 'You think it was some nutter on a clean-up campaign?'

'I'm not sure. Paloma was some bigwig's rent boy, according to his flatmate. He could have been wiped for security reasons.'

'Or jealousy. You know what these types are like – incontinent as the moon.' Fergus screwed up his greasy bag and potted it neatly in the bin. 'How's Little Boy Blue gettin' on?' This was his nickname for Atherton. It was not unaffectionate.

'I rang yesterday. They said the usual things.' He tried to be positive. 'It's bound to be a long job. It was a massive wound.'

'It shouldn't a happened to a bloke like him,' Fergus said. 'But then, I never thought he should be a copper. Restaurant critic, maybe. It's like seein' a raceharse pull a coal cart.'

'He's a good detective,' Slider objected. 'You're a Catholic, Fergus. Do you believe prayers are answered?'

'Always,' Fergus said firmly. He eyed his friend with large sympathy. 'Sometimes the answer's "no".'

'You're such a comfort,' Slider complained, and headed for the door.

Fergus called after him. 'D'you know what's headin' the bill at the Pomona in place o' *Sheepskin Slippers*? It's that big fat Vera doin' a strip, all dragged up in Egyptian like Elizabeth Taylor. *Two Ton Carmen* they call it. It's the last bastion o' good taste, that place.'

'Oh, you are awake,' Slider said. 'The nurses warned me not to disturb you if you were resting.'

'I can rest all day,' Atherton said.

'How are you feeling?'

'Excremental.'

Slider studied him from the doorway. 'You look like the Pompidou Centre.'

'And Honeyman sent a basket of fruit,' said Atherton, looking at the thing which lurked horribly in a corner, covered in brittle polythene and topped with one of those vast pale mauve bows beloved of florists.

'Honeyman's an idiot,' Slider said, fetching a chair to the bedside. 'Can't you give it to the nurses?'

'They won't take it. They keep saying I'll want it later, when the tubes come out. I keep telling them by then it'll be pure penicillin.'

'Maybe that's what they mean. Can I get you anything before I sit down?'

'Yeah. Wet my lips, please.' There was a container of saline solution and a crock of baby buds for the purpose. Slider performed the task neatly. 'You'd make someone a great wife,' Atherton said, to cover for the variety of emotions it made him feel.

Slider sat and made himself as comfortable as possible, wondering who they used as a model for these moulded chairs.

'How's Jo?' Atherton asked.

'Fine. Busy.'

'And you?'

'Ditto. We had a shout. That's why I didn't get in to see you yesterday.'

'You don't have to come in every day.'

'I do,' Slider said shortly. Atherton hadn't the energy to argue with him. He knew Slider blamed himself for the knife wound, because he hadn't let Atherton in on his thought processes, and therefore laid him open (ouch, change metaphor) left him vulnerable to the momentary mistaken identification which had let Gilbert get his blow in. Atherton had even, in his worst moments of despair, blamed Slider himself; but the truth was that it had all happened so quickly, even if he had found himself faced with a complete stranger when the door opened he wouldn't have seen the knife coming. But Slider felt responsible, and visiting every day was one small way of making it up. And Atherton liked to have him visit. It broke up the day a bit.

'Nicholls came yesterday,' Atherton said.

'He knew I wasn't going to make it. Did he tell you they've started getting the bill together for Mr Wetherspoon's charity concert for Children in Need? Nutty's going on in a fright wig and sequins singing "Hey Big Spender". He's billed as Burly Chassis.'

Atherton smiled painfully. 'Don't. It hurts to laugh.'

'Sorry.'

'When's that coming off?'

'The concert? September some time.'

'Maybe I'll be out for it, then.' Atherton sounded so doubtful that it seemed better to both of them for the subject to be changed. 'Tell me about the shout.'

'The shout?' Slider's mind was elsewhere and he sounded vague. 'Isn't it that painting by Munch?'

'Give the man a coconut,' Atherton said, secretly rather

impressed by Slider's knowledge. 'Not *The Scream* – the shout. Your shout.'

'Oh! Oh, it was a corpus. In a flat on the White City Estate.'

'Blimey, not again,' Atherton said. Slider told him about it. Atherton did not know Busty Parnell, and was faintly amused at Slider's seedy Soho and showbiz connections. What a Bohemian past his boss had had! He had heard of *Hanging Out in the Jungle*, of course – everyone had – and of Jeremy Haviland's suicide; but to Atherton it was Theatre History, it was like talking to someone who had actually met Flo Ziegfeld.

'Well, you've got enough there to be going on with,' he said. 'Seedy connections, mysterious lover, poison pen letters. You won't be bored for a week or two.' His voice cracked, and he licked his lips.

Slider looked at him carefully for a moment. 'What's the matter?'

'Nothing. Why?'

'Hey, it's me. What's the matter?'

Atherton hesitated, and then, with a hollow sense of helplessness he admitted, 'I'm afraid.'

'You're entitled,' Slider said.

Atherton shook his head slightly. After a while he went on. 'I've never been scared before. Not like this. When a bloke pulls a knife on you—'

Slider nodded. 'The adrenalin kicks in. Afterwards you think, "Shit, he might have killed me."'

'Afterwards. Not before. That's the difference.' He turned his head a little on the pillow, looking towards the shadows. 'It only happened to other coppers. Now it's us.' He licked his lips again. 'Aren't you scared?'

It was what Slider had been trying not to think about. But he owed Atherton that, at least. He looked it in the face and said, 'Yes. Shit-scared. I don't want to end up a notch on some stupid scumbag's belt.'

'So – what, then? Why go on?'

'The odds are on our side.'

Atherton closed his eyes.

Slider thought. Yes, the odds were on their side. But the odds were shortening all the time; and anyway, that wasn't it. So what, then? He couldn't do anything else, wasn't trained for anything else. But that wasn't it either. It was what had made him take the job in the first place, that made him stay with it. An inability to do nothing. There were those who, seeing two kids smashing up a telephone kiosk, hurried past, and those who had to protest. His body might have its own views, but his soul sickened at the stupidity and waste of crime, and if he didn't do something, his bit, to stop it . . . It wasn't exactly that he couldn't stop caring. That was perfectly possible, something he was on the edge of every day. It was that he couldn't stop caring whether he cared or not. *That* was the very, very bottom line.

He opened his mouth to share this revelation with Atherton, but Atherton was asleep again.

Freddie Cameron's bow tie of the day was claret with pale blue diagonal stripes, a bright spot in a dark world. Thunder clouds had come up, and an unnatural, yellowish twilight outside made the strip-lighted pathology rooms seem unnecessarily glaring. Slider introduced Hollis, and Freddie shook his hand.

'Permanent fixture?'

'I hope so.' Hollis looked around. 'Nice set-up you've got here. Last time I went to a post there was water running down the walls and the corpse was the warmest thing in the room.'

'High Victorian?'

'Low farce,' Hollis corrected, and Cameron smiled.

'I know what you mean. Well, there's still a good few of those dear old mortuaries around. You wait till you've attended an exhumation in one. That's when your faith is really tested.'

Slider looked around, missing the usual crowd that hung around post mortems. 'Where is everybody?'

'Holiday season,' Freddie explained.

'Surely not?' Slider said. 'They can't all be away at once.'

'Tell you the truth, old boy, pathology isn't the draw it used to be. And no-one specialises in forensic pathology any more. When my generation's gone, I don't know who's going to cut up your corpses for you. You know we've lost our only forensic odontologist, don't you?' Slider had heard that the Tooth Fairy, as he was called, had gone to Dublin, where, thanks to the EC, the livin' was easy. 'I tell the students, being a pathologist is a grand life. Easy hours, no stress – and dead men don't sue. Bodies may pong a bit, but it beats being called out in the middle of the night to deliver someone's baby. But they don't listen. To tell the truth, I think they see too many simulated messy corpses on the telly to sustain the thrill. The romance has gone out of it.'

'What you've got,' Slider said wisely, 'is *Weltschmerz*.'

'I thought that was a kind of German sausage. How is Atherton, by the way?'

'I hope that's a non-sequitur. He's coming along slowly, but it'll be a long job. The wound has to heal from the inside outwards, so it has to be kept open.'

'Ah,' said Freddie wisely. 'That must be a trial. Keeps it always before him, so to speak. How's his morale?'

'Shaky. But he's still very weak.'

'Is he allowed visitors? I might pop in and see him, if you think it'd cheer him up. Is this radiant female looking for you?'

Slider turned. 'Oh, yes, she's my new DC, a temporary loaner, though if I'm nice to her she might persuade them to let her stay.'

'You should have let her off this post, then,' said Freddie the chivalrous. He could never shake himself of the old habit of regarding women as delicate and lovely creatures to be protected and pampered, despite the fact that one of his daughters was a country vet and the other rode a Triumph Bonneville to work. 'Shall we begin?'

The body was stripped, and lay pale and faintly shiny on the PM table, like something made of high-quality plastic, an illusion aided by the teen-doll perfection of his figure. In life Jay Paloma had been lean and flat-bellied, and, apart from the nest of pinkish-blond curls at the root of the penis, entirely hairless. Even the legs were smooth – presumably the result of hours of agony with hot wax. Because of the leanness, the genitals looked unusually large by contrast, a curious effect Slider had noticed before. He wondered the Government didn't stress that point in its efforts to get the nation to lose weight. It would have had more effect than the health argument.

Freddie spoke into the microphone. 'The body is that of a male, apparent age thirty-five to forty years old, well-nourished, of medium build. Height—' He and his assistant measured. 'Height is five feet nine inches. Put that into Napoleons, will you, Carol?' he added for the typist. All metric measures were

Napoleons to him, just as all foreign currencies were washers. He stubbornly refused to be embraced by Europe.

'No sign of drug usage, no needle marks or tracks. Apart from the injuries to the head and face, which I will come to later, no apparent wounds, abrasions, or bruises. No surgical scars. Estimated time of death – now where did I put my notes? Ah yes. When I first examined the body at the scene of the crime, at – ah – 7.15 a.m. on Wednesday, it was cold to the touch and rigor mortis was present in the upper limbs, the trunk and the lower limbs as far as the ankles, but there was still some flexibility in the toes. There was post mortem staining present in the dependent parts of the body. The ambient temperature was 17.2°C and the body temperature 33°C. That was a liver stab, by the way. I avoided rectal testing because of the nature of the deceased's inclinations. The body temperature at 9.30 a.m. was 32.5°C. I estimate that the time of death was between fifteen and eighteen hours before my first examination at 7.15, that is between 1.15 and 4.15 p.m. on Tuesday.'

Slider caught Hart's eye. 'Hang on a minute, Freddie,' he said. 'Are you sure about that time of death?'

Freddie looked up enquiringly over his half-moons. 'You know better than that, old boy. Anything over four hours can never be certain. The variations and exceptions are endless. It's my opinion, but I wouldn't stake half-a-crown on it if you know better.'

'Well, we've got witnesses—'

'A witness takes precedence over the jolly old Three Signs, you know that. What time do you want, then?'

'Eleven-thirty on Tuesday evening. Not an eyewitness, but two separate witnesses to the door being kicked in and the sound of furniture overturned.'

'Eleven-thirty? That gives me not quite eight hours. Well, I'd have thought it was a bit short, but anything's possible. Now I look at him, he's thinner than I first took him for. Nicely built, but not an ounce of fat on him, so he could have cooled and stiffened very quickly, especially lying through the night in an unheated room. And of course,' he added with a bland look at Slider, 'he's shaved off all his body hair, so he's got no fur coat for insulation.'

'Shaved?'

'Or waxed. The things some people will do for love! Let's have him over, John.'

The examination continued. 'Hypostasis well developed on the trunk and lower limbs. Ah, you see here the evidence that our chap was a practised sodomite: hairless and smooth as a baby's cheek. Depilatory cream followed by Oil of Ulay, I suspect. Epithelium cornified, smooth and less elastic than normal, and there's a lack of sphincteric tone. No sign of venereal disease, or proctitis. Practised but careful. Ah, but here, do you see this? Some peri-anal bruising, and a couple of tiny haematomata. Our friend's had a bit of rough sex quite recently. Not immediately pre-mortem, though. Not part of the homicidal attack – twelve to twenty-fours hours before that, I'd say.'

'He went to see his lover the day before, apparently,' Slider said.

'Did he? You're not worried about this, then? Can we move on?'

'We haven't identified the lover yet. It could be important.'

'In that case I'll take swabs.'

Freddie came at last to the head injuries, and as he approached them he began to whistle quietly through his teeth, a defence mechanism which caused his typist considerable pain during transcription. 'Injuries to the head are consistent with having been caused by repeated severe blows from a hard object. The wounds are considerably overlaid and it is impossible to say with any certainty what the weapon might have been. The blows were inflicted with great force, sufficient to crush the skull.'

'In fact,' Slider said, 'it was our old friend, the frenzied attack.'

'Quite.' Cameron whistled on. 'Let's have him over again.'

'Ah, now, this is better. There appears to have been a single blow to the face, across the bridge of the nose, again with enormous force. The clean-cut edge to the wound here – d'you see, Bill? – suggests it might have been something with a straight edge or a square section. A metal bar, for instance, rather than a baseball bat or a knobkerrie.'

Slider made a note.

'The blow to the face was the first and fatal one, delivered with sufficient force to drive splinters of bone into the brain. Death would have been instantaneous. The rest of the blows to the skull were carried out post mortem.' Cameron paused. 'What's up, Bill? With all the blood down the front of the shirt and none down the back, you must have come to that conclusion yourself.'

'Yes,' said Slider, 'but it doesn't make it easier. If you sneak up on someone, it's usual to do it from behind.'

'Bit of a breach of protocol,' Freddie agreed.

'And there was no sign of a struggle, and no defence injuries—'

'True,' said Freddie. 'The fatal blow was undefended.'

'But if someone had kicked the door in, why didn't he see them coming? Unless he was drunk. Or drugged.'

'If he was unconscious through drink or drugs,' Freddie said, 'it could explain the rapid fall in body temperature and quick onset of rigor. Did he drug?'

'Not according to his flat mate, but she wouldn't necessarily know everything. Or even necessarily tell the truth.'

'Well, the blood tests may show something. D'you want the stomach contents analysed as well?'

'Yes, it may help.'

'I'll secure the whole thing and send it off, then.'

CHAPTER FIVE

Pom Deterrent

The ground-floor-level manifestation of the Pomona Club was a stuccoed wall painted with a mural of a tropical jungle prominently featuring a grinning snake and an apple. Entrance was via a side-alley, and the door sported a state-of-the art neon sign of an apple which flicked back and forth between being whole and having a large, deckle-edged bite out of it. Below the apple little red dots chased themselves round the border of a space which read alternately *Pomona* and *Cabaret*.

Despite the apple theme, Slider happened to know, because an amused O'Flaherty had told him, that the club had been named for entirely different reasons. Billy Yates, the owner, had had a long rivalry with a fellow businessman, Brian Hooper, who being from Sydney himself had referred to Yates's enterprise as 'that club with the Pom owner'. The name stuck, and Yates, ever a pragmatist, made the best of a bad job and renamed it the Pomona to make it look as though he had thought of it first. Despite his many business interests, Yates seemed to have a particular attachment to the Pomona, spending more time there than might seem warranted.

The neon sign was off now, of course, revealing the secret of its pseudokinesics in an unseemly display of unlit tubes and bulbs. The door below gave access to a steep flight of stairs: the club itself lived in the basement. Hart wrinkled her nose as she descended behind Slider. 'Mouldy place. How'd they ever get a licence?'

'God knows,' Slider said.

'I should've thought it would never pass a fire certificate.'

'Contributions in the right boxes,' Slider suggested. 'Friends in the right places.'

'On the square, you mean?'

'You might think that. I couldn't possibly comment.'

The club wore an insistent and insincere glamour, an air of having had just enough spent on it to make it appear to a casual or drunken glance to have had a great deal spent on it. It was gloomy now, lit only by the bar lights, and the reflection from the back-curtain to the dance stage, which was made of vertical shimmery stuff like giant Lametta. It smelled of cigarette smoke, spilled alcohol, disinfectant, cellar-mould, and a faint, spicy whiff of something that was either joss-sticks or a certain popular recreational tobacco substitute.

'What a dump,' Hart murmured, keeping so close behind Slider he could feel the heat of her body. Nervous, he thought; or perhaps she didn't have very good night vision.

They had not been unobserved. A door revealed itself over beyond the bar as an oblong of light, and a dark figure came through and quickly stepped aside so as not to be outlined. 'Can I help you?' a man's voice asked unwelcomingly.

'I'm looking for Mr Yates,' Slider said. There was a click, and fluorescent lights in the ceiling came on, pinning Slider and Hart like bugs on a table.

'If you're tryin' to ge' a job for your daugh'er,' the voice said with grim humour and a splendid array of West London glottal stops, 'forge' i'. She ain't got the tits for it.'

The voice belonged to a tall, very fit-looking young black man – the glossy, dessert-chocolate black of Africa – dressed in a suit of the same cheap-smartness as the club decor, and with his right hand tucked casually in under the left coat of his jacket. The hard eyes had already summed up Slider and Hart as not being dangerous, so the gesture was purely theatrical, meant to impress.

'Detective Inspector Slider, Detective Constable Hart. Mr Yates is in the back, is he?'

Now the right hand moved with the invisible-lightning speed of a lizard out from under the coat and down into a pocket. The alert pose became casual. A wide and perfectly false smile decorated the features. 'Oh, yeah, he'll be glad to see you. Always glad to see you lot, is Mr Yates. Come on through.'

So, Billy Yates keeps an armed guard at his side, Slider thought as he crossed the room. Now what has he got to be afraid of, I wonder?

The man led the way through into a narrow corridor. He knocked on a door, opened it and said, 'Mr Yates, it's the fuzz. Coupla detectives.' He stretched his arm to usher them in, favouring Hart with a salacious look. 'F'you want an audition, darlin', I don't mind waivin' the tits if you don't. Geddit?' he added with a grin of delight at his own wit.

Hart looked witheringly as she passed him. 'Jerk,' she said.

'Shut up, Garry, and get out,' a colder, older voice from inside commanded. Slider followed Hart into the tiny room, and the door was closed behind them. Billy Yates sat behind a cheap metal office desk piled high with papers. There were two cheap office chairs and a bank of filing cabinets on this side of the desk, and that was all. The room was so tiny there was only just room between the cabinets and the desk for the chairs. To open a filing cabinet drawer you would have had to lift a chair out of the way.

Yates was a big man who had once been muscular and was going slightly to seed. Still, he was big enough and strong enough to have taken care of himself, especially as, Slider calculated, in any situation he was likely to get the first blow in, and the first blow from him would be the only one in the fight. His face was big-featured, tanned with an expensive, overseas tan which Slider guessed he would sport all year round, and would have been good-looking if it had had a pleasant expression. But there was no smile in the mouth, no humanity in the eyes. It was a cartoon face, just lines drawn round a space, without animation, a representation of a human rather than the real thing. His hair was carefully coiffeured, his cufflinks large and gold, his aftershave filled the small room, but though his suit looked expensive, Slider's eye, tutored over the years by Atherton, saw that it was merely new, and would not last the pace. Cheap-smart again, just a better class of cheap-smart than his henchman's. Was Yates a man who was satisfied with what would pass muster, rather than the real thing, or did he dress down for the venue? If rumour was even half right, he had a wad the size of Centre Point, so he must be spending it on something.

'What can I do for you?' he asked. He waved a hand towards

the chairs. Slider sat. Now on a level with him, Yates's face waited for him without expression, his grey eyes stationary as oysters.

'Jay Paloma,' Slider said. 'He works for you—'

'Not any more,' Yates said sharply.

'Since when?'

'Since he didn't turn up to work. I don't give second chances. Not when there's a hundred people out there eager for his job.'

'When did you last see him?'

'Monday night – or Tuesday morning, rather, at about ten past four, when he left to go home.'

'Was he alone?'

'As far as I know.'

'And when was he due to come in again?'

'Seven Tuesday evening. Seven till four were his hours, with an hour and a half off. He didn't show up, and that was that as far as I was concerned.'

'No message or telephone call?'

'Nothing.' Yates shrugged. 'And after I'd taken a chance on him, given him the job when there were younger dancers I could have had.' And paid him accordingly, I bet, Slider thought.

'When you last saw him, did he seem in normal spirits?'

Yates only shrugged, picked up a cigarette box from the clutter of the desk, offered it to Slider and Hart, and then took one himself, making a slow business of lighting it. To give himself time to think, Slider thought, keeping silent. At last Yates said, 'As you mention it, he did seem out of sorts on Monday night. Hadn't got his mind on his job. Performed like crap. Fortunately Monday's a quiet night. But I made a mental note that he'd have to pull his socks up or get out.'

'Well, you'll be glad to know that you've been saved the trouble of making the decision,' Slider said, watching Yates's eyes. 'He's been murdered.'

There was no flicker, only a serious, considering look of inward thought. 'I'm sorry,' Yates said tersely. 'When?'

'Tuesday night.'

There was no response to that at all.

Slider went on, 'I'd like you to tell me everything you know about him.'

Yates made a dismissive gesture. 'I knew nothing about him, beyond his work.'

'Did he meet anyone here? Did you see him with anyone?'

'If I did, I wouldn't have made a mental note of it. The staff are supposed to be friendly to the customers, make them feel at home.'

'Who were his special friends amongst your staff? Who did he talk to during his breaks?'

'I don't know that he had any friends. I pay my staff to work, not to fraternise.'

'Well, perhaps I can talk to the people he worked with. Perhaps they'd be more forthcoming.'

Slider expected Yates to object to that, but after a slow, moveless look into Slider's face, he said, 'Do as you please. Just don't do it during my open hours. It wouldn't please my customers to have detectives hanging around asking questions.'

I'll bet it wouldn't, Slider thought. He was about to get up when, unexpectedly, Yates spoke again.

'There is something.'

'Yes?' Slider said encouragingly.

Yates seemed to be having difficulty in bringing himself to be helpful. At last he said, 'I do remember seeing him with someone just recently. For the last few weeks. Not every night, but a couple of times a week. Out in front – in the club. He's been sitting with a man, talking, during his break.'

'Did you know the man?'

'No. It wasn't unusual for Jay to talk to customers. But I noticed this one because he wasn't a fag.'

'How could you tell?'

For the first time there was a flicker of animation – a withering look. 'In my business you have to know. This man was—' He hesitated. 'He wasn't a customer. He wasn't enjoying the club. He was there on business of some kind.'

'Drug dealing, perhaps?' Slider said blandly.

The face went stationary again. 'I don't like what you're suggesting. I think you'd better go.'

Slider felt his headache coming on again. 'Oh, come off it, Mr Yates! You know and I know you get more dealers in here than Monte Carlo. I'm not here to investigate that. I'm not here to make trouble for you – but I can, if you won't help me.'

'I doubt it,' Yates said with such utter indifference that Slider wondered anew whose pocket he was into. All the same, after a moment Yates went on, 'But I've no objection to helping you. I'll give you a description of this man. About thirty-five, five-ten, well built, clean shaven, dark hair.'

'Would you know him again?'

'Maybe. Maybe not. He sat in a dark corner. I got an impression of him, rather than really saw him. He looked like trouble.'

'Trouble? In what way?'

Yates seemed to have difficulty in defining it. 'He was a professional. He was on some kind of business, and he was going to get it done, and if anything got in the way—' He shrugged. 'That's why I noticed him; that's why I kept my eye on him.' He tapped his nose. 'This was warning me.'

'And what do you think Jay Paloma had to do with him?'

'God knows. He wasn't screwing him, that's all I know.'

'Could he have been selling him drugs?'

'I've told you—'

'Without your knowledge or approval, of course,' Slider said smoothly. 'As I said, I'm not here to make trouble for you. But a man of your experience must have seen drug dealers at work. So off the record, could this man have been one?'

'He could have been the type,' Yates conceded. 'He had the look. That's all I can say. But Jay didn't use – not to my knowledge. I wouldn't have anyone who used working for me. Not worth the risk.'

'Someone waiting to see you,' Nicholls said as Slider passed through the front shop. The words brought a replay to his mind of Jay Paloma, nicely dressed and sweating through his aftershave with fear, turning up his eyes in appeal. *You let him down.* Cobblers, what could I have done? *Something. Anything. He came to you and you let him down.* And another mind-flash, of the pretty streaked-blond hair pasted into the splintered skull with pink ooze. Flash: the smell of sweat, not Paloma's dainty, fresh sweat, but the old accumulated stink of a man in shorts and khaki socks. Flash: Atherton's eyes widening in surprise and recognition—

'Bill?'

He pulled himself back. 'Yes – you said? Someone wants to see me?'

Nicholls watched him consideringly. 'You all right, pal?'

'Yes.' But Nicholls was an old colleague, and deserved better than that. 'That whack on the head I had must have knocked something loose. It'll be a while before it beds in again.'

'You came back to work too early.' Nicholls was serious.

'Good job I did, as it happens,' Slider said lightly. 'Where's this bloke?'

It was a slight, wiry man in his fifties, sallow and moley: his face was all over little tags and buttons, some dark, some flesh-coloured, as though he hadn't been finished off properly. He had a thick nose, a wide, lipless mouth, milk-chocolate-brown eyes behind large plain glasses, tight crinkly black hair turning grey. He was wearing grey flannels and well-polished black shoes with thick rubber soles, a blue anorak showing a peep of a pale blue polo-shirt, and a pair of new pale leather driving gloves, the sort with the knitted string backs. He was wearing the left one and holding the other in his left hand; his right hand showed the two first fingers stained rich amber, and a thick, plain gold wedding ring on the third finger. If he hadn't been under size, Slider would have put him down as a copper off duty.

'Mr Slider?' He offered a friendly smile with a very large number of small, uneven teeth. 'I hope you don't mind. Well, actually, I thought I might be able to help you,' he said in the mild accent of North Harrow. 'Benny Fluss is my name.' He pronounced it to rhyme with truss. He held out his hand, looking expectantly at Slider as though he expected the name to be recognised.

'Yes, Mr Fluss,' Slider said, managing with the grace of long practice not to notice the extended hand. 'What did you want to talk to me about?'

'Well, this awful murder, of course,' the man said, reclaiming his hand and comforting it by letting it play with his loose glove. 'Didn't Val – Miss Parnell mention me?'

'I'm afraid not,' Slider said. 'Do you think you might have some information for me? Let's go somewhere quieter, shall we?' He led the way to the nearest interview room and ushered the man in. He seemed nervous – or perhaps on edge was nearer the mark – but eager to please. A friend of Busty's? An ex-customer? Yes, perhaps that would account for the nervousness. A married man, fond of Busty but not wanting any trouble.

'Right,' Slider said when they were seated opposite each other, 'what do you know about this business?'

'Nothing about the murder, I'm afraid, but I am in a position to confirm Miss Parnell's alibi.'

'What makes you think she needs an alibi?'

The man smiled indulgently. 'Oh, I don't mean it like that. Obviously Val had nothing to do with it. Anyone who knows her would know that – and I've heard her mention you, Mr Slider, so I know you *do* know her. But I know how you chaps work. Everything has to be checked and verified, even if it's just to be able to put it aside out of the question. I'm here to put the record straight so that you can tick off that item and get on to something else. That will be helpful, won't it?'

'Any information which bears on the case is helpful,' Slider began, and Fluss jumped in again with eager garrulity.

'That's right. That's what I thought. So I popped straight along as soon as I heard about it, to save you the trouble of having to come and find me. Always glad to help you chaps – you're good to us, so we should be good to you. And I don't mind telling you,' he went on confidingly, 'that, awful though this business is, I can't help being a little bit excited at being involved even in a small way. I've always been interested in the law. It's one of my passions – almost a hobby, you might say. If you were to see my bookcase at home, you'd think it was a solicitor's! Benny the Brief they call me at our garage. That's my nickname, Benny the Brief. They all come to me with their little problems. I'm cheaper than a real solicitor, and I talk plainer English, ha ha!'

Now Slider placed the look of him, the neat appearance, the anorak, the shoes. And, like firemen, they gave each other silly nicknames which were often better known in the business than the real names: a nickname might go all over London if the idiosyncrasy it marked were extreme enough. 'You're a taxi driver,' he said. 'You're the one who brought Miss Parnell home on Wednesday morning?'

'Well done!' the man beamed. 'The detective is worthy of his hire! Yes, I'm the man who drove her home – and much more. I'm a very old friend of Val's, and I drive her everywhere. Whenever she wants to go anywhere, she calls me. I'm practically her private chauffeur.'

'That's very altruistic of you.'

'Oh, she pays the fare. Nothing funny about it, I assure you,' he said seriously. 'Not but what I wouldn't give her the odd free ride, being as we're such old friends, but she insists on it. "Benny," she says, "you've got your living to make the same as me." But she goes everywhere by cab, does Val.'

'So she told me.'

'Did she? She must have mentioned me then. She didn't? Oh. Well, I met her when she was working in the Nitey Nite Club, and there'd been a nasty case when a colleague of hers got raped by a mini-cab driver—'

'Yes, I remember,' Slider said. 'In fact, she mentioned that only the other day.'

Fluss nodded. 'It was a real shock to her. Well, I said to her after that, you can't be too careful. You make sure you always get a proper cab from now on. "Benny," she said, "if I could be sure I'd always get *your* cab, I'd be a happy woman." And that was the start of it.'

'How did you meet her in the first place?' Slider asked.

Fluss lowered his eyelids. 'Well, if you must know – strictly off the record – I was working "round the back" at the time.'

Slider knew what that meant: picking up tourists and taking them to a club on a commission basis. Touting was illegal for licensed cabbies, but – well, lonely Japanese reps looking for a good night out, a taxi driver with a living to make and too many cabs in competition, a club willing to pay £15 a head for customers – it was one of those victimless crimes everyone tried to close their eyes to. Knowing the Nitey Nite and knowing Val, Slider wouldn't be surprised if Benny had also been "going case" as it was called – driving a prostitute and her client from the club to a hotel and bringing the girl back afterwards. It was reassuring for the girl to know the driver was looking out for her, and the client would also know that he had been "clocked", and would thus be deterred from any funny business. If that had been the basis of their association, it might well turn into a lasting friendship.

'That's between you and the Carriage Office,' Slider said. 'I'm just interested in Val and Jay Paloma. So you've been driving her regularly?'

'For the last year or so, I've been the only person to drive her,' Benny said with a hint of pride. 'I'm on a radio circuit now – Monty's, you know?'

Slider knew. The full title was Monty's Radio Metrocabs; the garage was under the railway arches on the other side of Goldhawk Road, the owner one Monty Green, an expansive man with a figure like Pavarotti and the hackney carriage trade in his veins. Atherton called him Monty Verdi, an obscure joke that made only Joanna laugh.

'So she can always ask for me,' Benny went on. 'And for when I'm off duty, I've given her the number of my mobile. Any time, day or night, I've told her, you can call me.'

'What does your wife think about that?' Slider couldn't resist asking.

'My wife passed away, Mr Slider,' Fluss said gravely. 'Six months ago. Cancer of the liver.'

'I'm sorry,' Slider said. Of course, wedding ring on the right hand – some old-fashioned types still swapped hands to indicate widowhood.

'She went just like that,' Benny said, looking down. 'I suppose it was a blessing it was so quick. Thirty years we'd been married, and never a cross word. She was a wonderful woman.'

Slider waited a tactful beat and went on. 'So you brought Miss Parnell home on Wednesday morning?'

'That's right.' He jumped from Mourning Widower to Perfect Witness suspiciously quickly. 'Of course, it was booked for later that morning, to pick her up from her sister's at ten forty-five, but she rang me direct at six o'clock to say her brother-in-law had come home unexpectedly, and could I come and pick her up. She was in quite a state. The man's a brute, Mr Slider, not to mince words. I can tell you I was round there like a shot. It wouldn't be beyond that man to raise a hand to Val, same as he does to Shirley.' He gave Slider a significant nod.

'And what time did you get there?'

'About ten past six, it must have been. She was waiting outside on the pavement with her bag, which I—'

'That was quick,' Slider interrupted.

'Well, I hadn't far to come. I've got a room in Barlby Road

now, just round the back of the North Pole, you know? I sold the house when the wife died.'

'But it must have taken you some time to get dressed and so on.'

'I was already up, as it happened, dressed and shaved and everything. Well, I've always been an early riser, and since the wife passed on, I don't seem to sleep as much as I used to.'

'I see. Well, it was lucky for Miss Parnell, at any rate. And what time did you get to White City?'

'It would be just before half past. Twenty-five past, maybe. That time of morning there was no traffic about, so it was a quick journey.'

'And did you go upstairs with her?'

'I wish I had,' he said earnestly. 'I truly wish I had. I tell you, Mr Slider, I hate myself for putting her through that all alone. If only I could have saved her the terrible shock! But I didn't usually go up with her, you see, unless she had something heavy to carry, or she invited me in for a cuppa. And this time she just said, "See you later, Benny," and off she went like a bird.'

'See you later?'

'Well, I was to've picked her up to take her to work.'

'Did she seem upset about the business at her sister's?'

'No, not really. She knows the score there all right. She was angry when I picked her up that he'd virtually chucked her out, but she was more anxious about Jay, because he'd been rather down in the dumps lately. He seemed a bit under the weather on the Tuesday when I picked her up to take her to her sister's.'

'Oh, you saw him then?'

'Saw him, yes. He came to the door. In his dressing-gown, and not shaved – which I will say was not like him,' he added as if grudgingly admitting that the Krays were good to their mother. Slider gathered he didn't like Jay Paloma. 'Always neat and tidy he was as a rule, and kept the flat as nice as my wife kept our house. And like my wife would never have normally gone to the door in her curlers, Jay wouldn't normally have let anyone see him with a stubble and not dressed. So he must have been out of sorts.'

'Did he say anything about why he was out of sorts?'

'Oh, he didn't talk to me. Just answered the door and said he'd tell Val I was there, that's all. There was no conversation. But he looked, shall we say, a bit sombre. Val said he'd been quarrelling with his – *boyfriend*.' The slight hesitation and the emphasis showed what Benny thought of Jay Paloma's inclinations. Then he seemed to think better of speaking ill of the dead and added, 'Val was very fond of him. They'd been friends a long time, and he'd been good to her in a number of ways, according to Val.'

'Did you drive him, too?'

'I did not,' Benny said firmly. 'The arrangement I had with Val was special.'

'Oh. I understood Jay was very particular about taking cabs too,' Slider said.

'I wouldn't know about that,' Benny said vaguely. 'But, you know, I wouldn't be surprised—' He paused and glanced at Slider.

'Yes?'

'I'm sorry to have to say it, but I wouldn't be surprised if he wasn't involved in something shady that Val didn't know about, and it caught up with him. Sly, these people are. Acting a part all their lives, they get good at deceiving people. Val thought he was a snow-white lamb, but working where he did, and the types he must have been rubbing shoulders with every night – I wouldn't be surprised if he wasn't into something.'

'Do you have any idea what?'

Benny smiled apologetically. 'No. I'm afraid that's just supposition. No evidence. I shouldn't have said anything, really. I didn't come here to speak ill of the dead, just to assure you that you can cross Val off your list of things to check. I took her to her sister's and brought her back, and there she was the whole time, so she couldn't possibly have had anything to do with it.'

Slider raised an eyebrow, Atherton-style. 'You don't know that, do you? Unless you were with her the whole time, you don't know that she didn't go back to the flat at some point.'

'But she—' Benny looked absolutely dumbfounded, and searched Slider's face for information, his brows buckled with perplexity. 'But you can't think that! You can't think *she* killed him! Not Val. It's not possible. Surely you don't believe she had anything to do with it?'

'As a matter of fact,' Slider said, amused at the little cabbie's protectiveness, 'I don't. I was just pointing out the limits of your evidence. You're very fond of Val, aren't you?'

'I am fond, yes. Yes, I can use that word. I've always liked and respected her, and we've been friends a long time now—'

'More than friends, perhaps?'

Benny's sallow face darkened a shade with – embarrassment? Anger? 'I don't know what you mean,' he said stiffly.

'Don't you?'

'I don't see,' he said slowly, his face clearing and cooling, 'that it's any of your business. I came here to help, and I don't see why I should put up with impertinent questions about my private life. If that's the way you treat responsible citizens who try to help you—' He began to rise.

'I beg your pardon,' Slider said. 'I didn't mean to be impertinent.' Lovely word! 'It's just that every and any detail can help to fill in the picture, even when it doesn't have a direct bearing on the case. When you're groping in the dark for the light switch, even the position of a chair can help.'

Slider wasn't sure the metaphor really meant anything, but it seemed to do the trick with Benny the Brief. He got off his high horse with one bound, and was smiling again, and affable.

'Of course, I understand. You've got a difficult job to do – and a most unpleasant one, as I'm well aware. I've had enough friends in the police force to know that. Well, anything I can do to help, don't hesitate. And I hope my bit of information's been some use to you.'

Yes, that accounted for the rapid dismount – he wanted to be the one man with the discernment to understand the Copper's Lonely Destiny. There were people like that, fascinated by everything to do with the Job and longing to be associated with it in some way, outsiders who wanted to be inside. Sometimes they were invaluable and sometimes they were a pain in the neck. Slider was not yet sure which Benny the Brief would turn out to be, but his mother had always told him not to look a gift horse in the teeth.

CHAPTER SIX

Snow Use

Busty was staying in a hotel – a large Edwardian house at the near end of Hammersmith Grove. There was a short terrace of them: red brick with white copings, black-and-white chequered front path, stained glass panels in the door, elaborate wooden porch with pinnacles and poker-work which put Slider in mind of Hansel and Gretel. They all had names, the sort of names of which Edwardians were so fond, which almost meant something but not quite – Hillsleigh, Holmcroft, Endersby – and all, being too large to accommodate the modern idea of a family, had been turned into hotels. Busty was in The Hillsleigh, suffering from a mixture of shock and frustration, unable to face going to work, unable to go home, trapped in the lethargy of bereavement.

She welcomed Slider's visit as a relief. 'Is this social, or business?'

'Bit of both, really,' he said. 'Business mostly, though, I'm afraid. I want to ask you some more questions.'

'Would it be against the rules to take me for a drink or something?' Her haunted eyes pleaded. 'Just to get me out of here? This place is driving me up the wall.'

Slider glanced round at the awful institutional cheapness of everything in the reception area: the lozenge-patterned carpet designed to repel both stains and the eye; the bland floral wall-paper and framed prints calculated not to trip the taste circuits in any way whatsoever; the furniture intended to discourage sitting around. There were imitation parlour-palms which just failed to look like the real thing, standing in plastic pots in plastic Versailles tubs. Even the decorative bark mulch was plastic and almost exactly the wrong shade of brown, though Slider noticed someone had stubbed out a real cigarette in it. It was probably the most exciting thing that had ever happened in here. Poor old Busty would never stand a spell in Holloway, Slider thought, if one day here could drive her to distraction. 'Come on, then,' he said.

They went to the Hope and Anchor across the road, and Busty asked for a gold watch. Slider got her a double to save time, and himself a Virgin Mary, and they settled into a dim corner. The pub was of the same vintage as the houses across the road, and had apparently used the same interior designer. It was not much of a change, but it seemed to satisfy Busty, who sighed with contentment even before the Scotch touched her lips.

'I want to talk to you a bit more about Maurice,' Slider said. 'And I want you to be honest with me. Nothing you can say can harm him now, but it may help me to find who did this terrible thing. Do you understand me?'

Busty gave him a wide-eyed look. 'I got nothing to hide.'

'Don't try and stuff me, Busty. Hiding things from the police is second nature. And I've known you a very long time. But now you've got to go against nature and tell me everything. What was Maurice mixed up in?'

'Nothing that I know about.'

'I've had the hint from the Pomona Club that he'd been meeting someone in there a couple of times a week. Dark corner, private conversation. Now who would that be?'

'I don't know. Probably a customer trying to pick him up.'

'The boss says this bloke wasn't a ginger.'

Busty looked scornful. 'Billy Yates? What does he know?'

'Yates said the bloke was a professional, and he looked like trouble. Maybe a drug dealer.'

'He ought to know,' Busty muttered resentfully.

'Did Maurice drug?' Slider asked.

She kept her eyes on her glass, but she looked a little shaken. 'No. Never. He didn't like drugs.'

'What about poppers?'

She blinked. 'I dunno. Maybe then. I dunno. No, I reckon not. He hated drugs, Mr Slider. He got quite airiated about it. Said he'd seen too many good people go bad that way. He said—' She stopped abruptly.

'He talked to you about it a lot, did he?' Slider put in smoothly. 'Was he getting it for you, Busty? Was that what he was talking to this man for? You persuaded him to get you a little bit of white, just a spot for when you had the blues, or after work when you were really knocked out?'

'No,' said Busty.

'Against his better instincts, because he loved you. You wheedled him. He had the contacts and you didn't any more. Just a little spot of snow to get you through, who could that hurt? Everyone knows it's not addictive.'

'No,' she said stonily.

'And now it's come back on him, and you feel so guilty—'

She flared. 'No! I tell you *no*! I don't do that any more. Not since I've been sharing with Maurice. He hated it so much, he talked me out of it. He said we had better things to do with our money. We were saving up, Mr Slider, I swear to you. I could show you the savings book. The Halifax down the Bush. Saving for our retirement. So we could get out. He *hated* drugs. That's why—' She changed track. 'He wasn't buying drugs for me, I swear my Bible oath he wasn't.' But her face was as miserable as an abandoned dog's, and Slider took her sentences and repieced them.

'Who for, then, Busty? That was why he'd been feeling down, you were going to say. He hated drugs but he was buying them for someone. Why?' He studied her face. 'For the money. He was paid a commission, wasn't he? He was the intermediary and they made it worth his while, and the commission went into the savings account. He was doing it for both of you.' She was silent, staring into her glass. 'He was buying drugs for someone who could afford to pay him well, but who couldn't get them for himself. Maybe couldn't risk being seen buying them. Was it this friend of his, the VIP boyfriend he went to see on Monday?'

She looked up, a quick flicker of a glance. Surrender. 'I don't know who he is. That's the truth. Maurice never told me his name or anything about him, except that in his position he couldn't afford any scandal. So Maurice got the stuff for him. He wasn't going to. He said no at first but – but—' Her mouth turned down with misery. 'I persuaded him.' She started to cry. 'I said if he didn't get it, someone else would, and we might as well have the money as someone else. He didn't like it, but I persuaded him. He did it for us. And now—'

Slider handed over a handkerchief and she bubbled and

hitched into it for a while. When he judged she was back on line, he said, 'So how did it work? He got the stuff in the club, and then what? Brought it home?'

She nodded. 'That was another reason he didn't like doing it. He said it was putting me at risk. I told him not to be so daft. No-one knew it was there. And it was only for a few hours. He tried to arrange it so he always took it to his friend the next day. He didn't like it hanging around.'

In case Busty succumbed to temptation, Slider thought. He changed direction. 'He didn't go to work on Tuesday evening, did you know that?'

'No.' She seemed genuinely surprised.

'When you left on Tuesday morning, he was intending to go in, was he?'

'He didn't say he wasn't.'

'He wasn't ill?'

'No.'

'But you said he was upset because of this quarrel with his friend on Monday.'

She hesitated. 'Well, to tell you the truth – he was at first, when he was telling me about it. Getting it off his chest, sort of. But then he like cheered up. Started talking about the plan – you know, to get a place in Ireland.'

'You said you'd been talking about it on Sunday?'

'Yeah. He said on Sunday we nearly had enough, and he reckoned he could get hold of the rest of what we needed. But Tuesday morning he said it was all settled. All we'd got to do was find the place. He was even chatting to Benny about it, telling him where he was going to start looking for a place and everything.'

'So he'd got some more money on Monday, had he?'

She hesitated. 'He didn't say so.'

'But on Sunday he said he only needed a little more, and on Tuesday he said he had enough. So it sounds—'

'Yeah. Maybe. I dunno about that. All I know was, he was talking like it was all settled. "Val," he said, "we're going to do it." He was really cheerful about it. Just like a little boy,' she added with a sentimental look.

'So when you left, he seemed in normal spirits.'

'S'right,' she said, but then frowned. 'Only – I been thinking

– he mustn't of been quite himself, leaving them dishes in the sink. He always washed up straight away after himself. Very tidy, Maurice was, tidied up as he went. Nearly a fetish with him.'

'A late supper?' Slider suggested.

'Maybe,' she said. 'But you said he was sitting watching telly when it happened. He wouldn't normally sit down to watch without doing the washing up first.'

'Yes, your tame cab driver told me Jay was a diligent housewife,' Slider said. 'He came to see me this morning.'

'Benny did? What for?'

'Oh, to confirm your alibi.'

'Confirm my—? Cheeky sod! But I suppose he meant well. I should've let him know – he was supposed to be picking me up Wensday harpass five to take me to work, only it completely slipped me mind to cancel him.'

'Understandable.'

'I suppose he went round and saw all the cops there, and heard about it then. What did he say?'

'Oh, he just confirmed the times you gave me. He mentioned that Maurice opened the door to him.'

Busty gave a little snort of laughter. 'I don't expect he was best pleased. He'd have hoped to catch me alone. He's sweet on me, you see. Always turning up early, he is, wanting to chat. He even proposed to me a few weeks back.'

'Proposed marriage?'

'Yeah. His wife died about six months ago – cancer – and I will say he had the decency to wait a bit before proposing. But I've known a long time he was sweet on me. Maurice said – joking really – that I ought to accept, to give me security, but I wouldn't want to be married, at some man's beck and call night and day. You can refuse a customer,' she said, 'but refuse a husband and you've got hurt feelings for days after.'

'So you turned down the offer of matrimony?'

'Yeah, course. I told him I'd promised to stay with Maurice. Not that he really took it in. He still hangs round me just the same, hoping I'll change me mind. Poor Old Benny. I've known him for years, and he's been good to me, but the fact is, even if I wanted to get married, I couldn't get fond of him that way. He's a funny old duck; and my God, his plates don't half pen! That's one thing about Maurice, you could eat your dinner off him –

and drink your tea out of his shoes. Of course, being a dancer he's always been dead careful about his feet—' The tears welled up again as the present tense tripped her up.

Slider deflected her. 'So as far as you knew, Maurice was going to work as usual? And he didn't say he was expecting a visitor?'

'A visitor?'

'There were two whisky glasses in the front room. One on the coffee table and one down beside the chair.'

She thought about this, and shook her head. 'He never had visitors at home.'

'That you knew about,' Slider amended, and she looked disconcerted, but continued to shake her head in denial. 'His friend wouldn't have visited him there?'

'Not him! Too risky.'

'Was there anyone at the club he was friendly with? Anyone on the staff?'

'Not that I know about. He never mentioned anyone.'

Slider sighed inwardly. The trouble with someone like Busty was that you never really knew when you'd got to the bottom layer. She probably didn't even know herself when she was concealing things. It was just instinctive with people like her to give nothing away that you weren't certain the other person already knew.

'Well, I'd better be getting back,' he said. 'If you think of anything that might help me find out who this friend of Maurice's was, give me a ring, will you? Or if you remember the dealer's name, or anything else that might be helpful—'

'When can I go home?' she asked abruptly.

'You want to?'

She shrugged. 'All my stuff is there. And where else would I go? There's only my sister's, and I can't stay there. Trevor wouldn't stand for it, even if she had room. And there's no-one else. Maurice was all I had in the world apart from her.'

And Benny the Brief, Slider thought, but he didn't say it aloud. Benny's feet must be a deterrent indeed if even an ex-hooker couldn't stand them. 'I think you ought to be able to go home tomorrow. I'll check when our blokes will be finished there, and let you know.'

* * *

'All right, people, let's concentrate,' Slider said. 'Mr Honeyman would like this cleared up before he leaves—'

'I bet he would,' Mackay said.

'We could have a go at his dandruff, clear that up for him as well,' McLaren murmured resentfully.

'So let's give him the best goodbye present a Super ever had,' Slider went on, 'and get it sorted. I'll go through first of all what we know about Jay Paloma's movements. Yes, thank you, McLaren. Right: he was a performer at the Pomona Club, where there was a *frackarse*' – he gave it the Department pronunciation – 'on Saturday night, an attack by animal rights campaigners. Paloma was involved, not injured but may well have been upset by it. It was kept out of the papers, except for a par in Monday's *Standard*, which mentioned the club by name but not Paloma, nor the more interesting details of the incident. On Monday afternoon Paloma called at the station to see me, to tell me he was suffering from a poison pen campaign, which started six months ago with heavy-breather phone calls and escalated three months ago to threatening letters. It had escalated still further that morning – that's to say Monday – with a photograph of a badly mauled corpse.'

'Guv, the animal libbers,' Norma said, 'I suppose they were genuine? It wasn't part of the intimidation?'

Hollis, who was office manager, had the information. 'One of them checked out as a paid-up member, but only recently joined. The others seemed to be his mates, and they were all protest virgins. No previous campaign history, and no criminal record.'

'These types usually have enough form to seat a banquet,' Norma said. 'Maybe they were not all they seemed.'

'They didn't seem very much,' Hollis pointed out. 'It wasn't a very bright stunt, and it wasn't ratified by any of the baa-lamb brigades. Going by the interview transcripts, I think they were just a bunch of dickheads acting off their own bats.'

Norma nodded to that, so Slider continued. 'On Monday afternoon Paloma went to visit his regular lover, about whom we know nothing at present except that he is some kind of VIP who wanted to keep the relationship secret. They had a quarrel, according to Parnell. They also had somewhat rough sex, resulting in peri-anal bruising, according to the pathologist's report.'

'Because they'd quarrelled?' Mackay speculated.

'It might have been the way they usually did it,' said Hollis. 'We don't know.'

'On Tuesday,' Slider went on, 'Paloma got up and sat with Parnell while she got ready to go out. He was upset at first about the quarrel, but grew more cheerful as he began to talk about his plan to leave London and buy a boarding house in Ireland.'

'That sentence would make more sense the other way round,' said Norma.

'Parnell left the house at eleven-thirty, and she and the taxi driver Fluss are the last people we know to have seen Paloma alive. He was due to go to work at seven p.m. but didn't arrive, nor did he telephone to say he wasn't going in. At half past eleven p.m. we have two separate witnesses to the sound of the door being kicked in, and some kind of further noise suggestive of something heavy being knocked over. At six-thirty on Wednesday morning Parnell arrived home to find the door kicked in and Paloma dead. Any comments?'

There were shrugs all round. 'That's plain enough,' Mackay said for them all. 'Chummy kicks the door down and does him in. End of story.'

'Except for the minor question of who chummy was,' Norma added with delicate irony.

'Forensic says that from the size of the footmark,' Slider picked it up, 'we're looking for a very big man, probably over six foot, and powerfully built. The boot had a ridged sole of one of the usual man-made compositions, something like a Doc Marten—'

'Oh, well, that narrows the field a bit,' said Norma.

'So if we find a suspect we may get a bit of help there,' Slider concluded patiently.

'Guv, I can't believe no-one saw this geezer,' Hart said. 'I mean, with all them flats around – and half past eleven people are coming back from the pub. And what about the block opposite? If you heard a door being kicked in, wouldn't you go out on the balcony and have a look?'

'No,' said Anderson. 'Ninety-nine out of a hundred, the last thing they'd do is go out and look.'

'What about natural curiosity?' Norma said.

'What about self-preservation?' Anderson said. 'The immediate neighbours made sure they stayed inside where it was safe.'

'Yeah, but that's different,' Hart said. 'Across the other block it'd be safe enough to go out and have a butcher's. I know I would.'

'The estate's not that dangerous,' Norma said. 'People exaggerate.'

'The door was kicked in with one blow,' Slider reminded her. 'There may not have been that much to hear.' Hart shrugged, half convinced. 'By all means, interview everyone again. I'm always ready to give instincts a run.'

'I've been thinking,' McLaren said, and waited for the chorus of whistles and groans to die down. 'If this bloke went along there to kick the door in and take Paloma out, why didn't he do it in the middle of the night, when there was no-one around? Why choose half past eleven when there could be any number of witnesses?'

Slider looked at Hart. 'What's your thinking on that?'

'S'obvious,' she said. 'Middle of the night he would've stood out like a sore thumb. Half past eleven, pub letting-out time, he passes in the crowd, and if someone sees him kick the door in they probably just think he's forgot his key. Anyone hears a loud bang, they don't pay no attention, just think it's a drunken fight or something and forget it. So when someone asks did you hear anything, they say no, and mean it.'

Slider said, 'So the killer was a professional, to your thinking?'

Hart looked confused. 'Well—'

'Yes? Let's have it.'

'Well, guv, the choice of timing and kicking the door open looks professional. And the killing – the first whack across the bridge of the nose killed him instantly, that looks professional. But then he goes on to paste buggery out of the dead man's skull for no reason – that don't look professional. And when he stops to pick up the table and put the fag ends back in the ashtray – that looks plain daft.'

'Maybe he wanted to leave everything looking normal,' McLaren said.

'Oh, normal – with a dead body on the floor,' Hart said witheringly.

'He pulled the front door closed behind him,' McLaren defended himself.

'That was to delay discovery,' Anderson said. 'A front door hanging open in the middle of the night would arouse suspicion.'

'I can't see what the problem is,' Norma said impatiently. 'You've got someone with the foresight to choose the time of day for his murder and the expertise to know how to deal a killing blow. But then he gets carried away with excitement at what he's done and launches—'

She's going to say it, thought Slider.

'—a frenzied attack on the body. When he finally gets his breath back, he's not really thinking straight any more, if at all. Instinct takes over. He tidies up the table that got knocked over – maybe he had a houseproud mum – and closes the front door after him. I don't see why,' she concluded, 'you should expect a villain to be consistent – especially in an irrational situation.'

'You're talking about this bloke being professional,' McLaren objected, 'but you don't know he chose half eleven to be clever. Maybe he was dead stupid and never even thought about it. Maybe he had a beef with Paloma, and that just happened to be the time he lost his rag. Rushed round there, kicked the door in, and belted fuck out of him – just happened to get the first killing blow in where it landed, pure chance. That's much more likely.'

'And tidied up after himself?' Slider said. McLaren offered no thoughts on that. 'Let's move on, shall we? What about this drugs connection? Parnell says that Paloma was buying cocaine for his lover. Billy Yates says he saw Paloma talking to a man in the club who might have been a dealer.'

Hollis said genially, 'My uncle Fred might stick his wooden leg up his arse and do toffee apple impressions. Might doesn't feed the whippet.'

'Quite so,' Slider agreed. 'However, I have to say that I don't believe Parnell would have mentioned coke at all unless there was something in it. She and I have had a few run-ins in the past on that subject. Now it may be she's not telling me the truth, or at least not all of the truth – in fact, I'm sure of that – but I think we can be sure there's some truth in it. It's possible Paloma was supplying her, and she brought in the lover as a smoke-screen.

But on the other hand, she did say he was being paid well for it and putting the money away towards this B and B scheme she mentioned. I'm inclined to believe her. I don't think she's got the imagination to make that up.'

'It doesn't make the man in the club the dealer,' Norma said.

'No. But again, Billy Yates needn't have mentioned him. He certainly wasn't trying to be helpful to me, so presumably he was worried by this man and was hoping I'd act as pest control officer and rid the club of him. And if Billy Yates was worried by the man, there's something about him we ought to know. I wouldn't trust Yates as far as I could spit him, but I trust his instincts of self-preservation.'

'Guv,' Anderson said, 'how about this? Paloma said on Sunday he reckoned he could get the last of the money he needed for the Ireland scheme, right? He goes to see his lover on Monday and arranges to get another supply of coke for him. His lover gives him the cash. He goes into the club Monday night and buys the stuff as usual. Tuesday he knows Parnell's not going to be home, so he arranges to sell the stuff to some local distributor, probably for more than he paid for it. He's waiting in at home for the bloke to call, but word's got round that there's stuff in the flat, and before the right man can get there, someone else breaks in, grabs the snow and whacks Paloma. End of story.'

'There was no sign of anyone searching for anything,' Mackay said.

'If he was expecting to sell it, he probably had it sitting there on the table.'

'Why didn't he ring in to say he wasn't going to work? Ring in sick, or something?' Hart asked.

'He didn't care any more. He was leaving anyway, once he'd got this dosh,' said Anderson. 'Next day when Parnell comes home he's going to say to her, pack your bags, darlin', we're off.'

'Very beguiling,' Slider said. 'But where does the poison-pen campaign fit into this?'

'Maybe it doesn't,' Anderson said, wholesale. 'Maybe that was nothing to do with it. Given who he was and what he did, there's every chance there were people who didn't like him and wanted to scare him.'

Hart spoke up. 'Actually, boss, when you come to think of it –

you never saw one of the letters. And he never told Parnell about it, either, which you'd think he would. Maybe it never happened. Maybe he made it up.'

Slider looked at her. 'Why would he go to all the trouble of coming in to see me to tell me about it? He was certainly afraid of something.'

'I'd be afraid if I was going to pull off some dodgy stuff with a coke dealer,' Hart said. 'He came hoping you'd give him protection, put a copper on the door just for long enough for him to get away. Only he couldn't tell you the real reason.'

'We're really getting into Hans Andersen country now,' Slider said impatiently. 'We've got to get more facts. We need to find the man he spoke to at the club, and any other contacts he had there. If the man Yates spotted wasn't a dealer, who was he; and who was the dealer? Paloma had been working at the club for almost a year. He must have talked to other club employees. Who did he know and what did he tell them? Any ideas how we can get the information?'

'Billy Yates's staff won't talk to us,' Mackay said. 'It's more than their jobs are worth.'

'For jobs read lives,' Anderson concurred.

Hart snorted. 'You don't mean that big ponce Garry, walking about pretending he's got a holster under his arm?'

'Billy Yates has armed protectors, everyone knows that. They're not pretending,' Mackay said.

'Yeah, and they're going to go round shooting anyone that asks questions?' Hart said derisively. 'Do me a lemon! How long is Yates going to stay in business if he leaves a trail of corpses wherever he goes? If his boys carry shooters, it's to scare people. They're not gonna use 'em. Soon as they use 'em, Yates has got cops crawling all over his place, which is very good for business, I don't think.'

'That's the sort of attitude that can get you killed,' Norma said sternly.

'This ain't East LA,' Hart responded. She turned to Slider. 'I reckon I could get that Garry to talk to me, boss. He was fancying me rotten when we was there. If I come on to him a bit—'

Slider shook his head. 'I can't let you put yourself in that sort of position. If you lead him on and then try to back out, he might very well force you, or beat you up.'

'But, guv—' Hart protested.

'I think you underestimate the danger. He knows you're a copper, don't forget. He'd be glad to humiliate you. And if he got carried away, he might even kill you. Yates may be intelligent enough to know you can't go round offing people, but that's no guarantee Garry is.' Slider looked round at the others. 'Not Yates's staff, I don't think. But what about the other entertainers? They won't have the same loyalty, and I doubt whether they'll have the same fears. Yates wouldn't waste his energy on them. Find out who they are, and get to them, privately, away from the club.

'Get on to all the known users and dealers in the area and try to get a handle on it from that end. Find out if anyone did know about Paloma having coke on him at any time. And speak to everyone on the block, and anyone who was visiting that evening, and find out if anyone saw the door being kicked in. It's probably worth asking in the local pubs as well.

'Meanwhile,' he concluded, 'the killer doesn't exist in a vacuum. Someone knows him. Keep your ears to the ground. Ask around all your usual snouts. He came home in a state, probably with blood on him, and if he didn't tell his nearest and dearest why, they probably guessed anyway. You all know that ninety-nine out of a hundred crimes are solved through informers. Get out there and get at 'em.'

As the troops were dispersing, Hart waylaid him with a determined gleam in her eye. 'Guv, about that Garry—' she began.

Slider's heart sank, but he turned back to give her the benefit of the doubt. 'What about him?'

'I know I'm right about him. I'm sure I could get information out of him. He's just pretending to be the hard man. Honest, I know the type.'

'Well I'm *not* sure, so we'll just leave it, shall we?' Slider said.

'But you said you were always willing to go with instinct.'

'A woman's instinct, is that it?'

'No, guv, a copper's instinct,' she returned smartly.

She was so young and so confident she made him feel tired. 'How old are you?'

She stuck her lip out. 'I don't see what that's got to do with it, sir.'

'Of course you don't. One of the nice things about being young is that you think you're immortal. When you've seen a few colleagues go down, you know different. You're not in this job to get your head blown off, Hart.'

'I don't reckon to, sir, but—'

'Experience tells when it's worth taking the risk. For this, it's not worth it. Trust me.' He began to turn away again.

'You wouldn't say that to Mackay or Anderson,' she said sullenly.

His head began to throb. 'They would know better than to ask,' he said. 'If you want to prove you're the same as a man, stick a rolled-up sock down your knickers. I haven't got time to visit anyone else in hospital.'

'That's what this is about, ain't it, guv? You feel guilty about Sergeant Atherton and it's making you over-protective to the rest of us. With respect, you ain't got the right to lay that on us—'

'Don't give me that psycho-bollocks. This is not an episode of *Cracker*. And don't ever use those words to me again.'

'What words?' she said, taken aback.

'With respect,' he said, and left her standing.

'Am I intruding?' Joanna said, and he looked up from his desk to realise she had been standing in the doorway for some time, and he had been half aware of her and trying not to be.

'Oh, no, come in.' Joanna walked over and leaned across the desk to kiss him. She had been rehearsing at the Albert Hall for the evening's concert.

'Why so distracted?' she asked.

'I was afraid it was Hart coming back for a rematch.'

'Would you care to elucidate?'

He told her. 'I don't know why I got riled, except that she's so cocksure, and can't take orders, and wants to go swaggering into the jaws of death like Indiana Jones when it doesn't even begin to be necessary.'

'She's young,' Joanna said.

'I know. That's the trouble. God, they think anyone over thirty has lost touch with reality. It's part of my job to see they live to realise how wrong they are.'

'All the same, she's probably right – about you being over-protective. *Would* you have stopped Mackay or Anderson?'

'They're not female,' he said. 'It's no good looking at me like that. She was proposing to attempt to seduce a flash, gun-toting club hardman, and, having got information out of him, back out of having sex with him at the last minute. But anything he wanted to do to her, she couldn't stop him doing. It doesn't matter how feisty she is, or how well-trained, he's bigger and stronger than her, and that's the bottom line.'

'But isn't her life hers to risk?'

'No,' he said, 'it's mine. While she's in the Job and in my firm, she's my responsibility.'

Joanna looked at him thoughtfully. 'You came back to work too soon,' she said. 'No, don't glare at me, I don't mean your judgement is impaired, I just mean you look tired. And I bet you've got a headache.'

He tried to smile. 'Were you going to suggest having sex on the desk, then?'

'After the rehearsal I've just been through? Lupton and Bruckner? My arm's only hanging on by a thread. God, I hate the Albert Hall! You have to scrub twice as hard to make any impression. But I suppose making it hemispherical seemed like a good idea to her at the time.'

'Queen Victoria?'

'Mrs Hall. It was named in memory of her husband.'

He gave her a ferocious scowl. 'What do you want anyway, Marshall?'

'I was just going to suggest a spot of lunch. Have you got time?'

'I'll make time,' he said largely, feeling her different perspective on life like a blast of fresh air from a just-opened window. 'I'll take you to the canteen.'

'Gosh, you know how to spoil a girl,' she said.

The Special was steak and onion cobbler. 'Aptly named,' Slider said. It was in fact stew, with things on top that looked like dumplings but were actually a sort of hard pastry, having all the attributes of cobblestones except flavour. Joanna had the fisherman's pie. 'What's under the mashed potato?' Slider asked.

Joanna chewed thoughtfully for a moment and then looked down. 'Something white,' she said at last. 'With little bits of something pink.' She chewed again. 'I am eating, aren't I?'

she appealed for reassurance. 'It's so hard to tell without some sensory input, like taste or texture.'

'Never mind,' he said, 'you can make it up with the pudding – they do a wicked jam roly-poly and custard. Atherton says it's the best thing on the menu. You are going in to see him this afternoon, aren't you?'

'Of course. I thought I'd smuggle Oedipus in to say hello. Are you going to be home tonight?'

'Yes. I hope so. I think so.'

'I won't go for a drink, then, I'll come straight home.' She smiled at him suddenly. 'Nice, this, isn't it?'

He looked startled. 'Nice?'

'I mean, being able to plan to come home to each other, no tricky arrangements and subterfuges.'

'Oh, that.' He thought suddenly of Irene, like a low ache of misery, mooning about in Ernie Newman's overstuffed lounge and pining for her own kitchen. 'When this case is over I'm going to have to do something about that house,' he said. 'Change agents or lower the price or something.' It was enough apropos as a comment for Joanna to accept it at face value; but Slider was thinking that if the house were sold, Irene would know there was no going back. But if she was really unhappy with Newman? And if that relationship broke down, what about the children? They'd have to have somewhere to go, they couldn't live in a hotel. Maybe he ought to keep the house on as insurance for them? No, that was ridiculous, he couldn't leave the empty house there for ever just in case Irene changed her mind about Ernie. If she could stand him enough to run away with him in the first place—

Joanna's hand rested on his from across the table. 'Don't start worrying about that as well. You haven't got room. One thing at a time.'

He looked up, his focus clearing to take in her face, not Irene's, hers, Joanna's. A face so ordinary it was like looking in the mirror, you hardly even distinguished the features; but so important, standing for everything in the last few years that was good in his life, it was like looking at, oh, an authentic photograph of God or something. Skin and lines and hair, eyes and teeth and nose: what was it that made one set of them so different, that nothing in your life afterwards could be taken out of their context ever again?

'Are you sleeping with anyone tonight?' he asked as casually as he could.

'What, after the show? I hadn't booked anyone.'

'How about sex and a sandwich with me, then?'

'All right. My place, ten-thirty, on the sofa, bring your own coleslaw.'

A furious clearing of the throat whipped Slider's attention to the young PC standing at his elbow with a large brown envelope in his hand and a sappy grin slithering self-consciously about his chops. 'This came in for you, sir. Sergeant Nicholls thought you'd like it straight away.'

'Thank you, Ferris.'

Joanna watched him open it, smiling privately that a man of his age could still be self-conscious about being caught holding hands with his lady-love. And he'd probably use a word like lady-love, too, at least to himself.

Inside the envelope was the forensic report on the whisky glasses and bottle.

'Ah, now this is interesting,' Slider said. 'You know that we found two glasses, one on the table and one down beside the other chair?' Joanna nodded. 'The glass on the table has Paloma's fingermarks and lipmarks all over it.'

'Lipmarks?'

'Oh yes, they're quite distinctive too.'

'I must remember not to kiss my victims from now on.'

'Not with wet lipstick, anyway. The glass on the floor also has Paloma's fingermarks on it, but they're overlaid by various smudges and marks consistent with its having been held by a hand wearing a leather glove. And it has lip marks on the rim which do not match Paloma's.'

'So he had a visitor,' Joanna said.

'A visitor who didn't take off his gloves.'

'Unusual,' she conceded. 'Unless he had hives. I suppose the phantom tippler must have been the murderer, then?'

'It's a working supposition. Which suggests that Paloma must have known him,' Slider said. 'But that doesn't square with his having to kick the door in. It's not the usual way of announcing yourself socially. And why would you offer a drink to someone who'd just done that?'

'Well, look,' Joanna said, 'maybe Paloma used both glasses

at different times. He might have been sitting in the other chair earlier, put the glass down, then later wanted another drink and went and fetched a clean glass. Why not? I've done that myself. And if he was a fastidious sort of chap, the old, greasy glass might not have appealed. And then the murderer fancied a nip after he'd bumped him off, so he just used one of the glasses he found handy.'

'But the glass didn't have Paloma's lip marks on it,' Slider said. 'It had only one set of lip prints, on one side of the glass, and the rest of the rim was clean.'

'Maybe the murderer wiped the rim before he drank,' Joanna said. 'A lot of people would, quite instinctively, if they were drinking out of someone else's glass.'

'Hmm,' said Slider. 'But there's something else here,' he tapped the report. 'The whisky bottle has fingermarks on it too. Two sets. One possibly Paloma's, though they're not clear enough to identify with absolute certainty. The other set is over the top of them: a whole palm and five lovely digits, clear as day. Someone grabbed the bottle firmly in a manner consistent with either pouring or glugging from it – someone with an unusually large hand.'

'Didn't you say the footmark on the door was unusually large too?'

'Yes.'

'Then presumably they are a set. The glugger was the murderer.'

'Presumably.'

'So all you've got to do is find him,' Joanna concluded happily, 'and you've got your proof there all ready and waiting.'

Slider turned a page. 'Our mystery guest also left his fingermarks on the light switch. Several times.'

'It was night time,' Joanna pointed out.

'Yes, but the light was off in the morning. I suppose he must have turned it off as he left. And again on the front door. That was when he pulled it to, I suppose.' He turned back and read it all again. 'It's puzzling. Why did he drink out of the glass *and* the bottle? And why did he take his gloves off to pick up the bottle?'

'You want me to solve the whole case for you? He took a drink out of the glass because his nerves were shaken after killing Whatsisname, but that wasn't enough, he needed a good long glug, so he went for the bottle. But he couldn't get the fiddly cap off with his gloves on, so without thinking he took them off. *Voilà!*'

Slider smiled. 'You after a job or something?'

'Well, it's possible, isn't it?'

'Oh yes. There's simply no accounting for the stupidity of the average murderer – thank God, otherwise how would we ever catch 'em?'

He had just got back to his desk when Hart reappeared in his doorway. 'Guv?' He looked up. 'Sorry.' She gave him a wobbly grin. 'I dunno what come over me. Must be them testosterone pills I been taking. No, straight up,' she went on as he began to smile, 'I gotta shave twice a day now. And what you said about rolled-up socks? Don't need 'em. I can write me name in the snow just like anybody else.'

So he told her about the forensic report, as a reward. Hart was jubilant. 'Brilliant! If he's got form, we've got him.'

'Let's hope.'

'In any case, how hard can he be to find, over six foot, massive germans and plates the size of Wandsworth? You see that kicking someone's door in, you don't forget it in a hurry.'

'Off you go then,' he said indulgently, 'and jog some memories.' He stood up. 'I've got to see a man about a taxi.'

'How's that?'

'It just came to me. Busty Parnell said that Paloma went everywhere by taxi too. So he probably went to meet his lover in a cab, and if I can find the right driver, he can give me the address.'

'Brilliant, boss.'

'That's why I get the big money.'

CHAPTER SEVEN

Shades of Brown

The headquarters of Monty's Radio Metrocabs was, like every other taxi garage, cramped, chaotic and filthy. It consisted of two railway arches and the tiny cobbled yard in front of them. Under the arches was the repair and servicing workshop for the cabs, and the front right-hand corner was screened off with two walls of wood and glass to make a tiny office for Monty, into which he squeezed himself with his battered desk, his filing cabinets, and an old tin tray balanced on top of a kitchen stool on which the electric kettle and the coffee making equipment stood in a pool of sad spillings and half-melted sugar. There was no ceiling to his corner, and a single lightbulb dangled down, suspended on fathoms of fraying wire from the curved bricks invisible in the darkness far above. In the worst depths of winter a paraffin heater added its stink to that of Monty's cigars and the pervading odour of petrol, but did little to mitigate the cavernous chill. Every surface was tacky with oil, and overhead Metropolitan Line trains passed at regular intervals in a brain-bouncing, tooth-loosening thunder. It was not an office that welcomed visitors, and that was how Monty liked it. He liked his drivers out driving and making him money, not hanging around the depot complaining.

Across the other side of the yard in a new, brightly-lit and tropically heated portakabin, the radio side of the operation was worked by Monty's wife Rita and his mistress Gloria in a comfortable atmosphere of tea, bourbon biscuits, knitting, family photographs and refained gentility. They called the cabbies 'dear' and 'my pet' and asked tenderly after their wives' ailments, but ruled them with a rod of iron. They would not tolerate the word 'can't', and fined them for bad language on a sliding scale from a simple damn upwards. 'That's twenty pence in the Swear Box, my darling,' they would say primly when some benighted cabbie trying to find an invisible fare at a mythical address let loose with a *bloody* over the air; and such was the force of their personalities that the next time the transgressor was in the yard, he would go into the cabin and pay his dues. The box was emptied every week after the lucrative Saturday Night Swear, and the proceeds went towards taking disabled children on an annual adventure holiday.

'Isn't that doing evil that good may come?' Slider once asked Rita, and she primmed her lips and said, 'I don't suppose the kiddies mind, dear.'

Slider was always amazed by Monty's *ménage à trois*: he couldn't understand why he bothered. The two women were so alike that people often thought they were sisters. They were the same age, height and build, with the same solid, well-corseted figure and the expensively dull clothes of prosperous middle age. Both wore their hair permed and sprayed to the same style by the weekly attentions of the same hairdresser – Rita's was tinted mauve and Gloria's platinum. Both wore their glasses round their necks on a chain – Gloria's made of pearls and Rita's of little gold beads. Gloria's smile had more teeth in it – she had captured Monty by her vivacity, and was now stuck with it, Slider deduced – but otherwise there was nothing to choose between them. Perhaps that was why Monty hadn't.

The two women were the best of friends, and between radio messages chatted seamlessly in the manner of those who know each other's thoughts. They treated Monty with the same arch and half-affectionate exasperation as they treated the cabbies, corrected his manners, deplored his smoking, doctored his ills and chose his clothes. Slider couldn't imagine what Monty got out of it.

Slider tacked past the cabin, hoping to escape notice, though he saw through the brightly lit window that Rita turned her head, her jaws never ceasing to move as she talked to the public, the cabbies and Gloria, switching from one to the other as effortlessly as American TV programmes switch to adverts. Under the right-hand arch a black cab was up on the lift and one of the mechanics, Nick the Greek, waved a friendly spanner at Slider from the inspection pit as he crossed to Monty's office.

Monty removed a cold cigar from his teeth and struggled courteously to his feet. He was a short, wide man with a thick, collapsing face, despairing hair, sad brown eyes behind heavy glasses, and a full lower lip permanently deformed by having to accommodate huge Havana cigars. They were expensive, and the ladies tutted, so he hardly ever smoked them, just lit them and let them go out. That way they lasted.

He seemed glad to see Slider. 'Well, well, well! And what can I do for you today, young sir?'

'Hello, Monty. How's business?'

His face buckled with instant gloom. '*Well* bad,' he said confusingly. 'When is business anything *but* bad? Heads above, just – that's the best we can hope for. It's a wonder I can sleep at night.'

'Come off it, you old fraud,' Slider said. 'I see you driving about in a new Bentley.'

'It's not new, it's two years old,' Monty protested. 'I only got it to give my bank manager confidence, stop him foreclosing on me. I tell you, Mr Slider, I'm brassic. What with the cost of cabs, insurance through the roof, rates up fifty per cent this year, new Health and Safety rules coming off by the yard every week – it's as much as I can do to turn a penny. And Mrs Green is not a well woman, you know.'

'I'm sorry to hear that. She looks bonny enough,' Slider said, glancing towards the cabin.

'My mother,' Monty elucidated. 'She can't manage the stairs, you see, which means either putting in a stair lift, or making her a bedroom downstairs. Either way, it's all expense. And the mortgage enough to make you faint.' He sighed. 'I wouldn't wish this life on a dog, I promise you.'

So Monty lived with his mother as well as his wife and mistress, did he? Perhaps the one phenomenon accounted for the other. 'You know,' Slider said, 'five minutes talking to you does me the power of good. Makes the world outside seem so bright. You should work for the Samaritans.'

'You try getting cabbies to pay up at the end of the week, you'll soon know all about working for charity,' Monty said, and busied himself relighting his cigar. Honour satisfied, he went on more cheerfully, 'Anyway, what can I do for you? I suppose you're on this business of PC Cosgrove? Rotten bloody shame that was, pardon my French. Is there any improvement?'

'He's still in a coma, but stable, they say.'

Monty shook his head. 'Rotten business. He's such a nice geezer, too. He was round here, you know, just a few days before it happened.'

'Was he? What about?'

'Just chewing the fat. He used to pop in from time to time – have a bunny with Rita and Gloria, cuppa tea, time of day, that sort of thing. It was on his way home. How's his wife taking it? I feel sorry for her, another nipper on the way, can't be easy.'

'She's bearing up, I believe. But I'm not on that case – that's Mr Carver's. I'm here about something else – a murder last Tuesday. I want your help.'

'Right you are,' Monty said, looking intelligent. 'Anything I can do. Always happy to assist the boys in blue.'

'I want to trace the cabbie who picked up a fare from the White City on Monday, late morning.' He gave Jay Paloma's address and description. 'He went up to Town somewhere – I want to know where. It could be one of yours. This bloke went everywhere by cab – nervous type – so it's probable he telephoned for a cab and he may well have used your firm.'

'We can soon look that up,' Monty said.

'If not I'd like you to put the word about for me.'

'Fair enough. You're sure it was a black cab?'

'Yes, he didn't trust minicabs.'

'Pity he's dead, then. Can't afford to lose people like that – there aren't enough of 'em. Got a picture?'

'I'm getting them done now. They'll be round this afternoon.'

'Right. Let's go and look at the book of words.'

They went out into the yard together. 'Oh, by the way,' Slider said, 'I'm interested in one of your drivers, Benny by name.'

'Benny the Brief or Benny Bovril?'

'Benny the Brief. Is he all right? Reliable?'

'He's all right,' Monty said. 'He can be a bit of a pain in the neck – too much of this—' He imitated a yacking mouth with his fingers. 'But he's all right. Funny old sort – bit of a reader. Knows a stack about the law. The other drivers take the piss out of him, pardon my French, but they all go to him when they want to know something. Walking encyclopaedia. Is he in trouble?'

'No, no. I just wanted to know if I can believe what he tells me.'

'Oh, he's honest as the day, old Benny. Had a tough break a few months back – his old lady died. The Big C. Went just like that. Been married a coon's age, as well. He took it really hard – sold the house and everything in it, went to live in lodgings, said he couldn't bear to have her stuff around him, reminding him all the time. Worked every hour God sent. I said to him, "Benny," I said, "you'll crack up. Take a rest," I said. But no, he wanted to work. Kept his mind off, he said. He's eased off now, though – not been doing much at all, hardly turned in two tanners last week. Just as well, I suppose, or he'd come to grief, and I'd be sorry to lose him. Funny old bugger, but he's all right.'

They reached the cabin, and Monty climbed the steps and opened the door onto the Yardley scented, pot-plant-benighted bower. 'It's like the hanging gardens of Babel,' Monty muttered over his shoulder for Slider's benefit. The women's voices and the squawk of the radio were like birds' cries: Slider had a momentary vision of Rita and Gloria as brightly-coloured parrots swinging about the tropical branches. But they were nothing if not businesslike. When Monty explained Slider's quest, they consulted the day-book for him without ever ceasing to answer the phone and speak their mysterious incantations to the invisible spirits of the cabbies. But there was no record of a call to that address or anything near it, or for the name of Paloma or McElhinney.

Still, Slider was hopeful as he left the yard. Jay had been as bright and distinctive as his avian namesake, and if Monty circulated the query, someone ought to remember him.

Hart tagged on to Slider as he went past. 'Guv, I got a message for you, but I don't know if it's genuine or not. It sounds like someone's pulling our plonker.'

'What is it?'

'Well, this bloke said his name was Tidy Barnet. I mean, that's gotta be a joke, ennit?'

'He's a snout of mine,' Slider said. Barnet was his real surname. He had had an older brother whose nickname was Scruffy, so Tidy's sobriquet was inevitable. 'What did he want?'

'He just said to say,' Hart looked down at her pad to check it,

'Tidy Barnet says tell Mr Slider to ask Maroon. Does that make sense?'

'It does to me,' Slider said. 'He didn't say ask her what?'

'No, guv. That's absolutely all he said, word for word.'

'Right,' said Slider. They reached his room. 'Have those photographs gone round to Monty's garage?'

'Ten minutes ago. And I've got some good news and some bad news.'

'Bad news first.'

'Them fingerprints off the bottle – all negative. No match in the records. Whoever he is, he's got no recent form.'

'Damn,' Slider said. 'Given the MO, I wouldn't have thought that was his first attempt at violence.'

'Maybe he's too professional to get caught,' Hart offered.

'You'd better pray he's not,' Slider said. 'What's the good news?'

She grinned triumphantly. 'We got a witness.'

'Eye-witness?'

'I spy with my little eye, something beginning wiv B. A big black bugger in boots kicking the door in at half past eleven Tuesday night. Female living opposite. She does office cleaning at nights, and she's just got home, walking along the balcony feeling in her bag for her key, when she hears this wallop, looks across and sees chummy just kicked the door in and going in the flat.'

'You're sure it's the same flat?'

'It's right opposite. She pointed it out to me. Same floor and everything. No mistake, guv.'

'She must have been questioned before. Why didn't she say anything?'

'I looked up the notes, and one of the woodentops knocked on her door first time round, but she done the free wise monkeys. When she sees it happen, she just reckons someone's forgot his key, none of her business, right? But when they come round asking about murder, she gets scared. She reckons if she says anything, she's next on the list. So she stays schtumm.'

'How did you persuade her to unbutton?'

Hart grinned. 'You either got it or you ain't. Plus a few freats.'

'You what?' Slider was alarmed.

'Oh, nothing too pointed,' Hart said airily.

'What description did she give you? Did she get a good look at him?'

'Not really. Well, those flats are lit up like Colditz on a bad night, but he had his back to her, and she wasn't stopping to stare.'

'But you say she thought it was the occupant who had forgotten his key? She thought it was Paloma, in fact?'

'Oh, she never knew Paloma. Never knew who lived opposite. It's like that in them flats. You know the people on your own balcony – sometimes – but that's that. The block opposite's like the other side of a river and the bridge is out. Different country. Strange natives wiv peculiar customs.'

'Thank you, Michaela Dennis.'

'Who?'

'Skip it. So we've got nothing at all by way of description?'

'Well, she said he was black. And he was big.'

'The PC could have told her that.'

'Yeah, but I asked her how big, and she said like massive. As he went in the flat, he had to duck his head. Now, I measured and them doors is standard six foot six high.'

'If he's more than six foot six tall he'll be easy to find.'

'Yes, guv,' she said intelligently, 'but he needn't be that big. I mean, internal doors can be anything from six foot, six-three, six-four, yeah? Well, a bloke who's only six-two, six-three can get used to having to duck, and it gets to be a habit. Self-preservation. But there ain't that many blokes six foot three even, and she said he was big with it, like a weight-lifter.'

Slider nodded, thinking. 'Well, if she didn't see his face it's no good trying to get her to come in and look at some pictures. Still, I suppose at least it's further confirmation of the time.'

'That's what I fought. So what's this message, boss? About maroon. Maroon what?'

Slider thought about what had happened last time he went out in the field without telling anyone where he was going, and explained. 'Maroon is a person,' he said. 'Maroon Brown. She's a prostitute, lives in Percy Road.'

'Appropriate,' Hart said. 'Is that her working name?'

'Strangely enough, it's her real name. It's short for Mary Oonagh. She had an Irish grandma who brought her up.'

Slider told what he knew of the story. Maroon's grandma at age sixteen had got herself up the duff by a black stoker from a ship which had put in to Cork Harbour for repairs, and shortly put out again. Rather than face her family she had run away to London to have the baby. The war had just ended and the men were beginning to come home, and she had supported herself by working part time in a café and part time on the game. The baby, named Alice, had grown up to show a preference for her father's lineage, and at sixteen had followed family tradition by succumbing to the charms of a West Indian lorry driver and becoming pregnant.

'Of course, by the time the kid was born the father had already disappeared. So Alice did the same.'

'Leaving grandma holding the baby?'

'Quite. So grandma had her Christened with a fine Irish name, and shortened it to Maroonagh, but everybody either misheard it, or thought it was a joke, so she was Maroon Brown for ever more.'

'So how do you know so much about her, guv?'

'Oh, she gets nicked from time to time. I've seen her around, interviewed her a couple of times. She's not a bad sort.'

'And this snout of yours thinks she knows something about the murder?'

'So it seems.' He paused, weighing probabilities. 'I'm off to have a chat with her. If I take you along, can I trust you to keep your mouth shut?'

Hart looked wounded. 'Follow your lead in all things, that's my rule.'

'Ha!' said Slider.

The house in Percy Road – sounds like a film title, he thought – was one of those miniature grand houses built in the 1840s, semi-detached, three storeys including the semi-basement; where once a senior clerk, with a live-in cook and housemaid, aped the style of his immediate superior, who had much the same only bigger and detached. Now the house had fallen on hard times. It stood at the kink of Percy Road, alone of its type, surrounded by meaner dwellings; seedy and paint-lorn, it had sunk to the ignominy of division into a basement flat and four bedsits. Judging by the bell labels, all the occupants were toms. What would Mr Pooter have thought of that?

Slider gestured to Hart to stand close by the door where the overhang of the shallow porch hid her, and rang the bell. The curtain at the front bay window stirred slightly, and Slider felt himself invisibly considered. He tried to exude unthreateningness. The door did not open, but there was a feeling of activity inside. He rang again. After a further pause the first floor window at the front opened and a female face looked out – black but not Maroon.

'Whajjer want?' it enquired uninvitingly.

Slider stepped back a little and looked up. 'Is Mary there?' he asked.

'There ain't no Mary lives here,' the head said scornfully.

'Mary Brown. Mary Oonagh,' Slider said. The head drew back a little, and seemed to be conferring, if not with its own thoughts then with someone inside.

'You a mate?' it asked doubtfully.

'Yes, I'm an old friend. It's all right, it's not trouble, I just want a chat with Mary.'

'You better come in,' the head said at last. 'Push the door when the buzzer goes, and wait in the hall, orright?'

After a few moments the buzzer went. Slider pushed the door, gestured Hart inside with a finger against his lips, and let the door close again, flattening himself against it. Almost at once the bay window sash was put up, and a foot and leg appeared. He stepped out of the shelter of the porch to find Maroon halfway out, her leading limb reaching perilously over the short railings for the top step. She gave a squeak like a caught mouse when she saw him.

'Hello, Mary. Going somewhere?'

'Oh, bloody hell,' she said, trying to reverse her progress.

'Careful, now, you'll hurt yourself,' Slider said. 'Come on, love, I just want a chat. You don't need to go all Colditz on me. It's not grief for you.' She stared, wide-eyed, and struggled a little, unable to correct her balance so as to pull herself back. 'I think it'll be easier for you to come the rest of the way out,' Slider said. 'Here, grab my hand. And for God's sake be careful. If you fall on those railings you'll never play the cello again.'

'I don't need your bloody help,' she growled. But he helped

her anyway, keeping a firm grip on her upper arm when she was safely on the ground. She wriggled it experimentally, between fear and anger. 'Let me go, can't you? What was all that Mary cobblers? Nobody calls me that except my mum.'

'Reassurance,' he said. 'I just want to talk, that's all, I promise. Don't make it difficult for yourself.'

She was near to tears, and now that he was close to her he saw that she had been crying a lot recently, and he could smell how afraid she was. She had also been drinking. 'All right,' she said. 'Let's get inside. I don't want anyone seeing you here.'

Despite her acquiescence he kept hold of her until she had opened the door and preceded him in. She started like a terrified deer when she saw Hart lingering in the shadows, but Slider soothed her, introduced Hart, and ushered Maroon into the first room on the left. He half expected her to bolt for the bay window again, but she seemed to have resigned herself, and went straight to the mantelpiece to get a cigarette. The room had been the best parlour of the original house. It had a splendid marble fire surround, which had been horribly, carelessly chipped at some time, and also painted red, though the paint was now abandoning it in sheets. It housed a gas fire of extremely, not to say life-threateningly, mature vintage. The rest of the room contained an unmade double bed, a large wardrobe with a mirrored door, two basket armchairs, a chest of drawers, and a tatty chaise longue covered with dirty yellow damask. The room was wildly untidy, a mess of clothes, papers, empty bottles, crockery and glasses and other clutter.

Maroon lit a cigarette rather shakily. Slider sat down on the chaise longue and watched her. 'You must be in trouble if you were thinking of running away from me,' he said at last. 'Do you want to tell me about it?'

'I s'pose that's what you've come for. Oh Gawd.' Tears began to leak out of her eyes again, and she puffed rapidly at the cigarette as if that might staunch them. She had been quite good-looking once, but her nose and right cheekbone had been broken at some time, giving her a lopsided look, and though she was only thirty-two or three, drink, cigarettes and her general lifestyle were aging her before her time. She looked entirely West Indian, except for the higher cheekbones and slightly narrower face which was all she had inherited from her grandmother.

Her hair was closely plaited into windrows from front to back, finishing off with eight little plaited tails tagged with red beads. Her eyes were bloodshot and heavy-shadowed as she looked at Slider miserably, but without flinching. 'I had nothing to do with it, I swear to you. That's the honest trufe. I'd never do anything to hurt Andy. Christ, you must know that.'

Slider heard, comprehended, and made the mental adjustment without external sign; willing Hart, standing by the door, not to move or look at him. Not Paloma, then. He had been sent here for the flip side: she had information about Andy Cosgrove. 'If you had nothing to do with it, then you've got nothing to fear, have you?' he said.

She moaned and sat down on the end of the bed. 'You don't understand.'

'Is someone putting the frighteners on you?' Slider asked. 'You can't be scared of me, surely?'

Maroon looked up, and Hart saw that indeed, she wasn't afraid of him. How did he do it, she wondered? Must be pheremones. Maroon had already forgotten Hart. Her eyes were fixed on Slider with appeal, but she was going to come across. Hart almost held her breath, not to disturb the delicate balance.

'Oh Gawd, oh poor Andy,' Maroon said. 'How is he? Do you know how he is? I tried ringing the hospital, but they wouldn't tell me nothing. The word on the street is he's still in a coma. Is that right? Is he going to die?'

'I don't know,' Slider said, feeling his way with a sense of eggshells underfoot. 'They say he's stable, but of course they're very anxious that he should regain consciousness soon. The longer he's out, the worse it is.'

She put her face in her hands. 'If I'd known how it would end, I'd never have asked him to help me. But I didn't know. I thought he'd just – you know – start the ball rolling. Pass it over to your side. I never thought he'd go asking questions himself. Oh, my poor Andy!'

Her poor Andy? Slider's ears were out on stalks, but he spoke matter-of-factly. 'How did you and Andy first meet? I've often wondered.'

'When I lived on the estate of course.'

'The White City Estate?'

'Yeah. He arrested me for drunk and disorderly outside the

General Smuts one night. I was only nineteen. I was all right then – before I got this.' By 'all right' she meant in looks. She reached up and touched the broken side of her face delicately, as though it still hurt; probably it still did in her psyche. 'I got let off with a caution, and he come back the next day, when he got off duty.' She smiled shakily. 'Wanted to reform me – talk me into going straight. "You could get a job," he said. I didn't know whether to laugh or cry. I mean, me! What could I do? I been on the game since I was sixteen. I don't know nothing else. But he got to me. He was so—' She hunted for a word.

'Earnest?' Slider offered.

'Yeah. Like that. For him it was like, the whole world was a good guy really, you know? He wasn't long married then, and his wife was expecting their first. Little Adam.' Her face softened at the name. Blimey, she knows all the history, Slider thought. 'He was so happy, he thought he could change the world. Bleeding sunshine merchant. He even had me believing for a bit.' She nodded, her eyes round with the wonder of it. 'I tried getting a job, on the checkout down Gateway, just to please him. But I couldn't stand it, getting up every morning and sitting there all day, bloody customers treating you like dirt, yes-sir-no-sir while the manager looks down your front, dirty old git. And the end of the week, what'd you got to show for it? Peanuts. So I chucked it.'

'And what did Andy think of that?'

'Oh, I kept out of trouble in those days, so I didn't see much of him, unless I happened to see him walking down the street. No, it was later I got to know him really well. After I got away from Billy Yates.'

'Billy Yates?'

A look of great bitterness crossed her face. 'Yeah. Him. I'll tell you about him, but you can't use it.' Now she glanced at Hart, aware of her danger. 'You gotta promise me. He'd have me killed like you'd stamp on a beetle. D'you want to hear it all?'

'Very much,' Slider said.

'Lock that door, then,' she nodded to Hart, and got up and closed the window and pulled the curtains. Hart put the light on. Maroon crossed the room and put a rap tape on the cassette player, turning it up to a conversation-covering pitch. She was that scared, Slider thought. Hart had taken out her notebook, but Maroon looked at her sharply. 'Nothing written down. You can stay if he says. But you can't use any of this.'

'I vouch for Hart,' Slider said. 'Go on.'

Maroon sat on the bed and crossed her legs, putting the ashtray and cigarettes down beside her. Evidently it was going to be a long story.

'Billy Yates,' she said.

Billy Yates, it seemed, not only ran nightclubs, casinos and amusement arcades, he also ran a string of girls.

'Night after night you lie on your back thinking sixty per cent of this is for Billy Yates. I got quite good at sums. Take a fifteen minute blow-job: you're gobbling for Billy Yates for nine minutes.' She made a violent sound of disgust. 'But you know what was so creepy about him? He never did it himself. If he'd liked girls, if he'd come round now and then and had one on the house – management perks, like his boys used to – you could almost have liked him better. But he's a cold fish, Billy Yates. He never does it – never done it in his life, if truth be known. And it's not that he's the other way, either. He's not queer. He's just cold as a corpse. He looks at you like you're—' She shook her head. 'But I've seen him with his business pals, and it's all smiles and big cigars and slap-me-back old pals act. We did this trick once, me and this other girl, Jasmine her name was, at some posh hotel up west, up Lancaster Gate. We was supposed to spend the night with some business contact of Billy Yates's. See them come in together, you'd think they was brothers, arms round each other, laughing and joking. Only his eyes never smile. He's making nice to this Arab, and all the time his eyes are going round like a machine, checking everything in the room. Like he's taking photos. Click click click. The bed, the champagne, the lights, the fruity videos. And he looks at Jasmine and me, click click. That's all we was to him, two bits of gear for oiling up this deal.'

But it was unusual for Maroon to see Yates. Normally he ran his girls at arm's length, and that, in its way, was what they resented most. His 'boys' did all the hands-on work. They called themselves doormen or drivers or security guards, but Billy Yates just said, 'I'll send round one of my boys.' They were bouncers in the clubs, croupiers in the casinos, managers in the amusement arcades, and pimps to the girls; they were messengers and chauffeurs and bodyguards and sorters-out of trouble. They collected money and delivered rebukes. They were young, fit, tooled up, and saw themselves as an all-powerful elite. The girls hated and feared them.

'They could do what they liked, as long as they didn't damage the goods.' She shrugged. 'Some of them just wanted to get their end away, they was no trouble, just get on, do it, get off again. But some of them liked to hurt you. And they worked out ways to hurt you so it didn't show.'

Maroon worked for Yates's empire from 1982 until 1988. 'Six long years,' she said in a black voice. She was run by one of Yates's top 'boys', Jonah Lafota. 'We was his best girls, so we got Jonah for our pimp – only you'd never call him that, not if you valued your skin. Our 'manager' he called himself. He was supposed to keep us in order, and look after us, keep the customers from damaging us.' She reached up and touched her face again. 'It was him did this. I suppose I should thank him, because it got me away from Yates.' She gave a bark of ironic laughter. 'I'd kill him if I could,' she said, 'that's how much I want to thank him.'

It had happened one night when she was about to start work, and Jonah had come in and wanted to use her himself. She had protested she had someone waiting. 'I don't know what came over me,' she mused. 'You didn't argue with Jonah. But that night, I just turned round and answered him back. I think he was a bit lit up. Suddenly he just lashed out and hit me.' She demonstrated. 'Backhand, like he was playing bloody tennis. Sent me right across the room and hit the wall. Knocked me out cold. When I came to, I was in hospital with my face all broken.' She shook her head. 'Billy Yates was furious. If it had been anybody but Jonah, I don't know what he would have done to him. As it was, he just demoted him.' She shrugged. 'Me, I was let go. I couldn't work for Yates with this face.'

'You didn't go to the police?' Slider said, more to keep her talking than because he thought she might have.

She looked derisive. 'You kidding? Jonah would have killed me. I was lucky he hadn't killed me as it was, hitting me like that. Like I said, I think he was a bit lit up, because normally he was careful. He never hit people, or if he did he kind of pulled his punch, because he's a monster, is Jonah. Six foot six and built like a brick khasi, with hands on him like—' She demonstrated with her hands apart. 'So he'd gotta be careful.'

Hart stirred, and out of the corner of his eye, Slider saw her look towards him. Maybe they were here for the Paloma case after all. Maybe there was a connection that hadn't been suspected.

'Do you know where Jonah works now?' Slider asked.

'Oh, he's still with Yates. He's mostly at the Pink Parrot.'

'That's another of his nightclubs, is it?'

'Yeah. Down Fulham Broadway. Used to be a gay club, but it's more mixed now.' Maroon looked from Slider to Hart and back, the cosy confidence she had built up for herself evaporating. 'I don't want him to find me,' she said urgently. 'D'you understand? He'll kill me if he knows I've spoken to you.'

'You haven't told me anything against him yet,' Slider pointed out soothingly.

'He wouldn't care about that. If he even saw me talking to you—' She wrapped her arms round herself. 'You gotta promise me.'

'I promise you,' Slider said. 'I won't use your name. I'll find some other way. Go on now.' She still hesitated, so he primed her with the irresistible. 'Tell me about you and Andy.'

CHAPTER EIGHT

A Whale of a Tale

When Maroon was still in hospital with her broken face, Andy Cosgrove had come to visit her. He heard the word on the street, and came to see if he could help her.

'He was shocked when he saw what Jonah had done to me. He tried to get me to make an official complaint, so he could arrest Jonah, but I wouldn't. But anyway, after that he kind of interested himself in me. Andy helped me find somewhere to live and – well – he was around a lot and—' She shrugged eloquently.

'You became lovers,' Slider offered delicately.

Maroon was pleased with the euphemism. 'Yeah,' she said. 'That's it.' Reading between the lines, Slider guessed that from Cosgrove's point of view it was a case of the seven year itch. His marriage was no longer new, and his wife had begun to discover that being a copper's wife was not all roses, which had soured her temper. She had just had another child and sex was off-limits, and the baby was making the nights hideous. Cosgrove had succumbed to the comforts a grateful ex-whore was more than willing to offer. Slider was not surprised – it was a story he had heard many times before – but he was rather shocked that it was Andy Cosgrove, the Father Christmas of W12, who had sinned so callously against his wife. It seemed, however, that an affection had built up between Cosgrove and Maroon beyond mere sexual gratification, and he had done her a great deal of good. The affair had taken on a regular, almost domesticated pattern, and, his needs being satisfied, Cosgrove had begun to be a better husband at home too.

And then Maroon's sister turned up, come to the big city to seek her fortune.

'I didn't know you had a sister,' Slider said.

'Nor did I,' Maroon said.

It seemed that when Maroon's mother Alice had fled parental responsibility, she had headed up the A1, the Great North Road, which in those days had a romance and glamour to its name, and also led in the direction it was possible to get the furthest away from London. Over the years, Alice kept moving north. Occasionally when conscience bit or good luck came her way, she sent some money for her mother or a birthday card for her abandoned infant, and in that way she and Maroon's grandma kept in distant touch.

Eventually Alice reached Aberdeen, and feeling it impracticable to go any further north, settled down within handy reach of the docks. One day she found herself pregnant again. It was not at all in her plans to bring up a child, and as soon as the baby was born she hastened to her mother, who by then had moved back to Ireland, Maroon having left home. Alice arrived one day with baby Molly and left the next, in the early hours, without her. She had told her mother nothing about the baby's father except that he was Maltese – there was a large community of immigrants from Malta living in Aberdeen. Grandma, resigning herself to another surrogate motherhood, referred to the baby affectionately as 'my little Maltesa', and the nickname stuck.

'And you didn't know anything about her until she arrived on your doorstep?' Slider asked.

'Well, I never was one for writing letters, and Gran never got round to it,' Maroon said. 'Anyway, one day, about a year after I left Billy Yates, this kid turns up and says, hello Maroonagh, I'm your sister. She was just sixteen. Gawd, she was pretty!' Maroon's face softened with remembered delight. 'Brown eyes and hair like mine, but not dark like me, kind of honey-coloured skin, and sharp little features like a little cat. And she was bright, too, up for everything, always on the bubble. I loved her to death. All I wanted was the best for her. I never wanted her to go on the game like me. I wanted her to get a job and get married, do everything properly, like I never done.'

Everything would have been all right, if it wasn't for Jonah Lafota. He blamed Maroon for his demotion, and wanted his revenge on her, but felt that her close liaison with the local community copper made her a dangerous target. When Maltesa came to town, it looked like the perfect opportunity to make Maroon suffer.

'He went after her. I didn't know at first. He sweet-talked her, showed her the bright lights, told her how much money she could make as a high-class call girl, if she had the right manager. *Manager!*' She spat the word. 'When I found out, I was furious. I nearly snatched her bald-headed, told her if she wanted to throw her life away, she might as well go and jump off Westminster Bridge and get it over with. Of course, it was the wrong thing to say to Maltesa. She never would take telling. Got on her high horse right away. I tried everything I could, but she wouldn't listen. She said she could make a fortune in a couple of years, and then we could go off and live in Spain or somewhere. Oh, she was full of it!' Maroon said bitterly. 'Like any little kid dreaming of Christmas, it was all going to be so easy. And she could take care of herself, I needn't worry, she was up to all the tricks, no-one was going to take her for a ride.'

There was a heavy silence. 'What happened?' Slider asked at last.

'Jonah introduced her to drugs. She thought it was all part of the high life, and she could handle it. Of course she couldn't. Gradually she just – disappeared. Jonah made her work for her fixes, and she did things she didn't want to tell me about, so I saw her less and less. I pleaded with her, but it only turned her against me. She changed, that kid – her whole personality. It'd break your heart to see her moody and sullen like she was towards the end. I don't know what she was doing for Jonah at the finish, but he made sure she still got the stuff. She died in 1994. She was only twenty. *He* did that.' There was a pause while she lit another cigarette from the stub of the current one. 'She was a good kid at heart, just too full of spirit. Ready to try anything. She was easy meat to him. I'd have done anything to save her, but there was nothing I could do. After she died, I just wanted to run away. I think I went a bit mad. I drank a lot. I left the flat and moved around, bedsitters and that. There didn't seem any point in anything any more. And then Andy found me again.' She looked up. 'I hadn't told him anything. He didn't know what happened to Maltesa. He didn't know where I'd gone. I should've told him, I suppose. He was worried about me, bless him. Well, he found me, I don't know how. I told him everything, and – and I begged him to get Jonah for what he'd done to my sister. I didn't have any proof, you see. I must have been mad to try and get him involved. I should've known how it would end.'

'What did Andy promise to do?'

'First off he went to some boss man in your place,' she nodded to Slider, 'to ask for a proper investigation. I forget his name, but he was some high-up detective, Barlow or Barnet or some such—'

'Barrington?' Slider said, hiding his astonishment. How had he heard nothing of this?

'Yeah, could be. Anyway, Andy told this bloke everything, and this Barrington or whatever, he told Andy there was no way he could investigate it, and he told Andy to drop it. Absolutely forbid him to mention it to anyone. Andy was really shaken. He thought maybe this Barrington was in league with Billy Yates, maybe they was both masons or something, because Billy Yates has got loads of friends in high places – *you* must know that – which is why he's never got into trouble with the law. But anyway, Andy said to me don't worry, he'd go into it himself, and when he'd got the evidence, this Barrington'd have to do something.' She puffed rapidly on her cigarette; her voice was growing husky with too much smoke, taken too hot. 'I should've stopped him – except I don't suppose he would've stopped for me, not once he'd got the idea in his head. Stubborn as a donkey, Andy. But I never thought – I never thought—' She swallowed hard. 'Jonah must've got wind of what he was doing, and done him over. And he'll come after me next. That's why you mustn't tell anyone where I am. Don't write it down anywhere. And don't come here again – promise me!'

'Maroon—'

'And get Jonah!' she added fiercely. 'Forget the other, just promise me that! I don't care any more if he gets me, as long as you get him. I'd kill him if I could, but look at me—' She spread her arms. 'What could I do against a bloke his size? So you got to do it for me. If he ain't dead, I want him locked up, and throw away the key, for what he did to my poor Maltesa, and my poor Andy!'

When Slider swung the wrong way onto Uxbridge Road, Hart

turned to look at him, and wondered at the grim concentration on that usually benign face.

'Guv?' she said tentatively. 'Was that straight up, d'you reckon, or was she spinning a yarn?'

'I think she was telling the truth as she knows it,' Slider said, his voice vague from the depths of thought.

'But that stuff about Mr Barrington – he was the Super before Mr Honeyman, wasn't he?'

'Yes,' Slider said.

'Didn't he commit suicide?'

'Yes,' Slider said, reluctantly. Hart was silent. 'I don't know,' he answered her unasked question. 'I'd hesitate to think it for a moment. Mr Barrington had been under a lot of strain, but he never did anything to make me think he was corruptible.'

And yet, Slider thought, hadn't he always felt a mental question mark hanging like a dark cloud over the winding up of the Cate business? It was not something he would ever discuss, not even with Atherton, not even with Joanna: but Barrington had been very close to Colin Cate, had hero-worshipped him, and when Cate turned out to have feet of clay, Barrington was shaken to his roots. He had left the building without saying where he was going, returning hours later in a state of nervous exhaustion, without explaining his whereabouts. And it was during those hours that Colin Cate had been shot dead by a marksman with a rifle. Barrington, who had killed himself only a few weeks later, had been a notable shot in the army, and had trophies galore from his shooting club.

Was it possible that Barrington had been as bent as Cate? That his relationship with Cate was not that of the innocent patsy, which Slider had always assumed? That he had had a corrupt relationship with that other powerful local businessman, Billy 'The Pom' Yates?

'You're not to mention this, Hart,' he said. 'This is absolutely taboo, do you understand?'

'Sir.'

'I will put an investigation in train as to what, if anything, Cosgrove said to Barrington and vice versa, but it's a very delicate business, and I shall have to tread carefully. So I don't want any gossip muddying the waters. Not a word of this to anyone. If it gets out, I shall know it was you that spread it, and you'll be stuck on so fast your eyes will spin like a fruit machine, savvy?'

'Yes, sir.' They rode in silence for a while. Then Hart said, 'The other business, sir, the Paloma case – it looks as if it could have been this Jonah that whacked him, dunnit? I mean, Paloma worked for Yates, and there can't be that many six-foot-sixers with humungous plates knocking about.'

'It's hard to resist that conclusion,' Slider said. 'But what did Jonah have against Paloma?'

'If Jonah's one of Yates's hard men, maybe Yates told him to rub Paloma.'

'That just moves the question one pace sideways – what did Yates have against Paloma?'

'And where does Andy Cosgrove fit in?' Hart ruminated a moment. 'D'you think there's some drugs connection? If Cosgrove was trying to find out where Jonah got the stuff from, Yates might've started thinking he was a nuisance he could do without. And Paloma was supposed to be buying drugs for his friend.' She stopped, lost, and finally shrugged. 'I dunno. But I can't help feeling there's got to be a connection.'

'There's no fire without smoke,' Slider finished for her. 'Well, at least we've got some lines to follow up.'

'Talking of following, where are we going, boss?' Hart asked, taking the opportunity.

Slider looked about him. They were in Acton High Street. 'Why didn't you tell me I was going the wrong way?'

Atherton was looking much better. 'They've taken out some of the tubes,' Slider observed.

'I'm on liquids,' Atherton said. 'No-one looks their best with that much plastic around. You, on the other hand, look terrible.'

'I'm just tired. I've knocked off for an early night.' It was a quarter to eight, but Atherton knew the score and nodded. 'Joanna's got a session until nine, but it's only at Barnes, so she should be home by half past. I thought I'd have some grub ready for her.'

'Not the Seduction Special? Your spag bol?'

'It's not the only thing I cook. You talk as if I was a one-trick pony.'

Atherton looked wistful. 'I'd be glad to be able to eat hospital jelly and Dream Topping.'

'You will, Oscar, you will. The improvement from last week is amazing. Once they take those drains out—'

'Talking of drains, how's the case coming along?'

'We've got a suspect, one Jonah Lafota. Ever heard of him?'

'No.'

'Figures. He's got no record, damn him. And we've got no evidence against him.'

'So what makes him a suspect?'

'The fact that he's very big, and whoever kicked in Paloma's door had big feet, and an eye-witness says the kicker was very tall; and that he works for Billy Yates.'

'But you've got some fingerprints?' Atherton said. 'Then ask him for a set to compare. You've got him either way, then.'

'We'd be delighted to ask him, but we don't know where he is.'

'Can't you ask Yates?'

'Yates says he sacked him a week ago. Yates has a pleasant knack of sacking people just before they become notorious. We tried the address Yates gave us from his records, but of course Jonah wasn't there. We're watching the place, and we've put out word that we want to speak to him. So we're just on hold as far as that goes.'

'Yates must be feeling pretty uncomfortable, if he's got rid of this bloke so quickly. What reason did he give for sacking him?'

'He says Jonah came to work improperly dressed. No tie and a dirty shirt. He never gives warnings or second chances.'

'Nice man.'

'It's convenient, if you want to dissociate yourself quickly from anything that niffs a bit.'

'Yes, but you can't do that too often and retain your tingling-fresh aroma,' Atherton said. He studied Slider's face. 'What is it in particular that's bothering you about Yates?'

Slider hesitated; but it was so natural to confide in Atherton, and Atherton had been there all through the Cate business. 'This is in confidence,' he said. Atherton nodded, and he told him the story of Maroon, Cosgrove and Barrington.

Atherton whistled soundlessly. 'Old Andy Cosgrove? Who'd a thunk it?'

'Yes, even I hadn't expected that one. But – well, you know the temptations.'

'None better,' Atherton smirked.

'The worrying bit is the question of why Barrington told him to drop it.'

'You believe this Mahogany?'

'Maroon.'

'Whatever. After all, she's only a tom, and you can't believe everything they say.'

'She's pretty straight,' Slider said. 'She's one of the old sort, not like some of the foul-mouthed little bitches you get nowadays. I think as far as this particular business goes, she's telling the truth.'

'As she knows it.'

'Yes, that's the trouble. Barrington's dead and Cosgrove's in a coma, and who else would know what, if anything, either said to the other?'

'Well, you can't go tramping in asking people like Honeyman or Wetherspoon if Barrington was in league with the villains,' Atherton observed. 'In fact, I don't see that you can ask anyone on Barrington's side. What about Andy Cosgrove? Who would he be likely to confide in?'

'I've been thinking about that,' Slider said. 'The trouble is, you get a bit solitary and autonomous being a community cop. No regular partner, no-one you work with, and if this was a secret investigation anyway—'

'Did he have any close friends?'

Slider shook his head. 'Not in the Job.'

'What about his wife?'

'Ah, what? I don't know if he was used to confiding in her, but I wonder how likely it was that he'd chat to her about investigating the death of the addict sister of his prostitute mistress? And given that she's pregnant and spending all her time at his hospital bedside, I hardly like to ask her.'

'Well,' said Atherton comfortingly, 'the Cosgrove case isn't your baby. Why not hand what you've been told over to Mr Carver and let him worry about it?'

'Hmm. I suppose I must in fairness tell him what Maroon said. But if it was Jonah that killed Paloma, the cases must be connected.'

'I don't see why. You don't know it was Jonah whacked Cosgrove. You haven't the slightest evidence or indication. And Cosgrove might not even have spoken to Barrington. He might just have told Maroon that to fob her off.'

'How clear and simple you make everything seem,' Slider complained.

'It's lying here with a brain untrammelled by the daily grind. If you bring me all your evidence day by day, I'll solve the case for you without ever setting foot outside my own bed.'

'Thank you, Mycroft,' said Slider.

'Well, if I've got all the brains, it stands to reason you can't have any.'

'But you've got the looks, too,' Slider objected.

'You'll have to settle for Miss Congeniality,' Atherton said kindly. But suddenly he was exhausted. Slider saw it come over him. It was frightening to see the colour and animation drain so abruptly from his face.

'Are you all right?'

'Just tired,' said Atherton, as though a longer sentence would have been beyond him.

'I'd better go and let you sleep. Shall I call a nurse?' Shake. 'Anything you want?' Shake. 'All right. I'll try and get in tomorrow, but even if I can't make it, Joanna will come.'

He was almost at the door when he heard Atherton say sleepily, 'How's my cat?'

He turned back. 'He's fine. Eating like a horse. Well, eating horse, probably. Seriously, he's settled in very well. Misses you, though. He'd come and visit, but they don't let in anyone under eleven.'

'He's fourteen,' Atherton murmured, his eyes almost shut.

'I'll bring him next time, then, if I can find his birth certificate. They won't pass him otherwise. He doesn't look a day over nine.' No response. Slider looked gravely at his colleague's white face for a moment, and then went quietly out.

On the way home, Slider got out of the car at the phone boxes on the corner of Chiswick Lane and phoned Tidy Barnet.

'Can you talk?'

'Hang on.' A pause. 'Right, all right. You got my message?'

'Thanks, Tidy. It was the goods. Unfortunately it was the

goods on the wrong lorry. I'm not doing Cosgrove, I'm doing Paloma.'

'No names, Mr S. Not over the dog,' Tidy winced. 'You was lookin' for a certain party what smacked a certain iron 'oof, right? Well, the way I 'ear it, this certain other party from Wales, right? was the one what done it. Word is, it was a accident, party from Wales was elephant's trunk, right? Only meant to put the frighteners on 'im. Whacks 'im a bit too 'ard, and lo and be'old instead of frightened 'e's brown bread. But that's who it was all right, right?'

'So I'm looking in the right direction?'

'Right as ninepence.'

Now all I've got to do is prove it, Slider thought as he hung up. And find out what the hell is going on. Jonah – party from Whales, he thought further, with a derisive snort, as he climbed into his car. Tidy was a card all right. Right?

Slider was just coming out of the men's room when he met DI Carver about to go in. 'Ron, have you got a minute?' Carver grunted, which might have meant yes or no, and left Slider to follow him in. 'It's about the Cosgrove case. Is there any improvement, by the way?'

'Nah. He's still unconscious.' Carver turned on the tap and began washing his hands. 'It's over a week now. If he doesn't come out of it soon, they'll transfer him to the coma wing, and you know what that means. It's poor Maureen I feel sorry for. That woman's a miracle, sits by his bed hour after hour talking to him, in case he can hear her. How she copes with that and two kids as well!'

'I thought you ought to know, some information has come my way, about something Andy was apparently involved in,' Slider said. Carver made no reply. He began scrubbing his nails vigorously, and Slider gathered he was being aggressively uninterested in what Slider had to say – a warning off from his territory. Carver had been born with a grudge, and defended it jealously against any encroachment from the mellowing of age or the operation of human kindness.

Slider raised his voice over the ablutions, and recounted what Maroon had said. Before he could finish, however, Carver interrupted him.

'Look, Bill, Andy's a good cop, one of the best, and I don't think this sort of muck-raking is going to help him get well, do you? It's well out of order, to my mind, to gossip about him when he's flat on his back fighting for his life.'

Slider felt for a foothold. 'I'm not muck-raking, Ron, I'm bringing information to your notice that might help you find out who attacked him.'

Carver turned off the tap and straightened, meeting Slider's eye angrily in the mirror. 'Oh are you? Well thank you very much, but when I need your help I'll ask for it. I happen to know all about his affair with Brown already. It was all over a long time ago, and considering what poor Maureen is going through at the moment, I don't think it will help her to drag it all up again!'

Slider repressed the desire to smack Carver in the puss, and sought out his most conciliatory tones. 'Ron, I'm not trying to tread on your toes. You didn't let me finish. Maroon apparently asked Andy to investigate something for her, and if he did start asking questions it could have made him unpopular in certain quarters.' He gave Carver the details, leaving out any mention of Barrington, and was glad to see that Carver was listening intelligently.

When he finished, Carver said in a tone that was at least meant to be reasonable, 'Right. I see. Well, thanks for the info, Bill. I'll certainly take it on board. But if I were you, I wouldn't put too much credence on what a tom tells you.'

'You haven't heard that he *was* asking questions, then?' Slider said, disappointed.

'I told you, him and Brown was ancient history. He wouldn't put himself on the line for her. If she had any real information, he'd have passed it up to us in the proper manner, and since he didn't, you can take it as read he knew there was nothing in it. It was just a tom's grudge-talk. You said yourself she had it in for this pimp. No, Andy would have just said something to soothe her, that's all, and kept his distance. With Maureen in pod again, he's not going to do anything risky, is he?'

Slider nodded, unconvinced. 'Right you are,' he said. 'But if anything does come up, if you do come across anything that seems to bear on that line of investigation, you will let me know?'

'What's your interest in it, then?' Carver asked, without agreeing that he would.

Slider said the wrong thing. 'It's Paloma. I'm beginning to get a feeling that the two cases may be connected.'

Carver gave him his most boiled look. 'Oh, I doubt that. I doubt that very much.'

'All the same, I've had word from one of my snouts—'

'You've got your sources and I've got mine,' Carver said. 'Let's leave it at that, shall we?'

'But if—'

'I'll pass on anything I think you ought to know,' Carver said, heading for the door. 'Rest assured about that.' The door sighed closed behind him.

'Bastard,' Slider said quietly, but with feeling.

CHAPTER NINE

Custardy Sweet

There was excitement in the CID room. A lift had been taken off the front door of Jonah Lafota's flat, and now the comparison with the whisky-bottle print had come back positive.

'It's enough to bring him in, isn't it, guv?' McLaren pleaded. He had been watching the flat and felt he was due some reward for the boredom.

'How close is the agreement?' Slider asked.

'Sixty per cent. But that's because lift off the door wasn't much cop. With a proper set of prints off him, we can get it perfect.'

It was the first thing that even approximated to real evidence. 'You've still got to find him,' Slider pointed out.

Hart, who had just come in, said, 'Are you talking about Jonah?' She advanced to the middle of the group and grinned sassily. 'I know where he is.' When the clamour died down she said, 'I got it off a source of mine, that he's got this girlfriend called Candy that he's very hot with at the moment. Candy Williams, supposed to be a bit of a looker—'

'Looker, did you say, or hooker?' McLaren interrupted.

Hart made a rocking motion of her hand. 'She calls herself an actress, but basically she's done soft porn, magazines and films, and she's also worked for Yates. Table dancer. She's got a flat in that new block down by the river by Hammersmith Bridge – Waterside Court, I think it's called.'

'They're luxury flats,' Anderson said. 'The knocking business must be good.'

'Anyway,' Hart concluded triumphantly, 'apparently Jonah's been shacked up with her ever since Yates sacked him.'

'Who's your source?' Slider asked.

She turned to him, lowering her eyelashes demurely. 'I can't reveal my source's name. Fair's fair, guv. He's my snout.'

Slider gave her a long look. He suspected she had been hanging round Garry from the Pomona in defiance of his orders. He was going to have to have a heart to Hart with her on the subject as soon as they had time.

'All right. Give me five minutes to have a word with Mr Honeyman—'

'Oh, guv, talking of Mr Honeyman,' McLaren said, 'before I forget, the card's on your desk for you to sign. There's just you left, unless you want Jim Atherton to sign it as well.'

'I think he should, don't you?' Slider said. 'I'll take it with me, then, the next time I go and see him.'

While Slider talked, Honeyman listened at first eagerly, then with growing doubt. 'Oh dear, it's not very much, is it? I was hoping you'd manage to clear this one up really quickly.'

A quick result on a murder case would be a lovely final flourish on Little by Little's career. Slider stole a glance at his amazing Robert Robinson hairdo and his heart softened.

'I know we haven't got much, but Lafota looks good. One of my snouts has positively fingered him. Once we arrest him we can search his drum, take samples, pin him down. I think we can bring it home, sir.'

Honeyman raised hopeful eyes and wagged his tail. 'You think so? All right, but bring him in voluntarily if possible.'

'If possible,' Slider conceded.

Honeyman sighed. 'If Billy Yates wants to make difficulties—'

'Mr Yates seems to be trying to distance himself from Lafota, sir,' Slider comforted him. 'Could I have a word with you about something else? Something rather – delicate?'

Honeyman looked startled. 'Oh – er – yes, by all means.'

Probably thinks I want to discuss my matrimonial troubles with him, Slider thought, as he reached round behind him and closed the door. 'It's about Mr Barrington, sir.' Slider recounted a brief history of Maroon, Maltesa and Cosgrove. 'The difficulty is, trying to establish whether Cosgrove did speak to Mr Barrington on the subject, and what was said.'

'Why should you want to?' Honeyman asked, which was a

better reaction than Slider had feared. He had expected an indignant I-don't-like-what-you're-suggesting slap down.

'Well, sir, it occurred to me, if for some reason Mr Barrington did refuse an investigation, Cosgrove might have carried on under his own steam and buzzed about some people who decided to swat him.'

'What does Carver say? It's his case, after all.'

'He thinks Miss Brown is making it up. But I don't think she is.'

Delicater and delicater – rivalry between firms was not unusual, but it was never comfortable. Honeyman was thoughtful. 'I really think you would do better to concentrate on your own investigation, and leave the Cosgrove business to Carver. We won't achieve anything by duplicating efforts.'

'No, sir,' Slider said. 'But I have the feeling that the two cases may be connected – that Lafota may be in the frame for both attacks, and that Yates may be behind it in some way.'

'That's a lot of suppositions,' Honeyman said, but his eyes were distant, preoccupied. 'You were right that this is a delicate business. However, I am prepared to trust your instincts, and I will make some enquiries for you. I shall have to tread carefully, so don't expect overnight results. In the meantime, forget all about this conversation, concentrate on your own case, and don't do anything to get in the way of Carver's enquiries.'

'No, sir. Thank you,' Slider said. He was agreeably surprised at Honeyman's co-operation, and wondered with a renewed spasm of internal conflict whether his own doubts about Barrington were shared higher up. It was all too easy to succumb to a conspiracy complex. Honeyman's advice – or was it an order – was sound. He would do his best to forget about it.

He went back to give the good word to the troops, stopping off at his own room to pick up some papers. Prominently on his desk was the card McLaren had bought for Honeyman. He picked it up. On the front was a grinning pink cartoon mouse, holding a bottle of champagne in its paws. It had evidently been shaking it, Grand Prix style, because the champagne was gushing out behind a flying cork, and bursting bubbles and pink party streamers dotted the rest of the space. Across the top was the word CONGRATULATIONS. Slider opened the card. It had no printed message, but in the middle of the recto page, surrounded by the Department signatures, was written in careful capitals ON YOUR PREMATURE DISCHARGE.

'*McLaren!*' Slider roared.

In the confined spaces of the custody room, Jonah Lafota looked like Alice in W Rabbit's house. He was a huge man, not just tall, but massive as well, as if he had been built for a planet with stronger gravity. His muscles moved about in his thighs and upper arms as if on business of their own, and though he wore a fashionable double-breasted suit in a lamentable shade of light grey-green, it seemed to have been cut specifically to prove that you can't get a body like that into a suit. His hair was cropped close, but with the obligatory small thin pigtail at the nape of the neck; his ears were small and set very high on his skull, and he wore tiny gold earrings in the sparse lobes. His huge hands, lightly curled, hung like knobkerries down by his side. Despite his bulk, Slider guessed he would move quickly and lightly.

He was very black, and his wide nose had been further flattened by being broken and, Slider guessed, having the bone removed. Despite noticing this, Slider found it hard to take in his features, impossible to say whether he was good-looking or not, because all the eye would register was his sheer size. Slider had a moment of pity: what must it be like to live all your life with such difference upon you? Men longed to be tall and strong, but Jonah was a freak, a *lusus naturae*. What woman could he lie with without crushing her? What conversation could he join in with without bending down? Furniture would moan under him, doors admit him grudgingly, clothes and shoes reject him outright. What life was there for him, but to be someone's hard man, a blunt instrument for someone else's anger, but never a full member of the human race?

And then Slider remembered Jay Paloma, turned into something that would put Francis Bacon off his lunch, and hardened his heart.

'I'm Detective Inspector Slider, and this is Detective Sergeant Hollis. I'd like to ask you a few questions about Jay Paloma.'

'I don' hafta tell you nuffing,' Jonah said without emphasis. Sitting down he was about as tall as Slider standing up, which seemed to make his point irrefutable. Slider decided to ignore it.

'Do you know Jay Paloma?'

'Yeah, know him. He use come downa club.' He slurred his words, not as a drunk does, but in the manner of one who does not have to say very much to get his message across. He sat back on the small chair, his fists resting on the table, looking in a lordly way at the wall or the ceiling, anywhere but at Slider. He didn't seem nervous, angry or afraid. He didn't seem anything at all, really, except big.

'Which club?'

'Pink Parrot.'

'When did you last see him?'

'Jay? Dunno.'

'Roughly when? Give me some idea.'

'I don't see him there no more. He works downa Pomona.'

'When were you last at the Pomona?'

'Dunno.'

'Days ago? Weeks ago?'

'I go there sometimes. If Mr Yates wants me. I ain't been there a long time.'

Slider noted the use of the present tense. 'I understood that Mr Yates had sacked you.'

That produced a reaction. Jonah's eyes flicked towards Slider, and a sort of spasm clenched his face and his fists for an instant. He seemed to go through some internal struggle before saying, 'Yeah.'

'When was that?'

'Tuesday morning. I finished four o'clock. Mr Yates told me not to come back.'

'So Mr Yates was at the Pink Parrot?'

'He come round jus' before closing.'

'Was that usual?'

'He goes round all the clubs.'

'Every day?'

'Nah,' Lafota said scornfully. 'What jew fink?'

'Every week?' Lafota shrugged. 'So why did he sack you?' Lafota didn't seem to be able to answer that. His eyes were fixed on the wall beyond Slider and he was breathing like a karate exponent psyching himself up for a pile of house bricks. 'Was it for improper dress?'

'Yeah,' Lafota said at last, on an exhaled breath. Clearly

resentment was fighting with some other emotion. 'He said my shirt was dirty.'

'What did you do then?'

'I wen' home, didn' I?'

'To your flat in – Star Road? That's off the North End Road, isn't it?' Jonah shrugged. 'What time did you get there?'

'Half four maybe.'

'And what did you do?'

'Went to bed, man, wha' fink?

'Alone?'

Lafota clearly wanted to tell Slider to mind his own business, but an alibi was an alibi. 'Candy was there. My girlfriend. She been staying wiv me.'

'And what did you do for the rest of the day?'

'I got up about half one, messed around, had summing tweat, watched the telly.'

'What time did you go out?'

'I never went out, man.'

'Not at all?'

'I stopped in. Candy was wiv me. I stopped in and watched telly, went to bed about half eleven, went to sleep. Candy will tell you.'

'I'm sure she will,' Slider said politely. 'And what happened the next day?'

'I got up about half nine, and Candy and me went over her pad. She got stuff to do. All right?'

'Did you at any time go to Jay Paloma's flat?'

Lafota looked contemptuous. 'I don' even know where he live, man.'

'Oh, surely you do.'

'What is all this, man? Get off my back, right? I don't know nuffing about Jay, 'cept he use' come down the Parrot an' he don't no more.' He stood up, an effect like a bedside cabinet growing into a double wardrobe before one's very eyes. 'I come here, I answer your questions, all right? And now I'm going. You got nothing on me.'

'I'm afraid we have,' Slider said. 'We have your fingerprints, found inside Jay Paloma's flat, which you say you never visited. So I'm afraid I shall have to ask you to sit down and answer some more questions.'

He didn't sit down, and Slider felt the hair rise on his scalp for an instant; but he could see Jonah had been shaken. His brows drew together and his eyes dothered as he engaged in frantic thought – wondering what he might have touched, perhaps?

'I ain't answering no more questions,' he declared at last. 'And I ain't staying.'

'Then I'm afraid I shall have to detain you,' Slider said. He was surprised that Jonah had come voluntarily in the first place. Perhaps he was under orders from Billy Yates. If so, would Yates spring him, or continue to distance himself? It would be interesting to see.

Candy Williams looked both nervous and depressed. She was young – judging by the curve of her cheek and fullness of lip, Norma thought she was probably only about nineteen – and adequately pretty, though her face seemed puffy and her eyes red, despite the thick, disguising makeup, as if she had been crying a lot recently, or alternatively had been on a bender. She moved, Norma noted, with a certain upright inflexibility which did not go with the profession of dancer, table or otherwise. She wore a miniskirt and her long, young legs were bare, but she had on a large, baggy, concealing jumper. She had not seemed surprised when she opened the door to the police. Now she sat with passive docility in another interview room, her eyes moving anxiously from face to face, licking her lips occasionally. She would clearly like to be elsewhere, but just as clearly was under orders to do what had to be done.

'Your full name is Candy Williams, is that right?' Norma asked. Easy questions first, to get her relaxed.

'Clare,' she said. 'My real name's Clare. Candy's my stage name.'

'How sweet,' said Norma. 'And you're an actress, I understand?'

'Yeah, that, and I dance. Model a bit. Whatever.'

'An all-round entertainer. And you live at Flat Twelve, Waterside Court, Hammersmith?' A nod. 'You work for Mr Yates, don't you?'

She licked her lips. 'Sometimes.'

'Your last job was table dancing, at the Manhattan Club in

Clapham?' Candy did not dissent. 'Is that how you met Jonah Lafota? At the club?'

'Not at the Manhattan. I was at the Pink Parrot. Filling in.'

'Filling in as what?'

'Waitress,' Candy said.

'Topless?' Candy shrugged. Prostitution was the name of the game, Norma thought, but that was not what they were here for. 'How long ago was that? When you worked at the Pink Parrot and met Jonah?'

'About three months.'

'And you started going out together then?' Candy looked up for a moment, as if struck by the incongruity of the expression. Norma smiled. 'That's when you became his girlfriend,' she amended. 'I don't suppose you had much choice. He's not someone I'd like to have to say no to.'

Candy's eyes met Norma's. Her expression did not change, but contact had been made. We're all sisters under the skin, said Norma's smile, and men are all bastards. It's only a matter of degree. 'Does he knock you about, Candy?'

'He's all right,' Candy said expressionlessly.

'He isn't,' Norma said. 'Don't worry, I'm not going to give you away to him. Tell me about Tuesday last week. You'd been staying at Jonah's flat, is that right? Since when?'

'The weekend. Satdy. I went over Satdy afternoon. He was working Satdy night and Sundy night, but he likes to have me there when he wakes up. So I stopped on.'

'Were you there on Tuesday morning when he came home from work? And what time was that?'

'About half past four.'

'And what did he do?'

'He come straight to bed.' All this was easy to her, straight from the script. She answered without hesitation.

'What time did he get up?'

'It was about half past twelve when he woke up. I brought him breakfast in bed.'

'You were already up, then?'

'Well, I slept in the night, so I got up when he fell asleep.'

'I see. So you brought him breakfast, what then?'

'He et it. I got back into bed.' She shrugged to indicate the reason for that. 'Then we got up about half one.'

'And what time did he go out?'

Her eyes moved cautiously. 'He didn't go out.'

'He must have gone out at some point in the evening.'

'He didn't. He didn't go out at all.'

'But how would you know? You weren't there the whole time, surely?'

'We both stopped in. He was with me all evening, all night.'

'Come on, you must have been out at some point between half past one in the afternoon when you both got up, and half past nine the next morning when you went off to your place. That's twenty hours.'

The mathematics seemed to upset Candy, and she looked uncertain, but still she said, 'I was in the flat all that time. And Jonah was with me.'

'Every minute?'

'Yeah.'

Norma looked at her consideringly a long time. Candy shifted a little under the gaze, but returned the look defiantly. Norma changed tack. 'Tell me what you know about Jay Paloma.'

'I don't know him,' she said, easily again, back on script. 'I never even met him.'

'But you know who I'm talking about.'

'It was in the papers. Jonah's talked about it. He got murdered.'

'So Jonah knew him?'

'He worked for Mr Yates. Jonah's met him a couple of times, I think. He didn't know him well.'

'Why did Mr Yates sack Jonah?'

'I don't know. He didn't say.'

'He was upset about it, wasn't he?' Candy hesitated. 'He must have been furious. Did he take it out on you?'

'No,' she said, but absently, as though she was thinking about something else.

'Candy, I think Jonah had something to do with Jay Paloma's death. I think he's told you to say that he was with you, to give him an alibi for when he was at Jay Paloma's flat. That makes you an accessory. Do you know what that means?' No reply. 'It means that when we get enough evidence to charge Jonah, you can be charged with him. And we're going to get that evidence, believe me. It's only a matter of time. Jonah's going down. Surely you don't want to go down with him?' No answer. Candy stared sullenly at her hands. 'I've seen your flat – very swanky. Nice bathroom, nice kitchen. Soft toilet paper. You wouldn't like it in Holloway, believe me. It's a dirty, horrible place.' No response. 'Help me, Candy. If you tell me the truth, I can help you. You'll be all right.'

'You don't know Jonah,' she said abruptly, and then folded her lips tight, as though she hadn't meant to say as much.

Slider felt a certain sympathy with that. He spoke for the first time. 'If Jonah's inside, he can't hurt you, can he? Help us put him away, and then you'll be safe. It's the only way you *can* be safe. If he walks out of this police station, he's not going to be in the best of moods. Even if he thinks he's got away with it, he's going to be fed up with having spent all this time in here, and who d'you think he's going to take it out on?' Candy looked at him resentfully but said nothing. 'Just tell me the truth, Candy. He wasn't really with you all Tuesday evening, was he? He went out. Tell me what time he went out.'

Candy didn't hesitate this time. 'He was in all evening,' she said. But to Slider's ears it had a hint of wistfulness about it.

Billy Yates's brief was a quick-talking, smiling, rotund man called David Stevens. He had small, twinkling brown eyes and thick glossy hair, and exuded such enormous vitality he was like something out of a Pedigree Chum advert. He also had suits to die for, and the sort of wildly expensive red BMW coupé that successful pimps liked to drive. As he represented all the worst criminals on the ground, Slider knew him very well. The trouble was, Slider liked him, which made it harder to resist him. He thought Stevens liked him, too, but Stevens had the lawyerly knack of being able to think one thing and do another.

'How come you represent Yates as well as the scum of the neighbourhood?' Slider asked. 'Is there some connection I should know about?'

'You'll have to be careful what you say to me, or I might have to sue you for defamation of character,' Stevens said cheerfully.

'Definition of character, did you say?'

Stevens whistled soundlessly. 'Ooh, Bill, that's another hundred thousand. Mr Yates is a prominent local businessman of impeccable probity, who does a great deal of good in the neighbourhood and gives generously to charity.'

'Yes, of course, silly me, that's what I meant to say,' Slider said. 'And what can his interest be in Mr Lafota, I wonder?'

'Mr Yates takes an interest in all his employees.'

'Mr Lafota is unemployed,' Slider pointed out sweetly.

Stevens was unshaken. 'You didn't let me finish,' he said smoothly. 'The end of my sentence was – even when they have left his employ. Mr Lafota needed a solicitor – Mr Yates asked me if I would act for him. So here I am.'

'I can't say I wasn't expecting you,' Slider said resignedly. 'Though I didn't think you'd get here so quickly. Jonah hasn't even had his phone call yet. So tell me, how did Mr Yates hear that Mr Lafota was helping us with our enquiries?'

'There isn't much Mr Yates doesn't hear.' Stevens gave Slider a canny look. 'Now, Bill, don't be obvious! You can't bring in a seven-foot giant built like a brick shithouse unnoticed, y'know. Anyone could have told him that.'

'I suppose so,' Slider sighed. 'You're such a nice bloke, Dave, how can you square it with your conscience to spend your life trying to get creeps like him off the hook?'

'Not that old chestnut!' Stevens chortled. 'You must be feeling tired, old chum!'

Slider eyed him resentfully. 'Where did you get that tan? The Bahamas?'

'In my own little old back garden, mowing the lawn. It *is* summer, in case you hadn't noticed. And now I want Mr Lafota out. You've got sweet FA, and you know it, so you'll have to let him go. Much better not to struggle against the inevitable, as the actress said to the High Court judge.'

'Oh, gimme a break, Dave,' Slider said with faint, uncharacteristic irritation. 'We're not playing Scrabble, you know.'

Stevens only looked merrier. 'I know you want a result before Little Eric says bye-bye, but that's your problem, not mine. You've got nothing on my client, and I want him sprung.'

'I've got the fingerprints,' Slider pointed out.

'On a bottle of whisky, not on a murder weapon. Paloma bought his Scotch from the club, staff rate. Lafota's been in the store room there. The prints could have got on the bottle any time. You'll have to do better than that, sweetheart. It's not proof. It's not even evidence.'

'And the prints on the light switch, in the flat he claims he's never visited.'

'They're very poor prints, less than fifty per cent agreement.'

'It's enough to hold him on, while we look for something better,' Slider said.

Stevens shrugged. 'Temporarily. The Muppets will let me have him. You know that.'

'That gives me thirty-six hours. I'll take what I can get.'

Hart looked in. 'You still here, guv? I wondered when I saw the light on.'

'I was just thinking of going,' he said. He eyed her thoughtfully. 'Come in a minute, will you?' She came and stood before the desk, eyeing him perkily. Didn't these youngsters ever get tired? 'I don't generally interfere with my people's intelligence gathering, but then they know the rules I like to operate under. You're new to the ground, and you're new to me, and I have the feeling you also like life to have an element of excitement. This information you got on Jonah Lafota—'

She grinned. 'S'all right, guv, it wasn't Garry. Listen, just because I'm black, female, and I talk wiv a gorblimey accent, it don't mean to say I'm stupid.'

'I didn't think you were stupid,' Slider said mildly. 'I thought you probably felt you had something to prove.'

She became serious for once. 'You're dead right. You've heard of accelerated promotion? I got the opposite. People like me don't start from the starting line, we start from back in the pavilion.' Then suddenly she grinned again. 'And d'you know the worst fing of all? If I do get on, get promoted, even if I get commended, I'll never know if it's because I'm any good, or because some git's trying to prove he's not prejudiced. I can't win. *He* can't win. I hate positive discrimination. It's a bastard. At least with the old sort you knew where you were. If it wasn't happening to you, you knew everything was all right. Now they've invented the other stuff, you'll never know. You'll never, ever know.'

There was a short silence. 'You don't leave me with much to say,' Slider said. 'I was going to tell you there's no discrimination in my firm, but now if I tell you that, you won't be able to believe me.'

'Yeah,' she said with sympathy. 'It's like this—' She took hold of the skin of her cheek between finger and thumb. 'Once you got it, you just have to learn to live wiv it. You look tired, guv. An' I bet you ain't had anything to eat all day.'

Slider tried to look stern. 'You're not my mother.'

'That'll be a relief to my dad.'

Slider stood up, hesitated, and then said, 'D'you want to go and get something to eat? Now you've reminded me, I am hungry.' Joanna was away for the night, a concert in Leeds. He didn't want to go home to cold bread and cheese.

'Yeah, great,' Hart said easily.

'Right then. Oh,' he remembered, 'I've just thought, I ought to go and look at my house first. My old house – I'm not living there. I have to drop in now and then to make sure it hasn't been burnt down or taken over by squatters. It'll take about half an hour.'

'No problem,' she said. 'I'll come with you, if you like, and we can get a bite after.'

'Okay. There's a decent curry house not far from there. I'd be glad of the company, make sure I don't drop off at the wheel.'

He wouldn't, he was aware, have said that to Atherton, would not have felt the need to offer a justification. Was that another form of prejudice? He supposed it was, in a way, because he wouldn't have said it to McLaren, either – supposing he had ever been likely to invite McLaren's company. Why couldn't he treat Hart like a male colleague? He had never seen himself as a crusty old MCP – hadn't he always said Norma was the best policeman in the department? And that wasn't because she was a woman, but because she was the best. Ah, but then, had she been a man, would he have ever felt the need to say it? Bloody hell, this prejudice business was a minefield! No, be fair, he had only said that about Norma out loud when someone had attacked women in the police generally as being inferior in some way. And privately he thought about her no differently from his male troops: her physical difference was a trait attached to her like McLaren's eating habits or Mackay's football fanaticism or Atherton's finickitiness.

He didn't think he was prejudiced, not in any direction. He worried about Hart because she was a rookie and because she was a wild card – he didn't know what she might do. On the subject of which—

'By the way, who was your informant, if it wasn't Garry?'

'It was another bloke I met down the club. He's a regular, he knows everybody. S'all right, guv,' she added as Slider looked at her in alarm, 'nobody knew who I was. That's one advantage of being black and female, you can dress up outrageous so no-one recognises you. I walked right past that Garry in the doorway and he never clocked me. Mind you, he is as fick as pig-dribble.'

'And that's supposed to reassure me?' Slider wanted to forbid her to go there again, but in the wake of all this talk and thought about prejudice, he felt his hands were tied. After all, he wouldn't have tried to stop Mackay. He wouldn't even have tried to stop Norma.

CHAPTER TEN

Taking Hart

There was a slight fog, just enough to catch in the lights: the new halogen street lamps with their down-directed beams looked like a double row of shower-heads. The gibbous moon was an extraordinary colour, a most unnatural looking dark yellow. Lying on its back low in the sky, it looked like a half-sucked sherbet lemon.

'Where do you live?' he asked Hart. She had snuggled into the seat beside him, drawing her legs up and wrapping her arms round them. Her generation was so much more at ease with everyone than his had been. In her place at that age he'd have sat up straight and worried about pleasing.

'Streatham. I share a house. But I'm stopping with me mum and dad while I'm at Shepherd's Bush. They live in North Wembley.'

'Is that where you were born?'

'Near enough. Willesden.'

'So you're a northerner?'

'Am I?'

'North of the river. That accounts for why you seem so normal. Atherton has this theory that London north of the river and London south of the river are utterly alien to each other. He calls it Cispontine and Transpontine London.' It didn't mean anything to Hart. But then it hadn't to Slider until Atherton explained.

'You miss him, don't you?' she said.

'It was another complication in my life I could have done without.'

'What's this house we're going to?' she asked. So he told her. He meant to give her the briefest outline of the house situation, but her questioning was so adroit he found himself telling her more, about Irene now apparently having second thoughts and his worry about the children being brought up by Ernie Newman.

'It's not that I've anything against him, except that he's a boring fart. It's that they're *my* children, my responsibility. If anything goes wrong, it'll be my fault, but now there's nothing I can do to control the situation. I hate responsibility without power. It's – frustrating,' he ended mildly, suddenly aware of how much he was giving away.

'Yeah,' she said, in a tell-me-about-it voice.

He glanced at her. 'Have you got a boyfriend?'

'Not at the moment,' she said.

'It's hard for women in the Job – particularly in the Department. That's one of the unfairnesses.'

'S'right. And at least when you get married you can have a wife. If I get married, I've got to have a husband.' She made a face.

'Would you like to be married?'

'Not now. I want a career now. I like the Job, I want to get on. But I'd like to have kids too. I wanna have my career now, then when I'm forty-five ease off a bit and do the other. A bloke could do that. I can't. It's like *this*.' She tweaked her face again. 'So tell me about frustration,' she finished. 'The way I see it, we all got disabilities. It's like we're all cripples, one way or another. Blind people, people with no legs, they got to adapt. But when you got all your bits and pieces, you expect too much. We got to start thinking like cripples.'

'Count your blessings,' Slider said. 'They used to tell us that when I was a kid. There was even a Sunday School hymn.'

'If I was you, guv,' she said gravely, 'every morning when I got up I'd look in the mirror and thank Jesus I'm not McLaren.'

Slider laughed, and pulled off the A40 into the slip lane. 'Soon be there now. It won't take long. I've just got to make sure nothing disastrous has happened. Then we'll go for a Ruby. I'm assuming you like curry?'

'Do lemmings like cliffs?' said Hart.

When they got to the house he'd have expected her to stay in the car, but she got out when he did, so he didn't say anything. She followed him up to the front door. 'Nice,' she said.

He concealed his surprise. 'You think so?'

'My mum and dad'd love this.'

'They can have it,' he offered promptly.

'They couldn't afford it.'

'Neither can I,' he said, but he thought it just showed you, one man's meat is another man's McDonald's. Everything looked all right, no obvious broken windows or signs of squatters. He unlocked and stepped inside. The air smelled dry and stale, like packet soup. At first when he had come back it had seemed like his home, though deserted. Now he had been away long enough for it to seem alien to him: the spaces no longer fitted the geography of his eye's expectations. They say if you shut your eyes while walking you retain an image of where you're going to tread for eight paces, after which your brain loses confidence and you have to look again. It took longer to get unused to your old home, but he could no longer have confidently negotiated it in the dark. Not that it was ever completely dark. The street lamps filled it at night with a ghastly pinkish-yellow glow.

He left Hart in the hall and went upstairs to make sure there was no water where water should not be, and that the windows were all still locked. It was such a waste for the house to be empty, he thought, even though he didn't love it. And the mortgage hurt more now that he wasn't getting any use from it. Maybe, he toyed, he and Joanna should move into it. He had forked over those greens before, though, and knew the caterpillars. Even if he could live with Joanna where he had lived with Irene – and anyone could do anything if they put their minds to it – Joanna would hate it. He didn't suppose for a moment that she'd consent to it, so he had never even suggested it. He had put the house on the market and she had not demurred, so that was that.

Maybe, he thought, she had not demurred because she thought he would not consider it? She usually kept herself a firm pace out of his former life, deeming it to be his own business. Maybe he should have put it to her? Perhaps, like Hart, she would think it nice?

No, he couldn't be *that* wrong about her. But it made no sense to be paying for two properties. Maybe he should accept that he was not going to be able to sell it, and try to let it instead. But it would need a bit of capital spent, and who would provide that? Ernie was the only one with cash. Wherever he stepped, his foot landed in Ernie. The fact was that the easiest solution to everything would be for him and Irene and the children to move back in here. He shuddered. He hated being here, and prey to thoughts like that. Better get out fast and have a restorative curry.

He went downstairs again, switching off the stairs light at the bottom. The other downstairs lights were off, but there was enough coming through the glass door to see by. In the ghastly sodium dusk he looked round for Hart. She had wandered off somewhere.

'Where are you?'

She appeared silently in the doorway to the lounge, right beside him.

'Are you ready, then?' he asked.

'Mmm,' she said. She was very close, and as she turned her face upwards towards him he realised, suddenly and shockingly, that she wanted him to kiss her. Or, rather, that if he kissed her she wouldn't object, she would respond. He looked down, saw the gleam of her eyes, the full firmness of her lips, and he learned what a large variety of thoughts could bound through the head simultaneously – and at a moment when he was having enough trouble controlling his instant hormonal reaction, without having to sort a panic-stricken babble into order of importance.

She was *attracted* to him? He had never thought of himself as sexually attractive, though Joanna evidently found him so, but that was different, wasn't it, that was the whole bit, troo lurve? But as for Hart, oh my God, had he led her on, did she think that was what he brought her here for? Hadn't anyone told her about Joanna? He was right after all, you couldn't treat a female colleague exactly like a male colleague. Now what was he going to do?

The most horrifying aspect of the situation was that the lawless stirring in his loins was whispering that he could do it, yes he could, why not, he was a free agent wasn't he, why waste a golden opportunity? And simultaneously in yet another subsection of his brain he remembered that Kate had always got loin and lion mixed up and had long believed that loin chops had a much more exotic origin than the sheep or the pig.

Sometimes Fate takes pity. He did not have to discover how he would have got out of *that* one, because a shadow appeared behind the glass of the front door, and a key was slipped into the lock. It was Irene, of course. Apart from her, only the estate agent had a key. She said, 'Bill?' enquiringly, and a little nervously, as she opened the door. The front door obscured her view of them at first, but the hall was so small that once the door was opened flat against the right hand wall, he and Hart were immediately before her as she stepped in.

She stopped and stared at them. Slider saw immediately how it must look. He and Hart were standing very close together, all the lights were off, and the air was sulphurous with maculate conceptions.

'I saw your car out there,' Irene said falteringly, 'but there were no lights on. I thought – I wondered—'

Thanks a lot, Fate, Slider thought. Out of the doodah into the whatsname.

'We were just leaving,' he said. As an answer it left a lot to be desired – which was evidently also how Irene viewed Hart. Slider could see her bristling. 'I just popped in to check that everything was all right,' he said. 'This is Detective Constable Hart. My wife Irene.'

'How d'you do?' Hart said politely, but she did not move away from Slider's side. She looked at Irene curiously. The staging was all wrong, he realised: Hart was standing in a position of belonging, looking at Irene-the-outsider.

'Am I interrupting something?' she asked icily.

'Of course not,' he said. 'Don't be silly. As I said, we were just leaving.'

'Don't go on my account,' Irene said.

'Look, we've been working late and we were going to get something to eat, but I remembered I had to check on the house, so we stopped here on the way,' he said. He felt Hart stir beside him, and knew she was right. Never explain. It only made things worse – as if, paradoxically, it proved there was something to explain.

'Working late. Yes, of course,' Irene said, looking with operatic contempt from Slider to Hart and back. 'I should have remembered that's what it was always called. I was a policeman's wife for long enough.'

'Irene—!' he began, exasperated.

'Oh, I don't blame you,' she said bitterly. 'I've no right, when it was me that—' She couldn't quite say it. 'You're a free agent after all. I just would have thought that you'd – not in this house—' She choked and turned away. Slider felt a monumental annoyance that was only intensified by the knowledge that (a) she actually felt those things, despite the hackneyed words, (b) it was really he who was the guilty party, and doubly guilty because he went on letting her think it was she who had sinned first and (c) that she had hit on some of the same words, free agent, that he had been thinking himself only seconds before.

'Irene, will you stop talking like a Barbara Cartland heroine. Nothing is going on here.'

'It's none of my business if it is,' she said, maddeningly. 'I won't hang around here getting in your way. I just—' She dissolved into tears.

Slider pulled out his handkerchief and stuffed it into Irene's hands. 'Yes, what were you doing here, anyway?' he asked, trying for a mixture of briskness and kindness.

'I was just passing,' she said, muffled as she mopped, 'and I saw your car.'

'Just passing? From where to where?'

'Don't interrogate me!' she said with a flash of her old spirit. 'I'm not one of your criminals.'

'Sorry. But really—'

'All right,' she said angrily, 'I sometimes come here. When I'm feeling – when I don't feel right at Ernie's, I come here and just sit. It's my home, and I miss it, all right? I sit here and think – think that maybe we could get it together again, maybe you would forgive me and come back. Like a fool, I thought perhaps you missed it too. I see how wrong I was.'

'You were wrong,' he said, 'but not for this reason. WDC Hart is a member of my firm, that's all, and I don't think we should discuss our private lives in front of her.'

'I'm sorry,' Irene said, though he had no confidence that she believed him. 'Like I said, I've no reason to complain. I was the one—' She stopped again. He hated her to feel so very bad about her lapse.

'We'll talk,' he promised. 'We've got a lot of things to say.

But not now, not here. I'll ring you, all right? And we'll meet and talk.'

'All right,' Irene said, muted.

Hart seemed to shake herself free of her paralysis – or was it just curiosity? Everyone was nourished on soap operas these days. 'I'll go and wait in the car, guv,' she said, thought about saying goodbye to Irene and wisely thought better of it, and took herself off.

'She's a pretty girl,' Irene said.

'She's a colleague, that's all,' Slider said wearily.

'It doesn't matter,' Irene said. She looked at the handkerchief in her hand. 'I'll wash and iron this and send it back to you.'

'I wish you wouldn't talk like that.'

'I'll give it to you next time I see you, then.'

'Are you all right now? Can you drive yourself home all right?' The moment he said it, he cursed himself. She was going to say 'this is my home' and start it all off again.

But she just nodded. 'You'll phone me?'

'I promise.'

She started to go, and then stopped and said, looking up at him, 'I miss you, Bill.'

He knew he had to say, I miss you too, but wondered what effect it would have on her expectations; and in wondering hesitated just too long. She lowered her head, turned, and trudged off.

He locked the house up and went back to the car. When he was in, Hart said, softly and feelingly, 'Christ.'

And then some, he thought. He started the engine.

'I'm sorry, guv,' she said.

'It's not your fault. I'm sorry you came in for it.'

'D'you want to just drop me off at the tube or something?'

He looked at her, surprised. 'We haven't eaten yet. I don't know about you but I need a curry. A Madras at least, after that.'

She looked at him for a moment, and then grinned. 'Yeah,' she said. 'Me too.'

The taxi driver's name was Leonard Marks. 'Lenny,' he simplified it, offering his hand to Slider. He was a tall, well-built man with a large, handsome, fleshy face, thick wavy hair, and brown, steady eyes. Everything about him seemed calm, open and facing forward, like a lion gazing out over the veldt. 'Lenny the Lion, they call me,' he added on the wake of Slider's thought. 'From Sniffy Wheeler's garage in Homerton. Anyone'll tell you.'

'Right,' said Slider, accepting the bona fides. 'Thanks for coming in.' Monty had telephoned first thing to tell Slider he had found his man for him.

'It's the business all right,' Monty had said proudly. 'Good as gold, Lenny. Everyone knows him.'

'So you think you can tell me something about this chap?' Slider went on, tapping the print of Jay Paloma's photograph.

'That's right. It was Monday morning, last week, about half eleven – quarter to twelve. I'd done a book job to Paddington Station, but I don't generally like ranking up, unless I can see a crowd waiting, and there was nothing doing at the station rank. So I was cruising. I came down Edgware Road, round Marble Arch, down Park Lane. There was a fare outside the Dorchester, but I got overtaken – some smart-arse butterboy in a brand new cab who doesn't know the rules. I've got his number!'

He wagged his head significantly. Slider knew that to overtake – to take a fare who was signalling another cab – was a heinous crime, and no mercy was shown to the sinner. 'Go on,' he said.

'Right,' said Marks. 'So I get down to Hyde Park Corner and it looks like the Lanesborough Hotel rank is running, so I go round and put on. Anyway, just as I got up to point, your friend here appears.'

'He came out of the hotel?'

'No, he was a walk-up. But funny enough, I saw him in my rear-view mirror, paying off another cab at the corner. That's why I remembered him particularly. I wasn't really looking at him, of course, I only glanced, but I got that impression.'

Slider nodded. This man's impression was probably sure enough. 'You didn't see whose cab it was?'

'No,' he said apologetically. 'It was just a black cab. I didn't see the number or the company or anything. Well, anyway, this bloke comes up to my window and asks for Chelsea Embankment. I says to him, "Any particular part, sir?" because a lot of people call it Chelsea Embankment all the way along, from Cheyne Walk to Vauxhall Bridge. And he says, "Oh, yes, Flood Street, please."'

'How did he seem? What was his manner?'

Marks considered. 'A bit vague, maybe. Had his mind on other things.'

'Nervous?'

'Could have been. Maybe a bit. Preoccupied, is what I'd say.'

'Did you have any conversation with him?'

'Not a dickie. He just sat there looking out of the window. Anyway, soon as I turned into Flood Street off King's Road, he tapped the glass and said, "Anywhere here," so I pulled in, he nipped out, paid me, and walked away.'

'Did you see where he went after that?'

Marks smiled a slow, handsome smile. 'Well, as a matter of fact, I did. You see, I drove on down to the end of Flood Street, but the Embankment was chokka, so I did a u-ey and came back up to get back on the King's Road again. And there he was, standing on the steps ringing the doorbell. And as I get opposite, the door opens, and I see the householder all smiles letting him in. And I thought to myself, so much for all your cloak-and-dagger stuff, chum, changing cabs and getting out at the corner! Because it was obvious this bloke's a ginger, and the house he's visiting doesn't belong to Jimmy Nobody.'

'I don't suppose by any wild chance you saw the number of the house?' Slider asked.

'I didn't need to,' Marks said. 'I know the address very well. I've been there a few times, I know who lives there. It's Sir Nigel Grisham.'

'What, the MP?'

'Cabinet Minister,' Marks corrected significantly. 'Practically the Grand Old Man of the party. So how d'you like them apples?'

'Good God,' Slider said. 'You're quite sure about all this?'

Marks nodded. 'I saw him. I'd recognise him anywhere. Hurrying your bloke in, he was, hand on his elbow, peeping past him to make sure no-one was watching.' He mimed it graphically.

'But *you* were watching. If you were just opposite the house, surely he must have seen you?'

Marks shook his head. 'Seeing's not a matter of what's there, is it? It's a matter of what your brain takes in. And a black cab in London – well, it's part of the furniture, like a pillar box or a lamp-post. Your brain kind of edits it out. Unless you're looking for one, you just don't see it. I've noticed it time and again.'

'Sir Nigel Grisham,' Slider said wonderingly. Paloma had certainly been sinning above his station.

Marks grinned. 'Who's a naughty boy, then?'

'You're willing to make a statement about this?'

'Sure. Any time you like. Always willing to help. And I'll put out the word on that other cab, if you like, the one I saw your friend getting out of. Chances are he changed twice if he was trying to be clever, took his local cab to somewhere no-one'd think anything about. I'll see what I can do.'

'Thank you,' Slider said, 'but I don't think it's important. We needed to know where he went rather than how he got there.'

'I'll ask around anyway. It's no trouble,' Marks said, brushing his mane back with a casual paw. 'Anything you want, just ask for Lenny the Lion.'

As he went into the CID room, heads flew apart. The two closest were Hart's and Norma's, and Slider felt a low, depressing sensation that they had been talking about him, that Hart had been describing the marital scene on the doorstep. Or was that indigestion? He shouldn't eat Madras, or at least not after six p.m.

Norma and McLaren were back from searching Lafota's flat. 'We haven't got much,' Norma confessed. 'We've got a boot with a sole that matches the footmark on Paloma's door, but they're ten a penny.'

'Not in that size,' McLaren pointed out.

'True, but turning it up the other way, I doubt whether you'd find many blokes that tall under the age of, say, thirty, who didn't wear boots like that.'

'Every little helps,' Slider said. 'It all adds to the picture. Did you find anything else?'

'A packet of drinking straws in the kitchen cupboard,' Norma said, 'and I'll bet they weren't for Coca-Cola. Forensic is going over the place for any traces, but unfortunately he didn't leave any packets behind when he and Candy struck camp. Which for a careless man was awfully careless of him.'

'So it's back on the streets, then, boys and girls,' Slider said. 'Knock on those doors and ask those questions. If Lafota left his flat on Tuesday night to go to Paloma's, someone must have seen him. And people must be talking about it.'

'Guv, it must have been a hit, mustn't it?' Mackay said. 'I mean, why else did Lafota do it? He didn't have a beef against Paloma, did he?'

'Don't ask me – ask around,' Slider said. 'The staff and regulars at both clubs – the Pink Parrot and the Pomona – have got to be our best bet. I'm getting some uniformed help as of today, so I'll put them on the local stuff and you lot can concentrate on the clubs. I want everyone followed up and asked about both of them. Who did they know, where did they go, what did they do.'

'It's gotta be a drugs connection,' Mackay said. 'Stands to reason.'

'I hate to say it,' Norma said, 'but I agree. And my bet is that Yates is behind it; and if he is behind it, he's going to take a lot of winkling out.' There was a mutter of agreement.

'Nobody has special protection in my book,' Slider said firmly. 'If Yates has been a naughty boy, Yates is going to get his hand smacked. Meanwhile, we mustn't lose sight of the victim. We don't know nearly enough about what Paloma got up to when he wasn't tucked up safe at home with Busty Parnell. Although we do now have a line on his special boyfriend, for whom he was putatively acquiring the recreational sugar.' He told them about Lenny Marks's evidence.

Hollis whistled. 'Sir Nigel Grisham? Oh my oh my. That's bad news for the Government.'

'I never would have thought Grisham was an iron,' Norma said. 'He's got a wife and kids, hasn't he?'

'In the country,' Hollis said. 'And if this gets out he'll be spending a lot more time with them.'

'What about protecting a political career as a motive for murder?' Hart said.

'Don't get carried away,' said Slider. 'We've got Jonah on ice, remember.'

'Maybe we've been maligning him. How tall is Grisham?' Mackay wondered.

'Paloma could have been blackmailing him,' McLaren helped him out.

Slider said, 'I'm going to interview Sir Nigel Grisham myself—'

'And when he interviews people, they stay interviewed,' Norma concluded. 'Who're you taking with you, boss?'

'Hart,' he said. 'It's likely to be a delicate interview, needing subtle techniques.'

Hart was grinning broadly and the others were looking faintly baffled. It was good to keep your troops from growing too complacent, he thought.

Research into Sir Nigel Grisham's background proved he was eminently blackmailable. Besides the house in Flood Street he had a large country house near Chenies, in a part of Buckinghamshire long favoured by the upper echelons of government and the civil service for its pretty, unspoilt countryside and good fast roads into London. Grisham had married the daughter of a Cotswold landowner with the bluest of blood and the blackest of bank accounts and had raised four attractive children, the youngest just at university age. His Parliamentary career had been solid rather than fast-track, but in a Parliament increasingly filled by the callow and the indistinguishable, he had now in his early fifties attained an elder statesman status which was almost better than talent.

'And he's tipped to get Foreign Secretary in the reshuffle,' Hart said as they headed westwards – a simple phone call had established that Grisham had left Chelsea for his country house, or 'done a bunk' as Hart put it. 'A bum-scandal'd put paid to that, all right.'

'How do you know that?' Slider asked.

'Well, s'obvious. It's all right coming out of the closet if you're an actor, but the public don't like turd-burglars representing 'em at international summits.'

'I didn't mean that, I meant how did you know he was tipped for Foreign Secretary?'

She looked at him, wide-eyed. 'It was in the news. Blimey, guv, don't you read the papers?'

'When do I have time?' he countered irritably. 'I can't even get through all the stuff on my desk.'

'Yeah,' she said placatingly. 'Well. Anyway, the papers'd have a field day if it got out about him and Paloma, even without the murder. They don't like anyone in the Foreign Office to sleep around, ever since Profumo.'

'But that was prostitutes.'

'So was Paloma. And arse-bandits is even worse. It looks as though Grisham's got the wind up, anyway, making a run for it.'

'It is summer, you know. People do go out of London in summer. And he has a wife and children in the country.'

'He's bound to have seen Paloma's death in the papers.'

'Then he ought to think he's safe,' Slider pointed out. 'Dead men tell no tales.'

Hart only grunted, unconvinced. 'I bet he's in a panic,' she said. Slider agreed with her. If Grisham had seen Paloma's death mentioned in the papers, he must wonder whether he ought to come forward and disclose his relationship, or whether that would be exposing himself needlessly. Well, he was soon to find out.

Edge House, Grisham's country place, was closed off from the road by a high wall. The ornate gates were shut; through them was a view of a gravel sweep around a well-tended piece of lawn, to a handsome Palladian house in softly red old brick with an ancient wisteria climbing up one corner, and modern but tasteful single-storey additions on either side. A million upwards, Slider guessed, depending on how much land was attached.

'Lifestyles of the rich and shameless, eh?' said Hart. 'I've never been this close to the seat of power before. Are you sure it's all right to come asking him questions? We won't be slapped in the Tower for Les Majesty or summink?'

'Cabinet ministers have no special immunity, not like diplomats,' Slider said. 'He's got to account for himself just like anyone else. At least, if we can get past these gates,' he added, looking in vain for a handle.

'There's an intercom,' Hart pointed out. 'Shall I ring?'

'No, I'll do it,' Slider said.

She grinned. 'Afraid they won't let us in if they hear my accent?'

Slider frowned at her. 'Get in the driving seat.'

It was a woman's voice that answered when he rang; even

distorted by the intercom, it was middle-aged and cultured in accent. 'Who is it, please?'

'Detective Inspector Slider, Metropolitan Police. I'd like a word with Sir Nigel, if you'd be so kind.'

There was a pause. A conference going on, or simple caution? 'I don't know an Inspector Slider,' the voice said. 'You're not our usual security liaison.'

'It isn't about security, ma'am. I'm from Shepherd's Bush CID. I'd like a word with Sir Nigel on a private matter.'

'Well I don't know. It sounds very odd. Are you alone?'

'I have Detective Constable Hart with me. May I suggest you telephone my Area Commander, Mr Wetherspoon, at Hammersmith Police Station for confirmation of my identity?'

Another pause. It was like holding a transatlantic telephone conversation. 'Very well,' the voice said at last. 'Please come in, Inspector.'

There was a buzz and a click and the gates swung eerily open. Hart drove in over the scrunching gravel, and before they reached the front door, the gates had swung closed again with a solid electronic clunk. Someone must have been watching – there was a security camera mounted above the door – for the front door opened as soon as they reached it. A woman stood there, a well-preserved, well-dressed, well-coiffeured lady in her fifties, with a face schooled over a lifetime of public work to show no emotion. The eyes, however, were quick and anxious. They surveyed and summed up Slider and Hart with rapid professionalism.

'I'm Lady Grisham,' she said. 'Please come in.'

They walked past her into a lovely hall with a polished wood floor, a Sheraton side-table bearing a *famille rose* vase, and a staircase of airy beauty rising like an invitation to the delights of the first floor. The walls were robin's egg blue and weighted with old and expensive oil paintings; the air was cool and faintly scented with lavender. An ancient and outrageously shapeless black labrador waddled up with a clicking of nails and swung a polite tail, his blue-filmed eyes scanning in vain for faces through his own personal mist. Lady Grisham stood with her hands lightly clasped before her, elegant in a floral silk dress, pearls and a carefully-selected brooch, as she had stood on a thousand platforms and sat on a thousand committees:

being what was expected of her, waiting to cope. Slider felt a deep reluctance to be here. He felt like a vandal. He had come to smash this sweet order to bits; but he saw in her dark, unhappy eyes that Lady Grisham had been expecting this moment, perhaps for years.

'I'm sorry to have to disturb you like this,' Slider said when he had shown his identification, 'but it is very urgent.'

Lady Grisham was ready to fight a rearguard action. 'I know you have your duty to do, Inspector, but it really is a very inconvenient time. My husband is far from well, and he had a sleepless night. I persuaded him to try to take a nap in the library, and I really don't wish to disturb him just when he may have managed to get off to sleep. He has a very crowded schedule for the next few days, and in this present state of health—'

'It's all right, my dear.' The right-hand door which led off the hall, which had been standing slightly ajar, opened fully and Sir Nigel himself appeared. In tweed trousers, checked shirt, knitted tie, olive-green cardigan with leather buttons, and highly polished brogues, he was perfectly dressed for leisure in the country – if you were a public figure, that is. The old dog turned its head at the sound of his voice and staggered across, wagging everything in delight. Behind Sir Nigel was a glimpse of another lovely room, book-lined, with an Adam fireplace and comfortable old leather chairs. 'I wasn't asleep,' he went on. 'And I'm sure the inspector and his colleague wouldn't be here if it were not important.'

'But Nigel, oughtn't we to telephone Roger?' she said urgently.

'I don't think so. I don't think he can help at this stage. Won't you come through to the library, Inspector?' He looked bleakly at his wife. 'Don't let anyone disturb us, Annie. And no telephone calls.'

She met his eyes with some message, to which he shook his head just perceptibly; as if she had said, *run away, there's still time*, and he had said, *it's too late, there's no escape*. Slider was perfectly well aware that this was fanciful on his part, but he wished the minister hadn't called his wife Annie, and he wished the old dog hadn't tried to go with his master into the library and been gently, firmly repulsed. 'No, no, old fellow, not you. Go with missus, go on.'

'Jasper, come here,' Lady Grisham called. The dog pivoted stiffly and lumbered reluctantly to her, and Grisham closed the library door.

'Can I offer you sherry?' he asked, ushering them to seats.

'No, thank you,' Slider answered for both. He felt bad enough without drinking the man's liquor.

'You won't object, I hope, if I have one?' Grisham said. 'I usually do at this time. Sure I can't tempt you? Quite, quite. On duty, of course.' He made a slow bustle of getting out decanter and glass, pouring and putting away, and Hart flung a couple of urgent looks at Slider – *thinking out what to say* – but Slider let them pass him by. Grisham was trying to steel himself for the ordeal to come, that was all. Finally he came and sat down opposite Slider, took a large sip of the sherry, put down the glass and said, 'Now, what can I do for you?' in a bland and friendly manner as if they were constituents come to talk about road planning. But his voice wavered slightly, and he looked haggard. Lady Grisham had probably spoken no more than the truth when she said he was unwell and hadn't slept. His face, familiar from the television and newspapers, handsome in a presidential way, looked lined and exhausted; his mouth drooped wearily at the corners and his eyes were baggy with lack of sleep.

'I'm very sorry to have to broach this subject with you, Minister,' Slider said, 'but I imagine that you must be aware that Maurice McElhinney, also known as Jay Paloma, was found dead at his flat on Wednesday last week.'

Grisham was breathlessly still. 'Why should you think I would be aware of that? Am I supposed to know this—'

'To save you trouble, Sir Nigel, I should say that Jay Paloma was traced to your house in Flood Street on Monday afternoon last week, the day before he was murdered, and that you were seen to let him in and greet him in a friendly manner. And that he told his closest friend that he had spent Monday afternoon with his lover.'

Grisham started to tremble. He moved his lips a few times, but couldn't seem to speak.

'We have taken in custody one Jonah Lafota, who works at the Pink—' He stopped, because Grisham had gone quite suddenly to pieces. The meat of his face began to quiver uncontrollably, his mouth sagged so that a thread of saliva slipped out of one corner, his eyes rolled round and upwards. For a thrilling second Slider thought he was going to have a stroke or a heart attack, but it was only despair and grief. Grisham put his hands over his face and hunched forward, chewing at his brow with his fingertips, moaning quietly. Hart looked at Slider but he shook his head. Behind Sir Nigel's hands, the dog-like moans blurred into words.

'I knew this would come. Oh God, I've been such a fool. I can't bear it. I didn't mean it to happen. Oh God, I'm ruined. I'm finished. Oh God, what's going to happen to me? Annie. The children. They'll never live it down. It's horrible. I never meant anyone to get hurt. It was a mistake. I didn't want him hurt. What's going to happen to me? I'm finished. Oh God, I can't bear it.'

This went on for some time while Slider and Hart waited in silence, Slider feeling a familiar blend of emotions, pity for the writhing victim before him, relief that they were obviously on the right track, hope that he was going to come across with the goods. At last, when the paroxysm seemed to be waning, Slider got up, went to the cupboard where the sherry had been stored, sniffed out the brandy, and poured a large slug. He took it back to the cabinet minister, laid a kindly hand on his shoulder, and said, 'Here, try this. It will steady your nerves.'

Grisham removed his hands from his face reluctantly, but he knocked back the brandy and then busied himself with his handkerchief, wiping his eyes and blowing his nose.

'Another?' said Slider. Grisham nodded. After the second stiffener, he seemed back in control. He sighed, sat up straight, clasped his hands together in his lap for comfort, and said, 'I suppose I must tell you all about it.'

'It would be better if you did,' Slider agreed.

Grisham looked at him, half pathetic, half resentful. 'But I swear to you, I never meant any harm to come to him. You must believe me. I was as shocked as anyone when I saw in the papers that he – that he—'

'That's all right, sir,' Hart said gently. 'Why don't you tell it from the beginning? It'll flow easier that way. Just start at the beginning, and see how it comes.'

And, oddly, it was to Hart rather than to Slider that Sir Nigel Grisham told the tale. As though she would understand better. One minority to another, perhaps? But he told it, that was what mattered.

CHAPTER ELEVEN

Rich and Shameless

'I don't want you to think – I haven't lived a double life, you know,' Sir Nigel said. 'What I mean is, I haven't made a habit of—' He paused, and the words *this sort of thing* hovered unspoken. The trouble with the unspeakable, Slider thought, was that there were no words for it.

'You're a happily married man,' Hart said helpfully, and Grisham looked rescued.

'Yes, very happily. Annie is a wonderful person. Without her I could never have got where I am today. I love her very much. We love each other very much. It's important to understand that.'

'Yeah, okay,' said Hart, willing to be convinced. 'So where does Jay Paloma fit into it?'

'I don't know,' he said. He stared away bleakly. 'It was an extraordinary thing. It was not something I expected. I'm not – I haven't ever been—'

'Were there others before Jay?'

'No,' he said quickly. 'That's what I'm trying to tell you. Oh, I got up to the usual things at school, the way boys do, but it didn't mean anything. At that age it's just eroticism, not homosexuality.' There, the horrid word was out. Grisham seemed the better for it. 'As a teenager I had all the normal urges. I went out with girls. I planned to get married. There was nothing different about me.'

'So Jay was the first male lover you ever had?'

He hesitated. 'The first lover, yes. But I did – have encounters. Just a few. Over the years.' Hart nodded, easy, uncritical, simply interested, and Grisham unfolded a little. 'The first time was when I was in Frankfurt on a business trip. A group of us went out for the evening, rather overdid things, ended up in a night club. I started chatting to a gorgeous-looking female – well, she looked gorgeous in that light. I was rather drunk, you know, otherwise I wouldn't have—'

'Yeah, I know.'

'We ended up going back to my hotel room. I don't honestly remember all that much about it. But I suppose you can guess the rest.'

'The female turned out to be male.'

'Yes. And – well – he seemed to think I'd known that all along, and I was – I don't know – it was rather exciting in a strange way. So I—'

'Done it,' Hart finished for him. He looked at her carefully, to see if she were mocking or disapproving, and she made a tiny movement of her hands, shoulders and head which said as clearly as words, *c'est la guerre* – or, since it was Hart after all, *vese fings 'appen*. 'So that was the way it went after that, was it?'

'I didn't make a habit of it,' he said with a little sharpness. 'I felt very bad after that first time – mostly for being unfaithful to Annie. But over the years – the stresses of the job – I wasn't proud of myself, but I don't want you to think I was ashamed, either. We dedicate ourselves to public service, and we live a life of unnatural strains, terrible hours, long periods away from our loved ones—'

'Yeah, tell me about it!'

'Of course, you would understand.' And for the first time he looked at Slider, including him in the 'you'. Slider nodded slightly. 'Well, when you live that sort of life, something has to give in the end. And I think Annie preferred it this way, rather than – well, I never gave her a rival, you see. She has been the only woman in my life. And I was always discreet. What I did harmed no-one.'

'And it was always like that, was it?' Hart prompted. 'A casual pick-up in a club. Just a one-night stand.'

'Anything else would have been dangerous – and unfair to Annie. And it wasn't all that often, you know – once or twice a year. Half a dozen times at most. In any case, I've hardly had the time or energy in recent years. You can't imagine how ministerial work has multiplied in the last decade. I'd been living like a monk for years when I met Jay.' He paused at the sound of the name, as if re-realising the purpose of this cosy chat.

'So how did you meet him?' Hart picked up the thread easily and passed it back to him.

'One night, about a year ago, I was at my London house, alone and at a loose end. A meeting had been cancelled at the last minute and I suddenly had nothing I had to do. No-one was expecting me anywhere. I can't tell you what a heady sensation that was! It was the first time in months. Of course, I thought at first of coming down here, and I was on the point of telephoning Annie to say I was coming, when I suddenly thought, no, damnit, I'm going to take a little time for myself, be unaccountable for an evening—'

'Cut yo'self a little slack,' Hart supplied.

Grisham seemed charmed with the phrase. 'Cut myself a little slack, just so! That's exactly it! After being tethered head and foot for so long, the idea was intoxicating. So I went to the Pink Parrot Club.'

'How did you know about it? Had you been there before?' Slider asked.

'Only once, and a long time before, but I'd heard about it. If you go to clubs at all, you hear about others. And it was conveniently close. That's why I chose it, because it was the nearest.'

He seemed struck by the idea, and dropped into silent thought. Slider guessed what it was: by such random, meaningless decisions our fates are determined. If you listen very carefully, he thought, you can hear the gods laughing.

'And it was that night you met Jay Paloma?' Hart prompted after a moment.

Grisham came back from his distance, and seemed older, colder, greyer. The dance was over. This was the morning after. 'Yes,' he said. 'It was – do you know the expression *coup de foudre*?'

'Yeah,' said Hart, rather than break his rhythm.

'The moment I saw him, I was lost. And I knew it was the same for him. It wasn't like anything I'd ever felt before. Not even for Annie. I love her dearly, but this was something different. It was like meeting the other half of my soul after a lifetime of searching – except that I hadn't been searching. I hadn't even known I was incomplete. I fell in love with him, even though he wasn't a woman. It didn't matter what he was, what body he happened to be in. I just fell in love with *him*. Can you understand that?'

'Yeah, I can understand.'

Grisham shrugged as though the story was finished. 'So we became lovers. Whenever I could make time, we met. It was the start of a new life for me.'

'It couldn't have been easy,' Slider said, 'given how busy you were.' Grisham looked at him. 'And given that he was living in a place where you couldn't visit him, and that he was working as well.'

'You know all about it, I suppose.'

'I understand that you had – disagreements. About his working at the Pomona Club.'

'I wanted him to give it up,' Grisham said. 'If only he'd listened to me, none of this would have happened. I wanted him to give up work and move into a place nearer the centre, so that we could see each other more often. So that he could be more flexible about when we could meet.'

'So that he would always be available when you found yourself with time to spare,' Slider filled in.

'Is that unreasonable?' He addressed the protest to Slider, but then looked at Hart. 'He wanted to be with me as much as I wanted to be with him. I had enough money. I told him, he would never want for anything. I'd always been generous with him. Whatever he wanted, he only had to ask, he knew that. But he said he didn't want to be a kept man. He said it was humiliating. As opposed to what he did at the Pomona, I asked him? A kept man. How could he talk like that? When you love someone, you don't think like that.'

'So you quarrelled,' Hart said neutrally.

'Oh, not really quarrelled. We had arguments. Disagreements. It was something that came up from time to time. Mostly we were happy, very happy. But I did worry about the Pomona for other reasons, security reasons. And just recently – with the reshuffle coming up – I told him he *must* give up working there. If it got out, it would mean—' He stopped. 'Well, that's all over now,' he went on flatly. 'My career is over.'

Slider stopped Hart with a look and said evenly, 'Tell me about the cocaine that Jay bought for you.'

'Oh, you know about that, do you?' Grisham said with a bitter look. 'What do you want to know, then?'

'Whose idea was it? Did you ask him or did he offer? Did you use it together?'

'We didn't use the damned stuff! I've never taken drugs. I've smoked a little pot now and then, but only abroad in countries where it was legal. In my position you can't be too careful.' He did not seem to see any irony in the words. 'And Jay hated drugs, hated everything to do with them. He was passionate on the subject. I think if I'd ever suggested we took something together he'd have walked out on me there and then.'

'Nevertheless, he did buy cocaine for you.'

'Yes, he got it for me, under protest. He didn't want to do it. I had the devil of a job to persuade him. But it was – necessary.'

'What for?'

Grisham frowned. 'I suppose I have to tell you. At least then you won't think I took the beastly stuff. I don't want that slur laid on me, along with everything else. The truth is that I got it for a colleague. A fellow Member of Parliament. He was blackmailing me.' He looked from Slider to Hart and back. 'That's the sort of person we get in the House nowadays. Nice, isn't it? This – *colleague* – found out about Jay and me. He came to me and said that if it got out it would be the end of my career. At first I brazened it out. Told him to publish and be damned. But he said it wouldn't hurt *him* to spill the beans, and that if I wanted to make sure he couldn't do so without implicating himself, he'd tell me how. I couldn't think what he meant – I thought he was suggesting some disgusting *ménage à trois* – but it turned out that what he wanted was cocaine. He reckoned that Jay would know how to get hold of it, and if we formed his supply chain, he would never be able to split on us. A painless kind of insurance, he called it.'

'And did Jay know how to get hold of it? Slider asked.

'He found out. After a lot of persuasion. I gave him the money, he got the stuff and passed it to me, I passed it to my colleague and collected the cash. What he did with it I don't know. I hoped fervently that he would poison himself with it, but he hasn't so far.'

Sold it, probably, Slider thought, in single fixes to fellow ravers. At a profit. 'Do you know where Jay got it?'

'He found some contact through the club. That's all I know. He wouldn't tell me any names, and I didn't want to know them.'

'He actually bought it from someone at the club?'

'He wouldn't tell me any of the details. I suppose he thought it was safer for me not to know.'

'He was taking a considerable risk,' Slider said.

'I hated putting him in that position,' Grisham said, 'and he hated doing it, but he did it for me. That's the sort of man he was. He did it to protect me. Because I couldn't see any other way out. Oh, I've made such a mess of things!' He put his head in his hands.

'Tell me about the last time you saw him. The Monday, wasn't it?'

Grisham raised his head wearily, and obeyed. 'It was all arranged. We had the whole afternoon together, the first time in weeks that we'd had a decent amount of time. I can't tell you how much I was looking forward to it. But I could see as soon as he arrived that he was not in the best of moods.'

'How do you mean? Depressed? Worried?'

'I don't know quite how to put it. On edge, perhaps. Restless. He kept walking about the room, wouldn't settle. Did dance steps and stretches against the furniture. He did that sometimes to – to distance himself from me. Emphasising his independence.' This was addressed to Hart again.

'Why'd he wanna do that?' she asked.

'Oh, I don't know. He was upset about something and wanted to take it out on me. I didn't enquire too deeply because it didn't pay. I didn't want to quarrel with him, and I thought he'd just come out of it once he relaxed a bit. So I said what's wrong, and he said nothing, and I left it at that. But he kept picking at me, finding fault, wanting to quarrel. I let it all bounce off me. But then he picked up the newspaper and glanced through it and said, "Oh look, there's a bit about us in here."'

'I bet that gave you a fright,' Hart said.

'I can't tell you how my heart jumped. I thought he meant him and me. And when I looked at it, it was a news paragraph about some brawl at the Pomona Club. I – I'm afraid I just snapped. My temper was already frayed. He had been—'

'Winding you up?'

'Yes, winding me up. And I was always worried about the Pomona Club, and his connection with it. And I hated the fact that he went on working there in preference to a more civilised life where we could see more of each other. We had the most dreadful quarrel—'

'On that subject?'

'Mostly. It spread, as quarrels tend to, but it had its roots firmly in the Pomona Club. It ended with me giving him an ultimatum, and him telling me to go to hell, because he didn't need me. And he said if he got out of the Pomona Club, it would be for his own reasons, and he'd get right out of my life at the same time.'

'Oh dear,' said Hart, in response to Grisham's look of appeal.

'It was like having a bucket of cold water thrown over me. I stopped shouting and tried to placate him. I begged him not to say things like that. I said things should be whatever way he wanted. Well, he calmed down, and after a bit I thought the best way to make things up would be—'

'To go to bed.'

'Yes. Yes. But it wasn't like before. I was – I was angry with him. I wanted him to admit that he *did* need me, that it wasn't all on my side. But he wouldn't. In the end it was – rather horrible.'

Hence the rough sex. Slider could imagine it, rather more graphically than he liked. Grisham was afraid of losing Paloma, and fear made him angry. The one situation where he felt he had control was between the sheets, and he was going to prove he was master.

'So what happened after?' Hart prompted after a tactful silence.

'He left early. I'd arranged everything so that we could have a long time together. I begged him not to waste it, but he wouldn't stay. He looked at me so coldly.'

'And afterwards—?'

'Afterwards, after he'd gone, I wanted to punish him.' Grisham's voice was very quiet, and Slider was almost holding his breath. He had come to find out the cocaine connection and what exactly Jay Paloma had done on his last full day of life; but something else was coming, something unsuspected, and if Grisham were disturbed in any way he might realise what he was doing and shut up. 'I didn't want him hurt, you must understand that. Not hurt, just frightened.'

'Right, just frightened,' Hart agreed.

'To punish him for frightening me. And to make him see he couldn't leave me. After he left I had a lot of drinks rather quickly, and then I went out, I walked around – up and down the Embankment for hours – thinking what to do. And then I went to the Pink Parrot.'

'Yeah, 'course.'

'There's a man there – a sort of bouncer, I suppose, though he's always smartly dressed and carrying an expensive mobile phone. I suppose he might even be more of a manager than a bouncer. But he's huge, absolutely huge.'

'Yeah, I know. Jonah Lafota.'

Grisham blinked. 'You know him?'

'We've got him tucked up in custody, back at the station.'

'Ah.' It was a long, terminal sort of sigh. 'Then you know all about it.'

'From his end. Not from yours. You asked him to go and give Jay a smacking for you, did you?'

'No! I made it very clear I didn't want him hurt in any way. I gave Jonah money. To tell you the truth, even at the time I didn't really think he'd do it. He knew I was drunk – good God, it was obvious to anyone. He took the money and just grinned at me, as if he found the whole situation highly amusing.'

'Did he know about your relationship with Jay?' Slider asked.

'He'd seen us there together, in the Pink Parrot. And I expect Jay had told him. Anyway, I had another drink or two, and then I went home, and fell asleep like the dead. And the next morning, I thought it must all have been a horrible dream, except that I had a terrible hangover, and the money had gone all right. My anger was gone too. I just felt miserable. I didn't want Jay frightened, I just wanted him to come back to me.'

'Didn't you try to get in touch with Jonah?'

'Well, no.' Grisham looked a little dazed. 'In the clear light of day the whole situation was farcical. It never occurred to me for a moment that he'd do anything. I wouldn't have known where to find him, in any case, except at the Pink Parrot, and that's closed during the day. I did think about giving a ring in the evening, just to ask if he'd put the money away safely for me until I could collect it, but I realised that would only make me look more ridiculous.' He looked at Slider, pleadingly. 'I was quite sure he wouldn't do anything. I mean, why would he, even if he did think I meant it?'

Yes, why, Slider thought.

'In the afternoon I telephoned Jay's flat. I wanted to make it up with him. He didn't usually bear grudges. I thought I might even tell him about my little adventure, as a sort of joke. I thought it might amuse him – or at least prove how much I loved him. But there was no answer, so I supposed he'd gone out.'

'What time was that?' Slider put in.

'I left it until the afternoon, because he doesn't usually get up until about half past twelve. I telephoned at about half past one, but there was no answer. I was busy then for some time and couldn't get to a telephone, but I called again at about half past four, and again at six, but there was still no answer. After that I couldn't ring again because I had to go to the House – there was an all night sitting – but in any case I knew there'd be no point, because he leaves for work at about half past six.'

'Didn't he usually put the answering-machine on when he went out?'

'Yes. I did wonder about that. But he might have guessed I would ring, and didn't want me to be able to leave him a message.'

'Yes,' said Slider thoughtfully.

'And then the next day I saw it in the paper—'

'Yes,' said Slider again.

Grisham looked at him greyly. 'Can you tell me what happened? There were no details in the papers. I keep thinking – wondering—'

'We're still trying to find out exactly what happened,' Slider said. 'Jonah Lafota apparently went to the flat on Tuesday night, kicked the door in, and killed Jay Paloma with a single blow from some heavy instrument. There doesn't appear to have been any struggle, so it must have been quick. I doubt whether Jay had time to realise what was happening.'

'He killed him,' Grisham whispered.

'We have Lafota's fingerprints inside the flat, and we have a witness who saw the door being kicked down by him at half past eleven on Tuesday evening—'

Grisham sharpened. 'But he should have been at work at that time. Why wasn't he at work?'

'We don't know. I'm afraid there's a great deal we don't know yet.'

'But he's dead,' Grisham said. 'Jay is dead. That's the bottom line.' He rubbed his face with his hands, looking desperately tired now. 'What's going to happen to me, Inspector? Am I going to be arrested for murder? I never meant him to be hurt, I swear it. Will that make any difference? Mitigation, or whatever it's called. I loved him. I never meant him to be hurt.'

'It will be taken into consideration,' Slider said circumspectly. 'And the fact that you have co-operated with us, and haven't tried to hide anything, will tell in your favour.'

'Co-operated,' Sir Nigel said blankly. He shook his head slowly. 'I've been the most God-awful fool. And I'm responsible for Jay's death – I can't get away from that. I almost wish we hadn't abolished hanging. I ought to pay the penalty. It would be a relief, in a way.' His voice dropped to a whisper. 'I loved him so much.'

Slider could only take so much. 'I don't think it would be a relief to your wife and family to see you hanged.'

Grisham snapped out of it, though it was the frayed snap of very elderly celery. 'You're right. I must think of Annie and the children. I suppose there's no way of keeping any of this quiet? I don't want to escape my punishment, but the scandal would be a punishment to them, too, and they don't deserve it.'

You should have thought of that a long time ago, Slider thought, but not being one to kick a man when he was down, he didn't say it. 'That's not in my hands,' he said instead.

'Are you going to take me away?'

'I don't think that will be necessary. You aren't intending to run away, are you? What I'd like you to do is to make a full statement of everything you've just told us, with some extra details about times and dates that I'll ask you about. Then we'll leave you alone for the time being. Later it will be necessary to interview you again, perhaps here, perhaps at a police station, and the question of charges will arise. Your fullest co-operation will be in your best interests; and I'm sure

I don't need to advise you not to talk to anyone about any of this.'

'No,' Grisham said. 'You can be sure I'll keep my mouth shut.'

'Now I expect you'd like to have your solicitor present while you make your statement, wouldn't you?'

Grisham gave a faint smile. 'I imagine Roger's already on his way here. Roger Tagholm is my solicitor. Annie wanted me to call him when you first arrived, and I don't know my Annie if she didn't call him as soon as the library door closed behind us.'

Slider found Joanna by Atherton's bedside. Their heads were close together in absorbed conversation, but first Atherton looked up, and then Joanna turned her head and saw him, and they both smiled. 'It's the man himself,' Joanna said.

'Shall I leave?' Slider asked plaintively. 'You looked so cosy when I came in, I wouldn't want to be in the way.'

'We were just talking.'

'What about?'

'Jim has this theory that everyone in the world is a character out of *Winnie the Pooh*.'

'What I said,' Atherton corrected her, 'was that the characters in said book are such archetypes that you can categorise all the people you know by them.'

'That's what I said,' Joanna objected. 'And we were just arguing about which character *he* was.'

'I'm Christopher Robin,' Atherton said quickly. 'The wise outsider, the adjudicator who takes no part but sees all; the Great Narrator.'

'Also known as God,' Joanna said sarcastically. 'Whereas I said—'

'He's Piglet,' Slider said.

She looked delighted. 'Yes! You see it too!'

'I shall sulk,' Atherton said. 'I won't be Piglet. Joanna's Rabbit, of course—'

'You swine!'

'But you, Bill,' he went on solemnly, 'are hard to define.'

'He's Pooh Bear, living under the name of Slider,' Joanna said.

'But with just a touch of Eeyore, do you think?'

'Is this the best you can manage by way of intellectual exchange?' Slider asked.

'From where I'm lying, it's a Socratean Dialogue,' Atherton said. 'Do you know what the absolute worst thing about being in hospital is?'

'I'm sure you'd like to tell me.'

'It's the relentless baby-talk. At some point in history all the medical staff jointly decided that they could cope with the revoltingness of sick people if they treated them like subnormal seven-year-olds. "We're just going to pop you down to X-ray and take some pictures of your tummy."' He made a sound of disgust. 'They all do it. It's always "just": we're *just* going to do this or that – we're *just* going to cut your leg off – as if that makes it better. And "pop". Everything's "pop".'

'Pop?' Slider enquired mildly.

'Pop you down to theatre. Pop you into bed. Pop this thermometer in your mouth.' He assumed a whining falsetto. '"Would you just like to pop yourself over onto this trolley for me?" No I bloody would not!'

'You're feeling better,' Slider concluded. 'Your word-sensitivity's returned.'

'It never went away,' Atherton said. 'I just hadn't got the energy to talk about it. How's the case coming along?'

Slider frowned. 'I've got a whole lot of new information.'

'You don't seem too happy about it.'

'Because it doesn't make *sense*,' Slider said resentfully. He told them about Grisham. 'It looks like another couple of loose ends tied up, but it just makes things worse.'

'But you've got this Jonah bloke already, haven't you?' Joanna said. 'You thought he did it, and now Grisham says he paid him to do it. What's the problem?'

'As Grisham himself said to me, why should Jonah do it?' Slider said. 'Look, a man comes up to you in a club and shoves a wad of banknotes in your hand and asks you to go round and frighten a friend of his – why would you do it?'

'For the money,' Joanna said.

'A couple of hundred?' Slider shook his head. 'Not worth the risk, especially if you're working for Billy Yates. Besides, you've already got the money. The man's tired and emotional, and you're four times the size of him. If you want the cash, you've got it. You don't have to do anything for it. It's very unlikely the bloke will ever come back asking for it, and if he does, you've only got to smile menacingly and say you don't know nuthin' 'bout no money. What's Grisham going to do?'

'You're assuming Jonah's bright enough to think of all that,' Joanna said. 'What if he's really, really dim, and just does what he's told?'

'If he's merely obedient, why *kill* Paloma? That's just crazy.'

'He could have been drunk. Or lost his temper,' Joanna said.

'Or just over-enthusiastic,' Atherton said. 'You said he's huge – maybe he doesn't know his own strength.'

'Or maybe he'd always hated Paloma and was glad of the excuse,' Joanna added.

'And another thing,' Slider went on, 'where do the poison pen letters come in?'

'Maybe they never existed. You never saw any. Maybe Paloma just made them up.'

'But he was afraid of something,' said Slider. 'Maybe there weren't any poison pen letters, but he was afraid of something.'

'Maybe this, maybe that,' Atherton said sleepily. 'Anything's possible. Maybe Jonah didn't kill him.'

'Thanks,' said Slider. 'You said you were going to solve this case for me from your bed.'

'I can't make bricks without straw. Bring me more facts.'

'Facts,' Slider said crossly. 'What are facts? You think you know something, and then you turn it round another way and it means something entirely different.'

'Nothing is what it seems, and reality is up for grabs,' Atherton said sympathetically.

'That reminds me,' Joanna said, 'did I ever tell you my favourite Bob Preston story?'

'You have so many,' Slider said. 'Go on.'

'But this is a true story. You know Bob Preston, who used to be our co-principal trumpet? Right, well, Bob studied composition at university, and for his finals he had to write an original piece of music which would be marked by his professor. His professor was—' She named a famous English composer. 'He was so brilliant he scared the shit out of Bob, though he admired him tremendously. Anyway, when it came to it, Bob couldn't write a note, hadn't an original thought in his head. Complete blank. He was in despair, because everything depended on this composition. Then a street-wise friend gave him a tip. "Take a piece of your professor's own music," the friend said, "turn it upside down and write it out in your own handwriting. Your prof won't recognise it, but it'll fit his brain patterns well enough for him to think it's good. He'll love it, he'll give you top marks." Bob thought this was a brilliant idea, so he got hold of a Fantasia which he happened to know his prof was particularly proud of. He turned it upside down and wrote it out – and discovered that what he had was the first movement of a Sibelius symphony.'

Atherton shouted with pleasure.

'I never know whether to believe your stories,' Slider complained.

Joanna smiled seraphically. 'Everything I tell you is either true, or bloody well ought to be.'

CHAPTER TWELVE

Quinbus Flestrin

Slider faced David Stevens in the corridor outside the tape room.

'Look, Dave, you've got to get him to come across. It's not doing him any good, this refusing to say anything.'

Stevens shrugged his bouncy shoulders. 'I can only take my client's instruction. If he doesn't want to talk—'

'Have you explained to him about the change in the law over the right to remain silent?'

'Who d'you think you're talking to here? Of course I have.'

Slider struck off points on his fingers. 'We've got the footmark on the door, fingermarks inside the flat, an eyewitness who saw him kicking the door down. And now we've got Sir Nigel Grisham's statement that he paid Lafota money to put the frighteners on Paloma. There's no doubt we'll get custody extended.'

'I agree,' said Stevens easily.

Slider blinked. 'I've got enough to charge him.'

Stevens smiled. 'So charge him.' He was eyeing Slider closely. 'Charge him,' he said again.

'I want him to tell me what happened!' Slider burst out in frustration. 'Grisham only asked him to frighten Paloma. Why did he kill him? Was it an accident? Why did he wait until the next evening? How did he know Paloma was at home? Keeping silent now is pointless – can't you make him see that?'

Stevens grinned his predator's grin. 'Ah Bill, Bill, the great poker face! You've got doubts, haven't you?'

'Don't get clever with me. I just told you that.' He rubbed his eyes. 'If there's anything he's got to say in mitigation, he's weakening his position by not telling me now. *You* know that. Make *him* understand it.'

Stevens laid a hand on Slider's shoulder. His shirt was crisp, his suit unwrinkled, his aftershave a poem; and his eyes twinkled with that whole-hearted enjoyment of life only solicitors can afford. 'I will do my best, old son,' he pledged. 'Angels can't do more.'

Jonah, seedy, rumpled and smelling of sweat, lit another cigarette and coughed through the first drag. His eyes were bloodshot from smoke and lack of sleep. He glared at Slider defiantly across the table.

'I didn't do it, right?'

'You didn't do what?' Slider asked.

'I didn't kill Jay.'

'Then who did?'

'I dunno. How should I know?' All I know, 'e was dead when I got there, right?'

'That's not very original. If I had a fiver for every time someone's told me that—'

'Itsa trufe!' Now Jonah sounded frightened. His voice cracked a little. 'I never done nuffing to him. He was dead when I got there.'

'All right, tell me about it,' Slider said.

Jonah was no orator even when he wanted to speak. It was like pull-out toffee, getting his story, but assembled it amounted to this: he had driven from his flat to White City, timing it to arrive at about twenty past eleven when the pubs were turning out, so that he wouldn't be noticed. He went up to Paloma's flat, kicked the door in with one mighty blow of his right foot, went straight to the sitting-room, from which he could hear the sound of the television. Paloma was sprawled dead on the floor with his overturned chair.

'How did you know he was dead?'

'Aw, come on, man!' was Jonah's reply to that.

'Did you go right up to him and look?'

'Nah, I could see from the door he was dead all right.'

'So what did you do?'

'Nuffing. I never done nuffing. I just got out, right? It wasn't no business of mine.'

'Hmm. But you see, the people next door who heard you kick the door in also heard you knock over something heavy. They heard a thud, as if something heavy had hit the floor. Now what was that, I wonder, if it wasn't Jay Paloma?'

'I never touched him! I tell you I never touched nuffing!'

'Nothing at all?'

Jonah stared at him, eyes wide, his mouth open to repeat his panicky denial. But Stevens beside him stirred like the first faint dawn breeze ruffling the willows, and Jonah's mouth remained open and silent as he tried to capture the thread which had been spun for him.

'The bottle!' he cried at last. He might as well have pronounced it *eureka*. 'I was shakin', man, an' I needed a drink, so I grabbed the bottle. The whisky bottle on the table.'

'So you did go into the room, then? Just now you told me you stayed by the door.'

'Look, I just went to look at 'im, right? Like anyone would. I never touched 'im. And I was so shook up, like I said, I grabbed the bottle and took a drink, and when I turned round to put it back, I knocked the table over.'

'You knocked the table over?'

'Yeah.' Lafota seemed to feel relief at having reached sure ground. He looked at Stevens for approval. 'That's what these people must of heard, right? An' everyfing went on the floor. So I picked it up and put it back, and then I took off.'

'Why did you pick everything up?' Slider asked.

'I dunno,' Lafota said, floored by the question.

But in Slider's mind the scenario played true. What could be simpler for a man-mountain in a normal-sized sitting-room than to knock the table over? He might have done it at any point while he was whacking Paloma; or it might actually have happened as he said, when, shaky from the killing, he had fortified himself with a drink. It had the sappy ring of truth about it, that bit. The killing he had planned and visualised, but the mess as the table went over, spilling magazines, whisky and the contents of the ashtray on the floor, was something unexpected, and it threw him. In his panic, wanting to leave things as he had found them, wanting to leave no trace of his having been there – other, of course, than the dead body – the big lug had tidied up after himself, put the table back, rubbed the ash into the carpet so that no-one would notice it, entirely forgetting that he had left his dabs all over the whisky bottle. It was the sort of stupid thing a person would do, when they were not accustomed to thinking things out, and found themselves in an unexpected and frightening situation.

'So why *did* you kill him?' Slider asked at last, conversationally.

'I never,' Jonah said stubbornly. 'I told you. He was already dead when I got there.'

'All right, then what did you go to the flat for in the first place?' No answer. 'Why did you go to the flat and kick the door down?' No answer. 'Did you do it for the money?'

Jonah looked contemptuous. 'You call that money? I wouldn't spit on a beggar for that.' Stevens stirred, and Jonah glanced at him anxiously, and then said, 'I never killed him. He was dead when I got there.'

'But then *why* did you go there?'

Now Jonah looked sullen. 'I ain't saying no more. I never killed 'im, that's all. I ain't done nuffing.' He turned resentfully to Stevens. 'You get me out of here, right? They got nuffing on me.' And he folded his massive arms across his chest and ostentatiously closed his mouth.

Hollis was in Slider's room, reading something he held in his hands. He looked up as Slider came in. 'Any luck?'

'I ain't saying nuffing,' Slider said, going round his desk to sit down heavily. 'Now he says he found Paloma already dead when he got there, was so upset he took a drink of whisky, and knocked the table over putting the bottle back.'

'Really? Well, I don't know about you, but I'm convinced,' Hollis said brightly.

Slider gave him a look. 'It means he's talked his way out of the fingerprints.'

'It looks like an open and shut case to me, guv,' Hollis said comfortingly. 'I wouldn't worry. He'll come clean in the end.'

'With Stevens as his brief?' Slider said. 'What's that you've got there, anyway?'

Hollis proffered it. 'It's the additional forensic report.'

Slider took it. The lab had typed the anal swab ready for cross-matching if requested. Well, that should keep Sir Nigel straight and true to his story. There was no trace of any known recreational drug in the bloodstream, and the alcohol was low, 40mg per 100ml, so Paloma was neither drunk nor high at the time of death. And the stomach contents had been analysed as scrambled eggs and toast, eaten less than one hour before death.

'Well, that's consistent with the dirty dishes in the kitchen,' Slider said, throwing the paper down on his desk. 'No surprises there.'

'The hearty man ate a condemned breakfast,' Hollis said.

'A late breakfast, anyway,' Slider said. 'What else have you got for me?'

'Oh – this, sir.' Hollis passed over the envelope with an abstracted air of having forgotten he was holding it. It was large, square and stiff, and Slider guessed what it was before he opened it.

'Mr Honeyman's farewell party,' he said aloud. 'The official brass one, complete with speeches and presentation.'

'You're invited, sir?' Hollis said with a smirk. 'Congratulations.'

'Not so fast,' Slider said. 'I've got to take someone else from my firm.' He passed the invitation back. 'As the only sergeant still upright, that means you. If I've got to suffer, I don't see why you should get away with it. I'm not a well man, you know.'

Hollis bulged at him. 'Me, guv? They won't want me. I'm a new boy, hardly know Mr Honeyman.'

'Don't grovel,' Slider said coldly. 'You're It.'

'But it says black tie! My dinner suit's twenty years old. It's got twelve-inch flares and eight-inch lapels. The Fred West Wedding Suit look. I don't even know if I can still get into it.'

'Hire one,' Slider said brutally.

'Guv, listen, take Swilley. Give yourself a bit o' credit.'

'I wouldn't do that to Swilley,' Slider said.

'Hart, then.' Hollis seemed struck by his own idea a moment after voicing it. 'That's it – take Hart. Not only will it give you street cred, having a bird on your arm, but think how much it'll annoy the high-ups.'

Slider looked at him narrowly. 'White man speak with forked tongue. But you've got a point.'

'That's right, guv.' Hollis relaxed ostentatiously. 'She doesn't mind what she says to anyone, and she's cracking-looking.

And being an ambitious female, she probably won't mind going.'

'All right, you've made your point,' Slider said. 'I shan't forget, though, how you abandoned me in my hour of need.'

'That seems fair,' Hollis said happily, 'I won't forget it either.' He got as far as the door and turned back. 'Guv, I was just thinking – I suppose Lafota couldn't possibly have been telling the truth?'

'Meaning?'

'Well, you remember at the post mortem, the pathologist-bloke started off thinking the death were much earlier? It was you saying late breakfast made me think – well, it *is* more like a breakfast meal, scrambled eggs, in't it?'

Slider was silent. The wrong time of death? Two men on the scene? Could that be the answer to all the anomalies? There was something else, something that made Hollis's suggestion chime harmoniously rather than jar. He looked back through his mental filing cabinet, and Hollis waited, watching him. What the hell was it? Something he had noticed without noticing, right at the very beginning. Something about the room in which Paloma was found.

'You were at the scene before me,' Slider said at last. 'Were the curtains in the sitting-room open or closed when you arrived?'

'Open,' Hollis said without hesitation. 'The sun was shining in.'

'You didn't open them?'

'Not me.'

'Who was first on the scene? It was Baker, wasn't it? He wouldn't have pulled the curtains back. He'd know better than that.'

'Shall I check, guv?'

'Yes, do that. If the curtains were open—'

'Yes.'

'It isn't impossible that someone should sit and watch television at night with the curtains open, particularly in summer – with the long twilights people do sometimes forget to pull them. But—'

'Yes, guv,' Hollis said.

Slider met his eyes unwillingly. 'If there's anything in this, we're back at square one, you realise that. We'll have it all to do again. We'll have to go over every statement, re-examine the witnesses, re-interview all the neighbours with a new time of death in mind.'

'No nice goodbye present for Mr Honeyman, then?'

'Go and track down Baker. And if he says the curtains were open, you'd better assemble the troops to start looking at the statements.'

'Right, guv.'

'Oh – Hollis!'

'Guv?'

'That television programme that was on when we arrived at the scene. What channel would that be?'

'That's *The Big Breakfast*. Channel Four.'

'Right. Thanks,' said Slider.

Honeyman seemed ill at ease. 'Ah, Slider,' he said vaguely. He stared at and through him, frowning.

'You sent for me, sir?' Slider reminded him tactfully.

'Yes. Yes.' A pause. 'Oh yes. You've had your invitation to my farewell party?'

'Yes, sir.'

'And who are you bringing?'

'I thought Hart, sir, if that's all right.'

'Hart? Oh yes. Yes, good idea. Bring a little life into it. These do's tend to be stuffy. A lot of men together, slapping backs and talking shop.' He cleared his throat as though embarrassed. 'You know of course that I'm not leaving?'

'Not, sir?'

'No. Well, not this week, anyway. I had hoped we could bring this Paloma case home by today, but as we haven't – well, I couldn't go in the middle of it. Especially given the sensitivity of the Grisham connection.'

'I see, sir. So how long will you be staying on?' If the case went into extra time, what then? Would they just slip little Eric in the non-active filing cabinet years hence and forget him?

'I've asked for another fortnight,' Honeyman said. 'If there's nothing substantial by then I shall have to hand it on to my successor, but I did want to give it a reasonable chance. I look to you – er, Bill – to send me out in the right style.' He used

Slider's name with all the ease of a Victorian virgin naming a private part.

'I'll do my best, sir,' Slider said. 'So – what about the party?'

'Oh, we had to go ahead with that. There are some very senior people coming, and it's difficult to get them all in the same place at the same time. It would have been impossible to reschedule at this late stage.'

'I see.'

Honeyman looked at him almost pleadingly. 'And what is the latest movement on the Paloma case?'

Slider felt a cad to be hitting him when he was down. 'There seems to be some possibility of doubt that Lafota is our man, sir,' he said; and explained.

Honeyman's face, which had sunk at the opening words, rose again from the waves towards the end. 'Oh, I'm sure that can be got over. You must look into everything, of course, but there's no doubt Lafota was there, and he must remain our best suspect. And while we're on the subject,' he hurried on, as though afraid Slider might voice some more inconvenient doubts, 'I have some information for you concerning an enquiry you put to me.' He raised his eyebrows and gave Slider a significant nod. 'Shut the door, will you?'

Slider obeyed. Honeyman sat down behind his desk and gestured Slider to sit opposite him.

'This is confidential and very sensitive. I'm sure I can trust you?'

'Yes sir,' Slider said, a little intrigued.

Honeyman seemed to relax. 'I know you're a good chap. The thing is—' He hesitated, and, leaning forward a little, adopted an unburdening posture. 'Senior rank has its social aspect, and I'm not very good at being pally. It's held me back to a certain extent. But I've always believed in being open, and I dislike – yes, I dislike very much – the sort of keep-quiet-and-do-as-you're-told attitude that's rife amongst some of the higher echelons.'

Slider was now mystified. He could only look receptive and hope that the unburdening wasn't going to get too sticky. Deeply personal confidences tended to involve a morning-after hangover of the do-you-still-respect-me variety, which Slider had no wish to be on the wrong end of.

Honeyman sighed. 'I've been in the Job thirty years, all but,' he confided. 'I was never a high flyer. I was interested in police work, that's why I joined. But there comes a point when you have to decide whether you're going to have a career structure, or settle for being PC Plod and going out in a blaze of obscurity. And a career demands a certain amount of compromise. A certain amount of put up and shut up. Tact, diplomacy and the occasional—' He hesitated again, lost for the right word. Slider could think of plenty, but plumped for tact and diplomacy and waiting in silence. 'Fudge,' Honeyman said at last. 'Well, perhaps not quite that. A blurring of the outlines.'

'Yes, sir,' Slider said, to help him along.

Honeyman looked at him sharply. 'I don't mean abandoning one's principles. I don't mean doing anything wrong. But sometimes one has to be, well, pragmatic.' He stopped, internally digesting something, and then seemed to come to a decision. 'I've taken my share of stick over the years. When you aren't a high flyer, it's expected. But when it comes to being spoken to like that—'

'Sir?'

'Look here,' Honeyman said, 'I've been told to keep my mouth shut about this, but I don't see how you can carry on an investigation without all the information, and it is my personal judgement that you ought to be told. So I am going against orders. But this must go no further.'

'I understand, sir.'

'Yes, I think you do.' Honeyman scanned his face keenly. 'Cosgrove did put an enquiry to Mr Barrington. And Barrington did tell him to drop it. He had orders from higher up. There was – and is – a special Scotland Yard investigation going on into a very large drugs network. It is a very major investigation indeed, and they're hoping to bring down some very major players. The whole thing is very sensitive and very expensive, and if anything were to happen to disrupt it there would be repercussions at the highest level. The Drugs Squad has got undercover people in all over the place—'

'Including at the Pomona Club, sir?' Slider put in.

'Got it in one. That's why Cosgrove was warned off, and that's why I've been told to warn you off. Any snooping around the Pomona or Yates is likely to tread on certain toes, and it won't be tolerated.'

'Warn me off without explanation?'

'Exactly. That's what gets my goat,' he added with sudden animation. 'Don't ask questions, just do as you're told. What kind of way is that to run a department?'

'I appreciate your telling me all this, sir,' Slider said. 'Can I ask you – is Yates one of the big players they're after?'

'I can't tell you that. Oh, not because I've been warned, but because I don't know. But I suspect he is. There's something not quite right about friend Yates, or my name's not Eric St Maur Honeyman.'

Slider took that without a blink. 'It occurs to me to wonder, sir, whether Cosgrove was whacked because he was asking questions about Yates. His girlfriend said he told her he wouldn't be put off by Mr Barrington's warning, and that he'd go on asking questions on his own.'

'It occurs to me to wonder that too. But I've been told to keep my wondering to myself. Any questions that need asking will be asked by the great and good at Headquarters,' Honeyman said with undisguised sarcasm. A spot of colour appeared in each of his cheeks. 'But Cosgrove's one of *my* men. I may not have been with you long, but Shepherd's Bush is *my* ground and *my* responsibility. Well, that's it,' he concluded. 'You know as much as I do now. I'm not going to tell you to leave well alone. But I will tell you to be careful. Your career could be on the line if you foul the scent for the Drugs Squad. Those special posting boys are impatient of locals and arrogant as hell.'

'I suppose,' Slider said tentatively, 'you don't know the name of the undercover officer who's been targeting the Pomona?'

'If I did, I wouldn't be allowed to tell you. And if I told you, it would be strictly against orders for you to contact him.'

'Of course, I see that. It's just that, if we knew what he was up to, we could make sure not to get our lines crossed. It's easy to blunder into snares when you don't know where they've been set. We might already have caused some upset, simply by arresting Jonah Lafota. If only we could ask him,' he finished wistfully, 'I'm sure the officer on the ground would see the sense in keeping us informed.'

Honeyman eyed him through a blend of righteous indignation, years of resentment, and a touch of holiday rapture. 'I am absolutely forbidden to tell you Detective Sergeant Richard de Glanville's name,' he said firmly.

'Of course, sir. I understand.'

'It would upset Mr Wetherspoon very much if he were to hear you had approached DS de Glanville. Very much indeed.'

'I wouldn't dream of letting him hear that, sir,' said Slider. He and Little Eric looked into each other's eyes. It was a moment of contact, of tentative warmth between them. He wasn't a bad old boy, Slider thought, for an impossible bastard.

'Good, good. Well, off you go, then,' Honeyman said briskly. 'I'll see you at the party later on.'

'Yes, sir. Thank you.'

'At least they can't touch my pension,' Honeyman said as Slider headed for the door.

Slider sat down at his desk, hesitated a moment, and then picked up the phone and dialled Scotland Yard. 'Detective Superintendent Smithers, please.'

It rang a long time before a woman's voice answered.

'Pauline, it's Bill Slider. I didn't interrupt you in the middle of someone, did I?'

'Fat chance,' she said. 'I was in the loo, that's all. Is it trouble?'

'Why should you think that?'

'When else do you ever ring me?'

It was a deserved barb, Slider realised. He had known Pauline Smithers for most of his career, but her seniority, his diffidence, and Irene had prevented him from seeing much of her socially – which before Joanna might have been just as well. There had been a definite tenderness between them at one time.

'Congratulations on your promotion,' he said.

'Thanks,' she said. 'But you know I only got it because they're abolishing the DCI rank. They had to do something with me. Shove me up and shove me sideways.'

'Bollocks. You deserve it. You've deserved it for a long time.'

'You could have had it if you'd wanted it,' she said seriously. 'You've got the talent, and you haven't got my disadvantages.'

'Disadvantages?'

'Two of them. Front upper body, left and right.'

'From what little I know of them, I'm sure they're a positive asset.'

'Chivalrous but inaccurate. The point is, if I've got this far despite being female, you could have been a chief superintendent by now if you'd wanted.'

'I suppose that's it. I didn't want.'

'Then you're a fool, Bill,' she said briskly. 'Who d'you think you are, Peter Pan? You want to retire on that salary grade, do you?'

'It's not a question of money,' he began.

'Then you've got a Gandhi complex, which is worse.'

'I'm good at what I do,' he said. 'It ought to be possible to be rewarded – to get the promotion and the pay increases – without being moved into a different job that you wouldn't be so good at.'

'Yes, there's a lot of things ought to be different from what they are. You've just got to work with what there is. It's a fool who complains about the system when he can't change it.'

'I wasn't complaining. I'm happy being a DI.'

'You won't be for much longer, chum, when the kids start being promoted over your head, and you've got some spotty youth giving you orders. Still, it's no concern of mine. What did you want, anyway?'

That didn't sound very promising. 'I just phoned to congratulate you. How are you enjoying the new posting?'

'Don't stuff me, Bill. What do you want?'

'I need your help, Pauly,' he said meekly.

'I'd guessed that much,' she said. And then, more kindly, 'Are you in trouble?'

'I've got a case. It was difficult from the start, but now I've come up against official silences, it's escalated to impossible.'

'All right, tell me the worst.'

He gave her a rough outline of the case, and told her what Honeyman had told him. 'It occurs to me this undercover guy may have been the one Yates saw talking to my victim. I need to find that out so that I can strike it off my list. And I could use a little more information about what my victim was getting into. I'm groping about in the dark here.'

Pauline said slowly, 'And what do you want me to do about it?'

'Tell me how to get in contact with this de Glanville without blowing his cover or upsetting the brass.'

'But why ask me? I'm not in the Drugs Squad.'

'You're at the Yard. And you have contacts everywhere, I know you have. You've told me yourself plenty of times that you've had to play it sneaky to get on. The Ladies' Loo Network you used to call it. Female solidarity.'

'You're forgetting I'm brass myself now. Senior ranks solidarity – what about that? What you're asking me could get me demoted so fast I'd get friction burns on my arse.'

'But it's crap, this blackout. I'm far more likely to mess up their investigation through ignorance than if I knew where not to tread. Help me. Can't you help me?' There was a silence. 'Please, Pauly. I think I'm losing it.'

'I don't like it,' she said.

'It's in his own interest. If he was the man Yates mentioned, that could mean he's clocked him. He could be in danger.'

'I wish you wouldn't come to me with this sort of thing,' she said, and he knew from her tone of voice that he'd won. 'I don't mind helping you out, when it doesn't mean breaking the rules. But I'm in a vulnerable position now. You wouldn't believe the cabals that operate up here. And there are no women on the Squad, that's another thing.'

'No-one need ever know. You can do it. I wouldn't ask you if there was any way I could do it myself. And it's for a good cause.'

'Yeah. Your promotion. If only. All right,' she said at last, 'I'll try and get him to contact you. That's the best way. But if nothing happens, it's because I haven't managed it. Don't chase me up, or bother me, or leave me messages.'

'Hey,' he said, wounded, 'it's me.'

'And you owe me, after this.'

'Anything.'

'I won't hold you to the anything,' she said drily. 'But a bloody good nosh, anyway.'

'Just pick the date and the restaurant,' he said.

He put the phone down feeling happier. Women CID officers were so beleaguered that they tended to stick together and help each other out; and there was also that curious solidarity that women of all ranks show each other in front of the mirrors in the loo. Information he was confident Pauline could come by. The co-operation of the unknown de Glanville was a different matter. But he had done his best; now he could only wait.

CHAPTER THIRTEEN

There's Many an Old Tune Played on a Good Fiddle

The estate sat in its daytime quiet, all the kids in school, all the workers at work, just a few mums and tots about, and the occasional dog busily trotting its rounds. With the new universal affluence, even council tenants had cars, and parking had become a severe problem on an estate built for people who walked or went by bus. The roadsides were always occupied; the yards round which the blocks of flats were built had been divided up with raised flowerbeds and marked out into parking spaces, which were allocated to specific flats for fairness. Slider found an empty one easily enough, for in the daytime a lot of people took their cars to work, but in the evening the yards were full. It occurred to him to wonder where Jonah parked on the murder evening; and if Jonah wasn't the murderer after all, where had the murderer parked, and had anyone noticed an alien vehicle in their space?

As he got out of the car and locked it, he felt that inexplicable crawling of the skin that comes from being watched. He made a business of fumbling with the key and testing the handle to give himself time to look unobtrusively around, but he couldn't see anyone. The owner of the space, perhaps, debating whether to come out and challenge him? It was probably nothing, but being whacked on the head by a murderer had concentrated his instincts of self-preservation wonderfully, and instead of going straight up to Busty's flat, he did a walkabout, going up the stairs of the block opposite, walking along different balconies, looking out all the time for the tiny giveaway movement. But he saw nothing, and, chiding himself for over-reaction, he crossed the yard and went up to Busty's flat.

Busty answered the door to him with a blank look which endured for a moment before recognition tuned in. She was in full working fig – black skirt and a tight vee-neck mauve jumper with lurex threads woven through it. Her hair was fully coiffed and her makeup daunting, but behind it she looked sad. Slider thought that was really sadder than if she had looked haggard or grief-stricken or riven with despair. You could get sympathy, drugs or even – *absit omen* – counselling for desperate grief, but sad you have to do all on your own, and it goes on so much longer.

'Oh. Mr Slider. I was just getting ready to go to work,' she said.

'Hello, Busty. I thought you were poshed up. You look very nice.'

'Only will it take very long?' she asked, not responding to the compliment.

'Not long. I want to ask you some more questions. Are you up to going back to work?' he asked as she walked ahead of him to the sitting-room.

'I got to do something. Can't sit around all day. Especially not here.' She paused a moment at the door of the sitting-room like a horse baulking at water. 'I make meself come in here, but I still see him, you know, lying there.'

He put his arm round her shoulders. 'You're very brave,' he said. 'If it's any help, I think it must have been very quick. I doubt if he would even have known what happened.' Who had he said those same words to recently? Oh, yes, Sir Nigel. Jay Paloma had two mourners who had loved him sincerely. There were worse epitaphs.

'Thanks,' she said after a moment, and got out a handkerchief, carefully to dab her eyes. 'Don't get me going. I can't do me warpaint again.'

'Are you managing all right for money?' he asked her, wondering if that was why she had to go back to work.

'Yeah,' she said. 'I got me wages, and there's all the savings. Lucky Maurice put it in a joint account, so it come to me automatic. There was 'ell of a lot of it.' A thought struck her, and she looked at him with alarm. 'It won't be took off me, will it?'

'No. Why should it?'

'Because of Maurice buying the stuff for his friend.'

'I don't think that's going to come into it. Anyway, who could say that was where the money came from?'

She relaxed. 'Only he'd want me to have it.' A look of bitterness crossed her face. 'I've had his mum and dad on the phone. They want to take him back to Ireland to bury.'

'Ah.'

'Them what've never spoken to him in twenty years.'

'Yes. I'm afraid they are his next of kin. Did he leave a will?'

'Not that I know of. He wasn't expecting to get murdered.'

'No, I suppose not. Well, I'm afraid if they insist, the law's on their side. Does it matter very much to you where he's buried?'

'It's not the *where*, but I'd've liked to be there, to see him off. They won't invite me, though. Not someone like me.' She blew her nose carefully. There were little rings of white now on her nostrils where she had pinched the makeup off. 'What did you want to ask me, anyway? I got to get on, or I'll be late.'

'I'd like you to cast your mind back to the way the flat was when you came home that day. What I'm trying to do is establish exactly what time of day Maurice was killed.'

She stared. 'I thought you knew. Half past eleven at night, didn't you tell me?'

'I'm testing out a theory,' Slider said. 'There's a lot that doesn't add up, and it's possible we've been proceeding on the wrong assumption. Now you told me that Jay was very tidy – houseproud even?'

'That's right. It was him that did all the housework.' She looked round the room, and he looked with her. It was tidy, but there was dust on all the surfaces, and a cold smell of disuse. 'Everything was always spick and span.'

'What was his routine? What did he do when he got up?'

'Well, he'd have a cup of coffee, then he'd go to the bathroom. Always spent ages in the bathroom. Bath, wash his hair, shave – ever so particular about shaving, went over his chin with a magnifying mirror and tweezers after. And he had to do his legs and that.' She gave him a sidelong look and he nodded understanding.

'So all that would take him – how long?'

'An hour, I suppose. More even.'

'And he always bathed before breakfast? Never the other way round?'

'He liked to get clean first. Always wash and everything, get dressed then have his breakfast.'

'But that last day, the Tuesday, his routine was rather put out, wasn't it, because he got up to see you off?'

'That's right. Well, he'd've normally got up about half twelve, but he got up about eleven.'

'And what did he do?'

'Well, he made us some coffee, and he sat with me and drunk it while I finished getting ready.'

'In his dressing-gown and slippers?'

'That's right.'

'And he hadn't done his bathroom routine yet?'

'No. Well I was still in and out.'

'Quite. So when you left at half past eleven he would probably have gone straight to the bathroom?'

'Oh yes. Bound to. He wouldn't hang around dirty, not Maurice.'

'Which would take him to half past twelve-ish. And then he'd have breakfast?'

'I spect so.'

'What did he usually have?'

'Oh, all different things. Toast or cereal or something hot. Depended on how hungry he was.'

'Scrambled eggs, maybe?'

'Yes, he sometimes had that.'

'What did you have for breakfast that morning?'

'Me? I never had nothing. Just the coffee. I was going to have lunch at Shirley's, I didn't want to blow meself out.'

That would account, Slider thought, for two coffee mugs and the single plate and pot in the sink. It was looking possible.

'What about washing up? Would Maurice have left the breakfast dishes in the sink?'

'Oh no, he'd have washed up straight away. Never liked leaving things.' She looked at him, trying to follow his train of thought. 'Them things in the sink—'

'One plate, two mugs. If they were his supper things, why two mugs? Unless one was left from earlier in the day.'

'No, if he'd had a cup of coffee on its own some time, he'd

have washed up the mug. Anyway, he was sitting watching telly, wasn't he? He wouldn't have sat down and watched telly without washing up first.' Slider saw something dawn on her. 'And another thing, I've just remembered, and now you come to mention it does stick out – the bath towels.'

'Yes?' Slider thought. 'There were two stretched out on the shower rail.'

'That's right. Mine and his. He hung them like that to dry, and then later on he folded them up and hung them on the towel rail with the others. He'd never have left them like that all day.'

Slider nodded thoughtfully. Even people with strong routines could deviate from them. It wasn't proof of anything, but it was suggestive. The eggs might have been supper, he might have had a rogue cup of coffee earlier and been distracted from washing up the mug, he might have forgotten to go back and fold the towels. Any one of them – but all of them? Unless he had gone out on urgent, unexpected business, and been out all afternoon – then he might not have got round to completing his morning tasks. And Grisham said there was no answer from the telephone. But that could be evidence either way, in or out. 'Did Maurice ever forget to switch the answering-machine on when he went out?'

'I've never known him to,' she said.

Of course that wasn't proof either. He *might* forget. Or he might simply not answer for some reason. But it was another little grain to add to the scales.

'One last thing,' he said. 'The television was on when you found him?'

'Yes.'

'So whatever channel it was on must have been what he was watching when he was killed.'

'I suppose so.'

'My sergeant said it was set on Channel Four. Now, I've got here—' he felt in his pocket '—the schedule for that day, the Tuesday. Will you look at it, and tell me what there is on Channel Four that he might have been likely to watch.'

She took it, peered, crossed the room to her handbag for her glasses, and looked again. 'Well, the film, of course. He'd have been up for that. *In Which We Serve* – that was one of his favourites. He loved all that sort of thing, old black and white films, especially about the war.'

'Would he have known it was on? Do you have the television listings anywhere?'

'No, we don't get a paper or anything. But we got Teletext. And anyway, there's always some daft old film on Channel Four in the afternoon. Maurice knew that.'

'Let's see, that was on at one-fifty-five. Is there anything before that he'd be likely to watch?'

She peered. 'Hmm. I don't think so. He wasn't a great telly-fan really, except for the old films. He'd sooner read a book, he always said. Me, if I was home, I'd watch anything, especially the soaps, but he'd always tut at me and say it was rotting my brain and couldn't I find anything better to do. But he did like the movies.'

'All right, what about later in the day? In the evening?' She looked at the programmes rather hopelessly. He tried to help her along. 'What about the news? Would he have watched the Channel Four news?'

'Oh no, I don't think so. Well, there's not a lot here I could say for sure he'd watch. He wasn't really very big on telly, like I said.'

'Assuming for the moment that he was killed at half past eleven while he was watching television – what do you think he'd have been watching?'

'The film I should think. He quite liked Charles Bronson.'

'That was on ITV.'

'Yes. That'd be the best bet.'

'Not the documentary on Channel Four?'

'What, this one, about women in industry? Ooh no, I don't think so.'

'All right, thanks,' Slider said, taking back the schedule. Busty looked at her watch and he did likewise. 'Have I made you late?'

'Well, it is late. But Benny's not come yet. That's not like him to be late.'

'Perhaps he's waiting downstairs for you?'

'He always comes up and knocks. Wouldn't miss a chance.' She smiled a little. 'But maybe he saw you come up. He wouldn't want to intrude. He's like that. Very discreet, is Benny.'

'I'd better go and leave the path clear for him.' He walked to the door, and she followed him. 'Has he asked you to marry him again?'

'What, Benny? Nah. I wouldn't be surprised if he was working up to it though.' She sighed. 'I think I'll have to get rid of him. Stop using his cab. Now I haven't got Maurice to come between us, it could start getting awkward with old Benny. I mean, he's a nice bloke and everything, but it could get a bit embarrassing. And my eye, his feet don't half pen!'

Slider laughed. 'You make me nervous about my own. I shall go back to the station and investigate.'

'Oh no, you're not niffy,' Busty said.

He opened the door and stepped out onto the balcony, and, in his new caution, leaned briefly over the balcony wall to scan the area. Everything looked the same, safe and serene.

Busty came out, too, folding her arms across her twin peaks, blinking a little in the sunlight like a vast back-combed bushbaby. A wave of affection came over Slider. People like Busty were all right. They were never any trouble. They just got on with things.

'If there's anything I can do for you, Busty, you know just to ring, don't you? You've got my number.'

'Yeah,' she said. 'Thanks.' She seemed touched, and blinked a little more moistly. 'You're all right, Mr Slider,' she said, echoing his thoughts, and then leaned forward and kissed his cheek. 'Ta frevrything.'

Downstairs Slider got in his car, backed out of the space and drove off down the yard. He kept an eye on his rear-view mirror, but he saw nothing untoward, no sudden movements, or cars casually pulling out of parking spaces to follow him. Just plain, old-fashioned paranoia, he supposed. Everyone in the universe had that, according to Atherton.

In spite of his odd appearance – or perhaps because of it – Hollis came across as reassuring to members of the public. He sat on Mr Perceval's sagging sofa with his knees nearly up around his ears, his tufty, uncertain head appearing between them like an elf peeking out from the trees. There was a curious humility about him, as though he had come to learn: Plato at Socrates' feet.

Mr Perceval, who lived in the flat directly underneath Busty

Parnell's, was both reassured and flattered. It was a long time since anyone had wanted to learn anything from him. He had been wise in his time – he had actually led a very interesting life – but he was old now, and quite alone in the world, and he moved very slowly and whistled when he spoke because his false teeth were too big, so not many people had the patience to listen to him. His teeth were too big because his gums had shrunk, along with everything else. He had been a magnificent five foot six in his full manhood, now he was only five foot two. Where had his four inches gone, he wondered? He pondered the question sometimes as he moved slowly around his flat. The flat was too big for him now he was on his own, especially as he'd sold most of the furniture over the last few years, so that it was practically empty. He was like a shrivelled kernel rattling about inside a walnut shell. Back in history when they'd moved the calendar along to catch up with the rest of the world, people had gone out in the street and marched with banners shouting 'Give us back our eleven days!' He'd learned that in school. Sometimes as he walked about the kitchen, heating up his supper and setting out the tray (he still liked to do things properly, it helped fill the time), he would find himself chanting 'Give me back my four inches!' inside his head.

He'd left school at fourteen, though he reckoned he'd still learned more than they knew at eighteen these days. He was apprenticed to a violin maker in Ealing. Nineteen twenty-four, that was. He loved violins; it wasn't that he was musical, but he liked the feel of the wood, and the smell of the shavings and the varnish, and the slow, tender creation of something which was so much greater than the sum of its parts. They were all different, all beautiful in their own way, like women, and you had to know how to get the best out of them. When his apprenticeship was over, he went to Guivier's violin workshop up in Town. He'd met a lot of famous people. Sir Edward Elgar – he'd met him once. A real gentleman, he was, but sad, so sad it made you shiver. And that Yehudi Menuhin had come in once for a repair to a fiddle, and he'd chatted to Mr Perceval just as nice as you like. And although he wasn't musical, Mr Perceval had started going to concerts – well, it made sense, to see what it was all about, the work he put in. That was how he met his wife, Violet, at a concert at the old Queen's Hall. They went to the Proms together that summer, and one evening, after the concert, outside the Stage Door at the Albert Hall, Sir Edward Elgar had come out and passed right by Mr Perceval on the way to his car and had recognised him and touched his hat to him. A real gentleman. Mr Perceval was so pleased and Violet was so thrilled that later that evening he had popped the question to her, on top of the number twelve bus going home, and she had said Yes.

Three children they'd had, and would have had more, except that the war broke out, and though being the father of small children Mr Perceval could have got out of it, he didn't think it was right to. Violet agreed, and he joined up straight away. It was all right at first, they didn't send him overseas, so he was able to get back and see Vi and the kiddies now and then. They would listen to concerts on the wireless together. The old Queen's Hall got blitzed – that was a shock. Then later in the war he got sent out to the Far East. That was bad enough; but he ended up in a prisoner of war camp, and that was – well, you just didn't talk about it. Still, he survived, and you had to be grateful, didn't you? He lost most of his hair because of it, though, and nearly all his teeth. When he got home after the war, the first thing he did was have the rest out and get a nice set of false ones on the Beveridge, as they used to say then. Well, it was only fair to Vi. He looked a sight with all those gaps.

There was no place for a violin maker in the New Britain, so he had to begin again. Bicycle repairs he went in for. He reckoned with petrol rationed, everyone'd be using bikes, and he wasn't far wrong. Then he got interested in watchmaking, just as a hobby to start, but soon he was mending people's watches and clocks on the side, so to speak, and pretty soon that was the best part of the business. In the Sixties when everyone started getting cars, and bicycles went pretty much by the board, he dropped that side of it and started taking in wirelesses as well. It was just common sense and nimble fingers, he told Violet. There was nothing much to it.

Nimble fingers. You wouldn't think it to look at him now. He was lucky if he could make a cup of tea now without spilling it. And when you were old, people thought you were daft as well, that was the worst of it. He still had all his marbles, thank you, but they would talk to you that soppy way, like talking to a parrot.

Not that many people talked to him at all now. Vi was gone – taken suddenly, didn't even make it to his retirement. They'd looked forward to his retirement, doing things together. And the children were all gone too, Jim to Canada, Peggy to Australia. Kevin, the youngest, had gone out there too, but to Sydney – Peggy was in Brisbane. He hadn't heard from Kevin for sixteen years. Kevin never married. He never married, and then he just – stopped writing. Well, you had to wonder, didn't you?

And so here he was all alone in this flat. The pension didn't go very far, but he didn't want much at his age. If he'd saved a bit while he was working, maybe he could have gone out to Canada or Australia and been near the kids. He should have saved, really. But he didn't know that he'd really want to live abroad, even if it was Commonwealth. You were better off with what you knew. No, if he won the Lottery, he didn't know that he'd go. What he would do, if he won the Lottery, was go to a concert. He'd like to go to a concert again. Maybe one of the Proms – hear a bit of Elgar. He'd like to do that once more before he went Upstairs.

Hollis listened courteously, attentively, his hands still and no notebook in sight. And only when Mr Perceval had wound himself down and come to a stop did he raise the question of the bumps upstairs. 'It seems you mentioned when we talked to you before that you heard a noise upstairs earlier in the day – in the afternoon, sometime?'

'Ah, well, you didn't want to know about that, did you?' Mr Perceval said with a canny look. 'Young policeman, all impatience, wants to get on and get done with it. I'm an old fool and I speak too slow. He didn't want to know.'

'I want to know,' Hollis said.

'All interested in late at night, weren't you?'

'That's right. But now I'd be very interested in anything you could tell me about this other thing. A heavy thud, did you say?'

'A crash and a thud, I'd call it. Like something big and heavy falling over.'

'And do you remember what time it was?'

'Course I do. Twenty past one. I looked at the clock.'

'And why did you do that?'

The old man whistled a ghostly laugh through his vast china teeth. 'Clever, aren't you? 'Cause I thought someone might want to know, that's why!'

'Really? So what did you think had happened that someone might want to know about?'

But Mr Perceval only went on laughing to himself, his shoulders shaking. At last he stopped, sighing, and got out his handkerchief to wipe his eyes, a process of agonising slowness. When he had succeeded in getting the handkerchief folded and back into his pocket, he straightened his shoulders a little and said, 'Right, I'll tell you all about it, if you've got the patience.' Hollis nodded, and grew still and earnest again. 'Middle of the day, see, it's quiet. Everyone out at work, kids are at school. I like the quiet. I sit here and just listen. I got me library book, but mostly I just listen. You'd be surprised what you can hear. Metal frames, these flats are built on, did you know that?'

'No, I didn't.'

'Not from round here, are you?'

'No, I'm from Manchester.'

'I guessed that, from your accent. I was born and brought up in Shepherd's Bush. I saw these flats being built. Great steel frames, just like Lego it looked. And the metal carries sound, like the strings of a violin, you see, and the inside of the flats are like the sound box. I listen and try to work out what the sounds mean. Shut my eyes and visualise, see 'em walking back and forth, pulling out a chair, shutting a cupboard. Sounds were important in the jungle. It was all you had – nothing to see. Just the snap of a twig – and you got to know which direction it comes from. That takes practice.'

He paused, his eyes fixed, listening to something – in memory, perhaps. 'So anyway, this day you want to know about. *She'd* gone out, I knew that. I heard the front door slam. She's a heavy walker, and she will slam doors. *Him*, now, he's soft on his feet. You don't hear his feet, except when he goes over the creaking boards. I know where all of *them* are.'

'He was a dancer,' Hollis offered.

The old man lifted his head a little in attention. 'Was he? Was he? Now that's interesting. That accounts for the exercising, I suppose. Ballet, was it?'

'Something similar,' Hollis answered discreetly.

'He exercised in the evening, half past five to six o'clock. It took me a while to work it out, what it was. Anyway, this particular day, I'd heard him in the bathroom – you can hear the water rush out of the bath – and then in the bedroom – over that way – and then it all went quiet. Prob'ly in the kitchen. They got stone floors, the kitchens – fireproof, see? – so you can't hear walking about in the kitchen. Then about one o'clock I heard him come in above me. I was sitting in here, in the front room. There's a board about there.' He pointed to the ceiling near the door. 'It creaks when you step on it, no matter how soft-footed you are. He walked across, and then I heard the telly come on.'

'You can hear the television?'

'When it's turned up. *She* has it up loud. A bit mutton if you ask me. She'd had it on the night before. So when he turns it on, the sound's still up loud, you see? But then he turned it down. You know why? He had a visitor.'

Hollis felt his scalp prickling. They were on to something. He knew it. 'A visitor? How did you know that?'

'They've got a doorbell, just the right pitch to carry. He turns the telly down, crosses the creaker.' He pointed again. 'I didn't hear the front door open and shut. He doesn't slam like her. But then a moment later he comes back into the front room with someone else. I hear them come in, first the visitor, then him.'

'You're sure of that?'

'Two different treads. The visitor's a heavier walker. Visitor sits down over there, him upstairs goes over there. Anyway, then it goes quiet again – they're sitting down, right, chatting? Then about five minutes later *he* goes out and comes back in – gone to fetch something. He's not made a cup of tea – not gone long enough. Fetched something to show him, maybe.'

'Or fetched the whisky bottle and two glasses,' Hollis said.

'Oh, is that the way it was?'

'I don't know. I wasn't there. But there was a whisky bottle and two glasses on the coffee table.'

Mr Perceval nodded several times, piecing the knowledge into his sound-track. 'Right. Right. Then, twenty past one, it happens, a crash and a thud, just over there.' He pointed at the ceiling, and Hollis noted that he was indicating just about the position of the chair and the body. If Perceval had never seen the inside of Jay Paloma's flat, it was a good piece of evidence, because his own easy chair and television were in a quite different position. 'And then,' Perceval went on, 'some banging and trampling in about the same place—'

'What sort of banging?'

'Like DIY, but muffled. Like somebody hitting something with a wooden mallet, maybe, rather than a hammer. And he's moving his feet, the heavy-footed one, trampling about, like I said, but all on the spot.'

The repeated blows to the skull, Hollis thought. The frenzied attack. DIY was about the mark: Paloma had had the loft conversion to end them all.

'Then there's a silence, and then he goes out, back across the creaker, and there's nothing more. I didn't hear the front door close. He did it quietly. And then there's silence up there all afternoon. Which is why,' he said, fixing Hollis with a stern eye, 'I reckoned someone would want to know. Because I listened for him to go out of the room, but he never did.'

'Are you sure it was the visitor who went out?'

'Course I am. Different tread. Anyway, *he* was found dead up there, am I right?'

'Yes, he was, but not until the next day. He could have been killed any time. And we know – you know too because you heard it – that someone broke into the flat that evening.'

'He was already dead by then,' Mr Perceval said with calm certainty. 'Must've been. Else why wasn't he walking about? Why didn't he answer the phone when it rang? And why didn't he do his exercising? Always did his exercising, regular as clockwork.'

'That's a good point,' Hollis said. 'But why didn't you tell us all this before?'

'I told you, that young constable didn't want to know. In too much of a hurry.'

'You could have told someone else. Called at the police station. You should have come forward with important information like this, you know.'

'And would you have believed me?' Mr Perceval said. 'You were all stuck on half past eleven, and fair enough, with the door being broken down. If some doddery old josser came tottering in talking about creaky floorboards at twenty past one, you'd have shown him the door. Politely, all right, but that would have been the way of it, am I right?'

Hollis had to admit, unwillingly, that he was right. The ill-fitting teeth, the whistle, the slowness, would hardly have cut the mustard in the frenetic pace of modern station life, and without time and space to expand and justify his story, Perceval was barely believable. Even now, Hollis was wondering how you would ever present his evidence in such a way that a court would accept it. He was pretty sure the CPS wouldn't even want to try.

CHAPTER FOURTEEN

Honeyman: I Funked the Skid

Candy Williams looked frightened to death, but though her little chin quivered she faced Slider and Hart resolutely.

'I ain't got nothing to say. You got my statement. Why don't you leave me alone?'

'Hmm, yes, I know,' Slider said, 'but – can I sit down? Thanks. Yes, your statement. It's giving me problems, and do you know why?'

Candy didn't evince any desire to be told. She had sat down opposite him on the edge of a chair, her bony knees together and her ankles well apart, her hands clutched together in her lap. She looked about thirteen. She turned her face from him and stared at the window.

'I'll tell you,' Slider went on. 'Well, I knew you weren't telling the truth. And you knew that I knew, didn't you? I mean, nobody was fooling anybody in that interview room.'

'Candy, we're trying to help you,' Hart interposed sharply. 'Pay attention.' Candy's face remained averted, like a child refusing to take her medicine.

'The thing is this,' Slider went on conversationally, 'I know Jonah made you give him an alibi. I suppose he threatened you with all sorts of things if you didn't. I expect he gave you a few smacks as well, just to give you a taste.' Candy's mouth moved at that, a little, bitter downturn. 'So you lied about him being in the flat with you all that time. I don't blame you. But now something new has turned up, and that lie isn't going to help him any more. To help him you've got to tell me the truth.'

Now she turned her face back, looking at him, puzzled, trying to understand.

'You see, I don't think Jonah did murder Jay Paloma.'

She stared.

'But I can't prove it unless you tell me the truth. You've got to admit to me which bit of your story was a lie, so I can be sure the rest is true, do you understand?'

'You're lying,' Candy said, looking from one to the other uncertainly. 'You're tryna trick me. You're tryna to get me to drop him in it.'

'No. Absolutely not,' Slider said. 'Listen to me: Jonah doesn't need an alibi for half past eleven at night. But if you go on lying about that, I can't accept your evidence at all, on anything. You can't be his alibi for any other time. And that means you'll be useless to him.'

'You don't want him to think you've let him down, do you?' Hart suggested.

Candy began to sweat. She seemed confused. She looked at Hart and let drop an appalling facility of abuse.

'It's no good swearin' at me, sweetheart,' Hart said. 'I'm not the one on the spot. Big Jonah give you a job to do, and if you fuck it up—' She shrugged eloquently.

'You bastards,' said Candy. 'You pig bastard slags. What you tryna do to me?'

'Just tell me the truth, Candy. Tell me what really happened on Tuesday,' Slider said with gentle insistence.

She looked at him now, and there was appeal under the defiance. 'You don't understand. You don't understand *nothing*!'

'Then make me understand.' Slider became brisk. 'Come on, Candy, I'm trying to help you, but if you won't help yourself—'

He stood up, gesturing Hart before him. He thought it wasn't going to work – Candy let him get right to the door before she spoke – but at last she said uncertainly, 'Wait a minute.' He turned back enquiringly. She was chewing her lip, and there were beads of sweat like cloudy tears lying in her eye-sockets. 'Gimme a minute. Lemme think. I can't think!' she protested. Slider nodded to Hart to stay by the door, as if ready to leave on the instant. He took a step back into the room and waited, holding his breath.

'Are you telling me straight – about Jonah? That you don't think he did it?'

'Straight,' Slider said. 'I don't think he did. You'll be doing the right thing by him, telling me the truth.'

Her mouth turned down. 'I don't care about that black bastard. I hate him! Y'wanna see how much I care about him?' With a violent movement she dragged up her baggy sweater. She was naked underneath, and her small bare breasts flipped rubberily as the hem caught them. The sweater held up around her neck, she turned herself this way and that, like an art dealer tilting a painting to catch the light. Her narrow back and greyhound ribs were an impressionist sunset of black, red and yellowish green. She looked like a late Turner. 'He done this to me. He said he didn't hafta be careful 'cause I wasn't working.' She dropped her sweater and turned to look straight into Slider's eyes. 'He don't leave no marks, usually. He knows a lotta ways a hurtin' you without it showing.'

'You don't have to take this sort of thing, you know,' Slider said. 'You don't have to put up with it.'

Tears stood out suddenly in her eyes. She held her arms out from her sides, turning her palms up. 'What are you talking about? Look at me! He's four times the size of me. *How d'you fink I'm gonna stop him, you stupid, shit, fucking, man, copper!*'

She flopped down on the settee and put her head in her arms and sobbed loudly. Hart watched impassively, her arms folded. After a moment Slider sat down beside the girl and put a tentative arm round her, and she flung herself with a fresh burst to cry noisily on his shoulder. Slider waited. She was so small and bony and young, so young to be already one of the Lost and Damned. It wasn't the prostitution that bothered him. Unlike some of his colleagues, he had no problem with prostitution: providing it was all consenting, he thought it was people's own business. It was her hopelessness, the fact that so near to the beginning of her life she had decided that there was nothing to be had in life but money and the comforts it bought; that there was nothing to be done about anything, nothing to strive for or stand against.

Eventually she stopped, sat up, groped about her hopelessly for a tissue. The box on the coffee table was empty. Slider was about to part, sighing, with another handkerchief, but Hart the practical darted out and in again with a handful of bog roll from the bathroom. When the mopping up was done, Slider said to Hart, 'Make us some coffee, will you?' The tiny kitchenette was off the lounge, the door just beyond the end of the sofa: she would be able to both see and hear while in there.

And Candy Williams turned to Slider and said, 'All right, I'll tell you what I know, but it ain't much.' And she scanned his face for response, for approval perhaps, or at least for some sign that he was taking charge of her. She was born to be a victim, he thought. Chronically unable – either congenitally or because of her upbringing – to take responsibility for herself, she was there for the taking for anyone who would tell her what to do next, and by humping her, hitting her or buying her presents give some sense of structure to the terrifying formlessness of existence.

The first part of her story had been true. Jonah had come home from work at about half past four, his usual time after work. He hadn't been sacked by Yates. 'That was balls. He was just told to say that. It made him mad. He didn't want to have to tell anyone he'd been sacked. And not for wearing a dirty shirt. I fink Mr Yates said that just to put him on.'

'So he came home in a bad temper?'

'No, that wasn't then. All that come later. Listen.' She seemed distracted by his lack of understanding.

'All right, I'm listening. What did he do when he got home?'

'He went to bed, like always. We done it—'

'You had sex?'

'Whajjer fink? Then he went off to sleep. I fell asleep as well, but then the phone rang about eight o'clock. Not his flat phone, his mobile. That meant it was Mr Yates. He started talking to him, and it was yes, Mr Yates, no Mr Yates at first. Then he started to get annoyed. He got out of bed and was walking up and down and like clenching his fists. And then he kicked a chair out of the way. I knew I was in trouble then.'

'Was he arguing with Mr Yates?'

'You don't argue with Mr Yates,' she said flatly. 'But I could tell he didn't like it. He was saying why, and why's it gotta be done that way, and stuff like that. And when he finished he threw the phone across the room and shouted "Bastard!" And he looked at the clock and he shouted, "He waited till I was asleep, the bastard!" and then he threw the clock across the room an' all.'

'Why would Mr Yates do that? Wait until Jonah was asleep, I mean?'

'Just to make him mad. He'd know he'd be deep asleep at

eight o'clock and it'd be the worst time to wake him. He's like that, Mr Yates – especially with Jonah. He likes annoying Jonah, 'cause he knows Jonah can't get back at him. He thinks it's funny. He'll laugh out the other side of his face one day.' She looked seriously at Slider. 'Jonah'll kill him one day, I mean it, and I just wanna be around to see it.'

There were too many painful implications to that thought for Slider to comment on. He put her gently back on the track. 'Did Jonah tell you what Mr Yates wanted him for?'

'Did he! I got the lot. He ranted and raved about it.' She frowned, trying to put the story in order. 'Apparently this bloke come in to the club the night before – posh geezer – and give Jonah a load of money, just shoved it in his hand, four hundred, all in twenties – to go round this other bloke's house and give him a real fright. Like, maybe rough him up a bit, but nothing too bad, just scare him.'

'Yes, I know about that. I've had it from the posh geezer.'

This seemed to reassure Candy. 'Oh, you know him, do you?'

'I know him. And was Jonah intending to do what he asked?'

She looked scornful. 'Was he buggery! Jonah thinks it's all a big joke, seeing he's four hundred up. This bloke was well plastered, and Jonah reckons he's never going to remember next day where he left the dosh. Apparently he was swaggering round the club telling everyone, the great stupid bastard, and Terry – he's the manager, one of Mr Yates's spies – he tells Mr Yates about it. Because apparently this posh geezer's somebody really important?'

Slider gave a nod in response to the slight question mark.

'Well, anyway, apparently Mr Yates phones Jonah to tell him he wants him to do what this geezer asked after all. Jonah asks him why but Mr Yates ain't telling. He gives Jonah chapter and verse how to do it and when, and then he says – this is what really makes Jonah mad – he says that Jonah mustn't be working for him when he does it. So that's when he tells him to say he was sacked at four o'clock, and about the dirty shirt an' all. I bet it was that Terry thought that one up.'

'If Jonah hated the set-up so much, why would he do it? What was in it for him?'

'Well, he's one of Mr Yates's boys, isn't he? And Mr Yates would see him all right.'

'But he'd sacked him.'

'I told you, that was just the story. A course he was still working for him, only it hadn't to be official, so that if there was any trouble it wouldn't come back on Mr Yates. Like I say, he'd see Jonah all right. And if there was any trouble, Mr Yates's solicitor would get him out.'

This was a nice angle on Stevens, Slider thought. 'Go on. So what was the plan?'

'Well, Jonah was spose to go round there at eleven, so as to mix with the chucking-out crowds. And I was spose to give him his alibi. That's why he told me about it, see?'

'And what did you say?'

'I was scared. I said I never wanted nothing to do with it.'

'But if the plan was only to scare this man – where was the harm?'

She shook her head, folding her arms round herself as if she was cold. 'I see the temper he was in. I fought this bloke was gonna get a pasting, and I never wanted it coming back on me. I told Jonah I wouldn't do it, and he started shouting at me, but I was so scared I said I was going, and then he really went mad. He punched me in the stomach and knocked me across the room, then he picked me up and banged my head on the ceiling, and whirled me round and round over his head, and I fought he was gonna chuck me out the window. I was shit scared. I fought I'd had it. But he only frew me on the bed and jumped on top of me and started hitting me. That's when he said he didn't need to be careful 'cause I wouldn't be working for a while. But he was careful not to hit my face – nothing that wouldn't be covered by my clothes.'

She told it so matter-of-factly, as though she was describing the steps of a dance. Perhaps in a way that's what it was to her.

'Go on,' Slider said. 'What happened next?'

'Well, hitting me give him a hard-on, so he did – you know what. And then he wanted to go to sleep. But he said he couldn't have me sneaking off while he was asleep, so he tied me up to the bottom of the bed, and tied a rope round my neck and went to sleep holding the other end.' She examined Slider's expression.

'It wasn't so bad, 'cause he couldn't tie the ropes too tight, in case they left a mark. Only I was desperate for a pee, that was the bad bit. Anyway, when he woke up he untied me and let me go to the bathroom, and told me to bring him breakfast in bed.'

'What time was that?'

'About half past twelve. And then when he'd et it I had to get in with him 'cause he wanted sex again, and then he got up and had a shower.'

'And what time did he go out?'

'Not till evening, about half past ten.'

'You're sure about that? You're quite sure? You're telling me the truth now?'

'Yeah,' she said, and the word was a sigh, like someone accepting a sentence.

'He didn't get up until half past one, and he was indoors, in your presence, all day?'

'I should know,' she said succinctly. 'He watched the telly all afternoon. He started drinking as soon as he was dressed, and by the time ten o'clock come he was steaming. I was shit scared. If I could've run away I would've, but he never let me get near the door, and the one time he thought I was trying he thumped me again. Then about half past ten he got up and turned the telly off. He was so lit up and so mad by then, I thought meself, this is gonna turn bad, he ain't never gonna be able to stop himself. I mean, he's that strong he can break your arm just shaking your hand if he's not careful – and he wasn't in the mood to be careful. I thought he was gonna go out there and kill this bloke, whether he meant to or not. So he went, anyway, and he locked me in so I couldn't run while he was gone.'

'Did you try telephoning anyone?'

She shrugged. 'Who was there to telephone? I just waited. Anyway, about half past midnight he comes back, and I knew straight away it had gone bad. I never seen him like that before. He was jumpy and weird, laughing one minute, scared the next.'

'Did he tell you what had happened?'

'Nuh. He just said, "Candy baby, you and me's going for a little trip." And he reminded me what I had to say if anyone asked, and then he said let's go to bed.'

'And you went to sleep?'

She gave a short, unamused laugh. 'I wish. He was really wired up. I never seen him like that before. He was just humping me all night. I could hardly walk the next day. He fell asleep in the end when it got light, and then he woke up about nine o'clock and we left the flat about half past and come here.'

She came to a halt and was silent a moment, and then she looked at Hart, remembering where she was and who she was telling. 'When I saw in the papers, I thought he'd done it. He never said nothing to me, but when he saw me looking at the news about it, he just laughed, like a really weird laugh. He never said it wasn't him. I thought I was living with a murderer. I mean, he went out there and come back – and now you say it wasn't him?'

'I don't think so,' Slider said.

She looked bewildered. 'Then what the bloody hell's going on?'

'I don't know,' Slider said. 'Did he talk to Mr Yates at all, after he came back that night?'

'He'd been talking to him already, in the car, driving back after doing it. When he got in he said he'd got his instructions. That's all he said. And he never talked to nobody after that. He never left the flat, and that's the truth. I tell you, it was a relief when your lot turned up. It was like being shut in a cage with a mad animal.'

Slider tried to look solid and reassuring, though his mind was going round like a hamster on speed. What the hell was going on? 'You've done the right thing telling me all this, Candy. Don't worry, everything's going to be all right.'

'If you want to make a complaint against Jonah, we'll go all the way with you,' Hart put in.

Candy looked from one to the other. 'You don't get it, do you? It's not Jonah I'm afraid of, not now.'

If there was anything in the world that demonstrated the futility of human endeavour, Slider thought, it was a Function in a Hospitality Room. The characteristic feature of hospitality rooms is their inhospitableness; and a gathering for social purposes of a group of people who have nothing in common but business is bound to be dysfunctional.

'Why do I get the feeling I've been here before?' he muttered to Hart. She, he noted with a strange pang, was looking eager, as though expecting to enjoy herself. She had changed in the loo at the station, and was now extremely fetching in a black dress so short and so full-skirted she looked like a nineteen-twenties illustration of Violet Elizabeth Bott, but in negative.

'There ain't many females here,' she muttered back to him. 'Are you sure you should've brought me?'

'Quite sure,' Slider said. Having a pretty young woman beside him at a do like this was the only point of difference: the weary staff, the wearier canapés, and the choice between white wine that tasted like thinner and red wine that tasted like turpentine, were all too familiar. A rapid scan of the room, however, revealed that he didn't recognise a single face, which was a little odd. He couldn't even see Honeyman, though he supposed he must be lurking where the guests were thickest. He was still hovering uncertainly when a youngish man he didn't recognise approached him and addressed him in French, with the colonial accent of Croydon.

'Sorry?' Slider said.

'Oh, sorry,' the stranger said. 'I thought you were one of the French delegates.'

'Are we expecting French delegates?' Slider asked, puzzled.

'What?' said the stranger, upping the stakes to bewildered.

'Guv,' Hart said, tugging Slider's sleeve and gesturing towards the door. The parting of crowds had revealed the notice board – one of those fuzzy black slatted things with white plastic letters pressed into it. 'We're at the wrong bash.'

The management of the hotel, the board announced, was welcoming an international electronics firm to the Chiltern Suite.

'Oh, are you the police?' the stranger said, relieved. 'You're next door, in the Pennine Suite. All look the same, these places, don't they?'

Slider and Hart stumped next door. Directly in line of sight of the entrance was Ron Carver so deep in conversation with Mr Wetherspoon that he practically had his tongue down his ear. Slider did not find that immediately reassuring. A waitress with a hopeless expression offered a tray of filled glasses and Hart took one of white wine.

'Better not,' Slider said. 'You'll be running all night. Safer to wait and have a pint later.'

'I'll be all right,' Hart said. 'I'm black, enni? Guts of iron. Drink anything.'

Honeyman came up and formally shook hands with both of them. 'Nice of you to come,' he said. He teetered a little on his tiny toes – from inebriation, it was plain, as well as nervousness. 'And I see you've brought WDC – er—'

'Hart,' Slider supplied.

'Hart. What a good idea. Very dull, these affairs. Middle-aged men in suits talking shop. You'll brighten us up, er—' He had forgotten Hart's name again already. 'Pity there won't be any dancing. I'd have made sure I put my word in, stolen you from Slider here. *Droits de seigneur*, eh, Slider?'

Slider could feel Hart seething at this ponderous non-PC gallantry, and kicked her discreetly before she could jump down poor old Eric's throat. 'That's right, sir,' he said pleasantly. 'There's a good crowd, isn't there?' He glanced round at the assembled barons of F District. There were even some Area demigods – easily distinguishable because their dinner suits fitted them. Did they all know they had been brought here under false pretences, that the farewell was premature?

Honeyman intercepted the glance and looked even more nervous. 'Yes, very gratifying. The most senior ranks will be going to dinner downstairs later, after the presentation, of course, but meanwhile, I want everyone to enjoy himself. And herself, of course. Themself. Oh, you haven't got anything to drink,' he noticed, with obvious relief at being able to interrupt himself.

'I'm driving, sir,' Slider said quickly.

'Ah. Yes.' Honeyman blinked. Since when did the CID worry about that? 'Commendable. Commendable. Well, I must circulate.' He turned away, and then back. 'Er, Slider – that confidential matter we spoke about earlier? You didn't – er—' He cocked a significant eye at Hart.

'You said it was confidential, sir,' Slider said reassuringly.

'Ah yes. Good. It's just that – well, with so many senior ranks present – you understand.'

'Yes, sir, perfectly.'

When he was gone, Hart said, 'I fink he fancies you, guv. D'you want me to make myself scarce? I don't wanna be a gooseberry.'

'How would you like to spend your days tracing stolen cars?' Slider said coldly.

Hart grinned. 'All right, I'll be good. Who's that Mr Carver's so thick with? If he gets any closer they'll have to get married.'

'That is our Area Commander, Mr Wetherspoon,' Slider said impressively. 'Curtsey while you think what to say; it saves time.'

'Oh, is that Weverspoon?' Hart said. 'Yeah, I've heard a lot about him. He's getting up this charity concert, ain't he?'

'He was born getting up a charity concert. He's very keen on that sort of thing,' Slider said. A waitress arrived at his elbow with a silver tray of pieces of chicken tikka each speared with a cocktail stick. Slider and Hart both took one to get rid of her. The pieces were nicely calculated, just too large to put in the mouth whole, and just too small to bite without the remainder falling off the stick. They were also very hot. Hart evidently favoured the 'one go' approach. She chewed briefly and swallowed. 'I see you've got an iron throat as well as an iron gut,' Slider said.

Hart twirled the cocktail stick. 'What you sposed to do wiv these things, anyway?'

'No-one's ever come up with a satisfactory solution to the problem.'

'They can be lethal, you know,' Hart said. 'Wedding reception down our way, once, this bloke ate a bit of quiche or whatever without taking the stick out. His wife said, "'Ere, y've been and swallered your stick, yer daft get." "Oh blimey, so I 'ave," he says. They were just 'aving a good laugh about it when the stick goes right frough his windpipe and he chokes to death, before you can say vol-au-vent.' She eyed him defiantly. 'It's true. Put a bit of a crimp on the party, I can tell you.'

'I really needed to know that,' Slider said. 'Here—' And he relieved her of her stick and put it with his own in his top pocket, whence they would later, no doubt, return to haunt him. Wetherspoon finished with Carver, looked around, spotted Slider and started towards him. Significant? Slider wondered. Wetherspoon was a very tall, rather angular man, with grizzled, tightly curling hair that grew upwards above the temples, giving his head a strangely square look. He always reminded Slider, for some reason, of an Airedale terrier. It was rumoured of him that he had once, as a young man, smiled, but disliked the sensation so much he had resolved never to do it again. Some said that the one time he had smiled it had been at a woman, which had led to his having to marry her, hence his disillusionment. Slider, who had once met Mrs Wetherspoon, was inclined to believe the story.

'Ah, Slider – a word,' said Wetherspoon.

Slider obediently gave him one. 'Sir.'

Wetherspoon turned on Hart a smile that would have freezed the tassels off a stripper. 'If you'd be so kind,' he said. Men who packed his amount of fire-power did not need to specify the kindness. Slider jerked his head at Hart and she moved reluctantly away. 'Yes, Slider,' Wetherspoon continued when they were alone. 'You've made certain enquiries about Mr Honeyman's predecessor, in connection with a case.'

'Yes, sir.' Even allowing for Wetherspoon's designer charmlessness, Slider felt there was some little hint of disapprobation in the tone.

'The case is not, in fact, one of yours.'

'No, sir, but—'

'There are reasons,' Wetherspoon trod over him, 'very serious operational reasons, why your enquiries cannot be answered. In fact, your enquiries must not be pursued. Do you understand me?'

The words *yes, sir* hovered obediently at Slider's lips but he resisted them. 'I appreciate that it may be a delicate area—'

'No, I don't think you do appreciate,' Wetherspoon said. 'Mr Honeyman has passed on your thoughts to me, and I don't see that you have any evidence at all that your case and Carver's are connected in any way. It is for Carver to decide what is or isn't relevant to his own case. In any case, I have told him what I have just told you – that there must be no enquiries along the particular line you raised with Mr Honeyman. He understands that. Do you?' Slider drew breath to argue and Wetherspoon leaned his head a little closer and lowered his voice threateningly. '*Do you understand?*'

'Yes, sir,' Slider said.

Wetherspoon straightened up. 'Good. Now that that's out of the way, we can concentrate on enjoying this splendid party. But you haven't got a drink.'

'I'm driving, sir.'

'Ah. Very commendable,' said Wetherspoon, almost duplicating Honeyman's reaction. He glanced down at the glass of red in his hand. 'Pity though – I chose the wines myself. Do you like wine?'

'Yes, sir.'

'Good. Good. You don't have any sort of talent I haven't heard about, I suppose?'

Slider had lost him. 'Sir?'

'My concert, man, my concert. Singing, dancing, conjuring? Comic monologue? Play the piano, at all?'

'Not even slightly,' Slider said.

'Pity. Well, you must do your bit by selling tickets. Set a good example. I expect every officer, inspector and above, to sell at least twenty tickets. Friends, neighbours and whatnot. Get in among 'em.' He paused on the brink of a monumental descent into the vernacular, a jocularity aimed at winning the common soldier's heart. 'Bums on seats, that's the name of the game! Must make it a raging success. For the kiddies, you know.'

'Yes, sir,' Slider said. Wetherspoon gave him one more deeply unfavourable look, nodded, and went away. Slider felt the side that had been nearest him begin to thaw.

Hart reappeared. 'Trouble, guv?' she murmured.

'No, just being told there are things it is better for a detective inspector not to know,' Slider said. He looked across at Carver and saw Carver's gaze quickly averted. He'd have liked to know what Carver had been saying to Wetherspoon, though – and vice versa. 'I wonder if he was told the same thing. It didn't look like it.'

'Come again?' said Hart.

'Do you ever get the feeling that everyone else knows something you don't?'

'That's paranoid,' Hart said.

'You'd be paranoid if everyone was plotting against you,' Slider complained.

A waitress thrust another tray at them, and Slider took what appeared to be a cocktail sausage on a stick, but which proved – as he discovered when he bit it – to be merely a tube full of boiling fat, which instantly glued itself to the gums behind his upper molars and inflicted third degree burns. 'Bloody hell!' He grabbed Hart's glass and swilled desperately.

'Not your night, guv,' said Hart sympathetically.

'Why didn't I join the fire brigade when I had the chance?' Slider said bitterly.

The party ripened like a mould culture. Officers were getting drunk. The noise grew. Slider got separated from Hart. He got buttonholed by an agonisingly boring man from Hammersmith nick who seemed to know him a great deal better than he ought considering Slider couldn't remember his name and only recollected ever having spoken to him once, and who wanted to talk to him about crime statistics. He ripped himself free at last like sticking plaster, and began to push his way slowly but purposefully through the crowds, trying to look as though he was on his way somewhere, in the hope of avoiding any more conversations. He was beginning to get a headache.

And then suddenly Honeyman was at his side again, clutching two glasses of amber fluid. His cheeks were flushed and his eyes were shiny. 'Look here,' he said, 'I'm having a proper drink.' He proffered one glass. 'Join me? You weren't serious about that not drinking because you're driving business were you?'

Slider hesitated. Honeyman seemed to have become almost human. 'I didn't fancy the wine, sir.'

'Sensible man. Filthy stuff. But for God's sake, don't call me sir. Not here. Chance to let down the barriers for once.' He jerked the glass at Slider, swilling the liquid dangerously up the side. 'Whisky. Scotch, in fact. Took you for a Scotch man. Was I wrong?'

Slider took the glass just in time. 'I prefer a pint, sir, but I like Scotch.'

Honeyman leaned towards him with a fascinating smile. 'Between you and me, Wetherspoon fancies himself as a wine-buff. Hasn't a clue! Reads the Sunday supplements, watches the TV, takes it all as gospel. And the man's the most frightful bore about it. Never accept a dinner invitation to the Wetherspoons',' he warned solemnly. 'He's got a sign over his front door.' Honeyman drew it in the air. '"Welcome. This is what death is like."'

Slider wasn't sure whether he was supposed to laugh. 'I don't think I'm ever likely to be invited,' he said.

'No, I don't suppose you are. Welsh claret,' he added from a bitter memory all his own. 'Afghanistan Côtes du Rhone. Nuits

St Bogota. What was that advertisement? "Not a drop sold till it's five weeks old." Ah, this is more like. Well – cheers.'

'Cheers,' Slider said obediently.

Honeyman sank half his Scotch, glanced quickly round, and then looked at Slider. 'I suppose you're wondering what's got into me. I suppose you're thinking, my God the old fool's finally flipped his lid.'

'I wasn't thinking that.'

'The thing is, you see, that I'm suffering from a sort of last-day-of-term – oh, what's the word?'

'Euphoria?'

'That's it. Together with a dislike of being poisoned. And being talked to like a half-witted schoolboy. This is all strictly confidential, mind,' he added with belated caution. 'Where's that lovely young girl of yours? You won't repeat anything I say?'

'Of course not.'

'Being talked to like that. That's what gets my goat. I'm going to have another of these.' He drained his glass, looked around as if wondering where the bottle was, and then turned back to Slider. 'Talked to like an idiot schoolboy. At my own retirement party. After thirty years in the Job. It's not on.'

'No, sir.'

'So I wanted to tell you, Slider, that I'm on your side. You do what you have to, and I'll back you up. To the hilt. All the way.' He swayed suddenly, and had to shift his feet to regain his balance. 'Fuck it,' he said. Slider couldn't believe his ears. Honeyman looked at him almost gleefully. 'Didn't think I had it in me, did you? I know what you chaps think of me. But I tell you this – I'm a policeman, first and last. Not a politician. Not a businessman. Not a civil servant. And you are too. That's what I like about you, Slider. You're a good egg. D'you want that?' He gestured abruptly towards the tumbler in Slider's hand.

'No, sir,' Slider said, and gave it to him. Honeyman took a gulp.

'I'd like to bring this one home before I go. This case. Sir Nigel Grisham's involved. It's high profile now, you know.'

'Yes, sir.' High profile now, because of Sir Nigel – but who cared about Sir Nigel's friend, the dancer-cum-prostitute he paid for and exploited? Fame was all, fame excused all. Jay Paloma had been right.

'Do it for me,' Honeyman said, 'and I'll back you all the way.'

'I'll do my best, sir.'

'I know you will. Good man. Not many of us left. Not like that lot.' He gestured with his eyes in the vague direction of the rest of the world. 'Got to go. Presentation and speeches next, and then I've got to go and have dinner with *them*. Well, I won't be leaned on. They'll find out. I'll sweet-talk all they like, but I won't be leaned on.'

And with a nod he swayed away. Slider watched him go and wondered if it was possible to be drunk just on noise, because the world wasn't making much sense to him just then and his head was reeling, but he hadn't touched a drop. Not even the Scotch, more was the pity.

CHAPTER FIFTEEN

They Eat Horses, Don't They?

Hart had left her car at the station, so he drove her back there. 'Are you all right to drive home?' he asked.

'I only had two glasses,' she said. 'You were right. It was like urine re-cyc.'

'How would you know?'

'Anyway, I got to get changed, then I'm going up the canteen for a cup a coffee before I go home,' she said. She looked at him hopefully, but his mind was elsewhere, and he merely grunted. In his office he found a message asking him to call Det Sup Smithers, giving her home number. He telephoned Joanna first.

'What are you doing there?' she asked. 'I thought you were at the farewell party.'

'I was. But I've come back here to do some thinking.'

'Are you coming home? I was just going to have some supper. Oatcakes and cheese and a very large malt whisky. In the bath.'

He visualised it. 'Which one?'

'We've only got one bath.'

'Which whisky.'

'The Macallan.' But she had already guessed that he was going to say no. 'I've got no clothes on,' she added hopefully.

'I was just ringing to say don't wait up for me, I might be late,' Slider admitted.

'Oh.'

'Is everything all right?'

'Just peachy,' she said. 'Except that I've been getting funny phone calls.'

'What sort?'

'I say hello, they put the phone down.'

'How many? How often?'

'Three this evening.'

'Oh. Are you worried?'

'No, not really. It's annoying, more than anything.'

'Don't answer any more. Put the answering machine on,' he advised.

'What if you want to call me?'

'You'll hear my voice on the machine, and you can intercept.'

'But I'm not sure it's working properly.'

'I thought you were going to get it fixed. Oh, never mind now. Look, put it on anyway, and if I want to phone you – it picks up on the fourth ring, so I'll let it ring three times and stop, and then ring you again immediately.'

'All right. Are you on to something? Is that why you're staying late?'

'I wish I were. Every new bit of evidence I get seems to make things foggier instead of clearer.'

'It'll come to you,' she said. 'Virtue brings its own reward.'

'That's a misquotation,' he said.

'Just testing.'

He pressed the receiver rest to get a new dialling tone, and dialled Pauline's Richmond number.

'Pauline? It's Bill.'

'Oh, hi. Well, I've done it for you. Don't ask me how. He's going to ring you – but not at home and not at work. Give me your mobile number.'

Slider told her.

'Right,' she said. 'I'll give this to him, and he'll contact you and arrange a meet.'

'When?'

'He knows it's urgent,' Pauline said. 'That's all I can tell you. He's got to watch his back. Leave it to him. And – Bill? Be careful.'

'I always am.'

'No you're not. I heard about that attack on you, and your sergeant – what's his name?'

'Atherton.'

'That one. It's a dangerous game now. That's why our friend agreed to contact you. He wants to keep you out of it, to save his own skin.'

'I'll be careful,' Slider repeated. 'Pauline, thanks for doing this for me. I really appreciate it.'

'That's all right,' she said. 'All part of the service. D'you know why I never got married?'

'No,' Slider said, puzzled.

'I didn't think you did. When you've got this case out of the way, I'll hold you to that meal. But I warn you, it'll be a credit-card job.'

'Nothing's too good for you,' Slider said.

Almost immediately he put the phone down it rang again. He answered it and was greeted by silence. He thought for a moment it was one of Joanna's 'funny phone calls', but after a moment Irene said, 'It's me.'

'What's the matter?' he asked.

'Why should anything be the matter?'

'I know all your tones of voice. What's the matter?'

She seemed to have difficulty voicing it. 'I've been trying to ring you all evening,' she said at last.

'Well I've only been here about a quarter of an hour. I was at Honeyman's farewell bash.'

'I don't mean there. I was trying to ring you at home.'

He prickled with advance warning of a storm. 'Where?'

'Where you live, of course,' she said shortly. 'Sergeant Paxman gave me your home number.'

'Oh, did he?'

'I told him it was urgent. Anyway, why shouldn't he?' Irene said sharply. 'He knows I'm your wife. Is it supposed to be a secret?' Slider couldn't answer that. 'So I rang there, and a woman answered.'

'And you hung up, of course. That explains it. She thought you were a heavy breather.'

'Who is she?' The question was both naked and urgent. Slider dithered over what was best to do or say, what would hurt all involved the least.

'No-one you know,' he said at last.

'She didn't sound like a landlady.'

'You can tell that from "Hello"?'

'Bill, don't torment me,' Irene said. 'You're living with someone, aren't you?'

'I should have thought that was self-evident.'

'You know what I mean. You've got another – you've got a woman.'

No way out of it. 'If you must put it that way – yes.'

'It's that black girl, isn't it? That's why you took her to see the house. You're going to move in there with her.'

'Irene, for God's sake! I told you WDC Hart is one of my firm, a loaner until Atherton's on his feet again. I'd just gone to see the house was all right, that's all, and she happened to be with me.'

'You don't have to lie to me,' Irene said pathetically. 'Why shouldn't you have another woman? It's only natural. You're an attractive man. I couldn't expect you to be a monk for the rest of your life. I just wish you'd had the courage to tell me, and not make me find out that way.'

'Why do I feel I've strayed into a Celia Johnson movie? Watch my lips: I am not having an affair with Hart!'

'Well it looked like it, from what I saw. And you said you're living with someone.'

'You're the one who can tell everything from one word on the phone. Couldn't you tell that wasn't Hart?'

Irene made one of those extraordinary and devastating leaps of logic that women seemed to be capable of when sniffing out infidelity. 'Oh my God,' she said with the horror of absolute conviction in her voice, 'it's that woman at the pub, isn't it? When I had lunch with you. The one who came in, and you said she was Atherton's friend.'

'She is Atherton's friend.'

'Yes, and the rest. I *knew* she wasn't his type. My God! No wonder you seemed so put out when she turned up. I thought it was because you were ashamed of being seen with me.'

'Oh *Irene*—!'

'But why did you have to lie about her? You could have told me. I've got no right to complain, after all.'

'You were in the middle of telling me that Matthew wanted to go home. I thought—' That was a sentence too delicate to finish.

'Well, obviously,' she said bravely, 'there's no question of that now. I'm sorry I embarrassed you by mentioning it. I had thought that maybe it wasn't too late, maybe we might be able to get back together – for the children's sake if nothing else – but obviously it's too late for that now.' She drew a slightly quivering breath. 'If only I'd spoken earlier, maybe it would have been different. But I suppose you couldn't have forgiven me even then. I've made a mess of everything, haven't I?'

'It's not your fault,' he began, but she interrupted him.

'It is. I never knew when I was well off, that's what it was. And I suppose I didn't really think, when I walked out, that it was an irrevocable step. It was a sort of cry for attention, really, I suppose. I was just trying to make you notice me. I never thought properly about the consequences.'

'Oh, Irene,' he said helplessly.

'It's all right, I know, I've made my own bed and all that. Do you love her?'

'Look, I don't think—'

'You can tell me that, can't you? She's not much to look at,' she said dispassionately, 'so I suppose it must be love. Or was she just available? She wasn't really Atherton's girlfriend, was she? I'd hate to think you were getting yourself involved on the rebound. I mean, don't rush into something with the first female to come your way, just because she's desperate and you don't like being alone. It would all be such a waste if we both ended up unhappy.'

This was terrible. He was on hot coals. 'Are you really unhappy?'

She paused before answering. 'Does it matter if I am? I mean, if there's nothing to be done about it? If you've got someone else and it's serious, we're never going to get back together again. Or is it,' she added hopefully, 'just a passing thing?'

'It's serious,' he said unwillingly.

'How can you be sure? You can't have known her long. You've only just met her.'

It seemed an ideal moment to begin setting the record straight. 'I've known her a long time,' he said.

'What, because she was a friend of Atherton's?'

'A friend of both of us.'

There was a silence in which he could hear her computer grinding to a conclusion, but he couldn't think of a thing to say to interrupt the process. He wanted to tell her the truth, but couldn't break the habit of subterfuge which had built up around his relationship with Joanna. He found it intolerable that she should blame herself entirely for the situation, but feared bringing down her wrath on his head by confession. But they were adults, weren't they? And now that they had parted, surely the truth could be borne? It must be the best option, so that everyone knew where they stood, and a final and amicable arrangement could be made.

'Look,' he began – the most fatal, incriminating word a man could ever say to a woman.

'You were having an affair with her,' Irene said with chilling certainty. 'Before. Weren't you?'

'Look, I—'

'I *knew* there was something going on! I just couldn't fathom out what. But I told myself I was imagining things. And then, when Ernie started getting interested in me—' She found her anger. 'You let me feel guilty! You let me take all the blame, and all the time you were having an affair! You were sniggering behind my back with that – with that—'

'Irene, for God's sake, it wasn't like that.'

'How long? *How long?*'

'It doesn't matter. Surely it doesn't matter now. We've both got someone else. We've both got new lives. What does it matter whether—'

'What does it matter? You let me go through agonies of guilt about breaking up our marriage, and all the time you were messing around with that – that – *bitch* – and you ask me what does it matter? My God, she isn't even good-looking! How could you do it to me? It'd be bad enough if she was a dolly bird, but how could you betray me for that fat cow?'

'Don't talk like that. All that recrimination stuff is over—'

'Oh, don't you believe it, chum! I haven't started yet!' Irene spat, incandescent with rage. 'There's a few things going to be different from now on, I can tell you! I've been treating you with kid gloves, thinking I was the guilty party. Now you're going to find out a few realities of life. By the time I've finished with you, you're going to wish you'd never touched that bitch with a ten-foot barge pole. Your feet won't touch the ground, I promise you that.'

'Irene—'

'You'd better get yourself a lawyer, Bill Slider!' she yelled, and slammed the phone down.

Slider replaced his receiver and contemplated it in unhappy silence for a while. 'I don't think I handled that very well,' he said at last.

'You all right, guv?' Hart asked from the doorway.

He looked up sternly. 'Have you been listening?'

'Not me,' she said indignantly. 'I just got here.' She eyed him with interest. 'You look a bit down. I was just going off. D'you fancy a drink?'

He thought of Irene phoning up for a rematch and being told he'd gone down the boozer with Hart. Or even coming to find him and walking in on them. In any case, he had to be alone for when the Scotland Yard man rang. 'No, thanks all the same. I've got some thinking to do. You go on home. I'll see you tomorrow.'

When she had gone he sat a bit longer, staring at nothing, frowning in thought. And then he got up, making sure to grab his mobile, and went out. He was parked on the corner of Abdale Road – he couldn't get into the yard – and as he came out onto the street his mobile rang. There seemed to be no-one around. He stepped back against the wall and answered it.

'Yes,' he said into it.

'You were expecting a call from me,' said a voice. It wasn't a question.

'Yes.'

'I can meet you now. Mention no names. You know where they found the PC who got hurt?'

'Yes.'

'There. Ten minutes. Don't get followed.' He rang off. This was a very cautious fellow, Slider thought. Ten minutes didn't give him long to make sure he wasn't followed – no time to drive circuitously. He hurried to his car. He decided to park in Hammersmith Grove and walk the rest. He saw nothing in his rear view, nothing suspicious when he parked and got out. There were people about, but no-one seemed to be paying him any attention – or deliberately *not* paying him attention – and he had no sense of being watched. Besides, this was his home ground, and it seemed absurd to be taking all these precautions on these ordinary streets. He walked without elaborations down the quiet backstreets, only keeping an ear open for footfalls, and snatching a look behind when he abruptly crossed the road. There was no-one about.

When he reached the waste ground he felt more ill at ease. The lighting came only from the railway line above: there were deep shadows everywhere and blackness under the arches. He did not know what de Glanville looked like. Or sounded like, come to that – he was assuming the call came from him, but supposing someone else had got his mobile number, someone who had a grudge against him? There were plenty of those in his past, let alone the present case. He stepped onto the waste and kept close to the wall, and reaching the first arch backed just inside it and stood still, listening and watching.

He smelled him first. As soon as the man moved, and before the moving air brought a sound to his ears, Slider's nose picked up the cologne. Subtle, expensive. He put his back to the wall and looked into the darkness for the movement and said softly, 'Who's that?'

'De Glanville.' It was the voice on the phone – one worry down, anyway. 'It's all right. You weren't followed.' The voice came closer as it spoke, and now he appeared beside Slider in the entrance to the arch. Taller than Slider, but not by much; well-built without being heavy. A handsome, dark face with designer stubble making it look darker; thick, longish dark hair, brushed back and bronze-tipped and styled in a classy salon – or at least an expensive one. He was wearing the undercover cop's favoured blouson-style jacket, in suede – new enough for Slider to smell that now, too – along with dark trousers and black leather casual shoes with thick soles. He had a gold and jet stud in one ear, expensive and discreetly unconventional. The intelligent brown eyes were watchful in a face made firm by responsibility. A man who could look after himself and expected to win. To Slider he had copper stamped all over him. No wonder Yates had clocked him.

'Why here?' Slider asked.

'It was the only place I could be sure you'd know without my naming it. Mobiles are not secure. That's why I called this meet.'

Called this meet, Slider smiled inwardly. How they all loved playing cops and robbers! He had the strong desire to call de Glanville 'son'; but probably the danger de Glanville faced was real and desperate. 'You're going to tell me what's going on?' he said hopefully.

'I was in favour of telling you in the first place,' de Glanville said. He had a slight accent: Slider couldn't decide what. There was something about the 'e' in 'telling' and the 'th' in 'the'. 'I don't want local boys trampling all over my investigation, busting in on me and blowing my cover.'

'Believe me, I don't want to do that either,' Slider said patiently. 'If I know where the land mines are, I'll know not to tread on them, won't I?'

De Glanville smiled, a brief flash of very white teeth in the dark lower half of his face. Slider thought women would find him attractive. Perhaps it was necessary to his job. 'I've already had your oppo under my feet. What's his name? Carver? Why don't you people ever talk to each other?'

'Beats the hell out of me. Look what I had to go through to get to talk to you,' Slider said.

'True. All right. Let's get on the park. I'm in at the Pomona – I guess you know that.' He used 'guess' as a foreigner uses it, not an Americanism. Could it be that he was a real Frenchman? But he didn't quite sound French.

'Are you after Yates?'

'Yates is a player, but he's not the biggest. That's why we don't want him flushed out yet. It's his bosses we're after. But I had contact with the man you're interested in – Jay Paloma.'

'You met him in the club? Several times?' De Glanville nodded. 'You were spotted. Yates told me about you. He said he thought you were a dealer.'

'He was supposed to,' de Glanville said with a touch of complacency. Stand aside, redneck, and let the big city experts in. 'Paloma was buying snow – you know that, don't you? I'd seen him sniffing round a dealer I was interested in and for operational reasons I didn't want him hanging around that particular area, so I told him I'd supply him.'

'How did you get the stuff?'

'You don't want to know that. I knew who he was getting it for, so I supplied him for some time. I thought there might be some important connection that way. It did seem for a time that our big player might be an MP and using Parliamentary privilege to shelter under. But it turned out to be a false lead. So I dropped Paloma.'

'Wait a minute, let me get this straight. Did Paloma know who you were?'

'Not *who* – but what.'

'He was working for you, in fact.'

'Effectively. I got him the stuff, he passed it on to his bum-chum and reported back to me. I primed him with the questions to ask and what to look out for. But as I said, it was a dead end.'

'How did you persuade him to spy for you?'

'It wasn't hard,' de Glanville said with a short laugh. 'I was giving him the stuff at a fraction of the price, and he was pocketing the difference. He was perfectly happy. Plus I leaned on him a bit.'

'Really?' Slider said neutrally.

'I had the goods on him, didn't I? And you saw him: he was a bit precious – very dainty in his ways. He wouldn't have liked a spell inside with all those nasty rough boys.'

'Yes, that would scare him,' Slider agreed. 'When you dropped him, you told him you wouldn't supply him any more?'

'Of course. But he said he was getting out anyway. Saved enough of Grisham's money to go back to Ireland. I said that was a good idea. Didn't want him hanging around and maybe letting the cat out of the bag. Gave him a bit of a push in that direction, if you want to know. But as it happened, it wasn't necessary.' He shrugged. 'Best result all round, really, when he got topped.'

Slider nodded politely. 'I suppose you don't know who did it?'

'Nope,' de Glanville said. 'That's your business.'

'I told you that Yates had spotted you for a dealer, and you said he was supposed to. But it occurs to me that he might have blown your cover.'

'Because Yates sent one of his goons round to hit Paloma?'

'How the hell did you know that?'

'It's my business to know things. But I want Yates left alone. We're very close now. I don't want him spooked. And I want that gorilla of his sprung.'

Slider saw no reason to reveal his hand. He shrugged. 'If you say so. But what about Cosgrove?'

'Cosgrove was a worse problem to me because everyone knew he was a copper. He was clodhopping after Yates, and I had to get him warned off. I couldn't have him hanging round the club.'

'But do you know who whacked him?'

'Nope. I got him off my back, that was all the mattered to me. He hadn't been around there for weeks when it happened. But I doubt, frankly, if it was anything to do with Yates. Yates is too fly to put out a hit on a copper – and if he did, he'd do it more professionally than that. It had all the hallmarks of an amateur to me. But it's not my case,' he finished with a shrug.

'It's not mine, either,' Slider said. 'When did you last supply Paloma with any white?'

De Glanville considered. 'It was the Thursday before he was killed. Thursday night stroke Friday morning. I suppose he gave it to his friend on Friday or Saturday and a happy weekend was had by all.'

'And that's when you told him you didn't need him any more?' De Glanville nodded. 'So he knew before the weekend.'

'Certainly. Now I've told you everything you need to know. You'll stay away from the club and Yates from now on. I want everything to settle down again.'

'What will happen to him?' Slider asked.

'Yates? Why, have you got some beef against him?'

Slider thought of Maroon, and Maltesa, and Candy, and all the other pathetic toms nobody cared about. Thank you, Mr Gladstone. But they had rights, like anyone else, and what they did was not illegal, that was what got him. Prostitution was not illegal – living off their backs, like Yates and his gorillas, *that* was illegal.

'He's responsible for beating up a girl I know,' Slider said. All right, it was Jonah who broke Maroon's face, but it was Yates who made Jonah possible.

De Glanville hesitated, but then his face softened a little in sympathy. 'He's going down. Don't worry about that. We've got enough on him to send him away for ever and ever. As soon as we've sprung the trap on the top bosses, we'll clean up the scumbags like Yates.'

'And Jonah Lafota?'

'Him too.' Dark eyes gleamed in the darkness. 'My promise on that.'

'Thanks,' said Slider.

De Glanville looked out of the arch at the quiet night. 'It's safe enough. You can go now.'

Slider said, 'There is just one other question.' De Glanville looked at him a little impatiently. 'What *is* your accent? I can't place it. I thought at first it was French, but now—'

The teeth whitened across the dark face. 'What are you, Professor Higgins? Belgian Congo. Zaire. I was born there. My dad was in the diplomatic. But my mum's British.'

'Thanks,' said Slider gratefully.

He went a long way round to get back to his car, for safety's sake, but he saw nothing and felt nothing. He got in and drove. It looked after all as if there wasn't any connection between the Paloma murder and the Cosgrove case, except stupid concurrence. He didn't mind being wrong, but he absolutely hated Carver to be right, to say nothing of Wetherspoon. He thought about Carver and Wetherspoon at Honeyman's party. It hadn't looked terribly much like Wetherspoon telling Carver to back off and Carver saying yes sir, certainly sir. It had looked a lot more like Carver getting his hand down Wetherspoon's trousers, and Wetherspoon saying I'll pull strings for you, Ron, just don't stop loving me. But as Hart had said, that was just paranoid. Anyway, Cosgrove was not his case and not his business. He must put it out of his head entirely.

So he drove to the pub where Busty was barmaid, to ask her the only other thing he hadn't asked her – whether she knew Andy Cosgrove.

The pub was crowded, and Slider, scanning the bar for Busty, was surprised and amused to see that one of the bar stools was occupied by the trim, moley person of Busty's tame taxi-driver. What was his name? Oh yes, Benny the Brief. He had one hand wrapped round a half-pint jug and the other was supporting a lighted cigarette, and as Slider came up behind him he saw that his eyes were fixed adoringly on the heavenly shape of Busty Parnell, serving down the other end of the bar in a pink sequinned sweater, low-cut enough to leave everything to be desired.

'Hello there, Mr Fluss,' Slider said, remembering his name at the last moment. 'Drinking and driving? Tut tut.'

The little man started violently, and then smiled his crooked, multidentate smile as he recognised Slider. 'Oh, I only have the one when I'm driving, don't worry. I nurse it. I'm a great nurser. Can I get you one?'

'No, thanks, I just came to have a quick word with Busty.'

Benny looked pained. 'Valerie, please, or Miss Parnell. She's not – that horrid name – any more. That belongs to the past. That's all over. She's a respectable woman now.'

'Of course. I'm sorry,' Slider said, amused. 'It just slipped out. So you're still on duty, are you?'

'Not as such,' Benny conceded. 'But I'm keeping a clear head for driving Miss Parnell home when her shift finishes. That's a sacred duty to me, so you don't need to worry about me having too much, I can assure you.' He burbled on a bit, but Slider wasn't listening. Busty looked round at last and he caught her eye, and she came down to him with an eager look.

'Hello! Have you got some news?' she asked.

'I'm afraid not. I just popped in to ask you something. Could I have a quick word?' He flicked a warning glance Bennywards and she picked it up with commendable quickness.

'Come down the other end, then, where it's quieter,' she said. 'George, can you serve for me for a minute? Just five minutes. Thanks, love.'

At the other end of the bar she propped up the hatch and made a little quiet corner for them. Slider eased himself in beside her. 'I see you've got an escort laid on for later,' he said.

She made a face. 'Oh, I can't seem to shake him off. He's been ever so kind since Maurice died, can't do enough for me, but he gets on my nerves a bit. I'm thinking of setting George on him.'

'That's a bit cruel, isn't it?' George the barman was a low-browed, long-armed creature who looked like a genetic experiment gone horribly wrong. He was kindness itself, but his terrifying looks were too useful to the management for them to admit it publicly.

'Well, just to tell him he can't sit in here all evening nursing the same half,' Busty said. 'Anyway, what did you want to ask me?'

'Do you know Andy Cosgrove?'

'What, the copper? Of course. He got beaten up, didn't he, poor soul, and left in a coma. Just before Maurice got – you know.' She moved her head as though she could avoid the pain with the word.

'That's him. But I mean did you know him personally?'

'Everybody on the estate knew him,' Busty said. 'He hasn't gone and died, has he?'

'No, there's no change. You knew him to speak to?'

Busty smiled. 'Oh yes. Well, he used to go out with a working girl, didn't he? He always took a special interest in us.'

'Did you know Maroon Brown, his girlfriend?'

'Oh yeah. She used to live on the estate, did you know that?'

'Yes, I knew that.'

'And she used to come in here quite a bit. Met Andy here sometimes when he come off duty. Course, I haven't seen her lately.'

'So you knew Andy quite well?'

'Oh yeah. Like I said, he had a soft spot for working girls.' She glanced back down the bar at Benny the Brief and lowered her voice – unnecessarily – to say with a sporting grin, 'Old Benny thought it was terrible – about Andy and Maroon.'

'How did he know about them?'

'I told him, a course. He didn't half tut. Well, Andy's a married man, and Maroon's a full-time prostitute. And he didn't like me mixing with bad hats like that. He's a real old woman, sometimes, Benny.'

Slider was not interested in Busty's guard-dog. 'So when did you last see Andy?'

'Couple of weeks ago. Not long before he was done over, as a matter of fact. He came to see me at the flat one afternoon, when Maurice was out. Doing a bit of sniffing around, he was, not that he came straight out with it. But I know when I'm being pumped.'

'What did he want to know about?'

'Oh, I dunno. Something about Billy Yates and Maurice. I didn't get it at first. I thought he was after Maurice – you know, because of the stuff.' She lowered her eyelids daintily at the mention. 'But thinking about it later, I think he was hoping Maurice might have something on Mr Yates, to incriminate him. He had a down on Billy Yates for some reason, did Andy. It wasn't official police business,' she added cannily, ''cause he didn't come straight out with it. Just hinting around, you know.'

'Did you tell him anything?'

'And drop Maurice in it? What d'you think I am? Of course I didn't. Well, anyway, Andy stayed a bit and had a bit of a chat and then he went, and that's the last time I saw him.'

'Had he ever called on you before?'

'What, at the flat? No. No, he hadn't. Come to think of it, I suppose that must of meant it was important. But I didn't make anything of it, really. I mean, I know what you coppers are like. Always lonely, always wanting a chat.' And she smiled fondly at Slider, remembering.

Slider cleared his throat. He had enough woman trouble already. 'Can you remember exactly when that was – the day he visited you? You said it wasn't long before he was attacked.'

'That's right. It was the week before. On the Thursday or Friday, I think. Let me see.' She furrowed her brow willingly but evidently without much hope.

'You said it was while Maurice was out,' Slider prompted. 'Where had he gone, do you remember that?'

'Oh, to see his friend, of course. Wait a minute, yes, I've got it now. It was the Friday afternoon. And poor Andy got done over on the Saturday night. Well, there! With all the trouble over Maurice I never thought, but it was just the day before. It makes you think, don't it?'

'Why didn't you mention this to me before?' Slider said.

'You never asked,' she said with a touch of indignation. 'Anyway, it's got nothing to do with Maurice, has it?'

'No,' Slider sighed. 'No, I don't suppose it has.'

'Anyway, what did you want to ask me?' Busty said. 'Only I can't leave George holding the baby.'

'Oh, that was it. About Andy Cosgrove. It was just a loose end I wanted tying up.'

'And has it helped?' she asked, eyeing him keenly.

No, Slider thought, it hasn't. '*You've* helped,' he said. 'Thanks, Busty. When all this is over, I'll take you out and buy you a curry. Like the old days.'

'Only this ain't the old days any more,' she said sadly. 'In the old days everybody was shocked if a copper got hurt. Now it don't even make the front page. We didn't know when we was lucky.'

Ain't it the truth, Slider thought. On an impulse he laid his hand briefly over hers as it rested on the bar, and leaned forward to peck her on the cheek. 'See you, Busty.'

Outside, on the way to his car, he passed Benny's black cab. Or he assumed it was Benny's – he wouldn't expect there to be two Monty's Metrocabs parked down the side of the pub. It was interesting that he hadn't noticed it on his way in. It was like Lenny the Lion said – you didn't see black cabs unless you were positively looking for them. They were street furniture, and the brain edited them out.

He got in his car and just sat, wondering what to do next. He toyed briefly with the idea of going home, but knew he couldn't bear to. When he needed to think he had to be out; home had too many other connotations to be conducive. If he went home he'd have to tell Joanna about Irene and the phone call, and he didn't want to think about that yet; couldn't afford the brain-space, with so much else that needed to be sorted out. So there seemed nothing for it but to go and see Atherton. It was late, and even with flexible visiting hours the nursing staff might be unwilling to let him by. But he knew a back way in, and if challenged he could always flash his brief and claim official business. Which it was, in a way. Cot-case or not, Atherton was still his partner.

CHAPTER SIXTEEN

Waste Not, Want Not

He parked down the narrow service road behind the hospital, and when he got out and turned to lock the door, he got that prickling feeling again of being watched. It was just the loneliness of the road, he told himself, and the multiplicity of shadowy places. The backs of hospitals were always unlovely: all downpipes and dirty windows of frosted glass, and always a single mysterious plume of steam rising from somewhere into the yellow sodium-lit sky. He thought briefly of the waste ground, and de Glanville, and de Glanville's extensive caution. Well, he was after big players, and big players did sometimes get carried away. But they wouldn't be interested in Slider. His head was aching a bit, and he wondered if thinking you were being followed was a sign of brain damage. Perhaps he had come back to work too early. If he hadn't come back, this whole Paloma mess would have landed on someone else's desk and he wouldn't have Busty Parnell on his conscience. He should have taken more sick-leave. He yearned to be lying on a beach somewhere instead of here, slogging it out with this grubby mystery; but now he had taken hold of it, he couldn't put it down. Unless his head actually fell off, he would have to see it through.

His unofficial way in was across the back yard and past the dustbins. There was a metal fire door, one of those push-bar-to-open jobs, which was slightly warped and would only shut properly if you yanked it hard, which porters in a hurry often did not bother to do. If you just let it go to close by its own weight, it simply rested shut without the lock catching. So it was now. Slider worked his fingers under the rim and pulled it open. It gave onto a stone-floored corridor with dark-green glazed tiled walls lit by a single sulky bulb in the high ceiling.

To the right a much scarred metal door gave access to the incinerator room, where they burned the infected waste and the bits of people that people didn't want any more. Slider hurried past it with a superstitious shudder. At the far end was a pair of black rubber swing doors, and he pushed through these into a corridor of the brightly-lit hospital proper, with its white noise of air conditioning and its smell of you-don't-really-want-to-know-what-this-is-covering-up. Here was the goods lift and a series of store rooms, and a little further along a granite staircase with metal hand rails, alongside a branch corridor which led to the mortuary and the old post-mortem room. He had been there more times than he needed to remember, in the company of Freddie Cameron, which was how he knew this back way in. He clattered up the stairs, meeting no-one and reflecting how easy it was to bypass security in a hospital. But of course hospitals had not been built with security in mind. Who would ever have thought there would be a need?

Coming at Atherton's room from the wrong end, as it were, he didn't even encounter a nurse. He could see by the glass panel in the door that the light was on, and looking through he saw Atherton sitting up in bed; and in a chair beside the bed, chatting to him, was Hart.

He went in. 'What are you doing here?' he asked as Hart looked round.

'Just visiting,' she said. 'Why not?'

'It's late,' Slider said. 'How did you get past the nurses?'

'One of 'em's a friend of mine,' Hart said simply.

'Good evening. Yes, thank you, much better, thank you for asking,' Atherton said to the wall.

'I was going to ask if you minded being disturbed so late,' Slider said, 'but I got thrown off track. You're *looking* better.'

'You look terrible,' Atherton reciprocated. 'Are you having headaches?'

'Does Salman Rushdie have life insurance?'

'Has something happened, guv?' Hart asked, searching his face. 'Some new information?'

'Why should you think that?'

She grinned. 'Deduced it, din' I? You ain't bin home, and it's ages since I left you at the factory.'

'Pull up a chair,' Atherton said, 'and tell all. I need mental stimulation. Now I'm not drugged all day long, I'm bored to death.'

So Slider brought Atherton up to speed, and told them both about his interview with de Glanville and the truth about where Jay Paloma had got the cocaine.

'It's ironic,' Slider concluded. 'At one end of the chain there was Grisham being blackmailed into getting the dope from Paloma, and at the other end Paloma being blackmailed into getting it for Grisham.

'It's pafetic when you fink of it,' Hart said. 'When you remember, guv, how that Grisham was going on about true love and finding his soulmate, and all the time poor old Paloma was spying on him and putting his money aside so he could get enough saved up to leave him.'

'But it does look as though the drugs can be ruled out as a motive,' Atherton said. 'Obviously he wasn't whacked for bilking a dealer or anything. He wasn't really a threat to anyone.'

'It might still have been someone who knew he had the stuff and just wanted to nick it,' Hart said.

Slider shook his head. 'That won't work. There was no sign of the flat being searched; no sign even of anyone going through the victim's pockets. If some local low-life or addict did it just to get a single packet, they wouldn't have left without even looking for what they came for.'

'I suppose not,' Hart conceded unwillingly.

'Then what does that leave you with? Yates?' Atherton said. 'He's into some serious naughties somewhere. And he definitely sent Jonah Lafota round. Though we still don't know what he wanted Paloma done for.'

'*I* do,' Hart said.

Slider looked at her narrowly. 'Have you been hanging around that club again?'

'No, boss,' she said in wounded tones. 'I din't need to. I got my snout wound round my little finger now.'

'You're a bleeding contortionist, that's what you are,' Atherton said admiringly.

'I ain't been wasting my time,' she said with a sidelong look at Slider. 'My snout got it all off that ficko Garry. Apparently Yates knew Paloma had been scoring white in the club and he didn't like it, 'cause the dealer wasn't one of his. Well, we know

now it was one of ours. Anyway, Yates don't want any outside dealing on his patch, and he don't want any trouble spoiling the spotless reputation of his fine establishment. So when Grisham comes in and makes the fuss, Yates sees a way of putting the frighteners on Paloma, and if anything comes back at him, he lays it off on Grisham, because there's witnesses that the daft bugger give Jonah money to do it. Jonah don't like it, of course, because it's his spuds on the barbecue, but he's got to do as he's told. If Yates says it's Christmas they all sing carols.'

'Is that the way it was?'

'Yeah, and when we come in asking questions, Yates comes over all helpful and puts us onto the dealer to keep us off his back. Probably hoped we might scare him off the patch, as well.'

'Well, that ties up an end. But I rather think Yates is ruled out for the murder,' Slider said regretfully. 'I can't see him sending two men to do the same job. And if he'd had Paloma killed in the afternoon, he wouldn't have sent Jonah round in the evening.'

'Are you definitely accepting Jonah's story, then?' Atherton asked. 'That Paloma was already dead when he got there?'

'It agrees too well,' Slider said. 'Look.' He counted the points out on his left hand. 'For a start, Freddie Cameron originally put the death much earlier – between one fifteen and four fifteen. He accepted the later time because we had witnesses to the breaking down of the door, and an eyewitness outweighs the science of rigor. But that was his first opinion.' He extended the forefinger to join the thumb. 'Then there's the old man who lives underneath.'

'Sounds like the title of a children's story written by the Prince of Wales,' Atherton commented.

Slider ignored him. 'His evidence is very detailed. The visitor, the heavy fall, the trampling and banging as the body was repeatedly struck – it all agrees.'

'He could be making it up to get attention,' Hart said. 'Old man, living alone, no family—'

'We've all seen *Twelve Angry Men*,' Atherton told her.

'That's always a possibility,' Slider conceded, 'but he did point out the exact spot where the body fell, without ever having seen inside the flat. And his background and his explanation make it plausible that he was listening, and that he could distinguish what he heard. Hollis believes him, and Hollis is no monkey.

The old man also says that Paloma didn't do his practice at the usual time that evening; and we've got Grisham's word that he telephoned several times in the afternoon and got no reply.'

'Paloma could have guessed it was Grisham ringing and just not answered,' Atherton said.

'Of course. But add it to the rest of the evidence, and it starts to tell. Point – where have I got up to? Three?'

'Four, if you count Grisham,' Hart said.

'Four, then. There's the forensic evidence about the stomach contents. Scrambled eggs on toast eaten less than an hour before death. That ties in with the crockery left in the sink, and it could have been eaten any time. But Busty expected him to get himself breakfast after she left, and she says he always washed up immediately. So look at the timings: she leaves him in his dressing-gown at half past eleven. He takes an hour-plus to get shaved, washed and dressed – half past twelve, twenty to one. He cooks himself some breakfast and eats it. Puts the dirties in the sink to wash. Then he goes into the front room to put the television on—'

'He ain't done the washing up,' Hart objected.

'I have to guess here, but maybe he just popped in to check the time of the film. It was one he didn't want to miss, and they start at a different time every day. He and Busty didn't have a newspaper or a *TV Times*, but they did have Teletext. It's possible he just went in to check the time, meaning to go straight back to do the washing up before settling down. But at that very moment, the visitor arrives.'

'It makes sense,' Atherton conceded.

'They sit and talk, Paloma gets them both a drink, then at twenty past the visitor jumps up and whacks him.'

'But—'

'Bear with me,' Slider said, lifting his hand. 'See how this works out. Paloma's dead. So the washing up doesn't get done. The bath towels don't get folded and hung up as usual. He doesn't do his practice. He doesn't answer the phone. He doesn't go in to work. The television's on and tuned to Channel 4 for the afternoon film – a black and white wartime job of which he was very fond. Busty says if he'd been watching that night he'd have had it on ITV for sure. The curtains are open – if he'd been watching at night he'd have drawn them.'

'It's all circumstantial,' Atherton said.

'Yes, but it adds up. Nothing jars yet. All right, come eleven-thirty Jonah Lafota turns up to scare the bejaysus out of Paloma. He's drunk and furious about the whole thing. He kicks the door in and storms into the front room, where the telly's on. By the light of the screen he can't see much. So he turns on the light, leaving his fingermarks on the light switch. He sees Paloma lying on the floor. He walks over, sees the mess someone's made of the man he's been sent to scare, and realises the creamola he's in. He grabs a drink, knocking over the table, panics, picks everything up and puts it straight and leaves, remembering – for he's intelligent, our boy – to put the light off again as he goes, and pull the front door to so that it won't be seen until he's well away.'

'Brilliant, boss,' said Hart enthusiastically.

'Hm,' said Atherton. 'But Jonah's supposed to be professional. Why didn't he wear gloves?'

'Because he didn't go there to murder Paloma, only scare him; and having been scared Paloma wouldn't have brought charges, not even for the bust-in door. So there was no need to be careful.'

'It explains why there was gloved fingermarks on the glass and ungloved on the bottle,' Hart approved. 'The visitor at one o'clock came to murder, so he wore gloves. He had a drink with Paloma, and he used the glass.'

Slider nodded, looking from her to Atherton. 'We decided from the start that Paloma had been taken by surprise. There was no sign of a struggle. But how could he have been taken by surprise – and from the front – if the door had been violently kicked in? But if he was sitting having a chat with the murderer, who suddenly sprang up and whacked him across the bridge of the nose, killing him instantly – it fits all right. Lafota was telling the truth, Paloma was already dead when he got there, and the scrambled eggs were breakfast, not supper.'

'But who?' Atherton said. 'And why?'

'That, as somebody once remarked, is the question.' Slider rubbed his forehead. 'I think we need to sleep on it. We're missing something.'

Atherton caught Hart's eye and made a gesture towards the door with his head. She took the hint and stood up. 'Well, if it's all the same to you gents, I fink I'll go and have a chat with my mate. While I'm here. Got to keep her sweet or she won't let me in again. How did you get in, guv?' she added with interest.

'I've got a private route,' Slider said, 'but I'm keeping it to myself.'

'It's a secret passage,' Atherton said. 'Starts behind a concealed panel in the library and comes out in the crypt of the ruined chapel.'

'Garn,' said Hart, and departed.

Atherton looked keenly at Slider. 'What's up, boss? Is it the case?'

Slider hesitated, but it was habit to confide in Atherton. 'Mostly that. But now I've got trouble with Irene as well. At least, I think I have.' He told Atherton briefly about the phone call.

'You are a plonker when it comes to women,' Atherton said. 'How could you get yourself into such a mess?'

'Your own relationships with women are notably successful and well-managed, of course,' Slider said with a touch of resentment.

'I don't have relationships with women, that's the whole point. I flit like a butterfly from flower to flower. A little sip here, a little sip there, and—'

'Has Sue been in to see you?'

'Yes, she's been in,' Atherton said shortly.

'Just once?'

'Who's counting?' His tone was brittle. 'I keep telling you, there's nothing between Sue and me.'

'Yes, you tell me that, but you don't tell me why,' said Slider. If he was having his tender parts probed, he was going to probe back some. 'You and she were very hot, and then suddenly it all stopped. Why?'

Atherton was on the brink of snapping 'Is that any of your business?' when he paused and reflected that it just about was, or at least it had the right to be, and said instead, 'Look—'

'Ha!'

'What d'you mean, "ha!"?'

'Prevarication alert. When a man starts by saying "look", it's a sign he's wriggling. *Why* did you stop seeing Sue? Plain answer.'

'Because it was getting heavy. She was getting too serious.'

'*She* was?'

'You know what women are like,' Atherton said unconvincingly. 'You go out a couple of times and they start wanting to leave stuff in your bathroom. Then they want to know what you're doing every minute of the day. Before you know it, they're talking about looking for a flat together.'

Slider looked at him sadly. 'You're crazy about her.'

'I just don't want to get involved. Anyway, we're supposed to be discussing your problems, if you don't mind.'

'At least mine are positive problems, not negative ones.'

'Is that supposed to mean something, or was that a bit of your brain I just saw fall out of your ear?'

'It means,' Slider said, 'that if you're not "involved", as you call it, you're nothing. It's like saying life is difficult, so I'd sooner not be born.'

'Very profound.'

'You can sneer all you like, but what else is there? Bonking a series of bimbos you don't give a damn about? You might as well masturbate and save the money.'

'I'm quite happy as I am, thank you,' Atherton said with dignity.

'You aren't,' said Slider. They eyed each other for a while in tense silence. 'How are you, anyway?' Slider said at last.

'They're going to try me on solid foods next week,' Atherton said, not with unalloyed bliss.

'That's good, isn't it?'

'Theoretically.'

'Are you in much pain?'

'Oh, it comes and goes. No, it's a lot better now.'

'But?'

'I don't know,' Atherton said with evident difficulty, 'if I'll be coming back.'

'Oh,' said Slider. He sought careful words. 'That would be – a waste.'

'The thing is,' Atherton went on, looking bleakly at the wall beyond Slider's shoulder, 'I don't know what else I can do.'

'But you're intelligent. You've got A levels and everything,' Slider said. 'You'd easily get a job.'

'At my age? Anyway, it's the only thing I ever wanted to do, be a copper.'

'Really?' Slider said with some surprise. He had always thought Atherton became a policeman out of general indifference.

Atherton smiled faintly. 'My pose of languid insouciance is not meant to fool you, oh great detective. Since I was a kid reading 'tec novels, it's all I ever wanted. It disappointed my father and broke my mother's heart, but I always knew it was the one thing I could do well, and be happy at.'

'So why – er—?'

Atherton looked at him. 'I've seen bits of me God never meant to be seen. I lie here every day and look at *this.*' He gestured towards his wound. 'And I think, "I never want to be in this situation again." And next time it could be worse. I could be shot. I could get killed.'

'Oh, come on—' Slider began, but having screwed up his courage to say all this, Atherton wouldn't be stopped.

'It could happen. You know the chances. Seven officers killed in the last five years. God knows how many thousand wounded, some of them disabled or scarred for life. I don't want to end up with a plastic nose. And the thing is, they'll know. The villains. They'll know I'm afraid, and that'll make it all the more likely. I'd be endangering other people. I can't go on, Bill. I've – lost my nerve.'

Slider didn't know what to say to comfort him. 'Don't think about it now,' he said. 'Think about it later.'

'Thank you, Scarlett,' Atherton said, managing a smile.

'You're still under the weather. Everything will seem different when you're on your feet and out of here.'

'How do you cope?' Atherton asked, eyeing him.

Slider said, 'I don't really think about it until it happens.'

'You've had your share,' Atherton observed.

'Of course, it's your first time. That's always worse. And some coppers do take it harder than others. I suppose you've got more imagination, or something.'

Atherton winced. 'You make me sound like Patience Strong.'

'My advice would be, don't make any decisions on the basis of how you feel now. Get fit again, see how you feel then. Don't rush it. Run yourself in gently with a shoplifter or two, just to get your hand in, then move on to an underage burglar—'

'What's your interest in all this, anyway?' Atherton demanded.

'I should miss you,' Slider said.

It was the sort of moment when men get gruff. Atherton said gruffly, 'Well, you've got a new partner now. What's she like?'

'You've seen her. Slender waist, firm, pouting breasts, legs that go all the way up to her shoulders—'

'You could be describing me,' Atherton said, and the moment was past.

A nurse put her head round the door. 'I thought I heard voices. You shouldn't be here, you know,' she said to Slider. 'How did you get past the desk without me seeing you?'

He didn't want to give away his secret route in case he needed it again. 'I expect you were answering a call,' he said.

'I hope this is urgent, official business,' she said sternly.

'It was. I've finished now, though. I'll be off,' Slider said, obeying the insistently held-open door. 'I'll look in again tomorrow,' he said to Atherton.

'Don't bother,' Atherton said. 'Send me Hart instead.'

'You'd only burst your stitches,' said Slider.

Because the nurse was watching he had to go out past the desk and to the main lift, but he got out at the first floor and made his way back to the stone stairs. If he went out at the front he'd have to walk right round the hospital to get to his car and he was tired now. There was a smell of pallid food wafting up the staircase: the kitchens must be somewhere up this end. It was funny, he thought, how often the kitchen and body parts incinerator were close together. Mackay said it was a case of waste not, want not, and amplified the thought if given any encouragement – or even without it.

Slider pushed open the rubber swing door and found the corridor past the incinerator room was in darkness. Holding the door open, he looked for the light switch on the wall just inside, and clicked it. Nothing happened. The bulb must have gone. He didn't fancy groping his way down the passage in the pitch dark. But at the far end the metal door was slightly open – letting the rubber door close behind him to cut out the light, he could see two edges of the door outlined by the orange glow from the lamp-posts in the street. It was enough. It wasn't as if he could get lost anywhere.

The corridor was only thirty feet long, but five steps into it he suddenly got a very bad case of panic. The hair stood up on his scalp and he wanted to run. For an instant he stopped himself, manly-wise; and then he thought, yeah, what the hell, panic! And ran. At least, he flung the first running step forward, but that was all he had time for before the wall fell on him and knocked him down. He sprawled on the cold rubber floor, smelled a terrible smell of gas, felt someone looming over him; and a terrible, unmanning despair swept over him. This was it. He was going to die. And in his last moment, he thought of Atherton, so near but just too far away to help him.

The looming shape was gone. He wasn't dead. Someone ran past him. He dragged himself part way up, propped on one elbow, feeling sick. The outline of the metal door changed shape, there was a dark figure framed in it, looking out; looking back. A metallic scraping noise – whoever it was was forcing the door all the way out so that it stayed open. The figure ran back. Slider flinched; but it was Hart. He smelled her perfume on the gusted air before her.

'Sir, are you all right? Guv?'

'I'm all right. Get after him,' Slider croaked.

She was away again. He saw her darken the door briefly. He dragged himself into sitting position and leaned against the cold wall, glad of the little light, glad he was not in darkness. The nausea was passing, a numb, throbbing pain tuning in behind his head. He reached up shaky, flinching fingers and located the area of extreme tenderness around the lowest cervical vertebra, which woke to jangling when he touched it. The fact that he had flung himself forward had saved him from having his neck broken; amazing thing, animal instinct. He would never scoff at it again.

Hart came running back, and was on her knees beside him, her hands all over him. 'Nothing,' she panted. 'No sign of anyone anywhere. He's had it away down the road by now. Are you all right, guv?'

'I think so,' he said.

'What was it? Where did he get you?'

'He hit me with something. Back of the neck. My jacket collar cushioned it.'

'Who was it, guv? Did you see him?'

'No, he was hiding in the dark. The light didn't work. He must have taken the bulb out. Did you get a look at him?'

'No. Just a sort of dark shape at the far door. I must have scared him off.'

'Thank God you came.' He winced. 'Leave that alone. I'm all right, just leave me alone.' She desisted. 'Why did you come? What were you doing here?'

'I followed you,' she said. 'You left your mobile behind.'

'I did?'

'I just popped into Atherton's room to say goodbye, and he said you'd left your mobile. He told me about your back way in so I ran after you, down the back stairs. As I pushed open *that* door, all I saw was the dark shape as he scarpered out of *that* one.'

'He was standing over me, ready to finish me off. You saved my life.'

'Oh, that's all right. Any time,' she said, sounding embarrassed. 'Who was it, though? Someone to do with the case?'

'Unless it was a homicidal hospital porter, I should think that's a fair bet.'

'Sorry, guv. I'm a bit rattled.'

'How d'you think I feel? Give me a hand up, will you?' He got to his feet, leaned against the wall, and had an experimental moan. It felt good, so he repeated it. 'I'm too old for this sort of thing,' he said. Maybe he'd join Atherton in retirement. They could go shares in a chicken farm.

'Put your arm over my shoulder and I'll support you,' Hart said, slipping her lithe body into the operative position. 'Let me take your weight.'

'It's all right, I can walk,' he said.

'No, come on, guv. No sense in taking chances. I'll help you to a chair and then I'll go and find a nurse or someone.'

'What?'

'To have a look at your head. You'll need an X-ray or something.'

'Oh no you don't. I'm not getting caught up with all that again. I've done my hospital stay for this year.'

'But, guv—'

'He didn't hit me on the head, and nothing's broken. Just a bit bruised.' He tried an experimental rotation of the head and it hurt, but not by that much. 'I'm going home.'

'Suppose he's still out there?'

'You said he'd gone.'

'I could be wrong.'

'You can walk me to my car, if you're worried. But he won't attack again tonight.'

'How can you be so sure?' she said indignantly. 'If he really wants to kill you—'

'You don't know it's a man,' he said, to sidetrack her. 'It could be my wife taking vengeance.'

'Then she'd attack me, wouldn't she, not you?' Hart said with a cheeky grin.

He was glad to have distracted her, but he didn't want her continuing in this delusion. 'You take too much upon yourself,' Slider said grimly. 'Walk with me to my car, and then I'll drive you to yours, just in case. And from now on, we both avoid dark alleys. Will you stop flapping, WDC Hart! If he'd wanted to take on two of us, he wouldn't have run off when you came on the scene, would he?'

CHAPTER SEVENTEEN

State of Affairs

'All the same,' Joanna said, easing arnica into the spot, 'she had a point.'

'Atherton reckons she's got several,' Slider said. 'Ouch.'

'That'll teach you not to be facetious. What in the name of Jupiter did he hit you with?'

'It felt like a smallish building,' Slider said. 'But I wasn't knocked out, just groggy. And nothing's broken. It's just a bruise. I don't want to spend any more time hanging around a hospital if I can help it. I've got things to do.'

Joanna came round the front of him and sat down, knees touching his knees, face inches from his. She looked pale and tired and worried, and he suddenly had a very glad and lifting awareness of how much he loved her, which was reassuring in this world of uncertainties. 'Suppose he tries it again, whoever he is?'

'Well, being in hospital wouldn't help me, would it? I proved how easy it is to sneak in.'

'I was voicing a different worry that time,' she said. 'I'd moved on from (a) you might have delayed concussion to (b) there's a murderer prancing about trying to invalidate your ticket.' Her eyes were anxious. 'I don't want to lose you, Bill.'

She laid a hand on his knee and he placed his over it. This would be a good time, he thought, to give her something else to worry about. A nice go of stomach ache to take her mind off toothache. 'Irene knows about us,' he said.

It worked. 'What? You don't mean you told her?'

'It sort of came out.'

'Wait a minute, wait a minute, let's get this straight. When you say you told her about us, what exactly did you tell her?'

Her eyes widened so far her eyebrows made her scalp shift backwards. 'You told her everything?' He nodded mutely. 'Oh, bloody Nora, now what have you done?'

'Bloody Nora?' he said, amused. 'You sound like a policeman.'

'Laugh while you can,' she said grimly. 'Let me guess how pleased she was to find out the true state of affairs, if you'll pardon the pun.'

'She told me to get a lawyer,' Slider admitted. 'Her parting words before she slammed the phone down.'

Joanna jumped to her feet and paced about. 'Phone! It was her on the phone, putting it down when I answered! Of course, why didn't I guess?'

'How do women do that?' he marvelled. 'Yes, she was the phantom phone caller. She'd been trying to get hold of me – to discuss our getting together again, I imagine – and when she kept getting a woman's voice, she rang me at the office.'

'I don't know why you're being so flippant about it,' Joanna said crossly.

'It's less antisocial than crying,' he said, 'which is what I feel like doing.'

She sat down again abruptly. 'I'm sorry. I know you care about her – about them. But really, Bill, why on earth did you – I mean, what good did you think it could do her to know?'

'I just couldn't bear to hear her blaming herself for everything. Anyway, she'd have had to know sooner or later. It would have come out.'

'I don't see why.'

'Because whatever you think now, you and she are bound to meet from time to time in the future, and things slip out. You can't keep a guilty secret for ever. And the later she found out, the worse it would be.'

'After the divorce would have been good. I'd have settled for that.'

'I hate lying to her. I hate lying about you. I'm sorry, I didn't set out deliberately to tell her, but it just came out, and I can't help feeling it's for the best.'

'As if your life wasn't complicated enough already,' Joanna sighed. She leaned forward and kissed his forehead. 'You really are a clot, Bill Slider. She's going to have your balls for jewellery now, you know that? She'll divorce you for adultery, and it'll all be adversarial instead of amicable. She'll have the house off you, and every penny she can screw out of you, and refuse you access to the children on the grounds that you're an unsuitable influence.'

'Thanks.'

'I just thought I'd mention it.'

'Anyway, she won't. How can she, when she's gone off with another man?'

'But now she can say you drove her to it.'

'Oh, it doesn't work that way nowadays. The courts know what's what. It'll all be settled half and half in the end – these things always are.'

'But you'll have to fight for your half now, instead of being given it.'

He lost patience. 'What do you want from me?' he snapped. 'It's done now. Don't go on and on about it.'

She looked at him whitely. 'I'm just pointing out—'

'Perhaps you'd prefer me to go back to her? That would save you a lot of trouble.'

'Of course, your divorce is none of my business,' she said neutrally. 'You must settle it your own way.' And she went out of the room.

Slider sat and cursed, softly but fluently, and hit his knees with his fists a few times. Then he got up and went after her. She was in the kitchen standing over the kettle, waiting for it to boil.

'You haven't switched it on,' he observed. She pushed the switch in without answering. He put his arms round her from behind and kissed the back of her neck. 'I'm sorry,' he said.

She turned inside his arms and looked into his face carefully – to see if he meant it, perhaps – and then sighed and leaned into the embrace.

'I'm sorry,' he said again. 'I'm upset and worried. I shouldn't snap at you.'

She rested her head against his cheek. 'I worry about you. I wish we could just get away from all this.'

'I know the divorce is your concern too—'

'Oh, bugger the divorce. The divorce is a pleasant itch compared with having a maniac on the loose trying to kill you.'

'He won't try again,' Slider said soothingly. 'He'll have scared himself too badly by nearly getting caught.'

'Do you really think so?'

'Really,' he said. He felt her relax. 'Boy, I'm getting good at this lying, aren't I?'

She began to laugh. 'Oh, you bastard.'

He set her back from him and kissed her, and said, 'I'll be all right. I'm a survivor. It's Atherton you ought to worry about. He thinks he's lost his nerve. He's too sensitive to be a policeman, really. I think you should do everything in your power to boost his morale and get his pecker up.'

'Not until his stitches are out,' she said. 'Ah, but then! I want you to remember it was you who suggested it.'

He slept late the next morning, and went on dozing when Joanna got up, waking properly only when she came in with a breakfast tray. He dragged himself up. 'Let me pee first.' When he came back she had pulled the curtains, letting in the sunshine, and was sitting cross-legged in bed. He got in, and she settled the tray between them. Oedipus appeared from nowhere and jumped up on the bed, sat precisely with his tail round his feet, and closed his eyes against temptation. His purr gave him away, though. Slider felt like purring too. Scrambled eggs with Parma ham, toast, fresh peaches cut into easinosh slices, a jug of juice. He sniffed it. 'Squeezed?'

'For a treat. There's a grapefruit in there too.'

'Everything I like best. What's the celebration?'

'Oh, this and that,' she said. 'How's your neck stroke head?'

'It's been worse.'

They ate without talking much, and then she put the tray aside and they made long, slow love; the best for ages, which made him realise how much of their lives together was snatched between his duties and hers. Co-ordinating two schedules of unsocial hours took determination and dedication – but it was worth it. Afterwards they lay entwined and, eventually, talked.

'Shouldn't you be going to work or something?' she asked.

'I was just going to say that. What have you got on today?'

'Concert tonight in Newbury, but there's only a seating rehearsal. It's the repeat of the one we did in Leeds.'

'So what time d'you have to be there? Five?'

'Five-thirty. So I've got all day. I had thought of cleaning this place up a bit and doing some shopping. The joys of domesticity. You can help me if you like.'

'I'm on to you. You just want to keep an eye on me.'

'Do you blame me?'

'As soon as this case is out of the way,' he promised, 'I'll take the rest of my sick-leave and we'll go away somewhere. If you can get the time off.'

'Watch me. But what about the case? Did anything happen yesterday?'

So he told her what he'd told Atherton and Hart already. Going through it again was never a bad idea.

'So you know all about who didn't do it,' she said when he had finished.

'That's right. We've run out of false trails at last. Now we've just got to find who did.'

'It must be someone he knew, because he let him in.'

'People let in people they don't know,' Slider said. 'Meter readers, insurance salesmen.'

'You don't sit and drink whisky with the meter reader,' she said. 'Well, I do, but I'm unusual.'

'True. But then you do it in the nude. Paloma was fully dressed. I think it's fairly safe to conclude that he knew the visitor.'

'Could it have been his lover? Grisham? Come to try for a reconciliation? He pleads, Paloma resists, they argue, Grisham loses control and bashes him.'

'With?'

'Whatever,' she said evasively. 'Something he found lying to hand.'

'Whatever the weapon was, it was taken away, and Busty didn't say anything was missing.'

'She might not notice. Well, something he brought with him, then. A walking-stick.'

'Very gentlemanly, but not heavy enough. But anyway, we know it wasn't Grisham. He had an alibi. He was telephoning Paloma from his office in Westminster at half past one.'

'Why didn't you tell me?' she said indignantly.

'I didn't want to short-circuit you. I thought you might say something useful.'

'Everything I say is useful. So what about this weapon?'

'Whoever did the job, it had to be something small enough to be concealable when he left the flat, and heavy enough to be that small. Probably metallic. Possibly with a square edge.'

'Like a spanner?' she suggested.

'Yes, a heavy spanner would do it.'

'So you're looking for a man who owns a spanner. That narrows it down.'

'Ah, but he might have bought it specially.'

'True. So you've got to use your brains.'

'Don't say that as if it was a disaster.'

'Why not try a different approach,' she said, propping herself up on one elbow. With her short bronze hair tousled, she looked like a show chrysanthemum past its best. 'It seems to me you haven't considered the poison pen letters.'

'Not recently. But of course we thought we had the right man in Jonah, so the letters seemed incidental – if they existed. He didn't bring any in to show me, remember.'

'But I can't see why he would make them up. Assume they did exist – isn't it likely that whoever sent them was also the murderer? That it was an escalating campaign which went to its logical conclusion.'

'It's a possibility.' Slider sat up. 'The escalation is certainly there. Six months ago, according to Paloma, it started with phone calls; three months later the letters started, and increased in menace week by week. Of course, these things don't usually end in murder, but it's not unheard of. But who hated him with that sort of concentrated hatred?'

'Didn't he give you any hint as to who he thought it was?'

'He said he didn't know. I got the impression he had his suspicion, but he wouldn't say anything. At the time, I thought he suspected Grisham.'

'But why would Grisham—?'

'Oh, because of the Pomona Club – refusing to stop working there. But that was before I talked to Grisham. The man really loved Paloma; and I just don't see him as the kind to work in that underhand way. When he really lost it he acted very directly – rushing into the Pink Parrot waving fistfuls of quids. A poison pen is a different kind of character – slow, brooding, insidious and mean.'

She shivered. 'And now he's after you.'

'Well he won't get me. But what intrigues me is why did the campaign go so suddenly from the letters to murder? I'd have expected some build-up of physical attacks before the final one – broken windows, vandalism, arson attacks, that sort of thing. To make him suffer as much as possible before killing him.'

'Presumably he did something that speeded it up,' Joanna said. 'What happened in the days just before the murder? Could it have been something to do with that animal rights business?'

'I don't see what,' he said, frowning. 'That was a pukka AL job, though unauthorised, and none of them had any connection with Paloma – we checked. And the only person who was likely to mind about the publicity was Grisham, and we've investigated that. All the same,' he went on, putting his legs over the side of the bed, 'I think you're right. Something he did in the days before his death – over the weekend, perhaps – sparked it off. We've got to work out what.'

'You're getting up?'

'Mm. I have to go in,' he said absently, heading for the bathroom.

She saw he was off on his other plane. 'I wish I hadn't started you thinking. I thought we were going to go shopping together,' she said.

'Oh yes, let's have lunch,' he said vaguely over his shoulder.

'No, that was the Eighties,' she called after him; but he didn't hear her.

As he entered the CID room, Norma, without looking up from her desk, began to sing very softly an old CID melody.

They called the bastard Stephen,
They called the bastard Stephen.

The rest of the team joined in with increasing volume.

They called the bastard Stephen,
'CAUSE THAT WAS THE NAME OF THE INK!

'I gather Jonah Lafota has departed,' Slider said when they'd stopped.

'Not this life, unfortunately,' Norma said.

'Sprung last night,' Hart said resentfully. 'Pity poor Candy.'

'The fact is, ladies and germs,' Slider said, 'much as we may regret it, Jonah was telling the truth and Paloma was dead when he got there.'

'We can still nail him for conspiracy can't we, guv?' Anderson pleaded.

'And that filth, Billy Yates,' Norma added. 'We can't let him off.'

'I'm afraid there are bigger things afoot, and we are under orders not to frighten the rabbits.' Chorus of groans. 'But I am assured,' he raised his voice over the woe, 'that they will be going down and that deserts will be just. Eventually.'

'Mushroom time,' Anderson commented. 'Get your heads down, here it comes.'

Slider ignored him. 'So let's concentrate our minds on the problem in hand, which is still who killed Jay Paloma. We're back to basics. Whoever it was, it wasn't the invisible man, so let's get out there and ask questions. I can't believe that nobody saw the murderer arrive and – more importantly – leave. However calculating he was, he'd have been in a state of nervous tension, and maybe blood-spattered when he left. Someone saw him, they just haven't remembered it yet.'

They dispersed, muttering. He called them back. 'Oh, and some good news, to speed you on your way. The latest report from the hospital is that Andy Cosgrove's coma seems to be lightening. So there's a good chance he's going to come out of it.'

That at least produced a spatter of lighter expressions. McLaren, unwrapping a Topic bar, said, 'If he does come out of it, and he's still got all his marbles, he'll be a fool if he doesn't leave the Job. Once you've been in a coma like that, any little bump on the head can send you back down, and the next time you never come up again.'

Norma, who had a street gazette in her hand, threw the book at him.

Slider had all the documents of the case spread out over his desk, and when the phone rang it took him a minute to find it.

'Inspector Slider? My name's Larry Mosselman.' When Slider didn't react he went on, as if it explained everything, 'They call me Mr Atlas.'

'Sorry?'

'You know – Mosselman, muscle-man?'

'Ah! You're a taxi driver?'

'That's right. I thought you were expecting me to call. Lenny Cohen's been putting the word out that you've been looking to contact the driver who picked up a certain party on Monday the fifteenth?'

'You know Lenny, do you?'

'Everyone knows Lenny the Lion. We've played golf together once or twice, but he's a bit out of my league now. Well, he does a lot of nights, so he gets the practice.'

'You're not with the same company as him?'

'No, I work for Jack Disney's garage in Old Road, Hackney – just behind the Victoria Park?'

'Yes, I know it.'

'Anyway, in connection with your enquiry, I heard about it when I went in yesterday to settle up, and I think I might be the cabbie you're looking for. As far as I can tell from the picture, my fare was the same man, and I did put him down at the Lanesborough rank about twenty to twelve that Monday.'

'Did you see where he went then?'

'He walked on up the street, as if he was heading for the hotel entrance. That's all I saw, because I wasn't putting on myself, so I pulled away. But what made him stick in my mind,' Mosselman went on intelligently, 'was that when I picked him up, he'd just got out of another cab.'

'Had he? Well, we did suspect he might have. He was trying to be cautious, cover his tracks.'

'Not very good at it, though, if he let me see it,' Mosselman said. 'And Lenny saw me drop him as well. Mind you, he looked like a bit of a daft ponce, if you don't mind me saying so.'

'Talking of which, can you give me a description of your fare?' Slider said, to be on the safe side. He took down the details, which as far as they went fitted Paloma. 'And where did you pick him up?'

'Hammersmith Broadway, about ten past eleven. On the gyratory, outside the new building where the post office used to be. He was standing on the kerb, on the wrong side of the railings. He waved me down, but traffic was slow so I'd had plenty of time to clock him as I approached, and I'd seen him get out of the other cab and pay it off. Anyway, he got in and asked for the Lanesborough, and I took him there.'

'Right,' Slider said. 'Thanks. Well, it may not turn out to be important now, because we've found out where he ended up that day, but we're always glad to have the loose ends tied up. It all adds to the picture.'

'Right you are. Glad to help,' said Mosselman. 'Do you want me to come in and make a statement or anything?'

'I don't think it'll be necessary, but I would like to take your address and phone number in case we need to contact you.' He wrote to Mosselman's dictation, and then added, 'By the way, I don't suppose you saw the driver of the cab this man got out of?'

'No, I didn't see the driver, but I saw the name on the side of the cab. It was one of Monty's Radio Metrocabs.'

'Was it, indeed? Thank you, Mr Mosselman,' said Slider.

Monty was not in his hutch, for once. Winston, one of the mechanics, said he had gone to hospital.

'Nothing serious, I hope?' Slider said.

'Nah, s'just 'is check-up. It's routine, right? Like, 'e 'ad this 'eart attack, like years ago, an' they make 'im go, right, like, every six months, reg'lar.'

'I see. I'm glad it's nothing bad. Wouldn't want to lose another good man,' Slider said. Winston stared at him with his mouth open, and Slider hoped he was better in the motor mechanical field than he was at deciphering human speech. 'I'll just go and speak to Mrs Green,' he said clearly, and left the mechanic to work on that.

Rita was also missing, and the bower was surprisingly peaceful without her. Gloria gave Slider a toothy smile and invited him to sit down, offering him tea and biscuits with an eagerness that suggested she could not stand the near-silence. 'She's gone with Monty to see the specialist,' she explained when he asked after Rita. 'I think she wants to persuade him to make Monty give up the cigars.'

'But he doesn't really smoke them. He lights them and they go out. He probably just likes something in his mouth.'

Gloria wrinkled her powdery nose. 'They stink. I hate those

things,' she said. 'Is there something I can help you with, or did you particularly want Rita?'

'No, you can help me,' Slider said. He told her about Mosselman's information. 'I'd like to check the day book again, in case we've missed anything.'

But the day book produced nothing that looked remotely like Jay Paloma. 'He's sure it was this cab company?' Gloria said at last.

'He said he saw the name on the side.'

She shrugged. 'Then I suppose someone was doing him a favour.'

'But the cabbie saw him pay,' Slider said.

'Well, it couldn't have been on the clock,' Gloria said. She looked at Slider. 'It could have been Benny the Brief, I suppose. He was always round there, wasn't he, round the flat, 'cause he was friends with that woman.'

'It crossed my mind,' Slider said, 'but why wouldn't he have mentioned it to me?'

'Maybe because he didn't put it on the clock, and didn't want to get into trouble. Is it important? That wasn't the day the chap got killed, was it?'

'No, it wasn't. Probably it isn't important.' He thought a moment. Gloria was low man on Monty's totem pole, and had to toe the party line when Rita was around. This was a golden chance to get her views un-iced. 'What do you make of Benny Fluss?'

'He's all right,' she said indifferently.

'D'you like him?' She made a face. 'Tell me what he's like.'

'He's a boring old fart,' she said, surprising the hell out of Slider, who almost looked round for the Swear Box. She saw his surprise and blushed a little. 'Well he is,' she said defensively. 'Jaw, jaw, jaw. And never admits he doesn't know something. Makes it up as he goes along, and if you catch him out he bullshits and makes out he said something different. Can't be in the wrong, you know the sort; and patronising? Rita and me might be moron slaves.'

'I gather you don't like him,' Slider said mildly.

'Oh, he doesn't bother me, really. Don't see enough of him to get worked up. Monty thinks he's a hoot, plays him along, you know, to get him to talk. But there's a side to him I don't like.' She lowered her enormous, lavvy-brush lashes and looked at Slider sidelong. 'He was in trouble once, did you know?'

'Police?'

'It didn't come to that, but it ought to've, in my view. You see, Benny had a half-flat in those days – about ten years ago, this was.'

Slider nodded. Half-flat was the arrangement where two drivers shared the same cab, one driving days and one driving nights.

'Anyway,' Gloria went on, 'he found out that the other driver was seeing Gwen – Benny's wife, Gwen – while Benny had the cab. There was a terrible to-do. Benny went round to Sam's – Sam was the other driver, Sam Kelly – and beat him up. Did a real job on him. Terrible it was. Well, I know Sam was in the wrong, but Rita and me thought Benny went too far, and the police should've been told. But Sam wouldn't make any complaint against Benny, so I suppose he thought it was coming to him, but as soon as he was out of hospital he moved right away and we've never seen him since. But after that I could never really laugh about Benny like Monty does. I mean, it's in him somewhere, isn't it? And who'd have thought he could be that jealous about Gwen? I know they'd been married a long time, but I never got the impression he cared tuppence for her, seeing them together. It's a funny thing, jealousy, isn't it?' she finished on an academic note.

'It certainly is,' Slider said, substituting it at the last moment for how would you know?

He sat in his car and made the necessary calls. There were several of them, and by the time he got to the corner of Wood Lane, Hart was waiting for him.

'I'm spose to give you this,' she said, waving the warrant as she climbed in. 'What's cooking?'

'Benny the Brief,' he said.

'The tame cabbie?' she said with evident surprise.

'I've been thinking about time scales,' Slider said. 'Six months ago, his wife died. At the same time the silent phone calls start. Three months ago he asked Busty Parnell to marry him and she turned him down. From that point Jay Paloma starts getting threatening letters.'

'You think he sent them? What for?'

'Jealousy,' Slider said. 'The oldest, blackest, meanest emotion. He's been looking on Busty as his own property for years, but while he was married it never occurred to him to do anything about it. After all, he was comfortable as he was. But once he's a widower he starts to think he could have her all to himself, marry her and take her home for keeps. He's so confident of the outcome he sells the marital home so that they can get a new place together. He hasn't even asked her yet, but he's sure she'll jump at the chance of changing her unsatisfactory life for security and Benny's fascinating company. Only when the moment finally comes, she refuses him. She prefers to live with a painted popinjay who earns his living doing unspeakable things in a basement club.'

'Bit of a bummer,' Hart agreed.

'He can't hate her for it, of course: his hatred is aimed at Jay, his rival for Busty's affections.'

'So he starts sending poison pen letters, you reckon? I s'pose it makes sense.'

'I don't know whether he hoped to scare Paloma into leaving Busty,' Slider said, 'or if it was just venting his feelings. Bit of both, maybe.'

'The letters was posted from different places all over London, wun't they?' Hart remembered. 'A cabbie'd have no trouble sorting that side of it.'

'Yes, and living in lodgings rather than in a shared home he'd have the privacy to make them up.'

'So if it was him, what d'you think triggered the murder?'

'Jay Paloma was going to take Busty away from him. Jay had been saving money for them to buy a place together in Ireland – his dream plan. It might have remained a dream, except that he had reached a crisis in his life. He'd hated having to buy drugs for his lover, but now the supply was cut off he was probably worried about what would happen to Grisham. He must also have worried for his own skin – could he trust the supplier not to bust him? There was the paint-throwing incident at the Pomona which upset him; and the poison pen letters were getting him down. His quarrel with Grisham was probably the last straw. He was now so fed up with his situation that he decided their savings were enough for him and Busty to get out and put the plan into action. And Busty was happy enough to go along with it.'

'Yeah,' said Hart, staring forward. 'We saw Paloma going was reason enough to make Grisham mad, but we never fought about Parnell and Benny Fluss. Good one, guv.'

'I should have got onto it before,' Slider said. 'I should have picked up on the discrepancy in the statements. You see, Busty told me that on that last day, Jay was chatting cheerfully to her *and* Benny about his plan, but Benny said Jay didn't speak to him at all, and that he was low and depressed. I think Jay had probably told him they were definitely going when Benny drove him to Hammersmith the day before, and that was when Benny decided to do it. So he didn't mention that journey to me – in fact, he said he never drove Paloma – because in his own mind it was connected with his guilt. And he projected his negative emotions onto Jay the next day, and remembered him as being low and depressed.'

'Well, you would be, wouldn't you, if you was gonna get done that day?'

'Quite. Of course, all this is conjecture. But Paloma let the murderer in and sat and chatted with him, which meant he must have known him well; and Busty said he hadn't any friends, and never saw people at home. Also, Benny was the one person who knew Paloma would be at home alone. He drove Busty to her sister's, and he knew she would ring him to be collected from there when she wanted to come home, so there was no danger she'd walk in on them.'

Hart nodded. 'What about the weapon?'

'Joanna suggested this morning that it could be a heavy spanner. Something Benny would have to hand in his cab. Also we know the murderer wore leather gloves; and when I first met Benny he was wearing a pair of brand new ones.'

'The gloves'd get messed up.'

'And you can't get blood-stains out of leather. You can wash a spanner, though, as long as you haven't got a wife at home to ask you awkward questions.'

Hart sat thinking it through. 'D'you really think he'd do that, just for the sake of old mother Parnell?'

'She's not that old,' Slider protested. Actually, she must be about the same age as him. 'Anyway, he was obsessed by her. And jealousy is a strange thing.'

'It was a frenzied attack,' Hart said. 'If the first blow killed him, there was no need to bash his head in like that. It didn't make sense when we thought it was a pro job, but if it was jealousy – well.'

'That's what I thought. And given the way Paloma's head was battered, I think he could be dangerous. If he has moved from threatening letters to actually killing Paloma, the next step could be that he decides he can't keep Busty to himself any other way than by killing her – and then probably himself.'

'Yeah,' said Hart thoughtfully. 'I seen that sort a thing before.'

'We've got to get him banged up before he hurts someone else. But so far it's all guesswork. That's why we've got to have a look at his room and see if we can find something a bit more solid.'

'Like blood-stained gloves?'

'Or the makings of the poison pen letters – a pot of glue, some mutilated newspapers.'

'We should be so lucky!'

'And I've asked Norma to check his mobile phone account for the numbers he's called. We might be able to correlate something from that. Ah, this is it.'

CHAPTER EIGHTEEN

Hell Toupée

It was a stunted, two-storey house, one of a terrace built between the wars, and set below street level – there must have been a hillside there – so that you went down a flight of steps set into a bank to gain access. One flight to each pair, whose doors stood side by side, set back in arched porchways. Slider rang the bell, while Hart stood two steps up keeping a look out for homicidal black cabs, and eyeing the road as if it might bite her.

The landlady was a woman shrunk with age, with white wispy hair, National Health glasses, a thick nose, pendulous lip, and folds of heavy skin hanging loose about her face and neck like elephant's trousers. She wore a green nylon overall of the sort that Woolworth's assistants used to wear in the old days – for all Slider knew it might have been one, nicked in her heyday – and those tartan slippers with a fawn fold-back collar and a fawn bobble that boys used to buy for their fathers for Christmas back in 1962. She rolled a ferocious eye up at Slider and snapped, 'Yes?' in exactly the tone of voice in which she might have said, 'Bugger off!'

Slider got as far as introducing himself and showing his brief when she interrupted. 'Is *she* with you?' she said with a glare in Hart's direction. 'Tell her to get off the steps. I washed them this morning.'

Slider cut to the chase. 'I understand you have a Mr Fluss staying with you.'

'I've a lodger of that name,' she corrected aggressively, as though he had impugned her chastity. 'What's it to you?'

'I'd like to see his room, please, Mrs—?'

'Bugger off!' she snapped. Slider blinked. 'And it's Miss. Miss Bogorov.'

'Ah,' said Slider. 'Well, could you show us his room, please?'

She looked at him a moment longer, and then turned and went into the house without a word. One thing to be said about eastern Europe, Slider thought, it taught people not to argue with policemen. He beckoned to Hart and followed her in. The entrance passage was dark, and so narrow it might have been designed for a different race – which, in a way, it had, the working classes in the twenties and thirties being generally smaller and slighter than today's chunky breed. The smell of dust came up from the carpet as he trod; and mingled with a composite house-smell of dog, tea, cooked rice, metal polish and incense. The stairs were straight ahead, as narrow as the hall, with a dogleg passage going past them to the rear of the house. At the foot of the stairs, on the wall, was a rather beautiful icon with a beaten silver surround, of a melancholy saint with his eyes rolled up and his head so far over on one side he looked like a Guy Fawkes effigy without enough straw in the neck. The missing straw seemed to be leaking out through his body in hedgehog spikes.

Miss Bogorov, one foot on the stairs, glanced back and saw what he was looking at. 'Saint Sebastian. My mother brought it over.' Her voice for a moment became liquid. 'That's all I've got left of her things. Everything else got sold.'

'Over?' Hart murmured behind him, but he silenced her with a gesture. Now was not the time, and he was a Dutchman if he didn't recognise a deep vein of Russian melancholy just waiting to be mined, preferably across a table over endless tea. He left Saint Sebastian with a glance. Living with him, he reflected, was enough to make anyone scratchy.

'How many lodgers do you have?' he asked as Miss Bogorov climbed before him.

'Just the two. There's three rooms upstairs, but Mr Johnson has one for a sitting-room.' She turned her head all the way back and fixed him with a terrible eye. 'I live downstairs,' she said, to make sure he knew there was nothing louche about the arrangements. It occurred to Slider that here after all was Benny the Brief's soulmate, if he did but recognise it. He could marry her and move downstairs and they could swap Crying Shames to their hearts' delight.

Miss Bogorov reached the top, turned right and stood with her hand on the doorknob. The upper hall was dark and depressing, with a polished wood floor and a strip of patterned carpet down the middle. The walls were painted brown up to the dado and grubby cream above, and the doors were varnished dark brown with brown mottled Bakelite doorknobs. It couldn't have been redecorated, Slider thought, since it was built.

'Nearly six months he's been with me, Mr Fluss, and no trouble at all,' she said, looking from Slider to Hart and back as if searching for a clue. 'A very nice gentleman, respectable and quiet. With very proper views. Otherwise I shouldn't have taken him in. And Mr Johnson's been with me eight years. This is a respectable house. Trouble enough we had when I was a girl, and all through the war. I don't want any more trouble now. Remember that. This is my house. If you've got to do anything, do it quietly and don't make a mess.'

Then she turned the doorknob and pushed the door open, and stood back for them to go in, folding her arms across her chest and sinking her chin, in the manner of oppressed peasants the world and time over, when the commissars come to steal their pigs and slit open their grain sacks.

Slider nodded. 'Thank you,' he said pointedly. She sighed and went away down the stairs.

Slider surveyed the room. A single bed with a candlewick bedspread under the window. Cheap beige wall-to-wall carpet with a rug of nineteen-fifties vileness covering it in the middle – black with a pattern of red, yellow and green lightning jags. Very contemp'ry, he thought. A wash basin and mirror in the corner. A window so small and inadequate it seemed to be letting in darkness rather than light. An oversized wardrobe and chest of drawers using up the space. A pink basket chair on spindly legs jammed between the chest of drawers and the sink. A table and kitchen chair jammed between the wardrobe and the door. A low bookcase jammed between the foot of the bed and the wall.

The chest of drawers was five feet high, and a good four feet long, and drawers all the way. 'You start on that,' Slider said. The table was very small, its surface about two feet six by eighteen inches, and covered with marble – presumably it had been a washstand of some kind – and on it stood an Anglepoise lamp whose springs had gone, which was held in position by an ingenious arrangement of strings fastened to a hook on the picture-rail above. This, perhaps, was where the work had been done. Slider switched on the light and bent to examine the surface closely, hoping for a trace of glue or a stuck scrap of newspaper. But Miss Bogorov was too good a housekeeper, and the surface was perfectly clean. He went over to the sink. Here, perhaps, a bloody spanner was washed – too long ago, now, for any traces to remain in the waste-pipe. A Duralex glass held a toothbrush with a brown and shaggy head and a tube of toothpaste with a messy cap. He ducked his head this way and that to see if there was a lip print. There were marks enough on its surface. They would take it, anyway. He straightened up. What was that smell, a cold, old smell, almost metallic, which hung about the room?

'Guv?' said Hart at that moment. 'Have a goosey at this.'

He joined her at the chest – o would that t'were! – and looked into the top right-hand drawer which she had opened. Inside – amongst a useful litter of things like string, playing-cards, boxes of matches, Elastoplast, Sellotape, rolled crêpe bandages, the recharge lead from an electric razor, sundry loose 3-amp fuses, and a very old souvenir corn-dolly with Southwold painted across it which was losing its hair everywhere – sitting there mutely pleading for clemency was a bottle of Copydex, the sort that has a little brush attached inside the lid, and a pair of cutting-out scissors. Stacked neatly towards the back of the drawer was a couple of hundred white self-seal envelopes – 'the long sort' as Jay Paloma had put it.

'Of course, it don't prove anything,' Hart said in the sort of voice that expects to be contradicted.

'If only that dickhead Paloma had brought in an envelope,' Slider mourned, 'we could have done a match. Bag 'em up, anyway – oh, and the tooth glass. One way or another we've got to get something hard.'

'How were the envelopes addressed, again?' Hart asked.

'Printed labels. I suppose he had them done at a Prontaprint somewhere. Now if we could find which one—!'

'He'd have thrown any left away,' she said. 'Incriminating.'

Slider looked round. 'Keep looking for the gloves. I'll have a look at the books.'

The bookcase was so positioned that you had to crane round

the wardrobe to see the books at the end of the shelf. Very eclectic selection, he thought, using an Atherton word. Was eclectic right? Or was it eccentric? Or did they mean the same thing perhaps? Legal books, medico-legal books, a worrying collection of Arrow True Crime books, *Great Court Cases of History*, *F.E. – a Memoir*, Richard Gordon's *The Medical Witness*, Henry Cecil and John Mortimer, *The Layman's Guide to English Law*, a pocket Latin dictionary and four London A-Zs in various stages of decrepitude. Wedged in at one end of the top shelf and protruding slightly was a Basildon Bond writing pad. 'We'll have this as well,' he said, pulling it out with an effort. It brought with it a large format paperback which hit the floor with a thud before Slider could catch it. He picked it up. *A Practical Guide to Forensic Examination*. He put his thumb to the back and scrolled through it. Sets of black and white photographs, of clinical equipment, of weapons, close-ups of wounds, part-dissected bodies, and some whole-body shots of multiple mutilations. A brief sampling of the text proved it was a serious book aimed at the professional – a starter volume for the newly-appointed police surgeon, perhaps – which accounted for the unexpurgated photographs. Photographs? A thought struck him, and he examined the sets of photographs more closely. Plates seventeen and eighteen were missing, neatly razored out flush with the fold. He turned to the front. *List of Illustrations*. He looked up number seventeen: *The Waddington Case – Frontal View of the Injuries*. And number eighteen was the same case, the injuries to the head. A close-up presumably. What had Paloma said about the photograph that had been sent to him? A dead body, all beaten up, with its throat cut.

'I think we've got him,' Slider said, straightening up. 'This can't just be a coincidence. We've got him, Hart. Come and have a look.'

What *was* that smell? He heard a wooden creak and turned to look, just in time to see Benny the Brief in the doorway launch himself forward with his arm raised. Hart beat Slider's reactions off the mark by twenty years, hurling herself in hard and low like a rugby forward, hitting Benny amidships and carrying him by her impetus backwards to hit the door jamb. He rolled round it and fell out into the passage with her on top of him, hitting wildly but largely ineffectually (thank God!) at her back with whatever he was holding. Slider threw himself at them, grabbing Benny's business arm and slamming it to the floor with all his weight. The spanner – for it was he – jumped from Benny's hand and hit the floor, skidding along it with an interesting scuffing sound like an ice-skater on a rink.

'Get his other hand,' he panted to Hart, trying to get his knee over the leg nearest him and hold it down. Benny was bucking like a teenage horse, but completely in silence. Slider supposed he had had the spare breath knocked out of him. Between them they managed to get him subdued and rolled over on his face, and Slider sat on him while Hart got his handcuffs out of his pocket and snapped them on. Once he was cuffed, Benny fell silent and still, so still that Slider thought for one rippling moment he might have snuffed it. But when he was dragged up to sitting position, he proved to be alive enough to bare his tiny hampsteads and spit at them. His aim, fortunately, proved faulty, though Slider wondered what Miss Bogorov would think of spittle on her carpet. It seemed ungrateful after she'd taken him in and ignored him so nicely.

'All right, I'll watch him, you phone for the cavalry,' Slider said to Hart, and keeping a wary eye on Fluss he chanted the coppers' hymn of triumph at him. 'You do not have to say anything, but your defence may be prejudiced if you do not mention while being questioned something you later rely on in court . . .' It didn't quite have the swing of the old one, or the punch of the more informal 'You're fuckin' nicked, mate,' but it sliced the same way.

And at last he realised what the smell in the room was, the cold metallic ghost of the smell he was now getting hot and fresh in waves, the smell which, when he was sprawled on the hospital corridor floor, his nose had translated as escaping gas. It was Benny's feet, clad for sneaking-up purposes in a pair of tropical-swamp trainers. He could easily have qualified as the only man in history to get his money back from the Odoreater company. As Busty had said – and Slider could see now why she hadn't wanted to marry him – they didn't half pen and ink.

He was still doing the formalities, of course, when Joanna arrived to have lunch with him; she obligingly went out to fetch sandwiches so that he could eat at his desk, and came back with an inspired roast beef and mustard with salad in a granary roll.

'Where did you get this?' he marvelled. Sid's coffee stall only had white bread; the only granary Sid knew about was his grandad's wife.

'New sandwich bar just opened – you know, where the shoe repairers used to be?' Joanna put down another bag with an air of minor triumph. 'And they had a rather nice-looking banana cake. And I got you tea.'

'You're a wonderful woman. Your price is above rubies.'

'I haven't charged you yet,' she said. 'I'm thinking of adding on something for wear and tear to my nervous system.'

'I thought you were looking a bit peaky. But you should be glad we've got him under lock and key.'

'Only just. You could have been killed.'

'I was quite safe with Hart,' he said. 'You should have seen her! Across that room like Linford Christie. When we were reporting to Honeyman he asked her what steps she took when she saw chummy in the doorway and she said "Bloody long ones, sir." What a guy!'

Joanna eyed him. 'You know she's got a crush on you?'

'Nonsense,' he said through a mouthful of heaven. Of all sandwiches in the whole world, roast beef was his absolute favourite. 'I'm old enough to be her father.'

'That's the point.'

He swallowed. 'Anyway, I think she fancies Atherton. She seemed to be hanging around the hospital room last night.'

Joanna sat on the edge of his desk and took the lid off her coffee. 'Yes, and what *about* last night? I suppose that it was this Benny creature that thumped you?'

'Yes. I didn't see at first how it could have been, because I left him at the pub with Busty, waiting to drive her home when the pub closed. But after I left Monty's and before Hart and I went to his place, I rang Busty, and it turns out that after I left, she had a row with him, and told him she didn't want him to drive her home, that she'd get a lift from the barman.'

'How come?'

'Oh, he didn't like her chatting to me secretly up the other end of the bar. And I compounded my sins by kissing her goodbye – only on the cheek, but it was enough to rouse all his possessive instincts. She wouldn't have it, and virtually chucked him out.'

'So he, seething with jealousy, followed you with malicious intent? But how did he manage that? I mean, if you left before him—'

'I did, but I didn't drive off straight away. I sat in my car for a bit, thinking what to do next. I suppose when he'd finished having his row he came out and saw me.'

'And you didn't see him? You didn't notice him follow you?'

'I haven't seen him following me at any time, but he's been doing it for several days. That's how he turned up while Hart and I were going through his pad – he followed me all the way from Monty's. And he had his own front door key, of course, so he could let himself in quietly and creep up on us. Miss B, his landlady, shut herself in the kitchen and resolutely ignored the whole frackarse, even when the three of us were rolling about on the floor, and when the troops arrived with wailing sirens. We had to go and winkle her out to tell her we were taking him away – she didn't want to know. You'd think we were the *Cheka* the way she looked at us.'

Joanna took a sip of her coffee. 'So how did he square all this following people with earning a living?'

'He didn't. I should have picked that up, really, except of course that I wasn't looking at him for a suspect. But Monty told me, when I first asked if Benny was pukka, that after his wife died he worked every hour God sent, but that for the last couple of weeks he hasn't been turning in much money. Not surprising if he'd been driving about on his own business.

'Presumably with the "for hire" turned off, so he didn't get hailed.'

Slider nodded. 'Of course, a black cab is the perfect vehicle – pardon the pun – for spying on people. You're highly mobile, and you're inconspicuous. Nobody notices you, or thinks anything of it if they do. All black cabs look alike to a layman, and nobody ever looks at the reg number. You don't have to hide, or have an excuse to be there. And from the other side, nobody knows where you are supposed to be at any particular time. You're unaccountable.'

'Perfect for having extra-marital affairs,' Joanna said.

'Yes. I understand they do have a high divorce rate. Occupational hazard.'

She screwed up her sandwich bag and leaned over to drop it in his bin. 'Like musicians and policemen.'

'Talking of policemen,' he said thoughtfully. 'Fluss is on the brink of confessing to the Cosgrove attack as well.'

'*He* beat up Andy Cosgrove?' Joanna said in surprise. 'What on earth for?'

'The same thing, jealousy. Cosgrove visited Busty at her flat on the day before he was attacked. Fluss had got so obsessed by then he spent a lot of time hanging around just watching her door. He knew who Cosgrove was, and Busty had told him about Andy's affair with Maroon. Busty thought it was a charming story, but Benny disapproved strongly. So when he saw this lecherous reprobate coming out of his angel's flat, it was too much for him.'

'How did he manage to get him alone?'

'I haven't got to the bottom of it yet – I'm going to have another go at him this afternoon. He's still at the stage of hinting things, and only admits openly what he thinks I already know. But Cosgrove often hung around Monty's garage, and he'd been making enquiries about something he was investigating. All Benny had to do was to get a message to him that he had some information, and arrange a meeting. I think,' Slider said, staring reflectively at his banana cake, 'that he probably didn't mean to hurt him. From what he's saying at the moment, I think he probably only meant to frighten him off, possibly by threatening to tell his wife, but finding himself alone with the bearded pillager he lost his temper and laid him out. He thought he'd killed him, so he bundled him in his taxi and dumped him on the waste ground.'

'He must have been a little discomposed to hear that Cosgrove wasn't dead,' Joanna said mildly.

'Yes, and I do wonder whether pulling him in when we did might not have saved Andy from being finished off. That, and the fact that Ron Carver's been dealing with the case. If I'd been on both cases, and it had seemed that anyone was connecting them—'

'But you did,' Joanna said. 'You've had the feeling all along they were connected.'

He smiled ruefully. 'Yes, but that was just my dumb luck. I thought Yates was involved with both, and it turns out he was involved with neither. I haven't won any bouquets for that, you know.'

'You win mine,' she said. 'And I'm glad you're not going to be a sitting duck any more.'

'It may have served a good purpose. If he hadn't been following me around, he'd have been brooding over Busty's continued refusal to have him. I think she may have had a narrow escape.'

'I'm supposed to be glad about that? Sooner her than you, for my money.'

'But I'm paid to run the risk, she isn't.'

'I don't buy that. She got herself mixed up with the bloke in the first place. She should have had better taste.'

'You can be very harsh sometimes,' he complained.

She looked at him. 'I can't tell you what it feels like to think every time the phone rings it's going to be the hospital, to say they've got you there in more pieces than an IKEA flatpack waiting for an allen key.'

'You sounded just like Atherton then.'

She wasn't distracted. 'Though these days I suppose if the phone rings it's as likely to be Irene as anyone. What do I do, by the way, if she turns vengeful and arrives on the doorstep to batter me with a baseball bat?'

'She won't,' he said.

'You have no idea, Bill Slider,' she said solemnly, 'the strength of emotions you arouse in women. Well, I suppose I'd better go away and leave you to it.' He looked at her gratefully, and she smiled. 'I know. I don't suppose I'll see you before I leave for work tonight? No, I didn't think so. Oh well, at least after this you'll have some time off.'

'I promise,' he said.

'And watch out for your little WDC. Don't go sending out the wrong signals. I'm telling you she fancies you.'

'I'll prove you wrong,' he called after her. 'It's Atherton she's after.'

So he wasn't entirely surprised, when he arrived almost drunk with weariness at Atherton's room that evening, to find Hart there, sitting on the edge of the bed; nor to hear that Atherton was chatting her up – evidently inviting her to dinner at his place when he got out of hospital. Here it comes, Slider thought, the old infallible method. He got a female into his little bijou nest, laid a gourmet nosh in front of her, and once she got a sight of his cuisine, she melted into submission. How many women had he pulled that way? Well, about the same as he'd had hot dinners, by that reckoning.

'Are you fond of fish?' Atherton was saying.

'Yeah, we eat it a lot at home,' Hart said, unconscious of the approaching huntsman. 'My mum was born in Jamaica. They eat fish there all the time.'

'Well, you must let me cook you my special lemon sole,' Atherton said. 'I do it with lime and black butter, and it's absolutely delectable. I call it my Sole Raison d'Être.'

Slider felt it was time to intervene. 'You must be feeling better,' he announced himself.

Hart jumped up. 'I fink he's tryna get off wiv me. Is that all right, guv?'

Slider spread his hands. 'What have I got to do with it? I'm not your dad. Actually, I'm your debtor. I haven't had a chance to say this properly to you, Hart, but your prompt action in Benny's room probably saved both our lives.'

She looked pinkly pleased. 'I didn't even fink about it. It was just instinct.'

Slider looked at Atherton. 'She shot across the room like an actor hearing the phone ring. Old Benny didn't stand a chance.'

'Yes, I've been hearing the denouement,' Atherton said.

'One bit Hart won't have told you about, because I only heard it just before I left, is that Cosgrove regained consciousness this evening.'

'That's terrific. Does he remember anything?'

'They don't know yet. He'd still very dopey, of course, but at least he knows who he is, and he recognised his wife all right. They haven't been able to question him about anything yet.'

'We can only hope,' Atherton said.

Slider went on, 'Ron Carver's at his bedside even now, hoping he's going to disprove my contention that Benny the Brief did Cosgrove too.'

'But Benny's put his hand up for it!' Hart said indignantly. 'You put in a hard afternoon's work on him to get that confession, guv.'

'Mr Carver wouldn't let a little thing like that get in the way. He's got a whole line up of spare villains that he'd like it to be, and psychotics make false confessions every day of the week. He's praying the forensic team aren't going to find any traces in Benny's cab, but my money's on blood down the back of the seat.' He chuckled at the thought of Carver's rage when it did turn up. 'How that man does detest me, to be sure!' He oughtn't really to say things like that in front of Hart, but euphoria was eroding his native caution. She'd find out the truth of it sooner or later, anyway.

'Never mind,' Atherton said, 'I bet old Honeyman's pleased to get the Paloma case sorted.'

'As a dog with two willies,' Slider said. 'It might have been difficult to bring home without Benny's attack on Hart and me, though we had the lip print match, plus all the circumstantial, the discrepancy in his statements and so on. But now he's dropped himself in it, plus he's made a full confession, so it's all over bar the party-poppers. And Mr Honeyman can depart in peace, with a defiant digit in Wetherspoon's direction. Absolutely in confidence, but I gather the powers that be have been suggesting poor Honeyman's about as much use to the Department as a chocolate teapot, and that he couldn't bring a case home if it was strapped to his wrist.'

'It won't do you any harm either,' Atherton observed.

'Do I note a hint of envy in your voice?' Slider asked. 'Can it be that you are beginning to feel a restless urge to get back to work?'

Atherton smirked a little. 'Oh, well, I can't help feeling that if I'd been around we'd have got a result in half the time.'

'Bloody sauce,' Hart said indignantly.

Slider said, 'No, he really means he *can't* help feeling it. It's in his genes.'

'She doesn't yet know what I keep in my jeans,' Atherton reminded him. 'Besides, if our firm is going to be illuminated by her presence, I can't wait to get back.'

'Sadly, Hart is only a temporary loaner, as your replacement.

Unless I can get the new boss to buy her for us – assuming she wants to stay, that is.'

'You bet,' said Hart economically.

Slider refrained from asking why. Discounting Joanna's unwelcome speculation, did Hart want to stay for the joy of working in Shepherd's Bush, or for the heady prospect of getting into Atherton's boxers? Poor Sue, he thought, and wondered how Joanna would take it if Atherton did start something up with Hart.

But he had his own love-life to worry about. He hadn't heard from Irene since she slammed the phone down on him, and he was wondering whether he ought to ring and try to placate her, little as he relished the prospect. The alternative was to wait for the solicitor's letter – though he couldn't altogether dismiss Joanna's suspicion that she might get a visit from his ex-wife-elect, to rant if not to bash. Jealousy was a strange and potent thing. There had been times when he had wanted very badly to batter Ernie, and he wasn't even in love with Irene. Actually, he didn't know that Irene was in love with him, or ever had been, but there was that possessive demon that lurked in everyone, which said if I can't have you, no-one else is going to. What Atherton called *canis praesepis*. One way and another, he was going to have to pay for his sins. Perhaps Atherton was taking the wiser part after all by not getting involved.

'Actually, I have got a bit of news on that front,' he said, coming back to the present. 'Mr Honeyman sent for me this afternoon to tell me that they have named his replacement at last.'

Atherton sat up. 'Really? Fantastic. Who is it, anyone we know?'

'Oh yes, we know him. I should think everybody knows Detective Superintendent Fred Porson.'

Atherton's eyes widened. 'Oh bloody Nora! Not The Syrup! What have we done to deserve that?'

Hart was looking lost. 'Who's this? The what?'

'Fred "The Syrup" Porson,' Atherton elucidated. 'Famously foul-tempered and notoriously the bearer of the most unconvincing hairpiece ever to leave the back of a cat!'

'I crossed paths with him briefly when I was at Hampstead,' Slider said. 'We used to call him The Rug From Hell. He doesn't like it to be mentioned, so I warn you,' he said to Hart. 'Or looked at.'

'Trouble is, you can't look anywhere else,' Atherton said. 'But it's not just the rug: he uses words like a blind man swatting wasps at a picnic. Ernie Wise crossed with Mrs Malaprop. It's going to drive me mad. You know I've got a low threshold for language abuse.'

Slider was quietly pleased that Atherton was assuming he would be there to be driven mad. Talk of taking another job seemed to have been dropped. Things were definitely looking up.

'D'you know where he's coming from?' Atherton was pleading. 'Where's he been lately? Somewhere taxing, I hope.'

'He's been on a Commissions Office posting at the Yard,' Slider said. 'Traffic Planning Unit. So he'll be full of beans, raring to go, ready to get his teeth into an operational again. Ready to take out all his frustrations on us for being CO'd for three years.'

'Look on the bright side, guv,' Hart suggested. 'Maybe he'll be so glad to get out again he'll be in a sweet and pliant mood.'

'In the pig's eye,' Atherton said elegantly.

SHALLOW GRAVE

Cynthia Harrod-Eagles

Detective Inspector Bill Slider has always been keen on architecture – what Atherton calls his edifice complex – and The Old Rectory is the kind of house he would give anything to own. But the dead body of Jennifer Andrews, found in a hole on the terrace, rather spoils the view. It looks a straightforward case: Jennifer was a congenital flirt, and the hole was dug by her builder husband Eddie, who was violent and jealous. But questions remain unanswered. Why was Jennifer's body so unmarked? How did she reach her shallow grave unnoticed? And why would anyone want to be and estate agent?

As the investigation proceeds, it seems there is something rotten at the heart of the community surrounding the lovely old house. New suspects and motives keep crawling out of the woodwork, and when Slider finally gets a confession, it's from a wholly incredible source. To compound his troubles, he has a linguicidal new boss, more bills than a flock of pelicans, and a future ex-wife becoming less ex by the minute. In detection and in life, it seems, there is always more going on than meets the eye . . .

'Slider and his creator are real discoveries.' *Daily Mail*

BLOOD SINISTER

Cynthia Harrod-Eagles

Award-winning ex-*Guardian* hack Phoebe Agnew had a name for championing the underdog – and for attacking the police in print. When her trussed and strangled body is found in her chaotic flat, Detective Inspector Slider must demonstrate the impartiality of the law and find her killer.

On the day of her death the horribly undomesticated Agnew cooked an elaborate meal for someone. It may have been her old friend and reputed lover, the government advisor Josh Prentiss, but his powerful Home Office friends are pressuring Slider to look elsewhere. Unidentified fingerprints, a missing ligature, alibis offered when none is required – Slider is on a race against time to untangle the web of lies and hidden relationships. For Phoebe Agnew was concealing a secret, which someone is willing to kill – and kill again – to protect . . .

'Harrod-Eagles is a master of the telling phrase or the catchy put-down . . . reading her is a joy' *Irish Times*

GONE TOMORROW

Cynthia Harrod-Eagles

The stabbed body of a well-dressed man is found slumped on the swing in a children's playground in the heart of Shepherd's Bush – Detective Inspector Bill Slider's patch.

From the seedy pubs of Shepherd's Bush through the brothels of Notting Hill to the mansions of Holland Park, Slider and his team unearth the victim's sordid lifestyle of debts, drugs and dodgy deals, and it soon becomes clear that their suspect is a crime baron who will stop at nothing to keep his identity hidden.

However, Slider is not only up against a resourceful villain, he is also fighting a rearguard action to stop the case being taken off his hands and solved by incomers, and when it's all over he'll find the time to discover just what it is his lover has been trying to tell him . . .

'It's criminal how good Harrod-Eagles is when she puts old Bill to work' *Manchester Evening News*